EIGHT POINTED CROSS

MARTHESE FENECH

BDL Publishing

© Book Distributors Limited, Malta
Second Edition, 2020
First Edition, 2011

Eight Pointed Cross

Text © Marthese Fenech
Cover design by Andrei Xuereb and Jason Buhagiar
Map designs by Dr Stephen C Spiteri and Jason Buhagiar
Author photograph by Gordon Lau

Dear Reader,

I invite you to visit my website, marthesefenech.com, and subscribe to my newsletter, which serves as an extension to my books. From research, writing, and publishing to travel, adventure, and misadventure, I share what inspires me in hopes of inspiring you.

Oh, and there's also giveaways and free stuff.

To Mom—for constantly bursting into my room to offer me tea as I worked on this novel.

To Dad—for not constantly bursting into my room to offer me tea as I worked on this novel.

PREFACE

Though *Eight Pointed Cross* is above all a work of fiction, I have made every effort to remain as true to the history, cultures, and settings of the time as research and observation would allow. In cases where several authors gave differing accounts or interpretations of the same event or individual, I used the version that seemed most plausible.

With regrets to purists, I have favoured consistency in handling certain aspects of the novel. For example, Istanbul is the city of as many names as it has had masters: Lygos, Byzantium, Augusta Antonina, New Rome, Constantinople. At the time of Suleiman, the city was officially Konstantiniyye on coinage and government documents. In common parlance, it was already referred to as Stamboul, or Istanbul, which derives from the Greek phrase "Istinpolin" or, "in the City." Therefore, throughout the novel, the city is called Istanbul. The term for Mother in Turkish is *Anne*; however, to aid with pronunciation and to avoid confusing the word with the given name, I have added a final *h*, creating *Anneh*. Similarly, the correct spelling for the noble members of Malta's civil authority is *gurati*; for the sake of pronunciation, I have spelled it *jurati*.

Qur'an is a more accurate transliteration of the Arabic word for the Islamic sacred book; I have used that spelling when in an Ottoman character's perspective and Koran when in a Christian character's point of view.

Historical texts and maps identify an inlet in Malta's Grand Harbour as both Dockyard Creek and Galley Creek. To keep names uniform, I have referred to it as Dockyard Creek throughout the trilogy. Finally, Malta's first official saint, Publius, was canonized in 1634, about ninety years later than depicted in this fictional trilogy to allow for the church of St Publius.

Finally, an adjustment was made to the age of French knight Mathurin Romegas—in this novel he is about ten years older than he actually was in order to have him fully established as a master admiral and suitable rival of Dragut Raïs.

While researching *Eight Pointed Cross,* I travelled to Malta, Turkey, Italy, and France, where I immersed in these breathtaking places, their paces, their flavours, their scents, their vitality. In an attempt to experience what it might have felt like to be a defender during a siege in mid-summer Malta, I spent an afternoon on the open walls of fortress St Angelo under the most intense sun I've ever known. I was rewarded with severe heatstroke and a day spent in bed shivering, sweating, cramping, and convinced I contracted the plague. How the knights endured such heat in over fifty pounds of plate armour while being shot at for months on end is beyond me.

Heatstroke aside, Malta is my second home, and one of my favourite places in the world—four compass points of natural beauty, the smell of the sea in the air no matter how far inland one ventures, colour and life and church bells and *pastizzi*, and some of the most amusing, authentic people I've ever encountered. I am indebted to my Maltese friends, especially Andrei Xuereb and Jason Buhagiar, for their tireless work designing the novel's cover according to my concept, Ruben Xuereb, Mark Brincat, Franco Davies, Chris Abdilla, and Clive Farrugia, for being impromptu tour guides, language specialists, fencing consultants, researchers, drivers, and finders of awesome wine bars. It is an honour and a privilege to know them.

Istanbul is equally unforgettable. As I walked along the Golden Horn and contemplated how lucky I was to be in this most magnificent of cities, this living museum, something drew my attention from the shimmering water and across the street. There was a statue, majestic yet discreet, standing peaceful and dignified in the shade of Topkapi Palace. I had to go see who he was, this solemn man standing there with an open view of the sea before him and the pride of Istanbul at his back.

Of course.

It was Dragut Raïs, one hand on the globe, the other around a sword. All around us was perfect quiet. In the time that I stood there with Dragut, I think a moment of understanding passed between us.

As a first-time novelist undertaking a historical epic as a debut, I am most and forever indebted to the people who gave their time to offer suggestions and constructive ass-kickings.

I am particularly grateful to the brilliant David W. Ball, author, mentor, friend, counsellor, confidant, best-advice-in-the-world giver, and invaluable resource, who never once turned down a request for guidance. He is a person for whom I have unrelenting admiration and respect. I am thankful also to the incomparable Karen Connelly, celebrated author and editor whose no-bullshit approach forced me to produce the best work I could. And then, to try harder. I hope I have not let her down. My gratitude extends to writer Chris Humphreys, a pal and support, who interrupted his breakfast on numerous occasions to read my work and offer his feedback; John Heighton, a relentless champion of my manuscript; author Marsha Skrypuch, who invited me into her online writing group, without which I don't think I would have managed the last few passes of rewrites; I am especially grateful to members Eric Emin Wood and David Krauskopf for the time they spent reading and rereading scenes from my manuscript and challenging me to do better; writer Antanas Sileika, one of the best teachers I've ever had, a grammar genius who made studying syntax fun; Carol Rasmussen, an exceptional editor, always available to lend her expertise to help find the right words and omit the wrong ones.

I would like to thank Tony Mangion for his close reading of my manuscript and his attention to detail ensuring historical accuracy. Any mistakes that remain are my own. Dr Carmel Cassar and Dr Simon Mercieca have my great appreciation for their willingness to answer endless streams of history questions. I am grateful to Albert Vella and *Leħen Malti* for the opportunity to appear on the show and promote my yet-to-be-published manuscript to the Maltese Canadian community.

My friends at home and abroad have been the very best a person could hope for—simply having them in my life has made the already incredible experience of writing this novel all the more enjoyable. Allowing me to bounce ideas off them and vent about the unfairness of it all, constantly yet gently enquiring about how things are going, forcing me to take hot chocolate breaks—for this and so much more, I am forever grateful. It is said that those who take friendship from life take the stars from the sky. Well, I have the very brightest of galaxies.

I am blessed with a wonderful family. My parents, Alfred and Doris, to whom this work is dedicated, have always been exceptionally positive forces in my life, and embody the very best of what it is to be Maltese. My siblings are perfect role models for a little sister to look up to. My brothers, Dave, Steve, and Lou opened my mind to the wonders this world has to offer through their amazing pursuits, travel experiences, stories, and photographs; they have passed on to me a passion for life, a love of adventure, and a dangerous sense of curiosity; my sister Carmen's quiet endurance and dedication have inspired me to treat this manuscript like one of her many marathons.

Finally, but forever first, my loving thanks to Brad. Beyond his unwavering faith in me, beyond reading my manuscript numerous times, painstakingly searching out plot holes and comma splices, beyond his patience when I was tethered to my desk, deaf to the world around me, to dinner and dishes, beyond every kind gesture grand or small, his love inspires me. Before Brad, I did not know true romance, and could not write a convincing love scene if my life depended on it. Perhaps I still can't. But it's not for lack of knowledge. Every single day, Brad shows me the kind of love we read about, the kind I try to write about. Any scene in this book that depicts love in its purest form owes to Brad making that kind of love a reality for me.

Malta—Florence—Istanbul—Toronto
January 2004-June 2011

PRINCIPAL CHARACTERS

Malta
Domenicus Montesa, Maltese peasant
Katrina Montesa, his younger sister
Augustine Montesa, their father, a soldier-at-arms in service the Knights of St John
Isabel Montesa, Augustine's wife
Robert Falsone, Maltese peasant
Father Anton Tabone, *kappillan*, or parish priest
Angelica Tabone, his niece
Franco di Bonfatti, knight
Marcello di Ruggieri, knight
Gabriel Mercadal, *pilier*, or master knight, of the *langue* of Aragon
Girolamo d'Alagona, *hakem,* head of Malta's civil authority
Diana d'Alagona, wife of the *hakem*

Ottoman Empire
Demir, an Ottoman child
Al Hajji Hamid al Azm, Demir's father, a wealthy horse breeder
Yaminah, Demir's mother and Hamid's second wife
Ayla, Hamid's principal wife
Muharrem, son of Ayla and Hamid, half-brother of Demir
Jameela, a servant
Murad, Demir's best friend
Kemal, chief groomsman
Timurhan, a Sipahi, or imperial horseman

Historical Figures
Juan d'Homedes, Grand Master of the Knights of St John
Suleiman, Sultan of the Ottomans
Jean Parisot de Valette, knight
Dragut Raïs, corsair
Mustafa Pasha, Ottoman general
Sinan Pasha, Ottoman admiral
Giuseppe Callus, Maltese physician
Alonso Predal, *Protomedicus*, or head of the Maltese medical profession
Antoni Zammit, Maltese apothecary
Domenic Cubelles, Bishop of Malta
Mathurin Romegas, knight and commander of the galleys
Nicholas Upton, knight and Turcopilier
Nicolas Durand de Villegagnon, knight
Galatian de Sesse, knight and Governor of Gozo
Gaspard de Valliers, knight and Governor of Tripoli

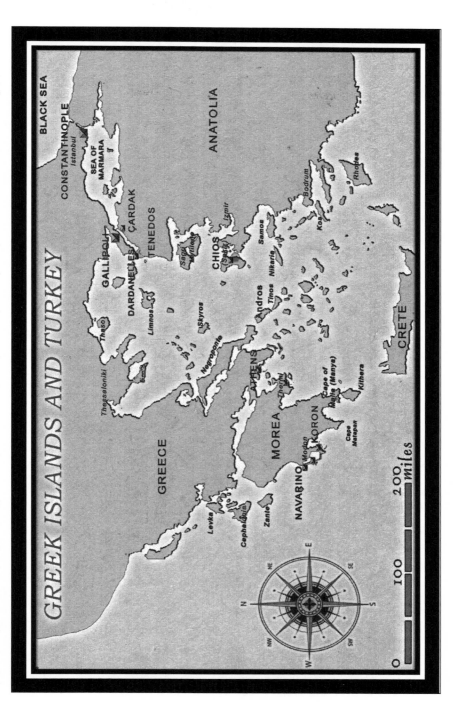

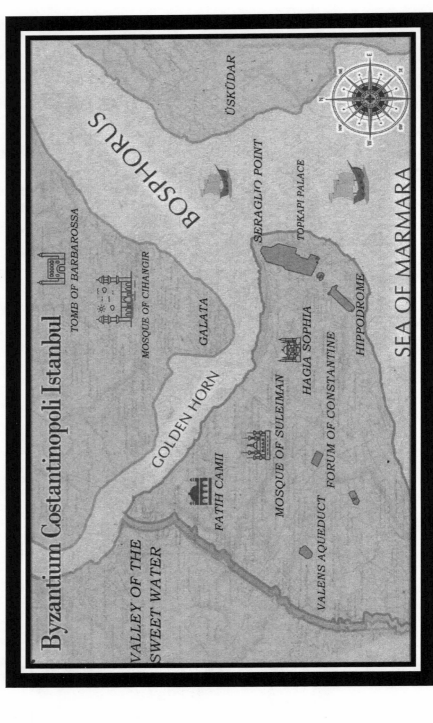

PART ONE

CHAPTER ONE

Malta, 1542

Immersed in a rare moment of quiet, the family does not sense the approach of the corsairs. They cannot see the North African slavers advancing over the island's rocky terrain and through the dark streets of the fishing village Birgu, now a mere fifty paces from the stone walls of the Montesa house. And they cannot smell the reek of the galleys, moored in a cove concealed by soaring headland. This night, the family senses only peace, smells only melting beeswax.

Domenicus sits on his father Augustine's lap. Winking candlelight creates shadows that move over his face.

"What story tonight, lad?" Pa asks. "Will I tell you of the battle for Rhodos, or of how good fortune blessed your mother the day we met?"

Across the room, Isabel gives a little smile without looking up from her embroidery.

"The story of you and Mama," Domenicus replies, resting his sandy head against Augustine's chest. The boy's hair smells of sea salt, dried into each strand after a mid-day swim. He sighs contentedly, as always feeling not the power in his father's strong hands but his gentleness, the easy smile in his eyes, the quiet dignity with which he carries himself. Other village men might brag and bully, but his pa never does. Domenicus often spends long moments staring at his own reflection in the surface of a puddle or the side of a pot, willing his features to develop as his father's have. Augustine's face is a smooth palette, glowing with the fresh sheen of a man mindful of indulgences. His jaw is sculpted into angles that meet at his chin, forming a countenance both beautiful and fierce. His dark hair seems forever windswept, heavy locks falling over his forehead.

Just as he opens his mouth, Katrina dashes out from behind a cedar chest. "We heard about you two yesterday! You haven't told us a battle story since forever." With an imaginary sword, she duels an invisible opponent.

Mama laughs, the pretty sound broken by a cough. She brushes away auburn strands that have strayed over her eyes, returns her attention to the needlework. Katrina plops cross-legged on the stone floor, looks expectantly up at Pa. He glances to Domenicus for permission, and once it is given, folds battle-scarred arms loosely across his chest and leans with his back to the wall.

"Rhodos. June, 1522. It was my twentieth year, and I stood staring out over the sea from my vantage on the walls. The air was alive with jasmine from the island plains, salt off the Aegean, and fear from a city in ferment." The small fire in the hearth flares suddenly, illuminating the whole house. It is a home like most in Birgu: bedrooms defined by sackcloth curtains separating straw pallets from the rest of the dwelling, one window casement panelled with oiled linen, easily removed to let in air.

"Two days following the feast of John the Baptist, she came: the Ottoman armada. Formidable. Beautiful. She was one hundred and three galleys strong, further strengthened by three hundred other vessels—triremes, brigantines, carracks, a tremendous fleet breaking the horizon." Domenicus loves his father's rich, deep voice, perfect for storytelling. "We soldiers, together with the Knights of St John, were positioned along the ramparts—" he pauses, distracted.

Domenicus looks up. He tilts his ear and listens closely but hears only the creak of crickets. "What is it, Pa?"

"Nothing. ...A stray dog, perhaps." Augustine passes his fingers over the small silver and turquoise eight-pointed cross, symbol of the Knights of St John, that dangles from a thin chain around his neck. "So. All men of Spanish ancestry were stationed at the bastion of Aragon, one of eight fortresses encircling the city. I had just returned from church, where every knight, every soldier, every citizen flocked once news of the coming siege had spread."

"Then," he continues, "Fra Gabriel Mercadal came to muster the men. The *pilier* of the Aragonese shook us: *Those who cannot bravely face danger are already slaves of the enemy! And not one among you is a slave!* His words echoed off the walls into the very heart of me."

"Were you frightened, Father?" Domenicus asks, though he has heard the story a hundred times and knows the answer.

"Not frightened enough. An army of one thousand sheep led by a lion is far more destructive than an army of one thousand lions led by a sheep. Suleiman the Magnificent led this attack—we faced an army of lions led by a lion." He leans slightly forward on his seat, lowers his voice for effect. "The Muslim pride marched ashore, hungry for Christian flesh."

Clearing her throat, Mama sets down her embroidery. "Time for bed, little ones. Papa can finish the story tomorrow. Or," she winks "perhaps he'll tell you of our adventures raising flowers in a reluctant plot instead."

As the three open their mouths in protest, violent commotion rumbles from the narrow village streets. Hooves trample cobblestone, rattling shelves, sending pottery jugs to crash and break on the floor. The four stand as one,

Domenicus and his sister huddling close to their father.

"*Slavers!*" It sounds like Nicolo, the cobbler.

"Corsairs!" shouts another villager. Domenicus is not sure which one. "Hide!"

"*Hide*," a Moor snarls in the pidgin dialect of the Barbary Coast, "And when we find you, we cart you to *El Djezair* in pieces!"

El Djezair. Algiers. Domenicus shudders at the name. *The Whip of the Christian World* they call it, *the Wall of the Barbarian.* He knows the stories. For centuries, Malta has been plagued by pirates, but none so efficient, so terrifying, as the Barbary corsairs from Algiers.

Smoke from the burning reeds of North African torches permeates his house and makes Mama cough—a deafening sound in this need for silence.

"Damn them," Augustine mutters. "Isabel, the candles. Domenicus, help me bar the door." Son pushes as Father pulls the heavy cedar chest across the floor. Pa finds his sword, and under cover of darkness, draws his family with him to the ground. He kisses the nape of Mama's neck.

Outside, whips snap on empty air, bite into flesh. With the sound of each lash, Domenicus winces as though the leather flog bloodies his own skin. His eyes fix on the door, and with shallow breath, he watches, waiting as each second brings the corsairs closer. Every shudder of the wooden door, every rattle of its hinges, sends pangs into his stomach. He wonders if they should hide in the dung pit, a hollow behind the house where the chamber pot is emptied. He hears the sobs of children younger than he is. Boys and girls make corsairs rich.

"I hate them," his sister whispers. "I'd kill them all."

Augustine crawls to a crack in the door unblocked by the chest.

"Pa, you're a soldier," Kat says, tone hushed. "Go fight them like you did at Rhodos."

Father looks over his shoulder. "I could no more prevail on my own against a band of corsairs than I could against an earthquake."

Domenicus moves slowly over cold stone to join his father. He peers out. Wailed entreaties for God's mercy rise with the smoke billowing from the scattered torches.

"I'll fight with you, Pa."

"And get yourself, your sister, and your mother captured. A good soldier must think, not simply act."

Tense silence returns.

"Resist at your peril, infidels!" The voice belongs to an Algerian slave trader. His authority marks him as captain of this corsair fleet. He is tall and full-bearded, wearing loose-fitting green pantaloons, the bloodstains on them sure indication that he *is* peril.

Paces down the road, the baker Emanuel staggers from his open doorway, his hands closed around his throat. Blood seeps through his fingers, onto his shirt and the dusty ground below. He falls face down, shuddering as he dies in a pool of his own blood. Treading over the body, a Moor drags Emanuel's wife from the house. Sarah is one of the many peasants who scratches out a livelihood by selling goods at Birgu's market.

"Dirty animal!" She smashes her captor square in the face with her elbow and, in his moment of blindness, tears away. The corsair roars with pain and chases her, catching a fistful of her hair. His nose a bleeding mess, he thrusts Sarah at the captain and tends his injury. Those already bound look on, hopeless. Sarah struggles fiercely, scratching, kicking, biting. She rakes her fingernails across her captor's bare chest, broad and scarred.

"Quiet!" he thunders. He blows two sharp blasts on a silver whistle. "*Yalla! Yalla!*" He pins Sarah's arms behind her back. She cries out, but will not yield, driving her bare heel into his shin. He reaches around her chest to squeeze one of her breasts with crushing force.

"This spitfire will fetch a handsome purse," the captain rumbles. "One heavy with doblas." Two turbaned corsairs emerge from Sarah's home carrying what few trinkets they could find, some majolica jars and a fat, headless Venus of Malta statuette.

"Waste no more time on trifles!" he barks. "To the anchorage. *Move!*"

Domenicus breathes deep. If the corsairs follow their orders, his family will be safe. He watches through the crack as slavers gather the captives. There are twelve, most of them children younger than his sister. The smallest are hoisted to men on horses. By the points of daggers, the corsairs force the prisoners to wherever it is the Moorish ships make berth.

"Put out your torches," the captain orders. Again, his whistle trills.

Domenicus glances over his shoulder as if to make sure his mother and sister are still there. He then fixes his gaze on the window. Shadows grow and pass across the translucent coverings, grow and pass.

Suddenly, a flash of bright orange.

A reed torch flies through the casement and lands on Katrina's bed, the sacking and straw instantly catching. The room comes alive with fire. To terrified gasps, Father snatches up Mama's embroidery and smothers the flames with it. She crawls over to a basin of water and throws it on the bed, choking the flames to silence. The safety of darkness returns.

Domenicus looks to his mother. Her hands are shaking. His own are trembling. But he has to be brave. Brave like his pa. He moves back to his spot by the door. Outside, a Moor leads a splendid white horse into the path of the departing corsairs. The animal's bare back is glossy, almost blue, in the moonlight. A semi-conscious woman is draped like a sack of grain over the man's shoulder, his yellow pantaloons streaked with blood.

The captain halts to seize the horse's rein and scowls at the Moor. "A minute longer, you would have been left behind, idiot." He swings onto the mount, gives it a gentle kick.

"I hit upon this sweetmeat just beyond the village," the corsair says, jerking his head at the woman thrown over his shoulder as he scrambles into step with his captain's new horse. "Her husband is dead. Skewered." He spits on the grainy cobbles. "Their girl-child got away."

The captain's eyes flash. "Girl-child?"

"The little mouse scurried into a field before I could grab her."

"Thou mewling hedge-born ratsbane! A girl is worth more than double any grown woman. Yet you, you errant toad, you bring me a woman."

The sobbing of the captives, the banter of the corsairs, and the hoofbeats of their steeds are soon swallowed by the night, the entire raid over within ten minutes.

Father stands. He pauses, looking up as if to thank God his family was spared. "Gabriel will be expecting me," he says, turning. He takes Mama's hands into his, squeezes them. "They're gone. We're still here. But I will not know ease unless you know safety. Come to your cousin's house." He unlocks the door and opens it slowly, sword raised, Domenicus peering around his waist.

At first glance, the fallout of the raid does not seem severe. There are a few small fires from discarded torches, but the houses are unscathed. Still, trails of blood mark the grisly passage of injury and death. One such trail leads to the baker Emanuel's doorway, where he lies sprawled across the step, his legs still inside the house. Pa crosses himself, saying he is not sure who is in more need of God's mercy now: the baker or his wife.

At the end of the street stands the lodging of Mama's cousin, the carpenter Bellizzi. In Maltese, he is known as *Ta'mastrudaxxa—the master carpenter*. To Domenicus and Katrina, he is Belli.

Pa raps on the door. Half a minute brings no answer. Then, with alarming suddenness, the door flies open. A thick man, bald and muscular, stands wild-eyed in the entrance, his hands clutching a hammer he is poised to swing.

"By the holy hairs of Pope Paul's sacred anus, it's you." Belli lowers his weapon. "But a corsair wouldn't knock, would he?" He grins, nudges his chin towards the road. "Go, Augustine. See your knights. And tell them next time Algiers decides to visit, they might get off their idle asses and offer some goddamn resistance."

EIGHT POINTED CROSS

CHAPTER TWO

Augustine takes an easterly path towards the scattered quarters of the knights. The small, square buildings of Birgu press together like gossipers in a huddle. The narrow streets wind and cross without order, each corner a bowshot from the next—a safeguard since the days of Malta's ninth-century Arab rulers. On these snaking lanes stand the residence halls of the Knights of St John. The rude exteriors come as a shock to fledgeling brothers, who hail from the richest estates in civilized Europe. While serving in Malta, these young men are assigned to one of eight halls, the *langues*, or tongues, depending upon their European homeland: Provence; Auvergne; France; Aragon; Castile; Italy; Germany; or England. The arrangement suits the knights well, allowing them to preserve fellowship with those who speak the same language. Although they are united under one banner—the eight-pointed cross—these men are patriots still and prefer not to mingle with brothers from other lands. Moreover, while the tongues of knights roll with the sophisticated dialects of the Continent, few will deign to learn Maltese, the speech of commoners.

Heavy hooves shake the ground moments before the mounted patrol appears. Two knights Augustine knows, Etienne and Armand, Frenchmen from Auvergne, round a corner astride Percherons brought from Norman stables. Moonlight glances off their armour, polished metal gleaming.

"News?" Augustine asks, speaking French.

"Nothing *new*," Etienne replies. "Corsairs landed under cover of an outcropping. Stole back to their galliots before the alarm was raised."

"Captives?"

"Father Anton Tabone reported a good few captured," Armand says grimly. "His own brother was slain, his sister-in-law taken. They were visiting from Mdina. By some miracle, their daughter managed to get away."

"God hid her with His little finger." Augustine continues past several other mounted detachments to the hall of Aragon, the residence of Gabriel Mercadal, master of the *langue*. Two Catalans guard heavy doors, each man

9

armed with an arquebus. Augustine requests an audience with their *pilier* and is ushered into the antechamber. Though the outer walls of the *auberge* are austere, inside, tapestries and oak furniture give silent testament to the Order's wealth. The foyer is washed in the moonlight that streams through lofty windows, making shadows stretch across the floor, creep up the walls. Augustine crosses to the corridor, the way lit by the blinking flames of fat votives in lanterns. A hint of cinnamon from the kitchen makes his mouth water. He has not enjoyed the rare, extravagant spice since his last campaign with the knights.

At the end of the hallway, Gabriel Mercadal descends a stair, his single eye squinting in the faint light. During the six-month Ottoman siege of Rhodos in 1522, he took a musket ball to the face. But the stubborn Spaniard was not in the mood to die that day.

"Dear friend," he says, greeting Augustine warmly. "You come to serve. Or is it for a mug of beer that you come?" The knight sends his page for his pipe. The seventy-nine-year-old clasps his hands behind his back and continues down the corridor.

"When do we depart?" Augustine asks.

"Would that my knights had your devotion," Gabriel replies, turning partway.

"My devotion? The Hospitallers are the most dedicated of all orders."

"I love you for your faith. But the Order is losing its order."

"Then we restore it."

Lengthy, silent moments pass. At last, the old man chuckles. "Would that my knights had your conviction!" He gives Augustine a good nudge. "Tomorrow, a caravan sets out to intercept Muslim merchant ships on their trade routes. That ought to twist Suleiman's scrotal mane into a tight knot, hmm?"

Augustine grins. "Indeed."

"The frequency of these raids has, at last, persuaded Grand Master Juan d'Homedes to increase fortifications. Knights have been consigned to the quarries. Your family could help out by taking over some menial tasks at the infirmary."

"Pleased to."

Gabriel smiles. "A welcome break from the heat." He peers down the length of the corridor, his brow furrowed, smile gone. "Where is that little whelp with my pipe?"

Augustine rubs his chin. "The corsairs that came tonight—was Dragut Raïs among them?"

"A man of that devil's skill and luck is not easily seen."

"His skill is not infallible, nor is his luck infinite."

"And neither is the night." Gabriel gives Augustine a playful prod towards the door. "Go. Rest. We leave at cock's crow."

***

Domenicus wakes before dawn and slips silently from Belli's house without waking the others. He passes over stubbly grass to the small stable behind the dwelling.

"*Peppone!*" he calls in a loud whisper as he starts climbing into the donkey's pen.

"Boy, how many times have I told you not to do that?"

Domenicus stops cold, stunned: *the donkey speaks!* He jumps back, gasping. His father emerges from the shadows, laughing his easy laugh.

"Pa! What are you doing in there?"

"I came here to sleep after my meeting with Gabriel. I did not want to wake you. We sail today. Now."

Domenicus wrinkles his nose. "You spent the night with the donkey?"

Augustine shrugs sheepishly. "We asses enjoy each other's company."

"How long will you be gone? When you come back will you teach me to use your sword?"

"Not too long. A few months." Augustine takes his sword from the wall against which he rested it and slides it into its scabbard, the stable filling with the sound of steel running against leather. "My sword is too heavy for you, but let's see if the smithy can't fashion one more suitable for a boy. Come. I'd rather not have to swim after the galleys." As they leave the stable, he adds, "Sir Gabriel wants you to help out at the *Sacra Infermeria*. They find themselves a bit short-handed."

This is wonderful news. Known Hospitallers, the Knights of St John built a hospital in Birgu equal to the best in Europe and deny entry to no man—count or commoner. Domenicus loves it there. The *Sacra Infermeria* is clean and cool and does not smell the least like horse shit.

Pa goes over his expectations. "You and your sister will attend mass, if not every day, at least on Sunday. Father Tabone will tell me if he does not see you."

"But what if we sit at the back?"

Augustine smiles. "Do not neglect your prayers. Say them true, from your heart, not your memory. As for your earthly duties, be careful not to scratch yourself fetching brambles for the fire, and when the flies grow too thick, it is time to shovel the dung pit."

Domenicus grimaces.

A few minutes later, with the bells of St Lawrence chiming in the distance, he waits in front of Belli's house for Pa. Villagers scrub dried blood off the walls and sweep debris into the street. The boy's gaze drifts in the direction of the baker's house. Two young men carry the body of Emanuel, his jaw and chin caked purple-brown. The slash is so deep his head dangles loosely, as though it will fall free any moment.

With a sharp intake of breath, Domenicus turns away.

***

In the dimness of the carpenter's home, Augustine gargles a mixture of honey and vinegar. He spits into a bucket, wipes his mouth on the back of his hand. He leans carefully over Isabel and Katrina, the two lying together on Belli's bed, heads tilted towards each other. Augustine does not have the heart to rouse them. As he turns to go, Isabel coughs into waking.

"I'm leaving for a time," he says.

"Must you? I miss you terribly when you're gone."

"And I, you, but the missing keeps food on our table." He offers his hand and she places hers in his, lacing their fingers together as they cross the room to the door.

"Your cough, it sounds angry," Augustine says, brow furrowing.

"I've never heard a cough that sounded happy," Isabel replies, smiling. Augustine brushes loose strands from her face. He brings his mouth to hers, knowing his stubble will soon end the kiss.

Isabel pushes his face playfully away. She slips her hands beneath his shirt, walks her fingers slowly up the slope of his back. Augustine closes his eyes, passes his hands over his wife's face, running his thumbs down the dip of her nose, pressing his palms gently against her high cheeks, tracing his fingers over the Cupid's bow of her slightly parted lips.

"What are you doing?" she asks.

"Pretending to be blind."

"Why?"

"A man without sight can only conceive a woman's beauty by touching her face. On this campaign, I will meet moments of darkness…" He runs his fingers down her neck, feeling the beat of her heart against his skin. "…Against shadow, your face will bring me to light."

***

The sun is up, already drawing sweat as Domenicus and his father take the dusty road to the harbour. The people of Birgu, hardened by relentless raids, go about business as usual. A peasant leads his donkey, panniers laden with potatoes, towards the market square, his wife following with a moneybox in her hands. Domenicus and Augustine veer west with the road, their way fringed by a patchwork of thirsty fields. The earth is parched to stubble, the soil so crusted and dry only thistle and cacti have the pluck to grow. Soon, ancient square buildings block the sun and make a narrow valley of the cobbled street. They walk the market, past woven rugs draped over lines, dull fabric piled atop tables, wicker baskets jumbled high, clay jars cluttered on mats, and continue together along the archway of the Order's treasury, past the hostels of the galley captains.

Ahead, Domenicus can make out the fortress St Angelo, standing in majesty at the end of the promontory. This great Norman structure commands an open view of the natural harbour and the ridged spits of land that contain it. The docking bay cuts inland, surrounded to the east by the key-shaped peninsula of Birgu and to the west by l'Isla, a steep, silvery outcrop marked by two windmills and a sequence of open hollows that run along the shoreline. Across the Grand Harbour, the rocky headland of Mount Sciberras rises high above the water, its slope dappled with dust-green shrub.

The wharf is dotted with traditional fishing boats pointed at bow and stern and painted blue, green, yellow, and red. Marking the prow of each sea craft is the eye of Osiris, a Phoenician symbol meant to ward off bad omens and protect anglers from sea monsters.

The last stretch down to the harbour is steep and must be carefully negotiated to avoid the snagging thorns of prickly pear. At its foot, knights and soldiers, slaves and villagers, throng the length of the dockyard. Domenicus and his father start down, hand in hand.

"Pa, why aren't you a knight? Why just a soldier?"

"Knights are the sons of great houses, men of noble birth from both lines. I am of noble birth from neither. Still," he smiles, "my common blood and I wish to serve the cross with the same devotion as those whose lineage gives the right."

"You *are* noble," Domenicus insists.

"I don't know about that. But I do know that if I were a knight, I would never have been able to marry your mother, and neither you nor Katrina would have been born. I would not trade you for any title."

"How come knights can't marry?"

"Because they must be bound without distraction to the Order. Perhaps also because they kill too many husbands, leave too many children fatherless, to become husbands and fathers themselves."

Domenicus struggles to digest this information, brow furrowing with the effort. "Is that noble work, killing husbands and fathers? Don't you kill husbands and fathers?"

"Perhaps it is not noble work. I can only hope God knows the intention is."

At the water's edge, dock timbers creak under the weight of soldiers carrying ammunition crates and powder kegs, water barrels and caged fowl. Warm air blends the scents of salty water and salty sweat, and ripples the surface of the Mediterranean burnished gold by the morning.

The open decks teem with activity, all hands securing ordnances, stowing provisions, inspecting spars. The long narrow warships, the galleys, shudder and groan, as do the oarsmen who must row them. Twenty-six benches carry two hundred and eighty head-shaven slaves, who together create the galley's signature stench. These men, either Muslim prisoners or Christian criminals, are naked, fettered, and seated on sheepskin. A bosun walks the corsia, the gangway between benches, testing the snap of his whip on empty air.

Thanks to his father, Domenicus is a minor expert on all things galley-related—from names and history to anatomy and stowage. The caravan will sail under the Napolitano Admiral Alessandro Ardone, who recently inherited the fleet from the renowned Admiral Bernardo Salviati. Ardone's galley, the flagship *Brezza*, bears mostly his Italian compatriots. The *Durendal*, named so for the sword of Roland, will carry knights hailing from the French *langues* of Auvergne, France, and Provence. The third warship, the *Atardecer*, will be home to Pa, and the Spaniards of Aragon and Castile. She is deftly carved with bas-reliefs and mouldings, her sails brailed along two curving yards. Her silk streamers catch high in the wind, banners fluttering like the ears of a hare. Her beauty masks the ugliness her oarsmen will endure, the discomfort her cramped decks will give her company.

Next, the chaplains embark, called to grant absolution before combat. The only group yet to board are the physicians and barber-surgeons hired to keep mariners groomed and deloused, and more importantly, to sew up those ripped open in battle. Domenicus is a long time watching these men.

Perhaps there is more than one way to serve the cross.

"Montesa, good of you to come." It is Gabriel Mercadal, approaching with a broad grin.

"Gone too long without some beer from one of your secret mugs."

The old knight laughs. "Clearly not much of a secret." He bends, eye to eye with Domenicus. "Will you be sailing with us? Shall I have the armourer fit you with a cuirass?"

"No, *Illustrissimo*. Pa says war is the territory of men."

"So it is. But when the day comes for you to venture into that territory, you will be just like your pa—as skilled a seafarer, as fierce a fighter, and as hardy a drinker. For now, it is the *Sacra Infermeria* that needs you. A Florentine will be expecting you at the gallery early tomorrow." Gabriel rises, gestures to Augustine. "Come, the *Atardecer* waits. One mustn't keep a lady waiting, even if she be fat and wooden." With a parting smile, the knight makes for his lady.

"You are the man now, Domenicus," his father says, crouching to kiss the top of his head.

And then, he goes.

CHAPTER THREE

Stifling air tastes of grit and dust. The earth is glazed red, pebbly and stippled with silver-green shrubs. It might not be very high, this rise, but it makes a taxing climb. When Domenicus reaches the brow, he turns. The fleet glides across the open blue, veering eastward, past the mouth of Kalkara Creek and beyond the jutting spit of Gallows Point, where sun-scorched bodies of convicts and corsairs dangle from nooses tied by knights, in grim welcome to those entering the harbour.

Domenicus pretends for a few moments that he can pick out his father on the deck of the *Atardecer*. He turns back to the road, edged by uneven walls that border fields the colour of tarnished-gold, meagre plots just beginning to show their promise. The creaking of wooden wheels lifts his head. A donkey-drawn cart jerks to a stop. A whip cracks.

"Move, you stupid beast." The gruff voice belongs to the farmer Grimaldi Farrugia. "*Haqq dik il-baghala ommok.*" *Damn your bitch of a mother.* The man's scowl digs trenches into his face, his hunched comportment indicative of the hostility with which he holds all the world. Long days in the sun and long nights at the tavern have conspired to parch his weathered face.

He casts his contempt on Domenicus. "Lazy scamp. If you were my boy, I'd beat you into crow fodder." Farrugia never had children, nor did he marry. And from his last statement, that is a good thing. Another leathern snap sets the wheels rolling and the poor beast of burden plodding unhappily along. Every bump pitches the farmer, provoking him to curse the animal and all its relatives. Domenicus thinks Peppone should thank God he ended up with Belli.

The boy passes the church of St Publius, an ancient structure standing lonely amid wild grass. In the year 60, Publius was the chief man of the island. The apostle Paul was shipwrecked on Malta and converted Publius to Christianity, ordaining him Malta's first bishop. Domenicus and his family attend mass here. But not the knights. Too small and rundown for them. Still,

15

in a village where most buildings are falling into ruin, the church is one of the few that is structurally sound. A bird has made her nest in the low steeple, and unlike the dull chime of the old bell, she brings life to the church with her song.

"Montesa, you ugly mutt!"

Domenicus spins round. A bare-chested boy runs towards him from behind a fat carob. His clothes torn and grubby, Robert Falsone has tied his shirt around his waist, exposing the ugly scars of a whip. His hair is dark and dishevelled, his big eyes brown and lively, cheeks bruised and smeared with sweaty grime.

"So, Falsone," Domenicus says, "no pirate stole you in the night."

The eleven-year-old throws back his head and laughs. "The bastards wouldn't dare."

"So why hide behind a tree?"

"Corsairs, I can handle. But Farrugia just passed this way… I didn't want that barking brute to make me weed his field. I'm already there six days a week. If he saw me, he would have sent me to his hopeless plot today too." Robert kicks a stone. "Let's go to the waterfront and kill pirates."

"I have to go home first. Coming?"

Robert nods. The two friends walk shoulder-to-shoulder, breathing air now strong with the smell of manure spread over fields.

"Guess what," Robert says. "Last night I found new hairs down there."

"Down where?"

He points to his crotch. "I counted. There are about twenty now. Want to see?"

"No!" Domenicus cries, pushing him away. "So. My father sailed with the knights today."

Robert snickers. "Off with the peacocks to teach the corsairs a lesson in preening?"

"Pa should never have told you what a peacock was."

"Well, just you pray they don't cross Dragut."

Domenicus swipes a dismissive hand. "That pirate is no match for the Knights of St John, protectors of Malta!"

Robert halts and faces him. "Listen here. Those arrogant foreigners don't care about Malta. They practically welcomed the corsairs into Birgu last night. Just like the day my father was killed. I'm surprised they didn't leave out warm milk and honey sweets. Today the knights go to fill their coffers by pillaging Muslim traders. Christian pirates, they are, and gold the only god they worship."

"Have a care—you'll get yourself into trouble."

"I'm not afraid of your knights. They're cowards." Robert squashes a shiny black beetle crawling over the dusty path, its shell crunching beneath his heel. "There. That's what I think of your knights." Domenicus picks up the dead insect with his thumb and forefinger, inspecting the broken black eggshell, its yellowish, oozing innards like yolk.

"They're not cowards. Pa told me about one knight, a Frenchman from Provence called Jean Parisot de Valette. He fought at Rhodos too. Once, his ship was captured by the corsair Kust Aly, who sunk it and put Valette in chains. The nobleman was a slave! He spent one year at the oar before the Order paid his ransom. And, he can speak seven languages, Robert. *Seven!* My father said Valette is the best knight in the Order."

Robert shrugs. "It doesn't matter about this Valette. The Order is nothing more than a flock of overfed peacocks that parade about like dandies and fuck tavern whores."

Domenicus and Robert find Katrina bent over a wooden trough, wringing dirty water from a blanket and squinting from the sunlight and the effort. Mama sits nearby, trying to salvage the embroidery that smothered the corsairs' fire last night.

"We're going to battle," Domenicus calls out.

"What about your chores?" Mama asks, raising her eyebrows. "The dung pit won't shovel itself." Domenicus is about to make a case for himself, when his mother laughs, revealing her hoax. "I suppose if I were a brave warrior, I'd rather kill pirates than shovel manure, so off you go. Will you take Kat—" she is cut off by a fit of coughing.

"Are you all right?"

"I'm fine, *Qalbi*—dear heart. Just the dust. Will you take your sister?" Domenicus knows it is an enormously unusual request for a mother to make, as the village adage goes: *girls must stay inside until the day they wed, and indoors they ought remain until the day they're dead.* If they do venture out, they shroud themselves in a black veil. But Mama is different. She refuses to appear as the shadow of a woman. Pa, who was born and raised on Rhodos, approves of her ways, even if they stir the blood of the neighbours.

"I'll bring Kat," Domenicus says, "if she wants to come."

"Of course I do!" She would go anywhere with him, and he doesn't mind. At night, he checks her bed for crawling things, and during the day, allows her to tag along to places no boy on this island would suffer a little sister to follow—like to the beach to fight corsairs. She quickly hefts the blanket but struggles to cast the damp bulk over the line.

Robert does it for her. "Sure you can handle a gun, *Qattusa?*"

"I'm not a cat, Falsone."

"Of course you are."

"Then you are a mouse, and I'll eat you up one day."

"You're going to marry me one day."

"I'm going to marry Peppone."

Katrina is first to make the rounded shore at the foot of Corradino

Heights. Languid swells hug the rocks in a salty embrace. Although not yet noon, the sun has baked the ground hot. Even so, it is a perfect site to battle corsairs—loads of ammunition and countless nooks for cover. Moreover, there are no sentries to spot them playing and spoil their fun. Katrina hates that more than anything.

"I'm a knight," her brother announces. "From the *langue* of Aragon."

Robert glances across his shoulder as he wades into the shallows. "If you're a knight," he replies grimly, "you'd better go hide in one of the caves. Leave the defences to the men." He drops to his knees and dunks his head, holding it under, releasing bubbles to the surface. He comes up, seawater running in golden beads down his face. Licking it from his lips, he gives Katrina's braid a gentle tug.

"So, Kat, your tail grew back." A few months ago, she decided that what made her a girl was her long hair, and if she got rid of it, she could grow up to be a man and have adventures. The epiphany came after Mama sent her to Belli's stable to feed the donkey. She began the transformation by sawing off her braid with the hatchet that was lying on the carpenter's bench. Lean and wiry and revealing no trace of femininity, she returned home with frayed, uneven hair, looking more like a boy than ever. She could not understand why her mother was so upset. Who wouldn't rather have a boy than a girl?

"My plan didn't work," Katrina says to Robert. "Now, are we going to kill corsairs, or what?"

Abruptly, he alters his demeanour, standing straight and soldierly before the empty bay. His bearing makes Katrina actually *want* to follow orders.

"All right men!" Robert calls. "Muslim galliots break the horizon! Prepare for the return of the dirt-eaters! Ready the cannons, prime the guns." He collects a handful of rocks and hurls them at the sea. "A direct hit!" He pumps his fist. "Look, the enemy ship is banking. I'll show those cretins the bottom with one more shot to the hull." Katrina paws through the rubble until she finds a stone worthy a cannon. She fires it off.

"You've sunk it!" Robert cries. "The murderous savages will drown! *F'oxx kemm ghandom!*" *Curse the genitals of their every relative!* "You there, Domenicus Montesa, pick them off with your arquebus if they try swimming to shore!"

Katrina busies herself gathering bullets for her brother's gun. She digs another large stone from its cradle of bedrock. Her eyes go instantly round. "A *scudo!*" She has unearthed a coin, one of the *scudi* introduced to the island by the knights. The visage on the faded metal is bearded and regal, very much the way she pictures God. She wonders if it is God.

"Put it in your pocket," Robert orders. Katrina obeys and immediately launches a cannonball at the enemy, now scattered along the waterfront. No stupid pirate is going to steal her *scudo*. At that moment, Domenicus turns to say something, and one of her large, jagged missiles slams into his face.

Fire sears in his flesh. The sun disappears, and darkness takes him.

Moments or days later, his little sister's frantic shouts bring him back to the light. He blinks open his eyes, but one doesn't seem to be working right. A flood of warm, sticky fluid weeps over his cheek. He presses his lips together, breathes quick short breaths through his nose.

"I broke his head! Oh God! I didn't mean to. I'm sorry!" Katrina's voice is distant, but near. Domenicus strains to focus, his sight fogged. He makes out only shadow, then, the peripheries of faces. And finally, Robert's slightly horrified expression, which quickly passes as he pulls Domenicus up. He staggers against nauseating pain, all the while trying to grasp how his sister could have knocked him off his feet. She spits on her sleeve and dabs his cheek, but even her careful touch causes him to yelp and shove her away.

"Come," Robert says. "We'll wash it out with seawater. That's the best medicine." The wounded knight sinks to his knees at the edge of a shallow pool, flushes his wound, and fights the urge to cry. After an initial, blinding sting, the saltwater actually tempers the pain.

Katrina chews her lip and hangs back. Domenicus can tell she is distressed by his silence, which she finds more frightening than yelling. He allows her some time to stew, finally giving her a nudge when he thinks she may very well eat right through her lip.

"I'll be all right, stupid. And I won't tell on you."

She is so overcome with guilt and sorrow and relief that the only thing she can think to do is throw her arms around him and squeeze.

In the distance, the bells of St Lawrence chime for vespers. Domenicus allows Robert to guide him up the slope and away from the cove. Katrina runs ahead, clearing the way of loose brambles and thistles, as tiny lizards dart across the path. The road is soon wider, flanked by flat buildings that break the sun. For Domenicus, it is a thousand leagues to his house. Robert walks him right to his front step.

"Take care of that battle injury, Montesa. You're needed back on the ramparts tomorrow."

EIGHT POINTED CROSS

CHAPTER FOUR

With dawn a moon shimmer away, Katrina slips barefoot from her house. She is practised at moving unseen, having done so many times to visit the donkey during the night. It demands a nimble step and held breath, but she makes it outside unnoticed. Her goal this time, however, is not the stable.

Katrina makes for the town square, the single *scudo* from the beach safely in her pocket. Most of Birgu is already awake and at work: the smithy firing up his forge, the butcher sharpening his blades, the baker heating his oven. Outside his hut, there is a line, growing by the minute. In a village where animal excrement and men's sweat are prevailing odours, freshly baked bread is a powerful tool to lure customers. Even so, Katrina has not risen for bread.

She reaches the market just as merchants are setting up shop. She knows exactly where to go—the same stall she and her brother often pass, with empty pockets and looks of longing in their eyes. Today, she has more than longing. Today, she has *money*.

Next to the clock tower is a small stand built with wood salvaged from a discarded galley. The counter is a sugary paradise of carob syrup, thyme honey, and most important, *qubbajt*—the sweet, sticky nougat coveted by every village child. The vendor himself is across the square conversing with the cobbler. His fat wife, however, snores on a stool, arms folded loosely across her ample bust, head against the wall, mouth slightly open, a spot of drool at the corner of her lip. Katrina coughs loudly. The woman starts, a croak of surprise in her throat.

At last, she takes notice of Katrina. And her bare feet.

"No beggars," she snaps.

"I'm not begging. I'm buying *qubbajt*."

"Buying indeed. Get lost, or I'll tell your father."

Katrina fishes the coin from her pocket and holds it triumphantly up. The old woman's scowl quickly changes to a merchant's grin, and the *scudo* disappears into her apron. A moment later, the wonderful, gooey, pistachio treasure disappears into Katrina's hand.

She runs all the way home, nougat sweating in her grip. Heart racing, she steals like a thief back inside her house and creeps across the cool stone floor. She sets the *qubbajt* on her brother's bed, covering it with a fold of his blanket. As she turns towards her own pallet, a hand catches her wrist. She looks down. Domenicus furrows a quizzical brow.

"Sorry about the rock," she whispers.

The sky is streaked through with orange, and under it, a straight road leads eastward, towards the foreshore of Kalkara where the three-storey *Sacra Infermeria* stands. Isabel peers at Domenicus, her soft features sharpened with concern. He squirms.

"Stop staring at me like that. You've cleaned it three times already."

"Were you able to sleep all right?"

"Fine," he lies. "Mama, you fuss too much."

"Astonishing a bird would fly right into your face."

"Dizzy from the heat," he lies again.

"I wonder if this little bird had bright green eyes," his mother says mildly, glancing at Katrina from the corner of her own eye.

As the clock tower heralds the seventh hour, a novice knight completing mandatory hospital service awaits the family at the loggia to save them trouble from guards. Access to hospital grounds is strictly forbidden to all but the infirm and those caring for them. As for women, the only ones allowed entry are nuns and laundresses.

Because the Order of St John of Jerusalem was founded as an Order of Hospitallers, each *langue* is appointed a day of the week to serve at the hospital. Today it is Italy's turn, though most have been assigned the quarries. A sixteen-year-old Florentine, Franco di Bonfatti, sets his face in dignified lines, holds his clean-shaven chin high, posture poised and perfect. He is sorely conscious his hair is inconsistently playful—short, soft curls that spring with his every movement.

Franco greets the family at the main entrance. He notices the woman is dressed quite boldly for conservative Birgu—head uncovered, arms exposed from elbow to wrist. Her features hold him, and he gazes at her high cheeks, her bright eyes, radiant below softly arching brows. When she gives him a smile, he becomes acutely aware of his idiotic gaping. He blinks rapidly, throws the woman's son a cursory glance.

"If you please," Franco stammers in Italian, gesturing for them to follow.

To walk through the gate of the *Sacra Infermeria* is to enter another world. The *cortile grande* is a large cloistered courtyard, trimmed with primroses, shaded by citrus trees, beauty at every turn. There is a manmade pond, dark water rippling with hot airstreams. The infirmary was built with stone cleaved on site, and the deep quarry that remained now serves as a rainwater basin to supply the hospital. In this edifice, the poverty of the village seems imagined. As they continue along the cobblestone path, Franco asks the family members for their names.

"Ladies, the bedclothes require sound beating," he says, falling in-step with Isabel. He looks over his shoulder and addresses Domenicus. "Our charge is meal service, boy."

"I think I'll come with you too," Katrina announces, tugging Franco's hand. He looks down, shocked a peasant would have the nerve to touch a knight. But disbelief soon dissolves into amusement.

"I'm afraid meal duty is for the men, little miss. Besides, I'm sure your mother would appreciate your help in the laundry room." He holds open the refectory door for Isabel to pass. Peasant or not, she is a woman—and a lovely one. "You know the way to the washing quarter, Signora?"

"Yes, thank you," she replies. "We'll take the work outdoors, to the *cortile basso*. Oh," she adds, looking back, "I have a great courtesy to ask of you, *Honorabile*."

"My courtesy is yours for the asking."

"Please have a physician tend my son's injury—" She begins to cough and walks off, her request going unfinished. Franco had been so captivated by the remarkable woman, he had not registered her boy's terrible gash. Now that the two are alone, the knight takes in the jagged abrasion.

"That is an angry wound," he says, stooping. "We'll have it looked at."

"The more people look at it, the angrier it gets."

***

A spray of seawater showers Augustine's face. He opens his eyes, licks salty mist from his lips. The Order's red and white banners catch high in the wind, a lively gust that fills the fleet's vast lateen sails. The *Atardecer* glides swiftly over the sea. Long and lean and slender hulled, she is a warship, driven by the motive power of slaves. The air carries the hypnotic thrush of the oars, which serves as both lullaby and wakeup call.

Augustine rubs a stiff neck and raises himself onto his elbow to gaze at the horizon. Beneath the large triangular sails, he feels more at home than ever, despite the discomforts of the voyage—the ache in his muscles from making a bed of the deck, the assault on his senses from the stench of sweating oarsmen, the stink of their excrement, which has long since saturated the planks. Under the Mediterranean sun, even the bits of tobacco in his nostrils do not temper the vile air of a galley.

Augustine watches the water. With any luck, the sea will maintain her calm. He turns his face from the briny deep, descends the companionway, and crosses the deck, moist timber yielding beneath his feet. He climbs another narrow ladder to the helm where Gabriel Mercadal pores over maps anchored in place by rocks. The captain adds the occasional scribble to open-faced logs, all the while managing a lively discussion with Pietro de Laya, his young first lieutenant.

"See reason, de Laya. Admiral Ardone's strategy is best. ...Wouldn't you agree, Montesa?" Gabriel asks, head down, back to the approaching soldier.

Augustine snorts with amusement. "You see better with your ears than most men with their eyes."

Gabriel laughs and turns. "Your footsteps give you away—light but sure, as though you are tracking rabbits in the Rhodian woodlands."

"And that," Augustine replies, "is why I always caught more than you."

First Lieutenant de Laya clears his throat. "So. According to Ardone's plan, his galley will force the Muslim merchantman into the port of Candia. The *Atardecer* and the *Durendal* will be hidden in wait, here—" de Laya taps the map with his forefinger. "A mistake. The *Atardecer* should drive the enemy into port. *We* are the marksmen. One drunken Spaniard is a more accurate shot than a galley full of sober Italians."

"Ardone is Admiral, and his word, final," Gabriel says. "Take heart. He will not engage the Muslim merchantman until she is trapped in the harbour. You may have first blood yet."

De Laya inhales noisily, nostrils flaring. He traps the air inside him until at last, he concedes with a sigh.

"Precisely," Gabriel replies jovially. "And, if I'm wrong, we can do it your way next time."

The first lieutenant shakes his head, laughing. "If you are wrong, Sir, we end up swimming with the Aegean fishes or worse, chained to the infidel's oar."

***

No matter how many times Domenicus serves at the hospital, its grandeur never ceases to impress him. As he trails Franco past storage rooms, past kitchen and pantry, he is awed by the wide corridor, the high reach of its ceiling, the smooth, clean walls, exquisite in their simplicity. A great mirror hangs on the western wall—not a tin mirror like the few Domenicus has seen, but a work of art, crafted from Venetian glass, framed in Athenian silver. He steps up to it, and for the first time, sees himself in sharp detail. He never imagined his wound to be so severe. His cheek is grated, leaking pinkish fluid, his eye dark red, flesh blue and yellow. No wonder everyone keeps staring at it—he wants to keep staring at it. He notes with proud satisfaction that he could be a soldier who has survived a terrible battle. The fading sound of Franco's boots on the stairs reminds him he is not a soldier, but a boy with a job to do. He runs to catch up. They pass through a chapel, the stone pillars at its entrance incised with cherubs, wings interlocking to create an angelic frieze. The focal arch bears an engraving of a ring encircled with rays, and surrounding the letters *IHS—In Hoc Signo Vinces—in this Sign, Conquer,* taken from Constantine's dream on the eve of the Battle of Milvian Bridge.

Beyond the chapel is a ward large enough to sleep thirty patients. Franco stops at its threshold and sends Domenicus for supplies. He is swiftly off to the *linciere*'s storeroom, pleased he remembers where it is. He returns a minute later, a tall, neatly folded bundle of tablecloths weighing him down as he follows the knight into the ward, where sixteen peasants await marvellous fare prepared and served by the noble sons of Europe's wealthiest courts.

Sunlight streams through lofty, narrow windows. Domenicus would love to press his hands against the glass panes. He finds it amazing that something, which appears invisible, could be so durable and so fragile at the same time. But he does not want to make himself look unrefined in a knight's presence, so he busies himself spreading cloths over bedside tables, pouring water, laying out utensils. Several patients gawk at him and whisper. One, a blacksmith, barks at the rest to mind their business. He beckons Domenicus, jokingly offering his bed.

"Such a battle wound," the smithy says, "warrants a stay for at least a month."

Domenicus likes this man and decides to play along. "This is just a scratch. You should see my opponent. It'll be a year before he's set right. Besides, my father needs me to run the house."

"Your father is Augustine," Franco cuts in, flipping out a tablecloth a few beds down. "A Spaniard, from Aragon." Domenicus did not think knights took much interest in their lessers and is intrigued by this one's familiarity with his pa.

"He was born in Rhodos, but his ancestors were Spaniards—they fought in the *Reconquista* and reclaimed Iberia from the Muslims," Domenicus explains. "How do you know my father?"

"A nodding acquaintance. I sailed with him while completing my novitiate. A true lover of the sea, and a truer pity he is not of adequate pedigree for knighthood." Franco di Bonfatti is the very picture of pedigree. "We quarried rock together also," he continues, filling a goblet with wine. "A blessing he speaks Italian, for I could not bear to hear nothing but this Arabic-sounding hotchpotch that is Maltese." The nobleman seems indifferent to the boy's birth as a Maltese. Domenicus shrugs off the slight.

Tables set, the meals soon arrive. At the top of each bed is a board scrawled in doctor-scribe with instructions for the patient's special diet. The chief man of the hospital, Bertrand le Grant, enters the room with a swish of his tunic. He is Parisian, a large man, cleft-chinned, and heavily browed, his scars evidence the Knights of St John are at all times ready to trade lancets for lances. He stands in the centre of the ward and, with a soft voice that belies his severe appearance, announces a name and a meal. Franco passes Domenicus a plate of vermicelli and points him to his patient.

The clap of sandals from the corridor turns his head just as his sister barrels past the doorway.

"Katrina!" he calls. She twists around, surges like a squall into the room. Her face is stark.

"Mother fell!"

Without thinking, Domenicus drops the plate to wobble and splatter across the table. He takes off after his sister, down a flight, and outside to the rear quad. There, on the cold stone, Mama lies motionless, spilt across the cobbles. Domenicus kneels, taps her cheek. He calls to her, distress pitching his voice higher. There is no response, no movement. He bends to listen for breathing.

Franco pushes through the doors. He slides his arms beneath Isabel's wisp of a body and picks her up, her sandals slipping off. Katrina quickly retrieves them.

"*Va bene*," Franco whispers, carrying Mama inside. He looks across his shoulder. "How long has she been unwell?"

"Days," Domenicus replies grimly. "But she'd tell you she's fine."

The knight places Isabel on a cot in a small, vacant room, which often doubles as quarters for menial staff. He kneels at her side, takes her wrist to check her pulse. His expression is bleak.

"I will find a physician." But Franco does not make it beyond rising. Mama blinks open her eyes. Her face is washed with confusion. Domenicus feels his own flood with relief.

"Signora, you fainted," Franco says, crouching beside her. "You will stay here the night."

"A very kind offer," she replies, rubbing her temple, "but I'm fine."

Domenicus and Franco exchange a glance.

"Please," Mama says, pushing herself up to a sitting position. "You will only get yourself into trouble, my lord. It's nothing, really. A chest cold. A moment of fatigue."

"I am quite certain I'll be in more trouble if I let you go. In the very least, allow me to take you by carriage to the women's hospital in Rabat."

"Listen to him," Domenicus pleads. His mouth and cheeks are rigid, but he feels the hardness in his expression soften when his mother smiles and says: "You fuss too much."

He is grateful Franco is not as quick to yield.

"Signora," the knight begins, "I cannot in good conscience allow a sick woman to leave."

"Then you can in good conscience allow me to leave." Mama has a way of making her say final. Even Pa knows he can't win. And so, all too soon, Franco yields.

"We have your word, you are all right?"

"My word."

CHAPTER FIVE

A white flash illuminates dark, swollen clouds. Thunder claps, as if to cue the storm waiting in the wings. The three-galley fleet struggles against capricious wind and mounting swells as deckhands work swiftly to down yards and lower sails. A fork of lightning cuts the sky in jagged lines. From the deck of the *Atardecer*, Augustine catches a second stick striking the mast of the *Durendal*. The oak splinters and cracks, and, with a terrible groan, the massive pole barrels down, sailors diving out of its way. It careens mercilessly onto the chained oarsmen, crushing them with its weight. Those gravely wounded die in their own filth.

The galleys are driftwood to the violent waves, each ship's construction tested as whitecaps crash over stems. Rain comes with equal vehemence, and soon, Augustine can make out neither the *Brezza* nor the *Durendal*. He can barely see beyond the prow of his own galley.

A hail of orders is bellowed from all directions: "Secure the rigging! Cover the powder! Lock the tiller leeward! Quick men! Bail! Bail! Bail!" Thunder tears across the sky with such ferocity the heavens will rip in two. Each rumble rolls through Augustine, pitting his stomach, shaking his frame. Hollered commands are no contest for the raging storm, almost all orders lost to eddying winds. Augustine is on his knees, using a waste bucket to bail water. For every one he empties, ten more are dumped onto the deck. Rain is relentless, rattling the planks, rattling the men. Wind lashes with the mercy of a whip. Water drains through the scuppers, only to rush back over the rails. The vessel rocks and pitches and sways, churning stomachs of even the hardiest. Beams creak and groan. The *Atardecer*'s spur veers round. The forceful rocking has most of the crew adding vomit to rising sea and rainwater. It is a cold, wet hell.

The stern lamp shatters. Only brief flashes of lightning provide illumination. Every hand free of chains bails frantically, filling buckets, cups, bowls, boots—anything that can hold water. Augustine hears Gabriel shouting orders, but cannot see him. The timbers are drenched, the planks slippery. He worries for his old friend, who would have trouble seeing had he *two* eyes. A second later, someone trips over Augustine's kneeling form and smashes hard against the starboard gunwale. He looks up, but in the blinding downpour, has no idea who fell.

Thunder rolls. Wind shrieks in his ears, invasive and rude. Concentrating on his task, he does not notice the pewter plate pitched into the air and sent spinning towards his head. The edge of the disc dashes his brow, cleanly slicing the thin layer of skin above his right eye, knocking him, still holding his bailing bucket, flat on his back, legs up in the air. His hand flies to his forehead. He presses the tips of his fingers against the open wound as blood seeps into his eye. Saltwater sprays his face, bringing a sharp sting. He gives his head a shake and keeps bailing.

Thunder rolls.

***

A tight road leads from the *Sacra Infermeria* through the village square, lined by the pale yellow glow of street lamps.

"Sleep at Belli's house," Domenicus says in a grownup voice, taking Isabel by the arm as Augustine would do if he were here. She does not protest—a sure indication she is not well. That she has not even mentioned his wound only lends further credence to his conviction. Katrina is also strangely quiet. Domenicus crouches before his sister. "Hop on," he says. "But don't choke me."

By the time they near the carpenter's lodging, the way is dark, dimly lit by candles in a few scattered windows. Catching familiar female voices, Domenicus looks to two such windows.

"...Farmer Bonnici and his wife Leonora, childless now," says the widow Carmelina Borg, a note of smug satisfaction in her tone. "And I know why." Domenicus slows his pace, tilts his head. Both women sit inside their own houses and converse through small casements paned with linen.

"The twins died in the famine," her neighbour ventures.

"That is the lie Bonnici tells!" Carmelina snaps. "Twins are not natural. They only come when a woman has lain with two men at the same time. Since God did not make the babies hoofed or horned, He punished Leonora by taking them..." Domenicus stops completely, intrigued by the widow's logic. Mama turns. Her features darken when she follows his gaze to the windows.

"Domenicus," she summons in a voice low and firm with displeasure. Her frown and narrow eyes startle him. She points to the ground before her, and he runs over. Mama crouches, looks directly into his eyes, speaks slow and plain. "A cruel story runs on wheels, and Carmelina Borg oils the wheels as they run. Do not make yourself a road to speed the lies along, dear one."

Domenicus looks at his feet. "I'm sorry."

"I know."

***

As suddenly as it struck, the storm that rocked the Mediterranean subsides. Massive waves become gentle swells lapping against the freeboard—the sea has thrown a tantrum and seeks pardon. Above, cables and yards flap loosely against the mizzenmast. The men are nauseated, some leaning over gunwales, retching intermittently. Fortunately, water in the bilge is only calf-deep. Augustine rises, a dripping, shivering mess of a man. He sloshes across the deck to the port rail.

"*Mire allí*! Look there!" he calls, pointing to the Italian flagship, bobbing lightly with the waves. From horizon to horizon, the *Durendal* is nowhere to be seen. As knights and sailors crowd the gunwales, Augustine whispers his own quiet prayer for the many souls aboard the missing French galley. He shields his eyes from the bright sun that now hangs between masts as he takes in the state of his ship.

"An easy day for deckhands," he remarks. "No shit to scrub. Certainly smells prettier."

Gabriel Mercadal, on his way up the slippery companionway, laughs wholeheartedly, placing his hand on the bannister to steady himself.

"Don't make me laugh! It hurts!" He giggles, approaching Augustine with a slight hobble. "You took a beating. What happened to your face?"

"Seems a plate thought I wasn't bailing fast enough." He runs the pads of his fingers over the slice above his eye. Gabriel lifts his tunic to reveal dark purple bruises.

"I too was punished. Knocked into the beam after getting tangled with some fellow."

Augustine's eyebrows arc at the revelation, but he does not declare himself *the* fellow.

"Don't look so concerned, man. My body has endured worse damage." Gabriel points to his empty eye socket and grins. "Shall I fetch Callus? He can sew you up proper."

Augustine chuckles. "Heavens no. As it is, the good doctor deems our company an overly coddled lot. I shudder to think what he'd say if I went to him with this little scratch."

From a small, portable altar, chaplains lead the ship's company in prayer. At its end, First Lieutenant de Laya brings a silver whistle to his lips and blows, signalling the oarsmen to action. In unison, two hundred and eighty slaves dip fifty-two heavy wooden oars. Sun catches in the water that pours from the blades, a hundred colours in each tiny drop. As the gap between the *Atardecer* and the *Brezza* closes with even strokes, the crew manages a breakfast of biscuits, the only provision not marinated in rain or seawater.

The two galleys align, manoeuvred by the skilful sweep of the *remi di scaloccio*. Augustine surveys the *Brezza* for damage but finds none. She appears unscathed: hull solid, mast strong, yards up, rigging tight. Her great sails are hoisted, hung out to dry. Neither does the crew look worse for wear, not a green face among them.

The Admiral of the fleet and captain of the *Brezza,* Alessandro Ardone, leans over the upper rail of his ship to address Gabriel. "Wonderful you Spaniards managed to stay afloat!" he hollers across the narrow strait sparkling between the warships. "Have we lost the *Durendal?*"

"No sign of her," Gabriel replies, tipped forward against the gunwale.

Ardone nods. "Mmm. We dock for repairs. Set a course for Porto Empedocle. There is an anchorage near the beach wall, not far. With some luck, we'll find the *Durendal* or her crew of French flotsam bobbing with the gulls." At the bosun's command, rowers heave the looms, sending the galleys to skiff over clear water. Bowsprits break the sea, making it splash and fizz and shimmer with the morning. Augustine pairs up with Tristan Galan, a young Aragonese, and together, they work expert fingers to refasten the lateen sail, carefully refitting spars with tackle.

Soon, the galleys round a bottleneck spit trending eastwards to the sea. There is a small sheltered port that teems with fishermen casting lines for cuttlefish, dipping pots for squid and octopus. The unbroken beat of the oars slows to a measured tempo. Sailors raise the rudders as the vessels near shoals. Seabirds wheel above the surface awaiting the right moment to plunge in with pincer-like beaks and seize an unsuspecting mackerel.

"Provisions!" Gabriel calls out to his crew, ticking off each item on a finger: "Fruit, vegetables, blankets, goats, chickens. Above all, as many water barrels as you can carry!" He leans towards First Lieutenant de Laya and lowers his voice, though Augustine overhears the captain's final request and smiles. "Fetch a cask of wine, will you? Two would be better."

The oar slaves remain chained to their benches. Each takes a turn to suck back long draughts of brackish water and replenish themselves with biscuits. Hands, buttocks, and thighs are raw with blisters, most of them burst, exposing tender pink flesh beneath, bleeding and leaking with pus.

Augustine takes a corked barrel from the bilge and crosses the gangplank. He is happy for a chance to stretch his sea-legs and have a look around Porto Empedocle, the southwestern Sicilian port serving as the gateway to the Greek-founded province Girgenti. A small village, Porto Empedocle is named for the Greek philosopher Empedocles, who flung himself into the volcanic mouth of Etna to prove his immortality.

Torrid African scirocco blows from the south, its heat oppressive. The blast of air is made visible by the wisps of dust looping and furling in spirals, like the ringlets of his wife's hair. A gust throws grit into his eyes, bringing tears, which quickly evaporate, leaving salty white streaks. Under his feet, the terra firma does not yield as readily as galley planks. His steps are rigid, stiff, as they take him along the hard, uneven ground leading up a gentle gradient. With each stride, he grows more comfortable, and before long, his legs carry him with ease.

Augustine passes through the town piazza, swarming with villagers and buzzing with a dozen dialects. He adjusts his hold on the empty barrel and starts up a hillside, dappled with daisies. Summer is in its infancy, giving expanses of sweetgrass time to thrive. As tall strands part to his stride, he thinks of his son and hopes Domenicus will one day caravan alongside the knights, so he too can visit places where grass carpets hills, not rocks carpeting more rock.

Soon, he makes the hilltop. Below is a lively shipyard, where brigantines and galleys lie careened, great timber whales. Hot air smells strong of chopped wood and resounds with the *thock* of the axes that chop it. Carpenters measure beams, trim frames, and saw planks as sailmakers stitch massive lengths of lateen into grand wings ready to catch the wind.

As Augustine descends to the brook, an appendage of the River Akragas, a remarkable sight captures his attention: the ancient ruins of the Punic Wars. The strewn, weather-beaten temples have the look of two thousand years, the air around them alive with spirits of a glorious past.

The riverbank is soft. A moment later, Augustine's heavy boots are off and set next to his barrel. The cool, damp earth is marvellously squishy beneath his bare feet. He rolls his trousers to his knees and wades into the stream for a drink. Every cold splash against his throat is a taste of heaven. Distant, muddled chatter fills his ears, but he is enjoying himself far too much to lift his head.

"*Oi! Laissez-en un peu pour nous!*—Ho there! Leave some for the rest of us."

He whips round. Etienne and Armand of the lost French galley approach heavily, each carrying barrels of their own. Augustine splashes clumsily onto the bank. The urge to ask twenty questions at once overwhelms him, leaving him capable only of a few nonsensical sounds.

"The *Durendal* is beached," Armand says, chuckling. "Sustained serious damage. The mast crushed a number of oarsmen, killing ten, wounding at least thirty."

"Perhaps," Etienne adds, "we'll swap our doctors with yours, to give ours a rest. We'll even take Callus if you promise to muzzle him."

At this, Augustine laughs, recalling the Maltese physician's sharp tongue. "So, what now?"

"The captains are deliberating a plan," Armand replies. "The Admiral wishes to depart this afternoon, but the shipwright doubts repairs will be ready in time."

Etienne issues a litany of curses. "Ardone, that flaming idiot! Damn to the briny depths whatever jolt-head put an Italian in charge." He stops for breath, squints at the brightness of the day. "Let's go. God knows our swag-bellied Admiral would just as easily leave without us."

Augustine uses his teeth to pull the cork from his barrel, and dips it into the sunlit brook, the Frenchmen doing the same. Drums full, the three start up the hill, Etienne treating his company to ever more creative insults aimed squarely at the Italian Admiral, and throwing in the man's mother for good measure.

CHAPTER SIX

Two weeks ago, his younger brother was buried in Mdina. And from the walled hilltop city, Father Anton Tabone's mule-drawn cart now struggles over a miserable, sloping road flanked by unkempt hedgerows and low stone walls.

Malta is small—seven leagues long, four wide. She is a rocky land, scarred with ruts and gullies, stippled with shrubbery and brambles. Soaring sea cliffs dominate the southern coast, coves and bays indent the northern shores. And in the middle of the island, standing in magnificence atop a flat summit is the citadel Mdina. Once Malta's capital city, Mdina is now home to the aristocracy, a lofty lot content to remain isolated high above the populace of peasants.

The priest looks over his shoulder. Great dust clouds rise from the path behind the cart. He glances at the reins resting loosely in his hands and then at his niece, who sits next to him. Anton's brother was the girl's father, killed the night the corsairs came, her mother abducted.

In all his years as a priest, Father Tabone has preached many homilies from his pulpit, yet unlike his colleagues, centres not on God's wrath, but His mercy, weaving proverbs of tolerance into the fabric of his sermons, earning more than a few raised eyebrows from his fellows. He is inclined to parables of the New Testament and loves to relate that of The Good Samaritan to parishioners. Anton is moved also by Mary Magdalene. So much so, he reminds his flock daily that only those without sin may cast the stones of condemnation—a message all but lost in Birgu.

For Father Tabone, mass does not end simply with telling the congregation to go in peace. He *is* the homily, lives the prayer. He shares what he can with those in need, and what he cannot, he shares anyway. A candle loses nothing by lighting another candle—it only makes the world a brighter place, he says. The priest consoles patients confined to bed, bringing the Word to those who cannot attend service. He comforts widows, visiting their homes with bread. A phalanx of dogs can often be seen trailing Father Tabone, for he is known to collect buckets of table waste left out by Mdina nobles and feed the scraps to strays. Should a fierce gale take a family's roof, he is there to help them rebuild. And on the first Friday of every month, he visits all the dungeons to hear confession. All dungeons save one, the one that exists beyond the village boundaries, the one he is not supposed to know about.

Anton was twenty-one when he entered St Sebastian's, a seminary built at the foot of Mount Tauro, the peak from which the ancient Sicilian city of Taormina takes her name. In his time there, he worked hard and lived simply. He entreated God to provide him with a parish where his presence would be needed, where he, as all good shepherds, could guard his sheep against hardship, or at the least, endure it alongside them.

In the days that followed his ordination, Father Tabone was sent to France where he worked as an assistant to the jovial French rector of St André's. Anton trained the altar boys, kept the books, milked the goats, and drank good wine. The duties were light and the town of Lourmarin sublime, hardly the challenge the young priest was looking for. Still, he was confident God would reveal His plan in due course, and so waited patiently, enjoying the perched pastoral village in the meantime. There, Anton Tabone lived in comfort surrounded by four compass points of natural beauty.

Then, he received word from Rome. He was to be assigned to the church of St Publius in his native Malta. Any other man would have baulked at the idea of leaving the exquisite French countryside for the destitute Maltese islands, but not Anton. France did not need him. He wanted to be in a place where he would matter, where he would meet challenges. In Malta, he would do both.

Father Tabone has never been at a loss for words. Yet now, he finds himself searching desperately for a way to console his niece. He rubs his thumbs and index fingers over the frayed leather reins. It is a jerky ride, wheels jarring as they slog over large stones, pitching the priest and his niece forward and back. He looks skyward. White brushstrokes of cloud pass across the endless blue as words across a page. *That's it.*

He gives his niece a careful smile. "All that you held dear was stolen from you. But I am going to give you something that no one will ever be able to take."

The girl looks up with vacant eyes.

"I'm going to teach you to read. It will bring you happiness. You can read of God's miracles, His humanity. You will learn of distant lands you could never otherwise see. Journey to the courtyards of France, caravan the sands of Egypt, sail the great water to the Americas. Every word is another gold ducat for the treasure of your mind. A treasure no one can steal from you."

For the briefest moment, her expression warms. "To read? Really?" Her astonishment soon gives way to a solemn request: "Uncle, will you teach me to write?"

"Of course," he replies. "I taught your mother to read and write, you know."

"Good. I will write her a letter every day, even if I have nowhere to send them."

***

In air so humid standing motionless draws sweat, Domenicus Montesa runs to the first of Birgu's three private pharmacies. An unusually slow day, few customers wait their turn—a blacksmith, his arm swaddled from wrist to shoulder with pus-stained bandages; the water seller's very expectant wife, fanning herself with her hand; the crone Carmelina Borg, eyes reproachful beneath her black *barnuża*. Domenicus wonders if she is here to buy a cure for meanness.

He takes a quiet seat on one of the two benches against the wall and picks at a newly formed scab on his knee until the crust tears and bleeds. The overpowering scent of medicinal herbs draws his gaze to shelves lined with ceramic jars, bone-white and painted indigo with symbols he does not understand. Decanters, jugs, and flasks, all imported from Sicily, sit alongside vases, spoons, and more flasks. A large decorative apothecary scale, burnished brass shining, rests on the counter.

Domenicus sighs, willing the pharmacist to take notice of him. It is an hour before Saverio Piccoli beckons. Domenicus rises onto the balls of his feet, grips the edge of the countertop.

"*Sur Mastru*, my mother needs medicine," he says. "She's very sick, worse every day."

The Sicilian apothecary raises an eyebrow, caterpillar thick. "Have you a prescription?"

"No."

"Has she seen a doctor?"

"Not really, no."

Saverio puffs out his lips and furrows his brow, shaking his head as though addressing a particularly stupid child. "So how do you know she is very sick?"

"She looks worse than half the patients taking up beds at the *Sacra Infermeria*."

The apothecary rests his elbow on the counter, and leans forward, placing his chin on his fist. "Since you are such an expert, you should know the rules. I produce the remedy when you produce the prescription. Now off with you. I have work to do." *Work to do?* This *is* work to do. Why does this ridiculous man not understand the importance of it all? Domenicus turns to leave, but the sight of the now empty shop is just too infuriating.

"There is nobody here! You *can* help."

Saverio ignores the entreaty, face creased with lines of pretended concentration. He twists the lid off a container. Sniffs. Twists it back on. He

35

carries on, playing with lids, sniffing at roots, until at last, Domenicus leaves, sandals clapping the slate floor.

Twenty minutes later, he stands at the counter of the second pharmacy in Birgu. Of the twenty minutes, most have been spent waiting for the apothecary to emerge from the supply room. When at last he returns to the counter, he scowls. "You're still here?"

"I'm not going anywhere until you help," Domenicus replies.

"Such big bluster from so small a boy. And one with no money."

"My mother is sick. We will pay you later."

"*Certo.* You are a child and have no understanding of the way things work. Go away and don't come back until you have money and a prescription."

"But—"

"*Esci di qui!* Go, before I take a broom to your backside!"

One apothecary shop remains, the farthest of the three from the Montesa house. A few paces beyond the Executioner's quarters, the small shop stands dwarfed next to the Palace of Conventual Chaplains. Sicilian-trained Antoni Zammit set up this pharmacy not long after the knights settled on the island. His is the only Maltese-owned and run in the village. Domenicus pushes open the door to reveal a space similar to the two he has just visited. Shelves, jars, crucibles, decanters, all a blur as he crosses the room, this time heedless of the villagers waiting on benches. Many raise their voices in protest, but he does not care. Behind the counter, the apothecary works his pestle to grind herbs.

Domenicus has had enough of being polite. "I need medicine. Now."

"To cure impertinence?" Antoni jokes, eyes on the powder in his mortar. Domenicus yanks the pestle from the pharmacist, setting off a current of shocked gasps that flows through the shop.

"No! My mother is sick. She needs medicine, *now.*" He checks himself and holds out the utensil, offering it back to Antoni in truce. "You must help."

"*Must* I?"

"*Please.* I mean *please* help."

"Have you a prescription?" Damn to the darkest pit of hell prescriptions and whoever invented them. Domenicus sighs miserably—all the answer Antoni Zammit needs. Yet, unlike the previous two apothecaries, Antoni is gentle in explaining his position.

"I'm sorry, lad, I can't sell you anything stronger than brewing-leaves. Your mother needs to be examined and diagnosed. A thousand illnesses can have the same symptoms. I would be arrested if I sold you anything that had an adverse effect. That kind of professional negligence would be considered murder if she were to die."

"She believes her life is in God's hands. And if she dies, I don't think God will be arrested for professional negligence."

"Unfortunately, I would not have the sway over a magistrate that God has," Antoni replies, not unkindly. "Why not bring the hospital to your mother? Call on the doctor. Where do you live?"

"We're staying with her cousin, Belli."

Antoni smiles at the name. "*Ta'mastrudaxxa*? The carpenter? He made my benches."

Domenicus is desperate not to leave empty-handed. "What sort of leaves do you have?"

"Camomile. It has beneficial properties, but none that will cure illness."

"I know. We tried camomile already. I made it myself."

Antoni nods. "I will send for the doctor."

CHAPTER SEVEN

Augustine bends over a bulwark, catching broken glimpses of his rippled reflection on the water's surface. A steady aft wind tousles his hair and fills the goose-winged lateen sails, a helping hand to exhausted oarsmen. Days sweep by with the same dull, steady rhythm of the oars. Porto Empedocle is several weeks and many leagues behind the armada, the galleys driven by the hard muscles of slaves along the heel of Italy's boot, over the Ionian, past Corfu and Prevesa, along Morea, hundreds of nautical miles eastward across the Aegean to the rocky coastline of Crete. Augustine turns to watch the oarsmen, their every gruelling movement executed with perfect synchronicity, making a scene both beautiful and horrible to behold. The sunburnt, blistered *schiavi* pull enormous looms, fifty-two wooden blades slicing the galley's way through the water.

As the sun melts into the sea, Tristan Galan, the young Aragonese on his third of three obligatory tours, stands next to Augustine and uses the upper rail as a buttress for his elbows. "Sail a thousand years and you will not catch that horizon," he muses aloud. "Imagine the world really was flat. What would it be like to spill over its rim and sail across the surface of the sun?"

"Terrifying and hot," Augustine replies.

"The sky fascinates me. You are learned. Do you know much about astronomy?"

"True knowledge is only realised when a man knows that he knows nothing."

Tristan grins. "Socrates?"

"None other."

"I do not want a dissertation," the knight says. "I wish to know, for example, what keeps the sky from catching fire? And who first discovered the earth was a great sphere and how?"

"Aristotle argued it was round. He witnessed a lunar eclipse and because of the circular shadow it cast on the moon, surmised the world must be an orb."

"I have seen Ptolemy's universe, the earth in the centre, sun circling on-axis around it."

"It is flawed," Augustine replies. "Aristarchus of Samos introduced the more plausible heliocentric theory of the earth and planets revolving around the sun."

"Did Ptolemy err also in making the earth bigger than the sun?" Tristan asks.

Augustine nods. "An Alexandrian librarian, Eratosthenes, made an estimate of the earth's size by studying the sun's reflection in a deep well on summer's solstice in the town of Syene. A Greek philosopher, Posidonius, made similar posits, using Canopus, the brightest star of Argo."

Riveted, Tristan smiles. "Tell me more."

"Let us pick up this discussion in a place where battle is not lying in wait."

"Alas," Tristan says, "so long as men draw breath, there will be a theatre of war."

"War and strife between opposites is the eternal condition of the universe."

"Democritus?"

"Heraclitus." Augustine and Tristan spend the night examining the heavy guns, securing them tight against their chocks.

Now, an hour before daybreak, a whistle trills, summoning the men to the foredeck. From his helm, Gabriel addresses the company.

"Men, brothers-in-arms, our spy network tells of an Ottoman trade ship en route from Cyrenaica. Dawn will bring her to the mouth of the Cretan harbour, where we will be waiting, as teeth inside that mouth." A hiss fills the air as Gabriel draws his sword. "The infidel will not rest until the Mediterranean is a Turkish lake. They forget the sea is *our* element!" He lowers his voice and grins. "However, should you happen to see St Peter guarding pearly gates, lower your sword and ask for some ale, for you are in paradise, where the breweries never close." A great cheer rises, one voice from over two hundred throats. Gabriel raises an open hand, palm forward. "Gentlemen, your last footsteps in this life walk you through heaven's door. Do not tread lightly."

Tristan leans towards Augustine. "A warrior poet."

"You should have heard him rally the boys in Rhodos."

"Astounding that our troubadour survived a bullet through the head. How did he manage?"

"Slept on straw in a crumbling tower for five weeks. There soaked enough of his blood into the stonework to make it a relation. By that time, the Turks had destroyed the bastion of Italy, and the fortresses of England and Aragon were but one stone standing upon another. We, the wall of Aragon, began to fail. Gabriel was back on his feet, directing our lines. There wasn't a knight or soldier or page that could look upon him, a hollow where his eye once was, and not be compelled to press on."

Two blasts from the bosun's whistle signal the oarsmen to a change in direction. Augustine places his hands on the gunwale as the craft follows the *Durendal* due south, away from the *Brezza*, the warship that will force the merchantman head-on into the two waiting galleys. Though not yet light, he can make out Candia's horseshoe harbour, guarded by the magnificent Venetian sea fortress, *Rocca al Mare*. Imposing ramparts stand strong in defence of the port. At the end of each spit stand lighthouses, beacons for tradesmen sailing to Crete, legendary birthplace of Zeus and refuge of Orion. Dominating the island is a mountainous spine rising high above the sea, piercing clouds. The rambling landscape, wooded with carobs and orange trees, slopes into black waters.

"Tell me, Montesa," Tristan begins above the din of final preparation, "Is it true about Gabriel Mercadal and his kegs?"

"Ask him. He is twice the poet when speaking of his beloved Spanish ale."

***

Too many days have passed since his father went away. Or perhaps, it only seems so because of the pressing need for his return. It is well past midnight, but Domenicus Montesa is wide awake. He tosses, he turns, and with every uncomfortable movement, straw pokes deeper into his back. He plots to steal a galley from the knights. Robert could help row. Domenicus considers swimming the distance. He is a strong swimmer. How far could his father possibly be?

He sighs heavily, miserable that every new idea is more ridiculous than the previous.

Mama has not left the house for days, not even to attend mass. What had been accepted as a chest cold, a moment of fatigue, has gradually immobilized her. Good on his word, the apothecary Antoni Zammit sent the doctor, but he came without notice while Domenicus and his sister were fetching brambles and Belli away at work. Mama was asleep and did not wake to the doctor's knock.

Domenicus is always tired, taking on the work his mother used to do on top of what was his to begin with. By the time first light blushes the sky, he has already made several trips to and from the communal cistern. Next, he heads to the marketplace where vegetable purveyors stand clustered in the shadow of the clock tower. After that, to the baker's, where he barters for day-old bread. He cleans out the chamber pots and sweats in the stable, hauling hay, clearing the donkey's stall of manure. After this, he fetches milk from Claudio Vella, a local goatherd.

Mama's expert eye is best for inspecting bedclothes for ticks, but somehow Domenicus manages—it just takes him twice as long. After checking on Isabel for the fourth or fifth time, he sews up any tears in his clothing, often bloodying small fingers in the process. Before the tower bell chimes noon, he makes up the hearth fire to boil water for dinner.

He is always tired but barely sleeps. Despite the demand of added chores and constant worry, there is one ritual that he will not skip no matter how weary he is, one that has become more sacrament than routine: every day, he treks to the dockyard, where he sits, awaiting the return of the galley bearing his father. The Order's warships come and go, but never the *Atardecer*.

His little sister works to keep both the carpenter's house and her own in order, sweeping grit from the floor, stuffing flat pallets with extra straw, shaking out blankets, pulling out weeds. She soaks soiled clothing in a trough of warm water, using wood ash and olive oil for soap. The laundry is scrubbed, pounded, rinsed, and left to dry in the sun. When the army of flies seems it will soon conquer, Katrina empties the household dung pit, dragging out buckets of fermented excreta to spread over the field behind Belli's house. She shoos goats from the tiny parcel and prepares the stew.

There is never enough water. To the cistern and back, she ventures, five and six times a day, carrying a heavy bucket on each arm. Should kindling for the hearth run scant, she treks a good distance southeast in search of brambles. This thorny brush seems the only plant able to thrive in the leas of uninhabited space. Because of the constant threat of corsairs coming ashore, Katrina carries one of Belli's daggers in a scabbard cinched around her waist. The endless gathering leaves her hands rough and bleeding. Domenicus wishes he could do everything and spare his sister the drudgery.

Now, he shakes off the slightly stale embrace of a thin blanket and paces the room. He pauses, held by his mother's face, her gaunt features severe in the dim glow of dying embers. The sight of her seizes him, overwhelms him. He needs to get out. After a moment, he crosses to the door and runs off, away from the house, away from it all. There is comfort in running, in creating distance between himself and his misery. He runs away from what he cannot control. The road is dark, deserted. His bare feet pound the cobbles of the narrow way, tiny rocks cutting his soles.

On a slope that overlooks the harbour, Domenicus finds a spot clear of thistle, where he sits knees to chest, listening to the stealthy noises of night: crickets chirping, waves battering the shore. Above, stars are pinholes in an endless curtain of darkness. The black sea is hardly discernible from the sky, the horizon invisible. There are two moons, one hanging above, one reflecting below. He turns his gaze to St Angelo, the castle's walls eerily beautiful with the glow of torchlight.

Dry thistles crunch under the weight of a heavy foot.

The boy's heart bucks, beats in his throat. Someone draws near. *A slaver?* His stomach drops as all heat abandons his body. Swallowing hard, he pulls his knees tighter to his chest. His heart pounds so loud, surely anyone nearby can hear it careening against his ribcage. Perhaps if he does not move, the savage might think him a heap of rocks.

A meaty hand comes down on his shoulder.

"I knew you'd be here, watching for your father."

Domenicus whips his head round. *Belli.* "I thought you were a corsair!"

"Good, you idiot. Dangerous here in the night. *Ejja*—Let's go." When Domenicus makes no movement, the carpenter sits on his heels. "You mustn't run off like this and worry your mother. You are the morning of her life." Belli rises, motioning with his head for Domenicus to follow. Brushing sand off the seat of his pants, he trails, racking his brain for a way to help Mama. He knows Belli is not an avid churchgoer. As a child, the carpenter went because his mother made him. As a man, he goes for the odd matching, hatching, or dispatching.

Domenicus decides to make a suggestion. "The apothecaries couldn't help. Why don't we buy a healing potion from the soothsayer Imperia? You have money."

Belli snorts. "That witch, *il-Bormia*? Yes, that we might burn at the stake *and* hang for witchcraft? They kill you twice for blasphemy! We are on the brink of Inquisition. Even priests are under the close watch of Bishop Cubelles, who vies to be named Inquisitor, yet you have the nerve to speak of soothsayers, they who try to play God."

"Physicians play God. They take fate out of His hands, place it in their own."

From the look on Belli's face, Domenicus can tell he narrowly avoided a smack across the head. "Don't be so stupid!" the carpenter growls. "God's healing powers work *through* physicians. Imperia is a *witch*. That bride of Satan stews kittens in snake blood. She eats puppy brains and lizard eyes."

Domenicus slumps under the weight of his failure. He does not understand. Imperia lives alone in a cave overlooking Malta's southernmost shore, where Domenicus and his father often go fishing. He has watched her tend sheep, never suspecting the woolly creatures might endure torment at her hand. For a kitten-stewing bride of Satan, Imperia seems to live a simple life. Still, Domenicus does not press the matter, turning instead to a subject Belli is always eager to discuss.

"Did you finish the table you were making for the knights? It looked nice. You never make mistakes. I don't think you do."

The woodworker grins. "*Qis mitt darba u aqta' darba*—Measure a hundred times that you only cut once," he says sagely. "The carpenter's adage. The table needs sanding. Almost done."

"You have skill in your hands. Mama too. I don't."

"Wait until your father teaches you the sword before you declare your hands unskilled."

To the east, a line of sapphire breaks the black, the ethereal symphony of night gradually replaced by the earthy cacophony of morning: crowing, braying, bleating. The sun comes swift, peering over the tops of buildings and spilling over their ledges. Domenicus and Belli walk the village byroads, which run crossways like tines of a crooked fork. As they round an elbow of stone that turns onto their street, Belli clears his throat. "Forget witches and apothecaries. I'll leave work early today, and take your mother to the women's hospital in Rabat."

"You know what?" Domenicus says, "One day, I'm going to build my own apothecary shop, and I'll be nice to anyone whose mother is sick."

They arrive on Belli's front step, and carefully, quietly, Domenicus opens the door, flooding the house with the morning. He crosses to his mother's pallet, sits at its edge. Belli marches across the room, unbuttoning his pants as he goes. Seconds later, urine hisses into the chamber pot, followed by a groan of relief. He makes a pillow of his shirt on the floor by the hearth and goes back to sleep.

Although her eyes are closed, Domenicus can tell Mama is awake. She puts her hand on his knee, gives it a weak squeeze. He takes her hand into his own and squeezes back.

CHAPTER EIGHT

The sun seeps gold along the horizon. At the helm of the *Brezza*, Admiral Alessandro Ardone makes a visor of his hand. He grins. A lone merchant ship marked Turkish by her banners navigates the open sea-lanes. According to the Christian spy network, she is en route to Istanbul following an exchange of goods with Benghazi traders. This ship is a fine jewel to add to the Order's treasury. She hugs the northern coast of Crete. The briny highways of commerce are established close to the shores, offering shelter in times of flash squalls and fresh water in times of empty barrels. Propelled by grand square sails, the merchantman veers south for the port of Candia, a city founded by ninth century Saracens, wrested from them by tenth century Byzantines, and procured by thirteenth-century Venetians as part of a prickly political deal involving knights of the Fourth Crusade.

At Ardone's command, the men of the *Brezza* are on their knees. From an elevated platform above the bow, two chaplains lead the crew in prayer, and with the sign of the cross, give absolution to all for the forthcoming slaughter.

"Make ready the guns!" Ardone calls, rising to his feet at the bow. "Lively now! Quick is the word, sharp the action! Hold fire and tongue until the merchantman is in range." It is ritual, this demand for silence. When the Italian admiral obtains the quiet he craves, he smiles to himself, savouring this moment of calm before the bloody storm. He takes in the curved line of the guns, the arquebus shafts gleaming with the morning, and his heart bucks with delight.

The *Brezza* is combat-ready, armed with a twelve-pound centre-line cannon that fires a heavy stone ball, two demi-culverins, several swivel guns, and more than two hundred battle-starved knights, craving the fiery taste of warfare. It is an ancient game played on a watery board, where the speed and turn of a ship are enough to make pawns of kings.

Orders pass through the ranks of soldiers and snap against the backs of oar slaves. The leathern pulse of the bosun's drum beats with a measured, even tempo. To this dull rhythm, slaves heave heavy oars, sweeping the vessel over the water like a falcon swooping in for her prey. The bosun stills his wooden hammers. Wings outspread, the *Brezza* glides on silence.

***

Across the water, Ottoman captain Avranos al Halil strides the cramped deck of his merchant ship and sets his hands on the rail. He is no stranger to sea combat, having fought as a gunner under Barbarossa against Admiral Andrea Doria and his Christian fleet in the battle of Prevesa. The defeat was a humiliating one for Christendom, as the Holy League surrendered with scarce a fight. Prevesa would be al Halil's last battle fought as a soldier, for after this Muslim victory, he retired from warships and took the helm of an imperial trade ship.

He stares across the water at a distant speck and sniffs, his senses keener than those of any hired lookout. By the grace of Allah, a strong westerly wind blows, and he catches the unmistakable whiff of a slave driven galley, the hard odour alerting him to danger. He squints. The threat is real. But who is she, this approaching craft? A thief of Christ, come to snaffle al Halil's goods? A murderous insurgent, with a mind for pillaging? Or a friend, allied in the name of the Prophet?

The solitary galley sweeps into full view, her red and white standards confirming the captain's fears that she is indeed a militant Christian vessel, one belonging to the Order of the Knights of St John, the most severe enemy of Islam.

"May the devil devour them." Al Halil brings a silver whistle to his mouth. Two trills, sharp and long. "The prize of the Sovereign Lord Sultan will not be taken plunder! Man the guns! Sharpshooters aloft!" The merchantman is not a warship. She is vulnerable. Still, al Halil is unwilling to excite the wrath of Suleiman the Magnificent. While rewards for pleasing the Padishah are plenty, punishment for failing him could see the captain's head hung from the gate of the *saray*.

Al Halil orders all expendable load jettisoned. Immediately, several slaves stowed in the rear hold are brought up to the deck and thrown into the sea as if the bones of dead fish. Those tossed overboard are Greek, Egyptian, and Dalmatian. All of them are adults, for they are not only heavier than child captives, but they are also worth far less. The few who can swim, paddle for shore. Those who cannot, panic and drown. The round ship, now fifty-six bodies lighter, is able to redouble her speed, though she is not a swift mover by construction. She is no match for a Maltese-built galley.

***

In the murkiness of the carpenter's home, Domenicus works the blade of a large carving knife through a potato, slicing it in two. He places each end on Mama's sweat dappled forehead to draw out the fever. Next, he dips a cloth in a basin of diluted vinegar, stinging fingers nicked earlier by brambles. Domenicus passes the damp cloth across his mother's colourless cheeks, draping it over the potato halves to keep them in place. Belli should be home soon; he promised to bring Mama to the hospital in Rabat. The village physician is also supposed to visit. With any luck, Isabel will receive attention from several doctors today.

As Domenicus awaits an arrival, he watches his mother's chest rise and fall. Having exhausted all earthly options, he kneels at her bedside, bows his head, and gives himself over to the divine, praying with all his might, praying God's will be done, so long as God's will agrees with his own.

✳✳✳

Augustine tightens his helmet and scrambles to the swivel gun, where Tristan greets him with a cocky smile. "Let's see about sending these barbarian bastards to sail across the surface of the sun."

Grunting with amusement, Augustine pours gunpowder from a ladle into the swivel's chamber, using experience as his measuring cup. With a moment to spare, he surveys the *Atardecer*'s living deck. The knights wear heavy surcoats emblazoned with the white cross of the Order, some donning backplates and cuirasses for extra protection against musket balls. The crew is in position, two men operating the centre-line gun, four the half-cannons and several, including Augustine and Tristan, the swivels. The others are positioned on the *arrumbada,* a perched platform above the prow, twelve-pound arquebuses braced against their chests. The gunwales teem with arbalesters and crossbowmen. Pikes, halberds, and swords, the silvery utensils of war, flash with the sunlight. Excess cordage and cables are neatly spooled, clear of the decks. The men of rank are scattered: Captain Gabriel Mercadal at his helm, whispering final orders to soldiers nearest to him, First Lieutenant Pietro de Laya amidships, echoing commands. An overseer walks the corsia, checking the position of his silent, sweating oarsmen, his whip a keen reminder to slaves to keep their feet off the chain rest. In this forced, anxious quiet, the rattle of irons is amplified tenfold.

The *Atardecer* is restless. From his position within the harbour, Augustine watches the *Brezza* stalk her quarry, closing in as the fat merchantman rounds the spit.

With a sudden and resounding boom, the *Brezza* fires.

✳✳✳

The iron ball crashes through the Ottoman ship's foremast. Yards securing her sails snap, cutting violently through the air. Instinctively, Avranos al Halil raises his forearm to protect his face from the cable. It sinks like teeth into the flesh spanning from wrist to elbow, his shouts lost to the bedlam unleashed around him. A volley of naphtha incendiary arrows ignites the mainsail.

"Douse the flames!" al Halil cries. "Steady now. Return fire!"

✳✳✳

Two Egyptian slaves tossed from the trade ship swim into the Cretan harbour, where a pair of galleys wait, red and white pennons a fluttering announcement of the crew's faith.

"Christians!" Dakarai cries, sputtering water. "They will take us!"

"And chain us to their oar," Jumoke huffs, paddling madly.

"Just swim, stupid! The enemy of our enemy is our friend." Dakarai kicks long, slender legs, propelling himself through the liquid battlefield. The exertion makes iron weights of his limbs. He swallows saltwater, stinging his nasal passage, burning his throat. He fights against the breakers, against injuries and an empty stomach. All around plays a deadly symphony: guns booming, rattling against their chocks, men crying out in a dozen tongues. Smoke billows out in a dirty orange plume that blocks the sun and throws shadows in his eyes. Under the force of cannonballs and scrap metal, the sea erupts in a saltwater explosion. Dakarai glances over his shoulder to make sure his friend has not gone under. Jumoke is a strong man, but weak swimmer. He coughs and dips. He comes up, heaving and swearing.

"Please God," he begs. "Please God."

"God wants you to swim faster!" Dakarai yells, catching Jumoke's wrist and tugging him along. A piece of broken plank spirals towards them, hitting the water with a splash, bobbing on its surface. Jumoke retches and wheezes, his body slipping under. He surfaces once more, gurgling prayers to Allah and Amon-Ra—with some luck, at least one deity might be listening.

As Jumoke prays for a miracle, Dakarai swims to one. The plank is large, but not enough to support them both. He grabs it and paddles back to his friend, pushing it at him. "Take it."

Jumoke accepts the board gratefully. It offers some buoyancy, but when he unloads his entire mass upon it, it sinks towards darkness.

"By the Prophet," Dakarai barks, tasting gunpowder. "Kick man! Kick!" The Christian galley looms, arrows from her deck hissing overhead. He sets his teeth, determined not to let exhaustion take him, not when he is this close.

***

Two warships converge on the merchantman: the *Brezza* blocks the stern, preventing escape from the rear, while the *Durendal* locks bow to bow, keeping her from moving forward. On the deck of the *Atardecer*, Augustine primes his cast-bronze verso. Tristan aims the swivel at the men of the merchant ship, sighting his targets between up-thrust thumbs.

"*Punto de blanco!*" he shouts, firing. Deposits of hardened powder inside the gun cause the iron ball to rebound from one side of the barrel to the other, leaving the muzzle at a slight angle from the centreline of the bore. The ball spins from the drag against the barrel walls and hurtles through the Muslim deck, the impact catapulting several robed men into the sea. Augustine works fast to scrape the crusted powder from the smoking bore before reloading. An

48

eddy wind brings dark, sulphur-laced plumes. He and Tristan cough and heave, gasping for clean air. None comes.

"We take her a prize!" Gabriel calls out from the foredeck. "Poseidon's floor needs no new furnishings!" Shots roar from the centre-line gun, the demi-culverins bellowing next.

"Oars, now!" Gabriel Mercadal hollers. "Starboard! Port! Pull! Pull like you're pulling an Italian off your sister!" The *Atardecer* lurches, wings beating double time, moving her into swift alignment with the Turkish ship. The bosun's tambour beats with the vigorous rhythm of combat, the oarsmen propelling the galley in harmony with this battle hymn.

"On the up-roll, *fire!*" Gabriel hollers. "Cripple her! Take her rudder! Hold for boarding!"

***

Domenicus slouches on a stool, watching Mama shift in restless sleep. The drawn curtains block out the afternoon light, making Belli's residence more mausoleum than home these days. The air is stagnant and heavy, weighing Domenicus down with its stifling heat. Exhausted, he is near hypnotised by his mother's breaths. A loud knock withdraws him from his trance. He greets the Sicilian physician as politely as urgency will allow.

"Smells like a galley bilge," the doctor says, wrinkling his nose. He wears the long white robe of his profession with pride and has markedly clean hands.

"She's sleeping," Domenicus replies in a low voice.

"Good. Nothing more irritating than a patient telling the doctor what the problem is."

"But don't patients know better what they're feeling if they're feeling it?"

"Nonsense. If all patients were doctors they wouldn't need me, would they?" He crosses the room, sets his black bag atop the bedside table, and bends over Isabel. "Who made the compress?"

"I did," Domenicus says cautiously.

The doctor glances over his shoulder, eyebrow arched with interest. "Why?"

"Because potatoes draw out sickness."

"So. It is not just patients who think they are doctors, but their relatives as well?"

Domenicus feels panic set in, worried he has done harm. "Should I take it off?"

"Let medicine to medical men," the medical man replies curtly, though he leaves the compress on Mama's forehead. The entire examination takes but a few seconds—cursory glances at her face and chest, a quick bend to listen to her breath. He produces a page from his satchel and scribbles something.

Domenicus cranes his neck to make out what is written but finds the words illegible—not that he can read well anyway.

"Move," the physician grumbles. "Your mother will be fine. A fever, brought by fatigue."

"Are you sure? Belli was going to take her to the women's hospital in Rabat today."

"Not necessary." The doctor drops the prescription into the boy's hands. "Have the carpenter take this to an apothecary."

"What's it for?" Domenicus asks.

The doctor sighs forcefully. "Vervain." He collects his things and turns to leave.

Domenicus races to the door and presses his back against it. "What will vervain do?"

"Good heavens, child! You try a man's patience. Get out of my way."

"Please, tell me, so we'll know if it's working."

"It will quiet her inconvenient fever. Unfortunately, not her inconvenient son."

***

From the *Atardecer*, Augustine looks across the water to the *Brezza*'s fighting stage, where Florentine knight Marcello di Ruggieri gives a ritual kiss to the white feathers of his arrow.

A volley, silent and deadly, soars through the great billows of smoke. A testament to di Ruggieri's skill, the first arrowhead notches a third eye in an Ottoman brow. Blood spreads like a smile over his temple.

***

"Grapeshot!" bellows al Halil. Two iron balls, connected together by chain, crash through the Ottoman bowsprit. Heavy guns bring flashes of light to the dark folds of settling haze, a boom accompanying each blast. At his helm, al Halil ducks, narrowly avoiding a torrent of metal debris. Bloodied and bruised, he uses his sash to bandage his forearm, deeply lacerated by the broken yard.

The few remaining sharpshooters prime their muskets and fire at the *Atardecer*'s moving targets, felling and wounding half a dozen knights. Despite the small victory, al Halil's decks are a mess of lifeless men, prow to stern, starboard to larboard. Smoke burns his throat, violent coughs shaking his form. His ship is lost, most of the crew too dead to care or too injured to do anything about it. Al Halil picks up a slain officer's musket and fires it hatefully at the Christian galley.

***

First Lieutenant Pietro de Laya never saw it coming. The musket ball breaks his flesh and sends him reeling to the deck. For a moment, the knight, just lately twenty-two, thinks himself dead.

50

Suddenly, the pain registers. Sweet, blinding pain. Dead men do not feel pain. The ball tore open his shoulder, rupturing his muscle, but damaging nothing vital. He howls in agony and relief.

***

The water echoes with the scream of fracturing timber. Augustine looks out from behind his swivel gun just as the *Durendal*'s iron-tipped beak slams into the trade ship, starboard bow. French knights use the grappling spur as a bridge and stream aboard the Turkish vessel, cutting down outnumbered sailors with swift strokes. From the *Atardecer*, Augustine and Tristan provide cover as these frenzied champions of Christ cut vicious arcs with Bilbaon blades. The air is misted red; Augustine tastes it, sickly sweet.

In this banquet of slaughter, knights feed on each other's manic will. Etienne Charroux spears a Moor, lifting him off his feet. Panic spreads through Muslim ranks, poisoning their lines. The Ottoman captain, however, stands fast on his deck, aiming and firing his musket until the furious stroke of a halberd knocks it clean from his hands. He manages to escape the blow with both hands still attached to his wrists, which Auvergnese knight Armand Debonnoel quickly binds together.

Within fifteen minutes, the rout is complete. The merchantman's deck is strewn with bodies, her planks slick with entrails. By the points of swords, knights subdue all survivors. The victors free all Christian captives, who cheer wildly for their liberators. Apostates, men who renounced their faith and adopted Islam to secure a more favourable position upon landing in Istanbul, are identified and immediately hanged from the rails, their bodies left dangling just above the water.

Augustine can't help but admire the spirit al Halil exhibits as he is marched over the spur and onto the *Durendal*. He speaks French, so his captor will be sure to understand. "To a barren scalp inhabited by an Order of lice," the former captain scoffs. He spits at the boots of Armand, the knight who leads him. "Suleiman would have done better at Rhodos had he rid the world of your banner."

"Shut your mouth," the Auvergnese growls, "Or I'll rid the world of you."

"Feed me your swill, swine of Christ. I will be in paradise that very moment, enjoying an eternal afternoon in the arms of a beautiful *houri*."

"Until then, you may take rest in the arms of your ugly compatriots." Armand drives his forearm into al Halil's back, jostling him forward as the rest of the Order's new acquisitions are chained to a prison without bars: the oar bench. Now that the trade ship is free of human cargo, she is relieved of her inanimate goods. The *Brezza*'s grapnels fly over the merchantman's upper rail and the Italian crew files aboard. Admiral Ardone grins broadly as crate after crate of bullion and silk and gems are heaved up from the bowels and carted onto the Italian flagship.

"A donation to the Treasury of St John from the Sultan's own Hazine!" he calls out merrily.

Augustine catches Ardone's boisterous laughter and al Halil's ensuing disgust: "As the goat that cannot govern his appetite and will perish from excess grain, so this relentless infidel grows fat on the goods of Istanbul and will perish in kind. May his belly explode." He spits again, earning himself a strike to the back of the head, courtesy of Armand.

"Now," Ardone booms, addressing all in his fleet. "A few good lads to sluice the planks!"

Aboard the *Atardecer*, Gabriel Mercadal approaches with some orders of his own, the first to secure the disabled merchantman for towing to Malta. He dispatches ten sailors to replenish the water casks and other provisions. As his commands are carried out, he pulls Tristan aside.

"A keg of beer. Be stealthy now." Tristan glances at Augustine from the corner of his eye. Augustine chuckles to himself as he wipes sweaty grit from his brow, rests against a bulwark. The bright sun has him drop his gaze to the sea. He squints, leans over the gunwale. Below, sharing a piece of timber, two young men struggle to stay afloat. Augustine finds a spool of rope and runs to the starboard rail, tossing down the line and shouting to them. They swim for the rope as it dangles just above the swells. One man passes its end to the other, the heavier of the two taking the line. Augustine hauls, digging his heels, gritting his teeth. The swimmer's toes grope the slippery ribs of the galley as he climbs up its side. He flops over the gunwale and kisses the planks. Augustine readjusts his hold, wrapping the rope several times around his hand, cutting off circulation to his fingers, turning them purple. His every muscle contracts as he pulls up the second swimmer, who has managed a foothold, hands scrabbling for purchase.

The timber is no doubt very slick, the swimmer equally exhausted. With a cry, he falls back into foamy water. He resurfaces and again grasps the line. His rescued companion meets Augustine's eyes, as though seeking permission to help. Augustine is more than happy to share the load. The bigger man coils the rope around his hands and heaves, as Augustine reaches far over the rail, catching the second swimmer by the wrist, hauling him over the gunwales by his britches.

He collapses on the deck, seawater puddling around him.

CHAPTER NINE

The air is heavy, the sky low. Hot airstreams sweep the scent of salt off a tired sea, but rather than bring relief, the lazy wind carries only more heat, like billows from a kiln. After an arduous morning, Domenicus slumps next to Robert on a large rock overlooking the dockyard. Without a tree to provide shade, the air itself seems to be sweating. Above, the sky is dull grey, the sun so strong it has faded a typically perfect blue easel into a colourless backdrop.

Domenicus passes his hand across his forehead. "Shouldn't you be working?"

"Ah," Robert grumbles. "It doesn't matter."

"But Farrugia pays you *money*. If he gets rid of you, you won't eat."

"*Il-lallu*, you're worse than my mother." Robert nudges Domenicus. "Here, I have an idea. You go work the field for that rat bastard. I'll do your chores and watch for your father."

Domenicus sighs, not in the mood for jokes. "Yesterday, Belli took my mother to the women's hospital in Rabat. The doctors there said the same thing the Sicilian said—she has a fever, brought by fatigue. Give her vervain, and she'll be fine. I don't believe a word of it."

Robert looks at his feet. He is silent for a moment. "Where's Kat?"

"Still outside the *Sacra Infermeria*, probably. We went to find a doctor to help Mama."

"And?"

"They wouldn't let us in," Domenicus replies. "The guard sent us away. Katrina said she'd stay until she could make someone listen."

Robert frowns. "But you both do work there. "

"Not for weeks now."

"They always gave you trouble at the gates?"

"Never."

"Kat should throw a rock at the guard's stupid head and take his key."

Domenicus makes a face at the remark, remembering his sister's unfortunately precise aim. He runs his fingers along the raised scar beneath his eye. "Take a beating more likely."

"Should I go wait with her?"

"No. You'll take double the beating." Domenicus looks with despondence at the empty horizon. "Robert, if I had a galley, would you help me row the oars until I found Pa?"

"I'd row them all, so you'd be free to take the helm."

"I believe you." Domenicus turns back to the sea, willing it to speed his father home. Colourful little fishing boats bob on choppy waters, carefully balanced anglers dipping nets, casting lines. He counts the boats. *Seventeen*. He counts the fishermen. *Eighteen*. Eight with rods, ten with nets. Of the eight casting lines, six stand. In the craft closest to shore, a father and son heave a net up onto their wobbly *dghajsa*. Domenicus knows the duo, local fishmonger Mario Briffa and his young son Henri. Sunlight catches in the water that drips from the ropes, making the fat droplets shine as glass beads slipping from a broken necklace. Another slow, stifling minute passes.

Today, like every other day, there will be no arrival of the glorious caravan galleys.

Today, like every other day, Domenicus sighs with resignation before going home.

***

Belli returns from his latest carpentry commission to find Isabel withered beneath a thin blanket, the sound of her laboured breath catching in the air. Domenicus rests on the edge of her bed, taking care not to disturb the pallet. His young face is etched with worry beyond his years.

"The vervain isn't working."

Isabel stirs, revealing creases imprinted in her cheeks by straw. She seems to have aged ten winters in as many hours. The sight is too much for Belli. He lifts his cousin carefully, carries her outside, glancing over his shoulder.

"Boy, fetch Peppone."

Domenicus does as he's told, emerging from the stable minutes later with the donkey harnessed, a thick blanket thrown over its back. Belli rests Isabel carefully on her abdomen. He sees the pain in her face and feels terrible, but she is too weak to sit up and support herself. He crouches before Domenicus, squeezes his shoulder.

"Come to the *Sacra Infermeria* tomorrow. Eleven bells."

At the hospital gallery, a lone guard halts Belli with an open hand. Narrow-eyed, the young man lifts his lamp, peering through the darkness at Isabel.

"You know this hospital is for men," he says curtly.

54

"Mercy. She is the wife of Augustine Montesa, a soldier right now serving on campaign."

"I am sorry," the guard replies in a voice not the least contrite.

Belli sighs. Then, with a great bellow of rage, he shoves the guard aside and kicks the door.

"S-Signore!" the youth stammers, recovering balance but not composure. "Do that again, I'll have you arrested. You will be whipped! Hanged!"

Belli kicks again, harder, and again, roaring. The guard draws his sword. "Stop! Stop, I say!" He squeezes the hilt but stays put. Belli strides defiantly towards him, despite being unarmed. The guard raises his weapon. At that moment, the loggia door opens and out comes a hospital *prud'homme*, a comptroller in charge of infirmary provisions.

"*Assez*! Explain this racket."

"An emergency," Belli says. "This woman needs immediate care."

"Woman? Surely you know this hospital is for—"

"*She is going to die.*" The *prud'homme* glances to the guard who shakes his head adamantly, then to Isabel, draped over the donkey.

"I will fetch the Grand Hospitaller." He turns on his heel, leaving Belli to wait impatiently. The guard stands in silence, visibly unnerved by the carpenter's hostile presence. For Belli's part, distress has replaced anger. If Isabel does not recover, Augustine will never forgive him.

He will never forgive himself.

The door whines on its hinges. Grand Hospitaller Bertrand le Grant emerges, toilet bucket in one hand, a lamp held by the other. He lifts the light to get a proper look at Isabel's face. "The laundress... she was here with—"

"A bed and physician," Belli interrupts. He knows he's already in big trouble and sees no point in faking good manners now. Le Grant gives him a rapid look-over.

"Leave the donkey with the guard. Bring the woman." The Hospitaller takes them through the covered passage and the gate beyond, which opens into the *cortile grande*. The grounds are eerily still, save the four or five crows perched at the reservoir, beaks rippling circles in black water. The hospital itself is as dark as its court, dim candlelight blinking between drapes. Belli feels his cousin fading in his arms as he struggles to walk steadily over dewy grass. Le Grant holds the refectory door open, after which he leads the way to a small, empty room, scented sharp with vinegar and lemon, washed in the faint glow of low-burning wall lanterns. Belli places Isabel on a cot next to a window.

"I'll fetch a surgeon," le Grant says, adding, "You are not excused for your violence against the guard. There will be consequences." The Hospitaller disappears into the corridor. Unperturbed by the reprimand, Belli crouches at Isabel's bedside. Her eyes are slits, chest rising and falling in erratic patterns.

She coughs dark phlegm ribboned with blood. Belli wipes her mouth with his hand.

Heavy footfalls sound from the hallway. A surgeon swoops into the room carrying a urine flask and a black leather bag of medical implements. As he places his hand on Isabel's forehead, he introduces himself as Fra Édouard de Gabriac. He presses his lips into a tight line and examines her gaunt, sallow face, her features severe, skin wan, in the unsteady light. He lifts her hand, his fingers working her wrist for a pulse.

"Has she been bled?"

"She has not," Belli replies. De Gabriac presses down on her abdomen with his palm. He spreads Isabel's knees and places the flask between her legs. The container soon fogs. He tilts it to a flame, dips his finger into the urine, touches it to his tongue.

"As I suspected," the surgeon announces. "The liver." He looks at Belli. "The liver produces the blood that feeds the brain. Her basilic vein should have been bled. Too late for that now."

Belli struggles to make sense of this information. "A sick liver would make her cough so?"

"Coughing is the body's way of trying to expel illness." De Gabriac dips a cloth into a basin of water, wrings it, and places it across her brow. "A compress to temper her fever."

"A wet cloth?" Belli asks, furrowing his brow at the absurdity of it all.

"Contrary to what most physicians will say, bleeding a patient is not the only way to moderate fever. Dr Callus recommends potato halves if one can spare a potato. Now, to operate."

Belli draws back. *Cutting her open?*

The surgeon frowns. "Your trust in me is not whole. You think me just some little cutter?"

"Of course not. But..." Belli's voice falters as he catches the glint of the silver scalpel "...it seems heathen. I do not know if her husband would consent."

"Then know that he would not consent to her dying." Édouard de Gabriac sets the rest of his instruments—a lancet, some needles, suturing thread, forceps, and probes—next to the scalpel, gleaming blue in a narrow shaft of moonlight. "Allow me to reassure you. I have studied with the most prominent doctors of the day—Johannes Quinterus of Andernach and Jacobus Sylvius at Montpellier. If she can be saved by human hands, I am as qualified to do it as anyone." He fills a silver bowl with a sedative solution of mandrake and belladonna, drops in a small sponge.

"This requires a few minutes to saturate," de Gabriac says. "I'll bring the operating table. Then, you must leave—you shouldn't be here as it is. There is a chapel, upstairs." With that, the surgeon is gone, swallowed by the dark hallway.

Belli takes Isabel's hand and presses it to his face. "Augustine will return soon. You are his life. Wait for him." The corridor echoes with a drawn-out screech. De Gabriac appears, pushing a long table that squeals horribly over the tiles. He drops his blade into another bowl, this one filled with brine. He puts his hand on Belli's shoulder as if to say, time to go. So it is on Édouard de Gabriac that he must now put his trust. The rest he will leave to God.

The surgeon tilts Isabel's chin and presses the narcotic sponge over her mouth.

She breathes in the solution.

EIGHT POINTED CROSS

CHAPTER TEN

A purple dusk turns the sea to a lavender field, the sky a meadow blossoming with faint white stars. Even the winds seem mauve. A smile blooms on Augustine's face. He wishes to swim in the glorious colours of twilight.

Music and mirth spill from the deck of the Italian flagship and sweep across open water to Augustine's galley. From the *Atardecer*'s gunwales, he spots Marcello di Ruggieri sitting atop a spool of rope on the *Brezza*'s poop deck, a lute in his hands, the lovely song floating over the waves evidence the young Italian applies the same deft touch to every instrument of string—whether strumming a lute or releasing a bow.

Above, red and white pennons flutter and flap against the flagstaff, the ensigns of the Order caught in the same air currents filling the *Atardecer*'s goose-winged sails. Timbers creak and groan under the weight of the men and the spoils. Oars thrum the vessel's passage as the giant bird's wooden wings beat, water trickling from their tips back to the sea. Then, the wings beat again. Towing the empty trade ship presents a gruelling task for the already severely taxed rowers, and the *Atardecer* falls behind because of the extra burden. Slaves issue streams of profanity in a dozen languages.

Augustine leans against the starboard rail, rubbing rough hands together. As cool fingers of wind tousle his hair, he thinks of his wife and children and contemplates his heart's eternal conflict—his love for his family at odds with his passion for the sea. But an eternal conflict cannot be resolved in one night. So, he breathes salty air and joins Gabriel at the bow.

"Beautiful, the shades of evening," the old Spaniard muses.

"Spectacular, the *via lactea*. I hate to darken its purity with words." He takes a pull from his flask. "This is why I will not retire."

Augustine follows Gabriel's gaze to the stars. "I understand. Who would want to give up such treasure? A copper sea as the golden sun sets upon it, a pearl moon broken by silver cloud."

"You do love the little things."

"There is nothing bigger than the little things."

The knight smiles. "Still, have you no desires? Are you to go down in history as the first man to be content with what he has?"

Augustine considers the question. "There is one thing. To sail under Mathurin Romegas. Forgive my vanities, but what pride to tell my son I've sailed with the finest captain the Order has ever known—" he catches himself "—*Two* of the finest."

Gabriel snorts. "A brilliant seaman... despite his being an infant and a Frenchman." The rivalries among different *langues* are usually light in nature; however, passions occasionally flare, none so incendiary as those of the Spanish and the French. Practice jousts fought in the bailey echo the louder clang of steel heard on the seas and fields of Europe, for even as Gabriel jokes, Spain and France are at war.

The old knight holds out a cup. "Some ale?"

"Naturally. That's why I make these caravans. Malta is dry of beer as it is rain."

"Because the only breweries that matter are in Spain." A moment of comfortable silence passes between the two men as they drain their mugs. The *Brezza* and the *Durendal* sweep ahead, gliding over the sea like silk over glass, two great moving shadows against the indigo sky.

"You'll soon see your boy," Gabriel says. "That pleases you. He is well-spoken."

Augustine nods. "A curious mind. He wants to know everything about the knights, their history, their politics. The night Birgu was last raided I was recounting the siege of Rhodos to my children. It's my girl's favourite. My son reveres the knights, but so gentle is his spirit, he prefers the story of my first encounter with his mother—as does Isabel herself. She thinks Rhodos too bloody for young ears. But I say we live in bloody times."

"How did you meet your wife, Augustine? Entertain a crusty old Spaniard. I, too, could use a lull from bloodshed."

"There is not much to it really. I needed help turning over a small earthy patch around my house." Augustine shrugs. "Isabel helped."

Gabriel frowns. "Hmm. No surprise your daughter prefers the siege of Rhodos."

"Well, no. I tell the story differently. Didn't think you cared for romance."

"Tell it properly. Tell it as you tell your children."

Augustine flashes a grin, grateful for the indulgence. He makes himself as comfortable as the cramped deck will allow, sitting with his back to the centre line cannon, knees drawn to his chest.

"To begin, I describe my dismay the morning of 26 October 1530, when our galleys moored on Malta. Our new home was a bleak, white rock—leagues from the Eden that was Rhodos. The island people swarmed the docks, curious, if wary, at our arrival. The men, bronzed by the sun, had faces neither cruel nor welcoming. I did not see women until I wandered deeper in and met a few, hidden behind black veils. I walked the entire village inside fifteen minutes. Where was I going to live? In a barn? A cave? But my path led to an empty house, which stood, or slumped rather, before a tiny plot. I wondered what I could coax from the earth—jasmine, some roses perhaps.

"As I chewed it over, a small grey donkey bumped me from behind. A man strode angrily over to claim the animal. *Peppone, do not disturb the newcomers*, he said. *They are a fearsome lot and would skin you as soon as look at you.* I laughed and assured him the only thing I knew how to skin was a rabbit. He went by Bellizzi. Some call him *ta'mastrudaxxa*. Others, just Belli. Maltese love nicknames. Here, my daughter cuts in. *Is that why Robert calls me* Qattusa?

No, I tell her, *he calls you* Qattusa *because you* are *a cat.*"

Gabriel chuckles.

"Belli," Augustine continues, "offered to help me restore the house. I asked him if he could handle a garden trowel as well as he could an adze. He said flowers are women's business and promised to return the next day with his cousin. In truth, I did not think much of it, expecting her to be rough, weary, and stooped like most other women I'd encountered. But when she arrived on my doorstep..." He pauses, remembering "...I was disarmed. *Prima facie.* She was fresh—that first breath of cool air after a lightning storm has chased away heavy oppressiveness. Her hair and face were uncovered, her eyes vital. The glorious figure beneath her frock took my breath. An unrelenting beauty." He closes his eyes, imagining the face that in all times of darkness has brought him to light. "A thousand poets writing for a thousand years could not put her loveliness to words."

"You speak as a man still mesmerized."

"I *am* a man still mesmerized."

"You are handsome," Gabriel says. "Was Isabel as taken with you?"

Augustine laughs. "If she was, she did not show it. But as luck would have it, she was unmarried—strange for a girl of twenty, by fifteen they are called old maids. Scores of men pursued Isabel, but her parents died of brain fever when she was a child, and living with her cousin took away the pressure to marry. So, she was free to help me create my Eden.

"I asked her why she refused the veil, why she insisted on doing things the world deems improper for a woman. She answered my question with several: *Was the Mother of God not a woman? Did the risen Lord not first appear to a woman? And the saints, brave martyrs of Christianity, are not many of them women? St Joan of Arc? St Catherine? St Agatha? What man then has the right to deem what is improper for a woman?*" Augustine spreads his hands. "Who am I to argue against the Mother of God?

"We sifted through rocks and pulled weeds. I loved every second. We spoke, mostly in Italian, and laughed, mostly at me. I told her about growing up in Rhodos, hunting rabbits, seafaring, swordplay, reading. Her questions were endless. It was amazing what she drew from me, things I'd long forgotten. She poked fun and tangled me up. I enjoyed it. Enjoyed her. And every time our project neared completion, I would find new chores to prolong our work. She caught on but did not mind. Then," Augustine continues, "one spring evening, we went for a walk, wandering fields and hills that rolled under a low, red sun. I was working up the nerve to take her hand when out of nowhere she kissed my cheek and ran off. It was quick and innocent. It made me ridiculous. I stood there a full minute, grinning like an idiot. We are in our eleventh year of marriage. And still, she tangles me up and makes me ridiculous."

Gabriel smiles. "My heart is happy for you. What you have with your wife is something rare indeed. I've never heard of love so pure. Certainly not in any marriage."

"The children adore Isabel, think she hung the moon. She taught my son to skip stones on water."

"You have a good home."

"All day our senses are nurtured. In the morning," Augustine says, "our house smells of blue skies and garden herbs. In the evening, of sunsets and wild thyme. At night, I swear you can smell the stars, sweeter than beeswax from our candles."

"Ah," Gabriel exhales, pushing himself up off the deck as quickly as joints stiffened by age will allow. "Soon those smells will surround you once more."

CHAPTER ELEVEN

Domenicus wakes with a start. He sits up, eyes straining to adjust to the colours of the day. He stares at the ceiling, the broken patterns of stone as he reties his drawstring undone in restless sleep. He thought the morning would never come. Now that it has, he crawls over his sister and, sandals in hand, creeps out of the house. The rising sun warms his face, lifts his spirits. Above, coral clouds move across the blue. Below, the ground is still cool from the night, fresh against bare feet.

The day is too new for a venture to the hospital, so Domenicus walks without a destination, eventually finding himself on the road to St Publius. Perhaps some divine intervention is in order.

Domenicus pushes open the gate, its hinges greased with only grit and time. He walks the cobblestone path, past the churchyard. Six steps daubed grey-green with pigeon excrement lead to the doors. His footsteps echo into the empty nave. It is small, fitting fourteen benches, each pew dimpled with depressions from two hundred years of parishioners taking seat. It smells like all churches—melted wax and incense and mould. Coloured light streams through a single stained glass window, illuminating swirls of dust and brightening the faces of stone saints that stand in corners. St Paul's nose is chipped, his right foot missing. Spider webs bridge St Mark's head to the wall.

Crossing himself, Domenicus genuflects, dropping to one knee as his father taught him. He sits on a bench three rows from the altar, eyes on the large crucifix hung to face the congregation.

"God, make my mother better. Please. I don't know what to do. But you do. Heal her like you healed Jairus's daughter and like you healed the woman who touched your cloak." Domenicus moves to the altar, places his hand on the nailed feet of Christ. "If you do, I'll never sin again, tell a lie, or pull my sister's hair…" At last, he abandons bartering for prayer, one tried and tested. "Our Father, who lives in heaven, hallowed is thy name…" Halfway through, his voice breaks. "Just make her better."

Moments later, he is out the doors. He lingers at the gate, wondering what else he might say to convince God to spare his mother. Footsteps and faint voices send him dashing behind a wide, stunted carob. He waits and watches, his slight frame concealed by the tree.

The parish priest, *Dun* Anton Tabone, rounds the corner in a swish of his black cassock. He carries a bucket of water and wears a simple wooden cross that dangles from a thin string around his neck. Trailing the priest is a girl Domenicus has never seen before. Her gaze is downcast. Domenicus cannot turn away from her. She is taller than Katrina, but like his sister and mother, wears no veil. Her skin is fair, her complexion honeyed milk. The girl's hair is pulled back in a plait that falls far down her back. Curly wisps slip out to frame her face.

The priest gives her a little smile.

Father Tabone is a good priest, kind-hearted and warm, Domenicus thinks, watching him. *Better than the old one.* For five years before being named *kappillan* of this parish, Anton Tabone was assistant to the former priest, a tyrannical, quick-tempered Sicilian, who had been a frightening presence, angry and unforgiving. Domenicus recalls villagers joking in private that the belligerent Sicilian scourged himself with demon entrails and had a Bible shoved right up his ass, not one Testament, but two. After the old despot's death, Anton Tabone was appointed *kappillan*. At this, the entire village heaved a collective sigh of relief.

Father Tabone stops now at the steps, points to the nest in the belfry. "These unholy birds think the stairs their privy. Give the steps a good scrubbing, will you? At nine bells, come to the vestry for reading lessons." *Reading lessons?* Domenicus can scarce believe that a girl—other than his willful younger sister—might have such an opportunity.

At her mechanical nod, Father Tabone puts his hand on the railing and crouches. "The Lord is close to the brokenhearted, dear one."

Domenicus steals one last look before slipping away. He meets his sister at home and helps her find their mother's ribbons. Mama loves braiding Katrina's hair with them but does not often get the chance, not with a daughter who is happier wearing grime than bows. Now, on the road to the hospital, Katrina plaits the ribbon into her tangled hair and does a poor, lopsided job of it.

"Think Mama will come home today?" she asks as a tiny lizard darts from their footsteps into the sanctuary of a rocky lee.

Domenicus shakes his head. "The hospital kept the smithy a week, and that was just for a burnt foot."

"That long? A whole week?"

Domenicus smiles for his sister's benefit. "Mama wishes she could stay a month. There, every day is Christmas and Easter and Carnival all in one."

"How?" Katrina asks.

"Think of it: meals served by knights, wines imported from *Franza*, feather beds... Even healthy men want to stay there. Think of Belli. Wouldn't he love watching the knights empty his bedpan every day?"

Katrina laughs. A second later, a brown and white goat with large pendulous ears and pointed beard charges towards them, a rebellious bleat in its throat.

"*Ejja 'l hawn!*" shouts a familiar voice. "Get back here, damn you!" Barefoot and shirtless, Robert Falsone chases swiftly after it, his stride sending dust motes into orbit. Rope in hand, he closes in on his fugitive, tackling the goat with both arms around its belly. It bleats furiously at being foiled.

Robert laughs. "Where do you think you're going, *mishut*? I don't like that ugly toad Farrugia any more than you do, but at least he doesn't whip *you*." He ties the rope loosely around the goat's neck and offers it some grain from his pocket. "Don't make war on me, friend. The whole world is not your enemy." He looks up at Katrina. "And you, where do you think *you're* going, with a ribbon in your hair?" He shakes his head. "What happened? Went to bed and woke up a *girl*?"

Katrina shrugs. "For Ma, I can pretend."

Robert furrows his brow, looks to Domenicus. "Where is your mother? Is she all right?"

"Belli took her to hospital yesterday," he replies.

"I'm sure they didn't dare bully him at the gates, those bastards," Robert says, lifting the goat with a grunt. "I'll be mending the fence that helped this miscreant escape. Look for me later."

At the hospital portico, there is no sign of the carpenter. Domenicus braces for the trouble he is certain the guard is going to give. The young man halts them, as expected, but greets them, as not.

"Montesa?"

Domenicus starts at hearing his family name spoken by a stranger. "Yes," he replies timidly.

The guard steps aside. "Hospitaller le Grant left orders to allow you entry."

Domenicus is stunned by this turn of good fortune. He passes through the gates into the cloistered courtyard. Knights on infirmary duty tend patients, who sit in the shade of orange trees. In the branches perches a choir of songbirds, a common sight in the *cortile grande*. Not so is Peppone. The donkey lies beneath a carob, his owner sitting on the ground nearby.

"Belli!" Domenicus takes off across the grass.

His sister trails swiftly behind. "Did Mama have wine from *Franza*? It's good, the best in the world." Katrina has never tasted wine but makes the proclamation with the authority of an expert.

Belli looks at his hands. "No, she didn't."

"How did the doctor fix what was wrong with her?" Domenicus asks.

"He didn't."

"Not *yet* you mean. He's still trying."

"No."

"What do you mean, *no?*" Domenicus refuses to believe a surgeon-knight of the *Sacra Infermeria* would just give up and send Mama home still sick. But before he can raise the point, he feels himself being pulled into Belli's embrace.

"Your mother is dead." The statement is so direct and so final, yet takes a moment to register. Domenicus suddenly weighs three times his body. Hardly able to breathe, narrow chest hitching from the effort, he is too numb to speak. He looks at the carpenter with unseeing eyes.

"But," Katrina says, her voice rising, "But..." She pushes Belli towards the doors. "Do something!" She pulls the ribbon from her hair, holds it out to him. "Give this to her. She likes it. Tell her she can braid my hair." Before Belli can act, Domenicus withdraws from him, the ribbon dropping from the carpenter's hand to the ground.

Domenicus speaks in a voice so hard and grim he frightens even himself. "*I hate her.*"

"Her life was in God's hands," Belli replies gently.

"I hate God too."

"God will forgive you that."

"God should beg *my* forgiveness," Domenicus lashes.

"God did not kill your mother."

Domenicus looks directly into Belli's eyes. "*You* killed her then. *You* brought her here. *You* challenged God. *You* took it out of His hands."

CHAPTER TWELVE

There is no hiding from the sun's face on the open deck of a galley. Augustine blinks away sleep and stretches muscles made stiff by night's cool air. Sugary pink clouds drift across the sky. He follows their path until his gaze falls on the starboard gunwales, where Dr Giuseppe Callus crouches, probing Pietro de Laya's bloody shoulder. Despite the distance, Augustine can see the entry wound is a mess of gaping flesh and exposed tissue. The knight grins, showing off the musket ball Callus dug out to anyone who passes by. The Maltese physician feels inside the wound for broken bone and bits of metal. Although his title is doctor and not surgeon, he has no qualms about soiling his hands on the guts of any man—from the lowest peasant to the loftiest noble. Augustine watches with interest as Callus douses the hole with alcohol and seawater. The knight stiffens and groans.

"A stroke of luck," Callus announces in Italian, the common tongue. "The bone has held, though from your carrying on, I don't know if the same can be said of your constitution. Now, if we can keep the wound from festering, it should heal nicely." He uses small forceps to pluck out tiny shards of the knight's armour, embedded in his muscle.

De Laya looks across his shoulder and smiles. "You do enjoy galley service. Is it so much fun to put us back together once we're broken? Or is it simply the pleasure of seeing us break?"

The doctor snorts. "At least," he says, passing his suturing needle through de Laya's skin, "these campaigns are ripe with opportunity to exercise my skills on the bodies of living, willing men."

"Indeed. Why, a knight could wake up to find his ass stitched over his face."

"Duly assembled at last," Callus laughs, tying off a knot. He dabs the puckered flesh around the sutures with alcohol. The knight turns his swaddled arm in a slow, painful windmill. After promising an extra ration of brandy to the doctor for his fine work, de Laya crosses to the companion ladder, stopping to show Augustine the musket ball.

In the kitchen amidships, cooks prepare breakfast, the scent of warm apples wafting from kilns onto the deck. Under the sharp watch of the overseer and his whip, the two rescued Egyptians walk the corsia, handing out wine-soaked bread to oarsmen.

Augustine pushes himself off the planks and approaches Dakarai and Jumoke, whose names he learned last night. "I might just keep you for myself when we arrive," he says in Arabic.

"Of course, Master," Dakarai replies.

Augustine waves his hand. "A joke."

"Not to us. You saved our lives. We are honour-bound to serve you in payment of this debt."

Augustine thinks of Belli. These two might be useful to the busy carpenter. Still, he shakes his head. "I've never been a slave nor suffered any to be kept."

"Servants then," Dakarai ventures. "All we have known is service, but always at the hand of a cruel master. You are not cruel."

"Nor am I a master. Perhaps there is work for you in a stable if its proprietor can afford hired hands. But," he adds, considering how cross Gabriel is going to be with him for making such an offer, "only if *my* master consents."

Dakarai squeezes Augustine's hands. "Your kindness will be written in the Golden Book."

"I'll present a request to the captain, but I promise nothing." He lowers his voice. "Also, for your own safety, you should declare yourselves Copts. For my part, I will keep your Muslim faith a secret. It could spare you the galleys, or worse."

Dakarai and Jumoke exchange glances, clearly troubled by the idea of abandoning their faith, even if merely for pretences.

"Apostasy?" Dakarai whispers. "Just yesterday we witnessed the hangings of those Christians who'd renounced their faith." Augustine can hardly argue the point.

"God forgive me," he says, "but I do not tell you to convert. Only to pretend."

"A quick inspection will reveal us," Dakarai says. "We are circumcised."

Augustine inhales, contemplates. "You will tell them your first master ordered you to choose foreskin or head—the one on your shoulders. Think hard on this, your lives may depend on it." He turns for the helm but stops when he catches Jumoke's irritated voice.

"Must you forever talk for me as though I do not own a capable tongue?"

"A little gratitude, please!" Dakarai snaps. "Would you rather be chained to the oar and forced to row for hours on end? Rather end up hauled to that festering hole Algiers and bastinadoed?"

"No," Jumoke grumps. "But I can speak for myself."

"Please. If your ass wasn't pointing downward, you wouldn't know how to shit."

Augustine laughs to himself as he heads to the upper rail. He leans forward and tilts his head, watching the blades slice through the water. White gulls cry overhead, dipping and gliding on the same wind that whips through his hair. It is a fine morning.

Soon he will be home.

***

Belli stands in his open doorway, staring out, but not seeing. Everything is the same, but nothing is as it was. Every day he makes things out of wood; today, he must make his cousin's coffin.

"I don't think God likes us." Katrina startles him as she approaches from behind. He turns, crouches before her.

"It seems that way, I know. But it is not so."

"Yes, it is."

"Signore," calls a vaguely familiar voice. The approaching woman is easily recognizable as Robert's mother Mea, despite her black shroud. Her toes twist and cross over each other, giving her a permanent limp. The widow's slight frame is stooped, slumping under the weight of a hard life.

Belli cups Katrina's chin and rises. "Very kind of you to come, Signora."

"I've been in prayer since I heard," she says, taking Belli's hands. Her fingers are like the cracked earth that carpets the island floor. "Isabel was a beautiful soul. That she refused modesty will not keep her from heaven." Belli ignores the remark, spoken without malice.

"How can I help?" Mea asks.

Belli leans towards her ear, drops his voice to a whisper. "I've been able to offer little more than senseless ramblings. It would be a tremendous favour if you'd stay here as I attend an important matter. Domenicus has uttered barely a word. Perhaps the shock is still too great."

Mea nods. "When my husband was killed... Do you remember? For months, Robert would run away, trying to find the corsair responsible. I had to lock my son in the well for three days."

Belli sighs sadly, remembering the day Robert asked him to sell him his donkey, so he could cover more ground. Domenicus appears in the doorway, arms crossed over his chest.

"At least Robert had someone to get revenge on."

"Be thankful your mother's death does not need avenging," Mea replies sagely.

***

On the outcrop overlooking the dockyard, Belli sits against the same rock Domenicus has occupied for months. Today the man, not the boy, sits in anxious wait for Augustine's return. The burden of telling the husband about his wife rests on Belli; their children have been through enough. He prays hard that Augustine will return today, in time for Isabel's funeral tomorrow morning.

As Belli made his way here, the Italian knight Franco di Bonfatti stopped him to offer condolences and to inform him the Grand Hospitaller has granted a pardon for his violence against the hospital guard. A fine was considered, as was corporal punishment. However, given the outcome, le Grant decided to let the offence go with a warning. A stern one.

Now, Belli leans into the rock, steeling himself for the words he must say to Augustine, for the suffering they will inflict. His stomach twists tighter with each passing moment. The afternoon slips away and, with it, the stifling heat, although there is no relief to be had: dusk comes without an arrival.

The chance for Augustine to say goodbye to his beloved wife fades with the sky.

CHAPTER THIRTEEN

Today Katrina will bury her mother. As the pale morning bleeds through a slit between curtains, she takes up Mama's brush, strands of her auburn hair woven among the bristles. Katrina leaves them where they are. She hopes her brother, Belli, and Robert are alone at church today. No one else knew her mother; no one even tried to. They wouldn't go because they care—they'd only go so they *look* like they care. And how unfair when the one who cared most, the one who should be there above any, cannot.

"What about our father?" Katrina asks quietly. "We... we should wait for him."

"We should," Belli replies. "We can't."

The door resounds with a knock. Katrina unbolts the latch. Franco stands in the colourless dawn, a stark contrast to his black livery. Although the morning is new, the air is thick. In surrounding houses, linen curtains are drawn to the side as neighbours peek out to watch the nobleman. On the road await two magnificent horses, heavy front hooves stomping their restlessness into the dirt.

Franco smiles gently. "You will not walk to church today."

Katrina sits behind the knight, her arms loose around his waist. She feels each hoof touch ground as the horse Phaedo picks its way through rocks strewn across the road that leads to St Publius. Villagers pushing load carts move aside, clearing the way for the mounted line.

Franco turns partway in his saddle. "It won't hurt forever, Katrina."

"Yes, it will."

"No, *cara mia*. My mother died when I was a boy, not much older than you are now."

"Was she sick?"

"She was trampled by a startled horse." Katrina is struck by the matter-of-fact way he says it. "There is a bridge in Florence," he continues, "the Ponte Vecchio. She ventured there one day, alone and on foot. A great noise frightened a horse. ...I don't think she ever even knew what happened."

Katrina meets Franco's eyes. "So, God doesn't like you either."

***

At the church gate, Father Anton Tabone receives Domenicus and his sister with a warm embrace. "Jesus said, *I am the resurrection and the life. Whoever believes in me will never die.* Your mother believed," he says. "She will never die."

Clang. The bell tolls. The morning bell—a mourning bell. A carriage halts at the gate. As Franco drops two *scudi* into the coach driver's expectant hand, Belli opens the rear door. There it is. Mama's coffin. Domenicus has to hold the sill to steady himself.

Clang. As parishioners make their way into the church, a cool wind chases clouds across the sky, an overcast canopy of great billowing edges. Robert and his mother climb the wide stone stairs. The farmhand wears his best clothes, his only pair of pants without holes and a lambskin jerkin that belonged to his father. His feet are bare. At his side, Mea hunches under the yoke of perpetual grief, each encounter with death further bending an already stooped frame. She kisses Domenicus on the top of his sandy head.

Clang. By now, the bell has rung twenty times. Belli and Franco pull the coffin from the coach. Domenicus is caught by the elaborate floral frieze carved across the coffin's side, and he remembers a day when Mama tickled him with just such a daisy.

Father Tabone leads the small procession up the stairs. The *kappillan*'s first steps inside the church silence the parishioners.

Clang. The bell has now rung thirty-two times, one for each year of Isabel's life. Domenicus blinks. Something within him wails: *It isn't fair!* He fights back the tears, fights them, fights them. But after everything has been torn away, and all that remains is useless resistance, he gives up. Down his cheeks they spill, three days' worth of unshed tears. The aisle is a narrow strait, the priest a watery blur. And the tears, a relief.

The coffin is set at the foot of the altar. Domenicus sighs against Belli's shoulder, his gaze wandering across the aisle. The farmer Giovanni Bonnici and his wife Leonora sit three pews from the altar. Father Tabone's niece sits on the bench behind them. She and Domenicus meet eyes. Hers are blue. He looks quickly to his hands.

The priest's voice falls distant. Domenicus imagines the afternoon his mother taught him to skip stones on the water. As the last one sinks to the bottom, Father Tabone calls him back to the present. "...And Simon Peter said to Him, *Lord where are you going?* Jesus answered, *where I go you cannot follow Me now, but you will follow later.*" The priest opens his arms, palms facing up. "Join me now in the prayer the Lord taught us."

The Lord's Prayer didn't do any good when it mattered. Still, Domenicus rises and recites the prayer mechanically. As the service continues, he drifts between past and present, between his mother sweeping cinders from the hearth and Father Tabone lifting the sacramental plate, between Mama catching spiders and the priest offering Eucharist. It all runs together—the elegy, the Amen, the carrying of the coffin to the churchyard.

An open plot has been dug into the stony earth beside the graves of Mama's parents, their shared plaque weathered and overgrown with weeds. Slanted shafts of sunlight break holes in the solid grey sky and light Father Tabone's face, wind rippling his robe as he raises an open hand.

"The Lord bless and keep thee, Isabel Montesa, wife and mother. His faithful departed."

Gravediggers lower the casket down to the earthen floor with a soft thud. In place of his father, Domenicus scatters a dozen lime tree leaves over the lid. As dirt fills the mouth of the grave, Father Tabone's niece moves next to him, closes her hand around his. He looks down at her fingers.

Her warmth remains on his skin long after she has gone.

Now, Domenicus slips his hand into his pocket, pulls out his mother's ring. It glints faintly in his upturned palm.

"For Pa."

EIGHT POINTED CROSS

CHAPTER FOURTEEN

With Gabriel Mercadal to his left, Pietro de Laya to his right, Augustine leans against the gunwale and takes in the state of the day. It is heavy and hot as the caravan galleys glide into the Maltese harbour. The guns of St Angelo fire in salute, announcing the convoy's triumphant return. Smoke spills over wide ramparts, below which oarsmen ease the galleys towards the pier.

Augustine squints as porters push through the growing host of welcomers to the edges of the docks. Knights draped in black habits stand out against throngs of drably dressed villagers. Stray dogs yelp, tails wagging as they lollop along the waterfront. Augustine bends over the rail, skims familiar faces in the crowd, looking for his wife among them. As the *Atardecer* shudders against the dock, porters rush forward to lower the gangplanks.

De Laya snorts, pointing at a dishevelled boy pressing towards the galleys. "Maltese children look as though they've been pulled from sewers."

Augustine narrows his eyes, chuckles at the sight of his son, unrecognized by de Laya. Isabel is going to give Domenicus the scrubbing of his life once she hears of this.

Gabriel too takes notice and nudges Augustine. "Go." The father shakes his captain's hand and takes off in a jog across the deck. He is first to disembark, crossing a plank that creaks under the weight of his stride. Excitement turns rapidly to concern: his son's face is not filled with boyish mischief, but unspeakable anguish. Augustine reaches Domenicus, crouches before him.

"What's wrong? Is everything all right?"

"No, Pa. Everything is not all right. Mama is… mama is…"

Augustine takes him hard by the shoulders. He notices a raised scar beneath his son's eye but is too distracted to address it now. "Mama is what? What is wrong with your mother?"

Before Domenicus can answer, Belli pushes through and takes Augustine's arm.

"You need to come with me now, Cousin."

Augustine will not budge. "Tell me what is going on. Tell me right now."

"Not here," Belli insists. "Just come away from the crowds. *Ejja mieghi.* Please, I beg you."

Augustine has never once felt the urge to hit the man. He feels it now.

"Goddamn it! You tell me! *What has happened to my wife?*" His shouting turns several heads, making further argument futile. Belli puts his big hands on Augustine's shoulders, stilling him.

"Isabel is dead."

The words strike like a bolt of lightning. Augustine does not move, does not speak. He no longer feels Belli's hands on him, barely makes out what the man is saying: "Needed surgery ... *Sacra Infermeria* .... Died in the care of the knights ... buried in the churchyard... so very sorry."

Unable to respond, Augustine walks away, leaving Domenicus and Belli to stare after him.

There is no way Isabel is dead. Why would God take her? Why? It can't be true. If anyone should be dead, it is the one who left for battle, not the one left safely behind. His tread is swift, to keep the pain at bay. Pain, too, is a swift mover. Hand over heart, Augustine staggers along the quiet street behind the *Sacra Infermeria.* When he can go no farther, he unloads his weight against the curtain wall that fronts onto the waters of Kalkara. The iron beak of a galley pulses past the mouth of the inlet. Such a sight has always swelled his heart. Now, it takes him from empty to hollow.

He walks for miles along the rugged coastline, finally reaching the headland of Mount Sciberras, its face bruised with purple contusions, cut with pink lines. Stray goats punctuate the quiet with random bleating as they thread their way through spiked baubles of prickly pear.

Augustine drops onto an ochre patch of dirt and hugs his knees to his chest, breath coming in long, ragged gasps as he rocks back and forth, back and forth. Slowly, everything wells inside him: his grief, his love, his loss, his Isabel, rising until he can no longer contain any of it—and he howls his pain, his cry echoing in waves off the rocks.

Eventually, Augustine takes the long road back to Birgu. He passes into the fat shadows of stone balconies, rounds the same corners three and four times, walks streets untouched by fading sunlight and streets coloured golden by it. He climbs stairs hewn from living rock, only to slog back down again, doing anything that might lengthen the walk home, ward off his awful reality. He is terrified of facing his children, who surely blame and hate him. Shadows grow long and weep across the cobblestones, spilling farther and farther, until at last, they disappear with the sun.

Somehow, Augustine makes it to the Publius churchyard. At the sight of Isabel's tombstone, her name carved on it, he loses control. He caves in on himself, collapses on her grave, eyes overflowing until the dirt beneath his face is soaked with tears. A slow parade of wind whistles through the trees. He breathes into the earth and weeps inconsolably. Where he lies is where he sleeps.

He wakes hours or days later to his wife's cousin crouched beside him. With a start, Augustine lifts his head. He cannot meet Belli's eyes.

"Go," Augustine says. "You should go. No, wait. First, I have forgiveness to ask of you."

"Forgiveness of me?"

"Had I been here, Isabel would be alive. She is dead because of me."

Belli takes him firmly by the shoulders. "*Not true*. Look at me. *Look at me*."

Tears roll down Augustine's dirt-streaked cheeks to the corners of his mouth. "I abandoned my son at the pier."

"You are consumed by grief. He understands. Come home."

"Home was in her arms. She *was* home. Home is dead."

"Augustine…"

"Go. Please, just go."

Belli rises. "Domenicus and Katrina are your home. Home is alive. And home needs you."

***

Robert Falsone is having trouble at the hospital loggia. Early the morning of Isabel's funeral, he sought out Franco di Bonfatti to ask about the ribbon Katrina lost at the *Sacra Infermeria*. The knight said he vaguely remembered seeing it on the grass in the courtyard and sent Robert to ask at the gate, where the boy now stands, miffed. Today, in place of a regular guard, a knight minds the entrance. He is a compatriot of Franco's named Gaetano, who laughs at Robert, and shoos him away. Robert refuses to leave, and Gaetano's amusement turns sour. He shoves Robert away with such force it sends him reeling to the cobbles. Undaunted, he approaches again. This time, the knight raises his hand to strike the boy across the face, but Dr Callus catches the guard by the wrist, staying the blow.

Gaetano jerks his arm violently away. "Mind your business, Magnificus."

"I am about to." The doctor crouches before Robert. "What's your story, lad?"

Robert rubs sore wrists, glances from the knight to the doctor. "Isabel Montesa died, and Katrina lost something of hers in the cortile grande. It's just a ribbon. I asked to retrieve it."

Callus rises to his full height. "Is this what your Order deems grounds for thrashing a child?" Without missing a beat, the doctor switches from Italian to Maltese, a tongue foreign to the guard's Tuscan ears. "This man's bowels are where his brain should be, and his brain in his ass." Few on the island have nerve enough to look a knight in the eye, let alone challenge one directly. But Dr Giuseppe Callus is all nerve. That makes him Robert Falsone's personal hero.

Gaetano scowls, a sure indication he senses the insult though he does not understand the words. He opens his mouth to voice his brewing anger, but Robert speaks first.

"It's all right, Callus. He didn't hurt me. Eh, think you can get the ribbon?"

"Done," the doctor replies, still speaking Maltese. "Unless, of course, this domincella here wants to wear the ribbon himself." Callus slides easily back into Italian. "Now," he says, nodding to Gaetano, "if you'd be so good as to open the door."

The knight goes white with rage, visibly furious at his own impotence against a mere doctor, a Maltese no less. "I will report this insubordination. Your tongue will be your noose."

Callus smiles. "Be sure to include in your report that you threw a boy to the ground because he asked to retrieve a grieving girl's only keepsake of her dead mother."

Seething, Gaetano unlocks the gallery door. Callus passes through, turning to wink at Robert, the grubby farmhand who stands taller and beams with the pride of an emperor.

***

In the falling twilight, Katrina sits on Belli's doorstep, waiting for her father. The galleys docked hours ago. Why has he not come home yet? Is he angry with her? With Domenicus? Will he go away again? She cannot bear the idea of losing Pa too.

Approaching steps turn her head. It is Robert. He reaches into his pocket and hands Katrina the blue ribbon dropped at the *Sacra Infermeria*. It is slightly frayed and very dirty. Her eyes widen with surprise. She takes the ribbon silently but gratefully.

"Your mother is the wind," Robert says. "You cannot see her, but will feel her always."

***

After midnight, Augustine reaches Belli's house, where he finds Domenicus and Katrina sleeping together on the same pallet. His gaze drifts to the sole empty bed, Isabel's silhouette still pressed into its straw. A murmur turns his head. Domenicus lies on his side, arm hanging off the edge of the bed, lips slightly parted, face tilted at an odd but strangely touching angle. Augustine kneels and feels his son's breath on his face. He stays this way for a time. It is almost an hour before he returns to his own house.

The air inside is stagnant and stale, as though a crisp breeze has been trapped inside these walls for a thousand years, its freshness spoiled and the air itself sour. The space would smell of sadness if sadness had a scent.

Augustine lights a candle and picks up Isabel's unfinished embroidery. In the halo of flame, he stares at it, every shaded curve, every line of thread. Hours later, he wakes to find the needlework on his chest. The candle has guttered in its own melted tallow, and the house is dark. He lifts himself from bed like a man flogged and parts the drapes. Morning sun streams in and catches floating motes of dust as fresh air whisks through the house.

"Pa," Katrina says in a low, throaty voice as she approaches the house with her brother. For the first time since returning to Malta, Augustine feels a glint of happiness. At seeing the hurt in his daughter's face however, the good feeling is quickly replaced by guilt. He goes at once to meet them.

"Why didn't you come home yesterday?" Katrina asks.

"Because I was scared," he replies.

She pauses, seemingly unsure how to respond to such an admission from her father. "We tried to help mama," she says. "The infirmary guard chased me away. No one would listen. I'm sorry."

He peppers her face with kisses. "Sweetheart, don't be sorry. Just be careful." He looks his son in the face. "Domenicus, forgive my actions yesterday. I was a coward. There is no excuse."

"You said in your absence, I was the man. I didn't do anything right. Didn't even pray right."

"It is a burden I had no right to place on you. Yet you proved yourself more man than any I have ever known." Augustine pulls his children close. "Our little family is going to be just fine, I promise. The three of us will be all right."

"What about Belli?" Katrina asks.

The father smiles. "Belli too."

CHAPTER FIFTEEN

January wind hisses through tiny chinks in the stone walls of the Montesa house. Across from Domenicus, Pa rests his elbows on the table, his chin on his fist. "Remember to stop at the rectory for Father Tabone's niece on your way to the hospital," he says.

"I won't forget," Domenicus replies. He stares into his cup, the honeyed milk recalling his mind to the girl's fresh face, which he has not seen since Mama's funeral. It is six months since he and his sister worked the wards of the *Sacra Infermeria*, and despite the passage of time, he bears a grudge against Édouard de Gabriac, the surgeon he holds responsible for killing his mother. His father has explained that de Gabriac did what any other in his place would have done. Still, Domenicus is convinced in his ten-year-old way that he needs someone to blame, and since he's too scared to keep blaming God, it may as well be the surgeon God was supposed to be working through.

Pa gathers his chisel, maul, lead, and erasing knife for stowage in his rucksack, which he will carry to the fortress St Angelo, where his day will be spent in the quarry, breaking back and stone. Soon after returning from the last campaign, he resigned from his position as a soldier of the Order and sought permission to work on the fortifications instead.

"Hurry up now. *Dun* Tabone's niece will be waiting." Father looks at Katrina from across the room. "It will be good for you to spend time with another girl."

"She's pretty," Katrina says. "Prettiest girl I've ever seen. Where did she come from?"

Pa chuckles. "From the moon."

"*Really?*"

Domenicus laughs at the way his sister's eyes pop.

Their father shakes his head. "Mdina, which may as well be the moon."

"Mdina? She's a noble?" Katrina asks, just as incredulous.

"No. She came to live here with her uncle. A corsair killed her father and took her mother." He slings his tool bag over his shoulder. "The priest is teaching her to read, you know. He said she flows through Bible passages like wine at Cana, able to read every word."

"Even Thessa—Thessa—Thessalonians?"

Pa nods. "Now, no make-believe battles with pirates today. I want you both home, straight as the sparrow flies. At least," he adds, as though reconsidering his severity, "for tonight." He passes through the open door and starts down the road, whistling softly under a vanilla sky.

Domenicus watches after his father, brooding. He and Robert had planned to spear a few corsairs this afternoon. A half-smile flickers across Katrina's mouth.

"Maybe he's worried another bird might fly into your face."

A bitter *Gregale* throws grit into the air and runs clouds across the sky. Beneath it, the ground is cold and moist from winter rains. Domenicus loves to slosh barefoot through the mud, but today decides to avoid the puddles. Upon reaching the rectory adjacent to St Publius, he raps on the door.

Katrina furrows her brow. "How do you expect anyone to hear that?"

"It's not civil to bang on a door. Especially a rectory door. This is God's house."

"God would want to hear," she says, nudging him out of the way and making a hammer of her fist. Seconds later, bare feet slap the floor, and Father Tabone's niece opens the door. Her hair is pulled tightly away from her face, revealing small features and large eyes.

Domenicus smiles. Where *did* she come from?

From the moon, Pa had said.

No, Domenicus thinks, *a place above the moon, above the stars. Heaven.*

"I hope I did not keep you waiting long," she says. "My uncle wanted four-minute eggs." She pronounces each word with a certain elegance, her voice practised, polite, perfect. She talks like a grownup. Domenicus likes it, likes the way her words string together like beads of a necklace. She is a living song, this girl. And he could hum all day.

"What's your name?" he asks.

"Angelica." *Angelica. Of course it is.*

Katrina takes Angelica by the hand and pulls her along. "At the hospital, there are knights, dozens. I'm going to make them teach me how to fight. I wish I could be a knight. Maybe I will be one. You and I are going to wash linens together. And we'll read together, too, one day, I hope. You don't wear a *barnuża* like the other girls. That's good. I don't like the other girls. They don't like me." The need for breath is all that stops her from carrying on. Domenicus jogs to catch up. He walks backwards to face them. Well, to face Angelica.

Soon, they are swept into the heavy foot traffic of narrow streets. Augustine once explained that the tight, winding lanes of Birgu were built by architects of a defensive mind: all village roads empty into the town square, a security measure to trap invaders. Now, the same security measures serve to trap prospective customers. Domenicus would like to talk to Angelica but knows better than to compete with his sister, whose voice rises above the pots and pans clattering at the back of a mule-drawn cart. She points out the town crier set to deliver news, the caged chickens clucking their discontent, the scented votives tinted purple and orange and green.

In the centre of the square, the crier lifts his parchment. "To the list of literature frowned upon by Rome, the Holy Church adds Boccaccio's *Decameron*, Erasmus's *In Praise of Folly*, and Machiavelli's *The Prince*. Possession is punishable by—"

"Birgu is busy," Angelica remarks, looking around.

"Do you like Mdina better?" Domenicus asks, falling in-step with her.

"Corsairs didn't come to Mdina and take my parents."

"I... I'm sorry..." he trails off, feeling stupid for asking. They continue in silence, past stalls of wicker baskets, woven mats, and brown pottery, scattered about the market floor. Roosters strut over cobbles, dogs sniff at piles of horse dung, hogs grunt and flop in the shade. There are tables covered in bales of dull fabric, and behind them, weather-chapped mercers armed with measuring sticks. Soon, the clucking of chickens and vendors falls distant. The narrow alleyway is a wind tunnel, strong gusts loosing tendrils of Angelica's hair as she works to keep her long skirt from flying up. Domenicus wants to help, but after his recent slip, is shy to offer.

"Wear pants," his sister says, looking down at her own legs. "It's easier to do things."

Angelica looks at her askance. "Is that not indecent?"

"Of course it is." Katrina flashes a grin and runs off. Domenicus is glad Angelica does not try to catch up. Today, he wishes the *Sacra Infermeria* were a thousand leagues away.

Today, he wishes he were a laundress.

***

A handsome knight waits at the portico. Angelica recognizes him easily as the young man who rode the lovely white horse to Isabel's funeral. He greets them each with an orange. She has never before been offered such beautiful fruit. The intensely sweet smell has her new friend Katrina already digging dirty fingers into the thick rind.

The Italian grins broadly and addresses Domenicus. "Your father sought me out this morning to advise of your coming to help us out. He said to expect a friend as well." His eyes flick to Angelica. "Would this be *Signorina* Angelica Tabone?"

"Yes, *Illustrissimo*," Angelica replies, offering the knight a polite smile and a curtsey. He pushes the large door wide, holding it open as he ushers them through the gate and into the *cortile grande*. Angelica often passes the wide loggia but has never been beyond it. Now, she finds herself in an Eden of white pillars swathed in green liana and fat, vibrant citrus fruit hanging from thin boughs like polished baubles. There is a rainwater reservoir, its glassy surface a mirror of orange and lemon trees, their leaves rustling with the passage of cool air. The knight leads them into the building through the refectory, a vaulted mess hall, towering and rectangular.

Although the Tabone family was of humble means, Angelica is no stranger to grandeur. In Mdina, her mother was a chambermaid in the houses of nobles who worked for the *Università*, the island's civil authority. They are a thoroughly snobby lot, about as cordial with their lessers as are the knights. At one time or another, Graciela Tabone worked for almost all the nobles, chapping her hands on the laundry of dukes and counts, bruising her knees on the floors of barons and viscounts. As soon as Angelica could hold a scrub brush, she joined her mother on her knees scouring these distinguished marble floors. It was exhausting work, and in her memory, the long days run together.

One day, however, stands out. That winter afternoon, Angelica and her mother were washing the floors of the *hakem*, the head of the *Università*. Angelica had just finished the antechamber and was starting on the next room, but in her inexperience, forgot to change the water in her bucket. Unluckily for her, the *hakem*'s young wife, Diana d'Alagona, was watching. Tall and striking, Diana was a woman of fierce beauty and fiercer temperament, whose vile disposition was legendary even among her peers. *If she were Queen of anything bigger than this house*, the bravest of guests joked when she was out of earshot, *she would make Vlad the Impaler seem a loveable dandy.*

In a fury, Diana snatched up the pail with one hand and Angelica's wrist with the other. She dragged the small girl into the open courtyard and threw the bucket of dirty water at her. Angelica was instantly soaked by the ugly brown splash. She gagged and choked and fought back tears. *If you think this water clean enough to touch my floors*, the noblewoman snarled, *it is clean enough to drink. Now back to work, lest I release your mother from employ.* Diana turned her heel and marched off, leaving Angelica shivering in the courtyard. That is until a Genoese gardener bravely snuck her some rags.

The knight's voice recalls Angelica to her surroundings. "Domenicus, your scar looks as though it might fade in time. Not been playing rough, I hope?"

Katrina takes the question, solemnly declaring, "I never threw another rock."

The Italian cocks an eyebrow. "A spirited thing, you."

She beams, sticky juice dripping from her chin. "I would make a good knight, don't you think, Franco?" Angelica starts at Katrina's informality and is relieved she's not the only one.

"Call him *my lord*," Domenicus hisses. "Or *Illustrissimo* like you're supposed to."

But Franco seems not to mind, laughing as he passes into the corridor. "If ever there comes a time when the world turns upside down and the Order allows women to join its ranks…" he halts at the laundry room "…I will be your top advocate."

Cool wind fills the sheets drying on the line. Angelica watches as Katrina nudges one of the laundry baskets with her foot, bends over it, inspects its contents.

"Beware the ticks. You don't want those little bastards in your clothes. And try not to touch any shit." Angelica has never encountered such liberal use of foul language and doesn't quite know how to respond. "They make cures from it," Katrina continues.

"From what?" Angelica asks, not sure if she really wants an answer.

"From shit. I heard two surgeons talking. They bake it and crush it into flakes. It's supposed to treat lesions. They only use the shit of healthy men though. Dogs too. Pedigrees."

Angelica furrows her brow. "How does that work?"

Katrina shrugs. "Seems absurd a leper would heal his lesions with shit, only to be shunned for his smell."

At last, Angelica allows herself to laugh. With a sweeping glance, she takes in the immensity of the *Sacra Infermeria*. "Are you the only laundress in this entire place?"

"No. You're here now."

"So it's just *us*?" Angelica feels a wave of panic at the notion.

Katrina winks. "There are old women and nuns. They won't work outside though. They think open air brings pox." She scoffs. "*I've* never had pox. They're always saying the rosary—one for each station of the cross. It takes two forevers. Then, they talk about all the sinners in Birgu."

"Are there a lot?"

"If you listen to what those crones say, everyone in this village should be rolled to hell in a barrel lined with fiery nails." Katrina's voice strains under the weight of a heavy blanket she struggles to drape over the line. She uses a wooden paddle bigger than she is to beat the cover, and with each mighty whack, the wool coughs nasty bits of debris. Once its fibre lungs are emptied, Katrina soaks the blanket in a trough of water, lye, ammonia, and verjuice. Angelica knows these sharp smells well.

"We leave it to bathe for a few minutes," Katrina says. She screws up her face. "I *hate* baths. Can't think of anything worse." She wrings sickly brown liquid from the first blanket, now double its weight. Angelica takes a sheet from the hamper. Fifteen minutes later, her hair a mess, hands dark red from scalding water, she still struggles to remove a bloodstain from that same sheet.

Katrina passes her a jug. "Cold water and vinegar for blood."

"Oh," Angelica replies, hot from the steam and the effort. "In Mdina, there were no bloodstains." She pours out a tub of brown-grey water, watching the liquid spill across the cobbles and turn the dust to muck. After a time, she glances up. "My uncle said *Montesa* is not of this island. Where is your father from?"

"Rhodos," Katrina replies. "His ancestors, from Spain."

"How come he doesn't make you wear a *barnuża*? And how do you talk so…so… You *curse*. Aren't you afraid of getting in trouble?"

Katrina laughs. "No."

"Why not?"

"Because Montesa is not of this island."

***

At day's end, Domenicus, who was on meal duty with Franco, meets his sister and Angelica at the loggia. The knight sneaks them some *kavati*, a coveted honey-sweet, for their labours and escorts them out. Dark swollen clouds hang low in the late-afternoon sky, pierced by arrows of sunlight fading above long shadows that creep across the road and sneak greedily up houses. The footpath becomes narrower until the trio can no longer walk shoulder to shoulder. Ahead, the church rises above the grass and weeds.

"Will you call on me again tomorrow?" Angelica asks, climbing the rectory steps backwards. Domenicus feels a wondrous thrill at the idea of tomorrow. He nods eagerly and keeps doing so until he realises he's been nodding longer than any person of sound mind should be. Angelica looks at him askance, her expression making his cheeks burn. She is wonderful.

I wonder if God would let me marry an angel.

Domenicus and his sister arrive home to find their father sitting with his back to the door. He does not turn to greet them.

"Pa? What's wrong?" Domenicus asks.

"You are on your way to becoming a man, and I have certain expectations of you." His voice is low, brooding. Alarmed, Domenicus thinks urgently back to the morning. Did he break something? Forget a chore? Nothing comes to mind. Then, he has it: his unfinished milk. It must have curdled over the afternoon and greeted his father with a sour whiff on his arrival.

Augustine rises from his stool. There is a sudden and bright flash, as though he has harnessed lightning with his bare hands. A spectacular sword lies flat across his upturned palms. "I expect you will make a fine swordsman." Domenicus sucks in a long breath he nearly forgets to exhale. A work of art, the sword is a smaller version of the one his father has carried since his youth in Rhodos—a diamond section blade, steel hilt, emblazoned with Spanish crests and foliage arabesques. The grip is fashioned from wood and wrapped tightly in black leather strips, the pommel bronze and etched with acanthus leaves. Domenicus closes his hands around it and, with deliberate, unhurried motion, lifts the sword, orange flame from a candle shining fire on burnished steel.

"Oh, Father..." he manages, holding the sword so the blunted tip points upward, eyes moving slowly over every inch of the beautifully tooled weapon.

"There is a scabbard for you," Augustine says, "So you can carry the blade at your side, as do all men of action." He motions for Katrina to move. "Let your brother take a swing." In the centre of the room, and with much enthusiasm but little precision, Domenicus carves a crisscross in the air.

"Again," his father prompts. "This time, hold the grip with only your right hand."

Domenicus repeats the pattern with the one hand.

"Not bad. Now, your left."

Domenicus senses the clumsiness of his left-handed attempt. Pa smiles. "Your right hand is your fighting hand. We'll strengthen your left—in case you lose your right in battle. But first, you will learn to think like a swordsman. In all battles, your mind is your greatest weapon. Sharpen that, and it will slice as effectively as a blade."

Domenicus sets the sword next to its leather sheath on the table and wraps his arms tight around his father's neck. Katrina scoots to the table and lifts the sword, an action clearly more arduous than expected. To its owner's horror, she drops it to the stone floor where it lands with a resounding clang. Her face goes red. She bends at once to pick it up, but Domenicus races over, beating her to it. Annoyed, he holds the sword to a nearby candle, inspects the blade for damage, turning it over to see both sides.

"A sword is a weapon," Augustine says, "an extension of its bearer. Not a toy, Katrina."

She frowns. "I know. I want to learn too. I can. I will."

"I believe you. I'll commission Malta's finest carpenter to make you one out of wood."

Katrina gives a low whistle. "Really? Malta's finest? Who?"

"Belli, you silly monkey."

"Silly *what*?"

"Monkey. A long-tailed quadrumanous species of Africa." Augustine laughs whole-heartedly at Katrina's expression. Domenicus can tell he used those words precisely to see the face she is making now. "It's an animal, sweetheart."

"Can he make me a bow instead?" she asks.

Most fathers would cuff their daughters for such a request. Hers only inhales pensively. "Maybe you can ask Franco di Bonfatti to teach you archery. He's a master. But don't bother him, Kat. Sir Franco is a good lad, but he is duty-bound."

Katrina shrugs. "I'll just make it his duty."

***

Angelica pins a freshly washed blanket to the line, smiling at Katrina's lively description of the sword Augustine gave Domenicus last night. Angelica just doesn't know what to make of this girl.

"It's glorious! Fit for the Grand Master," Katrina gushes as she wrings dirty water from a sheet, her forearms running with greyish suds, cheeks pink from rising steam. The hospital's heavy back door whines suddenly on its hinges. Out shuffles Censina, a broad-shouldered laundress with large grey eyes and coarse black whiskers above her lip. She drops a full wicker basket at Katrina's feet, gives her a hostile once-over.

"You shouldn't be working outdoors. Open air is the breath of the devil."

Katrina looks at the woman. "It's a little cold to be the devil's breath, don't you think?"

Angelica snickers, earning herself a sharp glance from Censina, whose pale features flush with anger. "*Katrina Montesa!* Replace your insolence with prayer. And roll down those sleeves! Must you run around half-naked?" The affronted laundress turns on her cracked heel, muttering to herself about exposed arms and the immodesty of it all as she hobbles back inside.

Katrina rolls her eyes. "They're all like her, the ones that work here. You'll see. Devil this and rosary that." She shrugs. A moment later, a smile blooms on her face. "Know what? I'm going to learn archery. The Italian will show me."

Angelica looks at her sideways. Katrina Montesa sure is peculiar. "Why?"

"Why not?"

"We're *girls*. Why would any girl want to learn archery? Why do you?"

"Because. Because I want to," Katrina replies. "Same reason you learned to read."

Angelica raises her eyebrows. It is true—for a girl in Malta, reading is no less absurd than shooting an arrow or flying to the moon. And Angelica learned to read.

***

In the afternoon, Katrina leaves Angelica alone to finish the last of the bedclothes and disappears with a basket down the corridor. Instead of taking the clean linens directly to the storeroom, she walks on, in search of Franco. The hallway takes her past offices, pantries, and quarters for menial staff, all to no avail. She encounters several of the daytime *barberotti*, surgical apprentices who mind the wards in shifts, but none questions her presence as she carries a great shield of laundry. After almost twenty minutes of wandering, she is ready to give up. On her way to the storeroom, she catches a familiar voice coming from the refectory. There he is, Franco di Bonfatti, wiping tables alongside other young knights assigned to mess hall duty. She stands quietly in the doorway until he takes notice of her, or rather, until he notices the big basket with legs, and comes over.

"Katrina? What are you doing here? Is everything all right?"

She peers over the top of the hamper. "Is it true you're a master archer?"

Franco tilts his head. "I don't know that I would call myself a *master*."

"I want to learn. I want you to teach me."

He looks at her in surprise. "Why?"

Must everyone always ask why? "I just do."

"You are brazen and presumptuous," Franco snaps. "Whatever would your father say?"

"He's the one who told me to ask you."

"Don't be ridiculous. Of course I won't teach you archery. I am a knight, and you are a girl. Now go on, back to work."

"But—"

"My answer is no." Franco turns back to the dining hall without waiting for her appeal. The ice in his refusal leaves Katrina cold, and as she walks to the stockroom to drop off the clean laundry, she broods over the situation. If her own father doesn't mind, why should the knight? Why should anyone mind that she wants to learn archery? She *will* learn. Just as she will read and write, and sail ships if she chooses and marry someone she loves and do everything else they tell her not to.

EIGHT POINTED CROSS

PART TWO

CHAPTER SIXTEEN

Istanbul
Gregorian: AD 1550   Hijra: 957 A.H

Demir wanders the wide corridors of the great house in search of his older
half-brother. The child peeks into every room: the kitchen, the storage, the
public quarters, the private, behind fat damask pillows and hanging Persian
carpets, all to no avail. With each flip of a cushion, each turn of a curtain, his
heart beats faster. Somewhere, Muharrem is waiting, watching, and every
second that Demir does not find him is a second closer to his older brother
winning.

It is not a game of hide-and-seek. Muharrem does not play with
Demir. Not games anyway. Muharrem plays tricks. When Al Hajji Hamid al
Azm, their father and master of the house, is away acquiring new horses for his
already thriving stables, Muharrem will sneak into the man's private chamber,
where dozens of fine weapons are on display. There are mounted scimitars and
broadswords, the blades sharp and inscribed with passages from the *Qur'an*.
There are crossbows and javelins, helmets and greaves, all ornate and finely
tooled. It is a bejewelled arsenal, gleaming with burnished emeralds and rubies.
Muharrem always goes for the prize of the collection: a masterpiece of curved
steel, a gift given by Dragut Raïs. The silvery half-moon gleams, its hilt gold
and silver, inlaid with topaz and ivory. Demir knows that Muharrem will take
the scimitar and hole up in some dark corner, waiting for his younger brother
to pass. He will spring from his hiding place, terrifying Demir.

If their father, Hamid, knew what his firstborn did in his absence, he
would have him bastinadoed—not for Demir's sake, but for Muharrem putting
his hands on the treasure. Demir has never told. The seven-year-old is certain
nothing in the world is worse than a tattler. Besides, Muharrem would only take
revenge.

Today, with Hamid away at Eyüp on business, Demir has decided to take preventative measures and find Muharrem before Muharrem finds him.

It is an autumn afternoon. The servants have tied back the curtains, allowing fresh air to blow through the long corridors and high-ceilinged rooms. The breeze carries with it salt off the three seas that meet at Istanbul, spices from the nearby market, and the prevailing scent of the city—her perfect roses, believed to have sprung from the sweat of the Prophet.

As Demir enters the women's quarters, he meets the Persian serving girl, Jameela. She is dressed from head to toe in indigo silk. Even in private, where she is free to unveil, she keeps her head covered to hide a disfigurement. Only her eyes are exposed, but they convey more of her than any other part could. They are a rich brown, flecked with amber, lit with warmth and humour. Demir worships her. A bright smile crinkles the corners of her eyes. Without a word, she points him to where he will find his brother. Surprisingly, it is not inside some chest or hidden passage or behind one of many hanging carpets. Rather, Muharrem is sitting in the foyer by the *mangal*, a hot coal brazier that fills the central hall with warmth. Demir is caught between relief and disappointment. He wanted to catch out his brother in his hiding place and scare *him* for a change.

Instead, he finds him bent over the *Qur'an*, and from the sweat on his brow, he is trying desperately to memorise an ayet. Muharrem reads aloud, stammering the words, not understanding the essence of a single one. By ten, boys who show respect to the tenets of Islam and properly practice ritual cleanliness are accepted to the *madrasah*. At eleven, Muharrem has already been denied entry three times. Demir feels sorry for him.

By three, Demir could recite the *al-Fatihah* flawlessly. He has since memorised most of the sacred book's passages. Demir is smart enough to know that Muharrem finds this a complete outrage. The older boy strikes out in any way he can, trying at every possible turn to scare his half-brother to death, or at least, scare him out of his wits. Now, Demir draws quietly near, attempting friendship yet again.

"May I help you practice?" he asks.

Muharrem glares at him. "You think you are smarter than me?"

"No. I like to help."

"Then go serve the beggars at the imarets."

"When I'm bigger, I will." Demir recalls the words of the imam. "The food most beloved to Allah is that which is shared."

Muharrem rolls his eyes. But in a blink, his expression changes. He moves over on the fat cushion and gestures for Demir to sit. Elated by the rare invitation, he flops next to his brother on the edge of the pillow.

Muharrem clears his voice. "You can recite any of the *Qur'an*'s passages on command."

Demir nods.

"Three seventy-five."

"Among the People of the Book are some who, if entrusted with a hoard of gold, will readily pay it back; there are others among them whom, if you entrusted with one silver coin, they will not repay it unless you constantly stood demanding."

"Well done."

Demir is overjoyed. His brother has never said anything nice to him before. Muharrem leans close. "Father told me about a special trick that good Muslims can do."

"What is it?"

"If you are truly an excellent Muslim," Muharrem begins, "one who has proven himself as such by say, memorising an ayet from the *Qur'an*, you can hold a hot coal in your hand and it will not burn you. The Prophet could do it. He could juggle them!" He shakes his head slowly, sadly. "I wish I could do it. ...But I just know you can."

Demir's eyes go round. "Think so?"

"Well, I've never heard the poetry of the *Qur'an* recited so beautifully."

"Can *Baba* do the trick?"

Muharrem nods. "Father is an exceptional Muslim. He has made the pilgrimage to Mecca *and* Medina. He had to do this trick first, so the imam could see he was worthy of the name Al Hajji. Go on. Take a lump of coal. It has to be a red one for it to be official."

Demir looks at his small hands, turns them over and examines his palms. Hot coal would really hurt if he turns out to be a bad Muslim.

"Come on," Muharrem urges. "You want to be like *Baba*, don't you?"

Demir flicks his eyes warily to the hot brazier. "I want to be an exceptional Muslim."

"Go on then. Everyone will be so proud of you. Father will throw a celebration ten times the one he threw for your naming ceremony. I'm sure Sultan Suleiman will attend, along with a hundred *Sipahiyan*. And Lord Dragut too." This seals the deal. All it takes to convince Demir to do anything, from taking a bath to coming in from the stables, is the mention of Dragut Raïs. Demir adores the legendary sea captain. He has met Dragut several times and pledged himself to him. Demir hopes above all else to rise to the rank of cavalryman in the Sultan's imperial army—a *Sipahi*, a fief-holding soldier of the elite mounted force. Hamid already owns parcels of land, here in Istanbul and in the boroughs beyond, granted by the Sultan himself. Demir is not sure, but he thinks some of it might qualify as a fief, and that would make him eligible to join the royal division.

If picking up coal is going to earn him a party that the Sultan *and* his cavalrymen *and* Dragut Raïs will attend, Demir will just as soon pick up twenty. He rises from the cushion and approaches the heating pan. His steps are taken slowly. Muharrem encourages him with nods, his eyes reflecting the red glow of the coals. Demir stands at the brazier, feels its heat. He hesitates. His palms are sweating. He closes his mouth, inhales through his nose. He reaches inside the brazier.

He yanks his hand back out. "I'm afraid."

"Don't be." Muharrem crosses to the heater and looks inside. "The coal will feel as soothing as... as the milk used to make the Sultan's pudding."

Demir smiles at the mention of pudding. Without thinking, he reaches into the open brazier for a second try. This time, he closes his hand around a red lump. It is a full second before the searing pain registers. He screams and yanks his hand away, but does not have the presence of mind to release the coal, holding it a second longer before dropping it onto the rug. The silken weave immediately catches, fuelled by the wind of Demir's flailing. The tender flesh of his hand sizzles and bubbles as he wails and clutches his wrist. He holds his burned hand to his stomach, bends over it. The pain is the worst he has ever known in his short life. His tormented cries fill the hall, the corridors, beyond. Meanwhile, the carpet fire begins to spread.

Muharrem steps calmly back. "I guess I was wrong," he says mildly, picking up the *Qur'an* still lying open-faced before him. "You are not an excellent Muslim. And you had better not tell anyone about your failure, or everyone will know you are a bad Muslim. Now stop your carrying on before somebody comes."

No sooner do the words escape his mouth than Jameela flies into the foyer. Her eyes catch fire, her flames far more fierce than the ones eating the rug. "Get water!" she yells at Muharrem.

"Get it yourself. And, you, worm of the earth, will address me with the reverence owing a man of my station"—*Baba* often uses this phrase and Muharrem loves it—"or I'll have Al Hajji take your other ear." The coldness and cruelty of his words leaves Demir numb, despite the intense pain of his burns. If Jameela is affected, she does not show it. She runs from the room, returning moments later carrying a bucket sloshing with water. She empties it on the small fire that hisses and crackles as it dies. The foyer smells of burned flesh and smoke. Only the sound of Demir's soft sobs fills the great vestibule. Jameela drops to her knees before him, turns his hand over to inspect the damage. He looks too. The burns are severe, his flesh blistered. He tries to stop crying. He has to be brave in front of Jameela, especially if he is going to marry her someday. But the pain surges through him, his hand throbbing, throbbing.

Jameela glares at Muharrem. "What have you done?"

"*Master.*"

"What have you done, *master?*" She spits the word.

He narrows his eyes, sticks out his chest. "Study the *Qur'an.*"

"Then better you study it harder, for its lessons are lost on you." Jameela looks back at Demir. "Come, sweet prince." Just as he manages to gather his wits, his mother, Yaminah, bursts breathlessly into the hall. She runs past Muharrem and straight to Demir, taking his burnt hand in hers. She gasps. Demir sees her horror and her struggle to compose herself. She hoists him off the ground and makes for the large fountain in the primary courtyard. Once there, she plunges his hand into the cold, clean water. Gardeners look on in curious concern. Yaminah catches one's eye.

"Bring my son a drink." The man rushes off. A minute later, Jameela emerges with a carafe of lavender oil, the gardener trailing with a jug of water. Mother takes it from him gratefully.

"Small sips," she says, holding the jug to Demir's mouth. "Take them slowly. And keep your hand in the fountain."

"For how long?" he asks.

"Ten minutes."

Demir grimaces. "But that's *so* long, *Anneh*." To a seven-year-old, ten minutes is forever; his mother may as well have said ten days. She kisses his hair. When it seems forever has passed, she takes his hand out from the water, and Jameela pours lavender oil over his wounds.

"Better?" Yaminah asks.

Demir sniffles, nods.

She takes his chin in her hand. "What happened inside?"

"I picked up a piece of coal."

"Why?"

"I don't know... Maybe I'm just a bad Muslim."

Mother furrows her brow. "A bad Muslim? What do you mean?"

"Good Muslims can pick up hot coals," Demir replies. His *anneh* and Jameela exchange glances. Jameela is Shiah. Demir hopes she will think this is Sunni custom.

"Truly?" the serving girl asks.

"Yes. *Everyone* knows that."

"I see," Jameela replies. A light wind ripples her silk robes, a gentle tide of deep blue damask breaking against the golden shore of her skin. "I am indeed very ignorant in the ways of my faith."

"*Baba* can do it. The imam made him do it before the Hajj."

"Who told you this?"

Demir feels his tongue trip up over the words. "I... I just know. Everyone does."

His mother sets her face in stern lines. "Lying is a sin. And lying to your mother is twice the sin." She looks him directly in the eye. "Who told you that good Muslims can pick up coals?"

Demir sighs. "No one. I made it up."

***

After evening prayer, Yaminah approaches Hamid in his dining quarters. She hates having to talk to him. He is a large and intimidating presence, especially to a woman of her slight stature. Even so, Demir's savage burns demand a confrontation.

She speaks without preamble. "Your son Muharrem hurt Demir." She presents the wounds to Hamid. Demir tries pulling his hand away. Yaminah tightens her grip on his wrist.

"It wasn't Muharrem," her son avows. "I did it to myself. I took the coal in my hand."

"Why?" Hamid's voice is a low growl.

"I don't know."

"*You don't know?*" Hamid whacks Demir hard across his raw and blistered palm. Yaminah cries out for the both of them, horrified that she held her son's hand in place for Hamid to strike.

"You almost burned down my house with your stupidity! You think the idiotic likes of you will ever grace the lines of the Sipahi? The Padishah would not waste a patch of dirt on you, let alone a timar!"

"I-I'm sorry," Demir stammers. Hamid raises his hand again, this time its backside, but Yaminah throws herself between them. The blow intended for her son lands forcefully against her temple, sending her tripping over a heavy rug. Hamid offers no word of contrition.

"Out of my way! Or it is back to Algiers, to the midden from which I plucked you."

"You are the devil," Yaminah gasps, crawling backwards. "*Shaytaan* himself." Demir runs to his mother's side. The pair shrinks under the chiselled, baleful glare of Hamid. Yaminah senses Demir gathering courage, standing his ground. She follows his stare to the poker by the brazier. Her son has never even stepped on an ant, but to protect her, he would use the poker. She will stop him. She does not get the chance. Hamid strides towards them and takes Demir by the throat.

"*Al Hajji Hamid al Azm!*" The angry voice comes from behind him, turning his head to the doorway. It is Ayla, his principal wife and the mother of Muharrem. Hamid checks himself, releases Demir. Ayla is in every way Yaminah's opposite. With dark hair, eyes, and skin, her features sharp, her bearing powerful, even her beauty is fierce. Ayla's voice resounds with total authority. "You violate the law of Allah when you strike a woman. The worst thief among people is he who steals from his faith, as you have stolen the name *Al Hajji* without paying its proper due." Hamid would have anyone else slow roasted for the remark, but before Ayla he shrinks, his voice lost of its thunder. Before Ayla, Hamid is a lamb.

He points defensively at Yaminah. "She accused *your* son of evil."

"Perhaps the charge is not unwarranted." Ayla crosses to the thick carpet hanging before a wall indentation and pulls Muharrem out by his ear. The boy squirms in her vise grip. "You see?" Ayla jostles Muharrem at Hamid, whose eyes bulge with new rage. Ayla steps gracefully between them, crouches before her son. "Walk not the earth as a liar, Muharrem. I offer you the chance to speak the truth. What role did you play in your brother's injury?"

Hamid, not so charitable, awaits no response. He raises his hand to strike Muharrem. Demir jumps to his feet and moves to his half-brother's defence before Yaminah can stop him. "Madam, Muharrem did not do anything."

The woman's severe expression softens. She cups Demir's chin in her hand and looks intently at his face. "Your eyes lie no better than your tongue, dear one." She bends to help Yaminah off the ground. "Take your child and retire to your quarter."

Yaminah gathers Demir and walks off, leaving Ayla to deal with Hamid and Muharrem. And deal with them she does; it is almost half an hour before she is finished with them. In the safety of her private chamber, Yaminah holds Demir close, and together they giggle.

Hours pass, the room soon bluish with the moonlight that spreads over Demir's face. He sleeps, hand bound with lavender flowers, breath coming easier. Yaminah cannot sleep, not with the sound of her son's painful wailing still very loud in her head. She lies next to him, brushes strands of his hair off his forehead.

Jameela has stopped in twice already, with fresh roots for his wound. During her second visit, she noticed the bump on Yaminah's temple. Now, the serving girl returns, this time with a small phial. Jameela sits at the end of the bed, careful not to disturb Demir, and touches lavender oil to Yaminah's bruise. She squeezes Yaminah's hand, kisses Demir on his forehead and slips off to her room. The mother smiles, knowing her son would have loved to be awake just then. Her son, the light of her life. He is so young, so fragile, so small, and yet she has not managed to protect him as a mother should. She will not let him leave her side, especially with that accursed bully around.

No, that is not the answer. What boy wants to hide from the world behind his mother's robes?

Yaminah glances to the window, the mosques beyond. The sky over the great *Fatih Camii* wheels with a drove of white gulls. They play on air currents, cut great slow circles above the golden crescents of the minarets. Soon, the muezzins will climb those minarets and give the call to prayer.

Yaminah lies propped up on her elbow, watching her son stir, feeling him breathe, and finally, she sleeps to dream of another life in another world.

EIGHT POINTED CROSS

CHAPTER SEVENTEEN

"Never cinch too tight. Do it just so." It is Kemal, slave and chief stable keeper. The Moroccan slips a finger between the leather strap and the beautiful Turkoman's belly to check the bind. Kemal bin Hamza Fâkih could cinch a horse blind, but always double checks, because a horse, especially one that graces the stables of Hamid al Azm, must be content at all times in order to fetch a handsome price. At least, that is the reason Kemal gives his staff of one hundred. The truth is that the stable keeper loves the creatures second only to God. Everyone who works the stables knows of Kemal's affection for the animals. Even Demir knows. The child spends more time in the stables than anywhere else. If Hamid was around more and paid any attention to his son when he was, he would kick up a storm over the boy's association with hired hands, but as it is, the man's neglect of his second-born is the most favourable gesture he affords him.

Demir watches closely for the thousandth time as Kemal instructs him in the ways of saddling a charger—placing the pad just before the withers, making sure the saddle is centred, fastening the cinch buckles snugly under the belly, minding that the strap does not chafe the horse's front legs. Demir is too small to do it himself, but sometimes, after the rest of the staff have gone for the day, Kemal will allow him to adjust the buckles.

Not today, however. Today, Demir may only watch, as there are too many hands about, changing straw, pouring grain, replenishing water, grooming manes. Kemal oversees a large staff whose sole function is to make sure Hamid's stables are pristine and his horses top profit-makers. He is Istanbul's best breeder, priding himself on some of the most superbly schooled thoroughbreds spanning the Iberian Peninsula to the Caspian Sea.

Twice the size of the house, these stables rival the Sultan's own at Topkapi. Only the main palace stable at Ahirkapi, the Stable Gate, is larger. Many of the Sultan's most prized steeds are the descendants of Hamid's own thoroughbreds. The stable in which Demir stands is more a palace for the princes that are his father's two hundred horses. Where their comfort is concerned, no expense is spared—they dine on the highest quality grain, drink fresh water from mountain springs, graze on the juiciest grass, train in the most immaculate meadows, wear reins inlaid with rubies, saddles of the finest doeskin. Their stalls are Spanish mahogany, costlier than stone but softer on hooves. A gold plaque inscribed with each horse's name and year of birth is mounted to the wall, high above the zigzag tiles meant to keep the animals from slipping. Demir wishes his bathing tub had those tiles.

The horse princelings have a full staff of courtiers as well. There is one groom for every two horses. There are ferriers to shoe them, and a special team of physicians to tend their sores and guard them against outbreaks. Every day, attendants scour the walls for fractures and jutting nails; if a horse is injured by human carelessness, heads roll.

Chief groomsman Kemal does not simply supervise. Right now, he is in the stall of a feisty Turkoman named Majeed, checking the beast's dung for worms and parasites before shovelling it away. He washes his hands then uses a tortoiseshell brush to untangle knots in the mane and tail, and takes a wooden pick to the animal's teeth. As he works, Kemal recites the Hadis, sometimes whispering them, other times singing.

Demir thinks Kemal is the smartest man in the world. He knows the horses better than most men know their own children. He knows which may romp together at turn-out time and which must be separated, which to keep entire for breeding, which serve better as geldings. He knows which tend to crib on the boards or eat sand, and which prefer a stall carpeted with wood shavings. He does not raise hand or whip or voice to command obedience, though he has raised all three against subordinate slaves, from whom he will tolerate no mistakes. Demir has noticed this and asked him about it.

Kemal had a ready answer: "Little master, horses are animals, majestic, noble, but incapable of reason. Humans who err have simply failed to use their God-given intelligence to choose rightly, and in failing to use something given to them by God, they reject Him. A good whipping will help them to choose rightly next time."

Demir understood, at least partly. But he doesn't agree. He is certain horses can reason. They are, after all, his friends, and he does not want to have friends that are witless. There is enough witlessness around the house with Muharrem living there.

Kemal has told Demir he is pleased that the boy aspires to join the royal cavalry. "A Sipahi," Kemal said, "is better than a foot soldier. *Atli er baskaldirmaz*—Horsemen do not mutiny." It is the adage of the imperial Ottoman cavalry, who share a spirited rivalry with the Janissaries, the elite infantry. "To be mounted raises the Sipahi *above* the Janissary."

Demir leans on the wooden gate and sighs. He wishes he could help. After two hours, Kemal finishes with Majeed and heads for the stall of Dionysus, the pride of the stable, and the light of Demir's life. There is a nobility about this fine Arabian, the bearing of a great warrior of old, Achilles or Alexander reborn. Demir senses the animal's majesty, feels as though he should bow to this lord of horses. Dionysus is a sleek, chestnut charger, muscular, beautiful, benevolent. The connection between boy and horse was instant. Demir was three when Dionysus was born. In four years, the horse became king, and Demir stayed a boy.

His heart swells in the animal's presence. Dionysus too seems pleased, stomping his forehoof and whinnying as he stretches his neck for only Demir to stroke. He loves him like a brother, a suitable bond, as Yaminah often tells Demir he is part horse. He and Dionysus have shared many special moments. One stands out in Demir's memory: the day this lord of horses carried a lord of men.

When Dragut Raïs was last in Istanbul he visited Hamid's stables. The renowned seaman was only here briefly, between his assault on Rapallo and his raid on Sousse. Dragut had recently been named *beylerbey* of Algiers and was interested in procuring a young steed. He, like Demir, was immediately drawn to Dionysus. Demir watched with a mixture of awe and dismay as Dragut drew his face close to the horse's muzzle and stroked its nose.

Kemal entered the stable, bowing low, from the waist. "*Salaam Alaikum*. I greet thee in the name of the Compassionate, Lord Turgut," he said, using Dragut's Turkish name. "It does me much honour to welcome you into the stable of Al Hajji Hamid al Azm."

Dragut touched his hand to his forehead then heart. "And upon thee be Allah's blessings. I think you will saddle this magnificent creature for me."

"Of course." Kemal prepared the horse, checking three times to make sure everything was perfect. Demir was caught between a smile and tears, thrilled that Dragut liked his favourite horse, but dreading the idea of losing him. Still, if anyone was worthy of Dionysus, it was Dragut Raïs.

The seaman squinted at the name on the plaque. He beckoned Demir. "Dionysus is your horse, I think. May I ride him? I will not without your blessing."

For an instant, Demir almost instinctively said no. But this was Dragut Raïs, *the Drawn Sword of Islam*, he is known. The man who Sultan Suleiman—King of Believers and Unbelievers, Possessor of Men's Necks—made commander of the imperial galleys. Dragut Raïs is the greatest ever to sail the sea. Who would a mere boy be to say the man could not ride Dionysus if he wished?

"Yes, my lord," Demir says. "Please."

Once Kemal had Dionysus saddled and ready, he opened the gate to Dragut. Upon mounting, the seaman offered his hand to Demir. "Will you come?"

Demir wanted to jump up and down with joy. Of course, he had to maintain his seven-year-old dignity. He set his face in solemn lines because this was a solemn business. He nodded and, with the help of Kemal, swung up behind Dragut. The seaman drove the great charger down the tiered grassy slope behind Topkapi Palace, the Sublime Porte. They trotted along the spine of the hill, dappled with flowers and studded with pavilions. The terrain was forested with great trees that broke the sky. Demir liked that Dragut did not whip the horse to obedience. He did not have to. Even horses wanted to please Dragut Raïs.

They reached the foot of the wooded hill and trotted to the rocks that gave onto the Bosphorus strait. The water sparkled with the afternoon, the sun reflecting in golden shimmies on its surface. The warm air carried the saltiness of the sea that stretched before them and the sweetness of the grass that rolled behind. The breeze moved through tall branches, rustled their leaves. Dragut reined the horse at the water's edge, turned in the saddle.

"Dionysus is a good horse. Sure-footed. Bred for battle. I would ride him into battle."

The idea of Dragut riding Dionysus into battle was almost too much for Demir to take. He had to do something special, something big. After his *anneh* and Jameela and Kemal, Dionysus was the most special thing he knew. He took a deep breath: "You can have him, Lord Dragut."

The seaman was silent for a moment. "It highly becomes a man to be so generous."

Demir was in ecstasy; Dragut had said Dionysus was a good horse and had called the boy a *man*—two marvellous accolades in as many minutes.

"But," the seaman said, "I think Dionysus would miss you, and be distracted for it. He might topple me from the saddle in the hopes that I would meet my end, so he could return to you."

"Do you really think so?"

"I know it," Dragut replies. "When you are Sipahi, you will make a formidable pair. The two of you will drive terror in the hearts of your enemies."

"I hope Allah wants me to be a Sipahi. I hope my name is good enough."

"If God and Suleiman are for whom you wish to fight, then your name matters no more than the colour of your eyes. Merit and courage forge a man's path to greatness, not the means of his birth. Else, I would be knee deep in goat droppings." Dragut went on speaking with Demir, asking his thoughts, giving him riding tips, talking about the world outside Istanbul. He just knew *everything*. Even more than Kemal. Demir wished Dragut Raïs was his *Baba* instead of Hamid, who was always cross, wore expensive clothes and jewels and perfume, and prayed only when he knew he was being watched. Dragut lived scripture and read poetry and dressed simply, in white robes and a beige turban. Although the seaman was easily fifteen years older than Hamid, their appearances told otherwise. Dragut was in his sixties and in excellent physical condition, every bit as lean and lithe as Hamid was fat and ungainly.

Finally, Dragut urged the horse on with a squeeze of his heels, drawing Demir from his thoughts. The animal picked its way carefully around the rocks, soon finding its stride on the smooth, cobbled way ahead. The cityscape mesmerised Demir. Hamid rarely let him outside the house. Now, Demir took it all in. They rode along the channel connecting the Black Sea to the Mediterranean. Horse and riders wound with the drowned valley of the Golden Horn. It looked warm and inviting. Demir wished he knew how to swim. He didn't know anyone who could swim. He wondered if Dionysus knew how.

Demir looked across his left shoulder. The seven hills above the inlet were ranged with mosques, countless minarets stretching for heaven like golden arms.

"*Al-Hamdu Lillaah,*" Dragut said, "Praise to Allah. It is a rare blessing to ride without being pursued or in pursuit." The sea captain wore the stories of his many battles in the scars that crisscrossed his skin. Demir asked about a raised line at his temple.

"Effendi, where did you get that?"

"At Sardinia, when I was captured by Giannettino Doria, nephew of the famous Andrea."

"Tell me."

Dragut chuckled. "Very well. You see Demir, luck turns to misfortune, misfortune to luck, but always and always, the wheel is turning. The scar you ask about comes from such a turn of fortune. I was there when the Christian knight Valette was captured by Kust Aly, a worthy captain who has furnished the ocean floor with many a galley, his benches with many a knight." Dragut smiled. "I met Valette. He impressed me. Of high birth, yes, but unlike most who fought under the banner of St John, his nobility did not lie in a title inherited, rather a quality inherent. A year later, at a prisoner exchange between the Order and the Barbary seamen, the Order of St John ransomed Valette."

"Did he give you that scar?" Demir asked.

Dragut laughed. "Perhaps he did. So turned the wheel of fortune that years after his release, Valette was present at *my* capture—the battle at Sardinia that saw my brow grazed by arquebus fire."

It is the custom of war, Valette said to me. He said it in perfect Arabic. I was pleased that we could now argue our faiths in the language of the Prophet. We will meet again, that knight and I…"

"How did you escape from Doria's galley?" Demir asked.

"Barbarossa appeared before the port of Genoa with two hundred ships sent by Sultan Suleiman. For three thousand five hundred gold ducats, my release was secured. The Sultan, bless him, placed too high a value on my service."

"I would have paid twice as much," Demir said in earnest. "If I had it, I would."

"Then you place twice too high a value on my service," Dragut replied.

Now, in the shadowy light of the great stable, Demir watches Kemal run his dark brown hands slowly down Dionysus's right foreleg, checking knees, cannons, ankles, once and again, before moving on to the left. Demir wonders if the horse really would have toppled Dragut Raïs from his saddle in order to return to the boy.

Looking at Dionysus now, he hopes so.

CHAPTER EIGHTEEN

Months later, Demir walks to school alone, taking the longest possible road to the *madrasah*. He knows peace during this walk, along the rocky shores of the Bosphorus, up, up, up a steep gradient that winds with the crenellated walls of the cannon gate, Topkapi Palace. As he passes the first court of the Abode of Bliss, he glimpses the Janissaries, the elite of the Sultan's elite, a thousand standing as one, in perfect stillness, perfect silence, the sun bright on their white felt bonnets. Demir is certain none even blinks. He wonders if he could stand unmoving for so long. What if he had to pee? What if *they* have to pee?

He crosses into the belly of the shadow cast by the magnificent Ayasophya mosque, its massive dome lit gold by the morning. Onward, his path takes him past the Hippodrome, built by Septimus Severus and embellished by Constantine to resemble the Circus Maximus of Rome. Demir cannot pass the Hippodrome without imagining himself astride Dionysus, leading his team to victory in a game of Cirit, the Sultan Suleiman himself watching from his gilt box. The boy heads down another sloping road, turns a sharp corner, up one more street, and at last, reaches his *madrasah*. He loves school, loves being treated like a grown-up, but even so, his nerves flutter as he walks the path to the building, adjacent a small mosque and ancient cemetery.

Demir has been admitted two years early because he had mastered the requisite skills. His classmates find it appalling that an infant runs among them. Muharrem does not defend him. In fact, he leads in the torture.

After Demir tested his faith with the brazier coals and failed, he set out to prove he was as devout a Muslim as any. He read from the *Qur'an* constantly, and though he was not always sure what the words meant, he sensed within them a kind of magic. He would recite passages for his *anneh* and Jameela and even Ayla, while Muharrem fumed.

Soon, the imam of the Firuz Aga mosque suggested Hamid present Demir to the *müderris* of the religious school for testing. Hamid was reluctant as Muharrem had failed to qualify for the school thrice and was now past the usual age of entrance. The man did not want Demir's intelligence to remind his neighbours of Muharrem's dullness. Hamid struck a deal that would save face. He told the imam he would allow Demir to be tested only after Muharrem was accepted. Three months later, Muharrem finally managed to meet the requirements for admission.

The first few months at the *madrasah* were awful for Demir. His classmates picked on him constantly. But, school has recently gotten better, thanks to Murad.

Several weeks ago, the boys convened in the cemetery outside the classroom. The tombstones were white, tall, and narrow, each inscribed with calligraphy and topped with a stone turban. Some of them were swathed in vines of big, beautiful roses, which added their fragrance to the warm air of spring. The students had devised a game, which was meant to test the courage of its players.

Each boy was to stand on a grave, eyes closed, and summon the dead man below, who would grab the boy's ankle and try to pull him in. Even if the dead man did not appear, the boy had to stand there for five full minutes to prove his courage. Demir knew this wasn't right, fiddling with the dead; if the instructor found out, he'd probably take a truncheon to their backsides. Still, the challenge would be worth the fear if it made the other boys accept him.

Two boys took their turns without being yanked in. Next, Demir was to go. He took a deep breath and stepped onto the plot. It was just a silly game. Talk to the dead all you wanted, yell, cajole, swear, it didn't matter, nothing was going to raise—

Something cold closed around Demir's ankle and tugged, hard. He screamed and struggled, falling to the earth before finally opening his eyes and turning to face the demon.

It was Muharrem. He was laughing. All the boys were laughing too, doubling over, holding their sides. They imitated Demir's screams and flailing arms. After a few more moments of ridicule, Muharrem went back to the *madrasah*, the others following, still laughing and making fun.

Demir lay on the grass, too humiliated to get up. His legs felt warm and wet, then cold and wet. In his fright, he had pissed himself. A boy walked quietly over. Murad Adalmış held out his hand to help Demir up. He looked at Murad's extended hand without moving, convinced this was just an extension of the trick. Finally, Murad sighed with impatience and, being larger than Demir, took him by the wrist and hauled him to his feet. He spoke with a slight lisp.

"Next time, don't be so stupid as to trust your brother. You are smart in the ways of the book, but in the ways of the street, dumber than an ox. I suppose that might be all right in paradise, and without any earthly sense, you're on your way there." Murad reached into the satchel slung over his shoulder and took from it a fuzzy orange fruit. He passed it to Demir, who eyed it with suspicion.

"It's safe," Murad said.

"You take the first bite."

Murad shrugged, took back the fruit and ate the whole thing. Demir decided that he liked this Murad. The older boy's face was pleasant, with small features uncharacteristic of most Turks. His eyes were bright and friendly and shone with mischief. Murad was soft all over, but strong. The others in the class were afraid of crossing him—he could thrash any one of them.

In the days that passed, Demir found he loved having a real friend, who was neither his mother nor a horse. Moreover, with Murad on his side, the others stopped picking on him.

Whenever they managed, Demir and Murad would sneak across one of the many Byzantine bridges spanning Haliç, the Golden Horn. They would explore the foreign quarter of Beyoglu and the streets of Galata on some mission or other, usually involving the break out of a prisoner from the Galata Tower, the fat stone cylinder, which has stood as overlord of the Bosphorus strait for over nine hundred years. These missions required planning and stealth and two very big imaginations.

After school today, the boys decide to explore the wooded lands of Pera. They have a few hours until evening prayer when they would be expected for ablutions. They pass into a covered way, flanked with shops and stands and smiths, its centre heaving with a crowd hungry for goods, and lined with vendors happy to feed it. The space boasts onion *gözleme* and sussapine pillows, here sandalwood incense, there Angora wool. The *muhtesibs* are out in full force. They are the Sultan appointed market inspectors whose job is to test weights and measures. The boys exit the *çarşi*, and walk the quarter's rough, congested backstreets, patrolled by stray cats and pickpockets. Beggars lie in corners and mules nose their way through the crowd. The pair passes into a thoroughfare and through a spice market, vivid with drums of saffron and cinnamon, paprika and curry. The splash of water and roll of laughter from nearby *hamams* fade into solemn prayer from the mosque. Soon, the sounds of the lively district die down. They walk a narrow footpath, leading exactly along the course of the busy Bosphorus. Across the strait is Asia. Demir wonders if the people who live on that side look and act differently than those on this side. He asks Murad, who rolls his eyes.

"Of *course*, they're different! They're *Asian*. Everything about them is different."

"But there's only a channel of water between us."

"People from different places are different from people who live in the same place."

"But what if they came to live over here, on our side? Would that make them the same?"

Murad shrugs. "Probably not."

This doesn't make sense to Demir. "But we're all people. Why does where we live matter?"

"The weather. It's because of the weather."

"Really?"

Murad shakes his head. "No, not really. Think of your father's horses. The Arabians are different from the Turkomans, who are different from the Tekés. They're all from different places, and they live together in your father's stables, but they're still different. It's just the way it is. *Malish. Maktub—Never mind. It is written.*" Onward they trek, the terrain green and lush, a breeze moving through the great boughs of cypress and willow that line the footpath. Boats cross the waterway, sparkling with the afternoon. They pass the small, unembellished mausoleum of Barbarossa. Murad points it out, as Demir has never been this far inland across the bridge. He is in awe, having heard the stories of this nautical legend, this mentor of Dragut Raïs. Demir pauses in wonder until Murad takes him by the arm and drags him on.

There is little foot traffic, just a few mounted patrolmen, marked by their blue şalvar, red jackets, and red conical caps. Finally, after another half hour of walking, the boys reach the base of the hilly forest. They decide that today they will be Janissaries on campaign in Belgrade. In reality, only Christian converts to Islam hold the position, but Demir and Murad can pretend. They march the woods, ducking for cover behind fat trunks and boulders, picking off any who oppose with perfect aim, and taking great care to do so silently, to keep the enemy from sensing their approach.

They hike deep into the forest, upward against a wooded gradient that becomes gradually steeper. Above, birds alight on branches, twittering without any concern over the fearsome *yeni çeri* below. The air flutters with butterflies that play on the shafts of light penetrating the leafy canopy. The soldiers continue their quiet advance. They sight a target: two Knights of St John. Spaniards. The young Janissaries prime their guns and take aim.

Suddenly, pretend musket fire is met by real bullets. Demir and Murad drop to their bellies in the soft dirt of the forest floor. They crawl behind a great rock.

How in the name of the Prophet has their game of make believe turned real? Surely, whoever is shooting can see they are children! *Maybe*, Demir thinks, *maybe we just imagined it.*

Another shot rings out. It is very real. The boys huddle close, terrified. Demir is hot all over and cold all over. He cannot see anyone, cannot hear words or commands. The forest is thick, obscuring their view. Who are the gunmen? There isn't a war on any of Istanbul's fronts. The Ottoman Empire laid the sieges; she did not suffer them.

He leans to Murad's ear and speaks in a whisper. "Should we let them know we're here?"

"And startle them into killing us?"

"What if we just start yelling, right now? We won't jump up or anything, but just make noise so they know someone is here."

"What if they *were* shooting at us?"

The thought hadn't occurred to Demir. The realisation seizes his heart. "Let's run."

Murad's severe expression is response enough. The boys stay put. Several tense moments pass. Another gunshot. This one comes much closer, lodging in a tree two paces from the boulder. Splinters fly from the trunk, shards finding a new home in Murad's cheek. He swears quietly as blood trickles from the cuts.

Suddenly, a gazelle leaps through the brush, close enough that Demir could grab its tail. It is a male, marked by long, lyre-shaped horns. There is another gunshot. And shouting from a half dozen Turkish throats.

Hunters! Demir starts to stand up, so relieved he could cry. Murad throws his arm over him to keep him down. "Stay still!" he hisses. "They'll be shooting in this exact direction now."

Three more gazelles spring from the brush. Three more shots. A cry escapes the smallest of the creatures. It crashes down the slope, rolling over itself in a mess of fur and hooves and horns. Demir's first instinct is to rush to the animal's side. But Murad holds him firmly in place.

The firing stops. The hunters come no closer. Demir is not sure if they even know they hit the gazelle. He waits, to be certain the siege has ended. Just as Demir is about to peer out from behind the rock, the forest thunders with new shots, though these are farther away, and soon fade. The painful cry of the wounded gazelle is closer and much louder now. Demir can stand it no longer. "I'm going. It needs help."

"Don't be so stupid," Murad says. "They'll finish it off any moment."

This time, Demir does not heed, squirming away from Murad and taking off down the hill. Murad groans and follows, grumbling as he negotiates his way down the slope, which is all thick, snagging roots, ignored in play, impossible in danger. Demir reaches the gazelle in moments. It is in torment. The bullet entered its rear flank—not a kill shot. The creature is small, probably the baby of the herd. Its big, liquid eyes tell of pain and fear. Demir approaches with gentle steps, his small hands spread out before him. The gazelle struggles to rise, only to collapse back onto the hillside. It stops wailing and seems to sigh, to accept its fate. Demir comes closer. The animal is small, two feet in height, its soft fur brown and white with a distinctive black stripe.

By now, Murad has caught up. "You are mad to go near that injured thing." Demir can attest that Murad is not afraid of any living person; the unpredictable nature of animals, however, makes him uncomfortable. It requires tremendous courage for him to approach the wounded gazelle now and Demir knows it. He is also aware that Murad does not want to look like a coward, so to let his friend maintain his honour, Demir says, "Stay back. We'd scare it more if we come at it together."

Murad gives a curt nod, but his eyes shine with gratitude.

The animal licks at the entry wound, blood soaking its light brown fur. It stiffens at Demir's approach and struggles once more to rise. Its legs wobble

111

beneath it, and it drops again. Something tells Demir to drop too. He crawls towards the gazelle, slowly, allowing instinct to guide him. He crawls, pauses, crawls a little more, and makes soothing sounds, like the ones his mother used to make when he needed comfort. At length, he closes the distance and places his hand on the gazelle's head, all the time fully aware that at any second the animal may deliver him a hoof that would seriously damage him.

Suddenly, a twig snaps and the gazelle goes rigid. Demir looks up. All he sees is the black bore of the musket.

"Move, boy," the hunter says. "I must finish him off."

"No."

"I know you think you are helping it, but you are not. It is suffering."

Demir does not budge. "He is suffering because you shot him. And now you want to kill him to end the suffering you caused. That's not fair."

"What is written is not always fair," the hunter replies. "Move."

"I won't."

The huntsman cocks his gun. "By the Prophet, you will yield."

"I will not. If you want the gazelle so badly, you will have to shoot me first." Demir spreads his arms to block the injured animal.

"Don't think I won't." He takes aim. Demir sees no malice in the man's eyes. Still, a gun is malice enough. The only thing that makes him sad about dying is that he will never become the Sipahi of his dreams. Perhaps Allah will grant him the title in heaven. He shuts his eyes, heart pounding in his throat as he waits for the blast. Instead of an explosion of gunfire, he hears different sounds: the gun lowering, the huntsman sighing, footfalls taken towards him.

"In the name of the Compassionate, I have not met another with your heart."

Demir slowly opens his eyes. "*Teşekkür*. Please, sir, do not hurt the gazelle."

The hunter crouches. He has boyish features, warm hazel eyes bright against tan skin, and the beginnings of a beard. He wears a turban adorned with a ruby. "I'm afraid it is hurt already."

"If I can get him to *Baba*'s stables, Kemal will make him better."

The hunter raises his eyebrows beneath the folds of his turban. "Who is your father?"

"Al Hajji Hamid al Azm."

"The horse master?"

Demir nods. "He has horses."

The hunter bows. "I am Timurhan Yusuf al Salih. Your father is the finest breeder in all *Der Saadet*. My own charger is from your stables, a Turkoman called el Saray. A marvellous creature. The one I will ride into battle once I complete training as an imperial cavalryman."

Demir's eyes grow round. "Imperial cavalryman? You mean a Sipahi?"

Timurhan grins. "Indeed. Now, let us tend your gazelle friend." He glances across his shoulder without fully turning. "And you with the bloody cheek would fare better to drop your rock."

Murad lets the rock fall from his hand. During the standoff between Timurhan and Demir, Murad had edged his way closer, hiding behind trees. He picked up a big, jagged stone and signalled to Demir that he would brain the hunter with it. Demir is hugely relieved that murder was not necessary.

Now, Timurhan is all tenderness as he bends over the gazelle and probes for the bullet. He tells Demir to hold the animal's head, Murad its legs, which he does with little hesitation but great fear in his eyes. Timurhan probes and prods. He takes his hunting knife from a sheath strapped to his leg and carefully begins to extract the bullet. By the end of the operation, his hands are a red, sticky mess of blood and fur. He wipes them on the grass, then hoists the animal across the back of his neck.

On the way to the bridge, Demir confesses his wish to be a Sipahi. Timurhan smiles. "If you succeed at the *madrasah*, and prove your worth as an excellent Muslim, there is a charger in your father's stables waiting to carry you into battle." *An excellent Muslim.* Demir recalls the last time someone told him to prove his worth as an excellent Muslim. Still, Timurhan seems more genuine than Muharrem. Muharrem would have shot the gazelle. Would have shot Demir too.

"Perhaps," Timurhan begins, "you will one day serve my uncle, Mustafa Pasha."

Demir and Murad gasp in awe, having heard much about the legendary Mustafa Pasha, commander of the Sultan's armies. Born into one of the oldest and most prominent of Turkish families, Mustafa is a descendant of Ben Welid, pennant-bearer of the Prophet.

Timurhan tells the boys what is expected of those who are chosen to enter the ranks of the Sipahiyan: the discipline, the skill, the exertion of mind and body, the responsibilities. "There are duties for a horseman of the imperial cavalry outside those of war. A Sipahi will ride with the Padishah on parade as his mounted bodyguard. It is a great honour. He is also responsible for the collection of taxes and, depending on his fief, is obliged to provide the army with up to thirty soldiers. And of course, he must spend time with his horse to develop a friendship, a rhythm, a trust. But I needn't instruct the son of a great breeder in the importance of a bond between man and horse."

"Do you play Cirit?" Murad asks, uninterested in bonding with an animal. Cirit is a mock-combat game, which nurtures the Ottoman's proud cavalry tradition. It is a game of showmanship and endurance. It is dangerous and thrilling, and in this game, as in war, the side spectators hope will win does not always prevail.

Timurhan smiles, adjusts the now subdued gazelle in his arms. "I play often. The games fill every bench in the Hippodrome. It is spectacular. If you wish, I will invite you to the next match. You can cheer for my team."

"Yes!" the boys chorus.

"I will play one day," Demir avows. "Murad will too."

Eventually, they make the bridge. At its apex, they watch the sun set over Europe, leaving Asia under a sky of pink and violet and orange swirls. Laid out before them, Istanbul is a living treasury, sparkling gold, silver and pearl. She is stunning, this city of as many names as she has had masters. Byzantium. New Rome. Constantinople. Konstantiniyye. Istanbul. *Der Saadet.* The Abode of Felicity. Founded by Byzas. Expanded by Constantine. Ruled by Osman. Conquered by Mehmet. This is the capital city of Islam and the centre of the world's greatest empire, a realm spanning the Arabian Peninsula to the border of Austria and from the Persian frontier to the littoral of North Africa. She has survived earthquakes and fires and Attila the Hun.

The city suddenly comes alive with the call of the muezzins: "*Allahu Akbar!*"

"Evening prayer," Demir says. "We will miss it."

The hunter shakes his head. "We will make our prayers on the rocks. East is east, from wherever we face it."

Once namaaz is complete, the three take back to the road, heading over a series of tight, undulating streets, passing the site of the latest work-in-progress of renowned architect Mimar Sinan, whose unrivalled vision and artistry have made Istanbul shine like the jewel she is. Over a year ago, he began construction on the *Süleymaniye Camii*, the magnificent mosque dedicated to the Sultan. Already it is taking shape, the courtyard laid, the foundations set. All around the quad spring roses and tulips. The gazelle spots the tulips and fidgets in Timurhan's arms. He whispers to it, coos, soothes it somehow. They turn onto another street, at the foot of a steep, cobbled gradient that leads to the Fatih mosque, named for Mehmet the Conqueror. It is the mosque where Murad's father worships, but Murad does not like going there. There are too many cats all over the place, hundreds, making the steps furry. Demir knows cats scare Murad the most. They, above all other animals, are unpredictable.

Now, Murad tells Demir he will see him tomorrow, thanks the soldier for not shooting them, gives the animal an awkward pat on its head, and runs to his door.

Demir turns to Timurhan. "Are your friends not going to wonder where you got to?"

The man shrugs. "They will probably think the baby gazelle had more spirit than I and managed to take me as a prize... I suppose they would not be too far off the mark."

At last, Demir and his new friend reach the house of Al Hajji Hamid al Azm. Kemal passes by the front gates on his way to the servant quarters just as the guard is opening the latch to Demir, who gushes with the details of the day to the chief groomsman.

"What are your plans for this animal, young master?" Kemal asks.

"To keep him, of course. We can put him in the stable."

"Your father will not allow it. He will have me slit its throat and cook its meat."

Demir is horrified. He works his brain for a plan. Just then, Hamid storms from the grand main door. Demir's heart sinks at the sight of his father. The man marches towards the gate in a rage, stumbling in his agitation, barely seeming to notice the small gathering in his great courtyard. His face is twisted up in anger.

Perhaps one of the servants has displeased him? If so, Demir trembles for the servant. Hamid has a fondness for devising ever-crueller ways of dealing with errant slaves. He has forced Demir to watch on several occasions. As Hamid crosses the courtyard, he notices his son.

Demir senses the danger and tries desperately to win his father's favour. "This is Timurhan Yusuf al Salih. He is a Sipahi in the imperial cavalry. He will be. His uncle is Mustafa Pasha! And he said you are the finest horse breeder in all of *Der Saadet.*"

Timurhan bows with all the grace he can muster while still holding the wounded gazelle. "*Salaam Alaikum.* It is with great honour that I meet you again, sir." Demir sees the bewildered glaze in his father's eyes. Timurhan clears his throat. "I am certain a man as busy as you would not recall a transaction with a simple cavalryman. I do not take offence. Allow me to say that you have raised not only the most magnificent steeds from the Ebro to the Levant but the best boy I have ever met."

"Of course I recall doing business with you," Hamid lies. His smile is friendly, his voice velvet. "Who would I be to forget the nephew of his lordship Mustafa Pasha, exalted descendant of the Prophet's pennant-bearer? It delights me beyond measure that the horse you purchased from my humble stable pleases you."

Demir blinks. It is a rare thing indeed to hear his father address anyone with reverence. In fact, the only other he can recall his father talking to like this is Dragut Raïs. "What brings you here now, good sir of the stirrup? If your desire is a perusal of the mounts, I will have the groomsman escort you through the stables at once."

Demir does not understand why Hamid has not taken notice of the antelope in Timurhan's arms. Perhaps the raki on his breath has dulled his senses. It disgusts Demir that his father is so liberal with the laws of Islam, which strictly forbid hard drink. It is *haraam.* If Timurhan notices the violation, he makes no indication. He speaks in his soft way.

"Thank you for your accommodation. Forgive me, however, for I have come to you with this wounded animal in hopes that you will open your stables and your heart to it, that it may know speedy recovery in your care." Demir is fully aware that his father must hate the idea of letting this wild animal into his stables, but knows also that Hamid is always a businessman—this small act will win him favour among the Sipahiyan. If the nephew of renowned general Mustafa Pasha echoes these endorsements to his uncle, it will increase

Hamid's already tremendous wealth. He soon relents. Demir cannot believe the luck this day has brought.

"Groomsman," Hamid says to Kemal, "show this fine lord of the saddle to the stables and provide him with a clean stall for this most graceful of Allah's creatures. Then, you will tend its wound."

"At once, effendi." Kemal turns for the stable.

Timurhan bows once more. "May the blessings of God be upon you and yours."

Hamid nods. "And upon you." Timurhan jogs to catch up with the Moroccan groomsman.

Now, father and son are alone together in the moonlit courtyard. Demir is about to set off after Timurhan, but Hamid takes him by the collar and draws his face close. His eyes are red and dangerous beneath his turban. "I will finish later what I could not start now."

"Yes, Father."

Hamid holds Demir a moment longer, finally shoving him away. The man barks at the blackamoor to open the gate, then stalks off into the street. Demir is glad to see him go. He knows it is wrong, but he hopes his father crosses the bridge and, in his drunkenness, loses his footing. Like most Turks, Hamid cannot swim. Demir abandons the dark thought and runs to the stables.

***

The boy is not the only one happy to see the back of Hamid. At a grated window on the third storey of the house, Yaminah watches with relief as her husband staggers past the guard. A sigh calls her attention to her lap, where Jameela rests her head. The serving girl is without her veil, something she will do only in the older woman's private room. Together, they occupy the divan, a low outcropping from the wall, cushioned with pelts. It is a cosy quarter, the floor soft and warm with deep rugs and flatweave *kilims*. Wall sconces give off wavering light, and deep blue pillows of brocaded silk, embellished with jewels and gold thread, soften the corners of walls painted rusty orange. Cones of sweet incense burn low, filling the chamber with the scent of cardamom.

Yaminah looks out through her window to the night sky and crescent moon. She strokes Jameela's straight black hair, stares out at the minarets, their own crescents lit by the moon. She watches a drove of gulls wheeling above. They look as tiny flashes of white light playing on fresh airstreams. Every so often, Jameela sniffles or sobs, the sound muffled by silk robes.

Yaminah rocks her gently. "You break my heart, dear one. Tell me what troubles you."

After a slow time, Jameela lifts her head. "I am but a grain of rice beneath your slipper. Why should I burden you?"

"Because I love you as a daughter, and you may call me *Anneh*— Mother."

116

Finally, Jameela pulls back and wipes her eyes, cheeks running black from the kohl and the tears. "Shall I prepare the mistress her bath?"

Yaminah shakes her head.

Jameela sighs. "If I tell anything, I must tell everything, and there will be no going back."

"So there is no going back."

Jameela glances around the room. She rises, slips to the doorway, looks left down the corridor, then right. She leaves the door ajar to hear any comings or goings and kneels before Yaminah. The serving girl drops her voice to a whisper so low it barely rises above the soft whinnying in the stables three storeys below. "It is... it is Al Hajji. Your husband."

Yaminah reads her eyes perfectly. "He wants to take you as a lover."

Jameela swallows. "I fear, *Anneh,* he has done already. In Algiers." She bows her head and kisses Yaminah's hands. "I did not want it. I am sorry."

"I'm not angry with you, sweetest one. My husband has many women. I am his second wife, and there are two after me. He has his boys too. The man is insatiable in the matters of the flesh. His tastes probably run all the way to the goats in the barn. But you, you are young to know a man."

"I am not so young," Jameela replies. "His fourth wife is younger. I'm already sixteen. Twelve when he first took me. I did not know what he was doing. Tonight he was drunk and made his usual advances. I resisted, giving excuses, feigning illness, but he would have none. Finally, he tried to force himself, and I pushed him over and ran. For that, he will put me out in the street."

"Does he often do this to you?"

"At first. But since he had my ear severed, he has not much summoned me to his bed."

Yaminah blinks. "Jameela, you told me you were attacked by a jackal."

"In a way, I was."

"You are right." Yaminah touches her servant's cheek. "Why did he do this?"

Jameela sighs. "I knew great pain that day and am not eager to renew the knowledge. Still, I cannot refuse you, my mistress, my friend. A time ago, the servants joked that Al Hajji's first wife, the mistress Ayla, was the true master of his household. A Greek gardener said once that the master is a eunuch whose manhood Ayla keeps rolled up in her prayer mat. One of the pageboys, a Bosnian named Ahmed, overheard the joke and told the master. Ahmed identified the gardener and told Al Hajji I was the one to whom the Greek was speaking. The master ordered me punished. I was fortunate, he only ordered my ear removed—to put an end to my listening to gossip. The gardener...he did not fare so well. The master had him chained to a wall and his tongue tied to a horse. A whack from a barbed rod sent the great beast galloping, ripping out the Greek's tongue. The sequence was repeated, though this time the cord was tied to his... tied lower. *A fine gelding for my stable,* Al Hajji

117

joked, as the gardener shrieked and bled and fainted. He was dragged behind the horse over the most punishing of roads, until what remained sickened even vultures. This won Ahmed the role of *garzóne*. But your husband tired of Ahmed too and had him put out in the streets. His throat was slit before sunrise the next day. Now, the same fate surely awaits me."

Yaminah is shocked to silence. She has had ample evidence of Al Hajji Hamid al Azm's cruelty, but this savagery is far beyond anything she could imagine. Her stomach churns with the awful knowledge, her head pounding with it. She has never been so full of hate. It makes her hot, makes her ill. She feels useless, unable to find words to comfort the serving girl she loves. Yaminah embraces Jameela, allowing her own tears to spill into the girl's black hair.

***

In the corridor outside Yaminah's door, a hanging carpet moves. Muharrem sneaks out from behind the heavy rug and steals down the hall.

CHAPTER NINETEEN

Malta

It starts on the sea, a soft, summery breeze that tiptoes over the water and wafts across the mouth of a cave, formerly a fortress in times of imaginary battle. Katrina and Angelica sit next to each other in its stone jaw, a copy of Boccaccio's *Decameron* lying open across their laps. Angelica's imprudent Aunt Giselle sent the book to the rectory from Italy, even though Rome deems the work immoral. Angelica hides it beneath her mattress.

"Let's read the one about the nun," she says. Of the volume's one hundred stories, she loves the tale that peals with the carnal wordplay of the stern abbess, the fornicating sister, and her lover.

Katrina smiles, bright against her deeply tanned face. She does not start reading just yet, turning instead to face Angelica. "I wonder what lying with a man is really like... It must be wonderful if it impels people—nuns, even—to such intrigues." She wrinkles her nose. "Seems strange though, the idea of a man sticking his—"

"Katrina! Don't be lewd!"

She rolls her eyes. "Come on, you really mean you've never even thought about it?"

Angelica goes warm. "How? I've never seen a naked man."

"I have."

"*What*? Who?"

Katrina spreads her hands. "I do live in close quarters with two men. It's an odd-looking thing, dangling there like a tail in the wrong spot." Angelica watches curiously as her friend scours the cave floor, stopping at a long, smooth rock that pokes through the dirt. Katrina digs out the phallic stone, holds it between her legs, and whirls around in a gyration of hips. She hoots with laughter, placing one hand against the wall to steady herself, the other to clutch her side. Mortified, Angelica covers her mouth.

"I need two pebbles to go under the long one," Katrina manages, leaning over in hysterics. This sends Angelica into a fit of laughter. Soon, she's howling too, pounding her fist on the dirt. Both girls lose control, laughing so hard they have to squeeze their thighs together to keep from peeing. They collapse against each other, laughing long after it hurts. Angelica wipes tears from her eyes and sits up straight, only to break into more giggles. And she cannot recall a finer moment.

Suddenly, hooves pound the terrain. Heedless, Katrina runs out from the cave, Angelica following her into the sun. She smiles instinctively—Domenicus approaches, astride a splendid black horse. Years earlier, the knight di Bonfatti presented the Montesas with Tramonto, the lustrous charger that carried the boy to his mother's funeral. Angelica shields her eyes as she watches the pair canter through frothy surf, water exploding under iron-shod hooves. Domenicus veers off the shoreline, pushing the horse to jump a stand of cactus.

"You're just showing off!" Katrina shouts, tunnelling her mouth with her hands. She turns to Angelica as he trots towards them. "An arrogant beast, isn't he?"

"The horse?"

"The rider." Katrina takes the leather reins from him. "Shouldn't you be at the Infirmary, learning how to cut people open? Or practising the sword, learning how to cut people open? Or gathering brambles? It's your turn, you know."

He grins. "There was precious little to do at the *Sacra Infermeria* today, so they sent me off. And if you'll recall, I fenced with Father until late yesterday. As for brambles, fresh ones are already waiting in the hearth. I even cleaned out the dung room—without any help from *you*." That his amusement only bolsters his sister's irritation makes Angelica laugh.

"Let me have a ride," Katrina says crossly. "He's not only yours." Domenicus yanks the reins back from her, but Angelica moves to catch his gaze, and he drops them.

"Forgive my rudeness, *Signorina*."

"Hello," she says. "Amazing how docile such a massive creature is under your control."

Domenicus beams. Katrina scoffs. "Get off, before the sentry sees us and spoils our fun."

"Henri would be right to chase you off. You should be careful reading in a cave. Dragut might catch you."

"Let him try."

"He *has* been trying," Domenicus says. Angelica knows he's right, but stays quiet. Over the past few years, the archipelago has endured small-scale attacks, masterminded by the seadog Dragut Raïs. "During his last raid on Gozo, his brother was killed. Pa said Dragut vowed revenge."

"So? Pa also said Dragut had a premonition he would meet his end on Malta." As brother and sister spar, Angelica craves a moment unwatched with Domenicus. As if reading her thoughts, he swings his leg over the saddle and hops down. Katrina mounts the animal easily, her legs not quite long enough to reach the stirrups, her boylike manner of straddling a horse most peculiar.

Domenicus seems to agree. "Why not at least pretend to be a lady, and sit side-saddle?"

Katrina grunts, and with a kick, drives the horse across rocky terrain. After a long, quiet moment, Angelica turns to Domenicus to break the now-awkward silence.

"So. Your sister's reading gets better all the time. Writing too."

"It is to be expected, with you for a tutor."

Angelica feels herself blush. "Would you like a *gbejna*?" she asks, bending to hide her face and to take a piece of white pickled cheese from its linen wrapping.

"In this heat, I probably taste like a *gbejna*." Domenicus pulls off his shirt, uses it to wipe sweat from his brow, then sets it on the ground, next to the *Decameron*. He picks up the book, peers at its cover. Angelica is relieved—for her, discussing literature is the perfect antidote for awkwardness.

"The prologue is devoted to Black Plague—something to interest someone with your medical ambitions. And one of the characters, Elissa, reminds me of Katrina with her sharp tongue."

"Oh?" Domenicus arcs an eyebrow. "And who do I remind you of?"

"I've yet to read about anyone like you."

He laughs. "Then you must read about Sir Arthur. Or one of his knights. I could be Lancelot. At least, once I prove my worth. For now, I might be reminiscent of a serf."

"What makes a serf less worthy than a knight?" Angelica asks.

"Nothing," Domenicus replies earnestly. "A knight has armour and more to eat, that's all." He shrugs. "Serf or knight, you'll come across someone. Not even monks read as much as you do."

"Books are my wings. I can fly anywhere in the world by turning a page, become anyone, say anything—" she cuts herself off. "It's silly, I know. You must think me foolish."

"*Pienso que usted es encantadora y hermosa,*" Domenicus says in Spanish. *I can think only of how lovely and pretty you are.*

Angelica narrows her eyes, but smiles. "Speak words we can both understand."

"I said I'd like to take you for a ride on my horse—he doesn't have wings, but he can fly."

Before Angelica can decline the oft-repeated invitation, Tramonto trots back to them with Katrina stooped in the saddle, arms wrapped around her abdomen.

"What's the matter?" Angelica asks, instantly concerned. Katrina dismounts, palms her belly.

"My insides are in knots."

Angelica glances at Domenicus and almost replies, *mine are too*. Instead, she says, "Go on home, Kat. Rest. The book is yours for tonight." After a few moments, Katrina straightens out. She takes the book with thanks and walks off, leaving Angelica alone with Domenicus.

He offers his arm. "May I escort you home, *Signorina?*"

She is more than willing, but with age comes formality, so for the sake of decorum, she puts up weak resistance: "No, no, you love to ride. Please don't deprive yourself because of me."

"But what if corsairs landed? Who would protect you?"

"It's midday. I hardly need an attendant." She hopes her refusal is feeble enough that he will try again.

"Oh," he says. "All right then…"

Damn it. Angelica opens her mouth, worried that silence will put an end to his efforts. "It's just that, well, the church is completely out of your way…"

He pats his horse on the muzzle. "Tramonto loves the grass that grows in the churchyard."

"Yes!" she says, painfully aware of her enthusiasm. "I mean, I suppose he could do with some grazing. He's awfully skinny." That settles it. Domenicus takes the horse by the leather shank and starts up the slope, Angelica trailing. Above, gulls play on the air currents warming with the day. Tramonto's large hooves *clip-clop* over loose stones, scaring a tiny lizard into a rocky cleft.

"Easy, easy," Domenicus whispers. "Take it slow." Ears laid back, the horse steps carefully around grooves, plodding with a gingerly gait. "That's my boy." Angelica finds the way Domenicus speaks to the animal endearing—most men would use a whip. But she is drawn by more than just his gentle nature: there is the ripple of movement in his deeply tanned shoulders, the trail of sweat rolling down his spine, and as he slackens his grip on the reins, she notices his hands, soft in their strength. She wants those hands in her hair, on her face, around her waist. Her breath becomes shallow. She swats the prickling stem of her neck. Domenicus turns to the sound of the slap.

"Pesky flies," she lies, wanting but unable to look away. His features are arresting, his eyes bright and vital, the sky after a summer storm. His left cheek is lined with a small, jagged scar. Angelica wants to kiss it, to kiss *him*. She feels her mouth on his. Her vision clouds, making her clumsy. She stumbles several times on rocks, sending them down the hill. Her skirt catches on cacti once, twice. Domenicus holds out his hand, but she tells him not to worry.

He raises an eyebrow. "Are you all right?"

"No. *Yes*. Yes."

"You are flushed."

"The heat." She fans herself in emphasis.

Domenicus gives his horse a hearty pat on the neck. "You see? You've made the top no worse for wear, and—" he turns and smiles at Angelica "—done a finer job than Miss Tabone."

A crooked path takes them along the village boundaries. It is a rutted land, steepled and dry. Domenicus sweeps his free arm grandly over piles of dung and the swarms of flies they attract.

"Egypt can boast her pyramids, Italy her Coliseum, Greece her Parthenon, but Malta... Malta has her epic mountains of animal shit."

"Egypt, Italy, Greece," Angelica recites dreamily. "How exotic."

"My father has seen the pyramids and the Coliseum. He's even been to places where leaves change colour with the seasons and float down from boughs to feed the earth."

"He made that up!"

Domenicus shakes his head. "It's true. The leaves turn gold and copper and brass, bright against the cinder skies of October. It happens in territories where winter brings blasts of snow."

"*Snow*," Angelica repeats. "A pretty word. What is it?"

"Soft white powder that blankets all the land," Domenicus explains. "It falls in distant northern realms, where you can see your very breath, where the air blows so cold it freezes the rain. And when moonlight touches the snow, it sparkles like a million blue diamonds."

Angelica furrows her brow. "Come on. You're just making fun of me now."

"Never."

"Then promise we'll go there one day, to this magical place where gold floats from tree branches, and the air turns rain into diamonds."

"I promise," he says. "You're like my mother, you know. Before she died, Pa would tell her all about the lands he visited. She didn't always believe him, either."

"Do you ever visit the churchyard where she rests? I never see you with your father."

"Not often," Domenicus replies.

"I've never visited my father's grave," Angelica says quietly. She has never spoken about the night her father was killed. But now, something pushes her to keep talking. She inhales, holds the breath inside her. At length, she speaks. "He had just saved enough to buy a cart, and that evening, suggested a visit to my uncle's parish. We arrived in Birgu and were met by invasion. A corsair rushed upon us, his pike levelled. Right away, my father offered to surrender cart and horse. Instead, the Moor caught my mother's arm and threw her onto the road. My father tossed the corsair what few coins he had in his waistcoat. Without a word, the Moor speared him through. My mother screamed and fought until stilled by blows."

Domenicus is silent for a moment. "He left you?"

"I made it over a wall and hid. …Even now, I can hear him breathing as he searched the field. A whistle blew, twice," she continues. "When I was sure he was gone, I climbed back over the wall. It wasn't real, even as I held to my father on the road. A knight found me and brought me to Mdina. The civil authority didn't know what to do with me. My mother has a sister, Giselle, usefully married to a gentleman of Rome. He didn't want the burden of another's child. My father had one brother, the priest. Uncle Anton sought permission from Bishop Cubelles to have me live at the rectory. At first, the Monseigneur objected, suggesting the orphanage at *Santu Spiritu* in Rabat, but my uncle pleaded, and the bishop relented." She pauses. "Aunt Giselle sends gifts—to make sure I'm comfortable, she says."

"Are you?" Domenicus asks.

"My uncle is kind, and I owe my happiness to him, but I would do anything to have my parents back. It's almost harder for me, knowing my mother might still be alive, but not knowing where she is. I've written her letters, but have nowhere to send them." Angelica looks at Domenicus. "I'm telling you this now only because… I don't know, maybe because you are safe."

"I'm certain your mother does nothing but think about you."

Angelica smiles. "She would have liked you. That's the best thing I can think to say about someone." As they cross the cobbles to the rectory, Domenicus stops. Angelica continues on but soon looks back. He nudges his chin to the flute poking out from her basket.

"Do you play?" he asks.

"A little, I suppose. It was my mother's. She would play the most beautiful song to me. I memorised it, but I'm not as good as she is…was…*is*."

"Will you play it for me sometime?"

"I'm not very good," Angelica replies.

"I'm sure you are."

They hold each other in an intent and silent gaze. Angelica finally breaks the stare. "I have to make lunch for my uncle."

"*Vous m'avez désarmé complètement.*" *You have completely disarmed me.*

Angelica laughs but does not request a translation.

Domenicus leads the horse towards the road but lingers at the churchyard. Leaving Tramonto to graze, he walks to his mother's grave. Already the headstone has the look of a hundred storms. He crouches and runs his hand over her name, tracing each letter with his fingers.

"Hello, Mama. I'm sorry I don't come to you often…" Tears gather at the corners of his eyes. "Don't think I don't think about you. I do. And I hope heaven's gardens please you."

At home, Domenicus finds Katrina sprawled on her pallet, bed curtain drawn partway. Alarmed, he crosses to her, puts his hand against her forehead.

"Your brow is cold," he says. "A good thing." She curls into a ball, bringing her knees to her chest, wrapping her arms around them.

"My *stomach* hurts, not my *head*."

"It's all connected. I can bring you water if you want."

"What I want is to be left alone," Katrina snaps, pushing him. "Go away."

Domenicus does not understand his sister's hostility. He rises angrily. "Poor whatever bastard you marry." He quits the house and goes to meet his father.

Beyond the labyrinth of streets, rising above the village buildings, the solid bulk of St Angelo commands the harbour fairway. The Norman fortress is the colour of strained honey, cut with windows that gaze out over the sun-soaked waters of Kalkara. A light wind rolls tiny ripples towards the open sea as visible dust wisps drift on air heavy with the smell of sweat. The clang of tool against stone rings louder with every step Domenicus takes. From a distance, the bastion is an anthill, its grounds crawling with activity. Labourers drive mule-drawn wagons loaded with pebbles and dirt and combed sand. Sun-bronzed men, powdered white with dust, fill the outer walls with rubble. A lone artisan works a chisel to carve an arched window frame, and beyond him, a draughtsman uses a bob on a string to check the plumb of the structure. The wall is slightly off level. He tosses up his hands, cursing a litany of saints and their mothers. Stocky, grunting workers lift massive blocks into place atop the walls. Builders prepare vats of mortar, as trowel-wielding masons spread layers of the paste over stone. Crews bathe newly constructed ramparts with water to keep the mortar from drying too quickly. Domenicus walks on in search of his father, past screeching winches and groaning pulleys, through rows of labourers, all of them chiselling and hammering, all of them sweating.

The dusty path takes him along a ditch that is being deepened to separate the castle from the town. Overseers hover near this trench, where Muslim slaves and Christian criminals quarry, muscles rippling with every swing of every pickaxe. Knights in black habits range the site, followed closely by young pages.

The tower bell will soon chime the dinner hour. Domenicus passes around rubble and stone, to the western bastion of St Angelo. A pain in his foot stops him briefly. He peers down to locate the rock lodged in his boot and bumps into a tall, regal knight, silver-haired and bearded like a patriarch.

"Pardon me," Domenicus says in Italian, the communal tongue. "My boot took a stone."

"A man should never be caught with his head down," the imperial Frenchman replies.

Domenicus smiles instinctively. He bows with reverence and, on rising, switches to French. "You are Fra Jean de Valette." Domenicus has imagined a hundred times the moment he would meet the revered Jean Parisot de Valette and is awed by the magnitude of his presence. Pa had mentioned that the knight was back in Malta, away from his governing duties at Tripoli, an outpost to which he was exiled for nearly beating a disorderly Maltese peasant to death. He has come to discuss matters of defence with Grand Master Juan d'Homedes. Valette is in his early fifties, but an excellent physique belies his age. His every movement is a show of dignity. At once, he is a soldier, a scholar, a linguist, a poet. A rare being, he is said to be a judicious man without artifice. He is the beating heart of the Order, the embodiment of its vows. And he lives to kill Muslims.

"You are no page," Valette says.

"No, *Illustrissimo*. I am Domenicus Montesa, son of Augustine. My connection to the Order is not of swords, but service at the *Sacra Infermeria*."

"Augustine Montesa fought at the wall of Aragon throughout the siege of Rhodos. He also sailed under Gabriel Mercadal. A shame your father abandoned his responsibilities as a soldier."

Domenicus feels his smile recede. *He did not* abandon *his responsibilities.* "With all due respect, my lord, my mother's death forced my father to retire."

"A vow is not made alterable to the whims of convenience," Valette says. "The sun will shine warmly upon your face one moment, be blocked behind clouds the next. The test of a man is his ability to weather the storm. The seal of a hero is on his brow." Without waiting for a reply, the Governor of Tripoli takes back to his inspection of the parapets. For a few moments, Domenicus stands alone on the wall, chilled by this icy man whom his father holds in such high regard. Valette spent a year chained naked to a Muslim galley bench, where to survive a single week is something of a miracle. To collapse from exhaustion is to be rewarded with flogging until near dead and tossed overboard to drown. A waking nightmare; a living death. Valette endured, and so, became steel.

Sighing sadly, Domenicus resumes the search for his father. He finds him perched on the third highest beam of a ladder, his attention on the freshly laid blocks of a new wall. Keeping the ladder sturdy with both hands is the Egyptian, Dakarai. Domenicus taps his shoulder, and the two young men exchange greetings, unnoticed by Augustine. Domenicus motions for Dakarai to step aside, and to amuse the slave, gives the ladder a good shake.

"Dakarai," Augustine grumbles without turning, "Keep it steady, man."

The Egyptian giggles. Domenicus shakes it again, harder. His father looks over his shoulder, his scowl turning to surprise. "What are you doing here?"

"Katrina is sick in her stomach, more so in her temperament. She sent me away." He releases the ladder as his father descends, and decides not to mention the encounter with Valette.

"Master," Dakarai begins, "I—"

"*Augustine.*"

Dakarai smiles gently. "No matter how many times you correct me, I refuse to address my rescuer so informally. And I know you have long since figured this out, but continue to remind me." He starts up the ladder. "Jumoke has gotten himself lost, I think. I will find him." Although the pair squabbles like hens, it is clear Dakarai does not like being without Jumoke for long. A lifetime spent locked together in slavery has made brothers of them.

Domenicus nudges his father. "*Master*, eh?"

"It has a nice sound. I think from now on, you and your sister will address me so."

***

In the dead of night, relentless pain wakes Katrina. Sweat dapples her brow. There is a war raging inside her lower abdomen, a war her body seems to be losing. One moment the pain is dull, nagging, the next it stabs, sharp and terrible. Her ankles and thighs feel bruised and swollen, the small of her back aches. She sobs quietly, her slight frame rocking side to side.

"Please, stop," Katrina begs, as though the pain is a physical being capable of reason. She herself abandons reason, turning frantically to God. *Make it go away.* She is convinced it is plague, punishment for reading illicit books. How fitting, she thinks, that reading the *Decameron* would actually summon plague. Maybe that was Boccaccio's plan all along.

The crotch of her trouser is wet. She slides her hand into her pants and feels a warm, sticky fluid. Mystified, she pulls out her hand and holds it close to her face. In the darkness, she cannot see what is on it. *What in God's name is going on down there?* Quietly, she slips from her bed, strikes a flame, and examines her hand. Her eyes bulge. "*Augh!* I'm bleeding! I'm dying!"

Augustine yanks open his bed curtain. "Katrina, what is it? What's wrong?"

"*I'm bleeding.*" She wipes her hand on her shirt, smearing it with blood. Her father takes the candle from her and lights a lantern. "I didn't do anything," she cries, worried bleeding from *that* part of her body might arouse suspicion.

"I know you didn't," he says, crouching to get a proper look at her pants. She looks down. Her inner thighs are streaked red. Domenicus draws aside his bed curtain.

"What the devil is wrong with you, Kat? Why are you bleeding like that?"

"Shut up, that's why!" she yells.

"Go back to bed, Son," Pa says. He turns back to Katrina. "How are you ever going to become an archer when the sight of a little blood has you in hysterics?" She hates that she does not know what is happening to her body—especially when her father seems to know.

"*What is this?*"

"It happens to all girls when they become women," he says. "It is a gift from God."

"A gift? So it only happens once, right? Or is it once a year, like Christmas? It better not be."

"Well... a woman bleeds this way for several days... every month."

Katrina almost chokes. Intensely aware of her femininity as never before, she pushes her father away. "I don't want a gift!" she explodes. "Why didn't *you* get it? Why doesn't Domenicus have to bleed once a month?"

"It's not God's plan," Augustine replies lamely.

"What *is* His plan? What purpose does gushing blood every month serve?"

"Father," Domenicus begins from his bed, "how can anyone bleed for several *days* and not die? Patients at the *Sacra Infermeria* often expire after mere minutes of bleeding."

"The purpose," Pa says, ignoring Domenicus and speaking to Katrina, "is so that when you are married, you can have children."

"Married? *Children*? I'm not ready for that!" But the notion has her thinking. After a few moments, she has it. "This is punishment because of the Grima rabbit!" Several months ago, a local butcher proposed a union between his eldest son Salvatore Grima and Katrina. To seal the deal, the hopeful bridegroom delivered a plump, skinned rabbit on a tray of flowers, its neck tied with curled blue festoons. Katrina shudders. Salvatore, unsmiling, sharp-nosed, cleft-chinned, twenty-seven-year-old Salvatore. *Father, he's horrible! I would rather marry the dead rabbit he left on our doorsill.* No father on the island would countenance such rebellion under his roof, especially from a girl. And yet while any other man would have beaten his daughter senseless for that kind of disobedience, Augustine only shrugged.

Politely turn Salvatore down then, he had said. Ignoring her father's wishes to refuse the proposal graciously, Katrina cut off the dead rabbit's head and had Robert leave it on the butcher's doorstep. Pa was furious. For the affront, he punished her, confining her indoors for three months, allowing her to leave only to empty the Grima waste pit every third week for the following fifteen, despite that the Grimas themselves only cleaned their dung hole twice a year.

Now, Augustine shakes his head. "You've been duly punished." He fetches Katrina several linen cloths from a cabinet. She glances warily to the pile stacked in his arms. "You will need a cloth to... you'll need to change it often...um...or else *it* could stain... Look at... you have to fold it and arrange it so—" He cuts himself off to give her a demonstration, folding the cloth into a compress.

Katrina yanks the pile angrily from her father and, issuing a torrent of imprecations under her breath, storms outside to the *bitha*. Tonight, she is not scolded for the stream of profanities. Through the window, she catches Augustine's voice as he addresses her brother: "I know you're listening, Boy. I know what your breathing sounds like when you're asleep. Leave this alone. For my part, I have no wish to further involve myself in these strange matters of womanhood and, for your own safety, neither should you."

CHAPTER TWENTY

Katrina stirs from broken sleep and kicks away her blanket. No blood on the straw beneath her, none on her clothes. Perhaps her ordeal is over. Rising from the bed, however, brings a startling gush. She changes the used cloth for a fresh one, scrubs the old and wonders if people on the street will take any notice of her transition to womanhood. She catches her reflection floating in the washbasin. She does not look any different and, apart from her discomfort, does not feel any different.

An hour of scrubbing and hanging laundry passes. The morning grows ripe. Katrina takes some coins from the square hole in the wall and, pulling her hair into a ponytail, makes for the marketplace. Her stride is awkward until the thick cloth adjusts to the shape of her body.

The town square is crammed with merchants and customers bartering over eggs and rabbits, yarn and candles. The air itself seems edible, smelling of fresh-baked bread and sun-ripened fruit. The hum of conversation hangs low, punctuated by barking and bleating. To this cacophony, merchants add their voices, hollering their wares. A scruffy dog, driven from a vendor's stand with a basinful of water, moves into a fight with another dog over a large bone. The dishevelled victor lies stretched out in the sun, gnawing his prize. Katrina buys some cheese and leaves the square to gather brambles.

Indiscernible chatter draws up her head. Three girls walk together, black veils pinned to their hair. They halt their gossip as they pass, each glancing at Katrina with smug contempt before breaking into laughter.

"Katrina Montesa is the seed of Satan," one says. "Mother says her father must be the devil. Any God-fearing man would tolerate such a daughter as he would thirst." It is Anne, spawn of that gorgon, Carmelina Borg. While Katrina does not mind being the subject of scorn, she will not suffer her father to be. She springs to action, catching Anne's veil.

"Your mother knows more about Satan than any good Christian should. Mention my father again, you'll know Satan just as well, do you hear?"

Anne covers her mouth as though she just let spill some horrible blasphemy. She yanks her shroud from Katrina's grip, tearing her own hair with unsuccessful effort. The two girls are nose to nose. Anne stiffens, unable to turn away. Her friends make no move to rescue her. Satisfied, Katrina steps back, allowing Anne just enough room to squirm away. The trio rushes off.

"*See?*" one hisses. "It's true! Your mother was right!"

Rolling her eyes, Katrina abandons the village and its idiots. She walks and walks, the leagues passing beneath her feet. The land is scarred with ruts and crevices. She ranges desiccated fields, threads clusters of prickly pear and picks her way through patches of thistle. About a hundred paces to the west are two uniformed men she takes for gendarmes. Despite the distance, she catches the glint of their guns, hears the foreign roll of their tongues. Probably shirking work to hunt falcons.

Katrina wanders farther southeast than she had intended and ends up on a low bluff overlooking the sea. Ochre earth and honey stones are strewn across creamy bedrock where only purple thistles and grey-green stonecrops borne in tight-spiralled rows have the pluck to grow. Imposing cathedrals of rock stand as the silent masterpieces of nature's architecture. The towers, the pillars, the steeples, the spires—spectacular stone ridges creating uneven lines against sea and sky. Pink and grey veins marble smooth cuts of sunlit rock, and beyond, the surf crashes against the base like white horses in a foamy gallop. One hundred and fifty feet above, two kingfishers soar, then, in unison, swoop down to pluck spiky mackerel from the sea.

Katrina breathes it all in. Here, gulls and lizards do not judge her. It is a place without human voices, a place of waves and wind and wings. A place of freedom.

It takes a great effort for her to leave. Fortunately, there is still plenty of time to gather brambles for the hearth and spare her brother the chore.

An hour later, Katrina passes once more through the boundary of the town. Before long, snug buildings give way to an open collage of rolling fields, a patchwork of silvery green and burnt gold. Parcels pelted from above with bird droppings are overgrown with thistle. Dividing these small plots are crumbling stone barriers, built with debris left over from the quarries. In this part of Birgu, the air is sharp with the smell of animal dung cooking under the afternoon sun.

Something else is cooking—something fouler.

"*Haffef* or I beat you senseless!" It is the farmer, Grimaldi Farrugia. Katrina forgets the brushwood, runs to the low stone wall. In a familiar scene, Farrugia kicks at Robert, who is on his knees digging little pockets in the dirt. Robert ignores the farmer. Katrina does not.

"Touch him, and the knights will hang you from the highest tree."

Robert looks up, but Farrugia speaks first. "Such big threats from so small a wench. Think your precious knights care a lick for this canker blossom?"

Katrina makes scythes of her eyes.

"I'll bet they pay handsomely to pluck a fruit like you, green though you are," Farrugia continues. He closes the space between them and takes Katrina roughly by the jaw. She feels his spittle. "I do like mine raw sometimes."

"Take your hands off me, you filthy tub of guts!"

"Back off," Robert says, wresting the farmer's arm away from Katrina. Farrugia strikes him full across the mouth, the blow sending the farmhand stumbling to the ground with a split lip and chipped tooth. He spits out the tiny fragment.

Farrugia fumbles to undo his belt to savage Robert as he has so many times before. Katrina stretches over the wall and yanks a fistful of his thinning hair. The farmer claws at her hands and curses, sending Katrina and the entire Montesa family straight to hell. Robert pushes himself swiftly off the ground and throws both arms around the man's waist, pulling him away from the wall.

"Kat, let him go," Robert says urgently.

She refuses, gritting her teeth, tearing at Farrugia's hair, cursing him with equal vulgarity. A blue vein fit to burst pulses in the farmer's temple, his face deep red. A rabid dog, he dribbles foam as Katrina pulls harder, pressing her foot against the wall for leverage. Farrugia's anger froths like boiling milk, his struggles impelling her to greater effort.

"Stop, gutter whore!" He closes a thick hand around her neck and with one brute shove, flings her to the road. She lands with a thud that jars her bones, her sandals flying off. Recovering quickly from the shock, she watches as Farrugia withdraws from the wall. He makes a fist and holds it under Robert's chin.

"Back to work, or by God's teeth, I will—"

Robert dismisses him with a wave. "Forget you. Augustine will kill you twice if he hears of this. Move aside."

Grimaldi Farrugia shrinks back, a lamb before a lion. Robert climbs over the wall without another glance in the man's direction.

Sitting on the ground in the same position she landed, Katrina looks up at Robert. He seems more man than boy. The years have formed him a face both beautiful and strong, his jaw defined and stubbly, eyes clear and bright under soft brows. There is something in those eyes, some conviction, that makes being near him effortless. His teeth are straight, luckily not badly damaged by the farmer's blow. Endless toil in the fields has left Robert lean and muscular, skin glowing warm with a bronze sheen. His dark hair is forever dishevelled, careless wisps ruffled easily by the wind. Watching him, his eyes, his hands, an odd sensation rolls through Katrina's stomach. It is a feeling she does not understand but has little time to consider. Robert hoists her to her feet, and as she bends to pick up her shoes, he retrieves her linen-wrapped bundle.

Farrugia gasps. "*Blood!* She's bleeding!"

Katrina looks down and around, long streaks staining her trousers red. She twists round. There is blood on the seat of her pants. *The damn cloth!* She is furious with herself. That is, until the light of realisation dawns on her mind: they do not understand the blood. *A wall is not the only thing a girl can use for leverage.*

"Jesus," Robert says. "You all right?" He takes off his shirt and ties it around her waist.

Katrina rubs her throat, thrusts her chin at the farmer. "Double his pay, and buy my silence."

"*Double his pay?* You mean to extort me? Thief! Criminal!" Farrugia cries.

"Report it to the gendarmes," Katrina replies coolly. "Also, Falsone will escort me home—you know, in case of ruffians. And you will pay him a full day's wage."

Farrugia glares at her. Trounced, he turns back to his field, and without a poor farmhand to bully, he hunkers down to his knees and mauls the dirt with his own fingers.

***

The clang of cold steel echoes off the ruins as Domenicus and Franco engage in spirited duel. Twice a week, so long as the Order's Admiral does not summon the knight for galley service, Franco meets Domenicus at these remote temples, where amidst the stone columns and confused rubble of Mnajdra, they joust, leaving their horses to graze in grassy patches where white snapdragons grow.

Domenicus loves the ruins, loves the whisper of history and ancient souls. Here, the eons melt away. Here, the pulse of the past beats strong and blends with his own. Here, something crosses over inside him. Here, he is a glorious warrior of old.

Behind his visor, Domenicus sweats as he lunges, swinging his sword with finesse, feet stirring a storm of dust. Franco sidesteps and deflects his student's weapon. Over the past eight years, the knight has accomplished all requisites of a novice—obligatory service at the infirmary and sailing three mandatory caravans—earning himself the right to go back to Florence, with a vow to return to Malta if summoned. Yet unlike his fellows, who itch to leave, Franco has decided to remain on the island, citing the poor relationship with his father as his reason.

The knight forces the young man against a wall. "How go your days at the hospital?"

"All right," Domenicus pants, trapped against the stone column. "The physicians don't allow me to touch the patients, not that physicians ever dirty their hands anyway. I take notes."

Domenicus responds to Franco's skilled swipe with a *balestra*, a jump forward finished off by a lunge.

Franco grins. "Impressive." He launches an attack of his own, the blades a blur of steel. Retreating, Domenicus quicksteps and wards off the knight's assault with a ceding deflection.

"*Eccellente*," Franco praises, disengaging with a circular parry. "Rest."

"Thank you," Domenicus heaves. He leans with one arm against a scored pillar, tufts and tangles of moss and weed at its base. "Today I witnessed an amputation. The surgeon sawed a man's arm off just above the elbow then cauterized the stub with silver nitrate."

"What do you hope to accomplish after all this?" Franco asks.

"I'm not sure," Domenicus replies. "A condition of the apprenticeship is to use my training to serve the Order. Perhaps aboard the galleys."

"As your father did before he retired?"

"With a lancet rather than a lance. My mother inspired me to ease pain."

Franco snorts. "You go ahead and ease pain. I'd rather inflict it on the infidel." The knight raises his sword. "Ready?"

Domenicus raises his own. The blades cross, slowly at first, a sequence of deliberate swipes and parries, swords flashing with sunlight as they slice through hot air. It takes a careful step to keep from tripping over the bones and rocks scattered about the ruins. Two blue thrushes perch on a fat stone pillar— an audience for the combatants. Domenicus swings mightily, but Franco sidesteps, his breath steady, no labour in his movement. Flustered, Domenicus swipes again, a grunt escaping his visor as he notches a coralline column.

"So. A hall in the Italian dormitory is being transformed into a small clinic," Franco says. "Should you wish to offer your assistance, I'm sure they could use you as a *barberot*."

"I'd like to find work at an apothecary shop… maybe open one of my own," Domenicus pants. He carries out a *raddoppio*—lunging and recovering, lunging again.

"Petition the Grand Master. But first, gain approval from the Protomedicus."

Domenicus swipes with a heavy in-breath. "Who is he?"

"Head of the medical profession. Alonso Predal. Perhaps you can meet him. Still, I think you should learn to kill men before you learn to heal them."

"I'm sure I'll kill my fair share *as* I learn to heal them." Domenicus executes a hanging parry, breathing hard, struggling for position. His boot heel slips, and he falls to one hand. "*Cazzo!*" The ground exhales a powdery breath. With a flick of his blade, Franco sends his opponent's weapon flying across the stone jungle to land on crushed rock that lies between twin tracks scored by ancient carts.

"Beaten again," Domenicus says. "I'll never match you."

Franco removes his helmet and smiles. "Probably not. But you are agile and quick. You predict my ripostes, and you think before you strike, which will save you from panicking into error." He sheathes his blade. "Never hesitate, for it is in that split second that your enemy will have your life. You will block ninety-nine thrusts, but if the hundredth penetrates, the ninety-nine no longer matter."

Domenicus removes his visor, strands of his damp hair slipping from the string tying it back, cheeks red from the effort and the heat. Wiping his brow, he goes to retrieve his sword. Franco takes a flask from his horse Phaedo's saddlebag. The two young men, worn by sun and exertion, take rest in Mnajdra's labyrinth. Tiny lizards dart over fallen columns, grooved and overrun with weeds. The earth is glazed red, a sharp contrast to the blue below. Domenicus looks out over the sea. Filfla, an uninhabited rock bleached by the sun and shaped by a million ages cuts the water and breaks the horizon.

On *torba*, the beaten earth, he and Franco sit opposite each other, backs propped against the pitted walls of antiquity. These interior slabs are notched with orange spirals. Baked clay models of human appendages are strewn about, skulls sitting in morbid display on stone shelves, eye hollows forever staring. In the midst of the bones, one cranium stands out, appearing strangely amiable, grinning even, as though happy for the chance to hear some good conversation.

Franco drinks long sips of water from his flask and passes it off as he wipes his chin with the back of his hand. "So. Where has that powder-keg sister of yours got to?"

Domenicus brings the flask to his lips, pausing before he sips. "Off reading in some cave."

"*Reading*? A girl?"

"You forget who you're talking about."

Franco smiles. "You're right." He is silent a moment, thinking. "I have books in my room at the *auberge*. I think More's *Utopia* would interest her. Of course, I found it maudlin and dull."

Domenicus arcs an eyebrow. "There's a book not occupying space in any church libraries."

Franco frowns. "I tell you, even in its infancy, this Inquisition is a nuisance."

"So, there is disobedience in you after all."

The knight chuckles. "When pushed, all men are capable of duplicity. And since I'm already in so seditious a mood, perhaps your sister might join us here tomorrow. By your leave, I will give her the book."

"Certainly. A book costs more than a month of hearty meals. Father can only buy one a year." Domenicus rests his head back against the wall. His eyes move over the lonely structure, built by a people only time would remember. He closes his eyes, imagines the sound of ancient tools working ancient stone. How those people must have drunk and loved and laughed.

"As there is no one around to see," Franco says, drawing Domenicus from his placid reveries, "I will finally give her an archery lesson. Do you know that in the years since our first acquaintance, she has never stopped imploring me to teach her? I think she sensed that the rock of my refusal was clay. I would love to know what that girl hopes to accomplish by learning the bow."

"My sister should have been born a boy. Weaponry fascinates her. She talks of nothing more. And she is not one to just talk. She is one to *do*. Wilful to a fault. Poor the man who marries her."

Franco laughs, and ticking off each action on a finger, says, "She reads, writes, curses… is there any other realm into which women should not venture that she is determined to conquer?"

"The sky. She is not happy to watch the birds. She wants wings of her own."

"I pray the sky is big enough to accommodate something so enormous as your sister's will."

***

It is an uneven coastline, dimpled and ridged. Katrina and Robert abandon the winding trail and start down the slope towards Corradino's western strand. From here, much of the island and her harbours fill a single glance. The farmhand stops walking and turns his face to the sea. A fisherman stands perfectly balanced in his tiny boat, one hand casting a line into the sleepy water, the other resting comfortably behind his back. Robert loves watching the anglers, so still, so serene.

Katrina dabs her sleeve to her tongue and wipes Robert's bleeding lip. He looks at her with vague uncertainty, but she smiles off his concern. "I'm not hurt."

"You are a crackbrain," Robert says angrily. "Everything will be worse now."

"Truly, you are a milksop. If someone is vile enough to shit in your hands, you mustn't be shy about smearing it in his face. Besides, that boar doesn't scare you, and you know it. He knows it, too. Anyway, my father would slit him navel to chin if I told him what happened."

"Augustine is a dove."

"*Il-lallu* Falsone!" she cries, tossing up her hands. "The bloody farmer doesn't know that!" Robert looks down. "I'm sorry. No one has ever defended me before. Not like that."

"Save your thanks. I just wanted to tear out that bastard's hair."

Robert surrenders the nook of his arm and allows her to pull him down the stony embankment to the seashore. The sun-baked rock is hot beneath his bare feet.

"Why don't you just leave the farm?" Katrina asks. "Find work in the quarries, or better, become an apprentice to a tradesman. You can do anything."

"I can't be a prince," he replies.

"If you build your own castle you can."

"A castle in the air maybe."

Katrina shrugs. "A castle is a castle."

"I don't need a castle. I'd just like to keep my own farm, tend the crops myself. A simple plot for my goat and me. I'd take a princess though. A beautiful one. One with proper manners."

"Why? So she can teach *you* proper manners?"

Robert flashes a broad grin and tugs on a few wisps of Katrina's loose hair. She tosses his shirt to the ground and chases him to the water's edge. He splashes into the sea and disappears under. Katrina kicks off her sandals and rolls her trousers up over her knees. She wades in after him and is quickly swallowed by the turquoise shallows.

"Swim off," she says. "I have to piss."

Robert cringes and laughs. "Perhaps my future princess can teach *you* some manners also."

They take turns going under to see who can make it to the harbour floor the fastest, each bringing a handful of sand to the surface as proof, once, twice, and again. Robert disappears a fourth time. Moments later, he comes up, water streaming over his face, a pearly pink shell in his hand. He passes it to Katrina.

"I love it!" she says.

He watches as she lolls lazily against the water's warm embrace, her body melding into the salty folds of the sea, water bubbling in silver pearls around her. She is a starfish, stretching out her arms and legs, staring up at high clouds as tiny rollers move over her and the slight current begins to take her. It is a great, moving bed.

"Careful," Robert calls. "You'll fall asleep and wake up in Sicily. And then you'll be stuck with Sicilians." He catches her ankle and tows her closer to land.

On the rocky shore, Robert makes Katrina laugh by standing upside down and walking on his hands. They dig snails from shallow pools and eat them. When Katrina isn't looking, Robert watches her reflection ripple and play on the surface of the water.

Afterwards, they sit side by side on salt-stained stone and dry off. Zerapha sea lavenders and golden samphires sprout from crevices packed with saline soil, bringing dapple colour to the beach. Robert lies on his back, arms bent behind his head. Rays of light catch in the drops of water rolling off his deeply tanned stomach. Katrina lies on her side, propped up on her elbow. Robert notices goosebumps on her arm, raised by a damp blouse against her skin. He reaches for his dry shirt and wraps it around her shoulders.

"I want to ask you something," Katrina says, sitting up.

"Ask."

"You found my mother's ribbon, the one I lost at the *Sacra Infermeria*. That was a beautiful thing you did. And I have never said thank you."

Robert feels himself blush at the praise, so foreign to his ears.

"But how did you know I left it there?" she asks. "And how did you get it? The guard would never have let you in."

"Does it really matter?" he asks.

"No. I just—"

"You're welcome." Robert smiles. At this moment, the whole world is his. He watches the copper sea, the gulls squabbling on its gentle tide. A lone galley, Christian pennons caught high in the summer breeze, strums the water, its bow surging the break. An hour murmurs by. The great, fiery ball dips west. Rosy-lilac hues dissolve over the surf, set rocks aglow, light up clouds, their weightless, billowing edges trimmed with shades of gold and purple. The wind seems to carry a thousand colours as it sweeps softly over land. It is naked beauty, alive and unfurling in all its purity.

"Heaven," Robert says. "It does announce itself."

Katrina draws her knees to her chest. "I wish I could drink the sunset."

"As long as you share some with me."

***

Augustine wipes sweat from his brow with a dirty rag, rolling stiff shoulders as he walks across low scaffolding and climbs down a ladder. The long day of cleaving, digging, and piling meets its end, the metallic voice of the pickaxe falling silent, the sharp din of tools breaking limestone replaced by indistinct conversations. He cleans his tools of the chalky powder still swirling about the quarry. Groaning planks above his head rattle with the heavy steps of descending labourers. Bits of stone spill from the ledge and rain onto his hair. He shakes the mess from his head.

Augustine tosses his rucksack over one shoulder, glancing to the top of a nearby ladder. Dakarai swings his leg over and begins climbing down, Jumoke three or four rungs behind. The grounds teem with workmen preparing to head home. Knights round up slaves and usher them from their daytime prison to the dank dungeons adjacent the fortress St Angelo. Augustine's palms burn from sweat seeping into open blisters, his feet swollen in heavy boots. Still, he is let no release: the site's chief designer approaches, waving for his attention. A stout man, his face is sculpted into a permanent scowl, his sun-beaten brow lined with a hundred worries. Augustine finds Antonio Ferramolino's appearance absurd, the mere sight of the *capumastru*'s bowlegs enough to bring a chuckle, especially when Jumoke comments that he can see the whole island and Gozo beyond through the wide gap between them.

"Montesa," Ferramolino says, "the knight Mercadal craves a word with you."

Augustine keeps his eyes off the man's crooked legs. "Something wrong?"

"Is anything ever right?" the *capumastru* snaps. "Are walls ever plumb? Ever sufficient in their strength? Go ask Mercadal, why don't you."

Augustine smiles inwardly to the sound of Jumoke's muffled giggles. A whip snaps, abruptly ending the Egyptian's fun.

Before long, Augustine finds Gabriel roaming the eastern ramparts, swept up in an assessment of the project's progress. Here is a man who will not sit on his laurels. When his plans come to fruition, St Angelo will be ten times stronger than the fortress of Rhodos, which he engineered to resist the armies of Ottoman Sultan Mehmet II, known to Europe as the Conqueror. Mehmet, the man who captured Constantinople and made it Istanbul, could not take Rhodos.

Gabriel passes his hand over the warm yellow stone, speaking to it as he does. "Summer will soon dry us out of construction. The mortar crumbles in this sun. Resume building in late September, quarry stone and stockpile supplies until then. By October, the fortress must be rainproof. She will be impregnable, with walls even Satan's fire could not breach." The knight looks over his shoulder. "I have a proposition, Augustine."

"Tell me."

"On our last voyage," Gabriel begins, a boyish smile flickering across his old face, "you told me that your greatest wish was to caravan with Romegas. He's setting out on campaign. There is a spot aboard his flagship that I've arranged for you to fill."

Augustine cups his chin in thought, exhales.

"Mmm. Not the reaction I'd hoped," Gabriel remarks.

"I'm grateful beyond words, but by not sailing these past years, I have been a good father."

"Domenicus is practically a man."

Augustine nods. "Yes, he is."

"And Katrina, no doubt will soon marry."

At that, Augustine snorts.

Gabriel ignores it. "It would bring me great pleasure to see you embark the Frenchman's galley—the kind a father feels watching his son reap that which he worked hard to sow."

"But you will not be there to muster the boys…"

Gabriel grunts, swiping his hand downward. "Horseshit. I offer my men a vision of heaven I cannot myself testify."

Augustine blinks. "I don't understand."

"Throughout history, commanders have justified putting their soldiers in peril by proclaiming how wonderful heaven will be once they're dead."

Augustine looks at him in surprise. "You would not speak words you did not believe."

"It is a cheap trick to dangle the reward of heaven before a man's eyes to entice him into battle. What right do I have to make death sound appealing?"

"Why are you saying these things, Gabriel?"

The old knight sighs. "I don't know…" he pauses, placing a hand on his belly. "Just making amends to God for using His kingdom to encourage boys to die." Gabriel smiles. "All I mean to say is that you do not *need* me, Augustine. Romegas is ten times the captain, even if I happen to be more poetic and better looking." He gives Augustine a nudge. "Talk it over with your children. Romegas sails in a fortnight. But make up your mind to this—as a blade unwielded rusts from disuse, as stagnant water loses its purity, so too does inaction sap the vigour of the mind."

***

Pausing in the shadow of the Montesa house, Robert hands Katrina the linen-wrapped cheese, soft now from time spent in the sun.

"Thank you for the seashell," she says, dallying at her door.

"Thank you for… just thank you…" He turns slowly away, stops. He plucks a yellow wildflower sprouting from a rocky chink and sends a smile over his shoulder. "For my mother." He starts for home, twirling the stem between his fingers. Katrina leans against the doorframe, watching after him until he passes beyond sight.

Suddenly, she recalls the red marks on her throat. How to conceal the farmer's handprint? She piles damp hair atop her head in thought. *Hair.* She plaits her tresses into two long braids that fall over her shoulders and goes back inside. A glance at her reflection on the side of a pot shows the braids are too thin. She undoes them, shaking her head to loosen out her hair. Now thicker, the waves hide the handprint nicely. Her attention turns to dinner. As she fills a deep pot with salted water, she remembers the brambles. There is no time to fetch kindling now. She runs to Belli's stable, returning minutes later with a sack of dry donkey manure. The dung soon smoulders in the hearth.

A half-hour later, cabbage stew is laid on the table. Augustine is quiet, dipping bread slowly into his bowl, as though every movement requires lengthy consideration. Domenicus chews absently, stirring the stew around his plate. He clears his voice.

"So Kat, Franco has asked you to join us at Mnajdra tomorrow, as long as Pa approves. At last, you have beaten the knight into submission."

"*Really*? He said that? I don't believe it! After all this time, he finally"—Katrina stops suddenly, waiting for her brother to reveal his hoax.

He laughs. "It's true. I hope he didn't mean to surprise you."

Katrina beams. "Fetch me at the old fortress tomorrow. Angelica and I will be reading."

Augustine looks up from his plate. The pensive fog clouding his eyes lifts with his gaze. As he opens his mouth to speak, there is a knock at the door. He rises and goes to see who calls.

Katrina is instantly tense. Carmelina Borg stands hunched in the doorway. Anne's hellion of a mother is cloaked in a veil, hard eyes peering above a peculiar smile.

Pa greets her politely but with some surprise. "Signora Borg, how can I help you?"

"I come with congratulations," she says, in a tone anything but congratulatory.

"Congratulations?"

At the table, Katrina exchanges a glance with her brother.

"Of course," Carmelina replies. "Is your daughter not newly engaged?"

He crinkles his brow. "I beg your pardon?"

The widow looks at him askance, tilting her head to the side. "You mean she is not betrothed? Mmm. How awful for you."

"What *are* you talking about, Signora?"

Carmelina peeks over Pa's shoulder and deliberately meets Katrina's eyes. "Everyone is talking," the widow continues, looking back at him, "about how your Katrina is always running with that Falsone boy. He's quite poor, even for Birgu. I mean, honestly, how could he possibly support your daughter, what with that frail mother of his he has to look after?"

Katrina feels her colour rising.

"Heed me, Augustine," Carmelina says. "Just today, someone saw the two of them *swimming* together and..." she crosses herself "...*lying* with each other on the rocks."

Katrina's breath catches in her throat. Blood rushes to her face. So intense is her rage, it frightens her. She does not know whether to holler her innocence at her father or hurl her bowl at the widow Borg. She wants to do both. She does neither. Pa remains quiet.

"A matter of shame," Carmelina persists. "And a disgrace to your good name. Imagine the scandal if she is with-child! This is what happens when you allow a girl to read. It opens her mind to demons." The woman heaves a theatrical sigh. "It's not your fault entirely; your wife is dead."

Katrina has had enough. She slams her fist on the table and springs from her chair. It hits the ground with a bang. Domenicus jumps up and hooks his arm around Kat's waist. She struggles against his hold.

But Augustine simply smiles at Carmelina. "It's quite all right, Signora. I know all about it."

The woman blanches. "*You do?*"

He chuckles. "Of course. Mea raised Robert well. Naturally, he asked my permission before taking my daughter to fornicate on the rocks."

Carmelina gasps, her sharp intake of breath serving only to encourage Pa in his fun. "I'm not at all worried about his supporting her either. He won't need to. Katrina plans to marry the carpenter's donkey. I do not imagine Peppone will have much more than shit to offer, but at least it burns nicely in a hearth. And while I'm sure your concern is sincere, and I thank you for it, I am quite certain you would not want to be caught on this of all doorsteps, consorting with Satan about his spawn." Augustine closes the door in her face, leaving the widow dumbfounded on the step and Katrina silent with disbelief behind him. He turns slowly, casts a grim look on Katrina. She broods for several moments. After what seems like an eternity, her father bursts into hearty laughter. "Girl, sit down, for the love of God. Do you honestly think I would believe a word that woman has to say? You would not do me dishonour. Now, let's to our dinner before it gets colder." He motions to the table. Quietly, Katrina sits down. Her brother too.

Augustine clears his throat. "So. I've been asked to make caravan with Romegas."

"Father," Domenicus says, "that's wonderful news!"

"Is it?" he asks, forehead creasing.

"Of course! You've always wanted this. When do you depart?"

"The galleys sail in two weeks. I had not planned to commit until I'd asked both of you." He folds his arms over his chest and leans back. "I admit this is not the response I'd expected."

Katrina kneels on her seat and reaches across the table to touch her father's hand. "If you seek our blessing, you have it. You have it tenfold."

"You want to be rid of me?"

Katrina shakes her head. "Never! But you've deprived yourself of your greatest love for us."

"You and your brother *are* my greatest love."

"Yes," Domenicus says. "And you have shown us that. But you miss the sea. Return to it."

"Besides," Katrina adds, "It will do you good. You are no longer so quick on your feet."

Augustine laughs deeply. "Well, I think I might just take the man up on his offer." He meets his son's eyes and rises. "Then I'll show Kat who is not so quick on his feet." Together, he and Domenicus pull her off her chair and tickle her. She squirms and howls with laughter until she can barely breathe, almost kicking her brother in the mouth.

Pa releases her abruptly. "Good God, Katrina," he says, staring at her with starting eyes. "What's happened to your neck?"

She looks up at him. "Oh, that? That's nothing. I'd forgotten all about it."

He frowns. "Don't waffle, girl." His tone is stern. "Did someone hurt you?"

"Of course not!" Katrina replies, with a musical laugh. "I was at the market today, and there was a woman selling lovely scarves spun from Italian silk. I tried one on, just to see how luxury would feel. I suppose my skin is averse to foreign fabrics."

Domenicus raises an eyebrow. "Since when do you care about silk scarves?"

"I thought," she begins tersely, "Angelica would like one." Katrina sees the uncertainty in her father's eyes. "I give you my word, and with all my heart, my word is good."

"I will hold you to your word because there is no uglier quality than that of dishonesty."

CHAPTER TWENTY-ONE

Édouard de Gabriac is the last man to have laid his hands on Isabel Montesa, hands that now pass a suturing needle through the flesh of an unconscious Greek notary, stabbed in the shoulder by a displeased client. The jewel-encrusted dagger rests on a nearby table.

Domenicus sits forward on his chair, scribbling every observation. Having tried his little sister's tactic of persistence, he finally won himself a taste of practical learning. He procured the opportunity by vowing silence, a small price to pay for such wealth of experience. Two days earlier, de Gabriac allowed him to help drain an enormous pus-filled abscess formed on a carpenter's hand—the result of a large, dirty splinter. Domenicus impressed the knight; so much so, de Gabriac broke infirmary edict by inviting him to assist with phlebotomy and the more troublesome amputation of a blacksmith's foot. The smithy had dropped his hot iron onto his canvas shoe, setting it ablaze, scorching his flesh. Gangrene set in and with it, delirium.

Now, the Greek notary's wound presents a far less problematic task for the surgeon, a master in the intricate embroidery of flesh. The surgeon dabs at the sutures with each pass of his needle. His hands run red with blood, some of it trapping under his neat fingernails.

"A beautiful dagger," he remarks, cocking his head in the direction of the blade. "Rubies, sapphires, emeralds… At least the criminal tried to kill his lawyer fashionably. Want it?"

Domenicus raises an eyebrow. "I can't steal from a patient."

"Consider it a gift from his disgruntled client. Besides, he won't miss it, where he's going." The surgeon looks up, reconsiders. "Of course, he might have liked to use it to cut himself free from the noose he will soon swing from… No matter. Take it."

Domenicus is not convinced. "Don't you have to report everything of note at your weekly meeting? I imagine the weapon used in an attempted murder important enough…"

"By the cobwebs between a Franciscan's legs, are you my apprentice or my conscience?"

"An apprentice to your conscience."

De Gabriac chuckles. "All right, since you are such a slave of the craft, tell me the four humours and their purpose."

Domenicus scoffs. "In what language?"

"Do not make a friend of overconfidence, therein lies the greatest risk of error."

"The humours. Hot and dry, cold and moist, or if you prefer, fire and earth, air and water. Should the humours fall out of harmony, the body becomes sick, therefore treatments are directed to raise or lower the humour levels to achieve proper balance."

"*Bien cuit*. Here is a harder question for you: if one day you find yourself caring for a patient, how will you respond when he asks—with terrible unfairness—whether or not he is going to die?"

Domenicus furrows his brow. "Does that not depend on the nature of the ailment?"

"No."

"No?"

"No."

"Do I tell him the truth?" Domenicus asks.

"No."

"No?"

"No."

"Why not?"

De Gabriac spreads his hands. "Because what *is* the truth? And how can *you* know it? You are not God. Besides, sometimes an ingrown hair can bring death, while a cracked skull might evade it."

"I'm afraid I do not know an acceptable answer."

"Because there isn't one. You must dodge the question. Say something noncommittal that satisfies the patient without giving him a definite answer. Although a surgeon is considered low and contemptible by most, to the patient he treats, he is the next thing to the Almighty. Whatever you say, the person will believe. If you say yes, the patient will spend his last days in misery, eventually willing himself to die because *you* told him he was going to—dying thus becomes duty, even if his state was not especially grave. Conversely, if he lives when you told him he would die, he will think himself invincible and never trust another doctor again. A surgeon's hands are human hands—only occasionally are they subject to divine intervention."

Domenicus rubs his forehead. "So much more to it than poultices and sutures."

De Gabriac nods. "While on the subject of study, you must have a look at the anatomical publication of my former colleague, Flemish physician Andreas Vesalius. The *Tabulae Anatomicae*. I brought you a copy." The surgeon ties the thread in a knot, pats the wound with a cloth. He wipes his hands and turns. "Oh yes, your book arrived from France today. I have it here for you now."

"How much do I owe you?"

"Nothing. I petitioned the Treasury Board for an allowance to buy new surgical tools. I always order them from my hometown, Toulouse. There is an exquisite bookshop—"

Domenicus cuts him off. "You bought the book with the Order's money?"

"Quiet. So, who is this girl anyway?"

"Have you never seen her? She is a laundress, here."

"All I see around this place are rotting limbs and black entrails. Fetch the book from my satchel."

Domenicus finds the surgeon's bag and bends to it. "*City of the Ladies.*"

"Perfect for a woman who can think," de Gabriac says. "But have a care that your mistress does not pick up ideas of becoming your master. Also, do not wave that book about in public. The Church frowns upon it. And where the Holy Office is concerned, it is best to tread with care."

"These ecclesiastics do not have much appetite for literature, do they?"

"Contrary," de Gabriac replies. "They demolish all the great works. With luck, they'll soon choke."

"What purpose does banning books serve?" Domenicus asks. "So few people can read."

"Rome believes certain stories drive literary citizens to offensive deeds."

"So if some fool tried to walk on water and drowned, would the Vatican ban the Bible?"

***

In the mouth of a deep cave, Angelica and Katrina sit together reading from an Italian translation of the *Odyssey*. An hour passes, each minute filled with the lively verses of cannibals and lotus-eaters, Circe and sirens. During a well-earned break, Angelica takes up her flute to play her mother's song. Warm strains of music fill the cave, echoing in alcoves, and pass into the light of day. It is a gentle song, beautiful in its sadness. With every breath, she wills the wind to carry the notes to Graciela Tabone, wherever she is... if she still is.

Across from Angelica, Katrina sits with her knees bent and apart, so much like a boy. She rolls up her pants and stretches out her right leg, her bare skin crisscrossed with scars from childhood games of war. Her hair is tied in a messy ponytail at the base of her head, loose strands falling over her eyes, stray wisps across her cheeks. Katrina rests her head against the wall, closing her eyes until the last note is swept to the sea. When she opens them, Angelica notices they are filled with tears. Katrina once mentioned that this song makes her think of her own mother. She blinks rapidly, taking up the book to hide her face.

"Franco is finally going to teach me archery," Katrina says, looking up. "I'm sure I'll be a deadly shot. Better than my brother. They'll be here any minute. Coming with us to the ruins?"

Angelica shakes her head. "Mnajdra is a long way to go. Dinner needs preparing."

Katrina nods and turns the page. She reads the same line twice.

"Where is your head today?" Angelica interrupts. "*Hold! For the man is guiltless, do not stab him with your sword* hardly bears repeating."

"I've begun my monthly bleed," Katrina says flatly. Angelica gives her a big hug.

"That's wonderful news!"

Katrina sticks out her tongue. "Do you have this thing?"

"Not yet."

"You're lucky."

"I don't know," Angelica replies. "You have to have it in order to become pregnant. I know girls who were married at eleven and started having babies by twelve."

"So? You wanted babies when you were twelve?"

"No... but someday I will."

Katrina wrinkles up her nose. "I'd rather die an old maid than have married at eleven. And I will not marry some ugly brute I don't love. I want the kind of love we read about, the kind that happens in Spain and Italy and France, the kind worth living for, worth dying for. I'm not marrying some dolt who leaves a dead rabbit on my doorstep. I don't care what the neighbours say."

"Maybe you *should* care what they say, for the sake of your father and brother. Your ways reflect badly on them."

Katrina frowns. "My ways? What ways?"

Angelica sees the hurt in her friend's face. "*Xejn*—nothing. I'm sorry. Augustine and Domenicus don't care a twig what anyone thinks." She smiles. "I like that you say things most people hardly dare think. I want to marry someone I love, too. I hope that's not too foolish a fantasy."

"Of course it's foolish, but who cares? My parents had love, so it can exist in Malta... even if my father had to come all the way from Rhodos to bring it here. And neither of us will settle for anything less, promise?"

"Promise."

Katrina takes on a solemn air. "A woman is a diamond, and being worn by a dull hand will keep her from shining as she could. Better to let her sparkle on her own." Angelica looks at her friend with new admiration and realises how very attached to her she is.

"I'm happy I have you."

"You'll be happier to have the man of your fantasies."

"Perhaps if I had him atop a four-poster bed and wearing nothing but a hungry look in his eyes." The two girls burst into laughter. Homer and his Odyssey are cast aside in favour of secret whimsies about true love and fiery passion and lifelong devotion, each fancy more absurd than the last. They talk of first glances, first kisses, and other firsts. They giggle and whoop until steps approach from the east. Katrina springs to her feet. In her excitement, she steps into a deep chink that throws her forward. Her body lands outside the cave with a heavy thud. The fall must have jarred her awfully—she makes no sound, takes no breath, her gaze fixed.

"Kat, are you all right?" Angelica asks, laughing as she emerges from the cave, expecting to hear Domenicus teasing his sister. But there is only silence. Angelica follows Katrina's frozen stare.

Corsairs. Two of them.

Angelica's mouth is instantly dry. Her heart pounds against her ribs, draining the blood from her face with every beat. Two turbaned men, one hefty, the other lean, carrying daggers, trek across the rocks. They stop in their tracks.

For a moment, the four only stare at each other. Angelica is first to act, yanking Katrina up by the nook of her arm. They rip across sandstone, bare-chested corsairs giving chase. Angelica gathers up her skirt to keep from tripping, sharp, sun-baked rock grating her bare feet as the sandaled men close in with powerful strides. The large one shouts something in the pidgin dialect of the Barbary Coast. Terrible scars disfigure his arms and chest.

"*Henri!*" Angelica hollers. *Why hasn't the bloody sentry raised the alarm?* Panic twists her stomach. "Henri! Ring the bell!" The wind carries her cries uselessly out to sea. She and Katrina struggle up the hill, in a confusion of crawling and running, panting and huffing. The ground is a treadmill of dirt and sand, slipping beneath their feet, sliding away, hampering their climb. Rocks bite deep into Angelica's palms. She curses the sentry.

A thicket of brambles catches her skirt and sends her reeling to the ground. She rolls over, tears at the fabric, gashing her fingers on the thorns. The lean corsair closes in, reaching to take hold. She scuttles on her backside, scooping up a handful of stony dirt and flinging it at his face. He staggers and swears, his blindness a chance for her to break away.

"*Ejja* Angelica! Faster! *Haffef!*" Katrina shouts over her shoulder, her shins barking against large rocks. The summit is near; if she could just make the hilltop and alert the sentry. Fifteen feet. Ten. A large, powerful hand closes around her ankle, but the man it is attached to receives a swift kick to the lip from her free heel. His hands fly to his mouth, blood from the split gushing red onto his blue pantaloons. He sets his dagger in his teeth and lumbers after her, his flabby, deformed chest jiggling with his movement. Katrina is far quicker, pushing through thistles that cut deep red lines into her legs. Terror leaves her numb to pain, deaf to all sounds save her own heart.

Angelica is close behind when her ankle rolls severely. With a yelp, she hits the ground heavily, legs in a tangle. She tumbles down the slope, grasping for anything that might stop her fall.

Before she can recover, the heavy corsair steps on her lower back, pinning her down in the dust. The earth swallows her cry. The slaver reaches around her neck, locks her head in the nook of his arm. Grunting, he yanks Angelica to her feet and marches southward, half dragging her behind. She digs her nails into his forearm to pry herself loose. No use. He is too thick, too strong. Time is scarce. Every second brings her closer to captivity, every stride to a galliot she cannot yet see. She smells it soon enough, the stink of human waste heralding its presence. Angelica fights fiercely against the man's grip, punching at him with balled fists.

"I'll die before I go!" she cries. The corsair draws the dagger from his yellow sash. The threat of his cold, sharp blade against her throat stills her instantly.

"*Henri*!" Katrina screams, "Henri, blast you! Ring the goddamn bell!" Bloodied, she is almost completely out of breath when she reaches the brow. The slender corsair closes in, his long, lean legs easily narrowing the gap between them. Katrina clips down the stony road, running on shallow breaths. Ahead, the watchtower's lofty, arched windows reveal no sign of vigilance. But, with the sentry post so near, and the village boundaries in sight, Katrina is certain her pursuer will give up. She glances over her shoulder. There is no trace of Angelica, only an empty dirt road swirling with disturbed dust. A faint cry is carried on the wind, drawing Katrina back to the slope, which the corsair who was chasing her descends, negotiating his way around ruts and cacti. Closer to the water, the fat slaver drags Angelica over the rocky terrain. Katrina is horrified.

"*Katrina*!" Angelica screams. "Do something!" Her captor mashes his hand over her mouth. She bites him, tearing open the soft flesh between his thumb and forefinger. She tastes salt and dirt. When her mouth drips with his blood, he lets out a roar and releases her. She trenches jagged nails across his scarred chest, ripping his nipple. Several of her nails break off, embedded in his skin. He hollers in rage, lunging, seizing her by the throat. Angelica claws at his eyes, but as he squeezes her neck, she grabs instinctively for his wrist. He lifts her off the ground, holds her inches above it, her toes reaching in urgency for the solid surface. Panicking, she fights to pry his unmovable hand from her throat. She feels the blood vessels in her eyes thickening. The colours of the world fade.

She is going to die.

And then, he lets go. Angelica falls onto her back. Fleeting relief comes with big, frantic gulps of air. The corsair snatches up her wrist and hauls her behind him. She wheezes and sobs and cries out, sick from the pain and the terror that dizzies her.

"Katrina, help!" Angelica trips over large stones. Breaking away is impossible now; landing her foot is agony, every ounce of pressure bringing terrible pangs. She falls onto her knees. "*Le*—No! *Let go!*" The slaver strides on, raking her bloody knees over hot sandstone. She drops to the ground and grabs for chinks in the rocky surface. "*Katrina!*"

"Keep fighting! *Isa!* Don't give up!" Kat shouts, taking up rocks, hurling them. She knows she might hit Angelica, but better to hurt her by doing something than kill her by doing nothing. The first rock lands wide, the second short. The third hits its mark—a glancing blow off the corsair's temple. He lurches forward but recovers his footing. Katrina rips pears from thick pushes, cutting her fingers on the spikes that jut from their rind. She throws, desperately trying to aim well.

"Angelica, don't give in!" Two more prickly pears fly. "Kick him! Bite him! Gut him!"

Sun catches in the hilt of the dagger secured in the corsair's sash. This is Angelica's only chance. She wraps her fingers around the grip, and gritting her teeth, wrenches the dagger from his belt and stabs blindly. She manages a clean, deep slice into his upper arm. At first, the pain does not seem to register with him, though his face goes wan. Without hesitating, she rips the knife from his flesh and stabs again, this time aiming for his side. He catches her wrist and wrestles the dagger from her, nearly snapping her bones in his massive hand. The corsair throws Angelica onto a plateau of rock, jarring her insides and bringing fire to her elbows. The impact causes her teeth to clamp down on her tongue. Tears spring to her eyes as blood fills her mouth. Some, she swallows, most trickling over her chin to mix with the slaver's blood and the grainy sand that sticks to it.

Before she can inhale, he is upon her.

"Fazil! What are you doing?" the younger corsair calls out as he approaches, narrowing his eyes warily. "This girl will fetch a handsome purse. That is more than we were looking for. Deviate not from the will of Allah. Come, the ship will leave without us."

"Go ahead of me," Fazil snorts, sweat dripping onto the pretty girl's battered face. "You forget the repairs, you stupid worm. They're not leaving yet." He pins her wrists to the ground with one hand, the dagger pressed against her throat with the other. He throws an irritated glance over his shoulder. "She has given me far more trouble than she's worth. I want payment."

"The captain will take your head when he hears of this."

149

"He is not going to hear of it, Emir. And if he does, I will lop off your head before his stroke falls on mine." Fazil releases the girl's arms, fumbles with her skirt. He digs his fingers into her thighs, prying apart her legs. She kicks furiously but finds only empty air. There is a loud grunt from the slope above, and Emir looks up at the noise. A great rock hurtles in his direction.

Katrina cries out in anger—she wasted a good rock on the wrong corsair. She runs as far down the hill as will safely bring her target into range. She pelts rocks and pears at Angelica's attacker. One hits his leg. Another just misses his head. The third ricochets off his shoulder and onto Angelica. Katrina swears, infuriated by her failure. Projectiles rain, several hitting the thin corsair, who stands nearby and raises his forearm to shield against the storm.

Katrina can barely lift her arm or bend her elbow, spasms making each throw more painful than the last. Her arm is soon numb, her body exhausted. Still, she heaves whatever she can find. A pear catches the younger corsair in the face. He shouts and chases Katrina back up the hill.

Angelica struggles against an unbreakable hold. She is terrified beyond measure, but beneath this terrible fear is rage, and from this rage, she takes the strength to keep fighting. She spits gritty red saliva at her attacker's face. It hits his brow and rolls down. Her skirt is up. She bites at his cheek but finds a mouthful of beard. She pulls anyway, ripping out hairs caught between her teeth. The corsair smashes Angelica across the mouth with his elbow. Everything goes white and hot.

The air is pierced by two blasts from a whistle. The North African galliot will soon take back to the sea. Fazil rips urgently at the string that laces Angelica's blouse. His own drawstring is loose, his pantaloons at his knees. His hand is a steel pincer crushing her side. The pain unlocks her legs. He stifles her cry with his meaty hand, her thrashing only feeding his urge. She scrapes ravines across his cheek with broken fingernails. He does not stop, numb to all but his purpose. He presses violently against her, tries forcing himself inside her. Recovering her voice, Angelica screams hysterically.

Gunfire echoes off the rocks. Gulls squawk and take flight.

Fazil slumps onto Angelica. His dead weight stifles her breath. Blood pours from the perfectly round hole in his temple and pools on her chest.

Blind to everything but Angelica, Katrina stumbles over stands of cactus, a trail of dark blood marking her swift passage over the creamy terrain. She is at Angelica's side in an instant. Her eyes are glazed, face pale and still, the rest of her buried beneath a dead man. She looks less alive than he.

Katrina senses someone else nearby and looks. It is the young corsair. His pistol is drawn, smoke furling from its barrel. Without words, he helps Katrina roll the large body off Angelica.

"*Hannini,*" Katrina whispers. "Look at me. Did he…did he…?" She cannot bring herself to ask and, overcome by helplessness, dissolves into angry, useless tears. Angelica's blouse is torn, her hair a dishevelled mess, the flowers braided into her locks now shredded, scattered. Blood is trapped under her fingernails, caked around her mouth, smeared on her cheeks. Katrina ties Angelica's blouse back together with the frayed strips of torn fabric.

Hooves trample the coastal rock. Franco rears his horse at the foot of the hill and jumps off, Domenicus seconds behind him. Sword drawn, Domenicus is first to rush upon the armed corsair.

"No!" Katrina cries. "Stop!" He halts, though his momentum carries him forward.

"Hold…" Angelica says, just audibly, "…for the man is guiltless." Franco cannot be bothered to wait for an explanation. He brings down his halberd in a swift crack, knocking the gun from the corsair's hand, and with lethal suddenness, raises his weapon to deliver a second blow, the deathblow.

"Wait!" Domenicus shouts, throwing his hands out. Heedless, Franco swings his halberd in an arc. The corsair hurls himself to the ground and rolls. The cutting edge finds grainy earth, missing his neck by a hair's breadth. He crawls over the dust, ferreting through loose dirt for something to deflect the imminent third blow. Franco closes his hands around the halberd's wooden shaft, the muscles in his arms rippling as he yanks. The blade, too deeply lodged, will not budge. Domenicus moves swiftly between them, using his body to shield the corsair from the knight.

"He saved them, Franco."

"Move."

"No."

Franco struggles with his halberd, kicking at the blade, wrenching uselessly at the shank. He remembers the sword sheathed at his side. "*Move!*"

"No."

A hiss fills the air as Franco draws his sword. "Out of my way!"

Katrina pounds her bloodied fist against the dirt. "Enough! If not for this man Angelica would be in a galley speeding towards Algiers." Franco fights to control his temper, fingers tensing and relaxing, tensing and relaxing, in time with the beat of his heart. He weighs his options. He could kill the corsair right now and do so without fear of reprisal. Knights often take matters into their own hands when they believe themselves justified. Oftentimes even when not. Against the sovereign Order, none has a voice. It polices its own, allowing no other judicial court to try a knight for a crime, whether insurrection in Paris, assault in Munich, or theft in Barcelona. Moreover, the killing of some wretched corsair is hardly a crime. Franco's only penalty would be falling into disfavour with his young friends. Katrina would never forgive him. What does it matter though, the favour of a commoner? Especially one with dirty clothes and an uncivil tongue in her head? Franco sighs. Whatever the reason, it *does* matter. All eyes are on him, watching as he decides the course of his blade. Will he bury it in flesh or back in its scabbard?

Finally, Franco sheathes the sword and silently fetches a rope from Phaedo's saddlebag. He binds the corsair's hands. "Where is your ship, filth? Speak!" Franco thunders in Italian, tightening the knot with each syllable. "*Parla, porco cane!*"

"Gently," Katrina says. "He does not know what you're saying."

Franco bridles. "It is not enough that I have allowed him to live, I must speak to him with prettiness also?"

Domenicus looks closely at Angelica. The blood on her throat raises alarm within him. Angry bruises begin to show on her face and neck. Her arms and legs run in a seamless fabric of purple contusions and bloody abrasions. Her lip is swollen and split. Domenicus crouches, wiping away her pink tears. She looks past him. He follows her gaze to her rescuer.

He is a handsome man, with a complexion of dark honey that tells of good health. Deep brown eyes are warm against the folds of a bright yellow turban and shine with intelligence and character. His beard is pointed, his face slender, chin sharp. For a man whose life is devoted to piracy, his look conveys childish innocence. He would more readily pass for altar boy than murderous plunderer. Domenicus mouths the words *Thank you.* Seeming to understand, the corsair touches his hand to his forehead, then heart.

Franco clears his voice. "*Dove* Henri *è?* That idiot sentry should have raised the alarm."

"Something awful has happened to him," Katrina says quietly.

Franco nods. "I'll go see." He leaves his halberd wedged in the earth, hoists the corsair off the ground and drapes him like a canvas of salt over Phaedo's hindquarters.

Domenicus offers Angelica his hand. After some hesitation, she takes it. Her legs are unsteady, her ankle a fierce blue. There is scarce a part of her without bruising or blood. Domenicus quickly fetches a linen cloth from his horse's saddlebag, tears it into even strips and kneels before her. He takes her swollen foot and binds her ankle as she holds his shoulders for balance.

"A temporary bandage," he says, looking up, "until you see a physician. For now, I am your crutch." He turns to his little sister, kisses the top of her head. "Would you get angry if I offered to help you onto the horse?" he asks, voice husky. "He likes you more than me anyway."

Katrina looks up into his face and smiles. "I love you, too."

The watchtower stands in eerie silence. Domenicus and Franco halt at its arched doorway and peer into darkness. They call out the sentry's name once, twice, again. The stone drum is still and cold and empty. Domenicus leans towards Franco.

"I think he's dead."

A noise, like fabric rustling, descends from the turret. Domenicus and Franco look up sharply.

"Well, *someone* is alive," Franco whispers back. Domenicus charges up the staircase, taking steps two at a time. In the archway that opens into the lookout, he comes to a halt. Franco runs right into him, both tripping into the room.

Henri, alive and well, fumbles with the drawstring of his pants. "S-Sir F-Franco," he stammers, eyes wide, back pressed against the wall. A young woman kneels before him. The scene takes a moment to make sense to Domenicus. Enraged, he knocks Henri down and kicks gravel at his face, blinding him.

"*Ahfirli!* Forgive me!" the sentry cries.

Domenicus bridles. "Forgive you? A devil was going to..." he halts his words, inhales. "The corsairs would have stolen these girls into slavery, and you, you slab of meat with eyes, you have the gall to ask for forgiveness?"

Franco shakes his head. "This is what happens when you give work of great importance to a Maltese." He points to the prostitute. "Get out of here Lilla, before I have you paraded naked through town on a donkey." Lilla straightens herself out and, with a swish of petticoats, nips down the stairs.

"Please," Henri begs. "My father will kill me!" Franco grabs hold of the sentry and jostles him down the spiral flight. He stumbles and trips and whimpers all the way, every two seconds looking over his shoulder at the knight. Franco gives Henri a final boot that sends him sprawling to the ground. He grovels at Franco's feet in a mess of tears and dust and snot. The knight lifts him by the scruff of his neck, holds him in place like a rabbit. "You and the Muslim filth draped over my horse will swing side by side from the scaffold." Domenicus knows Franco mentioned the scaffold merely to have some fun boosting Henri's terror. And it works, for the sentry wails. At worst, he'll be discharged, fined, maybe locked a week in the dungeon. The corsair, however, will not fare so well.

Katrina clears her throat. "What do you mean 'swing side by side'?"

The fun leaves Franco's face. "Surely," he begins, "you do not think the corsair will go free?"

"He killed his own companion to save a stranger," Katrina replies.

"He is *Muslim*." Franco uses the word as an insult. "He killed his companion to raid his pockets."

"You really mean to punish our rescuer?"

"You speak of this cur as though he is innocent!" Franco cries. "How dare you defend him? He is an infidel." The indignation thunders from him. "It is bad enough you want him alive, but unpunished as well? Forget you."

Katrina will not be hushed. "If you knights were doing your job instead of parading about in processions, corsairs would not have landed in the first place."

Franco bristles at the charge, eyes flashing with new anger. "Perhaps we should just let him wander the streets, as suits his fancy." He flicks a dismissive hand. "Enough. I refuse to bandy words with those impervious to reason. Make yourselves available—you will be summoned by a scribe of the Order to make a report. And you, *Signorina*, you will keep away from caves, especially since we knights, so busy with our parades, haven't the time to mind them. Stay at home. Tend your father's house, as is your duty." Franco mounts Phaedo, prompting him in the direction of St Angelo, sparing the corsair no bump in the road. Henri jogs beside the horse, stirring dust in his struggle to keep up.

Angelica stares after them. "*Mhux sew*," she says finally. "It isn't right."

"I will do whatever I can," Domenicus says. His promise is weak. What sway could he possibly hold in this matter? Against the Order, none has a voice.

Above, a white moon shares the sky with a red sun. It is spectacular, the east silver and ethereal with the moonrise, the west gold and glorious with the sunset. The great fiery sphere melts deeper into the western folds with each step they take closer to St Publius. Upon arrival, the sun is dissolved completely into the horizon, the waxing moon big and bright. Domenicus puts Angelica carefully down. She takes Katrina's hand, the two exchanging a look of silent understanding.

Domenicus takes Angelica's arm across his shoulders. "*Dun* Anton will be beside himself when he sees you. There are bruises, cuts. Your ankle is twice the normal size."

"He's not here. Left this morning for Zejtun to visit the widow of an old friend and observe vespers with her." Angelica wraps her arms tight around herself. "By the time he returns I'll have changed my clothes. I'll spare him details, but he must know the truth if he is to help free the man who saved me." *The man who saved me.*

"A Catholic priest would move to the defence of a Muslim corsair?"

"A priest whose niece was rescued by one." Angelica hobbles backwards up the steps.

"I am sorry for what happened..." Domenicus tips his face to hers, watches her eyes. "How can I help? What can I do? Come home with us now."

"...I'm all right."

"You are not all right." He cups her face, wipes salty trails from her cheeks. He wants to kiss her, kiss away her tears. "I will not leave you alone. Let me bring you to the physician's house."

"No, no. I don't want the entire village knowing what has happened before I can tell my uncle. That Sicilian doctor is a town-crier with a medical licence."

"Dr Callus then," Domenicus presses.

"Mdina is too far."

"Very well. I'll bring you to surgeon-knight de Gabriac. You needn't fear his talking to anyone. He speaks mostly French and deems common dialect beneath him," Domenicus says, trying for a smile. "Come. Please."

At last, she surrenders her hand.

***

Candles flicker and blink. Augustine sits at the table, listening carefully to the details of his daughter's near abduction. He chews absently on his stubby nails, gnaws dead skin around them. Franco di Bonfatti sits across from him, a shadow passing over the knight's fine features.

The door opens. Struck by twenty emotions at once, Augustine flies from his seat and lifts Katrina off the ground in an embrace. "Are you hurt? Are you all right?" Joyous relief turns swiftly to anger. "You are *never* going there again!" He looks to his son. "Where have you been? Sir Franco has been here an hour."

"We brought Angelica to the *Sacra Infermeria*. The guard at the loggia refused her entry. So, she and Katrina waited outside the gallery while I went in to fetch de Gabriac. He examined her ankle. He promised to bring her home in his carriage."

Augustine nods. "*Tajjeb*—that's good."

His daughter jerks her chin at Franco. "What has become of our rescuer?"

"The slave prison," the knight replies.

She glares at him. "Then here is my statement for your report: you and your Order are cruel and unjust."

"*Katrina!*" Augustine thunders.

"Father, he has imprisoned the man who saved Angelica from rape!"

Franco rises from his seat. "One honourable deed is hardly enough to redeem a man who has lived a lifetime of evil."

Augustine moves to Katrina's cause. "My lord, the love of a daughter forces me to ask if there is anything you can do to save this man's life? He has done me an immeasurable service. Alive, he can serve you."

"You rescued two Egyptians, and now you beg for the life of a Mohammedan slaver. What are you? Defenders of all things Muslim?"

"Mercy," Katrina says. "Show him the same measure he showed us."

"I did that when I left my halberd embedded in the earth."

"That was not mercy. It was misfortune—or good fortune."

Franco scoffs. "Do you know what would have become of you, *Signorina*, had the slavers taken you? A fate worse than death, that's what. Christian girls are stolen to Algiers, the very sanctuary of iniquity, where fat, rich Moors strip them naked and ogle them. You'd be purchased like chattel, made to trot behind your master's wagon, chains running from the cart to the iron collar fastened around your neck." Lack of wind forces the knight to stop talking and breathe.

"The corsair spared me from that exact fate," Katrina argues.

"Yet how many others has he condemned to it?"

Taking a cloth from the cabinet, Domenicus looks over his shoulder. "Really, must this man be punished for being born Muslim? We cannot help what we are born; God decides that for us. Heroes and villains are a matter of geography. All people trust their faith is the true faith. Who is right? None. Who is right? All. The blood of Eden flows in all our veins. We are all men. All men have souls—and our souls are the same size."

Franco slams an indignant fist on the tabletop. "*Blasphemy!*" He is startled by his own severity. "You do not stand at a pulpit, and I do not need your tutorage. Do you think this corsair would be arguing for *your* life if circumstances were reversed? Muslims are bloodthirsty killers with neither hearts nor souls. Do you know why they are brown? Because God painted their flesh to mark them, to warn us. Mohammed, in whose name they kill, took scores of wives to breed his own followers. From birth, they are taught to hate Christians."

"And what are we taught?" Katrina snaps.

"Girl," Augustine chides, "for the love of God, take the teeth out of your words."

Franco clears his throat. "I wonder if the villagers of this parish who have suffered losses at the hands of slavers would share in this passionate plea."

"The plea is not for slavers, but for a man who spared me from slavery."

Augustine sighs, and approaches with reason, rather than passion. "Sir Franco, after every caravan, scores of Muslims, both soldier and pirate, are brought back here as slaves. None is ever given trial. They are simply put to work where their hands are needed. Or, they are ransomed. Why should it be different with this man?"

"He was captured not on some ship during a campaign, but here, trying to snatch your daughter from her home. That's why the scaffold is an option the Grand Master will consider. And while any other knight would have lopped off the corsair's head, I, being *cruel* and *unjust*, stayed the desire. Because I did so, his fate is out of my hands. He has been turned over to the master-at-arms."

Unblinking, Katrina looks the knight in the face. "You still hold the halberd at his neck. The Grand Master would not sentence a would-be slave to death without reason. Do not give him that reason. Please. Just tell him the corsair saved Angelica."

Franco holds Katrina's gaze several moments, and in those moments, loses his will. "Your pigheadedness will be the end of me. I'll do what I can to see him spared the noose—but not a lifetime at the oar. I will, God forgive me, speak favourably of his deeds to the Grand Master. Naturally, d'Homedes will order my head examined. With any luck, your corsair is of a wealthy line. I'll fix the Grand Master's eye on ransom."

"Thank you," Katrina says, squeezing Franco's hand, making him blush.

"So," Augustine begins, pleased by his daughter's victory and changing the subject before the knight changes his mind. "What becomes of the sentry? Briffa will gut him like lampuki."

Franco shrugs. "What the fishmonger does to his son is his own affair. Henri will have a tidy fine to pay the Order—no doubt from his father's purse."

"Have you a replacement for the sentry?" Augustine asks.

"No, but we shouldn't be hard-pressed to find one. If there is one thing this island offers in readiness, it's solid young lads."

Katrina leans into Domenicus. Augustine overhears his daughter whisper, "Robert?"

"He hates the knights," Domenicus whispers back.

"He does not hate money." She goes to Augustine and bends to his ear. Across from him, Franco perks up, leaning forward on the stool, an intrigued smile on his lips.

Augustine strokes his goatee. "Sir Franco, do you know one Robert Falsone?"

"Falsone? The grubby farmhand?"

"He's not a grubby farmhand!" Katrina snaps. "He is a loyal and honest worker."

Augustine hushes her with a wave of his hand. "He would make a good sentry."

"Give him a chance," Katrina says. "You must."

"*Must* I?" Franco grins, folds his arms loosely across his chest. "All right. I'll suggest this Falsone."

Katrina flashes a big smile. "Pa, can I go tell him now? Please?"

Augustine shakes his head. "Leave the boy alone tonight. Tell him tomorrow."

Franco rises. "The hour is late. I am off." On his way out the door, he pauses at the threshold and turns, offering a polished bow. "Forgive me for raising my voice in your house."

"Ah," Augustine says. "Never mind. It's Katrina. Jesus would throttle her." As the door clicks shut, he motions for her to sit. "Come, Girl. Tell me what happened. Speak plainly. Not that it's even in you to mince words."

Katrina rests her head on his shoulder. "I lost my shoes. Also, we were almost killed."

EIGHT POINTED CROSS

CHAPTER TWENTY-TWO

With a deep sigh, Franco slumps onto the edge of his plump, feathered bed, his mattress the only luxury permitted in his room. He rolls his shoulders, runs long fingers through dark hair. Minutes are slow in their passing as he sits brooding. He barely hears his page Amedeo enter the bedchamber.

"My lord, you did not dine in-hall."

Startled, Franco gazes vaguely at the fourteen-year-old Venetian. "No, I suppose I didn't."

"Are you ill?"

"Not with a curable ailment."

Amedeo tilts his head askance. "Can I bring you something? Water perhaps? An orange? A physician? I will bring one." He wheels round and is off, like a shot.

"*Aspetta!* Wait," Franco calls, smiling. The page returns. "Bring me Marcello instead."

With a dutiful nod, Amedeo is off once again, the patter of footfalls fading down the corridor. Franco sprawls on his bed, elbows bent behind his head, legs dangling off the side. He stares at the high ceiling, rubs his eyes, closes them. He sits back up, taps his hands on his thighs, rises to pace the floor, only to lie back down again.

He takes in the state of his small, simple bedroom and suddenly longs for the opulence of the villa di Bonfatti. It is in a knight's private chamber that his vow of poverty is realised. Franco's room is militarily austere: four windowless walls that form a white shell encasing a bookshelf, desk, chair, and cot. There is a crucifix above the door and two wrought-iron lanterns fixed above the bed. A Bible rests on the small cherry desk, and next to this lambskin volume, a votive drips beads of purple wax into a silver plate. He watches a violet teardrop trickle down the cheek of the candle. Shadows bounce along the walls. He yawns, closes his eyes.

Every road in Franco di Bonfatti's life has been straight as the falcon flies, making inner conflict something as foreign to the nobleman as want. For centuries, the house of di Bonfatti has been a wealthy and powerful line, counting the ruling de Medicis among its friends. This aristocratic lineage made acceptance to the Order of the Knights of St John a virtual guarantee for Franco, Count Raimondo di Bonfatti's eldest born son. Early on, he knew the path to his Maker would be walked as a Knight of Justice through the realm of the renowned Hospitallers. Although at the time the pledge was made Franco was an infant and the vow not of his will, he never resented the Count's decision. Franco did not like his father, but it wasn't anything he cared to remedy. He adored his mother, but she died, and that wasn't anything he could change. He completed the work his tutors assigned, impressing them with an aptitude for mathematics, matched by a great capacity for theology.

He was handsome and rich, a man of means, his company eagerly sought by his peers. Nevertheless, he often turned down invitations to carouse the lively Florentine streets with his boisterous young friends in favour of spending evenings alone. When he did grace the town, beautiful women flocked readily to him, but none held his interest, none could bring him the simple pleasure that kneeling at a pew brought. Scarce a morning passed that did not see Franco seated inside the magnificent Santa Maria del Fiore cathedral, Brunelleschi's domed masterpiece. This encouraged his randy contemporaries to taunt, but the teasing fazed him none. He worked hard, prayed harder, and hated Muslims with equal vehemence. He tried to instil similar qualities in his young brother, Dante, but Dante was born a playful spirit with an open mind, one captivated by art and music and fun.

When the time came for Franco to shed the comforts of his family's estate, kneel before the altar, place his hand upon the Missal, and take the Order's solemn vows with his own mouth, he did so with an earnest tongue. In all his life, the only thing that stirred his passion was a single-minded ambition to be a thread in the cloth that wipes the stain of Islam from the face of the earth. This obstinate will made everything clear. Yet today, at the request of a peasant, he spared the life of a Muslim. Now, everything is clear as mud. Katrina Montesa has him perplexed.

The acetic scent of alcohol suddenly invades Franco's nostrils, and his eyes pop open. Marcello di Ruggieri is bent directly over him, grinning maniacally. They are nose to nose.

"Good God, Ruggieri!"

"I was just checking if you were dead," Marcello says.

"Dead?"

"You frightened your page awfully; he said you have an incurable illness."

"He misunderstood," Franco replies. "The boy frets like a hen. Where is he?"

"I sent him to fetch you a tonic with lemon." Marcello holds out his hand. "Get up, lazy wretch! Tell me, what vexes you?"

Refusing his friend's hand, Franco props himself on his elbows. He scrunches up his nose. "You smell like bad wine."

"It is bad wine. I stole it from the Castilians." Marcello shrugs. "Woody, but does the job. Have some, might loosen you up."

"Get me into trouble is more like it."

"What enters a man's mouth is not evil—only what escapes it."

"To drink is to put a thief in your mouth to steal your brain. Although, that assumes you have one." Franco gives a half-smile. "So, off hawking today? No one enjoys shooting things more."

"No one is a better shot. I never miss a target. And do not limit my meaning to birds."

"Have a care. Women are dangerous."

"You are the antidote for mirth," Marcello replies. "So? What makes you skin your teeth?"

Franco sighs. "I have a problem."

"Caught in a dalliance with a courtesan or three? I've told you how to avoid it."

"You are bound to end up in the *oubliette*, with all your carrying on. Worse, you will be defrocked, your name dishonoured, if you are found out in your wenching and revelling."

"The Grand Master could no more unknight me than I could unflower his mother. Anyway, how would I be found out? Do you think I bring women to d'Homedes' bedchamber?"

"When one of them turns up at the *auberge* door with a screaming bundle in her arms and your name on her lips, it will raise a few questions. But knowing you, you'll claim the conception Immaculate and the birth virgin. As it is, I'd be surprised if you didn't already have some offspring."

"I'm sure I have a few children looking out from other people's windows," Marcello replies.

Franco snickers. "Tonight, I will say three rosaries on your behalf."

"Off to the Vatican with you, monk!" Marcello cries, throwing up his hands. "Go, swim the Acheron and save the condemned souls adrift on a hell-bound boat."

"You truly are the cross of Christ, you know that?"

"By the useless hole of a Carmelite! You've always been too well behaved. Never did you join me in a drink when I stole spirits from my father's cabinet, never did you give me a boost so I could peep at naked ladies..." Marcello shakes his head sadly as he trails off.

"Listen, idiot. I need your counsel. Today I handed a corsair over to the master-at-arms."

Marcello furrows his brow. "Why go to the trouble? You have a sword."

"It's complicated. The corsair killed his companion, who was trying to rape a villager. He also spared Katrina Montesa, daughter of Augustine. In turn, she begged mercy for the corsair."

"Wash your hands of it. You've already turned him over. D'Homedes will find one use or another for the corsair. Even if it is simply to make crow sport of him."

"I vowed to at least try to have his life spared," Franco says.

Marcello flicks his hand dismissively. "Baugh. Shape this vow into a noose and tie it around his neck. Besides, who will hold you to a promise made to commoners?"

"No one. But they are more than mere commoners. They are friends."

"Knights are not friends with low people."

Franco shrugs. "I like them."

"They are beneath you."

"Yes, but their company is easy."

Marcello looks at him sideways. "I don't follow."

"You couldn't follow with a compass and a map," Franco says. "Perhaps I am drawn to them because their mother died when they were children, and having lost my mother, I feel a connection and a need to look out for them. Or, perhaps it is simply because they do not expect anything from me, not in the way of formality and bows and conventions. I can just be me. Sometimes it is too stiff around here."

Marcello arcs an eyebrow. "Too stiff? You *are* formality and bows and conventions."

Franco sets his face in stern lines. "I am cordial with the family of a soldier-at-arms in service of the Order. You bed prostitutes. Why should *I* be the one to justify myself?"

"Because my bedding prostitutes does not compromise my judgement."

"I'll appeal to the Grand Master, tell him what the corsair did," Franco says, more to himself than to Marcello.

"*You*? Appeal for an infidel?"

"Not for the infidel."

Marcello grins. "Ah, for the girl...."

"Yes... *I mean no*! No! Not for the girl."

"This is your crisis? Oh, you great bore. The solution is simple."

Franco sits up. "And what is it?"

"Let him hang."

CHAPTER TWENTY-THREE

Just before dawn, the cock crows. Katrina is already awake, having barely slept from her excitement over the sentry post. She wants badly to tell Robert, and rose several times during the night to sneak out and do just that, but then she would remember the corsairs and the awful look in her father's eyes, and lie back down.

Now that the rooster is awake, so the rest of the village must be. She rolls from her bed and reaches for her trousers. Still fastening them, she makes for Farrugia's farm. The dirt road is muddied with a few puddles from a midnight rainfall. She cuts through silvery glades, jogging the whole way.

Above, waves of cloud are capped pink and gold, the soft gilded ripples announcing a fine and fresh morning. Under this sky, even Farrugia's farm seems welcoming. A loud series of bleats pierces the tranquillity. Robert's runaway goat is busy demolishing a spray of hardy weeds. The animal's hooves stir dust plumes, which tiptoe in brown wisps over the dirt. Just ahead, astride his horse, is Franco di Bonfatti, conversing with Grimaldi Farrugia over the low stone wall. It is an odd scene, the lordly knight consorting with the lowly peasant.

Franco glances in Katrina's direction. He does not smile at her approach as she expected.

"It seems," he begins, "your loyal and honest worker has been taken into the custody of the gendarmes for theft and extortion. They came for him at his mother's house."

Katrina gasps as though she missed the bottom step of a staircase. Her head spins, her mind working to make sense of the terrible things her ears have just heard. She narrows her eyes, aiming her glare at the farmer.

"*Int qed tigdeb*! Miserable liar!" She tears for the wall, for Farrugia beyond. This time, he seems to know better than to take her for mere bluster and lifts his shovel in defence. Franco dismounts and catches Katrina by the waist. She struggles against the knight, calls out to the farmer. "What did he steal, you smarmy bastard?"

"None of your business, *mishuta*," Farrugia snarls, tightening his grip on the shovel. "Come closer, I'll bash out your brains!"

Franco turns Katrina around and bends to her. He speaks softly. "Robert is a coarse and illiterate farmhand. Poverty has practically predisposed him to theft." Were she not in such a rage, she might have paid more attention to the vindicated look in Franco's eyes. Now, with her own eyes flashing wildly, Katrina is blind to all but her fierce impulse to cudgel the farmer. She fights mightily against Franco's hold. He is too strong. Still, she manages to squirm round to face Farrugia.

"You won't get away with this, you slobbering beast!"

"Katrina," Franco chides. "You cannot accuse a victim of theft with perjury because you are friends with the thief."

"But there was no theft." None that Robert committed. If only she had not caught Farrugia shouting at Robert that day, if only she had not intervened. She could kill her tongue. "Sir Franco, don't you believe a word of it. It's a lie, and I can prove it."

The farmer scoffs. "Get away from here before I smash you."

Katrina flashes. "Try it, you damnable goon!"

Farrugia bites his fist, launching into an epic of Maltese blasphemies to vent his fury. He drops the shovel, hands going instinctively for his belt.

Franco puts a stop to it. "Take your hands off that belt before I beat you with it myself."

Katrina looks up at the knight. "It's my fault Robert is in this mess," she says. "Please help. You can fix this."

"Did you not just last night accuse me of being cruel and unjust?"

"I did."

The knight looks from the farmer to Katrina to his hands. He mounts his horse, pulls Katrina up behind him, and spurs the beast to a gallop.

Augustine quietly gathers his tools. He surrenders himself to thought and, turning his mallet in his hands, mulls over whether to accept Gabriel Mercadal's proposition. Augustine misses the sea, the taste of its spray. He longs to chase the horizon, to sail among the stars. Yet, the relationship between soldier and sea is not all romance. Campaigns are bloody affairs, and death sits in wait on the bowsprits. He looks at his son. Augustine's end would make orphans of his children. Moreover, the recent landing of corsairs has left him wary of a possible swell in Muslim mischief…

His daughter slams open the door and bursts into the house. Augustine places his hand over his chest in a start. "Where the devil did you run off to?" He clutches the handle of his mallet.

She beckons him madly. "Pa, Robert is in trouble! Come!"

"What have you done now?" Augustine asks Katrina sharply, following her outside.

Domenicus scrambles to catch up. "*X'inqala?* Where is Robert? What's happened?"

"Gendarmes took him," she says. "Farrugia has accused him of theft."

"We better move," Domenicus says. "Mdina is more than a few paces up the road. I'll ride to the rectory and bring Father Tabone to the *Università.* He'll speak for Robert."

Augustine nods. "Have Belli fetch the lad's mother. Mea cannot make the trek alone."

All start for the road, save Franco, who stands motionless before the house. Katrina turns to him. "Won't you help?"

Franco shakes his head. "These are civil matters. The Order has no jurisdiction."

Augustine approaches him, speaks in his easy way. "*Illustrissimo,* come now, you know the knights are the true masters of this land. Your presence alone will hold sway over any magistrate."

Several silent moments pass. At last, the cleverly worded appeal seems enough to convince Franco, who climbs onto his horse and nudges him in the direction of Mdina.

Tramonto pounds the ground, making the village a blur of obscure faces blending with rundown buildings. It takes great skill to drive the horse through the tight warren of crisscrossing streets at this speed. The mount gallops through a large rainwater puddle, splashing brown water on peasants quickly stepping out of the way. At the gate of St Publius, Domenicus pulls up the reins and dismounts in one swift movement. He races to the rectory door and hammers it with a closed fist. "*Dun Anton!* Come quick." After a moment, he raises his fist to bang on the door once more. Father Anton Tabone swings it open, his habitual smile replaced by a frown.

"Father," Domenicus greets him with polite urgency. "Forgive the hour."

"What do *you* want?" The priest's tone is cold.

"A quick word with you. Angelica, also."

"She cannot give it. She is in bed, recovering. Anyway, her place is indoors, where corsairs cannot find her, where she will be safe."

"Of course," Domenicus stammers. "But, that's actually not why I'm here…"

"No? Then why are you here, you selfish piece of audacity, if not to enquire about the condition of my niece?"

This is going all wrong. How can Domenicus ask for a favour now? He does not understand the priest's hostility. "Father, of course I am concerned about Angelica. I was up the night worrying about her. But right now, I need you to come to Mdina. Robert has been wrongfully imprisoned."

"You are no less a delinquent yourself who consorts with criminals," the priest snaps.

"Criminals? But Father, you *know* Robert. He is innocent."

"As you are of giving my niece books censored by Rome? If Robert Falsone is in need of a prison mate, I suggest you join him, rather than give my Angelica literature that will land her in a cell. Not to mention I am a priest! How would it look if my own niece was declared heretic?"

Disbelief chokes Domenicus to silence; all that escapes his throat is a squeak of protest.

The priest flashes. "Leave, now, before I inform the bishop of your taste in fiction." The *kappillan* backs into the rectory and shuts the door, leaving Domenicus dumbfounded on the steps.

Mdina stands on the summit of a flattop hill. This perched position makes the walled city that much closer to the sun, a flaming ball hanging over the rim of the world like a curious eye. It stares down unrelenting on Katrina and Augustine as they wait silently by the doors of the *Università* for Franco to hitch his horse at the public stable.

The ancient walls of the government building are draped with flowery climbers. A warbler alights atop a stone cornice, fans her tail, twitters her song. Katrina fidgets, digging her thumbnail into notched limestone. She turns to her father, her mouth working, lips parting as though she is about to say something. Instead, she exhales and says nothing.

"What is it?" he asks.

"*Xejn*—Nothing."

"It's never really nothing with you, is it? Come on, out with it."

Katrina swallows. "I—" Footsteps cut her off. Belli approaches, his muscular arm a support for Robert's mother Mea, swathed in her black *barnuża*. Katrina pushes against the main doors to enter, but Pa catches her arm.

"Patience. Give your brother time to arrive. And while we have a moment alone, you and me, listen and heed me. Be mindful of your words and the tone of their delivery. In fact, just keep quiet altogether. These are men of power, not as forgiving to insolence as di Bonfatti."

She groans at the warning and goes to meet Belli. Mea embraces Katrina, the girl's small frame lost to the folds of the woman's frock. "The farmer lies."

Katrina takes the woman's hand. "I know it. Everyone knows." She looks over her shoulder and smiles: Franco approaches. "You see? Even the knights know Robert is innocent."

Mea's expression turns hopeful, her eyes on the handsome knight as he draws near. The soles of his boots smack the cobbles, his black tunic swishing with his every stride. Domenicus is close behind, also on his way from the communal stables.

Katrina goes to meet her brother. "Where's Angelica? Is she all right?"

Domenicus waves her off.

"And Father Tabone?" Augustine asks, holding open the door for the others to pass.

Domenicus shakes his head, dejected.

It is a large foyer, teeming with activity. Barristers, notaries, tax collectors, and other administrators crowd the antechamber, all smartly dressed, all well-groomed, all occupied. Some sit, quietly scribbling in ledgers, faces lined with concentration. Others engage in lively discussions, the great space crackling with the fiery wordplay of a dozen debates. Katrina spots one of the *catapani* her father knows, a low ranking officer whose job it is to keep merchants from ripping off the public. Before Augustine has the chance to approach him, Franco stops a tall, portly official with a bright red beard. The man's stern appearance suggests higher authority. But whatever his status, it is rungs below that of the knight. Franco speaks without preamble.

"Fetch the magistrate."

"Regarding...?" the man asks.

"Does the reason influence whether or not I will be granted occasion? Or do you ask because you Maltese are a nosy lot concerned with affairs that are none of your business?"

The man's face flushes to the shade of his beard. Katrina thinks her father should have warned Franco to mind his words, too. Augustine steps forward before the civil servant puts them out in the street.

"Sir, our request concerns the imprisonment of one Robert Falsone, a farmhand from Birgu. We are here to speak for him. Do you know where we might find the magistrate?"

"Yes. I am the magistrate."

Augustine fires Franco a sharp look. "Will you grant us a quick moment, your Grace?"

The magistrate turns on his heel and starts up the staircase, stopping on the first landing. He turns and beckons the group. "A very quick moment."

With each ascending step, Katrina hopes against hope that their word is enough to free Robert, and she will not have to hurt her father with the truth. She tucks her hair into her collar and fastens the top button in an attempt to look like a boy. A lawman would barely take a young lad seriously, let alone a girl.

The magistrate leads the group through a corridor of offices, entering a large but simple bureau, its white walls bare, natural light sneaking in through a narrow part in crimson velvet drapes. He summons the *baglio*, the keeper of the prisons, to fetch Robert Falsone, and after rifling through some papers in a drawer, sits at his desk, its surface lacquered smooth and shiny. Folding his hands, the law lord takes in the group before him.

"So? Who are you people?"

Augustine introduces himself, starts naming the others, but the magistrate does not wait for him to finish. He snaps his fingers, points to Belli.

"You there, woodman. Speak."

The carpenter shifts his weight, visibly uncomfortable with being the centre of attention. "...Well, Sir, I've had enough dealings with Grimaldi Farrugia to know him capable of inventing these charges. He is the thief, a known one at that." Belli begins listing all the things the farmer is said to have stolen, from wood to shoes to honey sweets, but is quickly cut off for perpetuating rumours. Augustine speaks next, then Domenicus, each testifying to Robert's excellent character. The magistrate listens to the impassioned assurances of the accused's innocence with an expression of unwavering boredom. At length, he waves for silence.

"Not one appeal has been buttressed with substance. You lot have given me evidence to prove Falsone's innocence no more than you have provided a motive for the farmer's fraud." Katrina feels instant and terrible dread. The magistrate is right, damn him—all they've done is attest to Robert being a good person. And even good people steal.

As she wracks her brain for a way to persuade this impossible man without betraying her father, Franco leans over the desk, face to face with the public officer. Fortunately for Robert, sovereignty often outweighs rightness where knights are concerned.

"Worthy my Honourable Magistrate, I hate to remind you that if the Order does not see fit to imprison a man, your grounds to hold him are shaky at best."

The magistrate forces a smile, oyster tight. "With all due respect, *Illustrissimo*, I hate to remind you that by rights, the Order holds no sway over crimes of this nature. Theft committed by a peasant against a peasant does not fall under your jurisdiction."

"Listen," Katrina says, moving towards the desk, her long hair slipping from her blouse. If the magistrate cares that she is a girl, he makes no indication. But before she can continue, hurried steps bring someone new into the room. All heads turn. It is Father Anton Tabone, crossing the office with a rustle of his black soutane.

"Here on common purpose?" the magistrate asks, giving the priest a rapid look-over.

Father Tabone rests his hand on Mea's shoulder. "I will not forsake a parishioner."

The magistrate sighs. "Should I be expecting anyone else to speak on Falsone's behalf? The pope perhaps?" But neither priest nor pope will speak. The clank of chains resounds from the corridor, silencing further discussion. Seconds later, the *baglio* shoves Robert violently into the room. Manacled at the wrists, his arms are streaked blue with bruises, his back striped scarlet with lashes that crisscross from his shoulders into his trousers. His right eye is swollen, his lip, split two days before, reopened. Katrina can barely look. Mea sobs, cupping her son's battered face. Domenicus swears under his breath at the guard, quickly hushed by Franco's hand against his back.

The magistrate addresses the prisoner: "Many vow to your innocence. But did you not yourself confess?"

Robert nods.

"So these entreaties mean nothing, and you have all grossly trespassed on my time."

Katrina has had enough. "If he confessed, it was only to protect me." Her voice is small, and for the first time in her life, her bearing meek. The magistrate eyes her with distaste. She looks away from her father, steeling herself for the hurt she is about to cause him, and admits to everything: picking a fight with Farrugia, bullying him into doubling Robert's wage.

"It was all me. Robert objected. As for his confession, had he denied the allegations, the gendarmes would have demanded a reason for Farrugia's lie. What could he have said? He would have had to tell them what I'd done." She faces Robert. "No one would have believed him anyway."

The magistrate studies Katrina for an unbearably long time. He inhales, holds the air inside him. At last, he signals the guard to unlock the fetters. They crash against the floor with a clang that Katrina feels reverberate inside her. Robert rubs scored wrists, stepping away from the iron heap as Mea throws her arms around him.

Augustine extends his hand to the magistrate. "Thank you, my lord, for allowing sound judgment to prevail."

"Sound judgment indeed," he replies, labouring the words as he glances at Franco from the corner of his eye. The magistrate looks back at Augustine. "You, sir, are paterfamilias of your house. Better you teach your children manners before they find themselves tutored by a horsewhip. I suggest dangling your daughter in a well—a day or two usually straightens out wilful girls."

"Mmm." His grim countenance makes it clear he is deliberating that very course of action.

Katrina approaches her father warily. "I am sorry."

"You have done me dishonour."

"I know."

"I have never in my life felt shame. I feel it now. I don't like it."

"I am sorry."

"I know your actions were not dictated by malice. I know that you did not mean to hurt Robert or hurt me and that in your own odd way, you thought you were doing good. Still, extorting the farmer?" Augustine frowns, hardens his voice. "The men of this island are right in ruling their homes with the backsides of their hands."

Katrina inhales but says nothing. She loves her father, reveres him, but does not fear him. He never made her fear him. Now, she is afraid. Afraid he may take the road travelled by the other fathers, a road of whippings and beatings. More than this, however, she knows she has wounded him gravely, hurt his pride and scarred his trust in her. That she has let him down hurts more than any belt ever could. Her eyes water.

He sighs. "Tell me I did not raise a criminal."

"If there were words more powerful than I am sorry, I would use them. But there aren't. So I will say again, I am sorry. And I will show it. I'll do anything."

"Oh, you most certainly will. To start, I think Belli's stable and dung room are in need of cleaning. That chore will be yours for the next six months. I plan also to hand you over to Signora Falsone and have her put you to work. As well, you are not going to the *Imnarja* celebration." This annual festival of lights is something Katrina and everyone else in Birgu look forward to all year. It comes on the heels of the harvest at the end of June, making it a welcome break from the hard toils that fill a peasant's otherwise weary existence—a small taste of revelry, flavoured with folk songs and dance. Although miserable at the idea of missing the event, Katrina knows her punishment is deserved, and infinitely better than being put in the well for two days.

The sun makes a kiln of Mdina. Sweat glistens on Franco's forehead as he brings round the horses, their clunky hooves plodding the cobbles. Katrina stands quietly back, watching as Robert's mother takes the knight's hands into hers and squeezes them. He flinches almost imperceptibly at the peasant woman's unexpected touch.

"You are a good man, *Honorabile*," Mea says. "Robert is everything to me." She glances to the sky. "He is my son—my sun."

Blinking rapidly at the brightness of the day, Father Tabone approaches to offer Mea and Robert a ride back to Birgu. With thanks, Robert helps his mother up and into the cart but declines a ride himself. The priest then beckons Belli, who is heading to the Castilian *auberge* for a meeting with the *langue*'s master to discuss furnishing the formal dining hall. It would be the carpenter's most important assignment yet. Visibly nervous, he fidgets and wrings his hands as he settles in beside Mea. Father Tabone whistles to Augustine, who hesitates, glancing from the priest to Domenicus, neither of whom have exchanged a single word.

Augustine leans towards his son and whispers: "The matter of the priest's niece will be resolved." He takes a seat next to Father Tabone. A light snap of the reins pushes the small brown mule to action. Large wooden wheels joggle over stones as if finding them deliberately, the rickety cart pitching its riders from side to side. Mea braces herself against the edge and smiles shyly when Belli offers his arm.

Katrina, Domenicus, Robert, and Franco remain, all beaded with sweat, all eager to leave the hilltop city. Their steps carry them past villas and mansions and woody, clambering vines. Behind wrought iron gates stands the herald's loggia, home to Mdina's town criers. Soon, the small group passes into brief, cool darkness under the citadel's limestone entryway, and as they cross a drawbridge that spans a moat quarried six hundred years ago, Domenicus reaches into Tramonto's saddlebag for a water skin.

He peers at Robert. "You are in a bad way. Let me take you to the hospital."

"A good idea," Franco says, "The *Sacra Infermeria* is open even to the low people."

"Nah," Robert replies, ignoring the insult. "A dip in the sea will fix me."

Domenicus pats him gingerly on the shoulder, hands him the water flask. "If you won't see a doctor, let me at least prepare a liniment."

"Don't fret over me, you bitch of the *Sacra Infermeria*. It's nothing a tavern can't cure."

"I'd reconsider," Franco cuts in, swinging up onto his horse. He raises a dignified chin, looks down at Robert. "You'll be of even less use to me with dull senses."

"Use to you?"

"The watchtower at Corradino is lighter one sentry. The vacant post is yours to fill. Unless, of course, you'd rather continue labouring in your accuser's field."

Robert raises an eyebrow. "What's happened to Henri?"

"I'll tell you later," Katrina whispers from behind him.

Franco waves impatiently. "Well, what say you, Falsone?"

"Does a sentry have to make vows? Celibacy and the like? I mean, since he is part of the Order?"

Franco snorts. "My dear farm boy." He dabs at his eyes "A sentry post no more makes you part of the Order than entering a church makes you God. If positions were doled out that easily, Katrina and Angelica would be rising to knighthood because they wash hospital linens." Hand over heart, the knight chuckles. "No lad, the only vow you need make is one of vigilance."

Robert deliberates a few moments, more to keep from appearing overly eager than to give any real thought to the lucky opportunity. When sufficient time has passed, he nods.

"I take you on your offer. And I thank you for it."

"Make no mistake," Franco says, "you will not be hard to replace should you stumble in your duty. This land overflows with young men desperate for work. Still, on Katrina's recommendation, I sought permission from the master of Auvergne to employ you. Do not make me rue the decision." Each *langue* is accountable for some facet of the Order, and Auvergne is Marshal, responsible for the overall command of armed units.

"You will meet me at dawn tomorrow," Franco continues. "You will need shoes. Indeed, we cannot have a barefoot sentry." Robert glances at the knight's boots, fine calfskin marked by scarce a scuff, rounded tips poking through silver stirrups. For the first time in his life, his bare feet are a source of shame to him.

Turning partway in his saddle, Franco motions Katrina over and bends low to face her. "Have I proven that I am neither cruel nor unjust?"

"A million times. How can I thank you? Or rather, apologise?"

A smile finally spreads across the knight's face, breaking the solemnity that often tightens his features. "A lesson in Maltese to thank me, another to apologise." With a click of his tongue, he urges Phaedo to a trot, leaving a thick trail of dust in his wake. Before it settles, sister and brother each take one of Robert's arms across their shoulders, despite his protests.

"Good of Bonfatti to come all the way to Mdina," he remarks.

"Yes," Katrina agrees. "Very good of him."

"Makes me wonder about his motive since clearly, I've done something to ruffle that peacock's feathers."

"What are you talking about? But for him, you'd probably still be in prison."

"Yes, and I am grateful. It does not change that he sees me as an offence to humanity."

"Ah," Domenicus cuts in. "He's a knight. They're all like that. Franco means well."

Robert scowls. "Why is he always around? Does he not have knightly obligations? Vespers to attend? A page to bugger? Does he not have to help build a fortress where he and the rest of his lot can cower at the first sign of crescent banners?"

Katrina stops, the violent suddenness sending Robert to stumble forward. "Of all the ugly, ungrateful things to say! Franco has many duties, halfwit. He was kind enough to abandon them today for your sake."

Robert smirks. "You are sweet on him. A pity for you knights only give occasion to the wharf whores."

"That is what you say about the man responsible for your freedom?"

Until now, Robert was smiling. But at Katrina's last remark, his features darken. He is right to be cross, and she knows it. She chose her words poorly, especially after all he has been through because of her. Still, she can give no quarter, not just yet.

"Franco did not have to come here for you."

"He didn't come here for me. He came here for *you*."

It's true. And the awareness infuriates her. She storms ahead, taking her steps angrily. She makes it ten or so paces before Robert calls to her. She keeps going, marching downhill, eyes on the ground to keep from tripping over a stone and making herself a fool.

"*Qattusa!*" he calls again. She halts, annoyed that this stupid nickname is enough to penetrate her resolve. She stands silently, arms crossed over her chest, all the while knowing she has absolutely no right to be upset. Moreover,

Franco *is* often rude to Robert. Katrina has simply ascribed it to the knight's innate snobbery, nothing personal.

Robert limps over, and slowly, painfully, drops to his knees, cringing and groaning all the way down.

"Madam," he says, his grave tone on the slippery edge of the theatrical. "Forgive my shameful display. I am enormously sorry for offending you, fair my lady. In rue, I kneel before you on injured legs." When Katrina offers no words, Robert brings the backside of his hand to his forehead ostentatiously. "You withhold forgiveness? Then release will only come by suicide. Farewell my mother for me. And engrave in my tombstone the words: *Robert Falsone, halfwit bastard.*"

At this, Katrina feels her chin tremble. She fights to control herself, but the harder she tries, the funnier it seems, and she bursts into laughter.

"No, Falsone. Forgive me." She helps him back to his feet. "I am the halfwit bastard."

"Sometimes."

***

"The *auberge* of Aragon," Father Tabone announces as the wheels of his cart jar to a halt.

"God's thanks for coming to Mdina," Augustine says, stepping down. "Please think better of my son." The priest does not turn his head, affording his last passenger only a glance from the corner of his eye. Augustine places his hands on the cart's ledge and leans inside. "I do not believe you need me to remind you that it is the angry man who opens his mouth but shuts his eyes."

"Even open, the eyes of a father are sometimes blind." The priest hesitates a moment. He snaps the mule's reins, and the cart lurches forward. Augustine turns for the door.

Today, instead of the quarries, his work waits at the dockyard. He has been commissioned to assist in the dismantling of the great carrack of Rhodos, a massive vessel long past her prime. Before heading to the waterfront where she is being taken to pieces, he must render his decision to Gabriel Mercadal on the matter of the caravan. Augustine stands now in the fat shadow of Aragon's *auberge*, bracing himself for the *pilier*'s disappointed reaction. He wrings his hands like a child dreading a confrontation with a parent. Finally, he raps his knuckles against the heavy oak door, softly at first, then harder. Hinges creak a minute later, and Tristan Galan, the Aragonese who manned the swivel gun with Augustine aboard the *Atardecer*, stands in the doorway. The knight's face is grave.

"Montesa. Come in." Tristan props the door open with his foot as Augustine crosses into the grand entrance hall. "I sent my page to your house this morning. Nobody was there."

"I had pressing business in Mdina. Was there something you needed?"

Tristan stiffens. "My page was a herald of woe." He puts his hand on Augustine's shoulder. "Our warrior poet has fallen silent. Gabriel Mercadal is dead. Passed in his sleep."

Augustine blinks, not sure if he heard correctly. He *is* sure, but cannot believe. His knees go weak. So forcefully does this blow strike him, it knocks the wind from his lungs. "But... but... people like Gabriel don't die! How can a man who survives a bullet through his head die in his sleep..." His hands are clammy, face hot. "Just yesterday afternoon I met with him!" Augustine did not know such a rage of grief when his own father died. His entire body throbs as though it is a rapidly beating heart fit to rupture, pounding, pounding. Somehow, he makes it across the room, slumps into a chair. Tristan crouches before him.

"You were a son to him, I know."

Augustine looks to the staircase where the old knight often greeted him. "I have been a son to Gabriel Mercadal far longer than I was a son to the father who gave me life." A cloud of unreality settles upon him, and though Tristan's mouth is moving, he hears nothing. It all runs together: the shock, the denial, the rage, the pain. Gabriel is dead. Gabriel, the man Augustine loved as a father, the friend with whom he shared flasks of beer, the knight who took him under his wing, the poet who could inspire a disheartened soldier onward... Now, forever silenced.

With a mind bent on finding Romegas, Augustine trudges the dockyard in search of the renowned captain. The quay heaves with activity: warships and merchantmen sailing in and out of the harbour fairway, porters carrying crates of provisions to departing vessels, oarsmen hauling cargo off the newly arrived. The many decks of the great carrack are just as lively, Muslim and Jewish slaves toiling alongside Christian criminals and hired labourers, all working cleavers and axes to split her worm-eaten planks. The wharf smells strong of chopped wood and the sweat of the men who chop it.

Yesterday afternoon Gabriel Mercadal asked Augustine to help take apart the *Santa Anna*, the carrack of Rhodos. No longer can the enormous craft hold her own against newer, faster warships. In her halcyon days, the *Santa Anna* could store over four thousand tons of goods with stowage for half a year's fare. Now, riggers strip athwartships nets meant to keep falling masts from crushing crew. Workmen are busy cutting down the two forward masts that once held her vast square-rigged sails. Two knights roll a gun carriage away. A blacksmith sweats at his kiln melting boom irons. Wood cracks and splinters and clacks against more wood as axes and adzes reduce the once sturdy frames and hulking planes to nothing more than expensive kindling.

On the dock, Augustine threads through large spools of rope, his hand a visor against the sun. He pauses, eyes darting from one face to another, hoping to glimpse the captain in their midst. But he does not find Romegas; Romegas finds him.

"*Messier* Montesa," the Frenchman says from behind. Augustine turns. Romegas grins broadly, his little brown monkey babbling and crawling across his shoulders. The man is tall, solid, and bearded, and despite a jovial air, there is danger in his bright eyes. Romegas is a fire-eater—the only captain of the Middle Sea comparable to Dragut Raïs. Both captains of genius, both chess pieces on the Mediterranean board over which Suleiman the Magnificent and Charles V face one another, though neither naval man is either master's pawn. Christian and Muslim seafarers alike agree: if Suleiman has Dragut, Charles has Romegas, and the hands of these two admirals draw the lines of both empires. Romegas gives Augustine's shoulder a mighty squeeze.

"He was a true gentleman of the sea, that Mercadal, despite the misfortune of his being a Spaniard. Always a captain, whether at helm or at fort. Had he both eyes, he may have even rivalled me. God will appoint him a grand ship, packed to the gunwales with barrels of ale." He pauses, tries for tenderness. "*Je vous plains.* Mercadal thought the world of you."

Augustine nods. "The very reason I am here, now. To pledge my commitment to the campaign."

EIGHT POINTED CROSS

CHAPTER TWENTY-FOUR

In the middle of Mea Falsone's sixth recitation of the rosary, Robert comes home, spilling rose-pink light into the room as he opens the door. He brings with him the fresh smell of seawater. Mea beckons him to join her in prayer, but he declines with a wave of his hand.

"You pray enough for both of us. Besides, I don't think God visits Birgu this time of year. Too hot." Robert is not especially religious, going to church only to keep his mother from blistering him with hellfire sermons.

Mea tightens her grip on the wooden beads. "If He did not visit Birgu this time of year, you would not be here now." Her voice is stern. "Come, eat something. There is broth." The iron pot that hangs above the embers of the hearth is almost empty, the broth a mixture of salted water swimming with bits of carrot so fine they could be dust flakes.

Robert looks at her rosary. "Do you always cross yourself before you pray?"

"Of course."

"But what if you forget?"

"I don't."

"Have you ever finished your prayers and forgot to cross yourself?"

"I'm sure once or twice," Mea replies.

"So does that mean every thought you have after you finish praying goes to God? And then the next day, when you sign the cross to start a new prayer, does that count for yesterday, so you wind up ending the prayer before it begins?"

Mea furrows her brow. "Do you mock me? Or do you speak in riddles to test me?"

"Neither, sweet my mother," Robert replies, kissing her cheek.

"God hears all our thoughts all the time. Now, eat something."

Holes in the foliage roof reveal a sky cast violet with gathering twilight. Robert lies prostrate on the dirt floor of the single-roomed dwelling, his fist a buttress for his chin. He tips his face to look up at a sky broken by thatch. Mice squeak and scurry within the tangles of the grassy ceiling. A swipe from a hard gale is often enough to scatter the reeds and leave the house without a lid. For this reason, Robert dreads black clouds. He hopes to one day afford a solid roof for his mother.

It is for his mother's sake that he allows her to fuss over him now. Mea kneels beside him, gently dabbing the bloodied welts on his back with a length of brine-soaked linen. She wrings the cloth, water trickling pink into the bucket. A soft rapping at the door turns her head. She glances back at Robert, who shrugs. The last time unexpected visitors knocked, it was the *gendarmes*, come to take him away. Frowning, she tosses a black shawl over her shoulders and goes to see who calls.

Domenicus stands in the doorway, hoisting a pair of slightly worn leather boots. Robert smiles and pushes himself up off the ground.

"*You will need shoes. Indeed, we cannot have a barefoot sentry,*" Domenicus says, imitating Franco's condescension. He steps over the threshold and tosses the boots to Robert, who catches them and runs his hands over the black rawhide as though it were the finest doeskin.

"Where did you get these?" he asks, eyes glowing with gratitude.

"Robert will pay back every *scudo* you spent," Mea says.

Domenicus shakes his head. "I had an extra pair, *Signorina*, for riding."

"You are kind to call an old woman *Signorina*. Have some soup."

Domenicus smiles politely. "Thank you, I've already eaten."

"Augustine does not mind you leaving the house so late at night?" she asks, scraping the bottom of the pot with a long wooden spoon.

"My father is not home. I'm sure he's stayed late to help take apart that enormous carrack." Mea passes Domenicus a small wooden bowl, filled with the last of the broth. Tiny black shards from the pot float around the soup. "Thank you, *Signorina*. I swear I am not hungry."

"Child, how many times has your father filled my Robert's belly? Your mother, God rest her, sent us bread countless evenings. Please, I will be offended if you don't take it."

Domenicus accepts the bowl with thanks. "I was hoping," he begins between sips, "Robert might join me for a stroll this fine evening, to try out his new boots."

Mea glances over her shoulder. "A stroll? At this hour? A trip to the tavern you mean." She takes up her broom and begins stirring the dust. Robert, cross-legged on the floor, turns his new boots over, gazing at the heels and soles, barely scuffed. He leans far back to pull them on, whistling with pleasure. It is the first time he has felt the sensation of his feet inside shoes. He struts about, singing loud and off-key, pulling his mother to the centre of the room where he dances with her to music his voice supplies. Laughing, Domenicus hops out of the way, finding a place against the wall to lean. Robert spins Mea in a clumsy circle.

"All right," she says. "Off you go before anyone sees through the window."

"Sleep now, Mother." Robert takes the broom from her hands. "Sweep tomorrow."

She takes it back. "There is enough dust to sweep without rest for a thousand years. I want you home at a decent hour. I'll know if you're doing things you shouldn't be."

Snickering, Robert pulls his shirt over his head and steps out into the warm night. The sky is a great storybook holding the tales of a million stars. The moon shines bright on the road, lances silver across the stony terrain to light their way. When they are well out of earshot, he gives his friend a nudge.

"We are going to the tavern, right?"

"The White Horse awaits." Grinning, Domenicus pulls a flask from his shirt. "And here's a little something to get us there, courtesy of the *Sacra Infermeria*."

"Good. Bonfatti won't approve." Robert takes a long pull of brandy, wipes his mouth.

"Your dislike for him—for the knights—is misplaced. We have prospered under them."

"Yes, and that is why we have less to eat than their horses."

"But tomorrow you'll be sentry, earning more in a day than you did in a month breaking your back in that cretin's field. And you have Franco to thank for it."

"Oh Domenicus, when are you going to realise your love affair with the knights is one-sided? They would never suffer you to join their ranks. Even Malta's nobles occupy too low a rung on the aristocratic ladder to gain admittance. We are nothing to them."

"That isn't true," Domenicus says, taking back the flask. "The Order hires Maltese to build the fortifications. Belli is one of their chief carpenters."

"And if the knights lived on Corsica, they would hire Corsicans," Robert replies. The moonlit path takes the friends past crumbling towers of antiquity, tufts of spurge blossoming at their bases.

"Say what you will, but the knights gave me a father. If it wasn't for the Order, he would never have come to Malta, and I'd never have been born. Simply put, I am alive because of them."

"But that is hardly something they did consciously."

"I knew you would say that," Domenicus says, laughing. "All right, then. The knights are devoted. They spend their lives defending something, defending God."

"I thought you gave up on God when your mother died."

"I did. He did not give up on me."

"Very well, but how can you love the knights for defending God by killing Muslims then beg for the life of one yourself?"

"I don't care if that corsair worships loaves of bread. What he did has earned my love."

"Ah, but your knights would kill him *despite* what he did," Robert says.

"Look, the knights are worthy of our respect. They are educated, refined. The people of Birgu know nothing of the world beyond this village."

"How can anyone in Birgu know anything about the outside world when kept ignorant?"

Domenicus kicks a stone. "People keep themselves ignorant."

"Places of learning are reserved for the rich. Even you were too poor for the boys' grammar school in Mdina. Besides, who would sow the crops if we were all scholars? The knights, the nobles, the clergy, they keep their hands clean and the commoners good and dumb and dirty."

"Yes, well, the knights built a hospital to which noble or common, all men are accepted."

"Don't piss in my ear and call it rain," Robert says. "They expropriated and demolished houses on the foreshore to make way for it, without a care for the people living in them. They marched in and occupied this land as though it was owed to them. They impose merciless rule on people who were not their subjects in the first place. They defend nothing beyond their own interests. And most of all, they are cowards masquerading as men of substance."

"You're wrong."

Robert softens. "The Order gave you a father. I understand. Yet did it do anything to spare mine? Moreover, these knights come from the richest houses of Europe. They take vows of poverty with mouths full of delicacies. They do not know toil. Bonfatti is the son of a Florentine Count. Tell me, what could he, or any of the others, know about the life of a peasant?"

Domenicus sighs. It is true he has never been dealt a blow by the Order, unlike Robert, who has seen nothing but the backside of its hand. A loud hiss and rustling from nearby shrubs put an end to the discussion. Robert creeps towards the hedgerow to have a peek. Two cats, one mounting the other from behind, stop in the midst of their business to glare at the intruder. Robert beckons Domenicus and points to the felines, moonlight reflecting ethereally in their eyes.

Robert elbows his friend. "Now they have the right idea."

"Well, I'm not mounting you, so get that look off your face."

Laughing, the two young men finish off the brandy and cross the town square, faintly lit by the sheltered flame of a street lamp. A lone sheep lies in the middle of the road, beside a mound of stinking piles. On the other side of the midden, two hogs sleep side by side, grunting, grumbling. Robert pushes open the door to the White Horse, Domenicus following.

Inside, two courtesans stand shoulder to shoulder, arms crossed over their chests. One, a flaxen from Sicily, the other, a redhead from a nearby village, who heaves a sigh as she takes in the state of her workplace. It is after nine, and the drinking hole swarms with inebriated men, hooting and swaggering, their mirth bolstered by the lively tune of a fiddle. Those that sit smoke pipes, lazy grey plumes moving through air scented with hard drink. Half-empty bottles line shelves, clusters of white candles burn low, wall lanterns glow orange. Several patrons play cards, gambling with what small amounts of money they've hidden from their wives. They drink insatiably, laugh rowdily, and come up with ever more creative ways of degrading another's mother. Courtesans flounce before them, vying for attention. Some sit on the laps of card players, men conspicuous in their lechery. Among the gamblers is Pino Mifsud. He is here to win, and the pleasure girls know better than to bother with him.

The flaxen turns to her companion. "What is the chance the crown prince of France might stroll in here for a drink and whisk me away from this hellhole to his castle in Amboise?"

"A Jew would be named Pope before either of us leaves this rock," the redhead replies, scanning the room with distaste. Madeleine is a twenty-year-old from the small *paroċċa* of Zejtun. With her perfect teeth and waves of strawberry hair, she is quite unlike any other girl in the tavern. Her face is smooth, like a stone angel's, her nose slightly crooked, as though the sculptor's chisel slipped. She is tall, poised, her chest spilling from her green dress. "Still, a crown prince would sure be a nice change from this ugly rabble. And one night paying homage to a royal prick would yield enough money to feed my brothers for a year." At fourteen, Madeleine's parents died of pox. Left to care for twin baby brothers, she was swift in learning that lying on her back generated more than five times what she earned selling cumin at the market.

Madeleine's heavily powdered features brighten suddenly: two swarthy newcomers have taken seat and wine by the door. Young ones, handsome, probably virgins eager to discard the title and willing to pay for the opportunity. They will have money; they seem to be celebrating. A promotion? A betrothal? A convenient death? The dark-haired one with the bruised face is striking. Madeleine nudges her flaxen companion. "Perhaps some princes have come."

Robert is one big grin as a delightful redhead with an ample bust approaches. He glances to her hips, her chest, her face. There is nothing particularly beautiful about her, and yet she is a woman a man will look at, look away from, only to look at a second, longer time. She is fascinating. Her friend sits boldly on Domenicus, who does not resist. Robert bends his arms behind his head, leans back in his chair, and sets his foot on the tabletop, all in one fluid movement.

The redhead whacks together curled eyelashes. "What on earth happened to your face? You should have a care not to damage something so lovely."

Robert shrugs a shoulder. "Taming my mare. A regal Arabian. Scarlet, like you. Gave me a kick."

"Poor soul," she coos, running her fingers up the inseam of his thigh to his chest. "The beast must have hurt you terribly to bring such bruises."

"It's all right. I hit her back."

The young woman laughs, tossing lustrous ringlets over her shoulder before drawing Robert's face to hers. "I'm Maddie. Madeleine." She kisses him, slipping her tongue inside his mouth. He pulls her onto his lap and, as an expert navigator traces a course along a map, slides his hand over her thigh. Madeleine taps his goblet, confirming its emptiness.

"Some coins," she says, "to fill your cups."

He produces two and places them in her open hand. The money was for bread—he can almost sense his mother cringe. Maddie slides off his knee and beckons her quiet companion to follow. Robert watches Domenicus watch after them, a buckle appearing in the centre of his brow.

"X'ghandek? What's wrong with you?" Robert asks.

"I don't know. I've barely seen her face. She has not spoken a word. She could be mute."

"Is that not every man's dream, a mute woman?"

"Perhaps, but she is a whore. I would just be one of a hundred men."

Robert shrugs. "She is a servant of Aphrodite. She sells her body for her security, many a priest sells his soul for his. At least her trade is honest. What's more, she burns for you."

"The peril of my incendiary good looks," Domenicus replies, laughing at last.

Madeleine and her friend return to the table, each holding two tall cups of sweet rozolin.

Robert downs his drink, folds his arms across his chest. "Maddie, my darling, my lap awaits you, and there are far uglier ones in which to land." They giggle as she sits, her lips brushing his ear.

Domenicus reaches over the flaxen on his lap for his cup. He strives for a proper look at her face, but her hair is in the way. He glimpses the boundaries of her face, the tip of her nose, the end of her chin. The peripheries seem attractive, but whatever natural beauty God gave her is corrupted by powder and rouge and kohl. He squints through his alcohol-induced haze. She drops her chin and runs her hands along his inner thighs before nestling against him and pressing her back to his chest. His face is lost in her soft locks, the rest of him in her delicate fragrance. She takes his hands, placing them against her chest. The moment he feels her through the flimsy fabric of her dress, his hands stiffen. She leans back, resting her head on his shoulder, pressing her mouth against his neck, below the line of his jaw. He closes his eyes, gives in. Across the room, the fiddler plays faster and louder.

"Qed tfotti, ja xitan! You're cheating, you devil!" It is Pino Mifsud, eyes frenzied, fat veins in his temples pulsating. "No one wins four games straight, you fen-suckled swindler!" He stands crooked with fury, pointing at his plump, foreign opponent, who sits dumbfounded on a stool. The noise and music quickly die, the tavern's regulars all turning to see the reason for the uproar. Pino bellows his rage and overturns the table, sending it to crash upside down against the floor. Cups and cards and coins fly at surrounding patrons. The foreigner says nothing in his defence, just sits there, startled and sweating. He looks wide-eyed at Pino, at the upturned table before him, the mess of cards and cups at his feet.

"Mifsud," the barkeeper calls, his cloth-wrapped fist inside a mug. "No trouble in my place."

"The hell you say! This pig is a cheat!"

"No trouble in my place."

"To the devil with you! I will find a new place to take drink!" Pino thunders, storming out of the tavern many coins poorer.

"He'll be back tomorrow," a villager says, laughing.

In the rush of whispering that follows, Domenicus finally gets a close look at the face of the flaxen girl. He narrows his eyes. Whispered remarks become lively chatter, and soon the drunken laughter resumes. But Domenicus is silent. The flames of recognition burn his face. He has it: the prostitute is Lilla. *Watchtower Lilla.*

"Let's get out of here," he says, looking at Robert.

Madeleine jumps up. "That's the spirit!"

Domenicus sighs. He had meant for him and Robert to depart unescorted, but the huge grin on his friend's face halts any clarification. The four consorts quit the tavern. As they file out into the street, the night throws darkness into their eyes. They cross the market square, Robert with one arm around each of the girls, the three of them laughing and staggering in the pale light of a street lamp.

"My boots, my boots. I love my boots!" Robert sings, trying to skip, stumbling and almost bringing down Madeleine and Lilla in his attempt. Domenicus strides ahead.

"Slow down," Robert calls, voice bouncing off the buildings that edge the square. "My legs don't know how to be as long as yours."

Domenicus halts and turns partway, his expression not in the least amused.

"What's the matter with your friend?" Madeleine asks Robert.

He smacks her bottom. "I'm going to find out, my strawberry." After a night of drinking, his journey is a stumbling mess: he lifts his foot carefully, kicking it forward in a strange dance, slamming it down, making a complete nonsense of himself. Just as he is about to tip over, Domenicus comes to catch him. Robert looks at him with glazed eyes. "You saved me. My hero."

"Shut up."

"What's wrong?"

"It's late."

"No, early," Robert says. "All depends on how you look at things."

Domenicus grunts.

"Why are you running away?" Robert asks, struggling for focus and balance. "Is it because you want her to love you?"

"Not at all. I had thought her coy, but she was hiding her face because she recognized mine."

Robert squints, brow furrowing in his attempt to make sense of this.

"God's ass, man," Domenicus snaps. "She is the prostitute who was... *entertaining* the sentry when corsairs attacked Angelica and my sister." The stick of instant soberness whacks Robert across the head. He swings a glance over his shoulder at the two women, rolls his head back.

"So...you want Maddie? You can have her. Makes no difference to me."

"I want neither. I'm going home. Do what you will."

"I'll come with you of course." Robert leans heavily forward, about to fall.

Domenicus props him up. "Go on, have your fun. Here." He slips his friend two coins. "For bread."

Robert gives him a meaty pat on the shoulder before stumbling back to the women. He drapes an arm loosely across Madeleine's shoulder and allows the prostitutes to lead him into an alley, their voices and laughter echoing long after they disappear.

The clock tower tolls one. Birgu is tranquil. Domenicus walks the winding roads, now more than ever a confused maze. Flanking his path are flat-roofed buildings, black against an ink sky. In this calm, his thoughts are turbulent. He felt nothing for the prostitute, yet allowed her to put her hands on him. There is only one whose touch he has ever wanted. But he is afraid to tell her how he feels. Desire is easy; admitting it is not.

Domenicus rubs his eyes. Cloud has moved across the face of the moon, making his path difficult to discern. Though sleepy, he takes the long way home, trying to make sense of his emotions as he wanders the coast. He finds a flat rock and lies on his back, elbows bent behind his head. Airstreams move across his body, under his shirt, over his stomach. He loses count of the stars scattered along the great black rim and feels the world turn, wishing she were lying beside him feeling it too.

If he stays this way much longer, he'll pass out. He struggles up, and for a while, sits contemplating the silver sheen of the moon soaked sea. Wind whistles through chinks in the rocks, ripples the harbour's surface, raises goosebumps on his arms. He wants his bed.

Given the hour, Domenicus is surprised to see light inside his house. He takes a deep breath in hopes he might inhale sobriety with the crisp night air. Having forgotten his key, he raps on the door. A chair skids across the floor. Seconds later, the door swings open.

"Where in God's name have you been?" Augustine thunders. "I was sick with worry!"

Annoyed, Domenicus rolls his eyes, pushes past him. "Why? I'm a man, almost eighteen!" He stops then. If the cool air was not enough to sober him, the pallor in his father's face is. Domenicus has not seen this haunted look since his mother died. He reconsiders his hostility. "Forgive me, Father. I was out with Robert."

"Gabriel Mercadal is dead."

Domenicus blinks. "Oh God, I'm sorry. ...What happened?"

"Death came as he slept. Awake, Gabriel would have put up a fight. ...He is the second person taken from me without the chance for parting words." Wiping bitter tears, Augustine sits heavily on the cedar chest. Domenicus takes a seat next to him, watches as he passes his fingers over the eight-pointed cross dangling on a thin chain around his neck.

"Gabriel gave you that."

"The day we met." Augustine closes his hand around the silvery cross. After a few quiet moments, he tilts his head, sniffs loudly, breaks into a little grin. "I see you've become acquainted with spirits of an unholy nature." He cuffs Domenicus lightly across the head. "Heed. While I'm away on campaign, do not make this a ritual."

"You are going then?"

"It was the last wish of my dearest friend."

The Maltese air blows unseasonably cool tonight, finding its way easily through the oiled linens that make up the windowpanes. Augustine knows his son and daughter are asleep by the sound of their breathing. Alone, he stares at the last candle's flame, watching the tongue of fire lick upward. He bows his head, dropping his chin to chest. Fresh tears roll over his cheeks. Never did he imagine life without Gabriel Mercadal. To Augustine, the knight seemed Herculean. He closes his eyes.

Rhodos rises from the sea. A small boy treads lightly, almost silently, as he tracks a rabbit through the island's mountainous forest. He has already caught and killed two this morning, his sights now set on a third. A twig snaps to his left. He spins around, startled. Standing between two pine trees is one of the spectacular Hospitaller Knights of St John, easily recognizable by the white eight-pointed cross emblazoned on his scarlet tunic. The knight wears a similar but smaller cross on a thin chain around his neck. It is an exquisite pendant, burnt silver set with turquoise gemstones.

The child knows these masters of Rhodos well. He likes to sit on the rocks by the harbour where the great Tower of St Nicholas stands in majesty, dipping his small feet into the Aegean and watching the ostentatious caravans depart, red and white standards playing high on salty winds. He has never spoken to a knight.

I've seen you before, the boy says. *Usted es un Caballero.*

Yes, I am a knight. My name is Gabriel Mercadal. Who might you be, master hunter?

I'm Augustine Montesa. I can spell it for you. My father taught me. A-U-G-U-S-T-I-N-E.

Augustine—like St Augustine of Hippo? the knight asks.

The boy has never heard of the fourth-century Algerian saint but beams at the comparison nonetheless.

Tell me about your father, Gabriel says, sunlight spilling off treetops onto his golden hair.

He taught me to hunt. He was a master hunter. I'm not. Not yet.

The knight grins. *You are better than I am.* He eyes the brace of dead rabbits at the child's feet. *Will you catch a* conejo *for me?*

Augustine regards the regal man with a combination of shyness and wonder. He uses his foot to nudge the plumper of the two carcasses towards Gabriel. *Take this one.*

The knight chuckles gently. *You offer me the fatter one! Your parents will not be pleased.*

I don't think they'd mind so much. They're dead.

Gabriel crouches. *You are alone? Where do you live?*

In the hut my father built. Not far from here, just down the hill. I hunt rabbits and skin them. Once I caught a deer! A whole deer! But it was too big to keep for long. It turned and drove even scavengers away. He flicks his eyes to the sword sheathed at Gabriel's side. The Spanish imperial banner gleams from the hilt and pommel, heraldic crests embossed in the ochre hide of the leather scabbard. Augustine recognizes the insignia. *My father was from Aragon. My great grandfather's father was a hermangilda. He fought in the Spanish Reconquista.*

Gabriel bows his head. *Then we are brothers. Tell me, what happened to your parents?*

Mother died when I was born. Father not too long ago. His boat turned over in the sea during a storm. He couldn't swim...that was the only thing he didn't teach me... Augustine turns his attention abruptly back to the dead rabbits. *Here, I can show you how to catch these. First, you can't be so loud. Breaking twigs beneath your boots as you do will only warn them.*

The knight unfastens his necklace and secures it around the boy's neck.

For protection, Gabriel says. *Don't lose it. That is the eight-pointed cross of the Order.*

Augustine can hardly believe his good fortune. *I will never take it off. Never ever!*

The knight visits him almost every day, bringing food from the Order's kitchens, fine clothing fit for pages and squires.

And Augustine is alone no more.

One afternoon, he gathers firewood in restless wait of Gabriel's arrival. The pile is soon more than Augustine can carry on his back. He runs home and returns with an old lateen sail that, when folded properly, doubles as his bed. He makes a sack of the sail and drags the kindling to his hut with ease.

The hours this day seem slow in their passing, and every snap of every twig draws up his head. When Gabriel finally comes, there is a heavy book tucked under his arm. *The first order of business is to teach you to read. Then mathematics, theology, economics, philosophy, geography, and linguistics. Only when your mind is whetted, will we turn our attentions to the blade—if it is your design to kill a man in battle, you ought to know something about his land.*

Augustine's eyes grow round, his mind still held by the first order of business. *Isn't reading just for priests and rich men?*

Gabriel shakes his head. *Their advantage is mere ease of access. One's station is no reflection of one's intelligence. Some rich men are bumbling idiots, some poor rise to the greatest heights of artistry and philosophy. Take Leonardo da Vinci. He is the bastard son of peasants, yet is rich with skill few can fathom. At once, he is an esteemed artist, architect, musician, engineer, scientist, inventor...* The expression on Augustine's face halts Gabriel mid-sentence. The knight laughs out-loud at his overwhelmed young student. *Too much for a first lesson, I think?* Gabriel hands the splendidly bound treasure to Augustine, who accepts it readily. He sits cross-legged on the dirt and opens the book on his lap; his fingers apply a careful touch, as if the book is sacred and fragile. He has never even seen a book before, let alone held one close enough to smell its gilded pages. The knight settles himself on the ground next to the boy. *This is a book from the Order's own library. Thus, we will accomplish two tasks with once the effort — as you learn to read, you will unconsciously be taught history.* Augustine nestles his dark head against Gabriel's arm and breathes a sigh. The childish gesture makes the knight smile with undisguised affection.

It is dawn, the morning of Augustine's fourteenth birthday. Gabriel arrives, shakes the young man awake and orders him to come outside at once. The knight tosses a sword that lands at Augustine's feet and draws his own blade from its scabbard. Tree branches break the sun and cast shadows over Gabriel's face, making him seem fierce.

Take up the steel, he says.

Augustine looks askance at the knight. *You wish to kill me?*

Gabriel bites his lip to keep from smiling. *Not to kill you, to train you. You have just been shaken from sleep and have yet to gather your bearings. Battle does not wait to suit your convenience. It strikes at all times.* Now *is the best time to learn, now, when you are groggy and stiff. Happy Birthday.*

Augustine glances to the sword with uncertainty.

Take it up, Gabriel says, thrusting his chin in its direction. *It was crafted by one of the Order's smithies to my specifications.* Augustine bends to pick it up. As he hoists it, sunlight catches in the blade, making its steel flash white. Doubt turns quickly to awe. The sword is light, comfortable to hold. More a work of art and less a weapon, it is similar to the sword Gabriel carries – a diamond section blade, steel hilt, embossed with Aragonese crests, the bronze pommel embellished with floral ornamentation. The rosewood grip is wrapped in strips of black leather. Augustine closes his hands around it and slowly lifts the sword. Without word or warning, Gabriel swings at him, forcing a clumsy parry. *Be wily, be quick*, the knight instructs his startled student. Gabriel strikes again, knocking Augustine full onto his back. The knight offers his hand and hoists him back to his feet. *Always be on the ready.* He knocks him down again.

Dazed but fully awake, Augustine huffs with frustration. He recovers and rises again. The knight takes him by the shoulders. *Concentrate. The sword is an extension of your body. An appendage. Be light on your feet, nimble. Lose your conscious self, give in to instinct. Pretend you are hunting rabbits.* He swings again.

The blades cross.

Morning dawns on Augustine's sixteenth summer. The young man wrings his hands anxiously together as he struggles to keep up with Gabriel and his swift, purposeful stride. The knight glances over his shoulder, laughs gently at Augustine's outward display of nerves. Today Gabriel will present him to the Order's Grand Master, the Italian Fabrizio del Carretto, in the hopes that he will accept the fledgeling warrior as a soldier-at-arms.

I'm not of noble blood, Augustine frets as he and Gabriel hike the road to the Grand Master's palace. *Del Carretto will laugh at me and reprimand you for your foolishness.*

Gabriel flings a dismissive hand. *To serve as a soldier-at-arms you need not prove nobility.* He sighs. *Nobility. I hate the word. It is corrupted. You* are *noble.*

Not the kind of noble *that matters.*

Gabriel swings round and halts the young man. *Boy, shake that notion from your head this instant or so help me God I will beat it from you with a stick.* There is no smile to betray even a hint of jest. The knight's stern countenance startles Augustine into a fumbled apology. Gabriel waves him to silence. *The world sees you the way you see yourself. If you do not believe yourself to be a man of quality, neither will anyone else. We live in a world of paradoxes, where one can be noble without nobility. Those from rich houses may be bereft of virtue, while those rich with integrity may be without lineage. In both cases, noble men are without nobility. If in your heart you are ready to make a vow and serve the Order of the Knights of St John as a soldier-at-arms, then do so, without another thought wasted on pedigree.*

Augustine looks intently at Gabriel. *Thank you.*

They take back to the road and walk long moments in silence. Nearing the palace, Augustine nudges Gabriel and grins. *You weren't really going to beat me with a stick.*

Yes, I was.

Now, in the dim light of his house, Augustine opens his eyes. He brings his eight-pointed cross to his lips and kisses it. *Thank you, Gabriel. I will never take it off.*

CHAPTER TWENTY-FIVE

Dawn brings a knock to the Montesa's door. Domenicus stirs. He runs his tongue along the inside of his mouth, swallows bitter saliva and, suffering his first hangover, drags himself from his bed to the door.

Robert stands before him, a little too bright-eyed for someone wearing last night's clothes. The sky above is overcast, streaked white with cloud. Domenicus blinks despite the grey.

"Come outside," Robert says, adding, "Close the door, and give me your hand."

Domenicus gives him a dubious look instead, but eventually opens his palm, into which Robert drops two coins. Domenicus raises an eyebrow.

"She let you have her for free? She was smitten with you."

Robert laughs nervously. "Not exactly. It... just didn't work out. Too much to drink."

At first, Domenicus looks quizzically at him, but a picture soon forms in his mind. He struggles to suppress laughter, soon coughing from the effort.

"Stop," Robert says. "It's not funny." The solemn entreaty only makes Domenicus laugh harder. "I offered her the money anyway," his friend continues. "She pushed me over and left me with my pants at my ankles." This sends Domenicus into heaving paroxysms of laughter, making him helpless, hopeless. He holds his ribs to quell the cramps. Even the pain is funny.

"I'll find Maddie later, show her what I'm really made of," Robert says, smiling sheepishly. "Oh, and to add to my humiliation, my mother was waiting at the door. It's like she knew."

Domenicus wipes the tears from his eyes. "She *told* you she'd know."

"*You smell like a whore,*" Robert says in perfect mimicry of Mea Falsone. "*A pair of boots is enough to make you a sinner? Soles to compromise your soul. God's eyes are lidless. He sees all. To the confessional with you at dawn! You'd better have enough money for bread.* And so on. I just dropped face down on my bed and let her bite her fist and carry on until she tired herself out. Jesus, instead of fun from one woman, I got shit from two." With a little snicker, Robert looks to the road. "I'm off. Have to meet di Bonfatti at the watchtower."

Domenicus gives his friend a solid pump on the arm. Upon turning, his amusement ends. He stands fixed at the threshold, startled by the sight of his father, sitting on his hands at the edge of his bed. He is frowsty and dishevelled and seems to have aged ten years in as many hours.

"Morning," Domenicus says finally.

There is no reply.

"Father?" Domenicus crouches before him.

Augustine squints as though straining through a haze. A shaft of colourless sunlight catches in his green eyes. There is an almost filmy glaze in them, like heavy fog over a tired sea. He blinks several times, but the cloud does not dissipate.

"You know," he begins, "when I look into your eyes, I can see your mother staring through them back at me. God, there is so much of my Isabel in you. To look at you is almost painful."

Domenicus does not know what to say, so fragile is his father's spirit and so bruised by fresh grief. His mouth works, but words just do not. A strange sense of guilt takes him, makes him feel he should apologise for being this living vestige of his mother. Domenicus rises, squeezes the man's shoulder, and goes to heat a pot of water over the fire pit.

Having risen and dressed quietly, Katrina crosses the room, puts her hand against Augustine's cheek. "How can I make this better?"

"You can't," he replies.

"Then know that we both love and need you."

He looks down. "I do know that."

Katrina's hand drops away from his face. Domenicus sees his sister's sadness and leans to her ear. "He'll be all right."

She looks doubtfully at him, but a long list of chores forces her to leave the house.

Domenicus watches his reflection in the water warming over the hearth and searches his image for his mother's features. It is long moments before the first bubble forms and floats to the surface. There is a second, a third and fourth until he can no longer see his face. The water rolls, steam rising in swirls to the ceiling.

Domenicus brings a drink to his father and sits at the table, chin on fist, eye entranced by the white line rolling from his own cup. He burns to know what the priest said yesterday during the ride from Mdina to Birgu. A glance in his father's direction is enough to know now is not the time to ask.

"Go saddle the horse for me," Augustine says, drawing Domenicus from his silent deliberation. "Please," his father adds, more an afterthought.

"Shall I come with you to Gabriel's lying-in-state?"

"What about your work at the Infirmary?"

"I collect no pay for my efforts," Domenicus replies. "Missing one day will not matter."

"Missing two days will. You did not attend your apprenticeship yesterday. You must be dependable—this is the hospital of the Order of the Knights of St John."

"Very well. I will meet you after. I'll be at the *auberge* by eleven," Domenicus says. He stuffs his rucksack with a ledger, clean trousers, and a treasure he found on the beach—a treasure he is certain Angelica is going to love—and goes to the stable to ready Tramonto.

***

A warm, salty breeze whips through the arched window of the Corradino watchtower. Franco inhales. The air is thick, carries the promise of rain. He drops his gaze deliberately to Robert's feet.

"Nice boots."

"Aren't they?" Robert kicks up his leg to show them off.

Franco stands tall and straight, making no movement to indulge the new sentry. He folds his hands together neatly. "Did you steal them?"

Robert looks at him in surprise. "Of course not."

"Forgiveness, Falsone. You understand. Just seems a little curious that yesterday you were barefoot and today you wear boots fit for a cavalryman."

"A gift," Robert replies succinctly, "from Domenicus, last evening."

"Ah, yes, the tavern. I expected you to be lying face down in a gully this morning."

"I managed to crawl out," the sentry says, smiling.

Franco frowns, annoyed that Robert always meets his contempt with good nature. The knight places his hands on the warning bell. "Now, when you see something out of the ordinary—turbans, pantaloons, anything bearing the mark of Islam—you ring this alarm." He taps his fingertips against the brass. "You will be here twelve hours before you are relieved. Do not move from this spot while on duty." Franco barely looks at Robert, speaking more willingly to his own blurred reflection in the bell. "Arrive ten minutes before taking post. And I will be informed if you are late." The knight finally looks at his employee. "A decent marksman?"

"Never met a piss pot I couldn't hit." Robert has that infectious kind of smile possessed by those others cannot help but like. And it bothers Franco because he does not want to like Robert.

"Tell me plainly, if you were to handle an arquebus, could you hit a target?"

"I would first have to handle the arquebus. As a boy, I fought in make-believe battles with pretend weapons, but whenever I threw rocks, I hit my mark."

"All right," Franco says. "I'll give you a few lessons in aiming and firing a real gun."

Robert beams.

Franco snorts.

"What colour are my eyes, my lord?"

The knight furrows his brow. "They look brown." He shrugs. "Like dry soil."

"From the space between us, yes, they look brown. However, if you were to come closer and look me right in the eye, you would see an iris speckled with bronze, rimmed in deep purple."

"And this should interest me why?"

"Because from a distance a man might look upon something and at once deem it ordinary, dull. But if that man came in closer, he would be surprised at the difference between what he first concluded by a glance, and what he sees when he actually looks."

For a moment, Franco gives in and actually likes Robert Falsone. The knight fights the feeling and, gesturing abruptly for the sentry to follow, turns for the stair, moving with grace to flaunt his good breeding. Robert bounds carelessly after him.

Outside, Franco yawns a big yawn. Sleep was a long time coming last night. He acted against Marcello's advice and took the case of the corsair Emir Zayid al Tariq to the Grand Master, contending that a live Muslim put to work, however offensive his existence might be, would be more useful than a dead one. From Franco's passionate appeal, the Grand Master would never have guessed that the young knight did not believe his own words. D'Homedes told the Florentine he planned to do with this heathen what the Order does with all Muslim prisoners: chain him to a galley bench until either ransom or death frees him.

Franco lay awake brooding after his visit with d'Homedes. For Katrina, the knight finds it easy to lie. He moves to her causes readily, even those in direct conflict with his own. Yet as expert a liar as he has become, he cannot lie to himself. If she were to ask him to complete another such task, he would do it. For her, he would do anything. The twilight thoughts troubled him greatly. Even now, his mind is in a tumult.

"Did it take you long to learn?" Robert asks, startling Franco.

"What?"

"The gun. Did it take you long to learn?"

"Oh." Franco passes Robert the arquebus, which glints when the sun glances on the metal. With brilliant rays from above lighting their dark hair, the two young men look for a tender but fleeting moment like blood brothers. "No. No great skill is required for this weapon to be effective, so it's perfect for you."

Robert acquaints himself with the gun, passing his hand over its long narrow barrel. It is a simple piece made of a wrought-iron tube plugged at one end with a touchhole and a flash pan. He holds it against his chest and aims at a stand of prickly pear, clicking his tongue to imitate a cocking trigger.

"Now," Franco begins, "Rather than your chest, butt the gun against your shoulder."

Robert repositions the arquebus. "Much more comfortable."

"Good. Run your fingers over the trigger, the match tube, the jaws." Franco points to each part. "Pulling the trigger releases a spring that makes the jaws rotate. This brings the flaming end of the match into contact with the priming powder in the flash pan." He indicates some loose rocks. "Pile those and practice firing. Mind, corsairs don't stand still and wait to be shot."

Robert begins gathering large stones into a heap. Franco walks over to a cactus and rips off a pear, placing it atop the rock pile. He waves Robert up the slope. "Back, back."

Robert squats and loads the gun with a small iron ball. Franco notes the sentry's taut fingers and cautious movement. The knight is pleased, but will not admit his approval.

"Careful," he calls. "Keep the flame far from the powder, lest your face burn from the flash of your own pan." Robert rises to his feet and butts the arquebus against his shoulder. Franco hops out of the sentry's range. He strides across coarse terrain, stringing through patches of thistle and clusters of asphodel, blooming white and pink.

"All right sentry, let's see if you can't hit that pear." Robert hoists the arquebus back into position. On held breath, he takes aim. Franco squints behind him. The distance makes a pea of the prickly pear.

Finally, closing his eyes with the pull of the trigger, Robert fires. The blast sends him reeling back to the dirt.

"My God," Franco whispers against the boom still echoing in waves off the rocks.

Robert squeezes his eyes tighter. "Was it that bad?"

"By Christ, you've hit your mark."

***

Domenicus stands hesitating before the gate of St Publius. He doesn't know how he ended up here—he started towards the *Sacra Infermeria* and the next thing he knew, he was at the church gate. Something within has pushed him here, something that won't let him be anywhere else. Still, he wonders if waiting to talk with his father would have been a better idea. Despite his nerves, he opens the gate, his stomach pitting to the creak of rusted hinges. He walks around the rectory to the western wall, notched by a window curtained with colourless linen. He imagines Angelica watching as a melting sun floods the field with colour, turning it to a sea of red. He would swim with her in that field.

The window is easily within reach, but he decides to dig a few stones and lob them from a distance, just in case Father Tabone is the one who draws back the curtain. Domenicus finds a spot in the shade of a stocky carob, and as he feels its bark rough beneath his hand, remembers hiding behind a tree the first time he saw Angelica. He pitches a pebble, sending it to bounce off the window frame onto the grass. He tries again, this time missing entirely. He curses. The third stone smacks the pane with such a thump Domenicus is certain the glass has cracked. He considers making a run for it.

"Your sister is a far better shot than you."

He whips round, startled.

"Hello," Angelica says. Bruises run in discoloured streaks along her face and throat, blue and yellow reminders that he failed to protect her.

"The surgeon-knight tended you well?" Domenicus asks, his tone more formal than intended. If Angelica notices the change in his demeanour, she makes no indication. With a quick turn of her long skirt, she shows him her ankle, tightly bandaged with strips of linen.

"Why are you trying to break my window?" she asks.

"I…I'm not," Domenicus stammers, embarrassed by the stones in his hand. "I came to see you, to make sure you're all right. Seems like forever since we last spoke."

"Only two days since." Not quite the response he'd hoped.

"Well, I mostly wanted to thank your uncle for speaking on Robert's behalf," he says lamely.

Angelica takes his hand. Her fingers are cool, tense. "Forgive me, I've been on edge."

"Of course I understand." Domenicus reaches into his rucksack. "Here, I have something for you." He gives Angelica her mother's flute. The strain in her face instantly dissolves. Her eyes shine with surprise and gratitude.

"Thank you! This is wonderful! You are wonderful!" Now that's more like it. She plants a kiss on his cheek. The unexpected action throws Domenicus into total disarray. He touches his fingers to his cheek as if to hold her kiss there forever.

"You're welcome," he mumbles.

"Where did you find it?"

"I went back to the cave where you left it."

Angelica clutches the flute to her chest. "Thank you a million times!"

Encouraged, Domenicus resolves to profess his true reason for coming. "Angelica, I have something to tell you. I… I…" he falters, losing his nerve. "I can't understand why you told your uncle about the book I gave you."

"I never told him anything," she replies, a tight pinch above her nose. "Someone else must have. Domenicus, please believe me. He never even mentioned it." She pauses. "That means he's not sure. Let me check under my bed to see if the book is still there. If it is, will you take it?"

"My sister still has your *Decameron*. No harm adding another book to our sinful library."

Angelica's laughter plays like a dulcian. "Wait here," she says, turning for the rectory, walking with a limp painful to watch. The breeze of her passage

194

sweeps against his face. If she would let him, he'd carry her everywhere. Anywhere.

Minutes later, Angelica returns to the carob and passes Domenicus *the City of the Ladies*. He accepts the book willingly, stowing it in his rucksack.

"So," she begins. "Any news of the man who saved me?"

The man who saved me. "I'm still waiting for word."

A shadow crosses her face. "Do you think they'll kill him? I couldn't bear it."

"To kill him would be to deprive themselves two strong hands—the knights need men for the fortifications and the bench." Domenicus gazes at Angelica's eyes, which have lost all sparkle with talk of the corsair. At length, he finds something to say.

"Has your uncle confined you to the grounds? He was quite furious yesterday."

"He's added to my chores to keep me close," she replies, "but certainly not under lock and key. Even now, he's away, attending the lying-in-state of an old knight."

"Gabriel Mercadal. My father's best friend."

Angelica furrows her brow. "Then you should be there with him. You'll change those clothes first, though."

"I brought clothes," Domenicus says, looking down at his trousers, grubby from kneeling in the dirt to dig pebbles. "But...I... *Vous êtes tres jolie, et chaque jour je vous veux plus.*" *You are very pretty, and every day I want you more.*

"You know I don't speak French."

"I asked about your ankle."

Angelica narrows her eyes. "I don't think so. What did you really say?"

Domenicus works his mouth, but his tongue is dry and not cooperating. He clears his voice. "Oh. Just that... Damn it all. Here it is. I could not go another moment without being near you, hearing your voice. You're all that occupies my mind. I think I—" He cuts himself off. Angelica's expression is difficult to read. "What? Plan to enter a convent and marry Jesus?"

She looks away, glancing warily to the church. "You forsake propriety."

"What has propriety to do with anything?" He takes her hand.

"Everything." She pulls it away.

"But it's just you and me here," Domenicus says. "Just *us*."

"Let this go."

His heart sinks. "I fear, Angelica Tabone, that you are a breathing contradiction. How can you even speak of propriety when you ask me to hide books disfavoured by Rome? You take my hand one moment, recoil the next. This propriety of yours is imposed only when it suits your purpose."

"You don't understand," she says quietly. "My uncle is *kappillan*."

"Then under lock and key, you are."

"That isn't fair."

"You are not fair," Domenicus replies angrily.

"What would you have me do?"

"Admit that propriety has nothing to do with it."

"*Damn it, I was almost raped!*" Angelica cries.

Deeply stung, Domenicus is unable to formulate a response, and a fraction of a second later, heavy, ungreased wheels struggle over cobblestone as Father Tabone's cart draws near, a pack of excited stray dogs lolloping behind. Unwittingly, the *kappillan* of St Publius reins the argument as he reins his mule.

"*Dun* Tabone," Domenicus manages. "I came to thank you for defending Robert."

The priest raises an eyebrow. "Really."

"You are very kind," Domenicus adds. Father Tabone steps down from his cart and tosses the last of the slops to the dogs, tails wagging as they devour the discards of Mdina's noble tables.

"No lad, I am an angry man who opened his mouth but shut his eyes. If Grimaldi Farrugia lied about Robert, he lied about you too. The farmer came to see me early yesterday morning and told me he overheard you and Robert discussing a book you planned to give Angelica. I think for my part, I was upset about what happened to my niece on the beach, and just needed someone to yell at." Domenicus feels the colour draining from his face.

"Farrugia must have known your family would speak for Robert," Father Tabone continues, "and so intended to sabotage you. Who would believe a heretic defending a thief? I apologise for what I said to you. I preach only those without sin may cast stones, and then pelted several at you."

"Thank you, Father," Domenicus says. The book inside his rucksack is solid rock, weighing down the bag, digging the strap into his shoulder.

"Go now. Augustine is waiting." Father Tabone smiles warmly before retiring to the rectory. "Angelica," he calls, turning partway, "Good to see you on your feet. Make lunch, will you? I'll be off again soon. Some new babies need baptizing."

She hesitates, looks at Domenicus.

"To your chores, *Signorina*," he says brusquely, walking off without a parting glance.

Fifteen minutes later, Domenicus is naked behind a patch of tall shrubs, balancing himself on an unsteady foot as he steps into the leg of his black trousers. With a mind elsewhere, he mismatches the buttons of his doublet. It takes three tries to get it right. He slides his boots back on, stuffs the clothes he was lately wearing into his rucksack and, dusting himself off, takes once again to the road.

Domenicus knows a shortcut to the *auberge* of Aragon, which leads him past the Palace of Conventual Chaplains, round a sharp corner and into the shadow of the Executioner's house. Spirited laughter punctuates quiet.

Children run beside hoops, rolling them along with sticks taken from unattended kindling. The sun does not touch this street, blocked by stone buildings that make a ravine of the byway. At the end of the road stands the *auberge* of Castile, notched by large square windows panelled with Venetian glass. The way abounds with knights walking in twos and threes in all directions, the air alive with animated words spoken in a dozen dialects.

A quick left brings Domenicus to the *auberge* of Aragon, marked by the red and gold escutcheon above the door. It is a good minute before his eyes adjust to the darkness of the foyer, draped as it is in a black velvet shroud. He recognizes a few faces, most of them belonging to knights, some to their young pages. There are priests from scattered parishes and nobles from Mdina. Dignitaries standing for Emperor Charles add a splash of colour to an otherwise dismal scene as they converse with compatriot knights, who revel in the presence of the Spanish throne's representation. It seems less a solemn lying-in-state and more an opportunity to mingle with peers of the realm.

Domenicus is set to approach a familiar page and enquire after his father when he glimpses Augustine sitting on a chair in a corner of the antechamber. Domenicus passes through the throng and places a hand on the arm of his father's chair.

"I'm not to help bear the coffin tomorrow."

Domenicus frowns. "But you of all men were closest to Gabriel."

"The duty is reserved for knights alone. It is the Order's decree."

"Decree? Hang the Order's decrees!"

"Lower your voice," Augustine hisses. "Do not trumpet insolence in the ear of the Sovereign."

Domenicus scans the room for a knight of high rank. He finds the one with the highest—the pale, narrow-faced Grand Master, Juan d'Homedes. The old Spaniard stands proudly at the head of a thoroughly prominent body, listening to the soft-spoken Governor of Tripoli, Jean Parisot de Valette. Domenicus casts decorum aside with every step he takes towards the Grand Master. Before Augustine can stop him, Domenicus steps through the circle of knights, among them two Grand Crosses, the Bailiwick, the Turcopilier, and the Prior of Capua, most of these men members of the Sacred Council. He halts himself in the centre of this illustrious ring and faces d'Homedes, the only knight wearing a solid gold eight-pointed cross.

"My father has served the Order all his life. He has bled for it, left his family for it, lost his wife because of it, and now you deny him the simple honour of bearing his dearest friend's coffin?"

A pockmarked Castilian squire lunges forward to strike Domenicus, but the Grand Master stays his hand. "Gustavo! *Basta tranquilízate.*" D'Homedes turns to Domenicus. "Only knights may be pallbearers. It is custom."

"Has the Grand Master not the power to make an exception?"

The Spaniard flashes. "Do not fence with me, boy, I am the more skilled swordsman. Better you remember your station."

Domenicus scoffs. "I need rank to protest this injustice?"

"Enough out of you! My authority is absolute. Challenge it at your peril."

"Consider it challenged." With terrible suddenness, the squire lashes Domenicus full and savagely across the face with the backside of his hand. He reels, shaken by the force of the unexpected blow. His left eye throbs, fit to burst. Fury turns his childhood scar white against his burning red face. His cheek stings, his pride equally wounded. But he checks himself, allowing his expression to betray neither pain nor humiliation. Shocked murmurs ripple through the assembly. All eyes are on Domenicus. All but those of the Spanish dignitaries, whose eyes fix on Juan d'Homedes, watching, assessing.

"*Domenicus!*" Augustine thunders, striding over. The Grand Master eyes the father with reproach, before turning his cold glare back on Domenicus.

"If you wish to court the favour of your betters, do not entice their contempt," d'Homedes says. "It is fortunate for you, if a misfortune for him, that you are the son of Augustine Montesa, a man for whom I have a measure of respect. Your impudence is cause enough for severe punishment."

"You hold my father in high enough regard that you will spare his son, yet you will not allow him to carry the coffin of his friend."

The Grand Master bridles. "Disparage me again, and by Christ's wounds, the leathern tongue of a whip will know the taste of your skin. Perhaps a noose might choke the defiance out of you. In fact, give me one reason why I shouldn't send you to swing for this insubordination."

Pa inhales sharply. "Please, *Molto Illustrissimo*, I am sorry." Domenicus feels his father close a firm hand on his shoulder. "Grief has corrupted his tongue."

"Indeed." The Grand Master regards Domenicus icily. The young man does not apologise, only hardens his resolve, staring at the old Spaniard with steely eyes. "Yet still he stands before me unrepentant. Why, I should tie the noose myself. Guards, take him!"

"Please, Excellency," Augustine begs. "The survival of my house depends on my son."

All eyes are on d'Homedes, watching as he deliberates. A dreadfully slow time passes, and in this long silence, the hard fist of realisation smashes Domenicus in the chest. Better men have been hanged for less. And the look on the Grand Master's face indicates he is considering that precise course of action.

D'Homedes snaps bony fingers. "Gustavo, fetch the Montesas their horse." The squire bows dutifully and bumps past Domenicus, throwing him a smug glance. In that instant, Domenicus is consumed by an urge to rip off Gustavo's arm and beat him to death with it.

"Come, come!" a Spanish ambassador calls cheerfully from across the room. "A heartfelt apology to end this ugly row." He claps his hands. "Let's hear it, lad." Domenicus feels the back of his neck burning, hotter still when his father prods him with a sharp elbow.

"Well?" d'Homedes prompts. "Speak! Or has that lively tongue of yours fallen into a faint?"

"I…" Domenicus wants to go on defying the Grand Master and all his pompous sycophants, but a look in Pa's direction is enough to crush all that is left of his will. Besides, while some things are worth dying for, mere pride is not. "Please accept my apology, your Grace."

"For what exactly?" the Grand Master asks. "For your being a base-court malcontent with the manners of a barn animal?" Piping laughter erupts in the entrance hall.

Domenicus inhales, very much hating to be used for sport in this manner. "Yes, Sire."

"Say it."

"Pardon me?"

"Say it. Say: I apologise, *Molto Illustrissimo*, for being a base-court malcontent with the manners of a barn animal." The laughter grows louder, bolstered by jeers from the less restrained young men in attendance. Domenicus senses hot, angry tears stinging his eyes. He blinks them away.

The Grand Master gives no quarter. "*Say it.*"

There is no escape. Domenicus swallows and speaks in a voice so low it only just reaches the ears of those lining the walls. "I apologise, *Molto Illustrissimo*, for my being a base-court malcontent with the manners of a barn animal." The last word barely makes it out his mouth when the foyer breaks into vigorous applause and whooping, some grunting like hogs, others bleating like goats. The knights closest to Gabriel, Pietro de Laya and Tristan Galan among them, look on silently, visibly sickened by this tasteless display of boorish mirth at the lying-in service of their beloved *pilier*. Domenicus chokes back his fury, acutely aware above all that he has been reduced to nothing more than entertainment for a group of spoiled, infantile foreigners.

"Now go," d'Homedes sneers, "before I have second thoughts and order you to crawl around on all fours. I should have you flogged simply for admitting to being a base-court malcontent with the manners of a barn animal. And Augustine Montesa," he says, sending him a hard glance, "harness that little ox of yours, or next time, it will be to the slaughterhouse with him."

"Come, Son," Pa says quietly, starting towards the door. With a swish of his black habit, the Grand Master gives Domenicus his back. He can only stand there, silently seething.

Conversations gradually resume, whispered at first, but growing in volume with each passing moment. Domenicus stares after d'Homedes, dumbfounded that in one fell swoop, a disagreement could metamorphose indifference to resentment and finally to scalding hatred. He has never hated anyone before and had no idea the feeling could be so violent, so encompassing, so enough to make murder seem justifiable. He clenches his fists, his knuckles white. He holds the rage in his hands a few moments more. In the end, he relaxes his fingers and turns to follow his father. Domenicus makes it halfway to the door when a strong hand presses hard against the middle of his back. A glance across his shoulder reveals the knight Valette.

"You are wrong to excite the Grand Master's wrath," the Frenchman says sternly. "You narrowly escaped the gallows. He could have ordered you whipped—and should have done. If I were he, you would be enduring sound flogging this very moment, unable to protest, for you would be without a tongue." Had any other man made this declaration, Domenicus would have taken it as bluster; because Jean Parisot de Valette made it, Domenicus believes.

"It is not my intention to insult the Grand Master. Nor to disgrace my father. I am heartsick watching him grieve, now denied his only want."

Valette is not an unreasonable man. "You love your father," he says. "But you do him no favour by defying the Grand Master."

"If enduring a beating would grant my father's wish, I would endure it."

Valette wears a benevolence rarely betrayed by his grim countenance. "With all my heart, I believe you." He seems to reconsider his softness, a cold, hard gaze bringing frost to where there was just warmth. "Still, you are better to mind that tongue of yours if you have grown at all fond of it."

Swords of sunlight slice through an overcast sky and pierce murky puddles. Father and son walk the village gravely and silently, Tramonto *clip-clopping* between them.

"What is the matter with you?" Domenicus demands, turning to speak over the horse's saddle.

Augustine ignores him.

"*Father!*"

"*What?*"

"Have you nothing to say?"

"Please, Domenicus, have you not said enough already?"

"Forgive me for not wanting to see you suffer."

"Because at this moment, I am overjoyed," Augustine replies dryly. "You wish the Grand Master to make an example of you? You contested the man's authority right in front of dignitaries from Spain! You made him look an ineffectual weakling before men who represent the Emperor. I mean, my God, *what in the hell were you thinking?* Do you think I enjoyed watching a man degrade my only son? Do you think I would not suffer to see you led to the gallows for something so stupid?"

"You speak as though I was not justified."

His father flashes. "You were not justified! You cannot defy the Order."

"Did you not teach us to defend what is right?"

"Yes, what is right. There was nothing right in your actions today. You had better pray he does not reconsider his mercy. He'd do it too, you know, just to assert the authority you dared question."

"What makes him impervious to criticism? He is just a man, for Christ's sake. A man who shits in a pot, same as every other."

"A man who answers only to the Pope and God. A man whose authority is on par with the great monarchs of Europe. A man with the power to have you hanged," Augustine shouts over Tramonto's back. The horse snorts and flips his mane.

"What an honourable Order you serve, that hangs men for words," Domenicus says.

"You know the noose is looped for the insolence behind the words. For the last time, you cannot challenge the Order of Saint John. Those who do, wind up dead." Just as the words spill forth, the feuding father and son draw near the Executioner's house. Augustine thrusts an angry finger at it as if to say *you see?*

"I had always been proud my father served the Order," Domenicus says. "But today I have seen it for what it really is—tyranny in armour, and the Grand Master, a festering boil on the face of the Empire. How can you suffer yourself to remain loyal to an oozing pustule?"

"You are young and don't understand."

Domenicus is fed up being told he doesn't understand—first by his mother, then by Robert, then Angelica, now his father. "That is a weak argument! A feeble claim that will forever be the last refuge of a person wishing to end a quarrel."

Augustine sighs. "Look, there are times when yes, a situation does call for a person to push against injustice, but there are times also when that same someone would be better served by silence. It's not always easy, I know. The hard road and the right road are often the same road."

Domenicus kicks the dirt, sending loose stones to scatter and roll over the dust. "Everyone is so concerned with propriety. All of you should take up residence at a monastery, where no one ever speaks." He exhales in frustration, eyes dropping to the miserable road pounded by his feet. Dust motes come alive with every step. Soon village buildings give way to fields, a patchwork of dry land, and home is but twenty paces away.

"Did the squire hurt you?" Augustine asks gently.

Domenicus makes no reply.

"Perhaps an injury to your pride only."

Still, the young man stares straight ahead.

"So," his father presses, "Now you have chosen not to speak?"

"Only for fear I'd say something that might affront the horse, since every time I have spoken today I have offended someone."

***

Bent over a wooden trough in the growing shadow of the rectory, Angelica scrubs a heavy cotton shift until her elbows ache. The fabric begins to fray, the dye to fade, her fingers long since pruned. Efforts to keep her mind occupied or, in the least, off Domenicus, make her agitated in her chores. She huffs and sighs and plays everything over in her mind. And over again. Frustrated, she cradles her head in her hands, soapy water running from her fingers into her hair. She tells herself not to care, tells herself his behaviour was irrational. He misunderstood her rebuff. It wasn't even a rebuff, not a deliberate one.

Does he not see? She is the niece of a man who is not just a priest but the *kappillan*. Her every action is thus subject to the approval of a congregation of gossipers. Domenicus knows her life. And yet, this life has not stopped her from reading books sure to ignite disapproval from not only a few meddlesome parishioners but the Holy Church itself. Of course, none in Father Tabone's loyal flock knows about her books. She couldn't very well hide *Domenicus* under her mattress with them. Still, being a person who naturally presumes the fault lies entirely with herself, she reflects long and hard about what she could have done differently. For starters, she thinks, she should have been less guarded. Domenicus has never given her a reason not to trust him. And after all, he had only begun to say the very words that for ages she has longed to hear. His mere presence has always been enough to stir wondrous things inside her, things that loop and roll and flutter. He is the unspoken subject of every fantasy she has shared with Katrina. Angelica cannot help smiling, convinced now that Katrina must have known all along. It doesn't matter anyway because that's all they were, silly fantasies. She certainly wasn't expecting him to turn up today with a mind to make them a reality. Besides, romantic whimsies could not be farther from her thoughts these days.

She does not blame Domenicus for what the corsair tried to do, of course not, but she cannot help blaming him for being a man. A man could never understand her anguish, or that of any woman, after so gruesome an ordeal. She needs time, time to quiet all that raises chaos inside her head, time maybe even to feel safe again.

Domenicus *is* safety. And when he was standing there, stammering and struggling so sweetly, she wanted to kiss him. The power of so many conflicting emotions overwhelmed her. She didn't know what to say. So she said the wrong thing and in the doing, mortally insulted him, so bare was his soul and so sensitive to rejection.

Angelica's sore fingers recall her mind to her work, and she wrings greyish water from the same shift she's been absently scrubbing these past twenty minutes. The wind picks up, blowing the clothes already hanging on the line in a flimsy dance. A clothespin clamped between her teeth, she hangs two of three freshly washed cassocks, an alb, and a soutane.

The sound of steps turns her head. Katrina moves evenly through the wild grass, touching her fingers to the tips of the tall blades, her eyes on the priest's many garments. "So, your uncle has decided to move his vestry outside?"

Angelica takes the pin from her mouth and smiles, happy to see her friend.

Katrina embraces her. "I feel terrible I couldn't be here for you yesterday."

"Of course I understand. Robert needed you more." Just then, Angelica spots her flute, lying forgotten by the laundry basket. She feels her stomach pit when Katrina notices it too. "One of the parishioners found it and returned it," Angelica explains, sparing herself a lie with an evasion. She hopes Katrina does not ask whom and is twice relieved to hear, "That's wonderful. You were overdue a turn of good fortune. So, how is your foot?"

Angelica shrugs. "Better. The surgeon de Gabriac said it will be a while before I walk right, though."

"And everything else? I mean, after the corsair... I mean, all is well?"

"I think so." For a long moment, neither speaks. Angelica senses Katrina's uneasiness, sees the tension in her face, the not-knowing-what-to-say, and breaks the silence. "Shall we read?"

"I don't know. I thought you might want to talk."

"We're already good at talking," Angelica says.

"Oh. All right. So long as it's not Old Testament. I don't like being called *unclean*, especially over something God forced on me." A gust blows one of the sheets off the line and onto Katrina.

Angelica laughs. "I don't think the Almighty shares in your opinion."

Katrina squirms out from under the damp bed linen. "Why? He didn't write the Bible."

"*Katrina*," Angelica hisses. "You'll end up burnt at the stake."

"Come on."

"And they'll not allow you the mercy of suffocating from smoke. Heretics burn alive."

"I'm not a heretic!" Katrina cries.

"I know that. But you should still be careful, even in what you whisper. There is no worse death than burning alive. I know. I saw the burning of Father Gesualdo."

Katrina's eyes widen. "*Veru?* In all these years, you've never mentioned it."

"No, I have not. I don't like to think of it. My uncle said Gesualdo was a Lutheran partisan who tried leading a Reformation of his own. I'd really rather not talk about it."

Katrina nods, though Angelica can tell her friend finds departing the subject difficult. Even so, the two girls finish hanging the laundry in silence.

As dusk settles, Katrina watches her father pick absently at the food on his plate. Minutes are slow in their passing, made slower by a tense silence broken only when he or Domenicus converse in tight monosyllables.

"What is wrong with you two?" Katrina asks finally.

Neither gives a reply.

Katrina gives her brother's knee a poke under the table. "This wouldn't have anything to do with people on the street calling out *base-court Montesa* and making animal noises at me, would it?"

"*What?*" Domenicus fairly explodes, eyes flashing. "*Who?* Who did this?"

"I-I don't know," she stumbles, "One was a squire, I think, or maybe he was a page. There was a knight, a Spaniard. And some goon from the village. It was all very strange. I—"

"*Infantile bastards.* What else did they say? What did you say to them?"

"Nothing, nothing. I kept walking..." She shakes her head "What is this all about?"

"Not now," her brother says.

"But—"

"*Not now*," her father repeats in a growl low and hard with severity.

Katrina tries instead for a change of subject. "So, did you see Angelica today?"

"Why?" Domenicus asks.

"Well, someone found her flute and brought it to the rectory."

"Did she not say who it was?"

"Come to think of it, not really, no. She said some parishioner found it. My guess would be Dr Callus since he's always rummaging around in those old caves looking for treasure."

"Mmm."

"*Mmm,* what?"

"Nothing," Domenicus replies. The rest of the meal is eaten in silence.

An hour later, worn from a fruitless effort at conversation, Katrina blows out five of the ten candles and retires to a rough straw pallet. The two men soon go to their own beds and draw curtains, leaving Katrina to look on, mystified. Her struggle to make sense of the day's events serves only to keep her wakeful well into the night. She had always supposed that because of Father, the Montesa family was of the more respected in Birgu. Why then would people yell such derisions at her on the street? Sure, she has had unpleasant encounters with the widow Borg and her offspring, but this was nothing like that recent incident with Anne. Today, the Montesa *name* was loudly disparaged. This troubles Katrina, though not nearly so much as seeing her father at odds with her brother.

CHAPTER TWENTY-SIX

The mob in Birgu's square swallows Angelica. A grunting hog jostles her deeper into the crush of knights and peasants shouting jeers over the measured beat of a drum. In the centre of it all is a pyre. There is a young man chained to a stake, a gag in his mouth, his filthy clothing torn, his exposed skin lacerated and bruised. A hooded man rips the rag from the prisoner's mouth and packs it with straw. Twigs are stuffed into his tattered garments, brambles behind his ears. A practised executioner knows to position kindling so that the victim's head and limbs will catch at the same time.

Angelica is pinned between a blacksmith and a cobbler. They cram so tight against her she can feel every breath they take. There is a foully old woman, her stooped form draped in black, pressing hard against Angelica's back. She can barely breathe.

The bishop of Malta, seated next to the Grand Master, signals the executioner. The drumming stops, and he brings the torch to the labyrinth of dried reeds at the foot of the stake. The reeds do not catch at first, but a gust breathes life into the flame. The crackling hiss becomes a roar.

Fire sets in the prisoner's flesh.

Angelica feels the pulsing waves of heat against her face and closes her eyes, but sees through her lids. She covers her eyes but sees through her hands. The man is engulfed, writhing against his bonds, screaming. She knows his face. His beautiful face.

It is Emir Zayid al Tariq.

Angelica coughs until her eyes open. All is silent, dark. Her nightshirt and bedsheets are damp. At once, her body is hot and cold. She throws off her covers and paces. Heart pounding, she goes to the window, where she sits and stares at the glossy black sky until first light lines the horizon, and she is certain it was just a terrible dream.

***

The sun streaks pink across the pale sky, and though the day is quite new, the heat is already enough to dry the morning mists. Domenicus watches as knights in black habits file out from St Lawrence church following the funeral mass of Gabriel Mercadal, much-loved *pilier* of Aragon. A page leads the procession, hoisting the gold and red banner of Aragon. Grand Master Juan d'Homedes is a pace behind, his office marked by the ornate sceptre in his hand. Six knights, among them Pietro de Laya and Tristan Galan, carry the coffin, draped in black cloth. A pastor follows, his flowing robes rippled by hot airstreams, his acolyte walking slowly beside him.

A large group of peasant bystanders has assembled on either side of the cortège. Truly, the commoners could not care less that a knight has died— in fact, some are happy to hear it—but a procession is a procession, and that means a break from an otherwise dreary day.

From his place amongst the spectators, Domenicus scans the faces of the passing grievers for his father. Franco di Bonfatti walks beside an unfamiliar man, and behind them is the Italian Admiral Alessandro Ardone. Domenicus keeps pace with the moving line, picking his way through the horde of stationary onlookers, his eyes darting from face to face. He stops. Gustavo, the squire who slapped him, trails the Grand Master. Domenicus feels the same heat that burned his cheek yesterday. He considers pelting something at the Castilian, a rock, or better, a handful of dung. It would probably end up hitting the Grand Master. Not that that would be so terrible. Domenicus smiles briefly before abandoning the idea, which would surely earn him swift execution.

***

Clang. Augustine spent the night alone in a cradle between two high rocks at the tip of the peninsula, listening to tiny, black waves lap against the shore, his bare feet dangling just above the water. Now, the sea is the colour of the gemstones set in his cross, and the air carries the clear ringing of church bells. He rises, shaking out legs made stiff from long hours sitting. Yesterday, at the lying-in-state, Pietro de Laya approached Augustine about Gabriel Mercadal's final will. The knight had named Augustine heir to a tidy sum. De Laya asked him to stop by the *auberge* later today. But Augustine is uninterested in holdings and wills. For reasons he does not understand, finding his son is suddenly very important.

Clang. The funeral procession winds with the meanly kept streets. It travels beyond the bishop's palace and the armoury, past the convents of Castile, Aragon, France, Auvergne and Provence, before rounding a sharp corner and passing into the shadow of England's dormitory.

Clang. Augustine finds Domenicus wandering against the flow of the throng. The father wants to embrace his son but holds back.

"You came."

Domenicus shrugs. "I was looking for you. You've missed the funeral. And you will miss the burial if you do not move into the procession now."

"Gabriel will understand."

Clang. "I did you dishonour yesterday. You do not wish to show your face."

"You did yourself dishonour," Augustine replies. "And in truth, I wanted to stay away from all this, say farewell my own way, in the way I know Gabriel would like. He was never one for pomp and ceremony. ...But I am surprised you would show your face."

"You still believe I was wrong?"

"Not in your intentions, but in your actions."

Clang. The final toll.

"I'm not sorry for what I said to the Grand Master yesterday," Domenicus says. His eyes are soft, his mouth firm, making an expression both repentant and unapologetic. "What kind of son would not defend his father? Is it not to be expected? Even from a base-court malcontent with the manners of a barn animal such as myself."

Augustine grins. "I don't think you have the manners of a barn animal."

"Well, maybe sometimes."

"I owe you thanks. I was blind to your defence of me, seeing only your affront to the Grand Master." Augustine strokes his chin. "Perhaps it is an apology I owe."

"I'll take both," Domenicus replies, smiling.

"I must now ask a great courtesy of you." Augustine puts his hand against his son's back as they walk a tight road untouched by sunlight. Even in the shade, the air is close and hot.

"It is yours for the asking." At the entrance to the *Sacra Infermeria*, Domenicus rolls up his sleeves, his shirt damp from sweat.

"You know a caravan is a year away from home. In my absence, you will be the man. I need you to leave your apprenticeship and work the fortifications."

Domenicus falls silent. Augustine does not push as his son deliberates—he knows he is asking him to trade an education for a pickaxe.

"I suppose," Domenicus begins, "if order is to be kept among the Maltese and the knights at the quarries, they will need someone who can talk all tongues while you are gone." He grins. "That ought to yield a handsome reward from the Grand Master."

Augustine chuckles. "Come now, isn't working for that festering boil its own reward?"

***

For the first time in her life, Angelica dons a *barnuża* and moves like a shadow through the host of villagers. Eyes downcast, she walks slightly hunched, blending easily with other village women. Her steps take her from the crowded market square along a straight road, past the hostels of galley captains, beyond the Italian *auberge*, to the slave prison. These dungeons were quarried from the rocky foundations adjacent to St Angelo, paces from the shipyard. It is here that all Muslim prisoners condemned to the oar are housed. The dungeon's exterior, marked by the slow decay of time, has the look of a thousand years with its weathered stone. A heavyset Sardinian with a head like a ten-pound cabbage stands at the gate, rusted spikes crowning tall iron bars.

Angelica presents herself to the guard. "I will see a prisoner, Sir."

The Sardinian's belly jiggles with deep laughter that wracks his shoulders and rattles the ring of keys hanging from his belt. "Not a chance."

"Why not?"

"The dungeon is not accessible to villagers. Get lost."

Angelica straightens her back, pushes down her shoulders, and sticks out her chin, all in a vain attempt to appear older than she is. "Very well," she says loftily. "But Franco di Bonfatti of the Italian *langue* will be most displeased when I inform him that you denied me entry."

The guard smirks. "He'll get over it." He waves to the road behind her. "Trot, trot." The Sardinian kicks a muscular leg in her direction, intending to miss. Still, Angelica jumps from the path of his foot and throws him a dirty look.

Frustrated but not defeated, she heads to the nearby *auberge* of Italy, its façade facing l'Isla, the spit of land across the dockyard inlet. A soaring pillar, engraved with the image of the Sacred Host, trims an otherwise dull corner, and over the door's semi-circular hooding, hangs the black and gold shield of *Italia*. Angelica sits on the cold step outside the door and waits, patiently at first, but grows restless with each passing minute. She rises and peers through the large casement of Venetian glass. The entrance hall is empty. Fed up, she abandons the *auberge* for the market. She walks a skinny vein of road towards the heart of the village, where she is swept into a phalanx of knights and their escorts. Ahead, Franco walks beside another young man.

"Sir Franco!" Angelica calls. The two men turn.

"*Signorina,*" Franco says brightly. "How is your foot?"

"Better, thank you. Though a while before I walk with more grace than a three-legged dog."

The knight chuckles. The sun shines warmly over the tops of the flat roofs, spilling onto his dark hair, brightening his gold-flecked hazel eyes. "How may I be of service?"

"A great favour, one I pray you not repeat," Angelica replies.

His friend steps forward, burying an elbow in Franco's ribs. "Where are your manners?"

Franco smiles, gingerly rubbing his side. "Miss Tabone, allow me to present Marcello di Ruggieri, my greatest and worst childhood friend."

Marcello takes Angelica's hand and kisses each knuckle.

She feels herself blush. "I did not mean discourtesy, my lord."

"*Marcello*," he replies. "And you are free to shower me with discourtesy at your leisure."

Angelica looks at him askance.

"Never mind," Franco says. "He is too crooked to talk straight. Now, your request?"

"I need you to get me into the slave prison," Angelica says. "I wish to see the corsair, Emir."

The smile vanishes from Franco's lips. "Absolutely not."

"Please. I need your help. I would never involve you otherwise. I know you have no love for this man. I tried to go alone, but the guard refused me."

"Rightly so!" Franco replies.

Marcello pipes up. "Why do you seek occasion with a Mohammedan? He has no soul."

"Forgive me, *Honorabile*," Angelica says, "but the measure of a man's soul is determined by right action. This man's religion did not stop him from right action. I owe him thanks."

"He is spared the noose," Franco says. "That is thanks enough. I saw the Grand Master on the matter myself. Besides, even if I wished to grant you this favour, and I do *not*, your uncle would have me boiled in oil if he learned that I gained his niece entrance to the dungeons. How, moreover, do you even mean to speak to the corsair? You are not conversant in the tongue of the infidel."

"Words are not always necessary to convey meaning," Angelica replies.

Franco glances to the sky as though he is about to sigh and relent. Instead, he shakes his head. "No." His tone is final, putting an end to further protest. "That you would even ask this of me I find hugely disconcerting." The knight turns on his heel, leaving Angelica in dismay.

Marcello hesitates somewhere between staying and going. He leans towards her and whispers, "Meet me by the slave prison. I will be there inside the hour." He grins broadly, teeth flashing with the afternoon. "Fifty paces from the gate, there is a lone carob, fat and gnarled like the guard. Wait there. Go." Before Angelica can reply, he is off, his habit swishing as he jogs to catch up with Franco.

"Bonfatti, you dog," Marcello says, falling in step with Franco. "Is that the one for whom you had the corsair spared? If so, I understand. She is beautiful! I assumed the maiden you mentioned would be coarse as all the rest."

Franco frowns. "She is the girl that was almost raped. And, if you find the women of this land coarse, why do you frequent their beds?"

"Because I have no interest in frequenting yours. Anyway, she is stunning. A perfect flower in a plot of weeds. Tell me her name, so I might write it into a song."

"She is the niece of a local priest—a *kappillan*, actually, the head of his parish."

"That is her name? Hmm. Not very becoming," Marcello says. "Must be local."

"Her name is Angelica Tabone, idiot. Stay away. She is not some fruit ripe for the picking."

The two men reach the door of the Italian *auberge*. Behind it, St Angelo breaks the sun and casts a fat shadow over the dormitory. The clamour of metal tools working stone spills over the fortress walls and reminds Franco it is time for combat training. He heaves a miserable sigh, holding the door open for Marcello.

"You would think they would not force us to joust the day of a *pilier's* funeral. It is to take all afternoon, and we must don full armour in this heat."

"Ah, no one has ever drowned in sweat."

"Sir Franco!" The knight turns and squints, barely able to make out the form of young Amedeo Pistolesi as he marches the corridor, dark against the day. He meets the knights at the door. Piled in the page's arms are greaves, visor, sword, and cuirass. Amedeo, the only son of a Venetian duke, is eager to please the knight, obeying his every whim like a puppy.

"Sir Franco," the page repeats urgently, peering over the heap in his arms. "Time for the skirmishes. Italy faces Auvergne. Come, I will help you with your armour." The page looks to Marcello. "I will help you also."

Marcello winks at the boy. "I've been excused from training today. Sore back, you see."

"You have the devil's knack at deception, you do," Franco says, shaking his head.

Marcello looks up, shielding his eyes with his hand. "The sky is right for the hunt."

"For birds, I hope."

Angelica sits in a patch of grass, her back pressed against the trunk of a carob. She hugs her knees to her chest, glancing occasionally across her shoulder. Her stomach rumbles. She did not bother to break her fast this morning. The air coming off the water tastes of salt, intensifying her desire for food.

Dried out brambles crunch under the weight of a boot.

"*Signorina.*"

"My lord."

"*Marcello.*" The knight has a bolt of black linen against one shoulder, a satchel slung over the other. He extends his hand and helps her up. "Here." He holds the linen out to her. "Wrap yourself in this."

"Of course I will do as the nobleman bids, but why must I cover myself?" Angelica asks. "I am with you. The guard will not send me away."

"No, but he might tell your father. That would gain you sound beating."

"Hardly. My father is dead."

Marcello goes red and stammers. "I-I… I misspoke. Forgive me."

"You did not know. Moreover, you are right. I should conceal myself—my uncle is a priest." She takes the bundle from the knight's arms and drapes herself head to toe in the formless cloth.

Marcello rubs his chin, nodding his approval. "Stoop. Hobble when you walk."

"For the hobbling, I need not pretend."

"Ah yes, Bonfatti asked about your foot. How were you injured?"

"Turned my ankle."

"Well, I'd be happy to carry you anywhere you need to go."

Angelica feels her cheeks burning. "Thank you, no." She nudges her chin at Marcello's rucksack. "Something in there for me too?"

"This? No," Marcello replies. "Only cover, to keep Bonfatti from asking questions. Some hawking equipment. Of course, your company is welcome. Think of it, the two of us, waves crashing the shore, falcons wheeling above, sunlight catching in their grey-blue feathers …innocent misunderstandings."

"No."

"You don't like me, do you?"

At this, Angelica laughs. "I don't know you well enough yet to know I shouldn't like you."

The Sardinian seems not to have moved over the last hour, standing still against the barred entrance, arms folded across his wide chest.

"Unlock the gate," Marcello di Ruggieri orders.

The guard nods, his mien ever ingratiating as he yields to the knight. The rusted gate screeches, its latching greased with dirt and time. The Sardinian steps aside to allow a modestly robed Angelica passage. He catches her eye and narrows his own.

"Get a move on," Marcello snaps at the guard.

"Which of the prisoners does the noble lord mean to see?"

"One Emir Zayid al Tariq," the knight replies. "A corsair brought in a few days past." The guard leads them into darkness, down a long, tight staircase lit only by the moving ring of light cast from his lantern. Angelica's eyes strain in the gloom. The stench of urine and excreta assaults her senses with the force of a physical punch; it is a stink so fierce it stings her eyes and makes her nose run. She clings to Marcello, tightening her grip on his arm. At last, they reach the bottom step. With her free hand, she wraps her black garb around herself more securely to fend off the cold musty air creeping under her clothes. There are ugly sounds to accompany ugly smells. The squeaking, the wailing, the crunching of insects beneath her feet. Mice scurry over the hard stone, the ground thick with dirt, crawling with roaches and slugs.

The cell doors are wood, but for the small barred window at the top and the hatch on the bottom. Angelica wanders too close to a door. A prisoner's hand shoots through the bars for her veil. The guard pulls the looped whip from his trousers and snaps it on the filthy hand.

"Stay close," Marcello hisses, pulling Angelica towards him. At the end of the subterranean vault, the guard halts at the last door in the long line of cells. He raises his lantern to the keyhole with one hand, uses the other to unlock the door.

"On your feet, filth," the guard snarls upon entering the room. Marcello follows him inside, but Angelica hesitates at the threshold, no longer certain coming to this place was a good idea. A solitary prisoner, in the midst of prostrating on his pile of dirty straw, blinks at the light from the lantern. In four strides, the Sardinian marches the room and kicks the prisoner's side. "*Get up!*"

"Leave us," Marcello says to the guard. "If he tries anything, I will dispatch him." The Sardinian bows with what little grace he can muster and moves past the knight before handing Angelica the lantern and disappearing into darkness. Marcello leans against the wall, knee bent, arms folded, eyes alert.

Angelica crosses the cell, light bouncing erratically over the floor. She brings the lamp to the prisoner. His head is shaven, face covered in bloody grime. He remains on his knees, watching her as she draws back her hood, undoes her veil. She kneels on the straw beside him and touches his hand.

"Emir," she says, holding up the lantern so he can see her more clearly. The light of recognition shines on his face.

"Thank you," she says.

CHAPTER TWENTY-SEVEN

Eleven days pass, spent mostly in the hot, dusty quarries of St Angelo, and though it burns him, Domenicus has not attempted to see Angelica. He rests his pickaxe against a newly constructed rampart and leans over the fat stonework.

"Ho there!" he calls to Jumoke, standing on the scaffolding below. "How is your foot?"

The Egyptian looks up, squinting at the blinding sun. "Better."

"Ah," Dakarai cuts in, "He keeps his hairy paws dusted now."

Domenicus smiles. "Good." Ten days ago, Jumoke dropped a limestone block on his bare foot. Acting fast, Domenicus made a splint and swaddled the broken big toe in the cloth of his own shirt. Jumoke touted him a hero. It was not long before others agreed that the accolade was well deserved. Over the nine days following Jumoke's accident, Domenicus tended several men, suturing clean cut wounds, bandaging oozing ones. Anything more complicated than surface gashes or simple fractures he referred to the Hospitallers. This included one rather grisly incident, which involved a broken thighbone after a stonemason fell two storeys from the shaky crosspiece of a ladder. The workman's femur snapped, and serrated, bloody bone burst through his skin. In his hysteria, he tried shoving it back in but succeeded only in ripping more tissue, tearing his quadriceps and rupturing his femoral artery. Domenicus used both hands to apply pressure to the gaping wound to keep the man from bleeding to death. Desperate, he packed the injury with mud and tied a tourniquet to cut off blood flow. Two knights loaded the man into a cart and wheeled him to the *Sacra Infermeria*, where his leg was lost, but his life saved.

In the time between these injuries, Domenicus filled his days with cleaving, lugging, and dressing stone, and thinking about his father's impending departure. As a boy, Domenicus was given charge of the house but knows the responsibility was his in name only. Now, he broods, concerned about the management of money. Will he earn enough for food? Repairs? Or will he be

213

swindled and end up starved to death, lying face down in a gully next to his sister?

Domenicus wipes sweat from his brow with a dirty cloth and, with the clock tower tolling noon in the distance, leaves his pickaxe against a mound of rubble and joins his father for lunch. They sit on the outer ramparts overlooking the harbour fairway, Domenicus with one knee bent to his chest, the other leg dangling over the side. They watch small boats crossing the channel and gulls looping against the sky, and eat a meal of olive-oil soaked bread.

Augustine exhales thoughtfully. "Will you and your sister be all right while I am away?"

"Of course."

"Well, if you need something, anything, you know Belli is a pace away."

"Good gracious," Domenicus laughs, "Do you think you leave behind a boy or a man?"

"My eyes are a father's eyes. You will ever be a boy to me."

***

Tonight, dinner is at the carpenter's house. As Katrina sets a bowl before him, Belli leans over the table and smacks his big hand against Pa's chest. "God keep you safe, my friend. If not, may He provide me enough *scudi* to ransom your reckless Christian ass."

"With a bit of luck," Augustine replies, "God will provide you enough to ransom all of me."

There is a knock at the door, all but lost to Belli's laughter. Katrina answers it, momentarily puzzled by the caller, who she knows well but barely recognizes. It is Robert, a new version of him, squinting in the late sun, his uniform clean and pressed, hair in place, jaw shaven. Strapped across his chest is a fine arquebus that gleams with the dusk, and in his hand, a brilliantly shellacked bow, shining testament to the exquisite workmanship of the Order's weapon smiths.

"Come, lad," Pa calls, leaning back in his chair. "Join us."

"Thank you, no," Robert replies from the doorway. "I came to wish you well on campaign, and, if you'll allow it, to give something to your daughter."

"Kat, set another place," her father says.

As she crosses to the pantry for a bowl, she looks over her shoulder. "So, Falsone? What have you got for me?" She expects a turtle's shell or some other sea treasure washed ashore. Instead, Robert holds out his finely tooled bow. Katrina can only stare in disbelief at the lustrous work of art.

"You're welcome," Robert says, laughing as he steps inside the house. "I figure you'll need one if you're to become an archer." Katrina takes the bow as if it were made of glass, in awe of the curving line of its shiny belly, its deftly carved grip. She runs the flax linen string between her fingers, passes her hand over the stave, varnished smooth beneath her palm.

"It's perfect," she says finally. "The most perfect thing I've ever been given. ...But I can't accept this. It's too beautiful. It cost you more than you earn in six months."

Robert shakes his head. "It cost little more than a few coins, some time, some patience." He shrugs. "I made it for you."

Katrina bursts with pride. "It's amazing! You're amazing!"

"I think," Augustine cuts in, "the Grand Master will soon commission you to stock the Order's armoury." He rises and takes the bow. Narrow-eyed, he pulls the string to a half draw, then full. "This is really something, Robert. An ideal size, too. You've tillered it exceptionally well. The lower limb is nice and stiff. And the stave, good solid ash, is it?"

Robert nods.

"That cost you more than a few coins then. Ash is high quality—tough but flexible and takes a high polish." Pa redraws. "Remarkable."

"Thank you," Robert replies, blushing a little. "It's nothing."

"Give it here," Belli says, waving him over. He runs his hand down the length of the bow, upper limb to lower, over the riser, nock to nock. With a grunt, he rests the weapon on a nearby chair. Katrina senses Robert's tension rise as Belli prepares to give his professional opinion. The carpenter rubs his chin. "Flawless. A certified bowyer could not have fashioned a finer one. Nice touch finishing with beeswax and linseed oil. Falsone, I think there runs some carpentry in your blood."

Robert breaks into a wide grin as he leans his gun against the wall and pulls out an empty stool. Katrina puts her hand on his.

"Thank you," she says solemnly.

"Actually Kat, I owe you the thanks. Because of your help at my house, my mother has been able to rest a little. She said you'll make a good wife. ...The donkey will be lucky.",

***

The next morning, as in mornings past, Domenicus wakes at dawn to accompany his father to the docks. There is heavy foot traffic, villagers passing in all directions as if in harmony with the chiming bells of St Lawrence. Hogs sniff after chickens, small brown birds hop among loose stones, and down shadowed alleyways, shady men deal in commerce crooked as Birgu's streets.

"You know," Augustine begins thoughtfully, "you are at a ripe age to join the caravans."

Domenicus nods and kicks a small rock from his path. Maybe he should just enlist. That way, he wouldn't have to worry about running into Angelica.

"There is beauty out there, Son. Not so far away is Sicily's Peloritani Mountain chain. One week's journey, maybe two. There is Etna, the volcano

215

that rises up and up, an endless black wave broken by cloud." Domenicus cannot help but smile at his father's youthful spirit. "And Spain," he continues, "land of your ancestors. Your grandfather's village, a stone's throw from the Ebro, nested in the shadow of the snow-capped Pyrenees. Of course, there is Rhodos—my Eden, blanketed with light, coloured with a million butterflies. Everything is a portrait waiting to be painted. You would see it all if you served the Order, you know. Put your hatred for d'Homedes aside a moment. Would you be a soldier-at-arms?"

"I don't know."

"You don't know?"

"Honestly, I am neither skilled nor schooled enough to be a physician. My stone work is at best middling. I can't build a house or even a table. You saw the beautiful bow Robert made. I could never do that. Embroidery is for women, and even if it were not, it looks frightfully difficult. I'm not half the soldier you are...or even half the soldier my sister is! So there it is. I haven't the hands of a doctor or a mason or a carpenter or a soldier or even a woman."

Pa furrows his brow. "I watched you at the quarries. That worker, the one who broke his thighbone, he lives because of your hands."

"My hands did not save his leg."

"They saved his *life*."

"If I could only now splint the joint I've just broken," Domenicus says glumly.

"What are you talking about?"

"I've caused myself some injury. It hurts to be unrequited in my... affections."

"For the worker?" his father asks, smiling.

"No!" Domenicus cries. "For a girl... woman..."

"So that explains all this carrying on," Pa says, laughing gently. "First, you are not at all unrequited. The poor girl cannot throw herself at you. Her uncle is *kappillan*."

"I never said *who*."

"Your face has been telling the world *who* for years. You forget Anton Tabone is a priest, forced to take the place of Angelica's mother and father. Naturally, a man who vows celibacy does not expect to raise children. Moreover, his position compels Angelica to consider everything she does."

"I know that. I'm not stupid. It's just that I love her—" Domenicus stops. It is the first time he has spoken these words aloud.

"You've loved her since you were ten years old."

"It's different now."

"Of course it is. Falling in love is a volcano erupting—fire and heat and power. Only after the dust settles might you know love in its purest form. Not the exhilaration you feel when you see her. Not the desire to explore her body... Why the red cheeks? What I say is true."

"That does not make hearing it from my father any better," Domenicus replies.

"Come now. You think this feeling foreign to me? I know it well. At the sight of her, your heart caves in, your tongue trips, you are ridiculous, and yet, all is right with the world."

"Yes."

"Well, that is the thrill of being in love, which anyone can pretend he is. True love is what remains after the flame of being in love has flared. It is the steady glow of eternal embers. *That* love is worth waiting for, worth dying for. Be patient. You will have that love, the kind you take to heaven."

At the docks, four ornate bows point seaward. The galleys bob on swells licking up at low freeboards, red and white pennons flapping high in the morning wind. The quay heaves with knights in black *sobravestes*, soldiers, porters, and merchants. Deckhands inspect the tackle, checking and double-checking that the ropes are secure, ten pairs of practised eyes examining shrouds, stays, and sweeps. Gunners slide deck ordnances into their chocks and test the strength of the rivets. A helmsman adjusts the apostis, a boom rigged out over the side to extend the sail. Orders flow rapidly through the ranks as massive oars are carried onto the vessels. Porters hustle to load crates of food, barrels of water, and cases of ammunition. On the pier, a large host of villagers is gathered to watch a scene that would please even Portunus.

Pa has described harbours the continent and beyond knowing this same commotion, militant fleets throughout provisioned and armed for the hunt—a sport that makes predators and prey of them all, in a watery domain where the speed and agility of a ship can make quarry of huntsmen.

"Montesa, my pretty bullfighter!" Romegas calls jovially, his leather doublet swishing with every stride. For his size, the captain carries his weight ably. "I expect the men making this caravan to be men with strong beams, good solid spars, and no shit in their scuppers. Now quickstep to the gangplank, *Messier*. The sea parts to my sprit in ten minutes." Before Augustine can respond, Romegas is aboard his galley, moving into a brief discussion with a deckhand. The captain then turns his attention to the tiller, while his pet monkey, bounding from gunwales to corsia, does some inspecting of his own.

Domenicus turns at the sound of chains scraping over rock. Guards walk hundreds of naked, head-shaven prisoners from the dungeons to the wharf in double-file, their fetters rattling with every step. He surveys the ranks of slaves as they shuffle from a prison hewn from rock to one hewn from wood. The bulk of slaves are the *schiavi*, mainly Muslims occasionally joined by Christian criminals. Behind this group march the *forzati*, innocent men forced to row by way of a pressgang. Bringing up the rear are the *buonevoglie*, paid men who offer their service willingly. Free from fetters, they are the best treated of the lot, allowed to keep full beards and wear clothes to distinguish themselves.

Domenicus recognizes one of the *schiavi*. "That's him," he says, nudging his father and pointing. "The corsair Emir, the one who saved the girls." The slaves are marched aboard the galleys and chained to the benches. Arbalesters, arquebusiers, and archers take their places aboard the already congested decks, followed by hired physicians and last, the chaplains.

Armand Debonnoel, now first lieutenant, blows his silver whistle, signalling the porters to remove all gangplanks.

"Time," Augustine says, making no movement.

"Go, go," Domenicus replies. "I'll take care of everything."

"I know." The whistle trills a second time.

"*Papa! Papa!*" cries a familiar but breathless voice. At once, Domenicus and his father look to the crowd. The source of the yelling pushes her way through the throng.

"Sweetheart," Augustine says in surprise. "Is everything all right?"

"Sweetheart, indeed! And everything is *not* all right," Katrina fires. "You were just going to leave? Without even saying goodbye?"

"I said goodbye. You were asleep and did not hear. Forgive me. I hadn't the heart to wake you. I'm glad you're here, now."

Katrina draws an angry breath, brow furrowed. Then, she throws her arms tightly around him. He bends and kisses her messy hair. "I love you, too." The overseer cracks his whip, as though testing its bite against ship's mast. He snaps it before the eyes of the miserable oarsmen. Time to take up the heavy looms. The galleys shiver and quake. Augustine cups Katrina's chin, gives Domenicus a mighty shoulder squeeze, and goes.

The tambour speaks, and to its voice, the oarsmen arch their brown backs, wrench their arms, and heave the enormous *remi di scaloccio*, sunlight catching in the white spray dashed off the paddles. Sunlit jewels cascade from the stern cutwater and spill back to the channel as the wooden blades carve the armada's way through the water. With the guns of St Angelo thundering in salute, Domenicus watches his father climb the companionway and emerge onto the poop deck. The four-galley fleet glides out of the creek, over the harbour strait and into the sea.

Domenicus parts from his sister and walks the low-lying coast towards the quarries. Soon, steady hoof beats replace the distant sweep of oars. He looks up to see Franco riding towards him on his white Arabian, the horse of Bedouin nomads. Franco reins Phaedo to a halt.

"Greetings, my base-court malcontent," the knight says with a smile.

Domenicus cringes, the nape of his neck burning. "You heard about that, eh?"

"Naturally!" Franco chuckles. "It was an incident of some note. I'll give you that you are brave—I'd never defy the Grand Master. But then, I never had with my father what you have with yours." He pauses, as though teetering on the brink of deeper bonding. Instead, he changes the subject.

"Blast this heat. Time for combat training. Fortunately, I have some leave this afternoon, which I'll spend at Mnajdra teaching your sister the bow."

"Finally worked you over, did she?"

Franco laughs. "It is my pleasure." He bows in his saddle. But his expression changes swift and suddenly as the currents. "Oh, yes. I had an encounter with Angelica. Quite an obstinate creature."

"How do you mean?" Domenicus asks, not sure if he likes the sound of this.

"She approached me, asking to see that corsair," Franco tattles. "I refused her, of course."

"What? Why did she want to see him?"

"She said she owed him thanks. Anyway, he now propels the galley speeding your father eastward as we speak. And while on the subject of speed, I must be off." Franco snaps his reins and Phaedo is off, the horse's mane streaming silver wisps in the sunlight.

Domenicus stands alone on the rocks. He kicks a stone into the sea.

***

The day has finally come. The day she will loose an arrow. First, however, Katrina must do her chores. An hour of scrubbing an impossible limestone floor cramps her fingers. She pauses to pick out sharp bits of grit embedded in her knees, but stops, her gaze captured by her hands. They are small and chapped, black from grime, with a dark line of dirt trapped beneath each fingernail. She tries brushing off the soot with her fingers and when that fails, wipes her hands on her thighs, streaking beige fabric black. She looks at her hands again, turns them over and back again, and thinks of her mother, who had such beautiful hands, so delicate and slender, so clean. No matter how hard Mama worked, her hands never looked as used as Katrina's do now. She misses them, her mother's hands.

After a long moment, Katrina turns her attention back to work. The usual sounds of forenoon pass through the open door. Mario Briffa, the fishmonger, sings his bargains for sea turtles against the voice of goatherd Claudio Vella, selling fresh milk. Dogs bark and chickens cluck and sheep fuss. Wheels struggle over cobbles. Up the road, a shrill powder keg of a woman explodes at either her goat or husband. Her outburst is met by bleats, from either the goat or the husband. There is a splash of water as it empties from a bucket and hits the street.

Water. There is scarce enough at home to finish even half the chores. Off she goes to the cistern, two and three times, a bucket on each arm. Flushed from heat and exertion, she drains a full skin before shaking out the bedclothes and stuffing flat pallets with extra straw. At the carpenter's stable a half-hour later, she shovels the dung, spreads it over his tiny plot. Peppone's braying has her taking up a pail of grain to feed the horse and donkey. With the clock tower finally pealing noon, Katrina abandons housework and makes the long uphill trek to the coralline ruins of Mnajdra. Fuelled by excitement, she jogs almost the whole way, cutting through fields, ranging rocky terrain. It is just over an hour before she sees the tops of the white stone columns break the blue sky.

There are parallel ruts in the surface rock, tracks that cross and merge, suggesting the use of primitive carts by people the eons have long since forgotten. The southern sea cliffs are enormous, nature's dowry to those willing to venture close enough to the edge to capture the view. Sheer buttery rock faces, layered with substratum of pink and brown, plunge straight into the sea, as though God Himself sliced the cliffs with a great blade. Above, three peregrine falcons wheel, their pointed wings fully spread as they glide on warm air.

In the shade of a crumbling pillar, Katrina sits on a pillow of *torba* and catches her breath, knees drawn to her chest, eyes closed. At the base of the sea cliff, surf pounds and fizzes, its salt drifting upward on the breeze. She imagines her father breathing the same air, and wishes he were here to see her shoot her first arrow.

Hooves shake the ground suddenly. Bow in hand, Katrina jumps to her feet and emerges from the stone labyrinth. "My lord."

"When we are together alone, *Franco* will suffice."

Katrina smiles. "Thank you, Franco. What can I offer you in gratitude?"

"I did not agree to teach you for reward," he replies.

"I insist. Or does the noble think there is nothing a peasant might give him?"

"The noble thinks nothing of the sort. In fact, there is something."

"What's that?"

"One Maltese lesson for every equal in archery. At least then, I'll understand the insults I'm dealt by villagers," Franco laughs, patting Phaedo's hindquarter, sending the horse off to graze. He glances at the bow in Katrina's hand. "Where did you get that? Sneaking about the Order's armoury?"

She grins broadly. "No. Falsone made it."

The smile vanishes from Franco's face. "Mmm." He narrows his eyes, rubs his chin. "Hold it up. Ash? Not the best wood from which to coax a bow. And, it is too big for you."

"Too big for me?" Katrina is confused. Just yesterday, her father said it was the perfect size.

Franco nods. "Not to worry. I brought a more suitable one." He slips the smaller of his two bows over his head and holds the weapon up by its riser. "Pure yew, cut from the evergreens of mainland Europe. It is the best, most enduring stave for a bow."

To Katrina, the bows are identical. "I don't understand the difference between ash and yew."

"Think of a gown of damask as it compares to one of sackcloth."

"Oh." She is not sure what dresses have to do with wood. Fabric is obvious in its differences, she thinks, easily distinguished by beauty, texture, weight, durability. Wood is wood. Still, she supposes Franco must know what he's talking about, being a knight and all. Perhaps there are qualities in the stave invisible to her inexperienced eye that he can see. Maybe yew *is* the damask silk of wood. Yet, everyone at dinner yesterday seemed impressed by Robert's bow, even the carpenter Belli, who is not impressed by anything. Katrina does not raise the point. She sets Robert's ash bow gently down and reaches for Franco's yew. It is no smaller or lighter than the bow Robert made.

"So," she begins. "How fares our new sentry?"

"Hopefully better than as bowyer."

Katrina frowns. "I think his bow is lovely."

"It is a finger painting in the Sistine Chapel."

"Not a moment ago you asked if I'd snaffled it from the Order's own armoury. Why don't you like it now? Why don't you like *him*?"

"What's to like about an ill-bred pretender trying to be something he's not?" Franco asks.

Katrina feels her face flush. "Pretender? You go on as though you're different from the snobs in the Order when you, sir, are snobbery on legs. All you bloody knights think your hallowed touch is enough to turn shit to solid gold."

"Alas, every time I try doing that, I end up with soiled hands. No gold." There is earnest rue in Franco's tone, making Katrina laugh in spite of herself.

"Look here," she says, struggling for sternness, "Robert is better than you think. He's smart. He...he knows numbers. He can even do sums. And he lets me read to him. You try finding another man that would let a girl read to him. He's a curious mind, a dreamer."

"You are both dreamers, building castles in the air."

"Among all human constructions, they are the only ones that endure. Nothing can break a castle in the air."

"All it takes is a dose of reality," Franco replies grimly.

Katrina furrows her brow. "What is it with you? Is something the matter?"

"Nothing." The knight smiles. "Your friend is managing the watchtower fine, even for a farmhand of rather..." he twirls his hand as though searching for words less tart in flavour "...rather limited means." Franco slips his bow. "Come. Let me demonstrate my one skill before it gets any later. And, I want you to keep that," he says, indicating the yew bow she is holding.

Katrina's eyes go round. "But Franco—"

"Don't bother protesting."

"Franco! You give me too much!" Forgetting herself, she hugs him. Instantly, she feels his body stiffen. She withdraws, aware she has crossed the line. "Forgiveness."

"O-Of course," he stammers. "So, your bow has seen little service in battle, and that is a good thing. Any decent weapon-smith will tell you the wood of a bow has a living memory, and should always be drawn by the same archer." Franco points to a lone carob twenty paces from the ruins. "See that tree? I will lodge my arrow just below the branch jutting out on the left side." With lightning speed, he nocks a fleche and draws back his elbow until his hand grazes his face. Katrina holds her breath, hypnotized by his movement and poise. Head and body completely still, he pulls the bowstring across his jaw. His index finger firm against his anchoring point, thumb tucked into his hand, he aims, eyes no wider than slits, and holds position, as though feeling the power latent within the bow. Katrina exhales quietly, afraid even breathing might cost him focus. And still, he holds.

***

The sun bakes the quarry of St Angelo, raising its temperature to oven intensity. The culvert walls are achingly white, rays bouncing off stone and onto browned labourers. Domenicus works mechanically, muscles rippling with each plunge of his shovel. He dunks his shirt into a trough of dirty water meant for mixing mortar and wipes his face, chest, and the back of his neck. Refreshed, he wraps the dripping garment in a turban around his head. Water rolls to the small of his back. He does not stop for lunch, breaking only for water every few minutes. He digs alongside Egyptians Dakarai and Jumoke, who are quick to question his morose disposition.

"You are not yourself," Dakarai whispers. "Something vexes you?"

"Nothing I can control," Domenicus replies, grunting as he pushes his shovel into the near unyielding earth that surfaces the culvert floor.

"A woman, is it?" Jumoke asks.

Domenicus remains silent and notices the two Egyptians exchange glances.

"The minds of women are untamed," Dakarai says quietly. "Free as the winds that sculpt the dunes of Egypt. A man would have to travel until east becomes west then east again before he encounters one who is easy to understand."

"So, in a word, never," Domenicus replies, leaning against his shovel. He counts blisters that have formed, burst, and reformed on his palms and fingers. The flesh is red, raw, his salty sweat bringing fire. He crouches and rubs soft powder on his hands to soak up the pus.

Then, he thinks of what the knight told him this morning, and the sting returns.

***

At last, Franco releases the string, fingers slipping away as one. Motionless, he watches the arrow sail without the slightest deflection and penetrate the carob's trunk, just below the thick branch jutting out on the left, just as he said it would. He smiles. At his side, Katrina is elated.

222

"Incredible! I want to do that. I *will* do that. Teach me!"

"You cannot learn to do *that* in one afternoon. To master archery takes years. As well, perhaps some of my precision owes to the arrows. They were made by a fletcher of the house of de Medici." Franco can tell that Katrina has no idea who the de Medicis are, but they sound important, so she gives a low, impressed whistle.

"Let us start with the first and most important order of business," he says. "Correct posture. Stand straight." He moves behind her and bends slightly, his chin hovering above her shoulder. He catches the fresh scent of saltwater on her skin and is instantly uneasy. Her nearness affects him deeply, but he cannot coax himself to move. He knows he should leave. He knows he will not.

"Your feet… they should be shoulder-width apart, as though you just took a step."

Katrina strides out wide.

"No," Franco says, "A natural step, not one Goliath would make."

"Oh…" She blushes. "Sorry." She steps again.

"Good. Knees soft." Gentle wind sends strands of Katrina's hair across Franco's face. A wave in his stomach rolls against his spine. His hands, a moment ago sturdy and deft, now tremble. He swallows. "An archer's hair ought to be tied back. And when you shoot, you must not shift your weight. There should be an even amount taken on both feet and distributed between the ball and heel. You want the eyes of your string secure around the nocks at both the upper and lower limbs. And when you—" Franco notices that Katrina's eyes are closed, her open hand against her brow. "What is it?" he asks.

"There is so much to remember. I don't even know the words you're saying. I can't do this."

The knight tips his face towards hers. "Tell me something. The first time you opened a book, were you able to make sense of the letters on the page?"

Katrina shakes her head. "It took me ages to learn the alphabet. The skill came much easier to my brother. For him, reading just happened. Father was patient and worked hard to teach me."

"Well, there you have it. Today we attempt the letter *a* in the long alphabet of archery. Next time, *b*. Soon you will know not only the alphabet but the entire lexicon."

Katrina smiles uncertainly.

"Besides," Franco continues, "if you think after suffering years of constant harassment I would let you quit before even drawing the bloody string, you are quite mistaken."

She laughs, and the strain vanishes from her face.

"Now," Franco says, "let's see if I can't make a master archer out of you." He raises his chin. "Once your arrow is nocked, place your forefinger above the feathers, your second and third below. Curl them around the bowstring so that the first joint of all three are aligned. Do not pinch the arrow. Stop pinching the arrow." Katrina's knuckles are white from her grip. If the arrow were a living thing, it would be long dead from asphyxiation.

Franco laughs gently. "What did that poor fleche ever do to you?" He takes the bow and arrow from her and sets them on the ground. "Here, give me your hands." When she does not offer them up readily, he reaches for them.

"No... Stop," Katrina whispers. "They're dirty..."

Franco takes her hands despite her objection and runs his thumbs slowly over her knuckles. "Close your eyes." He massages each finger. "That's it. Relax." As he kneads out her tension, he feels his own growing. He keeps his eyes focused on only her hands, though soon finds they too captivate him. Even the dirt trapped beneath her fingernails is delightful.

What is it with you?

If only he knew. If only he knew why he would willingly torment himself by being alone with her when he cannot act, or why simply looking at her is enough to make him resent his vows. Does he even want her to return his gaze? What would he do then?

If only he knew. All he knows is how alive he feels when near her, how *awake*, and how badly he wants to touch her hair as the sun is touching it now.

Franco di Bonfatti has been acquainted with many women in his day, all of them beautiful and titled, elegant and rich. They flocked readily to him because he himself is beautiful and titled, elegant and rich. But to know one was to know them all, with their ruffles and their perfume and their curls and their obsession with all things external. They doted and cooed and fussed, and for all their pretences, were hugely boring, and so, prior to making his vow of chastity, he wrote off women altogether, deeming them frivolous creatures sorely lacking in conviction.

But this one, this uncouth, brash, insolent impossibility of a girl, is all conviction. She is indifferent to the things that make women of means swoon. And he so likes that, likes it all, her honesty, her sensibility, her spirit. Her dirty hands. Katrina Montesa is everything he is not, everything he wishes he could be, guileless, free. Her absolute certainty fascinates him. And terrifies him.

He stops massaging her hands. She opens her eyes and smiles. "Your face, so serious. You must suffer mightily at the hands of your peers. I'll bet there isn't a knight in all the Order so pure of heart, so committed to his vows, that forever he contemplates them."

"They are relaxed..." Franco blinks. "Your *hands*. Your hands are relaxed."

"Yes, thank you."

He clears his voice. "I talk of the alphabet and seem not to know it myself. I've skipped ahead from *a* to *b*. That is why you are having difficulty. I should have first introduced the parts of the bow, its limbs, rest, grip, nocks... Stringing is important too. You won't send too many arrows sailing without a string. We will start with that next time." *There must be no next time*, he tells himself, but quickly pushes the thought to some black place in his mind. For now, he wants simply to enjoy her company. "Since I've already muddled everything, we might as well try a full draw with an arrow."

"May I shoot it too?" she asks eagerly.

He throws his hands blithely up. "Why not?"

Katrina gives him a joyful smile and picks up the bow. As she raises the weapon and begins to draw the string, the knight exhales against her neck. Her shoulder shrugs to her ear and she laughs, spoiling an almost perfect stance. She lowers the bow and looks ruefully over her shoulder.

"I am sorry. It is easier to teach a goat. One of those has more grace. More sense, too."

"But less will," he whispers. "Now redraw."

***

Domenicus returns home from the quarries dusty and sweaty and utterly spent. He drops his tool bag at his feet, rubs his stiff neck. Cabbage soup bubbles in a pot over smouldering guanos, the valuable excrement of seabirds.

"Where did you get *guanos*?" he asks Katrina in surprise.

"Some idiot left it unattended in the back of his cart outside the White Horse tavern."

Domenicus gives his sister a wary look. "So you're a thief now?"

She shrugs and continues stirring the pot. "After an hour riding the White Horse, bird shit will be the farthest thing from the man's mind. You should know. Besides, it was either take the opportunity as it presented itself, or eat cold soup. There was no time to gather brambles. God will forgive me because I didn't tell a lie. And what is the greater sin, lying willingly or stealing in need?"

"If you did your chores, there would be no need to steal, and so, no need to lie."

"You are boring and practical." Katrina looks over her shoulder. "Oh yes, Franco wants you to meet with him later this evening. He said on the hill of Corradino at eight bells." The only thing Domenicus wants to meet with right now is his bed.

"Did he say why? I saw him early this morning, he mentioned nothing."

"Something about the Italian knights building a new clinic, I think." She pours soup into two bowls. "Or a pharmacy." Domenicus is only half-listening as he bends over the washbasin, splashes cool water against his face. He wipes his damp shirt across his brow and cheeks, palms smarting from broken blisters. Every movement takes great effort, his muscles protesting after hours on hours of hard labour. He sits heavily at the table and drinks soup straight from the bowl.

After dinner, Katrina makes quick work of the dirty plates and heads for the door in a hurry. Domenicus watches his sister from across the room as if through a fogbank. He doesn't think to ask where she is going. Exhausted, he closes his eyes and rests his head on folded arms to sleep the hours until his meeting with Franco di Bonfatti.

***

Tonight is the *Imnarja* celebration that Katrina is not allowed to attend. Under a sky that blankets land and water in shades of pink and orange, she and Angelica walk barefoot over warm, salt-stained rock coloured coral by the setting sun. Crayfish scuttle from their steps and disappear into rocky fissures.

"Ooh, look," Angelica says, pointing across the harbour. On the slopes and lowlands that embrace the bay, there is a spectacular cavalcade of light. The long road to the Mdina cathedral will take knights, priests, and villagers past the Grotto of St Paul in Rabat where they will stop for the *Imnarja*'s opening prayer. Those on foot carry lanterns, giving the ridged land a glowing periphery. Dangling from farm carts are little lamps that twinkle like fireflies. Latin hymns carry on the wind while a hundred moving lights bounce across darkening water.

"Come on, let's get a better look," Katrina says. "No one said I couldn't watch from the top of the hill."

***

At the top of that hill, Domenicus sits alone, back against a large rock. In the dwindling light, he strains to read the *Decameron*, resting open-faced against his thighs. At the sound of distant but approaching conversation, he looks up, furrowing his brow in surprise. He knew sooner or later, on an island this small, he would have to see her again—preferably from a distance—but he did not expect it would be so soon, or so near. Either way, she is here, now. Angelica Tabone. Lovely as ever.

"Strange," Domenicus says to his sister, "You don't look like Franco."

"Oh that," she replies. "I lied about that. Now you two pinheads can make up."

"Hmm. And here I thought lying was the greater sin."

"*Katrina*," Angelica says crossly, "You can't trick people into making up."

"Sure I can."

Domenicus places his book calmly on the ground. "Though it pains me to agree with your friend, she *is* right." He looks at his sister but feels Angelica's glare on him. Without neither word nor apology, Kat flashes a grin and runs off, leaving him to deal with the furious girl on his own. He is actually a little frightened, but determined to stand his ground—no matter how shaky.

"So," Angelica begins, "Why have you avoided me for almost two weeks?"

"You know where I live," he replies coolly. "If my absence troubled you so, why not knock on my door? Could it be because I am just some parishioner to you?"

"What?"

"You know what. You told my sister *some parishioner* returned your mother's flute."

"Yes, to keep her out of it," Angelica fumes. "*That* is how I've offended you?"

"Not exactly," Domenicus says. "Your *propriety* was far more offensive." Despite his bravado, he regrets the words the moment they leave his mouth.

"Enough! You did not give me a chance to explain! The instant you heard something you didn't like, you stormed off, knowing I could not chase after you. Not that I would have," she quickly adds. "How did you expect me to react to your advance when only two days before I was attacked? I was almost raped, damn it! Do you hear me now?" Domenicus looks down at his hands, ashamed at himself for making her shout that awful thing a second time.

"You're right, Angelica. I wasn't thinking. I'm sorry." He looks up at her. "I like you. A lot."

Her eyes go round with fury. "*What?*"

"I said I was sorry."

"That's not all you bloody said!"

"Let's address that first."

"Fine. What exactly are you sorry for?"

Domenicus rises to his full height. He inhales, holding the air inside several moments before exhaling. "For not protecting you. For not making you feel safe. For not saying the right things. I understand why the corsair has stolen your heart. I turned out to be a clumsy thief."

A pinch appears above Angelica's nose. "Is that what you think? I'm not *in love* with him, idiot. I am grateful he spared me an unspeakable violation." Domenicus has taken this too far. He allowed his wounded pride, his sense of rejection, to run him. He knows Angelica is not in love with the corsair. He's just sore that she went to a knight for help without even considering that maybe a lowly peasant such as he could offer assistance—the fact that he couldn't notwithstanding. More than anything, it pains him deeply that he was not there when she needed him most.

But before he can admit to any of this, Angelica speaks again: "Do you have any idea what my life would have become had I been raped? Who would want me then?" Her voice breaks, and she swings around, but Domenicus catches her elbow.

"Don't go," he says quietly. "I am an ass, a total, hopeless jackass." He bends to pick up the *Decameron* and waves the book like a white flag. "What can

I say? You make me a stammering wretch and…" he puts his hand on hers "*…Je veux vous baiser.*" *I want to kiss you.*

"Don't do that," she says sternly, unwilling to turn. "You make it impossible for me to hate you."

"That's good."

"Why, you absolute—"

"Shut up. I said a minute ago that I liked you. I lied. I don't like you." Domenicus senses another eruption, and so acts quickly, words gusting out on his breath. "Angelica Tabone, from the moment I saw you on the rectory steps I… I loved you. More when you came and took my hand the day we buried my mother. I have not known a second these years when being near you has not sent my heart careening against my ribs. And now, to say that I love you seems an injustice. What I feel is more than love. And if you say that is impossible, I say you are wrong. A new feeling has been created. It was just waiting to be felt." He stops, relieved to have finally laid his feelings bare. But in the silence that follows, a cold fear passes through him—his feelings are unrequited, and he has just made a real enemy of her, not to mention a fool of himself.

"Forgive me," he says, glancing to the road. "I should go." He makes no movement to do so.

At last, Angelica turns. "You're right about one thing. You are an ass." She reaches up and touches his cheek. "A total, hopeless jackass." Sliding her arms around his neck, she rises onto her toes and kisses his mouth. The kiss contains no ingredients, yet tastes sweeter than honey. Domenicus does not close his eyes. He wants to see—to be sure he's not imagining. When the kiss ends, he slips his arms around her waist and draws her closer. As she puts her head against his chest, he tips his face to the breeze and watches the trail of lights winding with the lands like a golden snake.

"Walk beside me always," he says. "Or let me carry you."

"I will follow you anywhere."

"*Estoy enamorado de ti. Je t'adore. Ti amo. Inhobbok.* I love you, in every language."

"And Domenicus Montesa, I love you."

CHAPTER TWENTY-EIGHT

Istanbul 1551

Demir sits in the stall with his gazelle, content just to be near him. The animal had arrived at the stables just after a beautiful Andalusian mare named Kalilah gave birth to a stillborn foal. Kemal paired the baby gazelle with the horse, and in the weeks that followed the adoption, the gazelle grew strong on his new mother's milk. Demir racked his brain to come up with a name for the baby, settling at last on Timu, in honour of Timurhan, the gentle hunter who brought the two together.

With his back to Demir, Kemal gives an ostentatious sigh, looks to the mare. "Oh, Kalilah, there is too much to do—cleaning, grooming, feeding. And now," he turns partway, glancing at Demir from the corner of his eye, "I am saddled with another chore: bringing the gazelle to the pasture."

Demir jumps to his feet. "Kemal, I'll take Timu to graze."

"I don't know…" The groomsman strokes his chin. "It is a serious business."

"I can do it."

Kemal appraises Demir. "Very well," he says at last. "I will allow it this once."

Demir beams. He leads Timu through the primary courtyard. The vibrant space bustles with servants, some tending the gardens, others using paddles to beat thick Persian rugs. Great palms nod over raised marble channels that swim with silver carp. A fat, tiered fountain bubbles and splashes, making exactly the sound Demir imagines water would make if it were giggling. The gazelle stops to nibble the tulips arranged in a perfect pink and yellow circle around the stone structure. Behind Al Hajji's house is an expanse of sweet, sunlit grass, a succulent green banquet for his thoroughbreds. Demir takes a turn through the tall blades, small fingers spread and passing gently over the tips. It is serene here, where soft strains of wind move over the pasture like breath through a duduk. He finds a patch of shorter grass and sits, watching the muscles rippling in Timu's long, curving neck as the animal swallows, sunlight catching in his light brown fur and flecking it with gold.

Since the gazelle's arrival, Murad has visited every day, and, once or twice a week, Timurhan the hunter stops in. Last week, the eighteen-year-old was officially entered into the ranks of the Sipahiyan. For Demir, the news was bittersweet; he was happy for Timurhan but knew he would see much less of him now. The new Sipahi will soon be leaving on a campaign expected to wrest the strongholds of the Knights of St John in retaliation for their taking of Mahdia. Timurhan told Demir the Sultan's objective for the expedition is Tripoli, to which the Order lays claim. Dragut Raïs, however, has a second objective: the islands of Malta, where his brother met his end at the Order's hand. Sultan Suleiman is right now preparing a great fleet, under the dual direction of admirals Sinan Pasha and Dragut. A decoy expedition is already sailing west to lure Admiral Andrea Doria to Sicily, away from the imminent attacks on Malta and Tripoli. Timurhan has promised Demir a detailed account of the assured Muslim victory, and the boy can hardly wait.

***

Today is a beautiful day, and the students of the *madrasah* have gathered in a field to play ball. Mursel el Emarat, Demir's teacher, invented this game, borrowing heavily from Episkyros of the ancient Greeks and Harpastum of the early Roman Empire. El Emarat's version requires ten players, perfect for his class size. He stands in the middle of the rectangular field marked by boundary lines and divided by a centre line. He holds a small follis, a round ball made from a pig bladder wrapped in deerskin. Each team, arbitrarily chosen, is made up of five boys. Demir and Murad are together with three others on one side of the line. Muharrem, in this game as in life, is opposite his younger brother.

"I trust you remember the conventions?" el Emarat asks his class.

There are murmurs of half-hearted assent.

"Very well," the teacher says. "Demir, restate the rules of play." It is clear to Demir that the *müderris* favours him above the others, despite his efforts to hide it. He wonders if he should pretend he does not know the rules of the game so that the teacher will pick someone else. But el Emarat would see right through him.

"One team tries to keep the ball on their side as long as they can, while their opponents try stealing it. Only the player with the ball can be tackled. At the end of thirty minutes, whichever team has made the most steals and kept the follis longest wins."

El Emarat nods. "*Iyi.* Children, do not see rules as restrictions. Use them as ways to develop complex passing combinations. Outsmart your opponent. This is a game of strategy, cunning, and trickery. Tactics first, force second. Julius Caesar used a similar sport to keep his soldiers on top form and battle-ready. Are we battle-ready?"

All the boys whoop and cheer. All but Muharrem, who wears a peculiar smile, betraying a hidden menace. The instructor tosses the ball high into the air. Murad and Muharrem jump for it at the same time, but Murad catches it first. He tosses it at once to Demir, who passes it off to Bekir. Muharrem charges, throwing both arms around the skinny boy's waist and taking him down in a full tackle. Bekir lands heavily on his back, biting down on his tongue from the impact. Muharrem snatches the ball away and throws it to his team-mate, Iskender. He pitches it immediately to Hasan who tosses it back. Demir is in a ready-to-pounce stance, feet shoulder-width apart, upper body leaning slightly forward, knees soft, hands loose. He watches the ball pass from one set of hands to the other and soon picks up a pattern: Muharrem to Iskender to Hasan, Hasan back to Iskender, Iskender to Sunduk to Muharrem to Iskender to Hasan, Hasan back to Iskender, Iskender to Yusuf to Muhurrem. For a full minute, Muharrem's team keeps possession of the ball, hands moving swiftly, bodies twisting and dodging their opponents. Yusuf has the follis and, just as Demir knew he would, he tosses it to Muharrem. As Muharrem's hands close on it, Demir tackles his brother and snatches the ball away. It is a great victory for the youngest boy on both teams. His squad cheers loudly for him, and he loves it, loves the acceptance and the praise. Even the instructor smiles. Muharrem's features are black despite the sunlight.

The ball is still in play. Demir quickly passes it to Bekir, who knows better now than to hold onto it longer than an instant. It is airborne once more, caught by Mehmed and from his hands, it passes into Kadri. Iskender pounces on Kadri, but the ball is already flying. Murad jumps and catches it, cradling it in both arms.

Then it happens, as if in slow motion: Muharrem runs full out at Murad and throws his shoulder, with all his weight behind it, directly into Murad's knee.

Everyone hears the pop.

The screams of agony. Murad's knee has been bent in a way it was never meant to go. He is on his back, rolling, howling, his knee already swollen, his shrieks lacerating.

Muharrem rises from the ground, dusts himself off, hanging back as both teams run over, crowding around the injured boy. The instructor is on his knees at Murad's side, soothing him as best he can, Demir at his other side. None of the boys knows what to do. El Emarat takes off his turban, unravels it, and begins binding Murad's terrible injury. As he does this, he sends Iskender for the *madrasah*'s custodian. Murad's howls settle into painful sobs and moans. Each one stabs at Demir. He looks from the large, tearful eyes of his best friend to the fretful eyes of his teacher, and inadvertently, to the cold, unfeeling eyes of his half-brother.

Suddenly, all Muharrem's cruelties run together—the brazier coal, the alum in Demir's soup, the lies about Dionysus perishing in a fire, the trick in the cemetery, the look on his face now. *This is a game of trickery*, the teacher had said. Muharrem *is* trickery, never more so than right now, as he stands casually to the side, watching Murad with amused contempt.

Without a word, Demir crosses the grass to Muharrem and punches him square in the face with eight years of pent-up fury. The bully drops to the ground, his face a bloody mess. Demir just stands there, admiring his handiwork. Muharrem is bawling, rolling, holding both hands over his nose as blood seeps through spaces between his fingers. Murad looks on, clearly distracted from his own agony by the unexpected pleasure of seeing his attacker bleeding on the ground.

The teacher and the students stare in shock at the gentle spirit who has never once raised voice or hand in anger. Demir can already feel respect from the spineless, the fickle, the ones who grovel to anyone with power in his fist. He does not care about them. What matters is that he has finally shown his brother what he's made of.

Demir knows he's in for it. Whatever *it* is, it will be worth it. A bastinadoing would be worth this.

His teacher speaks: "Allah does not love the aggressor, Demir."

"*Hocam*, if God does not love the aggressor, then surely He hates my brother, and I have done God's work. If I am wrong, if Allah does love Muharrem, and he is destined for paradise, I will gladly burn in hell."

El Emarat's eyes are scythes, his voice a whip: "Demir, inside. Wait for me."

With a polite nod, Demir strolls, *struts*, across the playing field, through the small cemetery and into the building. He sits where he always sits, cross-legged on the mat closest to the instructor's chair, and there awaits his fate. Whatever his fate, he will endure it. No, he will not. Demir is tired of enduring. He is feeling rather defiant today and sits up straighter. Over and again, he relives the punch that dropped his brother. It occurs to him that no one even made a move to tend Muharrem's bloody nose. Demir smiles.

***

Expelled. He is expelled from the school. Every servant in Hamid's enormous three-storey house knows it. His furious roar is enough to shake the delicate tulip-shaped *çay* cups on their glass tray just at it shakes every attendant, every scribe, every mother, to the quick. Everyone but Demir. For the first time in his life, he does not fear his father. He sees him as merely a bigger version of Muharrem. And today, Demir dropped that other fat bully to the ground like a sack of grain.

Now, Hamid is beating him, using his fists and whatever objects he seizes in his frenzy. Demir's passivity seems to incite the man to greater fury. "Have you prayed to *Shaytaan* for strength?" Hamid lashes. "Or have you snuck into my stores of Paphlagonia opium?"

Neither is true. Demir is simply resolved never to surrender one more tear, one more whimper, to his father or brother.

***

Upstairs, Yaminah gives her husband both. She sobs, pounding the door to her bedroom, begging someone, anyone, to unlock it. She can only cry and fear for her son, whose fate is in the big ugly hands of her husband. She worries for Jameela too, knowing the serving girl would jump to Demir's defence if she were anywhere near, despite the ten savage lashes Hamid dealt her with a barbed frond for refusing his advances a few weeks ago. Yaminah fights the lock and kicks the door. No one heeds. No one can.

When Demir came home earlier than usual today, Yaminah peppered him with questions, and before he could answer them, more questions came, because she had glimpsed his swollen, bluish-purple hand. She was shocked when he told her the truth in a very matter-of-fact way: he punched Muharrem in the face and talked back to the teacher.

Yaminah is not a stupid woman. No matter how awfully Muharrem had provoked Demir over the years, the boy had always remained docile as a lamb. Muharrem must have done something big to earn himself a punch in the nose. The thought of him writhing on the ground in bloodied agony amused her, as she knew it would amuse Jameela and Kemal and the rest of the servants when they heard of it. All of them have wanted a hundred times to punch the toxic little bastard in the face.

But then, Demir revealed the consequence: Mursel el Emarat had expelled him from the *madrasah*. Now, Yaminah was beside herself. Hamid would fly into an absolute rage. She considered not telling him, just going straight to the instructor and begging her son's pardon. Turks believe wholeheartedly in the second chance, why should el Emarat be any different?

But such a venture would be impossible. She had forgotten herself— movement outside her home was restricted. Freedom, though limited, was part of another life.

Anyway, if she did not tell Hamid, Muharrem certainly would. The horse master might not care about the blow—he might even be pleased because he always complained about Demir being too soft. But if the punch pleased him, the expulsion would not.

Yaminah thought rapidly. Hamid was away for the afternoon. A small gift. She could not allow him to get his hands on Demir. She needed someone who could control him. Someone he feared. Ayla. Yaminah loves Ayla, the way she stands up to Hamid, the way she leaves the house when she pleases. Surely, el Emarat would take Demir back if the mother of the boy he had pummelled came to school and requested his re-admittance.

Yaminah went looking for the older woman in the household harem, where she often sits gossiping and laughing with Hamid's younger wives and concubines. This time, Ayla was already out. One of the girls told Yaminah that Ayla was at the *imaret*. Hamid had allowed her to oversee the construction of several alms kitchens; for Ayla, it was one of her duties under the pillars of Islam, and for Hamid, a legal method of skirting taxes.

So Yaminah sat at the window, holding Demir close to her and watching the entrance gate. She did not move her eyes from it. Slow hours turned, but Ayla did not return.

And then, Hamid did.

***

After school, Muharrem sat on the divan in his room. He held a wet cloth over his swollen nose as instructed by the physician that came to the *madrasah* to tend that clumsy idiot Murad. Muharrem knew he would receive no pity from his mother Ayla, who seemed to lavish Demir with affection. She would tell him he deserved what he got, followed by a comment on Demir's patience in finally giving it to him. The notion only fuelled the fires of hatred for his half-brother. Muharrem knew he would receive no pity from his father either. Not because Hamid liked Demir better; in fact, that was the one thing Muharrem had over Demir—approval from *Baba*. But Hamid was not a man to pity anyone who lost a fight. Still, if Muharrem did not get pity, he would get pleasure from telling his father Demir was expelled from school for insulting the teacher *and* God. The thought of the punishment that would befall his brother somehow eased the pain and humiliation of his broken nose.

When Hamid arrived, Muharrem reached him first and told him everything. Well, not that he had broken Murad's leg, just that Demir had punched him in the nose and got himself expelled. *Baba* knew, just as well as Yaminah had, that gentle Demir would not smash Muharrem in the face for no reason. But he didn't care. The only thing that mattered to him was the punishment: *expelled*. That meant shame. Hamid shoved Muharrem out of the way and charged up the stairs to Yaminah's room. In one swift movement, he yanked Demir from her divan and strode from the room. Before she had even risen in pursuit, the key turned in the lock, and Hamid barked at the servants: *Go near that door and suffer the consequences.*

Now, in the foyer, Muharrem watches as his father continues the savage beating, sweating from his efforts, panting as he speaks: "I told you I would finish what I could not start in front of your cavalryman friend."

***

Demir's skin is broken in many places, and possibly a bone or two, but his spirit is unyielding. He savours the sweet, metallic taste of his own blood. His father can thrash him, but will never defeat him. Today, Demir is no longer a foal. Today, he is a charger.

***

It is long after midnight. Yaminah is wide-awake, desperately praying that Hamid has not killed Demir. The terror is going to drive her mad. She is the most alone she has ever been in her life and aches with longing for someone to talk to.

234

Perhaps, she thinks, there is someone. Last summer, Hamid's bookkeeper was called to the stables to take inventory—a process that always spanned several days. Yaminah had been watching and waiting months for such an opportunity. On the first day of the man's absence, she crept into his office and stole an inkstand. Two days later, she returned for a quill. The next day, she had just slipped some paper into the folds of her robe and was turning to leave when the bookkeeper walked in. Her heart almost stopped. Fortunately, her brain did not. She told the man she wanted his advice on textile trading. The pious bookkeeper, who appeared just as startled to find himself alone with another man's wife—and Al Hajji Hamid's, at that—dropped his gaze to the floor and told her to discuss it with her husband. She was glad for the abrupt dismissal and he for her abrupt departure.

Yaminah sits now at her window. It is the perfect night to compose a letter, the full moon giving off enough light for her to write. The inkstand sits bathed in a pale glow on the sill. For a while, she only stares at it. Maybe she has forgotten how to write. Maybe she has forgotten the tongue of her birth. She has been made to forget much about her former self. None in Hamid's household knows Yaminah is literate. But years ago, in another world, another life, a priest taught her.

The door is locked and will remain so until Hamid sees fit. Now is her chance. Now. She takes the quill, dips it into the ink. On held breath, she traces a line on the page. The line becomes a letter. The letter a word. The first few come with difficulty, both in thought and in act. She is a fountain that has been shut off a long while, the first few words trickling, but soon, sentence after sentence gushes forth.

My dearest daughter Angelica,

Nine years have passed since that awful night the corsairs came. I have been away from you longer than near you, yet have watched you grow. Every day I close my eyes and watch.

I have written you this letter a thousand times in my mind, but tonight the words will finally be put on paper. By day, all movement is subject to scrutiny. Even now, in the light of the moon, risk runs high, for the things I wish to tell you will reveal me a liar, a blasphemer, a coward—punishable in this household by death. But whatever the danger, the thought of letting you become only a memory frightens me more than torture and death possibly could.

The blows I sustained that night years ago knocked me from your world into another. I woke in the crowded bowels of a galley, its planks thick with sludge, the stench unbearable, clinging to me, seeping inside of me. It was a horror of which I will spare you the details.

At last—was it two weeks? Two months?—the galley docked. We had arrived. But where, I had no idea. As we were forced by sword tip up a ladder and onto the deck, I caught the city's name: Algiers. Hell. The Wall of the Barbarian, we know it, the Theatre of all Cruelty.

Yet, the city afar was dazzling. Beyond the harbour, great walls enclosed the capital and ran up a hillside grown with orchards and billowing palms. The houses within were whitewashed, shining so bright with the sun it was as if they were made of light. What a strange paradise.

We were ordered off the ship and towards the Kasbah. This is when paradise turned into the hell I had heard about. On the wooden stakes set into the wall, there were bodies, dozens, hurled down from platforms above and left to die in whatever position they happened to land. Parboiled heads mounted on spikes were arranged in a procession that spanned the fortifications. You, Angelica, were the only thing that kept me from running and somehow provoking my own death.

In the slave quarter, we were stripped naked and paraded before men who reclined on silk pillows. I was made to kneel before a large, lavishly dressed Bey—a man whose wealth commanded deference. The auctioneer probed and inspected my body, checked my head for lice. He put his hand inside my mouth to examine my teeth. I tasted his sweat. Finally, he addressed me: "Thou art the newest acquisition of Al Hajji Hamid al Azm, the most renowned horse breeder from Istanbul to Gibraltar. To the mistress of the bath, thou wilt make accounting for thy body, to the imams for thy soul. Thou wilt embrace henceforth the teachings of Islam. Conduct thyself well, and thine will be the blessings of Paradise. Poorly, and thou wilt weep tears of blood." A eunuch tossed my clothes at my feet and ordered me to dress.

I was to be Hamid's second wife. Yet, it would be months before I saw the inside of his house. He kept me hidden, confined to a shelter underground and sustained on couscous and water. My Maltese birth was to be discarded, along with my faith, my language, my customs. My history was rewritten: I was from a wealthy stock in Mers el-Kebir and our union was arranged by my father, who had recently sold Hamid a prized stallion. At first, I thought the choice was only between the greater freedom of a wife, if I converted, or confinement to the harem if I did not.

It was not so simple. Hamid wanted another child, and though his principal wife had provided him with an heir, she was unable to conceive a second time. He found me pleasing, and fit for the purpose. However, he had no wish to father a concubine's child. Therefore, if he could not take me as a wife, he would simply hand me over to the corsair who killed your father.

No matter my decision, death was coming. Graciela Tabone must die.

One day I will summon the courage to beg your forgiveness, and God's, for agreeing to convert. But as Hamid would have my body, never my heart, so his Allah would never have my soul. I would die before giving myself to the faith that brought the murder of your father, my forever love. I would be a parrot—reciting words with no care for their meaning.

During my time underground, Hamid had a eunuch instruct me in the ways of Islam. I learned the five Pillars—faith, prayer, fasting, alms, pilgrimage—all things that would make me Muslim on the outside. My tutor trained me in the customs of the household, the duties of a wife, the tongue of the empire. I was dressed as a woman of noble lineage. When I had been duly prepared, Hamid renamed me Yaminah. Then, he had his mute blackamoor cut the throat of my tutor.

Such is the nature of the man to whom I am now married.

And so came the day I took my first steps inside Hamid's courtyard, around which the great house was set. The grass was thick, and over it strutted such queer creatures! Peacocks and egrets and ostriches, all tame. I was not permitted inside the stables, which were enormous and, from the look of them, housed enough horses to mount an entire cavalry. There was opulence at every turn—even servants were finely dressed, their threads luxurious, their ankles and wrists jingling with bangles. They greeted me with deference, addressing me as Madam. *Serving girls led me to a beautiful octagon-shaped room, entirely marble, its domed ceiling cut with stars. There, they stripped me and bathed me in a bath of perfumed water. At first, I was alarmed—everyone knows bathing incites plague. But it is an unfounded fear. I've never known such pleasure of bubbles and warm water and fragrance.*

Yet, I was determined to flee. If I could escape to Tripoli, the knights would save me. I would bide my time. I bide it still.

Foolish me, trying to pick a lock with a wet fish. With no money and no means of transportation, where was I going?

I soon met Ayla, Hamid's principal wife. She was and continues to be kind to me. She is a striking and powerful Ottoman woman. Hamid quails before her. A man whose incendiary nature was forged in Satan's own kiln is afraid of a woman half his size. It is laughable.

My days were spent mostly in the embroidery or in the gardens. I befriended a young Persian serving girl, Jameela. She is a butterfly, beautiful, and so delicate, it is as though light is enough to bruise her. She is my companion and confidant. Still, I keep my past secret from her, for her own protection. She has suffered ineffably at the hand of Hamid, having lost an ear to his angry whims.

After a year, he entrusted the management of his Algerian stables to his chief groomsman, and we departed North Africa for Der Saadat—Istanbul. *Weeks spent at sea was a blur of coastlines: Tunis, Lepanto, Morea, Athens. At last, the craft swam into the Golden Horn. Istanbul is the most amazing city in the world. I did not think the hands of men capable of such creations. The city seemed to be made of gold and silver. Would that I could go on describing the beauty of this place, but it would take hours, and already the moon has begun to set. I will save those descriptions for the day we are reunited.*

My dear daughter, I am changed. My hair is dark with henna, my eyes with kohl. I am called Yaminah, but I am Graciela —here, she pauses. Graciela! How she relishes writing her true name!

This next part is going to be as difficult for you to read as it is for me to write. Soon after our arrival in Istanbul, I became pregnant with Hamid's child. You have a brother, Angelica. His name is Demir. To be called Mother again, or Anneh, *as it is known here, saved my life. It is my greatest wish that you will meet one day. It is impossible, but still, I wish it. I have taught him an old song on a new flute. If only he had been born to your father and me. He might as well have been, as he has nothing of Hamid in him, and for that, I thank God. Hamid's cruelty was passed on in full to his other son, Muharrem, whose name it pains me to waste ink writing. Let me say this on the matter: Demir brings much happiness wherever he goes, Muharrem, whenever he goes.*

I have kept my son ignorant of my true self, and so, his true self. He is young, but already shows promise of a capable horseman. He wishes to join the Sultan's cavalry, to become what is called a Sipahi, but he may only do so as a Turkish Muslim— She pauses again. *Turkish Muslim.* Her son is a Turkish Muslim, the very thing the Maltese fear and hate. The very thing *she* fears and hates. The thought claws at her. It shouldn't matter. It does matter. She wails inside. Demir is Demir, and she is his mother. But who is she? Graciela? Yaminah? Mother of a Christian *and* mother of a Muslim? She is a loving mother; that's all she can be. She continues writing —*I think Demir wants this position more for his love of the horses than of battle. It is not in him to hurt anyone. All who meet him adore him, Dragut Raïs among them. Yes, that Dragut, the corsair and bringer of death to Malta, the man odious to God. I should hate him, but I admit that in watching as he interacts with Demir, I do not feel hatred. Here, he is a lord of men, yet he places his prayer mat alongside those of slaves. I do not think the lords of the Order would kneel at a pew alongside even commoners. Angelica, it confuses me terribly. Everything I was raised to believe seems wrong. A Muslim mother loves her children just the same as a Christian mother.*

The Ottomans are a people of progression. I see it even through the windows of this house. Here, there is order. Sultan Suleiman, known to Europe as the Magnificent, known here as el Kanuni—the Lawgiver, codified the Koranic and Ottoman laws by which this land is governed. Under him, even Christians and Jews worship openly. Although the year in this world is 958 and the year in yours 1551, I think it is Malta that remains in the Dark Ages.

I am prisoner but confined to a prison of roses and marble. Here, I want for nothing. Nothing but you. No one means more to Graciela Tabone than you do. I can never express my love for you in a way that you will feel it as strongly as I mean it. I am two people. I am Graciela, your mother, and she is alive. This letter is written testimony. I am Yaminah, mother of Demir. I want to be one person, mother to you both.

Alas, the moon is sinking. The muezzin will soon climb the minaret and call the faithful to prayer. Sometimes I heed the call and perform namaaz, but most of the time cross myself and pray to God. And whether my prayers are said on my knees or level to the ground, they never vary: Father, keep Your protective hand over my Angelica as I would do. Keep her safe and guide her always. By Your grace, allow us to meet again. This I pray every day. And by His grace, we will meet again.

> *Your loving mother,*
> *Graciela Tabone*

She reads the letter over. When she is finished, she crumples it and tosses it to the floor. The paper ball rolls across the rug and bounces into the wall. If by some miracle, she can devise a way to send a letter, Angelica cannot know the truth, not all of it. The letter must be rewritten.

Dawn streaks Asia with gold, and night is broken by the voices of the muezzins. Yaminah bends, picks up the letter and smoothes it out. She folds it in half, again and again, until it is too small to fold anymore. She slips it inside the damask pillow that rests against her divan. Then, she says her prayer, exactly as she wrote it.

No sooner does she rise from her mat than a key turns in her door.

PART THREE

EIGHT POINTED CROSS

CHAPTER TWENTY-NINE

Malta 1551

The apothecary Antoni Zammit waves a prescription at Domenicus, who is at the opposite end of the pharmacy, sweeping gritty dirt tracked in from outside.

"Montesa, fetch me *mandragora*. There's a good fellow." The young apprentice rests his broom against the wall and crosses to the second of three huge shelving units, each with space for over sixty majolica jars, all labelled and arranged alphabetically. He removes one such container's lid and is assaulted by the ghastly stench of rotten apple—the signature smell of mandrake.

Antoni snickers, takes the jar. "How did you ever survive the wards of the *Sacra Infermeria* when this little root is enough to make you skin your teeth?" The pharmacist produces a small bottle from the cabinet behind him and passes it to the rheumatic farmer Giovanni Bonnici, waiting on the other side of the counter. "Brandy makes mandrake work harder."

Giovanni nods, but Domenicus knows there is no chance the poor farmer has enough money to buy even a sip of brandy, the preferred spirit of noblemen, let alone an entire bottle.

"Boiled water is just as good," he cuts in. "Will I write this out for you?"

The farmer shakes his head. "I don't read, lad."

"No matter. I can prepare it for you." Domenicus glances at his superior. "If that's all right."

Antoni severs a portion of the snarled brown root, which is said to shriek upon being pulled from the earth. "As you please—but not on my clock. I need you here, now."

Domenicus smiles at Giovanni. "I can come to your house after."

"Your help is welcome." The farmer attempts to say more but erupts into rasping coughs. He doubles over, placing one hand on the counter. Eventually, he straightens out, wipes his eyes, dabs his sleeve to his mouth. He drops a coin into the pharmacist's hand, and walks off, nodding thankfully, almost apologetically, at Domenicus. A sharp February gust blows into the shop with the opening door, flapping the brown folds of Giovanni's waistcoat like the wings of a sparrow.

"He won't pay you for your trouble," Antoni says, wiping his counter clean of spittle.

"It's just as well. I'll take my pay in experience."

The apothecary chuckles. He is silver-haired, some strands streaked with gold, a remnant of younger days. He is tall for an island-native, standing only slightly shorter than Domenicus, tall by any nation's standards. "Just don't kill any of my customers as you take your pay in experience."

"Never," Domenicus laughs. He leans against the counter. "You think I'm silly."

"No. ...Yes, perhaps a little. Still, I know it's not working with herbs that has you so eager to please."

Domenicus hesitates a moment. "...How did you ask your wife to marry you, *Mastru*?"

"There was no asking. Her parents gave my parents a nice goat. Why? Planning to propose?"

"I want nothing more. But I first need means to support a wife, children."

"Then you'll be waiting forever. No man in the history of the world has ever had enough means to support a wife and children." Antoni motions for Domenicus to lean closer in and drops his voice. "Have you even dipped your pestle into her mortar?"

"Good Lord, man. She's the niece of the *kappillan*."

"And my wife is the niece of a cobbler. What's your point, Montesa?"

Domenicus makes a face. "There's more than a little difference between cobbler and priest."

"Just avoid Father Tabone's confessional," Antoni replies. Domenicus is fully aware that little brings his employer more amusement than teasing the help. Even so, this apprenticeship is a blessing—and, came along by accident, in every sense of the word. During his time in the quarries of St Angelo, Domenicus saved the life of a stonemason who had snapped his femur in a terrible fall. The man happened to be the brother-in-law of Antoni Zammit, the only Maltese apothecary in Birgu. His shop was in need of another assistant due to heavy demand from not only the village but the hospital as well. Accompanying this need was Antoni's memory of a small boy who once stormed into the pharmacy demanding medicine for his ailing mother.

Domenicus lifts the end of a bench to clear dust balls collecting beneath, sweeps around a tall case. The many pieces of earthenware lining its shelves are drawn with Biblical scenes: Jesus healing lepers, bringing sight to the blind, raising Lazarus from the dead.

"Put down that stupid broom," Antoni bosses, pouring out a solution from a bottle with a bulging bottom and long neck. "Come. Watch. Learn."

Domenicus leans the broom against the wall. "You really think I can do what you do?"

"I'm mixing herbs, not turning water to wine. You are capable. My only concern is your lack of formal training. Have Augustine ship you to Sicily where you can study the science of pharmacy. You already have a knack for the art. That's where I studied, at Messina." Domenicus feels a pang at the idea of leaving. Antoni seems to notice, rolls his eyes. "Take Angelica with you."

"I don't think the *kappillan* would approve. Nor would a cobbler, for that matter, or any other man with authority over an unmarried girl."

"All the more reason to propose and appropriate that authority."

"Is formal schooling really necessary?"

"It's the licence that matters—you'll need it to open your own shop one day. Or to take this one over."

Domenicus nudges his chin at the mandrake. "Sell me another measure. And the brandy."

"All this talk of school and marriage making you ill?"

***

It is dark and dingy inside Giovanni Bonnici's house, the orange embers of the hearth the only source of light. Two sheep and a lamb lie together, a woolly heap in a black corner beyond reach of the fading warmth. Leonora sits on the floor, hands spread over smouldering ash, shoulders wrapped in an old blanket, one worn too thin to fend off the penetrating cold. Giovanni gives Domenicus a small onion. "You are kind to come."

He takes the offering, so as not to offend the farmer's pride. "Thank you."

"Augustine raised you well," Leonora says in a voice made hoarse by her swollen, mucus-lined throat. "Had our twin girls survived the famine, I'd give you one to marry."

Domenicus smiles gently. "Madam, you honour me." He gestures Giovanni towards the hearth. "Please, join your wife by the fire. Stay warm." Domenicus crosses the room and discreetly empties the contents of a small package onto the surface of a table. To his left is a water tank cut from rock, and next to it, the hovel's dung pit. Swimming in the tiny cistern are pieces of straw, bits of human waste, animal waste, and other debris. A good thing he brought the brandy. He senses Giovanni wandering over to watch.

"A generous bit of pulp from that small piece of root Zammit sold me," the farmer says.

Domenicus shrugs, mixing the crushed mandrake into a bowl of brandy. He pours the smelly concoction into two cups. "I can work a pestle and mortar, that's all."

"I didn't buy brandy... Surely you are not so skilled with a pestle and mortar as that."

Domenicus brings Leonora the first cup. She sips the brew, its ugly taste contorting her tired features, features that quickly flood with serenity— nothing like a spirit to warm the spirit. Giovanni skitters to a small square hole cleaved into the wall rafters.

"I'll pay you," the farmer says, reaching inside for the moneybox. He opens its lid, pauses, looks over his shoulder. His cheeks are coloured. "Perhaps... perhaps you might take the lamb?"

"Not at all. *Mastru* Zammit has already paid me for this visit."

Under a moon made pale by threads of cloud, Domenicus wraps his arms tight around himself to keep out the howling *Gregale*, the fierce Northeasterly blast that sweeps the straits between Italy and Africa. Above, the constellation Eridanus winds a white river through purple heavens. Head down, he leans into the stiff wind and broods over the idea of Sicily.

Soft light seeps under the door of his house, bringing Domenicus instant warmth. Inside, Katrina sits on her pallet, Angelica beside her, a sheepskin across their laps. Pa is at the hearth, bent over a pot with a ladle in his right hand. His left is dressed tightly in linen, a second skin since the loss of his pinkie and ring finger during his last campaign off the coast of Alexandria.

Domenicus drapes his arm across his father's shoulders. "What about the new fortifications?"

"There are many chinks in the island's armour," he replies. "The new fortress rising on the low ground where Mount Sciberras ends will stand on solid rock, impossible to quarry."

"That is no chink, it is an advantage," Domenicus says. "If it is impossible to quarry, it is impossible to undermine. Sappers will be toothless."

"True, but if the walls were breached, or if invaders were to bombard the interior, there would be no escaping through tunnels. From Sciberras, gunners would crush defenders."

Angelica pulls a stool noisily out from under the table. "This is ugly talk."

"The uglier the talk, the more interesting," Domenicus replies. "Besides, these are warring times. It is better to keep a war footing." He takes his seat and turns once again to his father. "I saw they've begun work at l'Isla too."

"On a site soon to be Fort St Michael. It will dominate the southern sweep of the harbour and provide diagonal crossfire with St Angelo. And as we speak, a great boom chain is on its way from Venice, meant to close the inlet mouth against attack. Each link is said to cost one hundred ducats."

Katrina brings soup to the table. "I'll have to steal one," she says.

"Good luck. Each link is twice your size."

After dinner, Domenicus asks his father to tell of his most recent campaign—a story he's heard several times, but enjoys more with each telling.

Augustine settles back in his seat, a cup of *rozolin* in his fist. "Dawn broke on conditions more perfect than any seaman could have dreamt, a fair and following wind, a lively crew, an excellent captain. And inside that first day swanning Neptune's realm, I knew my heart was not in it. I missed Gabriel Mercadal.

"As we neared Tripoli, I thought it time to give someone his due thanks." Pa glances at Katrina. Embers from the fire cast a warm light on one side of her face. "The slave was sat at the end of a bench closest to the gangway. I spoke in Arabic: *Your name is Emir Zayid al Tariq.*

"He was surprised, if wary, but nodded.

"*You would have to be a father to understand the service you have done me,* I said. He gave a quizzical look, so I reminded him of this service. The bosun's whistle shrilled then, ending our first encounter. I spent time with him, whenever an astern wind blew, and the galley could fly goose-winged before it. I snuck him food, a dried biscuit here, some salted meat there. Finally, after days of my talking and his listening, I asked him why he killed a Muslim brother for two Christian strangers.

"He tipped his face to the sky. *Allah does not love a violator of innocence. Fazil bin Ahmet was a violator of innocence.* This answer did not satisfy the question, but for the time being, I did not press him. When the fleet made temporary berth at Tripoli, I stayed aboard and asked again. He made no reply. A quiet month passed. One evening, as the armada hugged the coast of Cyrenaica, he spoke: *My blood is not the vulgar brew of the Moor, but the refined Syrian. You are a soldier, and you will know that thirty-two years past, Ottomans wrested Damascus from Egyptian rule. There lived a woman, the youngest of seven sisters, in the first village to be pillaged. Three men violated this woman, leaving her for dead. She survived, though not in spirit, and nine months later bore a child.*

I am the son of that rape. No man wanted her now, and her family sent her away. She settled near the Baradá River and raised me. She kept me fed and clothed and sheltered. She wanted to love me, but who could love a constant reminder of such a violation? When I was ten, she took her own life. I would not allow another girl to suffer that same fate." He pauses as Angelica wipes her eyes. She nods him on. "By the end of his story, I loved him. Truth be told, I felt more kinship towards this Syrian than towards any knight." Augustine looks again at Angelica. "You are tired, dear one. I'll finish another time."

"Please," she says, "I was only resting my eyes."

He gives her a doubtful smile.

"All right, I suppose I should go. I don't know if Domenicus told you, but I've recently found employ in Mdina. Rather, employ has found me. When Uncle Anton was collecting scraps for the strays, he asked around, enquiring if any parents were in need of a tutor for small children. The Protomedicus Alonso Predal has a son who will be attending the grammar school next year."

"Wonderful," Augustine says. "Teaching will be far more gratifying than scrubbing gruesome hospital linens." Katrina works in the Italian clinic's laundry room and sends him a stricken look.

"Well," Angelica replies, rallying to Katrina's side, "Unlike children born into privilege, hospital linens do not require lessons in humility. A laundress, moreover, can beat them with paddles if they resist."

***

It is cold and quiet and dark. Wind scours the narrow footpath bare and blows Angelica's hair across her eyes. Domenicus offers his arm, and she takes it, as much for the warmth as for guidance. A sharp whinnying breaks the silence, followed by a halting cry. The two start, swinging round just as the shadowy figure of a man reins his mare.

"Angelica Tabone!"

Domenicus glances quizzically in her direction. She shrugs. The stranger strikes a light and holds it up to his face, fine features lit by the warm glow of the flame. Angelica too instantly brightens, lit by the warm glow of recognition. "My lord!"

"*Marcello*," he replies, snuffing out the flame between a gloved thumb and forefinger. Domenicus raises an eyebrow. "Greetings, *Friend*," he says, voice clipped.

Angelica clears her throat. "Domenicus Montesa, I present—"

"Marcello, I gather."

"He's a close friend of Franco di Bonfatti," she says. "Strange you have not met before."

Marcello chuckles. "Knights do not often consort with villagers. Bonfatti is a bit of a renegade in that regard."

"If knights do not consort with villagers," Domenicus begins, "how is it you two have come to informalities?"

Angelica never told him of Marcello's sneaking her into the slave prison to see Emir. She quickly takes the question. "No informalities, my darling, only a nodding acquaintance. I met Franco on the street one morning, and he was in the company of Sir Marcello. I was caught in a crush on my way to the market and having a horrible time of it." She turns nervously to the Italian, who grins wide, teeth flashing in the moonlight. He looks to Domenicus.

"Montesa, eh? So, you are kin to Katrina?"

"You know my sister also?"

"None can achieve a whiter sheet. And you, you are the sharp young blade Bonfatti schools at Mnajdra? His promising swordsman?"

"I suppose that depends on how one defines promising," Domenicus replies.

"Well then! I shall have to join you at the ruins one day and show you my definition." Smiling, the Florentine gives his russet mare a solid pat on the neck. "My lovely Pleiades here needs her beauty rest, and I think the lovely Miss Tabone needs hers." Marcello extends his hand to Domenicus. The knight tips his head to Angelica and, with a snap of the reins, is off, leaving the two alone in the cold, quiet dark.

***

Augustine uses a shard of wood to pick his teeth. Across the table, Katrina rests her head on folded arms. "Father, finish the story."

"You have to be at work tomorrow before God is awake. Franco di Bonfatti was kind enough to offer you a paying job. It won't do to be late, Kat."

"What, to scrub gruesome hospital linens?" she says in mimicry of his slight at dinner.

"Ah, yes. Sorry about that." He pauses, rubs his salt and pepper goatee. "Katrina, you are literate. You too could find work as a tutor."

"No, I couldn't. I don't have one-tenth of Angelica's patience. Besides, what I do for money is fine for now. One day I will teach the women of Birgu the bow."

Augustine shrugs. "Whatever makes you happy." Any other father on Malta would have locked his daughter in the dung room for seeking work and making it seem his wage too scanty to provide. But not Augustine. A man of reason, he put only one condition on his daughter: she must save her earnings. His ability to reason has also made him mindful that Katrina's mulishness may keep her from marrying, and she will need these savings to sustain her if no man will. Sometimes he worries that he has erred in raising her to think freely. But he has planned for her future. He will protect her from starvation with the considerable sum that Gabriel Mercadal left him. Belli, moreover, promised Augustine he would leave Katrina and Domenicus his holdings and property since the carpenter never had children of his own.

"Finish the story," she says again.

He takes a long pull of wine and leans back against the wall, which snows limestone flakes as he presses his weight into it. "By mid-September, we'd raised the coast of Alexandria. The men were bored and combat-starved. Apart from training exercises, there had been no action. The burning itch for battle was upon them, and they were restless to scratch. Before dawn on the twentieth, it would be scratched to the bone.

"Romegas spotted a flotilla of three corsair galliots sleeping in an inlet, their curved sails bucking against the seaward draught. He squinted. The flagship banner, a red and gold proclamation of Islam, flapped from the mizzen. Below the crescent standard, the captain's own flag rippled with the same salty air currents. It was black damask, emblazoned with a monstrous wolf, jaws in a bloody snarl, teeth bare. Romegas broke into a grin as unsettling as his eyes were dangerous.

"*Vuk Mihailovic, the Wolf. The Torturer*, he said to an under officer. *We met before, at Tripoli. He managed to outrun me then. This time, however, the wolf and his pack are in a fine snare.* The *capitaine* commanded silence, the bosun immediately ordering men at oars to release the looms and remove their feet from the chain rests. Now, enforcement came not in the form of rawhide, but Toledo steel. The slightest rattle of shackles compelled quick beheading. Commands flowed in echoed whispers: arquebusiers forward, crossbowmen line the gunwales, archers steady on the *arrumbada*. At a swivel, I shared duties once again with Tristan Galan.

"Beneath a sinking moon, the galleys were porcupines of silver quills, bristling with spears and swords, pikes and halberds. Romegas took a place on one of two rowboats that went to assess the state of the galliots. They soon returned with the keyed-up Frenchman leaning far over the stem. *Stiff as corpses*, he whispered. *Preparing for the role they are about to step into.*

"It was time for the oar slaves to move. Careful blades tiptoed the fleet across the water. With the three corsairs in striking distance, Romegas gave the order for his galley to take the enemy flagship, anchored between her two Muslim consorts. *Forger en avant!* he shouted, striding aft. *Pull! Pull! Handsomely now!* It was clear most of the oarsmen had rowed for him in campaigns past. They seemed to know his method, his mind, and heaved together, gathering speed with a clean, even cadence. Larboard shifted to rest mode while starboard kept a powerful stroke. The galley slewed violently, and I was decked. One bank back-sculled while the other held her steady. *Together now! Double time!* As one, the slaves rose and fell, straining every muscle fibre, propelling the galley forward, closing the distance. With a final thrust, the massive oars sent her scudding across the water, head-on into the centre corsair. Wood screamed as the spur smashed through. Moments following this rude awakening, turbans began dotting all three Muslim decks. Shots coughed sporadically from enemy muskets. The stunned crew scrambled to order. Two others in our fleet were already down the throats of the remaining corsairs. Grapnels were tossed over gunwales, flaming tapers touched to culverin holes. One of the galliots was dismasted, another losing half her oars to a basilisk. Smoke hung low and held the scents of powder and death. A torrent of Muslim arrows was loosed, piercing the heavy plume, and with it, many Christian necks. I looked quickly over my shoulder to see if Emir survived the first volley. I did not see him at first; he was no longer on the bench. When I glanced again, I saw he had managed to roll under it. Moments later came the second volley, lethal in its speed, felling several in our number. Still, the advantage was ours, the Mussulmen torn from slumber by ambush as they were, the sun rising behind us, blinding them. But there is no certain victory. Overconfidence in battle is a stealthy betrayer.

"Sword drawn, Romegas led half the galley's complement in a screaming charge over the spur. An eye no doubt fixed on ransom, he went straight for the galliot's Christian-born captain, Vuk Mihailovic, a Serbian

248

apostate. No sooner had my feet touched the deck than a man in blue robes was running at me, pike drawn. I lurched from his path and watched as the point skewered the turbaned figure two paces behind me. My opponent was dead before he could even gasp in horror, his blood spraying my face, dripping from my blade. It was a spectacular fray, scimitars crossing with swords in a savage dance. Smoke snarled around the bodies of the dead and dying. And the noise, my God, the noise. It was alive, unrelenting. The guns, the screams, the steel.

"An Algerian came at me, his curved scimitar the very crescent of Islam. My new fight took me along the corsia between slave benches, up a companionway to the foredeck. I felled my pursuer on the stair and had a moment to breathe. A fleeting moment it was, for I jumped when I noticed a man, oar slave from the whip marks and shaved head, sitting in a wooden chair mere paces away. What in God's name was he doing sitting down when all hell was unleashed around him? I got my answer with a closer look.

"His face was grey, hands bound, bare thighs running crimson with the blood that dripped from the chair, pooled at his feet. Then I realized... He was the victim of an ancient Saracen punishment devised for errant slaves. Fixed to the seat was a sharp wooden spike, point up. The naked prisoner would be invited at sword tip to sit, and the mood of the sea determined how long the unfortunate lived, a usually calm Mediterranean often delaying death.

"The prisoner's eyes popped open, startling me a second time. He caught my gaze. *Mercy*, he croaked. But any attempt to remove him from the chair would have only augmented his torture, and he would have bled to death just the same. He shook his head, eyes shifting to my sword. *Mercy.* I understood. I crossed myself and swung. His head rolled onto the planks.

He is a casualty of war, I told myself, *and he is not dead by* my *hand.* I was slashed suddenly across my calf, by a large corsair climbing the companion ladder. He leapt onto the foredeck and rushed upon me. I parried clumsily, still trying to collect my bearings. He pulled a second scimitar from a back sheath and crossed his weapons, grinning at me through an *x* of glinting steel. He swiped. I sidestepped. My heel caught a puddle of the dead prisoner's blood and flipped me onto my back, knocking the sword clear from my hand. I was finished. My assailant raised one of his scimitars, but I managed to roll on his backswing. The huge blade was embedded in the plank instead of in my gut. In that moment, I was able to retrieve my sword.

"The fight was even. I drove him against the gunwales, slicing a diagonal line across his bare chest. Battle had moved to helm from the gangway, and steel crossed all around us. My opponent swiped at my wrist, cutting flesh and knocking the sword from me once again. This time, he acted quickly, swinging fast from a high guard. I jumped back, almost out of reach. *Almost.* He caught two of my fingers. Before he could send my head to join my severed digits on the deck, I was bumped by a heavy figure, and together we tumbled overboard. I hit the water so hard it may well have been solid land. My breastplate sank me swiftly. I had sustained a great loss of blood and had no breath inside me. I would drown. But that is not how I planned to meet my end. I struggled free from my anchoring armour, kicked, and made the surface. The man who fell with me was floating face down nearby.

"*Montesa!* a voice called from above. It was Tristan Galan, leaning far over the rail of the caravan flagship, dangling a looped rope. I got it over my head and under my arms. That is the last I remember of my rescue. I awoke to the barber-surgeon's call of *Sand! More sand!* He was busy wrapping my hand and having a difficult time of it. The planks ran slick with blood and entrails, making the surgeon's intricate trade ever trickier as he struggled to stay on his feet.

"Romegas stood over me, a grand smile on his bloody, gore-splattered visage. He waved Tristan over. *Galan! An extra ration of brandy for this unfortunately tarnished* maravedí. And off the captain strode, his monkey jabbering on his shoulder.

"The first-lieutenants of three in our fleet were given charge of the newly captured Muslim galliots, still in good enough repair to not require towing, damage gauged as nothing a little oakum couldn't mend. Christian slaves were freed from their fetters and replaced at the bench by men who were their subjugators. At once, the former slaves turned on the Wolf in vengeance for the hundreds of tormented leagues they had been forced to endure under his growling banner." Augustine looks Katrina straight in the eye. "Understand something. All men are capable of cruelty. Some just enjoy it more. Vuk Mihailovic was one. He would feign mercy, often allowing the most exhausted rowers reprieve from the bench to aid in sword making. The ship's smithy would hammer and fashion at his forge. Under captain's order, he would thrust the white-hot blade into the belly of his 'assistant.' There the steel would remain ten agonizing seconds, before being wrenched out and immersed in cold water. This savage method served twofold: to harden the metal while dispatching a slothful oarsman.

"Now it was time to strip the Wolf of his pelt. Despite the promise of a tidy ransom, Romegas stood back, unwilling to interfere with vengeance taken at sea. The larger of the slaves dove on the Serb, while others tore at his vestments. He was now naked as his former slaves, but somehow, all the more vulnerable in his bareness. They kicked him, stomped on him, bit him, bound him. A large Dalmatian hoisted him and, throwing his limp, bloodied body over one massive shoulder, strode to the foredeck. The headless body of the spiked chair's last victim was removed, replaced by the hysterical Vuk Mihailovic. The Wolf howled and writhed to the sound of his former oarsmen cheering on his pain. Romegas jerked his head in the dying man's direction and grinned. "*I always said that Serbian was a pain in the ass.*" It is here that Augustine usually ends his telling of the Alexandria campaign. Not this time. Now, he sighs. "Years of battle have hardened Romegas. That's not to say he doesn't possess a kindness, or that he is not likeable. He is good to his crew, treats the slaves without undue cruelty, but death, no matter how gruesome, does not faze him. I never want to be like that." Augustine searches his daughter's face and finds there an expression so earnest it makes him want to talk about the things he would rather not.

She touches his hand. "You lost more than your fingers that campaign, didn't you?"

For reasons he cannot understand, Augustine feels the sting of tears behind his eyes. "You see, I take life when I must, but find no glory in the act. I never did. I have said prayers for every man who ever died by my hand. Still, I feel conflict within me. Simply put, God is good, killing, bad. Why then do we kill in His name? Murder is murder no matter the banner, and to commit murder is to flout a Commandment of the Ten. Yet even as I am at variance with myself, even as I feel this discord, I know it is not the last time I will raise my sword against men of a different faith. I'll continue to grind whatever grist the mill requires. Sometimes that makes me sad, because a man I meet as an enemy in battle, I would just as easily meet as a friend in a tavern."

CHAPTER THIRTY

Enveloped by the pale dawn, Katrina waits outside the Italian *auberge*. Franco di Bonfatti's former page comes to let her in. The hapless Venetian, Amedeo Pistolesi, eyes up Katrina's dusty sandals. "I'll thank you to remove those... shoes."

It is the same greeting every day. Katrina bends to take off her offensive footwear. She follows Amedeo down a long corridor, past great chambers embellished with oak and walnut furnishings, high-backed chairs seated with fat cushions, and tapestries so huge their fringes brush the ceiling, their tassels sweeping the floor. Above the refectory entrance hangs the residence crest, *Italia*, stitched in gold thread. Amedeo halts at the end of the hallway, where the Italians maintain a small, newly built clinic. Its laundry room is simple as every other room is grand, containing a big round tub, two large kettles, hanging lines at the back wall, wicker baskets heaped in one corner, wooden paddles in another, and a table piled high with soiled linens.

This morning, Katrina will work alone and is happy for the solitude. After filling the tub with hot water, she climbs onto a footstool and uses one of the paddles to stir in the lye. She hops down to gather the dirty bedclothes, and though the tub stands mere paces from the table, the stink of urine and excrement from the sheets makes the distance a thousand leagues. She throws the heap into the water and, with the enthusiasm of a slave confined to the galley bench, takes up her oar. Steam dampens her hair, curling strands that have slipped from her bun and strayed to her cheeks. Her eyes sting, red and running from the lye. Long minutes of rowing bring fatigue to her hands, pain to her elbows, but worst of all, boredom to her brain. She sighs, imagining a life grander than this.

Her father was right: she *is* literate, and that is a rare gift for anyone in Birgu to possess. She stares into the ugly depths of brownish water and wonders if perhaps she is stirring away more than just the filth and grime with each pass of the paddle.

Last night, she planted a seed within herself when she told her father she wanted to teach archery to the women of this village. That seed has now taken root. There must be women of similar mind, women who, like Katrina, know the threat of battle is a cloud gathering rain, eventually to burst over the island. There may come a day the ranks of men are depleted, and it will fall on the women to answer the call to arms. Without training, they would be useless, tipping the balance of war in the enemy's favour. Katrina *will* do it, teach women the bow. Of course, she will have to do it on the stealth, for no father, no brother, no husband would approve. She could only teach women she trusts. But who in this gossip-mongering village might she trust? Her neighbours? No chance. Courtesans? They could not pay for lessons. Unmarried girls? Their fathers would beat them. Married girls? Their husbands would beat them. Perhaps she will round up a group of widowed orphan nuns. It doesn't matter. She has set her sights on a goal; the details can be worked out later.

The corridor resonates with heavy footsteps. She looks up to see Franco in the doorway, Marcello dawdling behind.

"Happy morning," Franco says, smiling at Katrina. "I wondered if later this afternoon you would have time for a Maltese lesson. After my recent months in Italy, I've forgotten everything."

With a grunt, Marcello pushes past his friend and swaggers into the room. He appraises Katrina with a big grin. "I met your brother last night. He is almost as striking as you."

Katrina feels her cheeks go warm and looks down. She notices a shadow on the floor. Filling the doorway is Ludovico dal Sagrà, the plump, pious master of Italy's *langue*. His eyebrows, connected by one long strip of thick, dark hair, are raised high against an already deeply lined brow.

"*Fra Marcello di Ruggieri!*" he thunders. The three jump. "What are you doing in here with the laundress?"

"F-forgiveness, *Illustrissimo*," Katrina stammers, "I had asked for help with—"

"Silence!" dal Sagrà barks, a tight spiral of rage, fit to snap. That the nobleman foams like some rabid dog makes Katrina want to laugh aloud, more so when she imagines a fat Italian dog with one big bushy eyebrow. "I give you work in a land where civilised labour is so hard come by, and you show your gratitude by distracting honourable knights from righteous thought? When you need assistance, you ask it from another laundress, not a man you might corrupt with temptation."

Katrina exchanges a glance with Marcello. The Florentine clears his voice. "Sire, my word, I am not in the least tempted by these coarse peasants. My horse is better schooled."

"That's enough out of you!" the Italian master roars, glare shifting from Marcello to Franco. "Do not let me catch either of you alone with this or any other village girl again. To the bailey for combat training. Don full armour, both of you. Ruggieri, for impudence, you will serve the *septaine*."

"Humbly, my lord," Marcello replies with a bow.

The *pilier* stalks angrily off, leaving the three in frightened silence. That is until Marcello collapses against the wall in a guffaw. Katrina follows suit, clutching her side and heaving with the release of long restrained laughter. Even Franco can't help a giggle.

"Damn it, Ruggieri," he carps. "Nice work. Full armour in the bailey. *Figlio de puttana.*"

"Sweat more in training, bleed less in battle," Katrina says. "A question of fluids, and which matter more to you."

"Mmm. Thank you for your wisdom, it will make today much better," Franco replies mildly, pulling his friend by the elbow. "Come on, before you get us into any more trouble."

Marcello straightens out. "Us? *I'm* the one dealt the *septaine*, curse Sagrà's ugly hind-end."

"The *septaine*?" Katrina repeats, brushing damp hair off her face.

Franco grins. "Confinement for seven full days of fasting. Ruggieri here can take nourishment twice, a fine fare of milk and water—a question of fluids, and which matter more to him."

***

Angelica sits with her back to a peach tree, cool dirt beneath her bare feet, a workbook lying across her lap. Swallows chirp from the boughs of fruit trees that line the Predal courtyard, which is the size of four houses in Birgu put together. Decorative vines nod over windows, climbers loop tall Ionic pillars, and garlands of cerulean and crimson flowers trim the walkway.

"I like your name, Manoel," Angelica says to her four-year-old student, a boy more interested in dirt than the alphabet. "Shall I teach you to spell it?"

"No," he replies, raking small fingers through black earth. "I'm hunting treasure."

"Treasure would be easier to find if you could read a map."

Intrigued, Manoel stops his expedition and looks up at Angelica. She holds out a quill in invitation, but the swing of doors turns their heads. Elisabetta Predal enters the courtyard in a swish of skirts and ruffled petticoats, every graceful movement a show of aristocracy. Her face is heart-shaped, a naturally fair complexion made fairer by skin whitener, smoother with sheep fat. Softly arching brows frame chestnut eyes. The auburn beauty wears a dazzling dress of yellow sussapine threaded with gold, and her hair, a pile of curls pinned atop her head, is weaved with strands of yellow pearls. Angelica's gaze falls to her own skirt, plain and beige. Part of her wishes she wore the lilac gown Aunt Giselle sent from Rome years ago. The young tutor is dull limestone next to a polished gem, and she is six again, scrubbing the floors of Mdina's nobles with her mother.

"My dear," Elisabetta says, her voice perfect and practised as a well-choreographed dance. "I thought you might enjoy a break from Manoel."

Angelica smiles. "Thank you, my lady, but we were just getting started."

Elisabetta, named so for the mother of John the Baptist, motions towards a glass table with her head. "The alphabet won't change over the next half hour. Come, join us."

"Us?" Angelica asks, looking beyond the lady Predal's shoulder to the doors. Before she might answer, another woman crosses the threshold and into the open quad. Maroon brocaded slippers, embellished with fine silver filigree, clap over the tiles of baked-clay. The noblewoman drops an uninterested glance on the peasant sitting in the dirt and the two catch eyes.

All moisture disappears from Angelica's mouth. It is the woman who could make Vlad the Impaler seem a loveable dandy, the woman who once threw a bucket of dirty water on a child servant in winter. It is the wife of the *ħakem*, Malta's most powerful son. It is Diana d'Alagona.

Angelica swallows, praying to God that she will go unrecognized. From the indifference on the noblewoman's face, God has granted this request. For all her cruelty, time has rewarded Diana with one kindness after another. She is still as beautiful now as ten years past. Her cheeks are high, her nose sharp but small, her eyes so dark there is little difference between the iris and pupil. Her hair, braided into a raven crown, sits atop her head in stark contrast to her milky face and neck.

Diana approaches Elisabetta in a cloud of exotic perfume and takes her arm. "Stop conversing with hired hands," she says, her tongue rolling in Italian. "You'll catch fleas."

Elisabetta stiffens visibly. "Really, Diana. Angelica Tabone is Manoel's tutor."

"Oh! How careless of me," Diana coos, glancing her over. "I mistook you a common gardener, sitting barefoot in filth and all."

Angelica smiles, rises, and dusts the soil from the seat of her skirt. "That's all right, Madam. *I* would have thought me a gardener." Across the walkway, an older Genoese waters a patch of young sprouts. He meets Angelica's eyes and makes a face behind Diana's back. Angelica looks down to hide her amusement, but soon looks again. The gardener is familiar. Pondering the connection, she slides her feet into her sandals and follows the two women to a glass table standing on white claw-foot legs. Elisabetta and Diana sit on chairs cushioned in clean pearl damask. But just as Angelica is about to take her seat, the *ħakem*'s wife raises a halting hand.

"Perhaps," Diana says, looking at Elisabetta, "a serving girl should bring a length of cloth?"

Angelica feels a burn at the nape of her neck. Elisabetta shakes her head. "Not at all. Have a seat, my dear." Angelica does as she's told, mindful to keep her back straight, shoulders down, hands folded neatly in her lap.

"Is that new?" Elisabetta asks, eyes on Diana's dress, a stunning gown of sarcenet, a shade lighter than her shoes and open at the sides, exposing an amethyst taffeta under-dress.

Diana nods. "Comes from Paris and costs twice the chandelier in our foyer. It is a blend of superb silks, no less breathable than a person of taste can or should endure." Her eyes flick to Angelica. "Anything cheaper than silk suggests certain crudeness, don't you think?"

Angelica's palms are moist. "It-It is exquisite."

"Yes, well, I suppose to a maid of such…em…limited means, a dress made of anything more luxurious than sackcloth would appear exquisite. But I say if it is not made of silk, it is made of spite and disgrace." A moment of uncomfortable silence passes. Diana touches her fingers to one of Angelica's curls. "A woman's hair is everything. I could spend the day brushing mine. If I could give a bath to each strand, I would. You have hair unlike any person I've ever seen before."

"Thank you."

Diana gives her a mean smile. "Coarse and bristly, a horse's mane."

Angelica looks down. She does not know how to respond. If only Katrina were here. Elisabetta frowns, but before she might put an end to the cruel game, Diana claps her hands twice. A jittery footman appears in the open doorway carrying a silver tray that glints with the afternoon.

"Trot, trot," she snaps. "Swiftly now, lazy thing." He places the tray carefully on the table, stands at silent attention.

Diana glares at him. "Awaiting a call to gambol and twirl for my amusement?"

The footman exhales and, with a quick bow, escapes inside, leaving behind the tray, arranged with three plates, an open jar of honey, a basket of fresh bread, peeled oranges and three cups, each brimming with a hot drink. Through rising steam, Angelica watches Elisabetta dip a spoon into the open honey jar, and lift the spoon high, allowing a thin gold thread of sweetness to catch with the sunlight as it trickles back into the container. The noblewoman notices Angelica watching, and smiles, sliding her the jar. "Sweetheart, take your drink with honey. It's from Toulon, said to be the very best in the world. If price is any indication of quality, truly this honey is fit for God's palate."

"Is Gozitan honey not said to be the best in the world?" Angelica asks. "Something to do with the thyme pollen and lemon, I've heard."

Diana clears her voice. "Swine that have tasted the swill of only one farm would think it the best in the world too."

Angelica takes the jar. The honey smells like liquid heaven, but she is afraid to show her pleasure. She is unsure whether to put a spoonful in her drink or spread it over the buttered cut of bread, both which she would normally do at home, but now, with Diana d'Alagona studying her every move, all the usual customs are fraught. Moreover, the idea of gooping the sticky gold all over the noblewoman's precious hair is insanely tempting.

"Elisabetta," Diana says, "Are you sure this girl is capable of tutoring your son? I mean, a jar of honey is enough to confound her. Perhaps these fancies are unfamiliar to the low people."

Elisabetta fires her guest a look of disapproval. "She is not a low—"

"Tell me, little tutor," Diana interrupts. "Where do you reside?"

"Well," Angelica begins carefully, "I live in Birgu, but—"

"See, Elisabetta? A village entirely populated with low people."

"In answer to your question," Angelica goes on, "I am from Mdina. I came to stay with my uncle in Birgu when I was a child."

Diana frowns. "*You*? Born in Mdina? This is the *Città Notabile*, peopled with courtiers. Where ever did you live?"

"Paces from the Casa Inguanez."

"How fun!" That mean smile again. "Were the casements of your little hovel panelled with oiled linen?"

"The rectory where I live now has glass windows," Angelica says lamely.

Diana tips her head to the side. "Rectory? You live in a rectory? Where do you sleep? With Jesus in the sacristy?"

Elisabetta clears her voice. "Any stories of court intrigue from your husband, Diana?"

"The legal affairs of everyday rustics bore me." Diana wrinkles her nose. "Rather, I am quite curious to know why the tutor's parents would leave Mdina, the jewel in Malta's crown, for *Birgu*, the armpit of the island."

Angelica has had enough. "The corsair who murdered my father and took my mother did not leave me with many options." She inhales sharply, amazed she made it through those last words without tears. Elisabetta, however, did not, and reaches over the table to take Angelica's hand.

"It is a pity about your parents," Diana says, bringing the cup to her lips. Then, as if struck, her eyes grow wide. She places the cup back on the table with a clatter. "I have it! It has been making me crazy! *Tabone*! At last, I remember. I believe it was my eighteenth year, the year I was wed. My husband brought in a new chambermaid. Graciela *Tabone*. I presume her girl-child was you."

"As surely as I am the girl you emptied that bucket of dirty water all over."

Elisabetta gasps at this allegation, but Diana beams. "Extraordinary!" She claps her hands. At the sound, the desperately obedient footman returns, only to be waved hastily back. Diana, now slightly more restrained, looks back at Angelica. "So, your husband allows you to work?"

"I'm not married."

The noblewoman arcs a heavy eyebrow. "Oh. Your... um... tolerable looks gave me to think that you would have had at least a few offers. You know, from goatherds, farmhands, and the like. Don't be a fussy thing—surely you do not have much of a dowry, what with your father dead."

Now she feels that sting of tears and greatly appreciates Elisabetta's attempts to come to her rescue. "Angelica is courting a lovely young man. He is learned, an apprentice to an apothecary."

Diana sneers. "Plans to support you on the wage of an apprentice, does he?"

"I… I should get back to Manoel," Angelica replies, beaten down by this unrelenting assault. She rises wearily and walks off, though she is unable to escape the voices of the two noblewomen.

"What in God's name possessed you to treat that poor child so horribly?" Elisabetta hisses.

Diana shrugs. "Do come on. You cannot let these grasping little villagers forget their station. Do that, and the next thing you know she will be replacing your body with hers in the marriage bed, and then what will you do? Take her place in the sacristy with Jesus?"

CHAPTER THIRTY-ONE

From his place in the watchtower, Robert watches Katrina run across Corradino Hill towards the sentry post as she does every day. Her arrival, as always, brings him a smile. Although visitors are forbidden inside the tower, she enters anyway, taking the tall spiral stair two steps at a time. Salty winds pass through the lookout porthole, ruffling his dark hair, passing over his face. Above, white-grey gulls climb to the highest blue reaches, where they dip and loop. He looks to the shore, a swirl of creamy pewter against a turquoise sea that shimmers under the five o'clock sun.

Robert senses Katrina behind him. She brings with her the scents of clean linens, clean breezes, and clean sweat. He glances over his shoulder, but his glance turns to a stare. She is no longer the rough, unkempt girl from siege games of yesterday, no longer the boyish twig who once chopped off all her hair. And though he sees her almost every day, today he sees something more. Something has crossed over in her. Something in him. The young woman who stands before him now, caught in a slant of sunlight, has features perfected by time, lustrous black hair, and skin the colour of singed gold, radiant against ocean green eyes. She is wonderfully alive. Robert looks at her now, really looks at her as if for the first time. She is beautiful. She scowls.

"What the devil are you up to?"

"Thinking," he replies.

"Does it hurt?" If her looks are delicate, her tongue certainly is not.

"No," he says, turning back to the window. "This is where I do all my big thinking. Do you ever just stop and watch the sky, Kat? I could spend hours. I watch as clouds are born, watch as they start their journey to some place new." He faces her once again. "Let's go catch snails."

She looks at him with rue. "I'm meeting Franco. Promised him a Maltese lesson."

Robert looks down, toes a pebble. "You'd rather spend time with him than with... the snails?"

Katrina lifts his chin with her fingers and looks into his eyes. "No. But I promised."

He scoffs. "Why does the lofty knight lower himself to the parlance of the rabble?"

She shrugs. "Perhaps he wants to better relate to commoners."

"Or to better spy on them."

Katrina makes a face. "No. It's a fair trade. He teaches me the bow."

"Hard to imagine a nobleman teaching a peasant anything but a lesson in contempt."

"He taught you the arquebus."

"Yes, after making a point to say any village idiot could use one," Robert replies.

"Well, there you have it. It's perfect for you."

He grunts. "Be good, or I'll tell Augustine to keep you in for Carnival."

Katrina snorts. "Try it." Of all things the Knights of St John brought with them to Malta, none has been so enthusiastically received as their aggrandizement of Carnival, three boisterous days of festivity to usher in the solemn forty of Lent.

The clock tower tolls in the distance and ascending footsteps echo loudly off the cylinder walls. Robert slings his arquebus over his shoulder just as the new shift comes running breathlessly in.

"Falsone," Marco Vella pants, "Forgive my delay. Please don't report it to Bonfatti."

Robert gives the boyish sentry an easy smile. "Not if you were two hours late. Just don't you tell him about my guest," he looks to Katrina, "who knows well she shouldn't be here." He turns to follow his guest down the stairs and out into the sun.

They sit side by side on some loose rocks. Katrina gathers a handful and arranges them over the dirt in the form of an R. She scoops up several more and makes an O. Robert watches with fascination as she spells out his name with the small white stones.

"Robert," she reads, tracing the word. She drops some pebbles into his hand. "You try."

He closes his fingers around them. "Better I keep to guarding the hillside, rather than trying to write on it."

Franco di Bonfatti arrives inside the hour, greeting Robert with a tight, humourless smile. The knight leans forward, pucker browed and squinty-eyed. "What's that on your face, Falsone?"

The sentry runs his hand over a stubbly cheek. "Time calls for a shave."

"Is that what it is? I thought it was the dirt."

"I have kindling to fetch." Robert rises, and with a parting smile for Katrina, walks off.

"Ho there, Good Argus!" Franco calls after him. "Make sure to unearth that chin. I want you presentable. You are in service of the Hospitaller Order of St John." Robert pauses briefly, strides on. With Falsone gone, Franco offers his hand to hoist Katrina to her feet. As he bends, he notices the pebbles spelling Robert's name and instantly feels a jealous pang. He had hoped the year spent back in Italy would have quieted this storm. It didn't. Nor did asking God to release him from this temptation, though he continues to ask, along with his contradictory entreaty that God keep Katrina unmarried. But God does not seem eager to lend His ear these days. He often ignores mothers who pray for the safe return of a son from war, husbands who beg Him to cure a wife's illness, beggars who entreat a scrap of bread; therefore, if the Almighty does not answer prayers of substance and weight, why would He answer prayers so petty and selfish? Still, Franco will keep asking.

When Katrina is not looking, he scatters the stones that spell Robert's name with the muddy tip of his boot.

***

The sentry stops at a lonely, unsown parcel to gather brambles, which, along with dust and stone, make for Malta's most abundant natural resource. The thorns that jut from the stems always tore up Mea Falonse's delicate skin, so Robert made the task of gathering brushwood his. Whether the gritty summer scirocco hisses or the icy winter Gregale howls, it is an errand he completes every day without exception. He swings his arquebus over his shoulder and uses it to break apart the savage brush. Brow glistening, he stomps the loose pile of twisted foliage with a booted foot. In the awful days before his boots, this was a chore far more painful to carry out.

Confident his mother will be pleased with all he managed to glean, Robert uses a length of twine to tie the thorny bundle together. He hoists it across his shoulders and takes to the road. A familiar bleating turns his head. He squints, breaks into a laugh. Grimaldi Farrugia's renegade goat tramps the dirt, four skinny legs stirring up a storm of dust. Robert approaches the animal, embracing it as he would any friend. He makes a leash of his gun strap and leads the fugitive back home. There, Robert calls for the farmer but is met by silence. Sentry and goat wander the field, past the old chicken shed still in bad repair.

"Farrugia!" Robert shouts, unloading the prickly yoke from his shoulders. He ranges the barren rows and recalls long days spent digging and watering. The earth is soggy from flash rains that poured furiously down days ago, and his boots are soon caked thick with mud.

"*Farrugia!*" he calls again, his voice jarring against the stillness. He treks the dirt to the barn, its walls streaked with the grey-green daub of pigeon excrement. Pushing open the door sweeps a breeze inside, where the air is musty and hot. An unusual scent of decay settles about him. He blinks rapidly, adjusting his eyes to heavy darkness as shadows spill across the gritty floor. Pale light streams in slender shafts through cracks in the roof, catching the dust as it swirls towards the ceiling. A strange sound comes from aloft, the sound of wood groaning.

Robert looks up. Hanging from a rope tied around a thick beam is Grimaldi Farrugia, eyes open, face mottled blue, tongue, swollen and purple and flopped against his chin.

***

Angelica passes into darkness as the horse-drawn carriage of the Protomedicus Alonso Predal crosses a covered bridge. "That's it, Biondina," he says to his horse, "A good, easy gait." The honey-coloured mare pulls them back into sunlight and plods a stony path, down a mean slope, away from the perched city of Mdina, away from its restrained atmosphere and the ghosts of four thousand years of settlement. Reins loosely in hand, Alonso glances at Angelica from the corner of his eye.

"That cow, Diana d'Alagona, was she rude to you?"

Angelica looks at him in surprise.

"She is positively ill-mannered," he says. "My blood curdles at her approach. I tolerate her presence only because her husband is *hakem*. I cannot fathom how my wife stomachs her company." Alonso leans towards Angelica. "I wish Diana's hair would fall out. Her love of it borders sacrilege."

Angelica smiles, delighted the two are united against a common enemy.

"Now," he continues, "To the more important business. Manoel. He is easily distracted. If it were up to him, he'd spend his days chasing lizards and catching spiders."

"The makings of a natural scientist, no?"

"Verily yes, but if my wife finds another insect on her pillow, another lizard in the pantry, her heart will stop." Alonso chuckles, bouncing in his seat as the carriage hitches over large stones and hidden ruts. "And having a wife so young meet such an end would reflect badly on my position, wouldn't you say?"

Angelica is not sure how to answer, so she doesn't. Biondina takes them past a hotchpotch of green and brown fields. A weather-beaten farmer tills his patch, his dishevelled wife carrying two pails of grain to the goats, pausing briefly to wipe away loose strands clinging to her sweaty brow. At Birgu's gate, Alonso looks across his shoulder at Angelica. "For the rectory, which way do I take?"

"If it's no trouble, *Magnificus*, I have business at the Zammit apothecary shop." There is no reason for her to visit the shop, but it is the only way she can think to introduce Domenicus and his aspirations to the Protomedicus without appearing pushy.

"Are you ill? That d'Alagona woman caused you a devil of dyspepsia, I think."

Angelica laughs. "Not at all. I thought I would pay the apothecary's apprentice a quick visit. I'd hoped to steal a walk home from him."

"I see. So would he be the lucky man to whom you are betrothed?"

"As soon as he works up the nerve to ask, he will be."

Alonso grins. "Your father would be happy with your choice. The apothecary Zammit tells me Domenicus Montesa is his best apprentice."

Angelica beams. "You know him!"

"Well, of him. His reputation precedes him."

"He'll like to hear that. All he wants is to build and run his own apothecary shop."

"Then all he needs is the Grand Master's approval. As I see it, Birgu's three pharmacies are not equipped to supply the public and the hospital. Have him write a letter and bring it to the Grand Master." Alonso tugs the reins, halting his mare. He steps down, walks round to the other side and offers Angelica his hand. As she reaches out to take it, he drops several coins into her palm.

"For today. And something extra for enduring that bride of Satan."

"Oh *Magnificus*, thank you! Will you come in? Domenicus would love to meet you."

"To visit the pharmacy unannounced is to give apothecary Zammit a terrible fright. I have already completed my annual inspection of his shop and renewed his licence, so he'd think me dropping in to spy. I will meet your Domenicus another time, I promise."

To Angelica's surprise, the shop is empty of customers. At the counter, Antoni Zammit absently grinds tobacco in his mortar. Domenicus crouches before a shelving unit, two jars at his feet, one containing roots, the other leaves. Neither he nor the apothecary looks up at the sound of the door.

"Can I help you?" Antoni asks, eyes on his moving pestle.

"Yes, please. Fill my prescription for an apprentice."

"Angelica," Domenicus says brightly.

"Go on, Montesa," Antoni says, nodding to the door. "Unless a bout of plague sweeps the island in the next half hour, I'll be able to manage on my own until close."

Angelica takes Domenicus by the hand and pulls him out of the shop. "I have good news! Alonso Predal wants you to take a written application for an apothecary shop to the Grand Master."

Domenicus furrows his brow. "Angelica, I'm not qualified to run a shop. I haven't even a licence to practice. Clearly, you did not tell the Protomedicus I have no formal schooling."

"Do you think setting up a pharmacy takes one day? By the time you secure the necessary approval, you'll have obtained your licence."

Domenicus sighs.

"What's the matter?" she asks. "I thought you'd be pleased."

"I am, of course, I am." He kisses her forehead and smiles. "Will you help me write this letter? Come, we'll do it right now."

Angelica sits at the table, a quill hovering over blank parchment. Domenicus slides his chair behind hers and rests his chin on her shoulder. He knows this will never work, but she seems so excited, and the last thing he wants is to hurt her feelings. Besides, trifles, such as the Grand Master wanting to make crow sport of him, can be worked out later. "How do we start this thing?"

"With flatteries, to grease the wheels of favour. When dealing with the head of a thoroughly arrogant body, you must employ near adulation. Something like, Most Illustrious, Judicious, and Revered Grand Master."

"Most illustrious and revered Angelica." He kisses her neck. "Does that grease your wheels?"

She laughs, pushes his face away. "Stop it. Your father could come home."

Domenicus brushes her hair aside, pulls her shift slightly off her shoulder and kisses the soft, bare sweep of flesh. There is a cluster of beauty marks at the base of her neck, random yet connected, like an uncharted constellation. She does not put up resistance this time as he runs his mouth over her skin to the hollow of her throat. An unquenchable fire burns within him, and the desire to take her to his bed, to love her in that way, is almost overpowering.

Suddenly, a frantic pounding at the door startles them both. Irritated, Domenicus goes to greet the unwelcome caller. It is Robert, stark white and wild-eyed, running a shaky hand through dishevelled hair. Domenicus steps back.

"What the devil—"

"He's dead. *Dead!*"

"Who? Who's dead? What's happened?"

"He was hanging in the barn!"

Angelica drops her pen into the inkstand with a splash and comes quickly to the door. "Robert, who is dead?" She takes his hand and pulls him gently over the threshold. His every movement comes stiff and rigid, as though he has forgotten how to walk. Domenicus closes the door.

"Farrugia," Robert manages. "He... The goat... I brought it back. That's all I did, just brought the goat, God blast it. Then, I saw the farmer, swinging by the neck."

Angelica covers her mouth. But Domenicus shrugs, palms upturned. "A celebration. Come, I'll pour the wine."

Robert fires him an appalled look. "Damn the jokes."

"I'm not joking. You should be glad he's dead. If he were murdered, it would not surprise me. Do you think he was?"

"I don't bloody know!"

"Did you report it?"

"*No*! Is your brain leaking? They'll think *I* killed him! I'll end up just like him! Only, with an audience."

Domenicus steps in front of Robert, places calm hands on his shoulders. "You must tell the gendarme."

"No, all I *must* do is be poor and die."

"Easy now. Tell me exactly what happened."

Robert nods. "I took the goat back to the farm, that bastard animal. I found Farrugia in the barn, hanging from the rafters..." His breaths come faster. "...They will think I did it. Christ, *I* would think I did it."

"Sit." Domenicus pulls out a chair. "No one is going to think anything of the sort. You are going to report it. That alone will prove your innocence."

"Lend me money. How much is passage to Sicily?"

"God's sweat man, he likely killed himself. If I were him, I'd have killed myself ages ago."

"I'm going to vomit." Angelica scrambles for the pail and slides it across the floor to Domenicus, who sets it at his friend's feet.

"I'm all right," Robert says. "I'm all right. I'll just let someone else find him."

"No, don't do that."

"You seriously think I should go to the gendarmes? I don't have good standing with them. Farrugia had me arrested for theft, remember? I know *they*'ll remember."

Angelica crouches before Robert and speaks gently. "Think if someone else saw you on his property and tells. Then you would really look guilty." She rises and brings him a cup of milk. He drinks it and, seconds later, throws it up.

"*Haqq ix-xitan*! Damn the devil!" Robert says. "I left my brambles in his field!"

"So what? Gather more," Domenicus replies.

"You don't understand. The gendarmes will wonder why a neatly tied bundle of brambles is there. And that damn Florentine Bonfatti heard me tell your sister I had to gather kindling."

"You and everyone else in Birgu. It is not an unusual chore." Domenicus puts a strong hand on Robert's shoulder. "Brambles or not, we are going to make a report. We'll go together. Now."

"And tell them what?"

"The truth."

"The truth will be twisted into a noose I'll soon swing from, you'll see."

***

The captain of the gendarmes lives just opposite the Cavalier of St James, and from Augustine Montesa's house, the only road that leads there passes Grimaldi Farrugia's farm. Robert halts mid-step. "Son of a whore. They've already found him."

Three officers in clean black livery carry a linen-draped body out to a wagon waiting on the road. Robert recognizes one as the officer who arrested him on Farrugia's false charges. Two identically uniformed men stand on the roadside, one with the seasoned air of senior rank, the other, marked a novice by his pimply youth. The pair questions Pino Mifsud, notorious gambler—defeated once, by some fat, cheating foreigner.

"...Just came to collect the money he owes me and found him in the barn."

"A suicide," the older officer surmises. "Couldn't pay his debt."

Pino grumbles.

"That should teach you to gamble," the youth scolds. "We should arrest you just for that."

The veteran officer gestures his colleague to stand down. "We're done here. Summon the scribe. Pino will make a formal report."

Robert is overcome with relief so strong it hurts. He exhales as though he's been holding his breath the last five minutes. Domenicus smiles and gives him a nudge.

The young cadet begins towards the house of the scribe, but stops, turns. "Wait. Wait a minute. Mifsud, were you carrying a load of brambles?"

The gambler shakes his head. "No. Why?"

"I recovered a bundle, flattened and tied. There," he points, "in the field."

Pino shrugs. "Maybe it was Farrugia's. Can I have it? He won't need it, and I haven't gotten round to collecting any."

The officer tips his head to one side, eyes crescents. "If you planned to hang yourself, would you go to all the trouble of collecting brush?"

Robert's palms are wet. Domenicus leans to his ear. "Pull it together."

The older gendarme takes notice of them. "*Hawn int!* Ho there!" he calls with a wave. "Falsone, that you? You worked for the farmer. Come here a minute." Robert casts a look of longing on the road behind him, wondering if he should just make a run for it, even as his legs carry him to the man-at-arms.

"Yes, I worked on the farm," Robert says simply.

The officer looks hard at him. "Farrugia once accused you falsely of theft. You don't work for him anymore. What are you doing here now?"

"Taking the road home."

"The road from where?"

"From my house," Domenicus cuts in.

"You went to Augustine Montesa's house straight from the Corradino watchtower?" the officer asks Robert.

"Yes," he lies, mouth dry.

The gendarme looks down at Robert's boots. "Your shoes are covered in mud. So is the dead farmer's field." He looks at Domenicus Montesa's boots. "Queer that yours are clean."

Domenicus laughs, gives Robert a shove. "The explanation for that is idiotic really."

"I will hear it nonetheless."

"Of course. We happened on a mud puddle, and Falsone here tracked himself through it. Mainly to upset his mother, I think. I have better sense, that's all."

"Mmm." The gendarme is a long time watching Robert's eyes.

"So, what happened here anyway?" Domenicus asks casually, trying to put an end to the interrogation. But the man-at-arms is too busy studying Robert; too busy listening to his silent language. Seconds are dreadfully slow in their passing.

At last, the officer blinks, releasing Robert from his stare. "It would seem a suicide happened here."

CHAPTER THIRTY-TWO

Early the next morning, Angelica finds Domenicus sitting in wait on the rectory steps.

"What's wrong now?" she asks, unsettled.

He smiles. "Nothing. I'm escorting you to Mdina."

"You'll be late for work."

"I'm at work already. The apothecary asked me to deliver a message to Dr Callus."

"What kind of message?"

Domenicus produces a rolled vellum. "The sealed kind." He winks and offers his arm.

The fields that flank the open road are lit gold by the new sun. This mostly unpopulated stretch between Birgu and Mdina is absent of human interaction, and as such, all the little, easily missed noises are amplified tenfold—grass rippling with the breeze, birds hopping among loose rocks, mice scurrying over low stone walls.

"You know," Angelica whispers, unsure why she is whispering but feeling she should be, "There is no school on Malta where you might obtain an apothecary's licence."

"Yes, I know."

She looks straight ahead. "You'll go abroad."

"To Sicily."

"Mmm."

"Don't worry, the Grand Master is going to deny my application anyway, so I won't need to bother with schooling."

Angelica looks at Domenicus. "Worry? Why would I be worried?"

"Oh... I don't know. It just seemed like the right thing to say."

"You think I don't want you to go?"

He breaks stride and faces her. "Do you?"

"I... Well..."

"What is it?"

"Is there a reason you haven't asked me to go with you? I mean, even if you don't go, even if we both know I couldn't, is there a reason you never asked?"

Domenicus furrows his brow. "Angelica, why are you asking me this?"

She looks down. "I don't know."

He takes her cheeks in his hands and looks into her eyes. "You once said you'd follow me anywhere." He smiles. "I don't want you to follow me. I want you right beside me, wherever the road takes me. And should that be Sicily, that's where you'll be, right beside me."

An hour later, they hike uphill to the city that stands on a pedestal, populated by people who think they do too. Angelica and Domenicus cross a drawbridge that leads over a deep moat flowing with rainwater and are quickly swallowed by the darkness of Mdina's great limestone gallery, spat out moments later on the other side. Sunlight makes Angelica blink, and as her eyes adjust to the brightness of the day, she catches a sight that halts her mid-step: twenty paces up the road, Diana d'Alagona strides through the iron gates of the Predal mansion. Angelica draws a sharp breath. She cannot possibly withstand another barrage of insults from this woman, one so skilled at finding every chink in a person's armour.

The gate opens a second time, and Diana emerges, wearing strong perfume and a mysterious smile. "A happy morning to you, my dulcet dear."

Angelica arcs an eyebrow. "What?"

Diana laughs. "*That* is how you address nobility?"

Angelica snaps from disbelief long enough to give a graceless curtsey. "M-My lady."

"Shame on you," the noblewoman says, wagging a heavily ringed finger, gems flashing with the sun, "Allowing me to continue on without an introduction to your fine young consort."

"Oh... This is Domenicus Montesa. You know him as the apothecary's apprentice."

Diana pays no further mind to Angelica, whose one apparent use has been exhausted. The woman's eyes move obviously over the peasant girl's fine young consort, however. Domenicus shifts his weight from one foot to the other, then, seeming to remember his manners, bows his head reverently.

"*Barunessa.*"

"I am Diana d'Alagona, friend to the Predals, wife to the *hakem.*"

Domenicus gives a low whistle. "The *hakem.*"

Angelica stiffens. She wants to cuff the back of his stupid head for showing the tyrant he's impressed.

"Well, Apprentice, you have chosen to tread a noble path yourself. It may not be head of all civil authority, but medical men serve a function." Her lightness of tone makes it difficult to tell if she is mocking him or being sincere.

"It *is* noble," Angelica says testily. "And earned."

Diana ignores her. "I have a great courtesy to ask of you, Apprentice. My husband often suffers bouts of nausea, you see."

At this, Angelica snickers. Diana fires her a vicious look. Domenicus glances from one woman to the other, plainly confused by their sparring. "What courtesy would the lady ask of me?"

"The courtesy of a house call. I would put in a favourable word on your behalf to the Protomedicus, of course. My praise would be greatly beneficial to one with your ambitions."

"Your confidence is appreciated," he replies carefully, "But your husband would be better served by seeing a proper physician. In fact, I am right now on my way to the house of Dr Callus."

The noblewoman touches his arm. "Is there no tonic you might dispense? No herb?"

"Not without a prescription, I'm afraid."

Diana shrugs. She turns to face Angelica. "So. Have you told your friend about our discovery most amusing?"

Although Angelica's mouth forms a smile, she narrows her eyes to convey her true sentiment. "No. I did not mention you at all."

"Discovery?" Domenicus asks, clearly confounded.

Diana peals with laughter. "Miss Tabone is too embarrassed to share the history of her humble beginnings, that's all." She lifts her chin. "I'll keep your secret, sweetheart."

"There is no secret," Angelica replies. "My mother was a chambermaid. Domenicus, you know that. Before she was taken, she found employ in the house of d'Alagona. I did too, for a time." She ends the explanation, deliberately leaving out the incident that made enemies of her and Diana, refusing to give the noblewoman the satisfaction.

There is a long moment of uncomfortable silence and averted eyes.

"I should go," Domenicus says finally. He glances to the noblewoman. "My lady, a pleasure."

"No, the pleasure was mine." Diana smiles a grand smile, offering Domenicus her powdered cheek. At length, he obliges with a stiff, awkward peck. He turns nervously to Angelica.

"And thank you for the pleasure of your company this morning," he says.

"No, the pleasure was *mine*," Angelica replies, drawing him to her for a big, theatrical kiss.

***

It is after dusk and, under a sky bruised purple by fists of storm cloud, Robert Falsone stands at the edge of an anonymous burial pit. The sentry's head and shoulders are misted with droplets of cold, gritty rain. He breathes in the stink of twenty rotting corpses, the smell rising from the deep hole in the ground.

Grimaldi Farrugia's sheet-wrapped body slides feet first into the ditch from the back of a wagon, the same one he was loaded into the night past. A lone gravedigger pitches a shovel of sea salt onto the decomposing bodies and turns to leave.

Robert does not know why he came here. He is not sad for the farmer's death. Still, something brought him here, to the edge of this miserable pit. And whatever that something is, it has him bowing his head in prayer.

***

Domenicus crosses a skinny bridge and presents himself to a Castilian knight at the portico of St Angelo. He requests occasion with the Grand Master, explaining his purpose to the guard and producing the application letter as proof. The knight skims the parchment. He whistles for his page, a Valencian no more than ten, who carps about the untimely nature of the visit as he ushers Domenicus into the castle courtyard. He remains silent, taking in the state of the fortress interior. His work on the fortifications never brought him inside the walls, stationing him instead in outer culverts and quarries. He marvels at the grand cavaliers, mighty buttresses, soaring pillars, ornate cornices, all fashioned by the skilled hands of local masons and artisans. The page crosses himself as they pass the fortress chapel, built a century earlier by the de Nava family. Domenicus slows his stride and looks out over the harbour. Torchlight splays orange ripples across the darkling surface. He squints, wondering if from this vantage he might glimpse the Sicilian coast. His father always could.

The page turns and beckons Domenicus impatiently on, through a long arcade, up a flight of stairs, onward against the gradient of several ramps, leading at last to the bailey. The inner ward is deserted, masons gone home, knights back to the dormitories. Standing at the far end of the open space is the magisterial palace of the Grand Master. The Valencian calls Domenicus to a halt at the portal, leaving him to wait on the steps, alone with his thoughts.

If they raced lunatics, he would place first. He is mad to come here, to ask a favour of the Grand Master. Juan d'Homedes will never put aside personal conflict and see the wisdom in approving a new pharmacy. Domenicus has heard from knights and officials alike about the Grand Master's long fall into senility. It is widely whispered that he has accomplished near nothing throughout his long reign. He refuses to improve defences at Tripoli and ignores Gozo. Many say his sole aim is to diminish the powers of the civil authority, and he has done so by instituting a second commune at Birgu, one completely subject to his will. D'Homedes took command of the coast guards from the captain of the village and handed it over to his seneschal. He has imposed new taxes and cut the salaries of soldiers. Despite this, Emperor Charles allows d'Homedes to continue unchecked because the two men are kin in mind and motherland.

Domenicus is mad to come here. Maybe he should just leave before exciting the wrath of the most powerful man on Malta a second time and earning himself swift execution. However, he is still standing there twenty minutes later when the Valencian returns. The page escorts him through a series of hallways, up a staircase, and finally down a corridor and into a large study.

In the flickering candlelight, Grand Master Juan d'Homedes sits behind an enormous desk. The marbled floor gleams so bright it appears slippery. The broad cherry mantel and tall walnut bookshelf betray no mote of dust. In a room so big with furnishings so grand, the slight man appears even smaller. His narrow face, sharp as a hatchet, looks up from an open ledger. The Grand Master's countenance is sullen, his mouth a knife-slash, his thin hair dull white. Colourless features darken with the recognition of his visitor, and he settles into a frown. The man is a chill, waiting for a spine to race up. For a skinny fraction of his former self, Juan d'Homedes possesses a formidable air. He snaps his notebook shut and nods to a high backed chair.

"Thank you, Excellency," Domenicus manages, taking a seat. "My lord... Sire... *Molto Illustrissimo...*" he stammers, feeling hot despite the icy glare coming from the old knight.

"I know who I am. What I don't know is what you want."

"I have a request... an application actually."

The Spaniard taps bony white fingers on his desk in a flat, even tempo. Domenicus quickly produces the parchment from his satchel.

"Shall I leave it with you, my lord?" he asks, eager to rise and go.

Juan d'Homedes takes the letter, holds it up to the candlelight, and reads aloud:

Illustrious, Judicious, and Revered Grand Master,

It is my most humble entreaty that the head of the Sovereign Order of the Knights of St John will consider my petition to build and run an apothecary shop somewhere within the limits of Birgu. Having lost my mother to illness, it is in her honour that I wish to devote myself to the health of those who reside herein.

For years I served patients and shadowed surgeons, primarily Fra Édouard de Gabriac, at the Order's own Sacra Infermeria. Excellent and Gracious Sire, I have been an apprentice in the pharmacy of Antoni Zammit, where I...

The Grand Master looks up from the half-read letter. "No longer a base-court malcontent with the manners of a barn animal, hmm? You could almost pass for a gentleman." He smiles, his lips clam-like, razor-sharp and tightly sealed. "For all your flowery prose, there is no mention of official qualification."

Domenicus shakes his head. "There is none to list as yet, Sire. I thought I would submit my request now. That way, once I am certified, I would be able to start building immediately. If you deny me, there is really no sense in pursuing a licence abroad."

"We don't need another pharmacy in Birgu. There are three."

Domenicus leans forward in his chair. "With respect, your Grace, Antoni Zammit's apothecary shop is constantly and dangerously short because of demands from not only the *Sacra Infermeria* but the needs of the village and smaller clinics as well. Physicians and surgeons are forever complaining. Just ask Édouard de Gabriac."

"Nonsense!" d'Homedes thunders, slamming the parchment onto his desk. Domenicus gives a start, as does the pie-eyed page lingering at the door. "Do not presume to tell me what is lacking in my Order. No hospital is better provisioned than the *Sacra Infermeria*."

"My intention is merely to bring your attention to the concerns of not only the village apothecaries but the Order's own medical force. A fourth shop would remedy this situation."

"Denied," the old Spaniard says flatly. "I am the Grand Master, and I am exercising the very authority you once dared question."

Domenicus narrows his eyes. "You reject my application for spite?"

D'Homedes scoffs. "You think the Grand Master of the Sovereign Order of the Knights of St John would waste his time spiting a peasant?"

"Move to reconsider. The apothecary Antoni Zammit is willing to draft a letter on my behalf, as is the surgeon, Sir Édouard. Even Dr Callus has offered."

"Callus?" the Grand Master snorts. "The man is unsalted. Better he minds his own business, and keeps his dissension in check."

"Callus aside, need alone will eventually force you to build a new pharmacy. I will pay for everything and build it myself. I'm not asking for a single *scudo*, just—"

"I have said no, and my word is final. Do not misunderstand my patience."

Domenicus gives a polite but indignant smile. "I will not trespass any longer on your time."

The Grand Master waves him off with a flutter of his hand. He rolls the letter into a neat paper cylinder, closing it in the desk drawer. As Domenicus rises from the chair, it occurs to him that the only reason d'Homedes granted him occasion in the first place was for the pleasure of denying his request. As he fades into the corridor, he hears the Grand Master growl at the hapless page: "In the future, refrain from bringing unsavoury villagers into my study, or I'll have you whipped."

Unsavoury villagers. Domenicus shakes his head at the disdain with which the Order views the Maltese. He walks through the hallway towards the stairs, eyes on the floor.

"What did I tell you about walking with your head down?"

Domenicus looks up. The imperial Jean Parisot de Valette stands before him. "What brings you inside these walls, Montesa?"

"An application, *honorabile*. I was looking to build an apothecary shop. I was denied. I haven't the necessary papers."

"Then you were denied with just cause. You cannot spur before you can ride."

Domenicus frowns, irritated by the Frenchman's gumption. "I don't think the papers would have made a difference. I wanted to secure approval that my schooling would not be for nothing."

"Schooling is never for nothing."

Domenicus sighs, provoking a severe look from Valette.

"You bear the mark of one who has lived a life too easy," the knight says. "I think the galleys might be the antidote for your arrogance. Was serving the Order not a condition of your apprenticeship at the *Sacra Infermeria*?"

Domenicus furrows his brow and nods. How in the name of God does a knight of Valette's renown know these insipid details about a commoner?

"Well, perhaps you should think hard on that oath," Valette continues, "for the Order will hold you to it. A sworn vow must be viewed as sacred. Moreover, a licensed apothecary who comes trained by the Order's own surgeons would prove useful on a galley. Any skill wielding arms?"

Domenicus can scarce believe the conversation he has become drawn into. Now would be a very good time to lie. But something in Valette's face, some danger therein, compels him to the truth, and he nods again.

"Trained by your father?"

"Yes, he taught me the blade, his lessons furthered by Franco di Bonfatti. He thinks I make a decent swordsman." Domenicus could kill his tongue, which seems to have taken on a life of its own. In his desire to impress Jean Parisot de Valette, he simply forgot himself.

"Good," the knight says. "Do not become too comfortable here. I may call upon you to fulfil your end of the bargain if pressed. *Sine die.*"

***

Diana d'Alagona sits at her vanity, staring at her reflection. She smiles, pleased with her face, but most of all, her hair. She undoes the tiara of plaits, allowing wavy locks to fall over her shoulders as she takes up her large, ivory brush. Time for her nightly ritual of one hundred strokes.

Three pillar candles stand on a silver tray, lavender beeswax melting in exquisitely strange shapes. Her dark eyes flicker with the flame; her heart burns with it. She makes one hundred brushstrokes, and in her distraction, very nearly strokes once more. She has not stopped thinking about the apprentice. Not that she's really tried. She plays out the kiss he shared with Angelica and replaces the peasant girl with herself, imagining how delicious that young man's perfect mouth would taste. Her own husband's mouth is small, his lips so thin, so useless in all areas but ones of legality. Diana pushes aside these irksome thoughts, concentrates on the apprentice.

First, she must do something about Angelica Tabone. Sure, the little tutor is pretty, beautiful actually, but she would be a novice in a sport that Diana is an expert. The noblewoman looks over her shoulder to her enormous bed. She breathes an extravagant sigh. The things she would do to him in that bed…

Heavy footsteps resound from the hallway, and the chamber door swings open, sweeping a sharp draught through the bedroom. Flames flicker and blink with its cold passage. Startled, Diana drops her brush to clatter on the tabletop. Girolamo d'Alagona, head of all civil authority and more important, head of this household, enters the room. He is large, a boulder of a man. The *ḥakem* furrows his brow. "What's the matter with you, Wife?"

She smiles sweetly. "You gave me a fright is all."

He crosses the floor and bends, peering at her face. "You are flushed. Taken ill?"

"No."

"You spend too much time out of doors with that silly mouse Elisabetta Predal. Open air is not good for you."

Diana nods to humour him. "Of course, you are right. I'll wear a heavier stole from now on." She takes up her brush and runs it through her hair, a task far more pleasing than consorting with her husband.

"I will send a footman to fetch Dr Callus," he says.

"Trouble neither yourself nor the good doctor," Diana croons. "If my cheeks are red it is from exertion brought on by my vanity." She waves her brush in his direction.

"Come to bed," he says, changing into a long white nightshirt. He sprawls out on the plump feather mattress, pats the spot next to him. "Exert yourself in other ways."

"When I've finished."

"How soon is that?"

She turns away. "I've just begun. You broke my tally. I was at six."

"Come to bed," he repeats, his voice harder, more insistent.

"In a moment."

"*Now.*"

She rises from her stool and goes to him. The sooner she complies with matrimony's horizontal duty, the sooner her husband will be snoring. The man is businesslike in these transactions, no kissing, no whisperings, the act itself a series of jerky motions in one unvarying position. He does not even break a sweat, though he does let escape the occasional grunt. And as always, she feigns pleasure. Yet this night, deception is easy, for while lying with her husband, Diana closes her eyes and pretends she is lying with Domenicus.

CHAPTER THIRTY-THREE

Angelica walks the quiet road from Mdina to Birgu. It has taken over two hours, but she hardly notices. She should go straight home to prepare her uncle's dinner, but she wants to see Domenicus, if for just a few minutes. It has been a perfect day. That horrible noblewoman Diana did not visit the Predal villa this morning.

Perhaps that is why Angelica's steps are lighter, why she twirls the stem of a crown daisy in her fingers.

***

The apothecary shop is unusually busy today. Patients come waving prescriptions for everything from fenugreek and ore cinnabar to infusions of bruised garlic to treat a lexicon of ailments: fevers, sties, vapours, and evil eye.

Somehow, the apothecary and his apprentice make it through the afternoon, herbs and faces, powders and tonics all blending together as contents in a mortar. When the last of the customers have been served, the two men lean against the counter and breathe relief.

"By the stone of Sisyphus," Antoni grumbles. "Must everyone get sick on the same day?"

"You've turned a week's profit this one day," Domenicus points out.

"A month's," Antoni replies jovially. He gestures towards the backroom. "Go rest."

But the shop door opens once again. Domenicus cringes at the sound. He had hoped for at least a five-minute interlude. "And so the stone rolls back down the hill."

Perfume, strong and familiar, fills the shop. Across the counter, Antoni is slightly wan.

"My lady," he says, his voice unusually reverent. "How may I help you?" Domenicus turns. It is Diana d'Alagona. She is striking, her dress scarlet and luxurious. Two ruby-encrusted pins keep stray hair off her face, her long tresses flowing over one shoulder in a glossy black waterfall.

"Apprentice," she says, voice silken as the threads of her dress. Antoni raises his eyebrows. She does not acknowledge him.

"H-Hello," Domenicus stammers, his surprise prompting him to a rather sloppy bow. "To what does Birgu owe the honour of your presence?"

"The *hakem*'s prescription."

"Prescription?" He stares dumbly at the paper nestled between her jewelled fingers.

She gives a pretty laugh. "For my husband's nausea, remember?"

"Oh, yes…" Her explanation gives Domenicus pause; there are at least three apothecary shops in Mdina. As though reading his mind, Diana clears her voice, waves the prescription.

"Seems the neighbouring pharmacies are short this particular medicine."

Antoni reaches over the counter and takes the paper from her. "*Buzbiez,*" he reads aloud. "That's easy. But the day has been busy. I'll have to check if there's any left. A quick moment, *Barunessa.*" He pulls aside the long drape hanging in the doorway and disappears into the backroom, the curtain sweeping back in place to fill his void.

Alone with Diana, Domenicus shifts uneasily. He quickly turns his attention to the jars on the countertop, replaces their missing lids. After a minute, he feels her intense gaze and looks up. "Are you all right? Your face is red. I'll bring you water." He turns for the back room, but she takes hold of his wrist.

"No. Stay. I'm fine. The ride from Mdina under an afternoon sun, that's all."

He looks down at her hand, wrapped firmly around his wrist. "The *hakem* allows you to ride without an equerry?"

Diana releases him promptly. "The *hakem* does not know every move I make." She smiles, dropping her voice to a whisper. "I buy the silence of the servants with *his* purse."

Antoni draws aside the curtain, fennel plant in hand. He wraps it in linen and holds it out to Diana, who drops coins onto the counter and flicks her fingers dismissively when he offers back the change. "Would the apprentice be so kind as to walk a lady to her horse?"

"Afraid not," Domenicus says flatly. "The shop has been overrun all day."

She sweeps her hand grandly at the vacant bench. "The shop is empty now. Besides, what if I were robbed? Ever would it lay on your conscience."

Domenicus sighs, taking the medicine. Diana slinks her hand around his upper arm and squeezes. He looks warily over his shoulder, hoping for a rescue from Antoni, but the bemused apothecary offers nothing more than a useless shrug.

***

Angelica turns onto the street where the Zammit apothecary shop stands, her fingers still twirling the flower she plucked an hour earlier. Beyond the spinning white petals, she catches a glimpse of Domenicus emerging from the pharmacy, Diana d'Alagona on his arm. Angelica feels her stomach pit, knees buckle. At once, she is hot all over, cold all over. Diana had flirted openly with him yesterday, but Angelica did not think for a second that the attraction was mutual. She will soon find out. She skitters behind a large farm cart, crouches, listens.

***

Domenicus allows himself to be taken by the hand, led across the road, past a cart and into a tight alleyway untouched by sunlight. "Signora—"

"*Diana.* Discard formalities when we are alone."

"I don't think it correct to be so familiar."

"Discard correctness also."

Domenicus is stumped for words. "So... The doctor diagnosed your husband's condition?"

"Truly, I'm not interested in discussing my husband's health."

"Then why come all the way here seeking his medicine?"

Diana halts with a sigh and faces him. "You are like a pony in need of tough schooling—a truly striking creature, but rather stupid. I came to see *you*. I paid a local doctor to forge the prescription."

"You're not serious." But he can see by her face that she is perfectly. He shakes his head. "I can understand a servant taking your bribes, but a doctor bound by the Hippocratic Oath?"

"Every man has a price: doctor, priest, knight. Even a disciple of our Lord and Saviour Jesus Christ. The Son of God, sold for a few pieces of silver." Diana touches his elbow. He watches with discomfort as her fingers walk up his arm. "I am here to present an overture. My house, tomorrow afternoon. I shall be free of my husband the entire day. In my private chamber, you will spend a few hours acting as my apprentice."

Domenicus swallows hard, unacquainted with such frank speech, especially from a woman. He feels himself blushing, but tries to mask his embarrassment with sternness. "You should be careful in your overtures. Here, even the cobbles have ears."

"I will give the cobbles a few *scudi* for their silence." Diana produces several coins, dashes them carelessly to the ground. She then presses herself against him, pushing him flush to the wall and, using the folds of her dress to conceal her hands, slips one into his britches.

Shocked, Domenicus takes her firmly by the shoulders and pushes her back. "Stop this."

"Why?" Diana takes his hand in hers, kissing his fingers. "Do you not find me beautiful at all?" She runs her tongue over his knuckles, her eyes on his.

Despite his anger, he feels himself stirring. "I'm not blind," he says, voice husky, hating the effect she is having on him. "What I see of you is quite beautiful."

"You are welcome to see the rest of me." She drops his hand and kisses his lips.

"*Stop*. Please." He turns his face away. The alley is empty. "Where is your horse?"

Diana laughs. "There isn't a man on this island who does not covet an invitation to my bed. Who are you to refuse?"

Enough is enough. "I am *not* interested, my lady—"

"*Diana*."

"*My lady*. I said no. You are married and to the *hakem* no less. I have already made an enemy of the Grand Master; I hardly need to earn myself the wrath of the *Capitano Della Verga* too. Besides, your fascination with me does not surpass your bed."

"Such is a happy sentiment for any man," she replies.

"I am in love with someone else."

Diana scoffs. "*Love?* I don't want your love, you arrogant animal. And if you're worried about your lovely little orphan finding out, you needn't be. I exercise the fullest discretion. The *hakem* knows nothing of my peccadilloes. You would not be the first, not the tenth for that matter. He, however, is not as careful. I know my husband tastes the fruit of other trees."

"I feel for you. I do."

"And I couldn't possibly care less. His affairs are his affair. My husband's title gives me claim to many things. Faithfulness is not one of them." She shrugs. "Run along now, before the apothecary's suspicions are raised."

Domenicus turns to go, still holding the wrapped fennel plant. Diana reaches for his elbow. He stops but gives the noblewoman his back. "I would think hard on this proposition, Apprentice, unless you wish to spend your days begging for alms in the street. I have very powerful friends, the head of all medical practitioners among them. A man of your ambitions has much to gain in pleasing me, much to lose in disappointing."

***

The taste of bile is strong in Angelica's mouth. She remains crouched behind the farm cart long after Diana d'Alagona has left, long after Domenicus has returned to work, long after her legs have cramped with fatigue. Finally, the twinge in her calves and pain in her knees force her to rise. She doesn't know what to do, whom to tell. Part of her wants to storm into the apothecary shop and confront Domenicus; the rest of her wants to chase the noblewoman down and tear out her hair. Either way, she has to do *something*.

She does nothing. A tumult has been raised inside her head that keeps her from thinking straight. So many questions now demand answers. Why did Domenicus not refuse Diana outright? Why did he take so long to say he was in love with someone else? What should have been an iron rejection was dough. Angelica swallows hard. Would he really go through with Diana's overture? The noblewoman, though clearly a shameless slut, is an undeniable beauty. She, moreover, will be experienced, skilled in a realm foreign to Angelica. Even so, Domenicus *loves* Angelica. Why would he go behind her back for so base an encounter? Why would he do that to her? She closes her eyes. Perhaps he would not be doing it *to* her. Perhaps he is thinking only of what he would be doing for himself.

Angelica plays the conversation over in her mind. There was threat in Diana's voice. Domenicus must have sensed the warning in her words. Low or lofty, people fear Diana d'Alagona. And she knows it. The snake will try to sabotage Domenicus in his aspirations. She could easily poison the Protomedicus with slander hissed from her reptilian tongue...

No, Alonso Predal is a man resistant to the noblewoman's venom.

That's it! Angelica will tell Alonso first thing in the morning. He'll know what to do, how to fix Diana d'Alagona. But the time between now and tomorrow seems impossibly long. And there is still Domenicus to deal with. Angelica's trust in him is implicit, but then again, this trust has never been tested. She thinks so hard it hurts, finally deciding to wait it silently out. It is on him to bring it up without prodding. She will act her regular self, behave as if everything is fine, thereby gaining the truth of his quality. On shallow breath, she crosses the way and pushes open the pharmacy door.

***

Robert walks home on a tired stride. He has not been himself since that gruesome discovery two days past. Dark thoughts consume him. He looks to his beloved sky to lift his spirits but sees only a meek sun fading behind filaments of cloud. The closest he came to heaven today was in watching a great osprey take flight.

As he nears his house, he catches a series of distant but familiar bleats. It is the goat formerly of Farrugia's farm, lately Robert's charge. He rounds a corner, eager to see his four-legged friend, but is greeted instead by one on two.

"Domenicus," he says, surprised.

"I'm in a terrible scrape."

"What's wrong? So long as it doesn't involve a dead body, it can't be all that terrible."

"The dead I can handle. The living are another matter entirely, especially when they themselves are quite deadly. Consequently, my predicament may involve a dead body. Mine."

"Are the riddles really necessary?"

"The wife of the *hakem* wants to sleep with me."

Robert feels his weary features come alive. "*What?*"

"She came to Zammit's shop late today with a forged prescription. She led me into an alley and demanded I go to her tomorrow."

283

"Will you?"

Domenicus hesitates before speaking. "I don't know what to do. If I went through with it, I'm confident Diana wouldn't tell Angelica, though I can't be sure—there is no friendship between them. However, *I* would know. It would hang over me, over *us*, for always. I love Angelica too much. I could never hurt her, whether or not she found out about it. And I so want to tell her everything."

Robert looks hard at his friend's face. "You seem unsure."

"Diana d'Alagona will interfere with my medical ambitions if I don't do as she wants."

"Angelica works for the Protomedicus. Naturally, she'd counter anything Diana could come up with to sully your reputation."

"Diana is the *hakem*'s wife. Her word would carry more weight than Angelica's. Also, it is to be expected that Angelica would speak favourably of the man she is courting."

"True enough."

"Robert, help me here. What would you do?"

"I will go in your stead. Diana d'Alagona is stunning. And vicious." He grins. "I'd let her hurt me."

Domenicus snickers, shakes his head. "Her beauty is trifling. Were she ugly, my predicament remains the same. Seriously, what would you do in my place?"

"Tell Angelica."

At first, Domenicus does not respond. Finally: "There is no way to win this. No matter what I do, Angelica will be hurt, either by my betrayal or my consigning us to a life of poverty."

"You have to tell her, and that's that," Robert says. "For the same reason you told me to go to the gendarmes. Think if she finds out somehow. Think if someone overheard Diana's request and relays it to Angelica or worse, her uncle. You will have made foes of Malta's three governing powers then— the Order, the *Università, and* the Church. Besides, is Diana d'Alagona really worth losing the girl you have loved for so long? And make your mind up to this: women sense everything. My mother knows every move I make, often before I make it."

***

Twilight covers land and sea in a heavy black blanket, making shapes and forms near impossible to discern from the window, where Angelica sits, brooding. She harks back to her walk home with Domenicus. He led all conversation, chewing over the weather, the state of the fields, anything to fill the silence. If she didn't know the truth, she would have found it odd that he never even asked about the obvious tension between herself and Diana. As it is, his lack of inquisitiveness made sense. Angelica upbraids herself for having not told him sooner about their history.

Initially, she did not want to give Diana the satisfaction of humiliating her yet again, even through a story. But as she thinks over today's events, Angelica wonders if she should have brought it up. At the time, she worried that if she mentioned Diana first, Domenicus would somehow catch on that she knew something, and therefore only admit to the noblewoman's advance because he had no choice. All Angelica knows is he didn't even broach the subject of Diana d'Alagona or anything that might be connected to her, no matter the degrees of separation. No talk of Mdina, of law, or chambermaids, no mention of apothecary shops, of prescriptions, or herbs.

Now, anger has replaced Angelica's concern about his aspirations being dashed. Domenicus had the chance to fess up, but knowingly, actively concealed Diana's proposition. That can only mean he intends to go to her tomorrow. And that he could barely look Angelica in the face only lends further credence to her conviction. Yet, even so, she stares out over the dark field hoping against hope that he will come to her window and make everything all right.

A slow time passes with no arrival. Just another bead of hurt in a string of many. Everything she thought about Domenicus Montesa is wrong. He is not the honourable man she believed him to be. He is no less a spineless bastard with a heart that beats deception. These thoughts are long hours consuming her. She does not make it to bed, falling into fractured sleep at the windowsill.

CHAPTER THIRTY-FOUR

Domenicus too has spent a restless night, though he is far from tired as he stands outside the rectory door, fist poised to knock, legs set to run. He does not understand his apprehension. It is the same feeling that swept him the day he came here to confess his love. Strange that after all this time Angelica Tabone still has the ability to make him nervous. But perhaps his apprehension makes sense after all—he has never before even considered deceiving her. He swallows hard and delivers the door a solid knock. Given the hour, he expects Angelica will answer and is surprised to see Father Tabone standing opposite him a moment later.

"You're too late," the priest says.

"Too late?"

"I'm going to take the liberty of assuming you did not come here to gaze upon my pretty face. My niece has already left for the day."

Domenicus smiles with unease. "You look well, Father. ...So, Angelica is not here?"

"Gone almost an hour."

"That's odd."

"As was her behaviour this night past," the priest remarks. "Her mood was black."

"Oh?"

"She told me to go fix my own supper. In nine years, she has never told me to go fix my own supper. I've noticed an unhappy change in her since she accepted work at the Predal house. You know my Angelica best. What's gotten into her?"

"Everything seemed fine yesterday."

"Mmm. A sure indication everything is not." Father Tabone nods to the road. "Go on. If you whip your horse, you will overtake her."

Tramonto closes the rock-strewn distance between Birgu and Mdina, four iron-shod hooves raising a thick brown cloud that marks the steed's passage. Neither the coarse pathway nor its flanking fields bear any sign of Angelica. Domenicus feels bad for working his horse so hard but cannot allow him to rest until they make the hilltop city. It is half an hour before the cathedral of Mdina breaks the sky from its towering perch. Domenicus digs his heels, pushing Tramonto for a final thrust against the mean gradient. At the crown of the rise, he reins, dismounts and, taking the cracked leather strap into his hand, leads the charger over the drawbridge and under the city's horseshoe entrance.

There is scarce any foot traffic, most of Mdina's population still breaking fast. Tramonto's *clip-clopping* hooves, the snuffle of his breath, are loud against the stillness of the fortress city. Local merchants set up shop in the town square, a cobbled piazza laid out before the cathedral doors. A hymn escapes the walls of a cloistered Carmelite convent, the haunting voices soon lost to the church bells, tolling in call to Matins.

Then, Domenicus spots Angelica, easily fifty paces ahead, passing through the Predal gates.

***

The noon hour has come. Diana d'Alagona lies on her side, elbow digging deep into a fat silk pillow, cheek resting in the bowl of her hand. Her eyes are fixed on the chamber door. She had a little fright in the garden yesterday evening, when, over marzipan and honey sweets, her husband dropped a comment about her visiting Birgu that morning. A barrister from the *Università* had caught a glimpse of her and mentioned this in passing to the *hakem*. She quickly invented a story about procuring silver from a jeweller and even produced a new bracelet as proof. Her testimony seemed enough to satisfy the lord of the courts.

Now, everything is taken care of: husband gone, servants plied with busy-work, a fine vintage waiting to be poured, nails lacquered, hair washed, perfume dabbed on every pulse point.

This scene belies the sentiments that vexed her only hours earlier. Last night, and for the first time in her life, Diana felt a pang of self-doubt. It occurred to her that the apprentice might indeed pass on her proposition. Now, however, her lost confidence has returned. The apprentice *will* come. His little orphan confirmed this at the Predal house over breakfast today when she mentioned he took ill yester evening. Clearly, he invented some illness as a guise meant to keep him from work and Angelica from troubling him. Diana is impressed. Domenicus Montesa is craftier than she gave him credit. She will reward his cunning.

Footsteps echo from the long corridor outside the bedchamber. Her heart races, flawless half-moon fingernails almost finding themselves at the mercy of her teeth. Like a bird preening its feathers, she primps her hair and quickly adjusts her position, taking a shape that accentuates the curve of her hip. She works to control her breathing, forcing an even rise and fall of her chest. Then, closing delicately shadowed eyes, she pouts her mouth.

Diana is ready for her guest. Each footfall resonates in her core. Then, there is silence—hanging, torturous, delicious silence. A hand closes around the doorknob. Her breath comes faster. The doorknob turns. It takes all her will to keep her eyes shut. She feels the light wind of the door opening. Someone enters the room. The door closes.

"My lady."

She opens her eyes. "Apprentice."

Domenicus Montesa stands with his hands loosely at his sides. His face is sun-kissed, light grey eyes luminous against golden skin. He is stunning. She beckons him with a slow curl of her forefinger. He crosses the room, stops at the edge of the bed. She pats the space before her inviting him to sit. He does, his back to her.

"I knew you'd come," Diana says.

"You left me little recourse."

She slides her hand under his shirt, over his skin, up the curve of his spine and feels his muscles stiffen beneath her fingers. "Take wine. It is superb, better than the best of Italian cellars."

"No, thank you."

"So, you told Miss Tabone you fell ill? Very resourceful."

Domenicus shrugs. "It will keep her away. Besides, that I'm here proves I am ill."

Diana digs sharp nails into his flesh, causing his back to arch. He looks with severity over his shoulder. "Because of you, I stand to lose not only the woman I love but my head with her, should your husband learn of this."

Diana rolls her eyes. "Oh stop. Just you keep quiet, and everything will be fine." She smiles, rises to her knees. "You are a beautiful thing."

"Let's just move on to business."

"Business?"

"Do not look so surprised. Is that not what this is? I need something you can help me get, and you have named your price. It is no different from the exchanges taking place right now in the market square—" Diana cuts him off, taking his face aggressively into her hands, kissing him hard on the mouth. This time, he responds. She slides her hands over his rippled stomach, runs her fingers along the thin trail of hair leading from his belly button down into his trousers. He inhales audibly. She pulls off his shirt, pausing to kiss his chest, and tugs at his drawstring.

"I want you. Now."

Before the apprentice might fulfil her want, the bedroom door opens a second time, sweeping in a new blast of air. This time, the Protomedicus Alonso Predal stands framed by the wood of the doorway. Diana's face contorts in horror. Domenicus smiles. He pushes himself up off the bed, puts his shirt back on, and moves next to Alonso. Diana tries in vain to control her shock. She sits up, straightens out her dress, smoothes her hair, Predal's eyes mercilessly on her.

Diana is left with one resounding thought: Domenicus Montesa is craftier than she gave him credit. She will punish his cunning.

"M-*Magnificus*," she stammers, placing both feet on the floor and rising. "I-I can explain… It's not what you think—"

"No, of course not. Knowing you Diana, it's probably much, much worse."

She lifts her chin and points an accusing finger at Domenicus. "It was *him*! He came here under false pretences, did me dishonour, did my husband dishonour!"

Alonso raises his eyebrows. "Is that so? How did he accomplish all that?"

"He… he said he came here seeking an audience with the *hakem*, that he might endorse his application for an apothecary shop. I told him my husband wasn't home. I gave him permission to wait in the salon, and the next thing I knew, he was knocking on my chamber door, the pig. He tried to force himself on me! He should be strung up—"

"Enough!" Alonso roars, startling Diana, a woman startled by no one. "Not another word! Your ability to lie convincingly has abandoned you, along with your soul, your heart, your good looks. I am here because I know the truth. When this young man rebuffed your advance, you threatened to use your position to sway me against him. You are a very stupid woman, Diana, to use me as a pawn in games of coercion."

The noblewoman straightens to her full height and narrows her eyes hatefully. "Alonso Predal, you do not hold one-tenth of the power my husband holds. He will strip you your title. What's more, you have no proof of these allegations. So go ahead, you grasping little worm, and tell the *hakem*. If it is a war you want, you will have one. But understand something first. My arsenal holds many a weapon. For starters, all I need do is tell my husband you are jealous of his status. You wish to use his marriage against him and enlisted this commoner here to assist you in your insidious plan."

Domenicus glances anxiously at Alonso. The Protomedicus, however, bursts out in laughter, his high-pitched giggle infuriating Diana, her fists balled at her side. She wants to smash him. Alonso dabs at his eyes and sighs, returning himself to a state of grimness. "You, my dear, are not the only one skilled in the art of war," he says evenly, pulling the forged prescription from his waistcoat pocket. "Naturally, I wouldn't be here if I didn't have proof."

"Proof of what?"

Alonso and Domenicus turn. Standing behind them is the chief man of the house, the chief man of the island, Girolamo d'Alagona. From the surprise in their faces, this was not part of their plan. The *hakem* breaks between Alonso and Domenicus. Diana shrinks back, a faded shadow of the formidable woman she lately was.

"Woman," he rumbles, "Explain. What are these men doing in *my* private chamber?"

Domenicus clears his throat. "Good Sir, if I may—"

"No, you may not!" the *hakem* bellows.

"Girolamo," Diana begins, struggling to recover from this second, much worse shock. "I—I..." She narrows her eyes, stands taller, changes her tone. "How dare you barge in here with accusations on your tongue? You awful, barbarous man!"

"I have made no accusations. I require an explanation. Then I will decide where is fit to lay the blame and with it, the tip of my sword."

Alonso bows to the *Capitano Della Verga*. "Signore, please, allow me to—"

"*No!*" Diana shouts, rushing forward, closing a hand around her husband's arm. "He will lie!"

Alonso smiles. "Lie? Madam, you are wrong. I was simply going to ask the *hakem* about his unfortunate stomach condition. I thought I might be of some service."

Girolamo yanks his arm from Diana's grip and swings round. "*What stomach condition?*"

Alonso wears a perfectly bewildered expression. "You suffer an ailment of the bowels, no?"

"No, I do not!" the *hakem* rages.

Alonso puts his hand on the apprentice's back. "Montesa, lad, tell His Grace why we are here." Domenicus fires Alonso a wary glance. The Protomedicus gives the young man's shoulder a rallying squeeze. "Go on, it's all right. Tell him how you came to me in concern over his condition."

Domenicus inhales. "Well... Most Venerable Lord *hakem*... Um..."

"Spit it out, damn you!" Girolamo roars.

"Your wife brought a prescription to the apothecary shop where I work. She said that you suffered terrible nausea and that a physician had ordered you special medicine. I was troubled and brought the prescription to the Protomedicus so he might treat you personally, given that you hold such an important office. And having studied medicine for some years, I knew it would take more than a little fennel plant to remedy the ailment your wife described."

Girolamo flashes. He speaks low, his voice hissing through clenched teeth. "I have no such condition." Diana feels her husband's eyes hard on her though he addresses the apprentice. "This apothecary shop, who runs it, Boy?"

"Antoni Zammit."

Girolamo closes the widening gap between himself and Diana "Visiting Birgu to buy jewellery from a silversmith, eh? You rutting cat!" He cuffs her full across the cheek with the backside of his hand. She reels but catches her balance. Through the tears that have sprung to her eyes, she sees Girolamo turn his fury on Alonso. "Strip Zammit his licence! He is banned from the profession forthwith! He can starve in the street."

"With respect sir," Domenicus cuts in, "*Mastru* Zammit is innocent. That, I will swear to, on my mother's grave."

"It is true," Alonso says. "Zammit will keep his licence and his shop."

Girolamo turns back to Diana. "Then who? Who dares to pluck the fruit of my tree?"

She thrusts her chin at Domenicus. Her husband charges at the apprentice. "*Bastard!*" Domenicus easily dodges the fierce but clumsy blow, Girolamo's fist connecting with only empty air. The misplaced force twists his body, giving Alonso the chance to hook his arm around the *hakem*.

"Your wife lies!" Alonso says, pushing the turbulent man to the wall. "She suborned a local doctor to write a prescription then went to Birgu to seduce this boy. When her charms failed, she threatened him. He came to me for help. Domenicus Montesa never touched your wife. I am here to insist she end these intrigues and leave him alone."

***

Early that morning, Domenicus had spotted Angelica passing through the Predal gate and called out her name. She turned. He was close enough to see her features flood with an odd blend of relief and anger as she crossed her arms over her chest.

"What are *you* doing here?"

"I have to talk to you," he replied.

"Oh you do, do you?"

He was cut by her sharpness of tone. "Why the hostility? And why are you here so early?"

"You, Domenicus Montesa, are in a position unsuitable to ask questions."

Brow furrowed, he took three or four tentative steps forward. "Very well. Then allow me a few words."

"A very few."

"Something happened yesterday, and I did not tell you sooner because I was afraid."

"And now you're not afraid?"

"Oh no. I'm still afraid, but I'll tell you nonetheless."

Narrow-eyed, Angelica tilted her head to the side and waited. Domenicus exhaled. "Diana d'Alagona came to Zammit's shop yesterday. She wants me to… She wants me to… She wants *me*. And she made it abundantly clear that if I did not give in she would damage my reputation, ruin my medical ambitions. But these ambitions are trifling if they come at the cost of deceiving you."

Angelica's severe expression remained unchanged. "Even though she assured you she would exercise the fullest discretion? That *your lovely little orphan* would never find out?"

The revelation took a moment to register. "What? How...? You *heard* what she said?"

"Every. Last. Word. You were right when you said the cobbles have ears."

"Why did you not put it to me sooner?"

"Because I had to see if you would act honourably. If you knew I knew, your actions would have been compromised."

Domenicus frowned. "Your trust in me is so fleeting that you would test my honour?"

"You gave me no choice. My trust in you was absolute until I witnessed your soft resistance to her advance. You put forth the most cursory of objections. A man of substance would have told me yesterday, but you chose to talk about clouds and grass. My trust in you was shaken by your own hand."

"That isn't fair."

Angelica bristled. "*Fair?* Do not talk of fairness after the night I spent! I would not wish such a night on anyone. What played out in my head was torture! Why did you wait so long to tell me?"

Domenicus withdrew into himself, shoulders tense. "So long? It is less than one turn of the earth since she came to me! By your own admission, you heard everything. I don't ever want to hurt you, but I also don't want to spend the rest of my days slaving in the quarries or worse. Diana d'Alagona could make that happen. I had to come up with a plan before opening the lid of this very dangerous box. And you, Angelica Tabone, have no reason to be cross with me. I am here, now, telling you the truth of my own volition, and you know it's the truth."

Angelica set her mouth, glanced in all directions. She took Domenicus by the hand and entered into the complex warren of laneways, one corner turning to two then three then four, and when at last they reached a shadowy crook free of doors or windows, she looked up at him and whispered, "So, what is your plan?"

He spread his hands. "I don't have one."

She sighed. "It figures. Well lucky for you, I do." Domenicus was relieved beyond measure: if Angelica had relinquished him in her mind last night, he knew she still loved him with all her heart.

"I'm going to tell Alonso Predal," she says. "We have an ally in him. He hates Diana. *That's* why I'm here so early, to catch him before he leaves. Now go. If Diana sees you here with me, it is ruined. This is a settling of scores over twelve years in the making. She will come to the Predal house soon, nine bells as usual. I'll make it known that you fell ill yesterday and are spending today in bed."

"Good idea. That will buy us time. Act fast, she expects me at noon."

"Have Zammit put you to work in the back room away from public view."

"All right." Domenicus turned. Turned back. "Angelica?"

"Yes?"

"Thank you."

She nodded and started off. He caught her elbow and turned her back around. "Angelica?"

"Yes?"

"For every second you remained wakeful, I am sorry. My apologies to your uncle also."

"Why?"

"Because he was made to fix his own supper for the first time in nine years."

***

Now, Girolamo d'Alagona, *Capitano Della Verga*, staggers on his feet. He places a trembling hand against the bedside table to steady himself, all the while fighting to control tears of rage, of pain. His unbearable agony needs an outlet. With a loud cry, he puts his fist through the door, tearing flesh from his knuckles. Despite the blood, the injury does not register. Right now, there is only one hurt he senses. And it brings his body more pain than any physical injury could do. His skin is the only thing keeping him from going all places at once. As he stands in his private chamber with the object of his wife's desire, a haze of unreality settles about him. He does not know whether to kill her, kill the boy, or kill himself. All he does know is that he wants to unknow this awful thing. An invisible hand has gripped the heart in his chest and will not let go, squeezing tighter with each passing second. He wants to die. He thinks he's going to. Malta's most powerful son has been rendered nothing more than a disconsolate cuckold.

He clutches his knotted chest and glances to the watery shapes before him, which were lately two men: "*Leave*," he manages. "*Now.*"

"You are not all right," Alonso says softly. "Your hand, it's a bloody mess. I can help."

"*I said go. Get out!*"

***

Diana sits at her vanity table, stroking her beloved locks, running her hand over the long glossy strands as if caressing a cat napping in her lap. Shards of broken glass, which once made up the huge mirror, lie all about the table and surrounding floor, the ivory brush she used to smash the looking glass flung into some dark corner.

She touches her scalp. And shrieks at the sensation of her baldness.

The moment Alonso Predal and Domenicus Montesa quit the d'Alagona house, Girolamo locked his philandering wife in their private quarter, returning an hour later with a quivering barber-surgeon forced at sword-point to cut off Diana's hair. Girolamo held his wife down as the barber sheared the hysterical woman like a lamb. For half an hour, the grand house

294

shuddered with her lacerating screams. And when it was done, the *hakem* once again turned his key in the outside lock without so much as a word. It will be long months before he allows her to move freely around the house, longer still before she gains permission to venture out of doors.

Tears stream down her face, over her bruised, inflamed cheek. Diana has never known these feelings of humiliation, vulnerability, ugliness. She wants to vomit. She stares at her once beautiful hair now lying limp across her knees as if at a murdered child. With each passing minute, however, her terrible grief is swallowed by ravenous anger.

Oh, how the apprentice will pay for this. And his little orphan, she will pay, too.

Diana will wear Angelica's hair as a wig.

CHAPTER THIRTY-FIVE

Tonight is the decadent feast before the dutiful famine. Tonight kicks off Carnival, three days of revelry and abandon to usher in the forty of Lenten sacrifice. Tonight the divide between rich and poor isn't quite so great. The market square is alive, heaving with peasants and nobles, knights and knaves, all of them drinking and dancing, laughing and singing.

Katrina is lost in the colour, the heady sights and smells of the piazza. The warm air moves with a blend of scents, the powdery-sweet and the salty, the smoked and the slow-roasted. It is as if a rainbow has burst and come down in a vibrant shower all over Birgu. Tinted lanterns hang from wires like charms from a necklace. Garlands of Sicilian carnations nod over ancient limestone walls amid brightly coloured candles that burn low and could just as easily be glowing fruit. Dazzling costumes transform this ordinarily drab village into the palace courtyard of some magical land. Some costumes are simple, some elaborate, depending largely on its wearer's purse. As though summoned from the pages of a hundred fairy tales, they are all here: sackcloth siren and silk pixie, bejewelled emperor and tattered buccaneer, feathered falcon and gossamer butterfly. There are dragons, and slayers to hunt them, ponies, and princes to ride them.

There are games of chance, contests of skill: knife throwing for the competitive, card games for the straight-faced. There are draughts and dice and cockfights. Anything that can be raced is, from small boats in the harbour and bareback horses along the Strada Reale to saddled pigs in the narrowest lane. Street performers turn somersaults, musicians pluck lively strings, fire-eaters swallow and spout flames, all for a crowd gasping its pleasure. Febrile enthusiasm passes through the square and, though twilight in mid-February, the closeness of so many in such a tight space draws sweat.

Katrina brushes away loose strands already clinging to her damp forehead. Earlier today, she decided that since Robert had planned to come as himself, she too would not bother with a costume. She pulls him now to the edge of the square.

"Look!" she says, stopping among revellers to watch a popular local dance, which plays out the capture of a Maltese bride by a Moorish corsair. When it ends, Katrina rises to the tips of her toes and, straining against applause, speaks in Robert's ear. "Come on, there's a card game we're going to play." She runs off, knowing Robert will catch up.

At the first vacant game table, Katrina sits on a stool and drops two coins before Reno Barberi, the portly dealer busy shuffling his deck. He glances up and appraises her with a loud snort. He then shifts his gaze to Robert, as if looking for permission before accepting Katrina's bet.

"One and Thirty, the game of Spanish royalty," Reno announces, taking her coins.

"Ooh," Katrina coos.

Robert crouches so that his chin is at her shoulder, strands of his careless hair straying against her neck. "The goal is to come closest to a score of thirty-one with three cards of the same suit. It's unlikely your first three cards will accomplish this, so you can face up and discard one card, replacing it with the top card on the deck," he says. "Continue discarding one card at a time until either of you knocks twice. After the knock, players are allowed one last discard. Then you both show your hands. Ace is eleven points, royal faces ten, the rest their number value. Closest to thirty-one of the same suit wins. Understood?"

Katrina frowns. "What's a suit? And a hand? You mean I show him my hands?"

"Perhaps reconsider trying your hand at cards."

"Which now? Left or right?"

"Good God," Robert snaps. "Let's go."

"*No.* Just be clearer with the rules, stupid."

Robert sighs, and of course, explains the game a second time. Eyes shining, Reno equals Katrina's two-coin bet and lays three cards face down. He takes three for himself and places the deck between them. "First discard," he says.

Katrina peels the corners of her cards up off the table. She glances to Robert. "If I have exactly thirty-one of the same suit, I win?"

"That's right."

"Then I win." She faces up her cards, ace, king, jack, all leering at the dealer. Robert gives a low whistle. Katrina grins, gathers the coins, rises from the stool. Reno reaches swiftly across the table and takes her wrist.

"Beginner's luck," he says. "A rematch. Double and half. Five *habba.*"

"Don't be an idiot, Kat," Robert says. "You were lucky. You'll lose what you just won."

She shrugs. "I'll be no worse off than I was five minutes ago."

Three games and twenty *habba* later, Katrina flashes her winning hand. Reno Barberi throws his cards furiously down without even looking at his opponent's. She smiles sweetly. "A rematch?"

Reno jumps up, his large, angry form turning over the table and forcing onlookers to hop back. Robert grabs Katrina's hand and yanks her behind him into the throng, through its narrow gullet, until the fat celebrating mass swallows them whole.

"You're just not happy unless things end in violence, eh?" Robert says.

"It's not my fault that great lumbering brute is too stupid to win his own game. He should be cheating, or in the least, smart enough to sense when his opponent is." Katrina stops walking and takes Robert's elbow. "Wait." She turns up his palm and drops half the prize money into his hand. "Without you, it would have been far more difficult to hustle that idiot."

Robert snickers. "You're just lucky he was too put out to look at your cards."

***

Walking past another such game table is Domenicus Montesa, wearing all black, masked across the eyes with a length of linen, a Bilbaon rapier sheathed at his side, fingers laced with an angel's. He gives Angelica's hand a little squeeze. Her hair is pinned and woven with white daisies, soft ringlets falling at her ears. Sewn to the back of her dress are wings, made from twisted reed and gossamer, catching with the warm light of hanging lanterns.

They thread the throng and end up in the centre of the square. Domenicus shrugs, bows, and asks for a dance. An easy wind blows northerly, shifting bright orange tongues of flame to lick seaward. Torch smoke furls and unfurls all around them, making it seem as though the village is set among clouds. The music is spirited, a peasant orchestra of fiddles and lutes, fifes and flutes. Their feet are a tangle as they try making sense of the complicated folk dance, at first putting in an honest effort, but after several ridiculous attempts, just poking fun at each other's missteps. Soon, the lively tune ends, and a slower one begins. A sole musician carries this song, striking the wire strings of his dulcimer with a soft, even rhythm. It is ancient and noble poetry, each note telling its own story. Domenicus pulls Angelica close and lowers his mouth to her ear.

"He denied her a wig."

Angelica smiles a dark smile that belies her attire. "The queen has lost her crown. And with it, her power. We should name her Samson. But we'd first have to blind her with hot pokers."

Domenicus arcs his eyebrows, pulls slightly back. "My, I shouldn't ever want to cross you."

The malice vanishes from Angelica's face. "No, don't say that. You must understand, she has done me many wrongs. Some I could forgive, but not the times she made my mother cry. I have so few memories of my mother. I cannot bear the ones of her in tears. Other than the corsair who killed my father, Diana d'Alagona is the only person I've ever hated." Angelica brings her forehead to his chest, closes her eyes. "Please, don't think I'm awful."

Domenicus kisses her hair. "I think you are amazing. And wonderful. ...And I think also of how I cannot wait to wake up next to you every day for the rest of my life."

She looks up at him in surprise. "Oh?"

He holds her face. "I've sent an application to the school in Sicily. Should I be admitted, you are coming with me. You see, I plan to work up enough nerve to propose. Naturally, being the milksop I am, I'll dither and dally, and trip over my tongue. But, by the end of it, you will know that I love you, I have always loved you, and I want to marry you." He pauses, watching her expectantly, unable to read her expression. "...So? What do you say? Say something. Anything. Just don't say no."

"Propose, idiot, and you will have my answer."

"Didn't I just?"

"No... Last I heard you were still planning to work up the nerve."

"Right, right." He takes her hands nervously in his and drops to his knee in the village square. Many dancing revellers take notice and lose their footing, stepping on each other's toes. Most stop moving altogether. Domenicus feels himself blushing. "Angelica Tabone—"

She can no longer contain herself. "Yes! Yes, I will!"

"But I haven't—"

"I don't care!" She bends and kisses him eagerly, right there in the centre of the square, right there in front of God and everybody, inspiring applause and whooping, along with a few disapproving *hmph*s from gossips delighted to witness the niece of the *kappillan* engaging in lewd public conduct.

***

At the opposite end of the square, Franco di Bonfatti and Marcello di Ruggieri join Gui de la Fon, a hot-tempered redheaded Provençal, and Cristoval Domingo, a Spaniard recently promoted from page, in a game of knife-throwing. The Frenchman and Spaniard actually throw their knives at the target board, unlike their respective countrymen, who are at war.

An hour later, Marcello has bested Franco, Gui, and Cristoval, two Parisian knights, the Prior of Barletta, a German page, and three Maltese villagers. Franco allows his victorious best friend to lead him to a seedy drinking hole swarming with men and prostitutes. Lilla, the flaxen from the watchtower, is among them. Franco meets her eyes, and she quickly looks away.

"I'll wait outside," Franco says, equally uncomfortable.

Marcello shrugs and disappears inside, leaving Franco to lean against the wall. The night smells of honey sweets and perfume, torch smoke and fresh bread, baked specially for those whose appetites are hearty with drink. It is a profitable festival for bakers. Smoke billows from street lamps, rolls from pipes, rises from fire pits set with rotating spits. Franco watches the costumed crowd. Tassels spin, capes twirl, satyrs leer, skirts swirl, all running together in a blur of colour. His gaze follows a magnificent but formidable dragon as it slopes and loops towards the foot of the clock tower. He squints, having caught sight of something more magnificent, more formidable.

She wears a simple shift, a plain skirt whispering to her calves, hair in a loose bun, strands in her eyes, no mask to cover her radiant face. Katrina Montesa is as striking as ever, cut like a fine jewel. The mere sight of her floods Franco with warmth, quickly iced upon glancing to her right. As usual, she is in the company of that offensive piece of peasantry, Robert Falsone. What is it about that illiterate rustic that so holds her attention? She is bright and beautiful, so high above him. She possesses the air of a noblewoman and, with a closet of extravagant threads and a few lessons in etiquette, would be well-matched a gentleman. *Well-matched a di Bonfatti*. Of course, *this* di Bonfatti knows he should leave her alone, if not for the sake of his vows, then the sake of his soul. Yet, even so, a slow, tentative stride closes the gap between them. Perhaps this is the night to confess his feelings. He can no longer deny them to himself; why deny them at all?

Franco never once resented his vows, having always felt them with a genuine heart, but somehow Katrina Montesa has managed to make him regret ever placing his hand on the Missal. Is that not enough then, to know he should quit the Order and make her his wife? He obviously cares more for her than he does his vows if he is willing to forsake them for her. Perhaps joining the Order was simply a catalyst to bring him to her. The year he spent back in Florence tending family affairs, she was everywhere, her hair the River Arno, her eyes the Tuscan grasslands, her laugh the bells of Santa Maria del Fiore. Franco thinks back to his notion of a few days past. He had wondered if God would even consider his entreaty when He often ignores requests of a far more noble nature. Perhaps it is simply that those who God chooses to ignore are lesser stationed. Why shouldn't that be true? If God would grant His favoured a loftier station, would He not give them His ear? Since God answered Franco's prayer and kept Katrina unmarried, clearly the two are meant to be together. Therefore, it is a union practically sanctified by the Almighty! Franco smiles with content, his chain of reasoning without a single weak link. His stride becomes increasingly purposeful.

A strong hand closes suddenly on his shoulder. Startled, he turns. It is Augustine, accompanied by that burly, uncouth carpenter relation of his. "Signore."

"Sir Franco, good to see you out enjoying yourself. Although," Augustine chuckles, "by your face it seems you are either enjoying yourself too much or not at all."

Franco laughs. "I've never been one for festivals. I only take part now to sidestep derision from my peers."

Augustine smiles. "A straighter arrow was never shaped. Ah, and speaking of arrows, have you seen my daughter about? I know she'd like to see you."

Franco's heart leaps at that. But he simply folds his arms loosely across his chest. An idea comes to him. This is the perfect opportunity to deal with the problem of Robert Falsone. Franco pulls Augustine away from Belli for a private conference.

"Forgive me, I know this might not be the right time, but there is a matter of some concern to which I must call your attention."

Lines set in Augustine's brow. "Of course. What is it?"

"Frankly, I am troubled by how much time Katrina spends with that Falsone boy, especially for two people who aren't even courting."

Augustine looks fondly at him. "My dear, dear Franco, no need to worry. I know my daughter is odd, willful. Because of this, Robert Falsone is one of the only friends she has managed to keep all these years. He is her *fidus Achates* and is as concerned for her honour as you or I."

"But, with all due respect Sir, I fear if she is constantly seen in his company, she will never find herself a husband, as most prospects will assume her the property of the sentry."

Augustine puts a gentle hand against Franco's back. "You do know if she heard you refer to her as property, you'd meet the devil."

"Joking aside, I wish only to open your eyes. The love of a daughter may have blinded you."

Augustine exhales a firm but calm breath. "While your concern is appreciated, and I thank you for it, it is not necessary. Katrina is master of her own threshold. Perhaps she will deem no man worthy to cross it, and never marry, or perhaps she will finally realize that she is in love with Robert."

Franco is aghast. "You cannot be seriou—"

"My lord, the night is in its infancy, as are you. Stop behaving like an old man. That's my job. Go, revel. Drink, laugh, taste the night. And if you see my daughter, ask her to dance."

As Augustine rejoins Belli, Franco can hear the carpenter muttering, "These pompous foreigners don't even try to disguise their bad manners. I'm a tradesman, not a cutpurse, yet he does not acknowledge me as I stand right next to you..."

Franco remains there, thunderstruck, watching after Augustine and wondering how in the world the man could possibly be so offhand regarding such serious matters. More than that, however, he is perturbed by Augustine's notion of Katrina being in love with Robert. Not because she might actually be, but because Augustine really is blind. How could so preposterous an idea even creep into his mind? Furthermore, how could a father think to condone such a catastrophic lapse in his daughter's judgment if it were true? Franco's contemplations are cut short by a hard poke to the middle of his back. Incensed, he turns.

"Why'd you leave, Bonfatti? I was looking for you outside the tavern."

"Oh. Sorry, Marcello. I saw someone I knew."

"Come, let's have a drink."

"You just had one."

"I just had three. And I want another. Presumably another after that." Marcello tugs on Franco's arm. "And you, you lily-livered ninny, you are going to indulge tonight if it kills us both."

Franco looks once more to the base of the clock tower. Katrina and Robert are no longer there. With a sigh, Franco surrenders to Marcello and allows himself to be led wherever the spirited Florentine wills. And that happens to be the stone elbow of some quiet street a good distance from the cluster of *auberges*. It is considerably darker here, save for the moonlight lanced across the ground, the fragile glow of low candles in windowsills. It is cooler too, away from so many revellers.

Marcello produces a full bottle from beneath his tunic, uncorks it, and tips it to his lips. He passes the libation to Franco, who waves in refusal. Marcello thrusts it at him, almost angrily. "Take the goddamn bottle before I beat you with it."

At first, Franco sputters and coughs, but with nodded encouragement from his friend, he knocks back another mouthful. Then another. And soon he finds he actually likes the taste, though not as much as the feeling that comes with it. He hiccups and giggles and grins.

Franco wants to see Katrina now more than ever. But how to get her alone? The sentry keeps a more vigilant eye on her than he does the coastline. Franco's gaze moves over the square, over the costumed couples swaying slowly together to the song of a single lute. *That's it.* He will do as Augustine suggested, and have a dance with her. Surely, Robert cannot follow her into Franco's arms. It will be just right, for as their bodies are close together, he will confess his affections, take his vow away from the Order and give it to her. And life will be good. Grand.

Of course, the initial consequences will be beyond measure. He will fall into disfavour with not only the most powerful Knighthood on the Continent but also his father, for the crest of di Bonfatti will be stripped from the *auberge* wall, thus ruining the chance for any other to gain acceptance to the Order, not to mention Franco will most likely be publicly flogged and shamed.

He doesn't care. It feels incredible not to care. For the first time in his life, the fallout of his actions does not matter to him. He is navigated solely by impulse and emotion—and alcohol. Pushing aside his prudence, he embraces this newfound recklessness. Never has he felt so light.

He is in love. Franco di Bonfatti, in love! And she loves him too, she must. Why else would she beg him to teach her the bow when she has a perfectly capable archer for a father? Why else would she give him lessons in Maltese, if not to prolong their time alone together? She has even *hugged* him. And there is no way she looks with the same intensity at just anybody.

"Well, it's about time you smiled," Marcello says, giving Franco a big grin. "Now let's enjoy this party as two drunken Florentines ought." Franco permits Marcello to pull him through the tight street until the music is louder, the laughter heartier, the air thicker, and the market square mere paces away. Just as they leave the stone ravine for the open quad, a strawberry haired siren catches Marcello by his elbow. She lowers her sparkling mask.

"Sweet Madeleine," Marcello says. "My favourite pastry."

"I had hoped you were craving dessert." Madeleine sweeps the knight back into the alley, without so much as a parting glance at Franco. He shakes his inebriated head and wanders off, watching the coloured lanterns, the glittering masks, the swirling costumes. They make him laugh, make him dizzy, make him think of the young woman who has captivated him.

A sobering sight stops him cold. *Katrina.* With *him. Damn it.* Franco pushes irritation aside and continues towards them, sitting together on a doorstep. Something catches on his boot. He twists around and looks down. The mask of a unicorn, stepped on and damaged, its silver horn bent, but still perfectly wearable. He picks up the mask and covers his face, pokes his way through the crowd to the street nearest Katrina and Robert. Franco finds a spot unlit by lanterns where he can watch and listen without being seen. Even if he is seen, he is just another fantastical creature in a host of many.

***

"...I wonder," Katrina begins, "If my brother proposed to Angelica. He's been talking about it for weeks, asking me what he should do, as if I know anything about romance."

Robert, who would normally crack a joke, does not even crack a smile. "A good thing Diana d'Alagona did not damage them beyond repair."

Katrina looks him in the face. "I miss you."

"What? Why? I see you every day. How could you miss me?"

"Because even when we're together, you're far away. It's not the same lately. You're not the same. Something weighs heavy on you. Tell me what."

"Nothing."

"You forget who you're talking to."

Robert sighs. He should know better. "I don't know why the farmer's death has affected me so, but it has. He was an awful man, one whose loss I hardly lament. It just seems death is always close. My father, my little brother, your mother, now my former employer. It's never a beautiful death, like the ones you've read to me from your books."

"Oh, Robert... I'm sorry. I didn't know."

"I never said anything. How could you know?"

Katrina rests her hand lightly on his. "Because I'm always listening, even when you're not speaking." Robert looks closely at her. His heart swells. Though overcome with emotion, he simply takes her cheeks in his hands and brings his lips to her forehead. If heaven were an eternity spent in one perfect moment from life, this would be that moment. Right now, he is so happy, he is jealous of himself. Right now, everything is right with the world.

***

From his place in the shadows, Franco feels his chest seizing. So simple was that kiss, so innocent, yet in it, the knight saw love: true, unmistakable love, and it brings him true, unmistakable pain. He is a battered animal tied to a post, yearning for escape but not knowing how to loose the leash that secures him. He curses his stupidity at thinking he could make Katrina his wife. Augustine is not the blind one, Franco is. Blind, for not having seen sooner what is so glaringly obvious now. More than this, he despises his weakness in the face of temptation—his willingness to throw away his vows, offend God, disgrace the di Bonfatti name for something so unworthy as that grubby bug of a girl whose only use is to arouse sinful thought.

Franco turns away, but in this compromised state, stumbles over himself, hitting the ground heavily. A litany of imprecations on his lips, he pushes himself off the cobbles and staggers to the nearest drinking hole. He finds himself an empty chair, slumps into it. His eyes, burning, move over the room. They take in an assortment of patrons, the exuberant and the brooding, the shifty and the straight, and the pleasure girls who could not care less about the mood of their customers so long as the mood of his purse is a generous one. Franco stops his survey suddenly, eyes caught, brain working. There, in a dark corner, is his chance to slip the leash tying him to his torment. Lilla struggles to wake the comatose Bavarian knight who must have procured her services. She looks up, as though physically touched by Franco's gaze. He motions her over. She hesitates, glancing to the big, sleeping German and back. At last, she crosses the grimy floor and joins the knight at his table. She folds her arms neatly over her chest.

"I know you, Bonfatti. I know you have no love for the nature of my commerce. I am not interested in being paraded through town on a donkey, so seeing as there are twenty other girls here plying the same trade, choose one of them to reprimand."

"That's not what I want."

Lilla narrows her eyes. "Then what do you want?"

"Your services, of course." Franco smiles, pushes the chair opposite him towards her with his boot. "Have a seat."

CHAPTER THIRTY-SIX

At the altar of St Publius, Father Anton Tabone closes the first mass of the day, reminding parishioners that during Lenten abstention, fasting to the point of frailty is not only needless, it is useless. To the answering murmurs of astonishment, he says, "God loves those who sacrifice in His Name, but He loves the hale and hearty also, for they approach His work with certain vigour."

The congregation, made up mostly of old women, shuffles blearily down the aisle, bones creaking and feet dragging. Anton smiles inwardly, unable to imagine even one of them approaching anything with vigour. When the last has filed out, he heads to the sacristy where the bishop's curate is sitting in wait. The tight whip of a man snaps to his feet at Anton's arrival.

"His Grace, the Exalted Bishop Cubelles, requests your audience, *Dun* Tabone."

The *kappillan* is surprised but not alarmed. Despite his curiosity, Anton knows better than to ask the curate why he is being summoned to the palace. The bishop's staff is a highly secretive lot, guarding a privileged word covetously, no matter how trivial. He wonders if perhaps Cubelles has finally decided to send St Publius a sexton. Or maybe Anton is to be reassigned to another *paroċċa*, conceivably one of Mdina's smaller chapels. Angelica would like that.

"Certainly," Anton says, voice muffled by the alb he is pulling over his head. He drapes it over a chair, smoothes out the wrinkles in his soutane. "When?"

"You're to come with me now."

Anton furrows his brow. "Oh. All right. I'll let my niece know."

The curate frowns, eyes reflecting a strange blend of displeasure and delight. "So, you failed to notice that she has not returned home from the revels. How unfortunate for you."

*****

Paces from the Italian *auberge*, Katrina watches as Robert leaves for the sentry post. Though the kiss was never discussed, Katrina thought about it long into the night. In fact, neither she nor he spoke much at all. She rested her head on his shoulder and listened to him breathe. They passed a quiet time together, sitting on the stone step long after the square emptied, long after the torches diminished, long after first light broke.

It is after dawn, and only now does she feel the slightest fatigue. At once, she is tired yet very much awake, her mind no less at variance than her body. Everything feels different. Even the thought of scrubbing linens all day does not seem so bad.

***

With the clock tower chiming eight in the distance, Angelica bursts inside the rectory, unmindful of the fact that she has been out all night. "Uncle Anton! I have news! Wonderful news!" She feels dishevelled and glowing, carrying her costume wings in one hand, sandals in the other. She flies into the kitchen, where the priest is sitting at their small table. His countenance is grave, halting her mid-step. Angelica has never before been afraid of her uncle. She is afraid now. He looks furious but remains silent, his grim quietude more alarming than any words could possibly be.

He points to the stool opposite him. "Sit." His voice is a low growl of displeasure.

"Oh, dear. The hour. I forgot myself. I am so sorry. I can explain—"

"*Sit.*"

She gathers up her skirts and does as she's told.

"Angelica Tabone, things are going to change around here."

"Forgiveness, please. I swear never to stay out like that again."

"Your staying out until after dawn is just a blade of grass in a very vast field."

Angelica leans forward, hands tightly folded. "What have I done to displease you?"

Her uncle's eyes flash. "It is twice the insult that you do not even know! For starters, you have not for one moment properly considered my role as *kappillan* of this parish, and that your every movement is regarded by the people of this village as a reflection of me."

"That's not true! All I've *ever* done is consider that very thing. I would never—"

"*Quiet.* I have always been lenient about imposing rules, allowing you to fly freely, believing that so long as I didn't cage you, you would fly right willingly. I have done this in error. You've kept ugly secrets from me. And not an hour ago, I was summoned to the bishop's palace where he dished me sound reprimand for your outrageous conduct." He slams his fist on the tabletop with such force it startles them both. "He threatened to strip my title!"

"*What?* Why?"

"I have failed as a shepherd, he said. If I cannot lead my own niece down the righteous path, how can I be expected to lead an entire flock?"

"Uncle, I swear, whatever he said I did, it is not true."

"No Angelica, it is all too true. You do not wear the *barnuża* as every other young woman in this village does. You run wild, going where you please, when you please, uncovered, unescorted. Henceforth, you *will* don the veil in public. You *will* ask my permission before leaving this house."

"But—"

"I'm not finished. The bishop is averse to your tutoring small boys, convinced that a woman in an authoritative role will only corrupt their sense of order. He even railed me for teaching you to read. Had I known your taste in literature, believe me, I never would have."

"Uncle—"

"*Be silent.* Above all, the bishop was most annoyed with your begging clemency for a son of Islam. Can you even imagine my mortification when His Eminence told me of your visiting a Muslim prisoner in the dungeon? That, Angelica Tabone, is beyond the pale. Do not look so shocked. Cubelles has a complex network of informants, you know that. Now tell me, how can you sit across from me, look me in the eye, and say you only ever think of how your actions reflect me?"

Angelica's hands are trembling, her stomach churning. There can be no lying, no denying. "Why...Why did the bishop choose now to take issue with you?"

"He shut his eyes to your misdeeds and my lenience for a long time, but could no longer. Not after receiving several reports from parishioners about the niece of the *kappillan* engaging in a wanton act of debauchery in the market square like a common harlot."

His words slap Angelica across the face. "That's what they called it? *A wanton act of debauchery?*" She rises angrily from the stool, sending it to crash against the floor. Tears blur her vision. "They can all go to hell! And Bishop Cubelles can drive them there in his gilt carriage!"

"*Angelica!*"

"No! I will not be made to feel ashamed because of last night! I did nothing wrong. So what if Domenicus and I kissed? Is a kiss not to be expected after a proposal?"

The priest raises his eyebrows. "Proposal?"

"Yes! He proposed last night. I see the villagers were so distressed by my debauchery that they left out *that* detail."

"A decent young man would have sought my permission before proposing to you."

Angelica narrows her eyes. "Permission? What for? You're not my father." She regrets the remark the moment it leaves her mouth. Her uncle sets his chin, a vain attempt to hide the terrible hurt evident in his eyes.

"I want to know what you were doing out all night. My vow of celibacy has not rendered me imbecilic in these matters. A simple kiss does not last until dawn."

"What answer could I give that would satisfy you?"

"The truth."

"Here is the truth: we talked. Planned. Waited for the sun to rise." A look of suspicion crosses her uncle's face, his unspoken mistrust paining Angelica to the core. "You don't like that truth?"

"Is it the truth?"

Slowly, sadly, she shakes her head. "To think, after all these years, you would side with a herd of hateful liars. When have I ever given you a reason to think low of me? Fine, I don't wear a *barnuża*. I go to the market by myself. And I even asked the knights to show mercy to the man who spared me rape. Yes, I visited that man, and the only reason I did not tell you was that I did not want to compromise you."

"You have disappointed me," her uncle says quietly. "Dishonoured me also."

Angelica sniffles. "And you have disappointed me..." Her voice falters with the hitch of her chest. "If you tell me to wear the veil, I will do it. Tell me to stay indoors, I will do it. I'll always do everything, anything, you ask of me. But what I will *not* do is pretend to feel shame for kissing the man who asked me to be his wife—especially to appease a mob of insufferable hypocrites and the robed imposter who leads them."

Father Tabone jumps to his feet. "You forget yourself! So help me God, I will not suffer defiance in this house, nor will I have my position of *kappillan* lost for things not of my doing!"

Angelica will not be cowed. "You will keep your position, Uncle. Tell the bishop you've disowned me, put me out in the street, and you may do it, for I'll soon be married and your burden no longer." She turns, turns back. "I hope your title is worth your solitude." She takes off tearful and barefoot, leaving her wings in a heap on the floor.

***

Katrina pins the last of the laundry to the line as a gentle wind fills the bedclothes and gives the air the scent of newly-washed linens. The afternoon breeze blows the corner of one sheet upward, sending it along her neck, over her chin to her cheek. Soon, the gust grows still, and in the silence that follows, Katrina closes her eyes. Against the blackness, she sees Robert, sees the boy returning a lost ribbon after Mama's funeral, sees the man bloodied and bruised after a night spent in prison for theft uncommitted, sees him presenting her a beautifully cut bow, sees him watching the sky. And all she wants is to be near him.

The clock tower peals the workday's end, calling Katrina back to the present. She opens her eyes, picks up the empty wicker baskets, and makes for the door.

Her heart jumps. She croaks, drops the baskets.

She never felt his presence, Franco di Bonfatti, standing there a living statue, watching her, half his body hidden behind one of the damp sheets pinned to the line. Something in the statue's eyes, some darkness therein, makes her uncomfortable.

"Good Lord," Katrina breathes, putting her hand to her chest. "You frightened me."

Franco crouches, plucks a crown daisy from the grass. "Have a flower on account." She accepts it gratefully but is not sure what to do with it. Her indecision must be written on her face, as Franco breaks into laughter. "I don't expect you to eat the bloody thing."

Katrina laughs too, though with some unease, and nestles the flower behind her ear. She bends to retrieve the baskets. On rising, she glances up at him. "I'm done for the day. Surely, you didn't find me simply to startle me, so is there anything you need before I go?"

The knight shakes his head. "Missed you last night at Carnival. Just wanted to say hello."

Katrina gives him a genuine smile. "You're sweet." Then, despite going thirty-six hours on no sleep, she sets out for the Corradino watchtower, leaving Franco alone between the bedsheets.

Katrina needs to see Robert, needs to be in his presence, where life is felt so deeply and perceived with uncomplicated sensibility. Yet today, unlike every other day, she does not run. It is not a fear of there being awkwardness where there was none before that slows her down. It is more a desire to take time to look at everything with new eyes, the way she looked at Robert last night and saw so much more than she ever saw before.

Soon, Katrina reaches the tower base. For the first time in her life, she hopes her hair looks nice. If only Angelica were here to primp her.

At the top of the staircase, she comes to an abrupt halt. The post is deserted, eerie in its emptiness. All is silent, save the waves breaking on the not-so-distant shore. She goes to the window, looks in all directions. Robert's absence makes no sense. In the years he has worked as watch, he has never once been away from his post. Could it be that he just went for a piss? No, sentries in service of the Order are not permitted to leave their place of duty, no matter the circumstance. Besides, there is a chamber pot. Perhaps Mea fell ill? No. Word would have reached Katrina by now, and the Order would have arranged a replacement to take over the tower. He had better not be playing some stupid game. She'll kill him. Anger quickly replaces concern.

Katrina grips the casement ledge and, leaning far out, calls his name, along with a few threats. Yet, as slow minutes pass, worry returns. Had Robert really planned a trick, he would have revealed his hoax by now. She turns fretfully from the window and looks down. A diagonal shaft of light streams in through the porthole and colours an arch on the stone floor. The salt-laced wind stirs gritty dust, sweeping it into a greyish vortex. On passing, it reveals several flung objects that glint with the afternoon. Katrina crouches for a closer look. She draws a sharp breath. *Coins.* The ten *habba* she gave Robert after the card game last night.

Something is very wrong. Those coins promised a week of meals; he would never be so careless. The scattered currency also indicates he definitely was here. A sense of dread pits in her stomach as she checks for signs of struggle, blood, scuff marks, anything. She looks around the small space once again, as if this sweep might expose something missed the first fifteen passes. Her search, however painstaking, is fruitless. All that is left of Robert Falsone in this watchtower are his scattered coins.

***

There is only one place Angelica Tabone can go to make things right by her uncle. The place where none ventures without first being summoned, the place she is heading right now. She turns a corner that leads to the street where the bishop's palace stands. Over and again, she rehearses in her mind what she will say to Cubelles if he grants her occasion.

At the gates, Angelica meets a guard, a tall man, muscular and dark, dressed in formal vestments that bear the insignia of the Vatican. His face is unfortunately comical, with fat, fishlike lips and hair like needles in a pincushion, making sternness near impossible to achieve—though not for lack of effort on his part. His eyes drop to the filthy hem of Angelica's lilac dress. She feels stupid, wearing such a gown at such an hour and without shoes.

"If you please," she says, pushing aside her discomfort, "I need to see the bishop."

"His Grace is not here."

"When will he return?"

"When it suits him," the guard replies, infuriatingly smug.

"I will wait all day."

"What is so important that a noblewoman robbed of her slippers or a peasant clearly confused about her station would wait all day for?"

"I'd rather not say."

"Then you will not see the bishop at all, whether he returns in five minutes or five days."

Angelica opens her mouth to protest but is stopped short by the *clip-clopping* of hooves over cobbles. She turns. A finely dressed coachman drives a bright white carriage trimmed in gold towards the palace gates. Angelica knows this gilt carriage. All of Birgu knows it, and none on Malta can match it. It is spectacular, an oak and brass masterpiece funded by the tithes of the diocese. The coach rolls on large silver-plated wheels, its rear hung with two magnificent coats-of-arms, bases touching, bodies tilted from each other.

Angelica bunches up her skirts and flings herself directly in front of the exquisite, ginger horse, causing the driver to rein abruptly. The mare rears up with a piercing whinny.

"What the devil is wrong with you?" the coachman barks at Angelica. Without a glance in his direction, she races, stumbling in her hurry, to the side of the coach. She rises to her toes and sets her hands on the ledge, something few would dare to do. There sits Bishop Cubelles, swathed in scarlet robes, fingers heavily ringed, his ornamented crozier, a staff in the shape of a shepherd's crock, resting across his lap. His hair is black and cut close to his scalp, a neatly cropped beard narrow along the line of his jaw as though a cart rolled over his jowl leaving a thin track from one ear to the other. His features are sharp, the most prominent being a large, pointed nose, making even his face seem accusing. Seated next to him is an attractive young man, who appraises Angelica with a mixture of contempt and intrigue. Before she might speak, that pucker-lipped curmudgeon of a guard rushes forward to shoo her away. He grabs her forcefully by the arm, but Cubelles waves him off, sunlight catching in his rings, making them flash with the flutter of his hand.

"Sergio, stand down." The bishop looks at Angelica, changes his tone. "I cannot imagine my attention so sought that a maiden would throw herself before a moving carriage to obtain it."

Taken aback by Cubelles' friendliness, Angelica curtseys. "If you please, your Grace, I wish to discuss something with you in private." She is fully prepared for refusal. To her great surprise, however, the prelate opens the carriage door and offers her his hand. The youth next to him smiles.

"Come, *Signorina*," Cubelles says. "I have a minute to spare as my nephew settles in. He is on stay from a seminary in Catalonia."

Wide-eyed, Angelica steps up into the carriage and sits, shoulders tense, against the luxurious velvet upholstery. Cubelles taps his crozier to the ceiling, where a portion of Michelangelo's *Last Judgment* has been reproduced across the upper panels. The driver snaps his whip and the rolling re-creation of the Sistine Chapel passes through the open gates.

For the first time in her life, Angelica gets a look inside the bishop's legendary courtyard. The lawns alone give her pause, thick and lush. Unblinking eyes of statues keep endless watch over gardeners busy tending the estate, alive with blossoms of every shade. The coach passes into shadow beneath a gothic quadripartite vault. At its end, stands the magisterial house, an edifice no less superb than the grounds before it. And all the while, most of Birgu lives in hunger beneath thatch ceilings.

At the main entrance, the driver halts. He opens the side door and helps the bishop down, then the youth, who is all too eager to give the coachman his bags. Now that the young Catalan's hands are free, he offers them to Angelica and does not let go of her even after she touches ground. The bishop notices, fires his nephew a cutting glance, and delivers him a few sharp words in Spanish. Unruffled, the handsome youth gives Angelica an ostentatious bow before departing with the driver.

Cubelles turns to her, but before he can speak, a curate, a sexton, and a sacristan are upon him: candlesticks are missing from the foyer, a cresset was tipped and splashed oil on a twelfth-century tapestry, villagers have come asking if attendance at Carnival has put their souls in peril. The bishop addresses each concern, and when the men have set off, he looks to Angelica.

"Your Excellency," she says, "Forgive my intrusion on your busy day."

"What troubles you, child?"

Something wells up inside her, and before she knows it, she breaks. "You cannot strip my uncle his title! He is a good priest, the best. He was kind enough to take me in, knowing well what an impediment I would be to his vocation. Punish me in his stead. I'll do whatever it takes to make things right."

"I believe you."

She blinks. "You do?"

"When I summoned Father Tabone here this morning, I had no intention of stripping him his title of *kappillan*. He is a good priest, you are right. Perhaps unorthodox in his approach, but a good priest nonetheless. Your larking about, however, makes him ineffectual in the eyes of parishioners. I took a hard line with him so he would take seriously my discipline, and in turn, make you take it seriously. I had hoped you would see the light, and so you have."

"Then why not summon me directly, your Grace?"

"Because Father Tabone was overdue a good chiding. He sometimes needs reminding that Birgu is a long way from Lourmarin. What they do in France is their business. Here, no man should allow a young woman to behave as you do. However, he has not completely failed as a shepherd. That you are here shows me he raised you with a conscience. You have begun the road to redemption. You will go to confession and take your penance. Thereafter, you will ask your uncle's permission before you venture out in public. Also, you will dress in a manner befitting the virtuous, not the slattern."

Angelica looks down, humiliated. Cubelles is cunning in his candour, steel in his tone of silk. Most whom he castigates do not realise they are being hauled over the coals until they see the scars.

"I had a mind to call Domenicus Montesa here too," the bishop adds.

Angelica feels the colour drain from her face.

"I decided, however, not to summon your future husband, largely because the reports I received from witnesses all point to you as the initiator. Besides, he has enough to worry about, having to keep that unruly sister of his in check."

"Future husband? You mean you know he proposed? And you did not tell my uncle?"

"It was not my place. Now, from here, don a veil and go to St Lawrence, where your confession will be heard. From there, begin your journey back to God."

CHAPTER THIRTY-SEVEN

The curtains are tightly drawn at the Falsone house, nothing out of the ordinary. Katrina raps her knuckles against the door. No answer. She knocks again, harder. Still no reply. Nothing at all. *That* is out of the ordinary. Mea never leaves the house, except to attend mass. Katrina presses her ear to the door. Something bumps her from behind. She jumps in fright, spins around. It is Robert's goat.

"You scared me, rot you," she snaps. But one look into the animal's big, luminous eyes and she softens. "What are you doing out here by yourself anyway? Where is your master? Where is Robert?" She looks to the sky. "God, where is he?"

Katrina abandons the hovel and winds up breathless on the doorstep of Italy's *auberge*. A Venetian page answers her frantic knock. She asks for the knight di Bonfatti. The pinched, pompous postulant turns up his nose. "The lord *Honorabile* is dining. Come back tomorrow."

"*Get him now!*"

The page flashes. "Of all the cheek! How dare you—"

"Look, idiot, this is an urgent matter involving a sentry of the Order. Interfere, and you can consider your knightly ambitions quashed. Now get Franco di Bonfatti this instant or I will come in there and get him myself." For some reason, the Venetian takes her for more than mere bluster. Her bearing commands deference, even though her station does not. Moreover, she *is* right; he must not hinder official business if he hopes to be named *Frater*.

"Just a minute," he grumbles, leaving her to wait in the dormitory's growing shadow.

Katrina paces, chews nails already severely bitten, glances constantly at the door, her distress augmented tenfold. It is remarkable how the urgency of the situation truly determines the length of a minute. Fifteen of those later, Franco comes outside. "What's the matter? You look terrible."

She starts at his voice. "Something has happened to Robert."

317

"What has?"

"He wasn't at the tower. He's not at home either. Neither is Mea. She's *always* home."

Franco rubs his chin. "Perhaps he went for a nap, seeing as he did not sleep last night."

"He wouldn't go for a bloody nap!"

"Maybe he didn't go to the tower at all. Maybe he went straight home to sleep."

"No, he was there. I saw his coins on the tower floor."

The knight looks at her sharply. "*Saw* his coins? Meaning you were up inside the tower?"

Katrina blanches at her inadvertent admission. Now what? Ah, fuck it. "Yes."

"Entrance is forbidden to all but sentries and knights."

"Consider the circumstance."

"Rules are not subject to the whims of circumstance. That is why they are called *rules.*"

Katrina furrows her brow. Is he serious? He must be. Joking is not in his nature. "Please, Franco. I am sorry I trespassed, but that's not important right now."

"It *is* important. I'm quite sure today wasn't your first time inside the tower. What's to say Falsone doesn't entertain other guests? Perhaps today he decided to entertain the wrong one. He wouldn't be the first sentry to do so. You forget the incident with Henri and the prostitute Lilla?"

Katrina bridles at the insinuation. "Look here, something bad has happened. What if corsairs took him? Every second we waste speeds him closer to certain death."

Franco spreads his hands. "If corsairs have him, death is a certainty."

"*What?*" Katrina wants to punch the knight for that remark.

"Easy. The alarm would have been raised, had corsairs landed." Franco pauses, inhales. "...Unless Falsone fell asleep at his post. You did keep him out until dawn."

Katrina's mouth is instantly dry. "Dear God, whatever happened to him is my fault."

"No, no, settle down. A pack of Muslim mongrels would never have left coins in the tower. Falsone is fine, I'm sure of it. I'll find him, if for nothing else then for the fact that he has a few questions to answer. He is employed by the Order and must be accountable for his whereabouts while on duty. Give me a little time to look into this."

Katrina looks closely at Franco. His expression seems sincere enough. "Hurry, please. I will not know peace until I know he is safe."

The *auberge* door closes, leaving Katrina with a sense of helpless dread. She debates going back to the tower, but Marco Vella will have taken post, and he is too afraid of Franco to let her in. She searches fields where Robert often gathers brambles. Unsuccessful, she tries the communal ovens, the waterfront, the churchyard, the taverns. She asks people on the street. None has seen him.

She goes back to Robert's house, hoping to find Mea. No luck. The goat is there, however, sprawled in a patch of dirt. This time, Katrina undoes her belt and makes a leash of it. She brings the goat to Belli's stable, pushing the animal inside the donkey's stall. When she arrives on her own doorstep, more voices than usual fill the house. Inside, her father, brother, Belli, and the priest are sitting at the table, rapt in discussion.

"Sweetheart," Augustine says brightly. "Kept you late at the *auberge*, did they?"

"Father, something terrible has happened."

All turn to look at her. "What's wrong?" She is not sure who spoke. "Robert is missing."

Domenicus furrows his brow. "What do you mean *missing?*"

"He wasn't at the tower or at home. Mea is gone too. And no one knows anything…" The worry, the exhaustion, all catch up, and Katrina feels tears gathering.

Father Tabone quickly rises, offering his chair. She shakes her head but somehow ends up dropping into the seat. Augustine crouches before her. "There must be a reasonable explanation."

Katrina wipes her eyes, streaking dirt across her face. "No, Pa, there isn't. Robert has vanished. All that is left are the coins I found in the watchtower." She sniffles. "Franco promised me he would do what he could to make sure Robert was safe."

Augustine raises his eyebrows. "Bonfatti? Coming to Robert's aid? That's rich."

Katrina gives her father an enquiring look.

"I had a strange encounter with him last night at Carnival," he says.

Father Tabone clears his throat. "Let us pick up wedding plans later when things here have settled. I should find Mea. She is fragile."

Pa nods. "Bring her back here."

Belli, quiet until now, rises suddenly and falls in-step with the priest. "I'm coming with you."

As the door closes, Domenicus faces Katrina. "When did you see Robert last?"

"This morning. He left me at my work."

"Did he say or do anything to make you think he was in trouble?"

Katrina shakes her head.

"A village peopled entirely with gossips, and no one has heard anything?"

"Whatever happened to him has happened in secret," she replies.

"The other sentry, Claudio Vella's boy, Marco—he must know something," her brother says.

Before Katrina can respond, the door resounds with a heavy knock. Augustine answers. It is Franco di Bonfatti, sombre in the shadowy dusk. Katrina's heart pounds, her extremities cold, clammy, her core twisted. Domenicus reaches across the table and puts his hand on hers. She barely feels him. As Franco crosses the doorsill, he and Augustine exchange brief courtesies.

The knight stands before Katrina, his face typically grave. "Falsone is all right."

She exhales forcefully, hand over heart. "Oh thank God! Where is he? What happened? The bastard, I'm going to kill him!"

Franco holds up a halting hand. "Katrina, stop. He is all right—as in, alive."

She sits straight up. "What do you mean?"

"He was arrested."

"*Arrested?*" she cries. "For what?"

"The murder of one Grimaldi Farrugia."

***

In the early twilight, carpenter and priest walk the quiet streets in search of Mea Falsone. There is no moon to light their path. February wind blows cold, throwing grit up into the air. One by one, flaming tapers are touched to street lamps, making the way slightly brighter. After an hour of fruitless wandering, Belli turns to Anton.

"I don't know where else to look. We've exhausted every corner of this village."

"Maybe that's just the problem. There is more to Malta than Birgu." The priest buries his hands deep in his pockets and leans into the gust. "Come, we'll fetch my cart and mule." The two men leave the thoroughfare for St Publius church, where Anton's dray is parked. They walk the first fifty paces in silence, consumed by thought. Belli decides to share his.

"Your niece loves you very much, you know."

The priest shakes his head. "I was wrong today. She came to me joyful and left tearful."

"You weren't wrong, *Dun* Tabone. These are dangerous times, times of inquest, times that see even priests burned at the stake. You were right to be firm. But don't you worry, Father. Domenicus will talk sense into her head. You know women—" Belli cuts himself off— "Hmm, I suppose you don't. How lucky for you. They can be... moody."

Anton smiles. "Thank you for the fascinating lesson in womanhood."

The road takes them through the town square, dark, deserted and swirling with debris. As they pass the church of St Lawrence, two women emerge, both heavily cloaked. One, the elder by her laborious movement, leans into the other. Given the hour and the weather, Belli and Anton approach and offer assistance. Upon closer look, Belli realises the older woman is Mea Falsone.

"Signora! God be praised," he says, crossing himself. "We have been looking everywhere for you. Thank heavens you are all right." However, peering more closely into her face, he sees that she is anything but. There is blankness within—not confusion, but a total lack of awareness. Her eyes are fully open, but she is unconscious. Her cheek is caked with dried blood, a dark purple river from temple to chin. The carpenter looks to the veiled maid at her side.

"If you please, *Signorina*, what happened here? Who did this to her? We are trying desperately to find her son."

The girl draws back her *barnuža*, revealing her identity. It is Angelica. Anton starts, clearly surprised.

"I went to see the bishop to beg his pardon that he might spare your title," she says to her uncle. "He ordered me to go for confession. It was late afternoon when I left the box. Robert's mother was at a pew. I spoke to her but could gain nothing more than ramblings. I returned to the confessional, but the priest was gone. I wanted to alert somebody, but I couldn't leave her alone, and I couldn't get her to come with me until just now."

"Where is Robert?" Belli asks.

"I do not know."

"How did she come to be at the church?" Anton asks.

"Again, I do not know. All I do know is that she needs care, now."

"Come," Belli says. "Let's get her out of the cold."

***

Domenicus has not drawn an easy breath since Franco entered the house with his horrific announcement. The knight has offered little information, saying all he knows is that a witness came forward—someone who saw Robert on Farrugia's property the day the farmer's body was discovered and deduced that since Falsone never reported anything, only one conclusion could be drawn. The witness said he felt it his duty to come forward and begged clemency for waiting so long.

"Who is this witness?" Domenicus asks.

"That is privileged," Franco replies.

"No, it isn't."

"I'm afraid it is," the knight insists. "I don't even know the identity."

"Yet you know for certain it is a he?" Domenicus presses.

Franco furrows his brow. "Your pardon?"

"You said the witness felt it *his* duty. So I'm asking you, do you know for certain this witness is a man?"

"Not for certain, no. But I think it a fair assumption."

Domenicus doesn't like how Franco has a perfect answer for everything. He wants to voice this feeling but thinks it may do more to hinder things than help.

"We have to do something," Katrina says, eyes rimmed red.

"We will," Domenicus says, squeezing his little sister's shoulder. He looks at Franco. "This witness, whoever he is, has erred. I know Robert is innocent."

"Oh? How?"

"Because... because Robert came here right after he found Farrugia's body. We were on our way to report it to the gendarmes, but they had already ruled it a suicide, so we left it. Franco, take me to the master-at-arms, I'll tell him this myself."

"The master-at-arms will dismiss you as a friend covering for a friend," Franco says.

"But I'm telling the truth."

"What matters here is fact, which has little to do with truth. The fact is he came here *after* finding the farmer. You do not know that Farrugia was already a corpse when Falsone first came upon him."

"Yes I do," Domenicus replies, voice hard.

Franco sighs. "I am not a judge. Moreover, I'm not even sure in whose custody Falsone finds himself. It might be the Order, but I doubt it, as I haven't been able to unearth much information. It could be that your civil authority holds him. I really don't know."

"Bloody find out," Domenicus snaps.

"Take caution in your tone," Franco snaps back.

"Enough," Pa cuts in. "We take this to every authority until we find out who is responsible."

The front door opens, and a sharp blast of air runs through the house, flickering candles with its passage. Father Tabone enters, Angelica trailing. Domenicus meets her eyes. Even from across the room and in failing light, he can see terrible distress in her face. This day has been long, punishing. All he wants is to throw himself into her arms, feel the warmth and safety of her embrace, but right now that is out of the question.

Behind Angelica and her uncle is Belli, with Robert's wisp of a mother in his huge arms. Domenicus rises from his chair, a thousand questions on his tongue, but is shocked to silence the moment Belli brings Mea into the light. Purple bruises unseen in darkness are now very visible, brutal contusions blotching her temple, cheek, and jaw. Katrina's hand flies to her mouth, but not in time to muffle her gasp. Franco shifts uncomfortably. Augustine swears under his breath. Belli lays Mea on a straw pallet, as Angelica and Katrina scramble to cover her with layers of sheepskin.

"Who would do this?" Domenicus whispers, brows drawn together.

"She needs a doctor," Belli says. "I'll fetch one from the *Sacra Infermeria*."

"*No,*" Augustine says abruptly. Domenicus looks at his father in surprise, as does Franco. "Leave the knights out of this. I'll take the horse to Mdina and call on Dr Callus."

Angelica looks up. "But the city gates will be locked by now."

"Not to worry. The porters will allow me passage." As Pa turns to go, Franco puts a firm hand against the man's chest, halting him mid-stride.

"Why leave the knights out of this?"

Augustine looks slowly down at Franco's hand and raises an eyebrow. "Because, my lord, we do not know what happened to Mea. We do not know where her son is. Until we do, we do not know who is friend and who is foe."

"Just what are you implying, sir?"

"I *imply* nothing. What I am outright saying is the knights could be behind this just as easily as anyone else."

Franco bridles. "That is absurd!"

Domenicus looks from his father to the knight, and back. Several tense seconds pass, dreadful in their length. Finally, Franco steps aside, and Pa is gone into the night. Domenicus joins Belli and Father Tabone at the table, sharing what little information they have gathered. He glances up, watches as Angelica wrings a cloth, passes it over Mea's face, cleaning dried blood from her cheek. His sister kneels next to Angelica, and whispers, "Does Mea know?"

"Know what?"

"Her son has been arrested for murder."

Angelica drops the cloth. "*Murder? Whose?*"

"Farrugia." Katrina blinks, wipes her eyes. "He was a suicide. This witness is lying."

"I know. I was here with your brother that day. Robert arrived in a complete panic after finding the body. I've never seen a person in such a state. There can't possibly be a case against him."

Domenicus is about to interpose when Franco, who had been standing disregarded in the shadows, now approaches Katrina, helps her to her feet.

"I should not linger. My presence is no longer useful." As the knight says this, Domenicus meets his gaze. "...Nor is it wanted, I think."

Katrina nods, tears running over her cheeks. "Oh Franco, please forgive us for our discourtesy when you have only come to help."

Franco takes her hands in his. "I did not mean to challenge your father in his home. I will amend myself to him. And I give you my solemn word that I'll find out everything I can, no matter how deep I must dig." Without parting words, the knight is swallowed by the night.

Domenicus moves behind Angelica and touches her shoulder tenderly, but furtively, before pulling his hand away and checking on Robert's mother. He takes the cloth, drapes it over Mea's brow. He crouches and, with great care, slips the woman's arms from her sleeves to inspect for bruising or fractures. She is out cold, undeniably so; a woman of her modesty would have otherwise kicked up a great fuss at having her arms exposed. Domenicus dilutes witch hazel with water to temper her contusions.

Despite the presence of so many in such tight quarters, it is quiet, save the crackle of the hearth fire and the chirp of crickets. Behind him, his sister sits slumped on the floor. He feels her eyes on him as he works through his fatigue, works with the air of a man invigorated. Angelica brings him a pail of clean water and a mound of fresh cloths. She uses one to wipe the sweat from his face. After a moment, she goes to her uncle and crouches before him.

"This morning," she whispers against the stillness, "I misspoke."

"I gave you little recourse," he replies.

"For how deeply I affronted you, I am sorry. You are the very best of fathers and Fathers."

"I love you, too. Now go help Domenicus. He needs you."

At the end of the second hour, Augustine returns with Dr Giuseppe Callus. The physician goes straight to the patient and squats at her side. He gives Domenicus an approving look. "I see you have things taken care of here. Anything broken?"

"Not that I could find, though I did not check her legs or ribs."

"Any vomiting?" Callus asks.

"Not in our care," Domenicus replies.

"Other discharge? Bleeding from the ears, mouth, or nose? A bowel movement?"

"No, *Magnificus.*"

Callus bends his ear to her mouth. "Her breathing comes without a hitch. Very good." He looks closely at her face and arms and probes around her neck down to her ribs. Mea's expression remains unchanged. All wait in tense silence, leaning forward. Callus looks at Domenicus. "Nothing broken in body, but spirit is another matter entirely. For the time being, there is no probe I might do to determine the extent of damage done to her wits. Arnica may help some. It is excellent for trauma of the senses." Callus glances to Angelica. "*Signorina*, I understand that you found her. What was her state? What did she say? How did she act?"

Angelica repeats what she told her uncle and Belli hours earlier. Callus listens intently, nodding and occasionally punctuating her story with a question. All of a sudden, a guttural gurgling calls everyone's attention to the pallet. Mea's eyes pop wide open, chest rising and falling with frantic gulps of air. She takes hold of Domenicus, squeezing his arm with pincer strength. He and Callus are the only ones in the house who remain calm.

"Mea," Callus says in a loud, clear voice. "Tell me what happened."

She blinks rapidly, eyes darting all over the room, mouth open, gasping, struggling for air as if she is drowning. Everyone crowds around the bed.

"Back!" Callus shouts. "Get back. Domenicus, not you. You stay." The doctor taps the woman's cheek. "Signora. Who hurt you?"

Her eyes roll back in her head, her body in violent convulsions. Callus puts his hands on her shoulders. "Stay with me, Mea. Who hurt you? *Who?*"

She meets his eyes, her tremors subsiding some, her voice a croak. "Men."

"What men? More. Tell me more. Think, Signora. Think."

"Bread... to the tower. They came for him there, these men. In black, all black. Set upon me with truncheons..." And she is gone back to the safety of her oblivion.

Domenicus squints. "Men in black..." He looks to his father. "Gendarmes?"

"Could be," Augustine replies. "Though gendarmes would have identified themselves as such, certainly not beaten a woman. Not to this state. Besides, Mea would have used the word *gendarmes*. *Men in black* means they are anonymous." He shakes his head, exhales. "My God, this is slippery. Who could Robert have crossed? That is the key to finding him."

Domenicus furrows his brow. "But there are only three possibilities— the dungeons of the knights, the church, or the *Università*."

Father Tabone shifts in his seat. "That might not be true," he says quietly. All eyes are on him. "There is one you did not mention. And you did not mention it because you do not even know it exists." He swallows, as though hesitant to continue but aware he has no choice. "I know only because of my position in the church, and I don't think the bishop knows I know."

"Spit it out, man," Belli says with mounting impatience.

Father Tabone nods, wrings his hands. "There is a dungeon beyond the city gates, quarried deep in the earth. It is sanctioned not by the Order, nor the Church, nor the *Università*, yet operates because of them all, and has since the days of Aragonese rule. It is a place people are put to await a trial that will never come for crimes that were never committed. They are the unfortunates who have somehow crossed the knights, the clergy, or the civil authority. They are innocent. The proof of their innocence lies in their very incarceration." There is a mixture of disbelief and outrage in the faces before Father Tabone.

Domenicus notices his father has gone pale. Augustine especially must be reeling from this news—he is a soldier in service of the Order, yet has never once mentioned this place. His mouth works, but he cannot seem to speak. "But... but..."

"How could such a place operate in secrecy?" the priest offers. "Because it is the one common thread among all three authorities. Each is bound to the other to keep it secret, for it is in the interest of each to keep it such, therefore, none will betray."

"But," Augustine begins, having finally regained his use of speech, "What are the families of these ill-fated told? Surely they cannot go on thinking a relative has simply disappeared."

"No, naturally not. The closest of kin are told that the relative has committed some sort of crime, usually something of a very serious nature—

rape, murder, blasphemy. The family is told the relative received his trial and was sentenced to die, but that the execution would not be public, to spare the family shame. The prisoner is, of course, not executed, as that would make a murderer of the authority which sentenced him to the secret prison."

Pa waves his hand. "Wait a minute. The Order has ruled Malta for twenty-one years, and if this place dates back to Aragonese occupation, how could the knights share ownership?"

The priest shrugs. "The knights were handed more than just the keys to the city upon arrival. Bringing the Grand Master and his henchmen into the know was probably the Church and civil authority's way of looking after their own interests."

At this, there is a shockwave of whispers. Angelica's face is ashen, her hands shaking. "You knew about this place, Uncle? You knew and have never tried to do anything about it?"

Father Tabone's shoulders sag. "Angelica, you want me to take on the three ruling powers? I would have ended up in there myself. I considered writing the emperor, but if the letter was intercepted, imagine the disaster that would befall our little family. Besides, I'm sure the emperor is fully aware of its existence already, or the existence of places just like it. Europe is scattered with them, these secret prisons."

Dr Callus, who has remained oddly silent, clears his throat. "So. It is true. I have heard whispers of it. Amazing what truths a person delirious with pain will reveal. I should pay closer attention to the ravings of my patients. Also, I must say, it is quite clear who is behind Robert's disappearance." Enquiring gazes shift from priest to physician.

"Who?" Domenicus asks when no one else speaks.

"The knights. Well, *a* knight anyway," Callus replies. "Think about it. What men would have the nerve to take a servant of the Order from his post without prior consent? Further, who would dare leave this post of vigilance empty, thus putting the whole of the island in jeopardy? If these *men in black* acted without the Order's sanction they would earn themselves a meeting with the gallows."

"But," Katrina begins, "the tower was empty. Would the knights not have arranged a replacement had they known they would be short a sentry the entire afternoon?"

The doctor shakes his head. "Make no mistake, there was a replacement—a knight or squire watching from a nearby vantage. Whoever is behind this would have considered that exact chain of reasoning. Whoever is behind this wants to distance himself as much as possible and to distance the authority responsible, but in the doing, he has put us closer to bridging the gap." Callus peers at Katrina. "I was told Bonfatti was here earlier. Where is he?"

"Gone," she says. "He said he would do his best to help find Robert."

"Your father tells me this Bonfatti has a low view of Falsone. Why is he so keen to help?"

"Maybe because he has a conscience."

"In which case he is the only knight in the whole of the Order so equipped," Callus says. "And I do not think his morality has anything to do with it."

"Then because he is my friend, and holds a high view of me."

The doctor grunts. "Ah, could this high view of you be behind Robert's disappearance?"

Katrina frowns. "Not a chance. Franco rallied to Robert's defence when he was imprisoned for a theft he did not commit. Why would he turn on him now?"

Suddenly, a violent clatter sounds from outside. All fall silent, barely breathing. Belli heads out at once to investigate. Augustine looks to the doctor, the priest. "Better we keep our voices down. There are fouler places to end up than the dungeons of St Angelo."

Minutes later, Belli returns, mystified. "Whatever made that noise is gone."

"A stray," Domenicus ventures, though he does not believe it. He rises. "I'm going to the fosse."

Angelica looks sharply at him. "The devil you are. You're staying right here."

"We do not know where Robert is. Perhaps he is in some secret prison, but perhaps not. I want to at least rule out obvious places, like the prisoner culvert at St Angelo."

Katrina rises. "I'm coming."

"Oh no, you're not," every man in the room replies in unison. Had this happened under different circumstances, it would have been comical.

Augustine stops Domenicus on his way to the door. "Careful, you hear? Whoever is behind this has gone to great lengths to cover himself, and should you find a loose thread and pull too hard, you will put yourself in terrible danger. To the fosse and immediately back."

***

Domenicus mounts his horse and starts for the fortress St Angelo, but with the streets too tight to gallop, he can kick Tramonto to only a trot. At the castle base is the deep culvert Domenicus helped to build. The fosse, as it is publicly known, is where prisoners are detained after corporal punishment. He reins Tramonto and jumps from the saddle. Torchlight flickers and blinks, licking upward from the crenellated fortress walls, creating erratic shadows across the culvert's thatch covering. At the ledge, he lies prone, straining to see through the foliage roof. A sweaty, bloody stench rises and with it, a few painful groans.

"*Robert*," Domenicus whispers urgently. Through the thatch, he can make out several known thieves, naked, lacerated, but there is no sign of

Robert Falsone among this beaten rabble, their fresh whip marks shining red in the torchlight. Beyond the ditch, past the walls, are the gallows. Ropes hang looped in readiness. Domenicus has never paid attention to the gallows before, having known none of the scaffold's victims personally. Now, with his best friend in some unnamed prison, the sight of a noose is all too unbearable. He averts his eyes. "*Robert,*" he hisses again.

"Who goes there?"

Domenicus squints through the darkness to the source of the gruff voice. A mounted patrolman draws near. "I'm looking for someone."

"You're not supposed to be here," the officer replies. "Leave, or I'll arrest you."

"Please," Domenicus says, rising, "Is Robert Falsone in there?"

"In ten seconds *you* will be in there and can look for him yourself."

Domenicus whistles for Tramonto. The horse knows its rider, seems to sense his urgency and is off before he is fully mounted, taking him swiftly beyond the patrol's sight.

Under the starless sky, the rider's mind churns with the winds. None of this makes sense. Why would Robert Falsone, former farmhand, present sentry, be at the heart of a conspiracy? He holds no rank, no office, no power. He has no title to usurp, no gold to steal, no wife to covet. Why would men of power concern themselves with a rustic? Especially one such as Robert, who leads a quiet, simple existence. If anyone has angered men of rank, it is Domenicus Montesa, having directly challenged the Grand Master of the Order. Further, surely the *hakem*'s blood still boils following the dreadful episode days ago. Both events went unpunished. Besides, had Robert gotten himself caught up in some kind of trouble, surely he would have told his best friend. Still, someone has taken great pains to hire black-garbed thugs to come for him, render his poor mother senseless, lock him in some prison beyond the village boundaries, fabricate a witness or coerce one, then cover his own tracks. It is too much to be a mistake. Domenicus comes up with nothing, and his heart is heavy.

The Montesa house is quiet. Domenicus returned to find Mea in Katrina's bed, Kat at her side, Pa waiting, and everyone else gone. Now, Domenicus is outside again, leaning against the stone shell of his father's house, staring at insects as they swarm in the halo of a lantern. Strange, he thinks, how drawn a creature could be to its killer. The door opens, and Augustine joins him out front.

"I put your sister in bed," he says. "Poor girl fell asleep on the floor."

Domenicus glances to his side without turning his head. "Robert was not in the fosse."

"We will find him."

Domenicus faces his father. "Have you no leverage? Can you not make an appeal to the master-at-arms for information?"

He shakes his head. "You bore witness to the extent of my leverage the day of Gabriel Mercadal's funeral. Besides, Bonfatti said it is unlikely the knights are holding Robert. I believe him."

Domenicus exhales forcefully, looks down. "That damnable Order infuriates me. And it infuriates you too. I saw your standoff with Franco earlier."

"I cannot hold against him that he defends his knighthood. Moreover, he has been a good friend to our family."

"Insufferable hypocrites. How do they live with themselves?"

"Easily," his father replies. "A man can always find a way to justify himself, just as he can always find a way to believe his own logic. A servant might steal from his employer but exonerate himself by attributing the theft to his scanty wage."

"In a way, I understand the servant's logic," Domenicus says.

"Ah, but this sort of logic extends from the lowliest attendant to the loftiest leader. How else do you think emperors sleep at night knowing they have sent young men—boys younger than you—off to be slaughtered for causes not their own?"

"And knowing this, you remain loyal to the Order?"

Augustine sighs. "I suppose I too am a hypocrite. Or not, for here is my justification: the Order brought me to your mother."

"And took my mother from you."

"Illness took her."

"With all my heart," Domenicus says, "I do not wish to argue the Order's value. Nor do I believe that the Order is behind this. What do the Knights of St John care about some illiterate peasant? Still, they must know *something*. Everything that has happened could never have without their sanction." He looks across his shoulder to his father. "I hate the Order. Yet, I understand why it has your love. It gave you a second father, gave you a life. But it seems whatever goodness dwelt within the hearts of the knights, died with Gabriel Mercadal."

"There is still honour there to be found."

"Yes," Domenicus replies, "in the heart of a soldier-at-arms."

***

Far outside the city gates, in some nameless dungeon deep in the earth, a heavy door closes with a hollow clang. He can only hope Katrina found his coins, the ten *habba* scattered on the watchtower floor, so she would know he had been there, and that the men who came for him were not corsairs, not robbers. He prays his mother is all right. His last memory is of her carrying a small basket towards the tower, a stick of bread poking out. Then, he was unconscious.

Robert Falsone, bruised and bloodied, slumps to the gritty floor. Unsure in the blackness if there is another prisoner in the cell, he presses his back against the cold wall, hugging his knees tight against his chest. After a time, he senses that he is alone.

The air is damp. The fabric of his shirt does little to ward off the cold, which puts an ache in his muscles. The stink of human filth is pungent to the point of taste, intensified by the darkness as if the darkness is the smell. Without sight, sound is amplified. Groans come from some dark place, heavy steps from outside the door. The keys dangling from the jailor's belt clink together. It is the sound of freedom, so close, so out of reach, as if liberation herself has come to taunt him.

Indeed, he is alone in the cell, alone in all the world.

CHAPTER THIRTY-EIGHT

Katrina is up the night grappling with Father Tabone's revelation. It is preposterous that such a prison could exist in total secrecy on an island this small. There must be another explanation. So, an hour before dawn, she creeps from her house to get it.

Franco had said there was a witness. That, at least, is something real. However, Katrina cannot simply go door to door, asking villagers if, between trips to church and the market, they happened to concoct a fancy lie about Robert Falsone.

The first thing she must do is find out which governing body is responsible for the arrest. On the surface, all signs point to the knights—to work for the Order is to be disciplined by the Order. However, murder is a crime against the king's law, which makes this a matter for the civil authority. Of course, there was no murder, but if that is the charge, that is the charge.

The knights and the civil administration will shoo her away the moment she comes around asking questions. The law lords are at least compatriots and may hear her out *before* shooing her away. As she takes the dark road to Mdina, she prays to St Jude Thaddeus, patron of hopeless cases.

It is over an hour before Katrina reaches the hilltop city, its walls lit gold by the rising sun. She races up the beaten trail and over the drawbridge. Without stopping for breath, she runs straight to the main door of the *Università*.

The antechamber buzzes with legal talk. A notary disputes a claim with a tax collector. Two of the four *jurati*, powerful nobles of Mdina, discuss affairs of state with several *ministrali*. All are handsomely dressed and neatly groomed. Even bureaucrats of low status are stations above Katrina Montesa. Now that she is here, alone, she has no idea where to turn. She decides to skip the lower-level officials and make straight for the *hakem*. She saw him briefly years ago while attending Candlemas with her parents in Mdina. But even if he deigns to see her this morning, she doesn't have a snowflake's chance in hell of winning

331

him over, not when the man's wife was caught trying to seduce Katrina's own brother. She begins to realise the hopelessness of her quest. There must be another way to find Robert. Perhaps Franco has news. She will go to his dormitory instead.

Although her mind is set on the door, her legs take her to the staircase she ascended once before on a similar purpose. She walks quickly through a long corridor of offices until she reaches the one at the end, and enters without knocking. The red-bearded magistrate sits at his desk, a writing implement nestled between his fingers. She remembers him—and his scowl.

"Who in the hell are you?" he snaps.

"Katrina Montesa."

"And what daisy field at the back of your mind makes you think you can just barge in here?"

"No daisy field, my lord, but a serious lapse in justice," she replies.

"What lapse?"

"Robert Falsone, a sentry in service of the Order, has been arrested for a murder he did not commit. In fact, no murder was committed at all. It was suicide."

"This is a matter concerning the knights," the magistrate says dismissively.

"No. It is a matter concerning us all."

"How's that?"

"Even if there was a murder," Katrina begins, fairly amazed the man is actually prodding her for more, "it would be considered a crime against the king's law, and therefore tried by local courts."

"Not if one in the Order's fold committed the murder. It certainly does not concern me. Go to St Angelo. This Falsone is probably detained there."

"He's not. And that's exactly why it does concern you. If he's not at St Angelo, and you're not holding him here, there is only one other place he can be."

"The confessional?" The magistrate suggests wryly. Smirking, he rests his bearded chin on his fist, making himself infuriatingly pompous. Katrina does not share in his amusement.

"The secret prison," she says, flatly.

The indifference lining the large man's face twists up into utter shock. His eyes catch fire and blaze. "*What? What did you just say?*" He jumps to his feet, knocking his chair over behind him. He launches himself like a dog at the door and slams it shut. In three strides, he is upon her, his towering bulk forcing her back. He takes Katrina by the shoulders, slams her hard against the wall.

"You foolish, foolish girl! This is dangerous, very dangerous." She feels his spittle and his fury and struggles against his hold. Any moment, her bones will snap in his vise grip. "I will have you locked up!" He pulls her away from the wall only to shove her back into it, knocking the wind from her lungs. She sees little lights all around her. The magistrate is going to kill her right here.

"I—I'm sorry," she stumbles.

He slams her against the wall once more. "Who have you told of this? *Who? Speak!*"

"No one! I swear it!"

The magistrate releases her. She drops to the floor, panting. He bends, face to face with her. "Breathe a word of this prison to anyone, and you will, I promise you, spend the rest of your worthless days there, do you hear me? As will every person you tell."

Katrina can barely make out his face despite its proximity, because of the tears blurring her vision. The law lord takes her by the hair, drags her back to her feet, slaps her face. "*Do you hear me?*" He slaps her again. "*Do you?*"

She manages a nod. At last, he lets go.

"Not a single word, now. There's a good girl." Katrina slumps back to the floor as the magistrate goes to open the door. "Guard!" he calls. At once, a large man with huge hands enters the room. "Escort this young lady from the building forthwith, and if she gives you trouble, whip her."

The guard takes Katrina's wrists into one of his hands. She yelps as he hauls her through the corridor, past the offices, down the stairs. She stumbles and trips, but the guard does not slow. Without a word, he pushes open the main door with his free hand and throws her onto the street, where she lands on her hands and knees, gashing her skin, jarring her bones, and knowing, beyond a doubt, that Father Anton Tabone's revelation is true.

***

Doctor Giuseppe Callus walks Mdina's thoroughfare, on his way to his brother's apothecary shop to load up on supplies. He sees a girl bent in a heap on the ground, shoulders wracking with sobs. He rushes to her side, brushes the hair gently from her face as he helps her rise. The doctor breathes sharply in.

Katrina Montesa, bloodied, bruised, shaking.

***

Augustine is outside when the cart stops at his house. He smiles, squinting from the brightness of the morning. "Dr Callus, come to check on Mea?"

"Not exactly." The physician steps down and helps Katrina to the ground. Augustine starts at the sight of his daughter, her bruises, her tear-streaked face.

"Mother of God! What happened? Who did this to you? I'll kill him!"

"Gently, gently," Callus says. "I've tended her injuries, though she refuses to tell me how she sustained them. I found her outside the *Università*."

Augustine flashes. "Katrina, why were you there? What did you do?"

She shakes her head. "I can't tell you. It will be awful if I say anything."

"It will be more awful if you don't."

"Perhaps," Callus begins, "This is a discussion for indoors. We can talk in the stable to keep from disturbing Mea."

"Get Domenicus," Katrina says.

"He went to see Franco," Augustine says, as he helps her up the road to Belli's stable, Callus trailing. Inside, the air smells of dung and wet straw. The donkey Peppone stomps a fore-hoof, as though unhappy to be sharing his quarters with Robert's cantankerous goat. Augustine sits next to his daughter on a mound of hay. He takes her hand gently, but addresses her firmly: "Speak."

After a long moment, she obeys. "I went to the *Università* to find out about Robert."

"*What?* Katrina! No! Tell me you didn't mention the prison. Katrina, tell me you didn't."

She looks down. "I'm sorry."

Augustine throws up his hands. "For Christ's sake, Girl! What would possess you? You have ruined everything! We had an ally in Father Tabone. He agreed to help Robert, and now... now you have sabotaged us. Not to mention put the priest in terrible danger."

"No, don't say that! I never even mentioned Father Tabone, I swear it."

"Perhaps," Callus interjects, "All is not ruined. Hear her first."

"I know I shouldn't have gone," Katrina says. "But as Domenicus went to the fosse to rule it out, so I went to the civil authority. When I mentioned the prison to the magistrate, he threatened to end me."

Augustine feels his heart racing. "This *magistrate*, he raised his hand against you?"

"Leave this, Pa. You'll only get yourself into trouble." The man shakes with rage. A calming hand rests on his arm. He looks up to see Callus standing over him.

"Listen to your daughter. She's right. Harm the magistrate, you only harm yourself. Then, you'll be no good to Katrina, or Robert, or anyone."

Augustine swallows. "I know that. Just give me a moment to be angry, will you?"

"Take as many as you need."

At length, Augustine looks to his daughter. "Attend. I love Robert, but I will not lose you or your brother because of this ugly plot. This is not like the last time he was in trouble with the law. Now, he is caught in the middle of something sinister. Many powerful men have much to lose if this prison is exposed. They will guard this secret with their lives, and will not baulk at the idea of ending yours or mine to keep it. Understand?"

Katrina nods. "I'm sorry," she says.

"Don't be sorry. Just be careful."

Dr Callus clears his voice. "We need to be of one mind in this one purpose. Tonight, we meet at my house. Midnight."

"I'll tell Franco," Katrina says.

"No," Callus replies sternly. "Only your brother, the priest, and us. The carpenter may join us if he wishes. We'll need Angelica to stay back with Mea. Above all, say nothing to di Bonfatti."

Augustine exchanges an alarmed glance with Katrina. "Domenicus!"

***

The dockyard waters sparkle with the day. It is a busy scene, boats crossing the harbour lanes, gulls wheeling above, bobbing below, fishermen steady in colourful dinghies, merchants sailing in, traders sailing out, scores of workmen labouring on the waterfront. The shipyard smells of the freshly chopped wood used on three new galleys being built to replace ones lost in storms. Domenicus finds Franco supervising deckhands as they reeve new halyards.

The knight looks up. "You should be more prudent."

"Prudent?"

"What idiotic impulse made you go to the fosse last night?"

Domenicus had intended to approach Franco with friendship, but the knight's hostility puts him out. "You mean something as insignificant as my looking into a ditch is noteworthy enough to reach your ears, but the whereabouts of Robert Falsone are impossible for you to dig up?"

Franco looks at him as if slapped. "I have had quite enough of Montesa rudeness. I've done nothing but try to help, and you have all responded with appalling insolence."

Domenicus suddenly feels terrible. "You're right." He meets Franco's eyes. "I am sorry, honestly. We expect you to find information that we cannot, and to find it double time. That's not fair to you. I apologise."

"I accept," Franco replies.

"Good. Now, about the witness. Are you certain there even is one? It's not a fabrication?"

Franco looks at Domenicus askance. "Fabrication?"

"It's just that, well, I heard something unsettling last night, after you left."

The knight cocks an eyebrow. "Oh? And what was that?"

"*Domenicus!*" He turns. It is his father, twenty or so paces away.

Domenicus squints against the sun. "What is it?"

"Your sister."

"What's happened?" he asks, running over, Franco following.

"She's had a little accident. I need you home."

Franco is all concern. "Is she all right? Anything I can do?"

Augustine smiles. "She'll be fine. Just took a spill while riding. Besides, I have no right to pull you away from duty. You've already been so generous with your time."

335

Franco acquiesces, though with noticeable reluctance, and starts back towards the shipyard. When he is well out of earshot, Domenicus leans towards his father. "What's this all about?"

"I came to save you."

"From what?"

"Yourself. In the name of all that is decent and holy, tell me you did not mention that prison."

Domenicus blanches. "No, I did not." He does not tell his father that he was all set to.

Augustine breathes relief. "Listen, your sister had an ugly brush with the magistrate."

"What? What did he do to her? Is she all right?"

"Yes, a few bruises, nothing too serious. This prison is obviously a dangerous secret if the mere mention of it would provoke a law lord to attack a girl. That's why no one linked to the knights or the civil authority can know that we know."

"I think we should just tell everyone about it," Domenicus says. "Tell the people of Birgu and beyond. It will bring a revolt, public outrage. They'd have to release everyone and shut it down."

His father halts mid-stride. "Don't even think that. The three powers would crush anything we said. They would crush *us*."

"What are we going to do then?"

"There is a meeting tonight at the doctor's house. Twelve bells on the darkness."

***

Midnight in Mdina. Domenicus catches the distant toll of the clock tower as he crosses into Dr Callus's lodging, a small stone cottage that stands on one of the city's many crisscrossing byways. Medical volumes line his shelves, along with artefacts from his treasure hunts: broken bits of pottery, ancient coins, fragments of a skull, and a large femur—the favourite of his youngest patients, because he tells them it is the toe bone of a dragon. Domenicus believed until he was eleven, Katrina, nine.

The doctor's guests sit together on the floor by the hearth, their voices hushed. Callus is no stranger to secret meetings and knows well how to conduct one. He drains the brandy from his cup, looks to Father Tabone.

"Tell us everything you know about the prison."

"It is old, built in the time of King Alfonso. I have never been there. Only a select few are supposed to know it exists—the bishop, the *hakem*, the Grand Master, their very close favourites."

Katrina rubs her neck. "The magistrate."

Belli throws up his hands. "If we don't even have an idea where this place might be, what good is this meeting?" Domenicus can't help agreeing, but stays quiet.

"I said I've never been there," the priest replies, "not that I have no idea where it is. The bishop has referenced it more than once while engaged in what he thought was a private conversation. The prison lies beyond the village, somewhere between Birgu and the southeastern sea-cliffs."

Katrina squints as if looking back to a vague memory. "Would there be guards?"

"Of course," Father Tabone replies.

"In the open, do you think?" she asks.

"It's possible."

"I don't know if this is worth anything," she says, "but a time ago, on my way to the southeastern coast, I noticed two men I took for gendarmes, just sort of idling about. There was a good distance between us, but I saw they had guns. I thought they were hawking." She inhales pensively. "Oh yes! And I heard them talk. Their speech was neither Maltese nor Italian. If it were French or Spanish, I would have recognized it. It was a tongue I had never heard before."

"Greek? German? English?" Father Tabone suggests.

"I wouldn't know."

Augustine runs his hand along the raspy line of his jaw. "Well, it makes sense that the keepers of this prison would not employ Maltese. Too risky."

Domenicus nods. "Say, then, this is the location. What now? Have we abandoned the idea of finding the witness?"

"Perhaps," Callus begins, "there is no witness. If the prisoners are innocents, what need is there for witnesses?"

Domenicus considers the doctor's point. "To keep up the pretence. Who would readily believe a family member committed a crime without the word of a witness? Besides, the more layers, the less likely the conspirator will be found out."

Belli coughs. "Piss on the witness. I say we set the prison ablaze."

Pa jogs the carpenter's ribs with his elbow. "Talk sense, man. You think the guards are going to stay to free the prisoners?"

"No, but we can smoke out the guards and go in ourselves to free Robert. I have an axe."

"Leaving the rest to die?"

"We'd get them out too," Belli replies. "You are a man of action, Augustine. You've fought in sieges, in smoke and flame."

"What if," Domenicus ventures, "we exchange a dead body for a live one?" The suggestion piques interest, all eyes now on him. "With your help," he looks at Callus "we can take a corpse from the *Sacra Infermeria* and leave it in the dungeon in place of Robert."

A grin plays on the doctor's mouth. "Hmm, this idea, it's not the dumbest thing I've heard."

"How do you plan to make the exchange?" Augustine asks. "Moreover, whoever went to the trouble of having Robert locked away will surely notice if he's suddenly back in Birgu. If we manage to get him out, he will have to leave Malta forever."

At first, no one speaks. At length, Domenicus clears his voice. "He will go to Sicily. I'll be there shortly to commence my studies. He'll stay with me."

"No, Son. Think this through," his father says. "First, how will he board a ship unnoticed? Second, if he does leave Malta, what becomes of Mea? Third, he cannot stay with you in Sicily. The hall of residence is open strictly to students. And above all, you'll only be there a few months. He will be there for the rest of his life."

Katrina, quiet until now, speaks up. "I will go with him."

Augustine furrows his brow. "Kat—"

"I love him. I have always loved him. I will go with him. And if Italy is not far enough to keep him safe, I'll go with him to France, to Germany, to Denmark. Anywhere."

Augustine is silent a while. "You really are serious."

"Perfectly."

"Then if we get him out," he says, voice thick, "you will leave with him."

Domenicus rises angrily. "*What?* Father, you can't let her go! Forbid her! *I* will take care of Robert. I'll see that he is settled abroad."

"This is not your decision to make," Augustine says gently.

"It's not hers either! She's *not* going!" Domenicus faces his sister. "I will not allow you to run off to some strange land you know nothing about. You'll starve. You'll get yourself killed."

"If Angelica's life were threatened, if she had to leave Malta to save herself, you would not go with her?"

"Of course I would!"

"Why is this different?"

"Because it is. Because you're my little sister." His eyes water, but he swallows hard. The last thing Domenicus needs right now is to become a blubbering mess. "How do you plan to get to Sicily? To survive? Trading on your keen wit and good looks?"

Belli cuts in. "She'll do fine with the money I set aside for her. It's enough to support them until Robert can find work." Katrina looks at the carpenter in surprise. He shrugs. "I'm not going to leave my holdings to the donkey, am I?"

Now that the argument has ended, Dr Callus speaks up. "So, the cadaver idea is out. What about a living diversion?"

Katrina shifts from sitting to kneeling. "If the guards were kept busy, one of you could sneak into the prison and get Robert out."

"Busy with what?" Father Tabone asks her.

"...I don't know." She looks down at her hands. "A couple of courtesans."

Augustine narrows his eyes. "Just who would these courtesans be?" Katrina does not look up. "Me. And maybe Angelica."

"Not a chance!" Pa thunders.

Domenicus is equally adamant: "Absolutely not." Their sentiments are echoed by everyone else in the room. Everyone but Dr Callus.

"They wouldn't have to actually *do* anything with the guards," he ventures. "Just distract them for a few minutes. This is not a stupid idea."

"Yes, it is," Father Tabone snaps. "Stupidest thing I've ever heard in my entire life. Besides, are the guards just supposed to believe two courtesans happened to be looking for customers in the middle of nowhere? They'd never fall for it."

Callus snorts. "You put too much faith in what these guards would and would not do. They are men after all, and what man wouldn't enjoy some attention from two beautiful girls?"

"All right, assume they do fall for it," the priest says. "Katrina and Angelica will not intend to go through with the transaction. What happens when the men decide to take what was offered?"

Belli slams his fist into his open palm. "I break their skulls."

"You'll do no such thing," Augustine says. "There won't be a need. My daughter and my son's future wife will not play the role of whores." His tone is hard, final.

"Then," Callus sighs, "we are right back to where we started."

Domenicus sighs miserably. "So Robert is there until he dies."

Katrina slaps his face. All are shocked to silence, especially him. After a few moments, he nods. "You're right. I'm sorry. We won't give up."

His sister continues the discussion, offering no apology. "We have associations. Why not make use of them? Father Tabone, you are our eyes and ears in the Church. Domenicus, Dr Callus, you are acquainted with Alonso Predal, head of all medical practitioners and senior official in the *Università*. He helped you once. He can help you again. He is a good, honest man from what I hear."

"Too good, too honest," Domenicus says, "to know anything of this place, and he wouldn't have had a chance to overhear anything as you did, Father Tabone."

Katrina looks down, speaking more to the floor than to anyone in the room. "We have an ally in the Order, even though you all refuse to see him as one. Franco has proven himself a loyal friend to our family. And, he is privy to information we could never access. I don't understand why he has suddenly fallen into disfavour with us. He wants to help. Why should we slap his hand away?"

Callus uses a poker to revive the flame dying in the hearth. The newly invigorated fire lights the doctor's features, reflects in his eyes. "I don't trust him."

"With respect, Dr Callus, your distrust is based strictly on his being a knight."

"Can you think of a better reason to distrust a man?"

"Yes, an *actual* reason," Katrina says.

Domenicus shifts restively. "This should have occurred to me sooner, but Franco was the one who delivered news of Robert's arrest. He also told us there is a witness. If everything is so covert, how did Franco unearth these details?"

"Because he's a knight!" Katrina snaps, fully riled. "This is precisely why I think we could use his help. You're repeating what I just said, only putting it in a negative light."

Belli sucks his teeth. "I still say we set the place ablaze. You all know I'm right."

Callus smirks. "Even a broken clock is right twice a day."

Augustine waves for attention. "We're talking in circles. Do we involve outsiders or not?"

"Franco is not an outsider," Katrina insists.

"Neither is he one of us," Pa replies. "And you forget—I am a soldier and part of the Order. I can poke around too, you know. I say we use our connections without their knowing. Agreed?"

"Agreed," reply all but one.

"It's a mistake not to include Franco," Katrina says.

"I'm sorry, Kat. It has been put to vote. You must adhere to its outcome. Now," Augustine continues, "has any member of the Church been slighted by Robert?"

Father Tabone shakes his head. "None. Believe me, I would have heard about that."

"The *Università* then? Has he crossed a *jurat*? The *hakem* himself?"

Domenicus takes this query. "Impossible. He's never in Mdina to cross anyone."

Callus folds his hands. "That leaves but one governing body. The one Robert serves. The one he hates above all others. The Order of the Knights of St John."

***

Lilla sits on a stone slab beneath a windmill, its blades turning languidly with the late night breeze. After a time, a cloaked man hikes the narrow footpath towards her, the dirt beneath his feet broken by thick roots. He moves with vulpine furtiveness along rocky terrain to the tip of the promontory.

Franco di Bonfatti drops a velvet purse at Lilla's feet, coins rattling against each other. She bends and sweeps it off the ground. It is heavier than any purse than she has ever lifted. "Fifty *tarì*!"

He nods. "Passage back to Catania."

Lilla smiles. "For a few minutes with Marco. Easy money." She rises, presses herself against the handsome knight. "I thought you wanted something else when you called me over." She slides her hands under his cloak. "That too would have been easy money."

The knight pushes her away. "What you've done for me is far better."

"What exactly have I done for you?"

"Secured me a witness."

"What do you mean?" she asks, a tight pinch above her nose.

"I needed to get Robert Falsone out of my way, but there were no grounds for his arrest. By catching you in the watchtower with Marco, I was able to force him to sign a document naming Robert as the murderer of that farmer who killed himself a few weeks ago."

Lilla steps back, smile gone. When the knight solicited her to sleep with the sentry Marco Vella, she thought it was some strange prank. She should have known better. The lofty knight thinks himself heights upon heights above her kind. Even when he told her she was to act shocked and penitent when he barged in on them, she assumed it all part of the game. Or maybe she ignored her suspicions because of the tidy sum Franco had offered her.

"Why are you telling me this?"

The knight waves her off as though she is an overly inquisitive child. "Because you are beneath caution. Beneath even contempt."

"So what does that make you, who hired someone beneath contempt?"

Franco grabs Lilla by the wrist and twists it. She yanks her arm away, his fingerprints burning red on her skin, and stumbles over a patch of thistle, tearing her petticoat and landing heavily on her backside. Her eyes are on Franco, even as she crawls backwards.

He laughs at her. "I'm finished with you. No need to fall on your back for me."

"You have no honour."

He shrugs. "Go tell the Grand Master."

"And be paid Robert Falsone's wages?" Lilla rises warily to her feet and wipes bloodied palms on her dress. She snatches up the velvet purse and without another word, gathers up her skirts and bolts.

CHAPTER THIRTY-NINE

Franco greets her at the *auberge* door with a frown. "Did I not tell you I would bring word?"

"You did. I'm not here seeking word. I have it to give. Meet me at the ruins, one hour." She turns for the road without giving Franco a chance to respond.

"Katrina, wait!" he calls after her. But she does not. Instead, she runs to Belli's stable and fetches Tramonto. With no time to saddle the horse, she rides bareback. Once beyond Birgu's boundaries, with only open fields between her and her destination, she pushes the beast to full gallop.

The tops of white stone columns soon break the sky, the ruins bright against the reddish earth on which they stand. Katrina halts her horse, dismounts. The air is fresh at the edge of the cliffs, and carries the scent of sea and sky, having touched both. It is a peaceful place, a scene contrary to the one in her head. Every step taken towards the pillars fills her with guilt for betraying her family's trust. But as much as they care for Robert, they do not love him the way she does. She cannot sit idly by as they shun someone who can help. Anyone who has ever truly loved would understand.

Stones scatter suddenly within the ruins, stopping Katrina in her tracks, freezing her breath. Franco emerges from the coralline maze, bringing her much relief, if a little disquiet, with his unexpected appearance.

"My lord," she says, feeling formality in order. "I did not expect you to overtake me."

"I watched your approach," Franco says. He tilts his head, peers through a narrow gaze. "You did not fall off your horse the other day, did you?"

"No, I did not." Katrina looks the knight in the face, focusing hardest on his eyes. They never waver. "Can I trust you? Truly trust you?"

"With your life," he replies. "But really, you have to ask?"

"Right now," she sighs, feeling herself already on the brink, "I don't even trust myself." She takes a deep breath. *God forgive me.* "There is a secret prison, beyond Birgu." Franco flinches visibly—an action Katrina takes for scepticism. She needs a way to convince him. "Sounds absurd, I know. But none of the governing powers is holding Robert—not openly anyway. He obviously didn't just disappear when he was arrested for murder."

"I don't think it's absurd," Franco says. "In fact, I know such a place to exist."

This shakes the earth beneath her feet. "Why did you keep it from me?"

"A number of reasons. The first, and forgive me for it, I didn't think Robert Falsone important enough to end up there. This prison is for those who pose a serious threat—dissenters, conspirators, reformists, would-be assassins, and the like."

"But if these men are guilty of such things, why should they be hidden away? Had Robert killed the farmer, he would be tried and executed publicly. Were he even merely a suspect, there would still be a trial. The very fact that he's been hauled off in secret is proof of his innocence." She halts briefly, consumed suddenly by Franco's earlier omission. "You know, I am greatly vexed that you withheld the existence of the prison."

"I've already given you one reason for that. Here is the other. I am honour and service bound to guard this secret at all cost. The conspiracy of silence is meant to save you Maltese from yourselves. Imagine if the populace caught word. There would be a revolution, blood in the streets."

"Rightly so!"

"No, Katrina, think about it. Average citizens needn't worry about ending up there. How often do peasants have dealings with knights?"

"What about the civil authority? The Church?"

"You think Falsone wronged a clergyman or a law lord?"

"I think the Order is behind this," Katrina says flatly. "Why else would you be the only one capable of unearthing any information?" Franco frowns, crosses his arms over his chest.

"You've spoken to the civil authority on this matter?" he asks.

"The moment I mentioned it, the magistrate attacked me."

Franco looks with severity at Katrina. "Girl, you dabble in things beyond your ability to comprehend. If you carry on in these idiotic investigations, you will bring yourself to ruin."

"What are you saying? To just give up on Robert?"

"Yes."

The ice in his response has Katrina retreating several paces. "Why do I have the feeling you know more than are letting on?" The knight flashes and, in two strides, closes the growing distance between them.

"Because, Child, you are suspicious and distrustful. I have been working tirelessly on Falsone's behalf, following every possible lead. You could at least pretend to be grateful."

Katrina stands her ground, refusing to be intimidated by another man of power. "And you could at least pretend to be on our side."

"I *am* on your side."

"Then why are you so hedging in your responses?"

"You are not asking questions. You are levelling accusations."

Katrina sighs. "Very well. How did you learn of Robert's charge? And of the witness?"

"I inquired as to the whereabouts of the sentry and was given the charge and the existence of a witness as my answer. When I pressed for more, the master-at-arms denied me."

With renewed hope, she takes hold of Franco's arm. "So he knows where Robert is?"

"Katrina, let me handle things inside the Order. I worry for your safety. And the safety of your father, your brother, your friends. You saw what happened to Robert's mother. Worse can happen to your father, your brother, your friends." Katrina feels her foundation crumble. How many must be put in danger for this cause? She would trade her life readily for that of Robert Falsone. Would she be so quick to trade the lives of everyone else?

"Tell me what to do," she says finally.

"Let me seek out the identity of the one behind this."

After lengthy deliberation, Katrina nods.

"Heed now. This cannot be done in a day. A fortnight perhaps." Franco pauses, considers. "Yes, meet me back here, two weeks today. Noon. In the meantime, keep quiet."

"I promise," Katrina replies. "I'm betraying my family by being here with you now. Please don't be angry with them. We vowed silence. A vow," she quickly adds, "that has nothing to do with a lack of trust in you." If Franco senses the lie, he makes no indication.

"Two weeks," he says.

She turns. Turns back. "I'm glad I came to you."

"I'm glad, too."

***

It is late Sunday afternoon. Domenicus sits alone at home, no idea what to do with himself. Yesterday, he and Belli brought Mea to the women's hospital in Rabat, where she would receive better care than at the Montesa house. When the doctor of the ward asked what had happened to her, they told him she had fallen down a flight of stairs. This morning, Domenicus visited the comatose woman at the hospital. Her bruises looked much worse; a sure sign they are getting better.

Now, he sits staring at the kitchen table, his eyes moving over the crisscross of lines nicked into its surface. He flicks crumbs across it, runs his hand through his hair, sighs. He has spent the last few days wracking his brain, trying to come up with something, anything, to help his best friend. And try as he might, he cannot help but be a little angry with Robert. From when they were children, Domenicus warned him to curb his severe declarations about the knights. He did not heed.

A knock sounds at the door. Domenicus is grateful for a distraction. It is Angelica, making the distraction a wonderful one. For the first time since Carnival, they are together alone. Without a word, she throws her arms around him, buries her face against his chest. He says nothing, content to hold her, to feel her body against his. He kisses her hair and holds her tighter. A moment of purity amidst all this corruption.

The moment passes all too soon. Angelica looks up at him. Domenicus sees weariness in her eyes, sees her fighting fatigue. She brings her hand to his cheek. "I have an idea."

He takes her hand, steps her over the threshold and closes the door. "What is it?"

"We have agreed that Franco di Bonfatti cannot be our connection inside the Order. There is, however, a knight who can be."

Domenicus furrows a curious brow. "Who?"

"Marcello di Ruggieri."

"You have got to be joking."

Angelica shakes her head. "He'll help us, I know it."

"He is Franco's best friend. If we went to him, he would tell Franco."

"You are wrong about him, Domenicus. Marcello *can* help."

He sighs, crosses his arms. "I'm listening."

"I know you did not warm to him. And yes, on the surface, he embodies everything about the Order you despise, but behind the arrogance is a genuine man. And I know he will help us because it would not be the first time he has gone behind Franco's back for me."

Domenicus is not sure he likes this. He tries to push aside his own petty jealousy to hear her out, but this proves difficult. "I thought you were but nodding acquaintances."

Angelica rolls her eyes. "There is nothing between us, I swear it. Let me explain."

"Explain."

"I needed to see the corsair—the one who saved me. I knew he was being held at the dockyard slave prison. I tried getting inside on my own, but the guard turned me away. I ran into Franco and Marcello on the street, and I asked Franco to help me gain entry, but he refused. Marcello secretly offered his service. Because of him, I was able to thank Emir personally. To this day, Marcello has never mentioned it to anyone. This, Domenicus, is how I know we can trust him."

The subject of a *corsair* being the man who saved Angelica is still a sore one with Domenicus. And now, he cannot help resenting that she never told him about Marcello di Ruggieri sneaking her into the prison. The knight was obviously not motivated by the plight of the corsair. The randy Florentine has quite a reputation for womanizing. Domenicus cannot ignore it.

"Why did you keep this from me? It is very clear what his intentions were. How is this any different from when Diana d'Alagona approached me?"

Angelica bridles at the comparison. "It *is* different and you know it. Regardless, you must not let your feelings influence you now. Be angry with me later. For the moment, I think we should enlist Marcello's help."

"And I think you should stop dismissing me as though I am an idiot child."

"Well, then, stop acting like one."

Domenicus frowns, turns away. Angelica takes his face in her hand and guides it gently back towards hers. "I'm sorry, all right? I should have told you. And yes, if things were reversed, I would be furious with you. But right now, we mustn't quarrel. You are welcome to reproach me later. For the time being, however, let's put this aside and work to help Robert. Agreed?"

"You forget we are sworn to keep the knights out of this."

"Marcello is not like them. He has already proven that if he swears secrecy, he will keep his promise. I think he would sooner say no to us then say yes and later betray us."

Domenicus sulks. "You know an awful lot about a man you claim is a nodding acquaintance."

"Stop it," Angelica says crossly.

He does. "Before proceeding, we should seek permission from the rest of our little knot. We cannot go behind their backs and confer with a knight."

"Your sister will make an issue of it. She was explicitly forbidden from mentioning any of this to Franco."

"So what do you suggest?" Domenicus asks.

"I'll go see Marcello," Angelica says. "I was not there when you swore your oaths of silence. It, therefore, does not hold me. This way, you will not be in breach."

"I think whatever we all agreed to at that meeting includes you."

She shrugs. "In all the commotion, you forgot to tell me."

Domenicus sighs. He knows when he is defeated. "I don't like this. I think it will go badly with Ruggieri."

"And I think it will go worse if we do nothing."

***

Franco paces his room. One time in his life emotion dictated his actions. One bloody time. And it will be his undoing.

He thought he was prepared for Katrina's confrontation; he was at the Montesa window the other night, listening as that meddlesome priest exposed the prison. A rat startled the knight into knocking over a pail, forcing him to run off. Franco knew eventually, Katrina would be coming for answers. Still, hearing her actually speak the words was unreal. He had flinched and was certain he betrayed himself in that movement, but she seemed to take it for disbelief. And as he looked at her, all he wanted to do was touch her.

Now, Franco leans forward on the edge of his bed, feet planted on the floor, half a mind to go report Father Tabone to the bishop. However, the knight would be found out in his eavesdropping, and the Montesa family's suspicions confirmed. Franco finds he is absurdly wounded by their distrust—they are right to suspect him, but it hurts that they were so quick to do so. They should be honoured he would even deign to speak to them.

He shakes off self-pity, focuses on his own idiotic handiwork. Why, why, why was he so stupid? From birth, anything he ever wanted, his wealth and title guaranteed him. He was therefore not prepared to meet obstacles in fulfilling his desires. Robert Falsone was the first he'd encountered. It killed Franco to be denied the one thing he wanted most, and on account of a peasant no less. So, he reacted with terrible and irrational suddenness, failing to give all details their due attention. Specifically, that guilt would torment him without mercy.

In his dimly lit room, the knight watches shadows move along his wall and contemplates all the other things he could have done to Robert—had him arrested and hanged outright, pushed him off a cliff. At the time, murder seemed too great a sin. Now, atoning for murder would be easier than facing the consequences of his clumsy plotting.

Downstairs in the vestibule, a great clock tolls the eighth hour, startling Franco from his trance. He needs time to come up with a new plan. He is pleased he has at least bought himself two weeks—not long enough, considering the complex nature of his scheme, but better than having to deal with daily requests for information. Still, he swore to Katrina he would return to her with word. *Let me seek out the identity of the one behind this,* he said. So, he is on a quest to find himself.

Franco lies back, propped up on his elbows, and closes his eyes. He sees Robert before him, sees the sentry on his first day working the watchtower. Sees him smile his infectious smile. Robert Falsone is innocent. A big part of Franco wants to confess, to present himself before the Grand Master and tell the truth. That would bring light back into his life, for so long as he hides beneath his shroud of lies, he will be in darkness. Besides, there is no sin so terrible that God will not grant absolution.

The Grand Master, however, may not be as quick to forgive. Few in the Order's number know of the prison's existence, and any time it is to be used, the Grand Master must be made aware. Otherwise, it would be overflowing with men who did not jump aside fast enough as a knight strode by. Franco is in such good standing with Juan d'Homedes the Spaniard did not even question the knight's desire to use the prison, let alone his knowledge of it. In all probability, the old man did not hear a word of the rehearsed lie—he would have nodded the same had Franco entered his study to announce the hour.

The knight opens his eyes. Candles burn low, almost guttered out in their own melted wax. He rises, his mind resolved: he will go see d'Homedes now and take whatever punishment is dished out. He walks two paces. Sits back down.

He can't do it. He cannot ask the Grand Master for Robert's release. Franco will be publicly expelled from the Order and named *putridum et fetidum*. He will lose everything: his knighthood, his title, even his life, but worst of all, his honour. Whatever is left of it. Besides, d'Homedes will not release Robert. The Grand Master could not risk the boy opening his mouth.

Franco chews the meat of his thumb. He will go himself to the dungeon, order Robert released. The prisoner would be so grateful, he would not think to question the reason for his confinement. He would simply give thanks for his release from it. Anyway, Robert Falsone is just a stupid, illiterate peasant without a clue as to who is behind this … this misunderstanding. Moreover, Franco could be the hero, tell Katrina he secured the discharge.

That's it. His mind is made up: he will have the sentry released tonight. Now. He stands once more. Makes it to the chamber door. Stops.

Robert Falsone is *not* stupid. He would know Franco is behind everything. The knight does not move, hand on the doorknob, mind churning, emotions erratic, alternately flooding him with anger and guilt, hostility and fear. He could buy the sentry's silence, freedom the currency. He will even throw in some gold pieces to pretend none of this ever happened—enough to live a comfortable life abroad. And, Franco will give Katrina up, knowing fully who has her heart.

He will never give her up. He goes to his desk, puts his head in his hands, and considers his original plan. Why, why, why was he so stupid? In his drunken rage and blinding heartache, the plot seemed brilliant, flawless. Damn Marcello di Ruggieri and his accursed bottle. Franco should have never named a charge—the very thing meant to distance him from the sentry's disappearance now connects him to it. He had intended to reveal later that Robert had been executed for the crime.

Franco lifts his head, taps his fingers on his desk as he works out his thoughts. In a month, maybe two, he would have made the tragic announcement. The Order governs its own; everyone knows that. Franco would have told Katrina and Domenicus that Robert's hearing was not public, as the Order's proceedings never are. Of course, Katrina would have been devastated, and it would have pained the knight to deliver such terrible news. But in her sorrow, he would have been her greatest comfort. And with Robert "dead," she would no longer be blind to Franco's charm.

He sits up straighter. Perhaps the tragic announcement can still be made. And if Katrina remains blind, he will simply deliver her to Robert…

where the two of them can be together until the end, separated for life by cell walls a foot thick.

That's it, his mind is made up.

CHAPTER FORTY

Angelica wastes a morning trailing Marcello. The Florentine is popular among his peers, and constantly in their company, whether attending matins at St Lawrence, at the shipyard overseeing the construction of new galleys, or returning to the *auberge* for lunch.

An hour passes with Angelica sitting on a nearby bench outside the dormitory, the sun hot on her black *barnuẓa*. Finally, Marcello di Ruggieri emerges, alone. Angelica rises, thinking this the perfect moment to approach him. But the knight is quickly off, his stride purposeful and swift and taking him down a tight alley that turns onto another and another after that. It is difficult for Angelica to keep up and keep her distance at the same time. She sweats beneath the yards of fabric and wonders where he could be going in such a hurry. Then, in the shadows of a dead end, she finds her answer. It is a woman. She draws back her hood, shakes out her long, red hair. She is pretty, but not in a conventional way. And there is no mistaking the look in Marcello's eyes when he sees her.

"Madeleine."

The prostitute smiles brightly. "You received my note. I'm glad."

Marcello kisses her brow. "Not as glad as I am that I taught you to write."

Madeleine takes his hand. "Is it safe here? We could sneak back inside that abandoned barn. You know, where the old farmer killed himself."

Marcello runs his mouth along her neck. He looks up and over his shoulder. The windowless back side walls of tall houses conceal them.

"We are safe enough," he says.

"Good, because I want you now." With that, they are upon each other. Madeleine lifts her skirts and takes him inside her with a sharp breath, right there against the wall. Their love is passionate, frenzied, yet tender. Angelica can scarce believe her eyes or her ears. Not because Marcello di

Ruggieri is enjoying the company of a prostitute, but because he seems to have genuine affection for her. He taught her to write. To *write!*

Angelica turns away. She certainly cannot approach him today, not after what she has just witnessed. She needs first to collect her bearings. What's more, the encounter has given her an idea.

***

Under cover of twilight and cloak, the Italian lord is led down a flight of rock-hewn steps, deep into the darkness. The hefty Greek jailor, Costas Kiriakoulias, unlocks the door to a cell, executes an ungainly bow, and makes way for the nobleman, who takes the lantern and enters. The air inside is acrid, stinks of urine and vomit and fear. The prisoner withdraws against a corner as though the soft nimbus of the lamp causes him pain.

"Leave us," the visitor says in Greek. The heavy door sweeps in a gust as it shuts, making the flame blaze brighter. Taking care that only the peripheries of his face are exposed, he lowers the lantern to get a good look at the prisoner.

The light of recognition dawns on Robert Falsone's face. "You. No surprise."

"*Prosit,*" Franco di Bonfatti replies in Maltese, before slipping smoothly into Italian. "Means *congratulations* in the tongue of commoners, correct? Katrina taught me the word during one of our many private lessons." If the remark at all baits Robert, he makes no indication.

"So? Now what?" he asks, as though enquiring about the weather.

Franco arcs an eyebrow. "You are awfully steady for someone on such shaky ground."

"You expect me to scrape and grovel and beg? No chance, pig. I'm not afraid of you."

"Perhaps you should be. If I will it, you die here." Franco makes his voice a whip but hates that it has not the lashing effect of one.

"And what is your will?"

At first, the knight does not reply. He cannot. For reasons he does not understand, tears burn his eyes. "… To be you."

Robert furrows his brow. "What?"

Franco throws back his head and lets out a roar that falls somewhere between a hysterical laugh and a bellow of rage. "All I want is to be you! You have nothing. You have *everything!*"

Robert gives Franco a flat, measuring look.

"You … you don't believe me?" The knight's voice is small, childlike.

"I believe you fine," Robert replies. "But tell me you did not come here seeking pity."

"I don't want your pity."

"What do you want, for Christ's sake?"

Franco sighs, feels his strength leaving him with his breath. "I want her. That's what I want. That's all I want. ...And she wants you."

"So that's why I'm here? Because you are unrequited in a love your vows do not permit you to fulfil anyway? It is laughable."

"You are in a position unsuitable to find anything funny."

"What am I supposed to do then? Sob? Wail? You will never hear a cry escape me. I understand you are pained, but I am no more to blame for your broken heart than are the trees for your faulty brain." This is not going as Franco had hoped. He wanted to see Robert broken, begging, it's true. The knight pushes down his growing agitation. Even in the faint light of the lamp, he can see that Robert is starving and emaciated, and finds some twisted comfort in that.

"Don't you see?" Franco says. "It *is* your fault. But for you, she would be mine."

"She is not mine, idiot!" Robert cries, rising, his voice jarring in the empty cell.

"Then you do not see. And that is precisely why you do not deserve her."

"If you are in love with Katrina, why don't you just tell her?"

This throws Franco. "...Tell her?"

Robert shrugs. "Think. Whether I am locked away here or free on the outside, if her heart beats for you, it beats for you. Perhaps she does feel as you do but has stopped herself out of respect for your vows. She deserves to know that there's a choice. And if that choice happens to be you, kindly let me go. I won't tell anyone about this place. No one would believe me anyway."

Franco is taken completely aback by Robert's logic, especially because it makes perfect sense. The prisoner is right now offering his subjugator a way out.

It is all too easy—must be a trick. Franco narrows his eyes hatefully. "You're only telling me to tell her because you know she loves you! If I let you out, you'd go straight to the Grand Master's palace and tell him everything."

Robert's shoulders sag. "Have it your way. But before you leave, I'd like to know what they think happened to me."

"That you've been taken on capital charges. That a witness signed a statement naming you Grimaldi Farrugia's murderer."

Robert smiles, a formidable weapon in this verbal joust. "You've been busy."

Franco flashes at the accusation. "Are you suggesting I had something to do with the old man's death?"

Robert spreads his hands.

"He was a suicide!" the knight cries. "I'm not a murderer."

"No, just a liar and a scoundrel and a coward. But no, not a murderer."

Franco is suddenly furious beyond control. He does not know what he meant to accomplish tonight beyond ascertaining that both men are equal in their misery, but whatever it was, he has done the opposite. The fact that Robert Falsone still has the upper hand, even now, enrages Franco to lethal heights. Somehow, Robert is no longer the prisoner. Somehow, he is freer than Franco. Robert is free where freedom matters most—his conscience. For a man of honour, which Franco lately was, it is worse to be outside the cage with a conscience in irons. And Robert Falsone knows it. He is the caged bird that torments the cat with song.

There is no restraining Franco's fury. He unleashes years of hatred on Robert, hitting him full across the face and sending him to the ground. He kicks him in the chest, steps on his arm, bending it in a way it was never meant to go. Robert takes the assault without crying out, his silence only driving Franco to greater madness. He kicks him again and again, landing his boot in the prisoner's stomach, groin, face. White with rage, Franco swoops down, seizes Robert, and yanks him to his feet, propelling him against the wall, knocking the wind from him. He closes a fist tight around his neck and squeezes. Robert's eyes spring wide. The two young men are nose to nose. A thousand threats run through Franco's brain, a thousand ways to further hurt the prisoner's already broken body. His breath is rapid, teeth clenched, eyes stinging, heart racing. He holds Robert against the wall, squeezing and releasing his throat, squeezing and releasing.

Finally, Franco lets go. On his way to the door, he pauses, casts a final look on the prisoner, a wheezing, bleeding heap on the ground.

"Oh. Your mother is dead."

And the cry Robert vowed Franco would never hear escape him echoes in every corner of the prison.

CHAPTER FORTY-ONE

Four days later, Franco di Bonfatti's lie, meant only to further distress Robert, comes true. Mea Falsone dies. The woman is without company when she passes. The attendant assigned to her ward notices her lifeless body in the morning and immediately informs the physician. He is baffled by her death, as she had been showing improvement these last few days, her bruises going painfully dark, yellowing, fading, her breath coming deeper, less ragged, her sudden and violent tremors occurring infrequently. She was on the road to recovery.

And now, she's dead.

The resident physician deems it death by broken heart. Giuseppe Callus deems the physician an idiot. Callus strongly suspects her death was caused by internal bleeding, a result of injuries sustained during her attack. The chief of the women's hospital says this so-called *internal bleeding* is yet another of Callus's unfounded notions. To bleed, by definition, is to discharge blood, his superior says. The woman clearly died of a broken heart—her son abandoned her and left her with nothing. What else was there for her to do but die?

The debate ends there.

The news hits Katrina the hardest. She is inconsolable, barely able to function. Domenicus too is deeply grieved and spends hours at her side, trying to help her through her own sorrow and in doing, ease his own. Both speak only of Robert. Mea was all the family he had on this earth, and now she is gone. His pain will be cataclysmic.

Katrina, along with her brother, her father, Belli, Angelica, and Dr Callus, stands now at the edge of an open plot in the churchyard. Father Tabone sings a soft elegy, as gravediggers lower the coffin into the ground. Mea's resting place is next to that of Isabel. The friendship denied these two women in life will be theirs to cherish in heaven.

Katrina is exhausted by grief. She has long surrendered to it, yet still it comes, unrelenting. As she leans now against Augustine's arm, she thinks of her own mother's funeral, the comfort Robert brought her. She thinks of the ribbon. Tears roll in steady streams over her cheeks. Robert cannot attend his mother's funeral, let alone be comforted. He does not even know she is dead.

Clang. The bell tolls.

***

Lilla sits at the dockyard, feet dangling above the water, a ticket to Sicily in her hand. She cannot read, but stares at the writing on the paper, memorises every curving line, every curlicue. This is all she has hoped for, all she has worked for since being abandoned by the Greek sailor at the Maltese pier years ago. She will be in Catania in less than eight weeks. She will be home. This should be the happiest moment of her life.

Yet it is the most miserable.

Lilla bought her passage home with the life of an innocent man. She looks at the travel paper in her hand and has half a mind to drop it into the sea. But what good will that do anyone? She would be stuck here, Robert would still be locked up, Franco would still be free to do as he pleases, and those who love Robert will forever be left with terrible questions.

So she will give them the answers. Of course, they will not believe her, a wharf whore, but she will try nonetheless. And if at the end of it all, her word is not accepted as true, she will know that her intentions in the telling were, and her conscience will be clear.

And then, she will just have to try harder.

***

Later that morning, the Grand Master sits at his desk to a sealed vellum. He breaks the wax and reads the letter. After lengthy consideration, he summons Luis Cabanyelles, a young Valencian page, and sends him on an errand to fetch the knight Franco di Bonfatti.

The boy makes for St Angelo's inner courtyard where knights train in hand-to-hand combat. He arrives at the bailey and pauses to take in the action, framed by four lines of men in burnished metal. Armour glints silver under the hot Mediterranean sun, where visors are lowered, pikes raised, swords unsheathed. For the next few hours, the men of Italy must meet the men of Aragon with broadsword, rapier, mace, and halberd. It is a primitive art, depriving the knights of their contemporary arquebuses. Luis watches the fearsome assembly with a mixture of wonder and aspiration. It is near impossible to know one knight from the other by their armour. Luis looks to their shields. There are three dozen flashing with the afternoon, a heraldic crest here, a fleur-de-lis there, a patron saint, a mighty tree, a unicorn, a dragon of curled lines, a red lion roaming the African plains. At last, Luis spots the crest of di Bonfatti, and behind it, the man belonging to that crest. Franco wears Maximilian armour, named so for the famous German Emperor. The plates are ornate, tooled with large round shapes and bold fluting.

Franco steps out from the crowd, his sparrow-beaked visor lowered, square-toed sabatons tinny against the ground, and meets his opponent, Cristoval Domingo of Aragon. Both men clasp arms and press the flats of their blades to their chests in salute. A heartbeat and it begins. Franco advances easily, the tassets in his lower body armour allowing for smooth movement. He swings his two-handed sword, striking the Spaniard's blade. Luis glimpses Marcello di Ruggieri at the edge of the scrimmage and moves next to the knight he adores. Marcello once allowed the page to face him in a practice duel. The knight took it easy, swinging wide, yielding position, curbing force, yet even so, Luis nursed terrible bruises for a week. And in all his life, could not recall a finer experience.

Now, Marcello tunnels his mouth and shouts insults at Cristoval to distract him. But the Spanish knight is deaf to them. He pivots on his front foot, sidesteps, and launches a counter-attack, nearly trapping Franco against the wall. Franco swings wide, breaking time. He recovers, ducking a fierce swipe of Toledo steel. Cristoval has the advantage, and uses it, lunging at Franco, who swiftly parries, and sweeps his blade in an arc onto the younger man's shoulder. Shaken, Cristoval takes his body out of line, stepping promptly back and thus giving ground. Franco advances and Cristoval takes a high guard. The swords cross, a blur of steel, of sparks. Attack. Deflection. The savage dance keeps on, neither man leading, neither following. To Luis, Franco is the master, a natural and gifted swordsman, but Cristoval is a thinker. The bailey is a board on which he plays the joust as a game of chess—an exceptionally fast-paced game of chess.

Checkmate. A sudden flash of sunlight in Cristoval's blade blinds Franco, and in that brief but critical moment, the Spaniard slams the flat of his sword against the Florentine's head. He collapses hard to the ground. His compatriots gasp, having never seen anyone best Franco di Bonfatti. It is a lousy way to win a skirmish, a lousier way to lose. Still, it is just as well; a flash of sunlight in an opponent's eyes on a real battlefield would produce the same result, and it too would count.

Cristoval extends his hand to help Franco to his feet, just as Luis dashes across the castle courtyard to deliver d'Homedes' summons.

"Sir Franco, his Excellency the Grand Master requires your presence."

Still sitting, Franco lifts his visor and looks at Luis as though straining through fog. "Now?"

"Yes, my lord." The page waits a few moments for the knight to collect himself but soon notices Franco is taking a long time. "Sir? Forgive me, but the Grand Master gave express orders."

Franco gives his head a shake, dropping his visor back over his face. "What?"

Luis looks askew. How hard did Domingo bash him? The page begins to repeat himself, but Franco waves him off.

"I'm coming. I'm coming, just trying to gather my wits."

Marcello bends over him, smiling wide, teeth flashing with the afternoon. "To say you're gathering your wits implies you actually have some. Now get up, Luis doesn't have all day."

Despite the intense heat cooking him inside his armour, Franco leaves his visor down. It is a good thing too—he can only imagine the awful pallor of his skin. He has never known such simultaneous turbulence of mind, heart, body, and soul. He struggles to collect his thoughts, more to control them. Has he been found out? Did someone blab? *Of course, someone blabbed.* The only question is *who.* That silly strumpet Lilla? That snivelling sentry Marco? They have nothing to gain from Franco's ruin. But there is no chance of confronting either of them now, not when his every step brings him closer to the Grand Master, the very man he has spent the last week avoiding.

For a time, Franco made himself believe things would return to normal. Now, disaster is upon him. Perhaps it is time to admit his offence and accept his fate. He is everything Robert Falsone called him: a liar and a scoundrel and a coward. It has torn him apart, deceiving everyone he knows, making up new lies to cover the old, and he is almost relieved that he has been found out. Having two faces is a heavy, wearisome business.

Franco stands outside the Grand Master's study, oblivious to the path that brought him here. But now, at this great oak door, he is very aware. Luis Cabanyelles knocks, a soft sound that resonates inside Franco like a roll of thunder. Seized by fear, his first instinct is flight. The page bows and departs, leaving Franco feeling desperately alone. He raises his visor—a covered face before the Grand Master is grounds for sound reproach—and on held breath, crosses into the enormous room.

"... Spotted a flotilla prowling the Mediterranean. Spies say Turkish—" Juan d'Homedes looks up from his discussion with Jean Parisot de Valette, knight, and recently named lieutenant to the Grand Master. Franco's stomach pits: the situation has just become worse. Even if Juan d'Homedes considers some level of mercy, Valette will surely talk him out of it. A stern man, he does not countenance weakness, no more than he tolerates debauchery. Valette would send Franco to the gallows for the complex mess of his creation, which could put the Order at war with the Church and the *Università*, and the people of Malta at war with all three.

Before the Grand Master, Franco bows low and from the waist. "*Molto Illustrissimo.*" He looks to Valette with equal deference. "*Honorabile.*"

The Grand Master scowls, clearly in a foul disposition. "Franco di Bonfatti. I have summoned you on a grave matter." Franco scrunches his toes in his sabatons. His mouth is dry as sand, a strange feeling when every other part of him is wet with sweat. He swallows, clears his voice.

"Sire?"

The Grand Master motions with a sweep of his bony hand for Franco to sit. He takes the empty armchair beside Valette, whose presence at this moment is most unnerving. It is like being before God and St Peter, but somehow, worse. Franco inhales, bracing for the inevitable explosion from the Grand Master.

Instead, d'Homedes produces a folded parchment of calfskin, its red seal broken. He slides the vellum across the desk. Franco takes the paper into his hands. He knows the lettering.

***

Hours later, in a not so distant chamber, another seal is broken, another note read. It speaks of an urgent matter but does not name it directly, claiming the unwritten content very dangerous. It tells its reader where he must go and when. *Speak of this to no one*, it says. Marcello di Ruggieri is anxious for tomorrow. The letter is intriguing. The signature at the bottom more so.

It is signed, *Angelica Tabone*.

***

Marcello is the first to arrive at the place designated in the note. It is leagues from Birgu, a grassy plain, untilled, forgotten, lying somewhere along the southeastern line of the island, but not quite at the cliffs. Twice he thought he had misread her directions, but somehow, managed to find this place, marked by a lone residual boulder. The day is warm and the air of forenoon sweet with the wild grass it rustles. Marcello's mind churns with the wind and the curiosity. Whatever could have prompted Angelica Tabone to request a secret liaison? She knows he is attracted to her, infatuated even, but she is betrothed. What is she after?

Whatever it is, he will soon find out. Marcello dismounts Pleiades and leaves the horse to graze in the big field. He sits with his back to the huge rock and waits, arms bent behind his head, legs stretched out. He does not wait long. She approaches from the north. He rises, happy to see her, if oddly timid. "Angelica."

"My lord."

"*Marcello*. I would think after sending me a note requesting a private meeting, you would at least address me by my Christian name."

"Fair enough."

Marcello shifts his weight from one foot to the other. He wants her, wants her badly, but the thought of actually having her makes him feel something strange, something he has never really felt before. ... Is it *guilt*? Yes, he thinks it so. And he holds this feeling directly responsible for the action that ensues—an action he can scarce believe, an action that makes him consider admitting himself to the *Sacra Infermeria* for dysentery.

Marcello makes a very serious face and speaks in a voice equally solemn. "*Signorina*, I am flattered, believe me. I think you are beautiful. God knows in my younger days I would have jumped at this opportunity. Hell, I would have jumped at it a few months ago. Now, I cannot. You are betrothed and I am ... well, suffice it to say I could not live with myself if—"

"Whatever are you talking about?"

He furrows his brow. "You did write me that note, did you not?"

"Are you saying you think I asked you to meet me because I want you to … I want you to … I want *you?*"

"Don't you?"

"No!" she cries.

Marcello is mortified. The back of his neck goes prickly hot.

Angelica wrings her hands. "Oh, Marcello. I am sorry. I did not mean to mislead you. I am fond of you, but I did not ask you here for… *that.*"

The knight snickers. His snicker becomes a chuckle, and then a laugh, whole-hearted and deep. "I am an arrogant animal. Forgive me. I should have known better than to question your virtue."

Angelica laughs too. "Please, do not ask forgiveness. My note was vague. I'm sure if I were in your position, I would have thought along similar lines."

Marcello wipes his eyes and smiles and sits down again. He pats the spot next to him. Angelica sits beside him, draws up her knees. He gives her a nudge. "So? Why the private meeting? I hope not simply a fancy to embarrass the piss out of me."

"No, never."

"Then…?"

Now, her smile vanishes, and she becomes very serious, very solemn.

Marcello di Ruggieri returns to the *auberge* in a daze. Of all the reasons he had imagined for Angelica's request to meet him, the actual one had never occurred to him. There was no way it could have. Now, faced with the true reason, he wishes all she had wanted was a romp in the field.

Could it be true? Might such a prison really exist? Marcello, for one, has never heard of it. Does Franco know about it? Impossible—he would have told him; they tell each other everything. Still, Angelica was quite adamant that he not mention anything to di Bonfatti. The entreaty confused Marcello some, as he has always known Franco to be a good friend to the Montesa family and their acquaintances. Marcello paces his room. He is not ready for bed. There is too much on his mind and he will only lie sleepless, which he hates. So, he leaves the *auberge* and wanders the streets.

The night is black, the air slightly chill. He walks alleys that crisscross without order, but eventually empty back into the main square. It is where all the streets meet and from where they all depart, like points of a star. He strays to the curtain wall behind the *Sacra Infermeria* and watches torchlight dance on the dark waters of Kalkara, listens to small swells lap against the rocks below. He thinks hard about Franco di Bonfatti. What would make Robert's friends look on him with suspicion? True, Franco has been distracted lately, sullen, but his mood often swings, worse than any woman Marcello has ever known. Still, a capricious temper is not suspicious in itself. Marcello has teased Franco about harbouring feelings for Katrina Montesa. Perhaps they believe Franco saw the sentry as competition. Marcello sighs heavily. He is angry at Angelica for telling him all this, for burdening him with worry. He was happy in his ignorance, happy in his friendship with Franco, happy in his status, in his dalliances with his forbidden sweetheart Madeleine.

Now, everything is ugly and clouded and uncertain. Marcello shakes his head. One certainty remains: he owes Franco his loyalty.

Marcello resigns his anger against Angelica. He still likes her as much as the day he went behind Franco's back to take her into the slave prison. But he cannot do what she wants this time. He cannot spy on a fellow knight, on his best friend. When he took Angelica to see the Muslim prisoner, it had done no harm to anyone. This is different. He must tell Franco everything. If the tables were turned, Franco would tell him—he has proved his loyalty a thousand times if once. Who would Marcello be to keep this from his friend now?

The knight returns to the *auberge* and makes at once for Franco's private rooms. He knocks on the door. There is no answer. He shrugs. Bonfatti's closed door has never stopped him before. Marcello turns the knob and pushes the door wide. The room is dark and cold, no body heat, no warmth from candles. The air is unscented, clear of any smell that would otherwise herald human presence. He goes to the bed, prods it. It is made, unslept in, and from the dust on the pillows, has been so for quite some time.

.

CHAPTER FORTY-TWO

For the first time since the day they buried Mea Falsone, Katrina leaves the house. She blinks rapidly, adjusting to the sun as she carries two buckets to the cistern. Despite the brightness of the day, she passes like a shadow through the village. She has aged thirty years overnight, finding difficulty doing the things a girl her age should manage easily. She fills her buckets and begins the trudge home, each breath coming like a sigh.

Katrina was devastated when her mother died, felt all those awful things, confusion, anguish, anger, a torrent of emotion that was both painful and numbing. But Mea's death somehow seems more tragic. Katrina recalls the words Mea spoke to Domenicus shortly after their mother died: *Be thankful your mother's death does not need avenging,* she had said. Mea Falsone's death needs avenging. Katrina is heartsick with this awareness, more so for Robert, who lost both his parents to violent ends, and may never take his vengeance for either.

Her thoughts make her heedless to her surroundings, to the chickens clucking along the cobbles, and the dogs that chase them, to the goats complaining with loud bleats, and the villagers that complain with louder ones. After a time, however, Katrina senses a presence keeping her pace. She tries to ignore her unsought companion but to no use. Fed up, she stops altogether, hoping the veiled form will just pass.

Instead, it speaks: "Katrina Montesa."

She starts at hearing her name spoken by a stranger. "Who are you?"

"Keep walking."

Katrina surprises herself by obeying. A glance from the corner of her eye reveals nothing of her companion's identity. It is thoroughly unnerving that she cannot see the features beyond the folds of the hood. "Who are you?" she asks again.

"A messenger, if you will."

"What is your message?"

"One of truth."

"One of riddles," Katrina says, impatient.

"In a way," the stranger replies. "I know the answer to the riddle keeping you up at night."

Katrina's palms are instantly sweaty. Her grip wanes on the buckets. "What? What are you talking about?"

"Robert Falsone."

She drops the buckets now, water splashing onto the dusty ground. Her eyes are wide, expanding with the puddles.

"I will tell you everything, but not here in the open." The stranger's total calm does little to ease Katrina's growing desperation.

"Where?" she pleads. "When? Tell me now, you must. Please."

"Meet me tonight at l'Isla, ten bells on the moonrise. The second windmill."

Katrina narrows her eyes. "How do I know you are a friend? How do I know you haven't been sent by someone to give me the slip?"

"You don't know. But you have little choice, I think."

"I have enough to say no."

"Then you leave Robert to certain death." The person starts to leave. Katrina reaches out, catching the stranger's arm by the elbow.

"No, wait. Tell me what you have to gain by doing this?"

The cloaked figure turns partway away. "I'll see you tonight, Katrina Montesa." Hearing her name roll off this stranger's tongue a second time fills Katrina with great foreboding. "Come alone, or I will not emerge, and you will never hear from me again."

The day is impossibly long, each hour slower in its passing than the one before. Katrina is not afraid, only anxious to meet the person who claims to know a truth buried so deep not even a knight in the Order of St John can unearth it. Who is this messenger? Katrina deliberates the rest of the afternoon, her mind a jumble of names connected to Robert, names distant from him, making it through most of Birgu. Finally, around the dinner hour, she gives up.

As the first stars appear, she catches an unexpected break: her father and Belli depart for Mdina to confer with Dr Callus, and Domenicus leaves to meet Angelica, who stopped by earlier with an urgent request to see him. Katrina supposes neither her father nor brother will return soon, which means she can leave the house late without having to sneak out or invent a story.

At last, she walks the curve of the Grand Harbour to the second windmill at the tip of l'Isla. She squints at the lone figure sitting on a stone slab.

"Pardon me, but are you ... are you the person I'm supposed to meet here?"

The stranger slips her hood, shakes her head to straighten her flaxen hair. Katrina peers closely at the young woman. "I know you. You were the one with Henri in the watchtower when corsairs attacked my friend and me."

"My name is Lilla."

"I must ask a courtesy of you, Lilla. Please meet whoever it is you're meeting some place else. I have a very important engagement here, and if the person sees you here, it will be ruined."

"It won't."

"Yes, it will," Katrina insists. "I was given precise instructions." She reaches into her pocket, feels for a coin. She holds it out to the prostitute. "Here, it's all I have. Just go, quickly. The person I am meeting will be here at any moment."

Lilla glances from the coin to Kat's face and back to the coin. She pockets the offering and smiles. "The person you are meeting thanks you for your generosity."

Katrina takes a second to process this. "It's *you?*"

"You were expecting Aphrodite? Sorry, I am but one of her labourers."

Katrina does not know what to say. She is not sure whom she was expecting but probably would have been less surprised to see Aphrodite herself sitting in wait on the stone slab. No matter. At least the first mystery is solved. Now for the second and more important.

"I've done exactly as you asked. Tell me what you know."

Lilla nods and moves over to give Katrina room to sit. "I think this is going to be difficult for you to hear. I think you won't believe me."

"You would be surprised at the things I've been hearing lately, and the things I've come to believe. I don't think there is anything you can tell me that will shock me."

But she is wrong. Probably the most wrong she's ever been. And as Lilla heaps horrible detail atop horrible detail, disbelief feeds outrage until Katrina's fury is a monstrous beast. She shifts, rises, paces, sits back down, rises again. The sky is black, but her fire is enough to light the entire village.

When at last Lilla is finished, every aspect laid bare, right down to the *tari* Franco di Bonfatti paid her, a wave of fear almost knocks Katrina down. And what she fears is her own unbelievable rage. *Franco betrayed me. Franco lied. Franco was my friend. Franco carried me to my mother's funeral. Franco spoke for Robert in Mdina. Franco knew Mea. Franco is responsible for her death. Franco betrayed me. Franco lied.*

And Franco knows everything *because* I *told him everything.*

Katrina is numb all over. The words just keep cycling: *Franco betrayed. Franco lied. Franco knows. Betrayed. Lied. Knows.* Over and over, the words echo inside her, building, building, until at last, she runs to the waterfront and throws up.

***

The night air rustles the leaves of the great carob outside the rectory. Angelica sits with her back to the tree, Domenicus beside her. He rests his head against the thick trunk, his moonlit face tilted to the sky, eyes closed. Angelica wants badly to console him but does not know what to say. Her plan to involve Marcello di Ruggieri did not go the way she had expected. She apologises to Domenicus, who has been mostly silent since she first told him the news.

His voice is thick. "I have never felt so helpless in all my life. My best friend has been spirited away to some unknown hell, and I can't do a thing to help him. If he were at least charged openly, I could visit him, but I don't even know where he is. Christ, I don't even know *if* he still is."

"Don't say that. We will think of something." Angelica loathes the uselessness of her words.

"I am tired of thinking," Domenicus replies. "Time calls for action."

"To act without thinking is to shoot without aiming." She looks at his face. His eyes remain closed, but a tear squeezes through and rolls down his cheek. He does not brush it away.

"How much longer do you think Robert can stand? He is strong, but even he must be despairing by now, so many days since he's had contact with anyone." Angelica takes his hand in hers and kisses it. Domenicus sighs, finally opening his eyes, red and weary.

"Belli was right. Maybe we should just find this place and set it ablaze."

***

Katrina wants to kill him. As she lies awake in bed, the desire consumes her. Her first instinct after leaving Lilla was to run straight to the Grand Master's palace and tell him everything. But for once, Katrina allowed a cooler head to prevail. Had she gone to the Grand Master she would have accomplished but a lifetime in a cell next to Robert's. She has learned from past mistakes. This time, her line of attack will be methodical, not emotional. As testament, she has not said a word to anyone, not even her father or her brother. She wants to tell them, especially when she sees the dejection in her brother's face, but so long as she is the only one fully in the know, she is the only one fully in charge of the approach.

She peers through the darkness to the ceiling. It occurs to her that Lilla may very well be inventing the entire story. Perhaps Franco wronged her in some way, and she is striking out. With a headshake, Katrina dismisses the idea. There were too many intricacies for Lilla's story to be a fiction. It astounds Katrina that Franco would be so careless as to divulge all the details of his plot to anyone. But it serves him right. His arrogance, his thinking a prostitute beneath caution, will be his downfall. Katrina's mind is all over the place, her emotions no less scattered. At once, she feels anger and relief, pain and numbness. But the underlying hatred never varies.

She marvels that Franco was able to weave such elaborate embroidery of deceit within such time constraints. Hiring the prostitute, catching Marco Vella in the act at the watchtower, notifying the men who were to come for

Robert, having Marco stationed nearby watching the coast, all of this organised and set to go before Katrina turned up at the *auberge* that morning for laundry duty. If it were not so vile, it would be impressive.

She is furious with herself for trusting Franco, for revealing to him that her family knows of the secret gaol. By her big, stupid mouth, she has put more people she loves in danger. A chill passes through her as she recalls meeting with Franco at Mnajdra. Easily, he could have pitched her over the precipice and declared it an accident—it would not be the first time she wandered too close to the edge of a cliff. It is lucky that she is the only dupe who trusted Franco and fell for his promises of dedication to Robert's cause. Of course, he is dedicated to it! He is its bloody mastermind.

The last time she saw him, he told her to meet him at Mnajdra in two weeks. She will keep the appointment.

Katrina wants to kill him. And tonight, she kills him a hundred times.

The next day passes much the same, the days that follow all running together. Most of her time is spent thinking about how to deal with Franco di Bonfatti. She considers just showing up at the *auberge* and confronting him outright. He would deny the charge—especially when she refuses to reveal the informer. Or he might fly into a rage, dangerous as a wounded wild boar. Lilla had mentioned she thought Franco was mad. Katrina does not think he is mad. He is too cunning. Perhaps she should rethink her plan to keep their meeting at the ruins. But there is not much of a choice. If she deviates from what he expects, he will be suspicious.

A few days remain between now and then. If she acts quickly, cleverly, she might be able to get Robert out of that deplorable place and be off to Sicily with him before Franco is the wiser. The knight would never find them. Besides, it is not as though he can ask leave from the Grand Master to go look. And so Katrina goes now to the only place she can think of in a time like this, to tell the one person she knows will tell no other.

She goes to see her mother.

The churchyard is quiet, lit with the afternoon and thick with grass and wildflowers. Katrina kneels at Mama's grave, traces her fingers along its stone face. She talks at length to her mother, which is easy, and then to Mea, which is not. Kat is responsible for the woman's death, and cannot bring herself to continue. Instead, she does the worst thing she can do. She recalls the day Franco came to Mdina to speak for Robert. *You are a good man, Honorabile*, Mea had said to the knight. *A good man*. Katrina weeps and apologises and makes promises and weeps some more. And after an hour, she rises and goes to keep those promises.

CHAPTER FORTY-THREE

Before dawn the next day, Augustine and Belli are set to depart for Gozo. Several months ago, word of the carpenter's skill with an adze had reached the island's governor, the knight Galatian de Sesse, who offered Belli a handsome sum to furnish his entire study. Pa has decided to go along and get the carpenter settled.

Katrina would normally raise a mighty fuss at the idea of her father leaving at a time like this, declaring it a sin, even if only for a few days, but at the moment, his going away is practically divine intervention. It will be easier to rescue Robert without Augustine around to protect her. Still, for the sake of pretence, she feigns distress, stopping her father at the open doorway.

"Pa, do you have to go?"

He nudges his chin towards Belli, who is waiting outside in a small farm cart loaded with supplies, his donkey reined and ready. "Yes, Sweetheart. Belli needs me. Just until he is settled."

"He doesn't need you. He can handle anything. *I* need you. Robert needs you." She almost does too good a job of convincing her father to stay. He steps back inside the house. Katrina curses herself.

Domenicus comes unknowingly to the rescue. "Kat, be fair. There is nothing Pa can do for Robert here, now. All any of us can do is think. He doesn't need to be in Birgu to think."

Katrina wants to hug her brother for giving such an effective speech. Instead, she sighs and gives her father a sad, resigned look. "Go on, Pa. I know nothing can be done for Robert right now. I just feel better when you're around." That last part is not an embellishment, for truly, no matter how bad things get, simply being near him makes her feel everything will be all right. "Go on. Belli won't fare well alone against the knights. You know how they cross him when they speak in foreign tongues. He'll go mad without you to translate."

The carpenter's large form suddenly fills the open doorway, blocks the early morning light. He waves Augustine to get a move on. Pa looks to Katrina for permission. She nods. He puts a gentle hand against her back as they walk together into the dawn, Domenicus trailing.

"Stay out of trouble, the two of you. I'll be back soon. No poking around, understood?"

And with a light snap of the donkey's reins, they are gone.

***

The footsteps wake him, footsteps made by someone trying to keep them unheard. Domenicus squints through the darkness. A moment later, the creeping figure passes into the diagonal shaft of moonlight that streams through parted curtains.

"Where do you think you're going?" Domenicus asks his sister.

She freezes in her tracks and looks towards his voice. "I thought you were asleep."

Domenicus sits up, fully clothed. "I haven't slept properly in days. The slightest sound, like, say, someone sneaking out of a house on tiptoes, is enough to wake me."

"I understand. But do something for me, will you? Pretend you were sleeping."

"Of course I won't." He rises, crosses to the door to bar her from leaving.

"I have to go. You cannot stop me, and you cannot come with me. I promise I am not going to get into any trouble."

Domenicus meets his sister's eyes. They are lit with determination, and he knows argument is futile. She has worn this look before, and then, as now, her way triumphed. Still, he cannot give in so easily if he wishes to maintain some semblance of order in this house while his father is away. He puts on his sternest face. "You are not going anywhere. Certainly not without me."

Katrina speaks with perfect calm. "Put yourself in my place, and Angelica in Robert's, and then tell me again I'm not going anywhere."

Damn her ability to do that. "Can you at least tell me where you're going? If something happens, I want at least to know who I am to kill."

She smiles. "I am going to see someone who can help Robert. This man is a trusted friend. That's all I am going to tell you. Now, kindly move."

"Let me follow you. I'll keep my distance, but be close enough to keep you safe."

"No."

Domenicus sighs. He said it himself: time calls for action. And if his sister can make that happen, he must allow it. "Go. And by God, be careful."

"Thank you." She buttons her cloak and disappears into the night.

***

370

Katrina stays off the main road, choosing instead to trek through the field. It is a frightening business that serves more to scare her than make her feel safe. Although she has been to and from Mdina a thousand times if once, tonight she is unnerved. Katrina usually enjoys the nocturnal song of crickets, but right now finds it a horrible sound made by ugly black beasties. There is the occasional hoot of an owl, which pierces the night and makes her jump. And worse, the constant squeak of mice. No, *rats*. They must be rats. A sudden change in wind direction whips her hair across her face, brushing loose strands against her arm. She slaps at herself, convinced a flying cockroach has just alighted on her shoulder. She spends an hour like this: nervous, tense, jumping at every noise, upbraiding herself for her stupidity. Her foot catches a rut, which sends her to eat dirt. She spits and coughs and gets back to her feet and runs. Lucifer himself is trailing her. She swears she can hear his hooves tramping behind, certain the earth is groaning beneath his hated feet. Of course, she's not about to turn around to confirm this. No need for a face-off with the Prince of Darkness.

Finally, the black silhouette of Mdina's great cathedral breaks the indigo sky. Recharged, she quickens her pace and takes the path at a sprint. She makes the perched city out of breath and sweating, crosses the drawbridge and runs straight for Dr Giuseppe Callus's stone cottage.

***

Fifty paces down the road, *the Prince of Darkness* breathes relief at seeing his little sister arrive safely on the doctor's front step. Katrina none the wiser, Domenicus turns to leave.

***

"You were right about Franco," Katrina says when the physician opens the door.

Callus shrugs. "I know." He gestures to one of three sheepskins spread before the hearth.

She sits, instantly warmed by the glowing embers. "But how? How did you know?"

He passes her a cloth to wipe her face and a blanket to drape across her shoulders. "We doctors spend a lot of time looking at foul insides. After a while, we develop a sense for them."

Katrina nods. "You are the only person I could come to. Thank you."

"Your father will have me killed if anything goes wrong. *I* will have me killed."

"It's my idea, so don't worry."

"Nevertheless," Callus says. "I should be objecting, or at the very least, not taking part. I am only going along with this because Robert Falsone's life depends on your success. Also, I am fully aware you will go through with it with or without me, and I'd rather it be with me."

371

Soft rapping sounds at the door. Callus crosses the floor and lets Lilla in. The breeze of her entry breathes new life into the hearth, grey ashes flaring red. Once she is comfortably settled, the doctor takes his seat on the floor with them. "We plan everything tonight, work out the smallest details. By God's will, the three of you will be off to Sicily by this time tomorrow."

***

Off to Sicily by this time tomorrow. Off to Sicily by this time tomorrow. Off to Sicily. The words roll over in Katrina's mind the way the wheels of the doctor's cart roll over the road, making for a very bumpy ride back to Birgu. Lilla sits up front, beside Callus, Katrina behind them, her back to theirs, her legs dangling off the end.

If she is off to Sicily this time tomorrow, she will not be able to say goodbye to her father. The thought fills her with terrible sadness. She loves him deeply, and her leaving will hurt him deeply. But he will understand her need for haste, and he will forgive it.

As soon as she and Robert are settled, she will write. Perhaps, in time, her father can visit her. He would like that, a chance to venture abroad once more. It is long since last he travelled. Domenicus will come too, with Angelica, who will be his wife, likely the mother of his child by then. Katrina's nephew or niece. She smiles inwardly at the idea. It won't be so bad. It will be grand.

Tears begin gathering. She will likely never see any of them again.

Katrina awakes in a fortress—the great bastion at the tip of Corradino, which has withstood a thousand sieges by a million corsairs. And under Commander Robert Falsone, the defenders always triumphed. She smiles at the childhood memory. But the warmth of the moment quickly passes, the cold reality of morning now setting in.

She chose not to go home after the meeting in Mdina because she knew her brother would pepper her with questions, or worse, insist on helping. Still, she didn't want Domenicus to think she got herself murdered, so she scrawled a note at the doctor's house and slipped it under the Montesa door. Now, she wraps her arms around drawn-up knees and wishes she had thought to bring a blanket.

Most of her day is spent sitting in the mouth of the cave, gaze fixed on the sea. As the hours pass, the water transforms from the pink of dawn to the gold of morning to the green of afternoon to the copper of sunset. A great bank of cloud that had been growing steadily fatter throughout the day now covers most of the sky, its puffed body blushed, its rounded, billowing edges lit gold.

Heaven, it does announce itself, Robert said to her once, as they lay on these very rocks and watched the same sunset. That day seems so long ago and in another world. Soon, the air begins to move and disperses the clouds. Colours fade, leaving star dotted blackness in their wake. It is time.

Katrina rises, rubbing muscles made stiff by hard ground and damp air. She sets out from the cave and takes an exterior path to the meeting place, the dirt patch outside the Couvre Port on Birgu's lower east side. Once she arrives, she crouches amid the shrubs and waits for Lilla.

***

"Don't look so awkward," Lilla instructs her new friend. "Own yourself, girl. Don't slouch. Stand taller. Walk with grace. No, not like that. Grace, I said, not to strut about like a duck. Good God, are you a boy chasing chickens or a woman on her way to seduce a man?" Lilla waits until they are beyond the Cavaliers of St John and St James to fuss properly. "If you give the guards any reason to doubt, it is over. And right now, you are giving a thousand reasons."

Katrina huffs. "Well, it's not like I go around seducing men every bloody day."

Lilla puts her hands on her hips and appraises her hostile companion with a critical eye. "Men like breasts. Make yours look bigger."

"How am I supposed to do that?"

"Squeeze them together. Like this." Lilla sticks out her chest and pushes her arms inwards in a way that, amazingly, looks very natural. Katrina tries copying her, but the effort is written all over her face, her features just as awkwardly compressed as her bust. The attempt has Lilla shaking her head. "This is not going to work."

Katrina drops her arms. "Maybe these men don't care about that stuff."

Lilla raises an eyebrow. She smiles, like a big sister instructing a younger one on the ways of the world. "My dear, *all* men care about that *stuff*. But never mind that now; let's work with what you do have." Lilla peers at Katrina's face, lit by the enormous moon hanging overhead. It is a lovely face, even without powder and paint. Her hair is black, lustrous, falling a long way down her back. Her neck is smooth, formed in graceful lines, a grace absent from her carriage, which is childlike and a little rough. Everything about Katrina Montesa is fresh, pure. Nothing about Katrina Montesa will do—if she is going to be a prostitute, she has to look the part. Lilla takes her by the shoulders and turns her around. She reaches into her satchel for a few pins and places them between her teeth. Using her fingers as a comb, she brushes Katrina's hair. It is as soft as it looks.

"You remind me of my mother when she would brush my hair," Katrina says. "I'd object, of course, and two seconds into it would surrender completely." She glances over her shoulder to smile at Lilla, who smiles back as she finishes combing through the few tangles. With expert hands, Lilla piles Katrina's hair in a pretty mound atop her head and uses the pins to keep the elaborate structure in place. She licks her finger, coils loose wisps around it until they curl. The ringlets fall at Katrina's ears. Lilla reaches back into her rucksack and takes out a cosmetic brush, some powder, and a small jar. She dusts Katrina's eyelids with kohl, rubs a daub of tinted animal fat into her cheeks, paints her lips, dabs scented oil on her neck and wrists. Lilla smiles at her perfumed magnum opus.

"Splendid. You look like a whore."

Katrina touches her fingers tentatively to the top of her head. "I feel strange," she says. "Heavy. Is all this really necessary?"

Lilla nods. "You have to look the part, but more than that, you have to be unrecognizable to these guards if things go bad. They will be looking for a pleasure-girl, one with red lips and fancy hair. Now, for your clothes."

Katrina looks down. She wears a simple beige blouse and long skirt. "My clothes?"

"They could do with some ruffles, but we don't have time for that." Lilla presses a finger to her lips, eyes moving over her companion's small frame. She loosens the string crisscrossing over Katrina's chest, creating a deeper neckline. Lilla slides the blouse off her shoulders and down.

She grins. "*Now* you look like a whore."

"Thank you, I think."

"Callus is waiting. We have to meet him at the rock."

Katrina squeezes Lilla's hand. "You are a good person."

Lilla squeezes back. "There is no such thing."

***

Where are those bloody girls? This plot must be carried out under cover of night, and before it is too long into the guards' shift. Giuseppe Callus, armed with a hatchet, has been crouched behind this boulder since before daybreak, and it is now after moonrise. Throughout his almost sixteen-hour vigil, he's watched four sentry changes. They work in pairs for alternating four-hour stretches. From the distance, he can see they are armed. There is also no surface structure. The prison is underground, in every sense of the word. The guards seem to gain entry through a trapdoor of some sort, though it is difficult to tell from the distance between them and the doctor's vantage. The entryway was used only twice throughout Callus's watch.

The day passed slowly and without incident. No important comings or goings, no visits from the authorities, no new prisoners being brought. Only once did the doctor feel the stirrings of trouble. Imperia, the soothsayer exiled from Birgu, wandered by with her goats. She lingered a touch too near too long. The guards simply turned their attention to the skies, pointing at any bird flying low enough to make a good target. One of the men even took a shot. Callus found himself strangely amused—to be a guard at this prison, one must double as an actor also. It was during the hawking theatrics that he was able to catch bits of conversation. Their tongues rolled with the distinct dialect that could only be Greek. *Damn it.* They had better be conversant in Italian, because Katrina is unlikely to speak Greek, and Lilla far more unlikely.

It was all the dialogue Callus heard for the day. The long, drawn-out silence makes him uneasy. The guards of this prison are a disciplined lot, quiet, focused, austere. He begins to worry for the success of the plan.

It *will* work, he tells himself. It has to. A beautiful woman is overpowering. Two, twice so. Now, if only they would arrive. In the darkness, he is unable to make out much beyond the occasional flash of a guard's gun in the moonlight. Exhausted, he turns away, leans with his back against the rock. He crosses his ankles and closes his eyes. No sooner does he nod off than he is startled into waking by approaching steps. He keeps his eyes closed, certain that any moment he will feel the cold end of a gun pressed against his head. Instead, he feels the cold end of a finger.

"Doctor," whispers Lilla.

His eyes pop open. "Jesus."

She smiles. "Nope, just Lilla."

Callus shakes his head, grins. "What kept you?" Lilla nudges her head towards her companion. The doctor peers at the girl. "*Katrina?*"

She shrugs. "Somewhere beneath the layers of sheep fat."

Callus gestures the two women into a low huddle behind the rock. He gives them a full report. At the end of it, Katrina looks at him sceptically. "Do you honestly think they'll believe that we just happened to be walking through this field at this hour?"

Lilla shakes her head. "We'll tell them we're a gift from Bonfatti for a job well done."

Callus shakes his head. "No, no, no. Not for one second would they believe that a knight would be fool enough to send prostitutes here. When *il-Bormla* happened by earlier in the day, the guards pretended to be hunters. You will approach them as though they are. You will make no mention of a prison, guards, or knights. Say your father found you out as prostitutes and sent you away. You just need a little money to get started on your own."

Lilla rises, dusts herself off. "Let's get a move on."

Dr Callus gasps with recollection. "Damn it! Wait. We have a problem."

Katrina furrows her brow. "We have several."

"The guards are foreign," he replies. "Greek."

Katrina throws up her hands. "*I don't speak bloody Greek.*" Her hissed whisper is almost a shout. Callus waves her to lower her voice.

Lilla smiles. "It doesn't matter—lust is the lingua franca."

Callus sighs. "If the situation weren't so complicated, I would agree. But given what we're up against, we can't afford a single miscommunication."

Katrina speaks in a voice of panicked agitation. "Now what do we do? Act out our story?"

Lilla puts her hand on Katrina's shoulder. "No, we tell them. *Miláo Eliniká —I am fluent in Greek.*"

Callus and Katrina exchange incredulous glances.

Lilla shrugs. "That Athenian sailor who left me at the docks had his uses."

Katrina throws her arms around Lilla but draws abruptly back. "This is really asking a lot now. These guards are supposed to believe we just happened to pass by, *and* can speak Greek?"

Lilla sits on her heels and folds her hands. "It will be fine. Listen, I'll do all the talking because you know nothing about my line of work and your inexperience will expose our fraud. I'll approach them with Italian, which they very well might know—especially if they communicate with knights and law lords and clergy. If, however, they don't, I will switch to Greek. If they question me, I simply tell them about the Athenian sailor I lived with in Sicily. Agreed?"

Katrina nods. She reaches into her pocket and holds out a ribbon to Callus. It takes a moment, but he recognizes it as is the frayed, silken strip he helped Robert find at the infirmary years earlier.

"If the worst happens," she says, "And you can't get him out, give this to him." She turns, turns back. "But get him out."

***

No actual prostitute would be armed with a cumbersome bow and quiver of arrows—despite her skill. Instead, Katrina feels beneath her long skirt for the dagger strapped to her upper thigh. She prays to God she won't have to use it. The reality of the situation is upon her, and she can no longer hide her fear. The guards are going to smell it as strong as her perfume. Tonight, she plays the role of a whore. No, she scolds herself. Tonight, she must *be* the whore. Every man has a price. And Katrina's currency is flesh. Or, the promise of it. Still, she cannot control her nerves.

"Lilla, I ... I'm scared. I've never ... um ... I've never been with a man before. I think they'll know just by looking at me."

"No, they won't. You are not the girl you are used to seeing. Besides, I won't let anything happen to you, all right? If you feel threatened, run. I'll take care of them both."

Katrina blinks. "You can't thrash them both on your own. You'll need my help."

"Thrash them? No. I once handled two men at the same time—the *hakem* and the magistrate, right in his office at the *Università.*" Katrina's eyes grow round at the revelation but most of all, the matter-of-fact way Lilla reveals it.

***

The guards notice them straight away. "Lost your way?" one asks sharply in Italian.

Lilla gives a musical laugh. "I was about to ask you the same question."

The second, a heavier-set guard, clears his voice. "We're not lost. We're camping out. Best hawking done at dawn." He smiles at the pretty girls, who smile back readily. The other man does not smile at all. He is every bit the opposite of his colleague—rail-thin, dark, abrupt. He turns to his partner, a larger man, fairer and more forthcoming, and addresses him in Greek. Neither has much the look of a formal guard, their attire simple, faces unshaven, hands dirty. Naturally, their unkempt appearance is meant to give the illusion of hunters. On closer inspection, however, the thin man's stern countenance and perfect posture betray his occupation.

"I don't trust them, Costas," he says. "What woman is out at this hour? And in *this* of all places? They're spies, sent by our employers to make sure we are doing our job."

"Relax. Look at them. They're whores. Let's have some fun, Spiro Agelakos. The only thing these two want to spy is a stiff Greek phallus and a few coins."

Spiro's features cloud. "I hate being paired with you, you know that? In all the auxiliary, you lack discipline."

Costas looks hurt. "You hate being paired with me?"

"Why do you think in an entire shift I speak more readily to the field mice than to you?"

Lilla understands every word and takes stock of the situation. It is not so bad. This Spiro Agelakos is reluctant, and that is a good thing; he will be for Katrina since he does not want anything. The other, Costas, seems very keen. And Lilla has slept with much, much worse. She speaks in Italian to keep her linguistic skills a secret. She must arouse their interest in her other talents with the tongue.

"Let me tell you the truth," Lilla says, interrupting their quarrel, her voice deliberately loud so the doctor might hear. "My father discovered me today. And he found out from a fellow baker, a man I had recently … worked for. Pa was going to kill me, truly. But I ran off, my sister in tow. We are on our way to the eastern caves." She touches the back of Costas Kiriakoulias's hairy hand. "That is why you two are such a fortunate find. Your pleasure in exchange for a few coins." She walks her lacquered fingers slowly up his arm. Her touch stirs him—she can see it in his face. "So? Would you boys like to help two lost girls find their way?"

Costas looks to Spiro, reverts to their native tongue. "See? I told you. Come on, you great bore. What could possibly happen? It will take, what, five minutes? Ten? It will be good for you, loosen you up some. I want the flaxen. You take her sister. She's quiet, perfect for a sap like you."

Lilla heaves a grand sigh. "Well? Interested in a little romp, or should we move along?"

Spiro indicates the empty field with a dismissive flick of his hand. "Move along."

Costas bullies the smaller man with his great bulk, begins leading the girls into the bushes. "Excuse my friend, he's just an idiot. Of course, we are interested. And if he would rather stand off to the side, I will take you both."

***

Finally, with the four deep in the brush, Dr Giuseppe Callus is able to act. He moves furtively over the ground. There it is, the door, more a lid, to the dungeon. He opens it, slowly, very slowly, yet even so, it creaks on its hinges. It is not at all loud, but to Callus, it sounds like ten thousand shrieking demons.

***

"Did you hear that?" Spiro hisses in Greek, looking at Costas, who has reclined against a patch of dirt in a clearing surrounded by cacti, his muscular arm around Lilla's shoulders.

"Hear what, you great turd of Peloponnesus? Your manhood shrinking further in on itself?"

It is all Lilla can do to keep from laughing. She bites her lip, passes Katrina a silk scarf, takes out her own. Katrina looks up at Spiro and motions him to the ground. "Sit, will you? You're making me nervous standing there."

He wears an expression of undisguised suspicion, eyes narrow, brow creased. "What are you up to with those scarves?"

"Your pleasure, of course," Katrina replies. She rises to her knees, takes Spiro's hand, passes her fingers gently over the bumps of his knuckles. At length, he acquiesces and sits down beside her. Costas is already all over Lilla, one meaty hand up her skirt, the other pulling her dress down over her shoulder. She moans loudly, to cover any noise the doctor might be making with the door or with stumbling down the stairs.

***

And stumble he does. The stair, if it can even be called that, is narrow and steep, hewn unevenly from crude rock, the steps crookedly spaced. Twice during his descent, Callus loses his footing, twice catching his balance at the last moment. By the time he reaches the bottom, he is a rapidly breathing, sweating mess.

The enormous moon outside is the only source of light, casting a pale silver gleam along the dungeon corridor. There are ten, maybe twelve cells on either side. The doors are wood, a tiny hatch on the bottom, an even smaller barred casement near the top. Large dead cockroaches are sewn together by glistening cobwebs.

The corridor is suddenly plunged into total darkness. A cloud must have passed over the moon. Callus gropes in the darkness, the wall scalloped and slimy beneath his fingers. Finding a prisoner not meant to be found is hard enough with a severe time constraint and little light. Now, the light has stopped, but time has not, and in the blackness, he has no idea how to proceed.

***

Lilla secures the knot binding her scarf over Costas' eyes. If only that accursed Spiro would let Katrina do the same, they could knock out the guards with a good bash to their heads, get Robert, and get away. But Spiro Agelakos is too wary, damn him. Lilla works harder on Costas, performing acts that make her an expert in her profession. She drives him to the threshold but always stops, to make his groans all the louder and entice Spiro to want to experience whatever is making his companion call out God's name with a passion fit for one at a pulpit.

***

Giuseppe Callus huddles low to the ground. He hears the rats and feels the roaches and keeps going. The wind sweeps the clouds off the moon, which streams pale light once again through the partly open door. He manoeuvres himself through the tight passageway, stopping at the cell farthest from the stair. He lifts the hatch and peers inside.

"Falsone, you in there?"

Nothing. This one must be empty. He tries four more with the same result. It pleases him some that this hellhole isn't full to capacity. Or perhaps it is, and the prisoners are too worn to make themselves heard or too dead to bother trying.

***

Spiro seems content just to lie on the ground with Katrina next to him. She hates every second of it, but with a glance at the noisy heap of arms and legs at her left, she is fully aware that her situation could be much, much worse. Eventually, the noise has the desired effect on the stoic Greek guard, and Katrina's predicament becomes worse. Spiro leans in and kisses her on the mouth. She recalls how wonderful Angelica made a kiss sound, how delicious and exhilarating. For Katrina, there is nothing delicious about it. She detests his raspy tongue, and her first instinct is to bite it off. For the sake of Robert, she stills her urge and allows the guard to continue in his. She endures his thin lips, endures his hands in her hair, endures him.

Spiro is at her neck, pulling her blouse farther down, brushing her shoulder with his lips. It gives her shivers—the bad kind. She hates just lying here, letting some strange man do as he pleases with her. She shuts her eyes, shuts him out. That is until she feels him loosening his pants. Her eyes pop open. Clearly lost in his desire and oblivious to her distress, the guard slides his hands up her legs, slowly lifting her skirt. She gasps. A second later, his pants are at his ankles. Spiro is fully aroused and begins parting her knees.

Instinctively, Katrina takes his wrist to stop him. The guard looks into her eyes and seems to read her terror. He pushes himself hastily off the ground.

"*Costas*," he hisses, doing up his pants.

The big Greek is visibly rapt in his haze and uses one hand to lower the scarf, which gives him noticeable trouble, his fat fingers struggling with the complex knot. Costas manages to pull the blindfold partway down. He scowls.

"I'm busy, *vlaka*."

"Fine, stay here. I'm going." As Spiro marches off, Katrina struggles desperately for the strength to stop him, soothe him, and bring him back to her, because she knows what is at stake. But her relief at having him away from her is so powerful she cannot bring herself to move.

Lilla motions her to action, but she cannot budge. So Lilla calls out to Spiro. "Come back! My sister is a prig. I will take care of you, here, now!"

But he does not return.

***

Callus opens the sixth hatch, hears low, despairing moans made by an unfamiliar voice. An awful sense of guilt sweeps him. Would that he could free this prisoner too. But he cannot. Not now. He moves on. The seventh door. He lifts the hatch, squints again into blackness.

Suddenly, Callus takes a swift kick to the face with a force that sends him onto his back. He swears under his breath and rubs his bleeding cheek. Must have been mistaken for a guard.

"Falsone," he hisses, "That damnable foot attached to you?"

"Yes," the voice replies from inside the prison cell. "Yes, it's me! Open the hatch again."

Callus obliges. "Just don't you kick me again."

"Who are you?" Robert reaches his hand through the opening. The doctor takes it in his.

"It's me, Giuseppe."

"Callus!" The name escapes as a joyous sob. They clasp arms through the small square hole. The doctor feels as his hand is drawn and held to Robert's stubbly face, feels tears rolling over his fingers.

"All right, all right," Callus soothes. "Everything will be all right. I'm here. Katrina too."

"She's here? Where?"

"She's ... outside. Safe, behind a boulder," Callus lies. "I wouldn't allow her to come down."

"How did you find me? How did you get inside? You know I didn't kill the farmer, right? Bonfatti invented that. He is behind it all. And my mother, is she all right? He said she was dead, and at first, I believed, but he is a liar." Robert pauses, quickly adds: "He was lying, right?"

Now is not the time for such terrible tidings. Callus hesitates but a fraction of a second. Still, it is a fraction too long. "Callus? What is it?"

"I have to get you out," the doctor says. "Move away from the door. I have a hatchet."

***

Spiro cannot shake the girl's eyes, her petrified expression, from his mind. She has never been with a man before; her face revealed her innocence. Thank God Costas did not insist on having her, for that look would have only driven him to greater lust, and he would have taken her by force. It would not be the first time. God, how Spiro hates being paired with Costas. How he hates Costas.

Seconds later, Spiro arrives at his post. He can still hear the flaxen moaning from here. The guard stops his ears and looks to the night sky, trying to distract himself with the constellations. The great Dipper spills its contents across the black rim. Not a full minute passes that he grows bored and glances to the prison door. And to his utmost horror, sees it ajar.

***

Callus takes his first swing, notching the door. He struggles to yank the hatchet from the wood. This is going to take a lot longer than expected. He prays the girls are faring all right. He readies the second blow, adjusts his grip on the handle, takes a deep breath. On his backswing, the door at the top of the stairs opens violently against its hinges. He falls to his belly. "*A guard.*"

"*Go!*" Robert hisses. Callus remembers the ribbon. He reaches into his pocket and passes it swiftly through the hatch.

"We will not give up on you. She will not give up on you." With those parting words, the doctor closes the hatch and rises. He knows there is nowhere for him to hide. He is trapped and has but one escape: direct assault. Callus puts the hatchet in his pants and goes to meet whoever comes.

***

Spiro takes each step cautiously. No peasant knows of this place, so he need not fear a breakout attempt. It is much worse than that—one of his superiors must have come to find him and Costas missing from their post. Whoever it is will be furious and probably imprison the Greeks in this very hellhole. Costas will deserve it, but Spiro will not. For the life of him, he cannot understand why Costas is employed by the keepers of a place that requires iron discipline. Perhaps that is precisely why Costas finds himself in its employ—to fool the odd passer-by, because who in his right mind would leave that fat idiot in charge of anything?

Spiro's thoughts shift quickly back to the more unsettling riddle: Who has entered? Could it be the Grand Master? The *hakem*? Spiro prays with all he holds dear that whoever this visitor is, it is not someone of the Church, for none tends to be quicker to anger, quicker to dole out ungodly punishments, than the bishop and his cronies.

"Sire?" Spiro calls into the shadow. "Pardon me, I just slipped off into the bushes to relieve myself." He makes it to the foot of the stairs, heart pounding, mind racing.

Then, everything goes black.

***

The guard is unconscious before he hits the ground. Giuseppe Callus stands over him, rubbing his fist. The doctor sprang from the darkness and punched Spiro square in the face, knocking him out cold. He lies sprawled on his back, blood lit bluish by moonlight running over his chin, onto his clothes.

The doctor in Callus worries the guard might choke on his own blood, so he sits him up against the wall, and is off like a shot up the stairway.

***

Katrina inches away from Lilla and Costas. It has been three minutes since Spiro rose and stalked off, and she has yet to recover. She struggles to gather her bearings, knowing she must go at once to Dr Callus and Robert's aid. But what can she possibly do? She's just a stupid little girl who can't compose herself when composure is dire.

She remembers her dagger. She could kill the guards and free everybody locked up underground. It would look like a robbery, done by common ruffians. No one would ever suspect Katrina or Lilla or Callus. Of course, missing prisoners would alert the authorities that it was no robbery, not in the strictest sense of the word anyway, but who cares? She and Robert would be on their way to Sicily by then.

Katrina waits a moment, watches Costas, whose eyes are closed, lips parted. She slips her hand under her skirt, feels for the hilt, closes her hand around it. She doesn't know if she has the stomach to go through with murder. But it wouldn't be murder, she reasons, it would be a soldier killing another in war. This *is* war. She herself declared it on those who keep Robert prisoner. She grits her teeth, pulls the dagger from its sheath, careful to keep it from making any noise that would alert Costas. The curved blade, stone whetted and sharp, gleams with the moon. As Katrina advances, she catches eyes with Lilla.

Suddenly, Callus crashes through the bushes. "Still you rob me my honour? Not a day after you disgrace our entire family!" He takes Lilla by the hair and wrenches her off the startled Greek, who moves quickly to cover himself. Callus takes Katrina forcibly by the wrist, yanks her to her feet. He throws Lilla in front of him and shoves the girls forward. Neither needs to feign alarm.

***

Costas can make out nothing of the man but his silhouette. Shocked, he gropes for his gun to shoot the intruder, more for ruining his pleasure than anything. But then he would have to kill all three of them, and he is in no mood to dig three graves. Spiro would be no help, no help at all.

Ah, let the father recover his honour with the savage beating he is going to give his daughter. A pity though, Costas was enjoying her. After lying another minute in the small clearing, he does up his pants and rises. With the scarf still loose around his neck, he goes to tear a strip off Spiro, who damn well should have seen this lunatic hurtling forth and dealt with him accordingly.

Honestly, what kind of guard is Spiro Agelakos anyway?

***

Once clear of the bushes, Katrina, Lilla, and Callus break into a sprint. Kat pushes through the pain, running barefoot over rocks and thorns. Finally, when they create good distance between themselves and the prison, Dr Callus slows his stride. "I hope I did not hurt either of you."

Katrina waves off his concern. "Is Robert all right? What happened?"

Callus describes what transpired in that dark place. Katrina feels tears sting her eyes when she learns of Robert's questions, his concern about Mea.

"The ribbon," she says, voice broken, "Did you give it to him?"

"Yes."

"Do you think the guards will report this?" Lilla asks, breathing hard.

Callus shakes his head. "No. The guards can't do anything or tell anyone because they'll get themselves into very serious trouble."

"What do we do now?" Katrina asks.

Callus sighs. "With all my heart, I do not know. We won't be able to try anything that reckless a second time."

Lilla takes Katrina's hand. "I think … I think the only thing left to do now is for you to confront Franco di Bonfatti."

***

Costas has no idea how long Spiro has been unconscious. The large Greek holds a torch and takes it all in: the blood caked to Spiro's face, the notch in Robert Falsone's cell door—silent testaments to a failed breakout. His brain works to understand the scene before his eyes. Then, it hits him: the whores were a distraction.

Minutes later, Spiro shakes his head, brings his fingers to his swollen nose and winces. Costas sets the torch in an iron cage and offers his hand, but Spiro slaps it away.

"Look what you caused! Do you realise what this means? Someone was down here!"

"From the look of you it would seem Hercules was down here," Costas says mildly.

"This is not funny! Peasants *know* about this place."

"So? We find them. How hard could it be to track down two prostitutes?"

"Do you think they're going to be flouncing around every corner tavern now? They will go into hiding. Likely they are not even prostitutes! The dark one has never been touched."

Costas grins. "The other was experienced enough."

Spiro waves him off. "The fact remains that we do not know who these conspirators are."

"We question the prisoner," Costas says. "The one they tried to break out. He would know his rescuers. He will identify them."

Spiro throws up his hands. "Or else what? We lock him up and throw away the key?"

"Then what, in your infinite wisdom, do you propose we do?"

"I don't care what *you* do. What *I'm* going to do is report you."

383

Costas narrows his eyes hatefully. "You're going to do what?"

Spiro sets his chin. "You heard me. I am going to the Grand Master's hall. From there, I will go to Mdina to see the *hakem*, and after that, to the bishop's palace."

With all his heart, Costas believes Spiro, a man not one to bluster. And so, Costas swiftly changes his demeanour to one of total contrition. He drops down onto his knees and begs mercy. "My wife and children will starve on Cephalonia without me to send money. If you bring me to formal charges, I will not only be without work but will swing from the scaffold. It is a fate I brought upon myself, but take pity on my family." He grovels, looks up with pleading eyes.

"You don't even have a wife and children! I hope you don't. Now, if this was the first time you compromised us, I would be moved to silence, but it is not, so I am not." Spiro wipes some of the blood from his face, turns on his heel and begins up the stair.

He does not make it past the third.

The shot echoes off the walls, in every alcove, every niche. Spiro sprawls forward on the stairs, a lead ball to the back, his slender form writhing. Costas approaches slowly, smoke furling from his pistol. He turns the wounded guard over and smiles. "Costas Kiriakoulias is a hero, they will say. He thwarted a breakout." He primes his gun. "But poor, poor Spiro Agelakos..." Costas puts the weapon to Spiro's chest, which hitches as his life leaves his body "... killed in the escape attempt." Spiro's eyes are wide, horrified. His mouth moves, no words escape. Costas fires, point-blank. Another flash of light. Spiro's body shudders from the blast, his blood splattering his killer in the face.

A moment later, Costas turns the key in the seventh door. It opens, complaining on rusted hinges as it does. His immense form fills the doorway. In two strides, he reaches the prisoner, lifts him off the ground by the throat and slams his body hard into the stone wall.

"Now, who shot my brave partner and caused his tragic death?"

CHAPTER FORTY-FOUR

The fourteenth day has come—the day Katrina has longed for and dreaded. The day she must meet Franco di Bonfatti.

He seems to have taken as great care to avoid her as she has to avoid him. In fact, she has not seen him once, not a chance meeting on the street, nor an encounter at the market square.

Katrina waits now at Mnajdra, her horse grazing on wild grass. In case things go bad, she has the carpenter's dagger strapped to her thigh, and after the night with the guards, she knows she is not afraid to use it.

But Franco does not show up. For two hours, Katrina waits under a burning sun. She begins to lose her nerve. He must know something. Somehow, he has learned of the breakout attempt. But how? From one of the guards? From Lilla? Perhaps the courtesan gave up the information for a few more *tari*. No, Katrina thinks, ashamed. Lilla put herself in as much peril. More.

Katrina shades her eyes and squints, still hoping Franco might turn up. He does not.

She has but one choice: the Grand Master of the Order. It is the only way. She will tell him of Franco di Bonfatti's involvement and of the guards Costas and Spiro. She will swear before God and Grand Master that no one else knows about the prison. In exchange for her silence, she will ask only for Robert's release. It is a terrible danger in which she places herself, and surely the Grand Master is going to have her executed, but it is a necessary danger.

Katrina mounts her horse and snaps the reins. Tramonto passes over fields that roll like grassy waves, towards Birgu, towards St Angelo. The fortress guards will never let Katrina inside, even if she announces her intention to see the Grand Master. *Especially* if she announces her intention to see the Grand Master. And even if she is granted occasion, her brother has already made enemies of Juan d'Homedes, and he will know Katrina and Domenicus as kin and dismiss her before hearing a word.

An idea comes to her: the fortress guards may not let some random peasant inside, but if she were with a knight, they would have no choice.

Within fifteen minutes, she is outside the door of the Italian *auberge*. The quartermaster answers her knock. He is a spindly man who jumps when greeted by Tramonto's enormous head. He looks to the beast's left and scowls.

"Who do you think you are, skipping work the entire week? You are dismissed."

"Fine. I need to see Marcello di Ruggieri."

"Concerning?"

"Franco di Bonfatti." The quartermaster raises his eyebrows, and after telling Katrina to wait, he closes the door on her face. She sits on the stone step. Half an hour passes. Part of her is afraid Franco may pop outside the *auberge* and see her sitting there. Another part of her hopes he will do exactly that. She wonders if she should just go to St Angelo alone. It would be more productive than what she is currently doing. She rises, gives Tramonto's shank a tug.

"Katrina!"

She looks to the right. Marcello di Ruggieri approaches, falconer equipment in a bundle tucked under his arm. He walks alongside Amedeo Pistolesi, Franco's former page.

"Thank God," she says. "I had just about given up."

The knight furrows his brow. "Given up? What do you mean? Katrina, are you all right?"

Tears well in her eyes, spill over her cheeks. Amedeo looks from Katrina to Marcello and back. Without a word, the youth slips swiftly off.

Marcello wipes Katrina's face carefully with his sleeve. "What is it?"

She looks up into his eyes. "I need your help. I have to see the Grand Master."

"What for?"

"You wouldn't believe me if I told you, and I wouldn't blame you. Just believe me when I tell you it's urgent, and you are doing a good thing by helping me."

"That's not enough for me to tell d'Homedes. Give me more."

"I wish I could."

"In that case, I'm sorry, I cannot help. I wish I could," Marcello says ruefully. After a moment, he tilts his head. "Angelica came to me recently. Does this have something to do with that?"

Katrina's knees go weak. "What are you talking about?"

"She heard some ridiculous tale about a secret prison—"

"Oh, dear God."

"So that is what this is about?" Marcello takes her by the arm and leads her to a dead end. "Do you realise the trouble you will bring upon yourself if you go to the Grand Master with this?"

"Then find Franco."

Marcello frowns. "Franco is not here."

"I can wait."

"No, you don't understand. He is not on Malta."

Katrina is instantly dizzy. "*What?*"

"His father has taken ill. It's been days now since Franco left for Italy."

Stunned, Katrina places her hand against the wall to steady herself. "How could he do this...?

Marcello stiffens. "He hardly *did* this. It is not his fault his father is dying."

She shakes her head but does not clarify the remark. "How long will he be gone?"

"It depends on how long the count has to live. Could be a week as easily as it could be a year. Franco is only obligated to return to Malta if summoned by the Grand Master."

Katrina's legs give out. She sits down hard, right there in the middle of the street, and buries her face in her hands. Marcello bends and hoists her back to her feet. "All right, let me humour you. Say this prison does exist. Say Falsone is confined there. What has Bonfatti to do with it?"

"I don't think you want to know. Whatever I tell you, I cannot untell."

"Tell me."

"This will not be easy for you to hear." Katrina hesitates before continuing. "Whatever Angelica told you is true." She gathers what remains of her nerve and gives Marcello di Ruggieri the entire story, from Robert's disappearance to Franco's betrayal to the breakout attempt. The knight remains mostly silent. It is not every day he receives news this grievous, but he handles the story surprisingly well. Still, Katrina can sense Marcello is deeply pained at the idea that Franco could be behind this.

"You are the only person who knows the entire story from all sides," she says. "You may even know sides that I do not, from your meeting with Angelica."

Marcello nods grimly. "And I wish I knew none of it."

"Do you believe me?"

He swallows. Without a word, he leads Katrina to the public stables and secures Tramonto. She has no clue where he plans to take her but goes anyway. The typically jovial Florentine is morose. They end up walking the waterfront, steps taken in silence. At length, he turns to her. "I wish Franco had come to me before putting this madness in motion. I would have talked him out of it."

"Maybe he didn't want to be talked out of it."

Several pensive moments pass. At last, Marcello clears his voice. "What exactly do you plan to tell the Grand Master?"

"The truth."

"If I had my hand full of the kind of truth you have, I would take caution in opening it."

"How am I supposed to do that?"

Marcello halts his stride. "You mean to go before the Grand Master of the most powerful knighthood on the Continent with a charge not against only one knight, but against the entire Order, as well as the Church, and the civil authority. I refuse to take you where you want to go until you consider what you risk. You are a peasant and a woman, and in the eyes of titled men, highly dispensable. The Grand Master will never release Robert and punish Franco simply because you vow to keep silent. He will only see you as a threat to a shaky covenant among the three governing powers, and will treat you as such."

Katrina shakes her head. "He does not have to punish Franco. I only want Robert freed. We will leave. No one will know."

"To go to the Grand Master with this is to pass the death sentence not only to yourself but to your family and closest friends."

Katrina knows he is right. And she is heartsick with the knowledge. "Tell me what to do."

Marcello breathes deeply. "I will go to the Grand Master."

She takes hold of his arm. "What? *No!* You cannot risk yourself too."

"Heed. There will be no other direct attempt to free Robert yourself. And Franco is out of reach. I do believe that if he was here and you appealed to him, he would break and secure Robert's release. Knowing Franco, I am sure he wants nothing more now than to go back on what he did. But he is not here. I am. So I'll go to d'Homedes."

"With what?"

"A young lad was taken in error to the secret prison, and the men who came for him beat his mother so savagely she died from her injuries. I'll ask for Robert's release under the condition that he agree to terms of exile." Katrina sees the logic in Marcello's plan but feels terrible guilt.

"Your friendship with Franco will be ruined."

"Let me worry about that. Besides, Franco will be grateful I cleaned up *his* mess for once."

For the first time in a long time, Katrina smiles. "You are a good man."

"I am a whoremongering scoundrel."

They leave the wharf, walk a hundred paces to St Angelo and together, cross the narrow bridge that spans to the castle's portico. Marcello ushers Katrina past the guards and inside the thick fortress walls. She follows him up several ramps, over wide ramparts, through the empty bailey to the Grand Master's palace.

"Wait here," he says.

***

Grand Master Juan d'Homedes is not in his study. In the corridor just outside the office, Marcello finds Luis Cabanyelles, the Valencian page who adores him. There is a formal meeting of the Sacred Council, the boy tells him. Reports have surfaced of a Turkish fleet sailing west. With thanks, Marcello approaches the great chamber where such conferences take place. The door muffles the lively discussion on the opposite side. He tilts his ear to the heavy oak.

"...A formidable army and a swarm of barbarians are upon the point of rushing upon our island." It is the unmistakable voice of Jean Parisot de Valette, lieutenant to the Grand Master. "These infidels, my brethren, are the enemies of Christ, and it must be decided whether our holy faith and the gospel must or must not give place to the Koran."

"You jump to conclusions." It is the Grand Master Juan d'Homedes. "Such an expedition as the one you speak could not possibly be directed against Malta. It is on Sicily that the Turks will unleash their fury. Else, they are sailing to join their allies the French, in an attack against Spain."

Another knight speaks up, one Marcello does not recognize by voice. "Monsieur le baron, I come here in my own galley from a voyage to the Morea. I confirm your lieutenant la Valette's concerns. The Turkish armada is indeed on her way to Malta and Tripoli."

"You are off beam, Fra George St Jean," the Grand Master replies sharply. "What's more, any Frenchman who addresses this council with information contrary to my opinion is a liar and a traitor." This is met by spirited protest.

"*Silence!*" d'Homedes thunders. Marcello shifts uneasily as he waits for a pause.

"Allow me a word, Excellency." It is the newest Governor of Tripoli, Gaspard de Valliers. Marcello knows d'Homedes has no love for this knight—a moral and temperate man, admired by his fellows and thought to be ideal for the office of Grand Master. Because d'Homedes caught wind of this sentiment, he relegated de Valliers to Tripoli where he would not be a threat to the old Spaniard's position. Tripoli, a grain of Christian sand on a Muslim beach, is a hard place to be. In the city where Jean Parisot de Valette had kept order by bending men to his will, Gaspard de Valliers failed.

"Sire," de Valliers begins, "It is imperative that you strengthen defences at Tripoli. She is weak. She will fall easily."

"You are Governor," d'Homedes replies, "and if the land under your jurisdiction is weak, then I say you are not much of one. However, on the recommendation of the Viceroy of Sicily, I will send you two hundred fresh fighting men."

A distinguished knight of the Order, Commander Nico Durand de Villegagnon, clears his voice. He is a well-respected knight who distinguished himself as a brilliant mariner during an ill-fated campaign against Algiers ten years earlier. "With respect, I was at the Court of France a few weeks ago.

There, I was given rigorous warning from Constable de Montmorency, nephew of the late Grand Master de l'Isle Adam, and from Grand Prior de Lorraine. These are gentlemen of France, Sire, who venerate the Order. An attack on Malta and Tripoli is imminent. Further, reports have reached Messina from the Levant naming Dragut Raïs and Sinan Pasha as commanders of the Sultan's fleet."

The Grand Master scoffs. "And you, Sir, are either the dupe of the Constable, or you intend to make us yours."

"I am sorry you see it that way, your Grace. However, I think it is in our best interest that we alert the Maltese to a probable attack, in order that they can prepare."

"Out of the question!" d'Homedes fires. "They will be alerted to nothing. I will not have pandemonium in the streets because of some unfounded French surmise. And anyone who defies my order of silence will be whipped." There are forceful sighs and grumbled objections, but also finally a break in discussion.

Marcello raps on the door. A guard opens it, and the Florentine enters the hall. The room is gathered with knights of the highest rank: all eight *Piliers*, two Grand Crosses, the Admiral of the Order's fleet, the Turcopilier, and various commanders and senior officers. It is a scene of imperious countenances and grim stares. The Italian master, Ludovico dal Sagrà, glares with undisguised contempt at Marcello, who shrinks under the *pilier*'s baleful stare.

"My lords," Marcello says, bowing low.

The Grand Master peers narrowly at him. "Ruggieri, you interrupt a meeting of the Sacred Council. What matter could possibly be so pressing?"

Marcello feels perspiration on his brow. After everything he has just overheard, what in God's name makes him think this is a good time to approach the Grand Master? He'd been so busy steeling himself for a confrontation that he had not considered the effect of the current dispute on the Grand Master's already volatile temper. "F-forgive me, *Molto Illustrissimo*, the matter is of a confidential nature. I would much rather divulge the details in a private setting, if you would oblige me, Sire." Marcello senses his *pilier*'s hot gaze burning holes through him, but he will not meet the man's eyes, steadying his gaze only on the Grand Master.

"If the matter is private, you should know better than to announce it in a public forum."

"With respect, Excellency, a meeting of the Sacred Council is hardly a public forum."

The Italian master now makes himself impossible to ignore. He rises from his chair and addresses Marcello in a voice sharp and cutting. "Di Ruggieri, for speaking with insolence to the Grand Master, you will serve the Quarantine." The Quarantine is the forty-day version of Marcello's last punishment, the Septaine—confinement to the dormitory, fed bread and water.

Marcello swallows and takes the excessive sentence with thanks. "A punishment well deserved, my lord." He bows again to the Grand Master. "Forgive my impertinence, I meant no offence. Please excuse me, but I am obliged to reiterate the inflammatory nature of this matter is such that your Grace would prefer the particulars be revealed in private." Marcello decides right then that if the Grand Master presses him harder, he will simply make something up and approach d'Homedes with the truth later. But the Grand Master insists no more.

"Very well. I will return to my study when this council is adjourned. Wait there."

Marcello gives a reverent nod. "With gracious and humble thanks, *Molto Illustrissimo*."

The knight sits cross-legged on the floor of the hallway outside the old Spaniard's office like a boy awaiting an encounter with a fearsome schoolmaster. He finds reason to smile, having known his share of cantankerous schoolmasters. However, a schoolmaster could not do the damage to a small boy that the Grand Master could do to Marcello.

He is quickly yanked from his reverie by the clapping of boots against the floor. He jumps to his feet and stands at attention. Juan d'Homedes looks with some confusion at the knight, as though wondering why someone would be waiting outside his study. However, the cloud quickly passes. He opens the door and invites Marcello inside.

"You seemed to have upset the delicate internal balance of your *pilier*," d'Homedes says.

"I misspoke. The punishment is justified."

"Perhaps. But I talked him down from the Quarantine to the Septaine."

Marcello brightens at this unexpected turn of fortune. Perhaps this will not go as badly as he expected. "Thank you, Sire! I am unworthy of your compassion."

The Grand Master sits, indicates a chair for Marcello to follow suit. "I am in a good mood."

That is excellent news, seldom heard, and all the more unexpected given the hostile tone of the Sacred Council. Marcello prays for the grace to say the right things and keep from altering the Grand Master's good mood. "Your meeting went well, I trust?"

"I have successfully allayed the fears of the council. There are rumours that a Turkish fleet sailing under Dragut Raïs and Sinan Pasha is heading for our shores. It is idle talk, nothing more. There has been a preliminary attack on Sicily, and this new fleet is on its way to finish the job. That, or it is heading to Toulon, to join France in an offensive against Spain. Hostilities have broken out between the two kingdoms, but none against the Order. Besides, Malta is a fortress." He leans comfortably in his chair and smiles. Marcello doesn't think he has ever seen the man smile before. It looks odd on his face, misplaced somehow.

"Now, my fine Florentine, for your matter most furtive."

***

After what seems like fifteen years to Katrina, Marcello exits the magisterial palace. She is immediately upon him. "What happened? What did he say? Was he angry with you? Will he free Robert?" She looks closely at his face. It is grim, set in weary lines. "Are you all right?"

Marcello leads her away from the doors and across the deserted bailey. "I've been served the Quarantine."

"What? Why?"

"I spoke out of turn and angered my *pilier*. The Grand Master reduced the sentence to the Septaine. But after what I had to say, he restored the original penalty."

"But ... what does this mean for Robert?"

Marcello sighs angrily. "Robert stays where he is. It is a sad business about the prisoner's mother, d'Homedes said, but better dead than to survive as a cripple only to die from starvation. As for Falsone, it is too much to risk to have him released, exile or not. It could bring disaster, no matter where he is. It is unfortunate for the boy, but sometimes one must be sacrificed for the greater good. The Grand Master's words, verbatim."

Katrina is stupefied. "*The greater good?* That son of a bitch!" She is almost screaming. "Well, *I* know about this place, and will not rest until everybody else in Birgu does too!"

Marcello grabs her and draws his face up close to hers. "Do that Katrina and end up dead ten times inside the first hour. One of the Greek guards was murdered a few nights past. The Grand Master deemed it a robbery attempt gone bad. *Common ruffians*, he said, *thinking they were robbing two hunters*. A stroke of luck for you, but if d'Homedes were to learn that peasants know about the prison, it would not take him or any of the other authorities a moment to figure out what really transpired. You honestly think they could not trace it back to you, your family, your friends?"

"Which ... which guard was killed? How? We didn't do it, Marcello, I swear."

"The murdered guard was Spiro Agelakos. His fellow made the report, saying the two of them came under attack by three brigands. He played dead to elude them, but the other tried to stop them and took two bullets. One at close range. Tore his heart to shreds."

Katrina is struck dumb, horrified beyond measure. She is too numb to cry, barely able to draw breath. Finally, after several moments of shocked silence, she manages a few words. "The guard—Costas—he is lying. He did it. He turned on the other. ..."

"You see the value these men place on life? Do you see? Now stop this madness, or *your* heart will be torn to shreds! Your only hope is to wait for Franco to return and appeal to him. I will make it my personal mission to see that he secures Robert's release. Franco will listen to me, to you."

Katrina's voice falters. "Appeal to him now, in writing."

"A letter will not have the same effect—it may keep him away longer. We have no choice. *You* have no choice. And if I hear of your uttering a word of this to anyone who does not already know, I will, I promise you, kill you myself to spare you the torture you will face at the hands of the authorities, do you understand?" Then, after threatening her life, Marcello puts his arms around Katrina and allows her to sob against him until she is utterly spent.

CHAPTER FORTY-FIVE

Istanbul

Demir walks alongside Murad, whose steps these days are taken slowly and with the aid of a crutch. He may never again walk independent of it, from the damage sustained by Muharrem's blow to his knee. The streets are narrow, with many turns and blind alleys, rising and falling like great cobblestone waves. Every minute or so, Murad stops to rest.

It is late April. The air is warm and fragrant, and Istanbul abuzz with talk of war. Within the great walls built by the Emperor Theodosius, discussion spills from every barbershop and tavern, runs rampant in the sheltered maze of the Grand Bazaar: *Malta is infected by the Order; she must be bled.*

"Timurhan will kill five hundred knights himself," Demir gushes.

"Five hundred? That's a lot," Murad says. "Are there that many in the whole of the Order?"

"I'm sure *Shaytaan* spawns at least fifty knights a day from his shit."

"A hundred."

The boys laugh. After a long, careful amble, they reach the first of eighteen gates to the Grand Bazaar, which spans sixty-one streets and houses over eight hundred shops. Often, the pair cuts through the *Kapali Çarşi*, a shortcut home from school.

Demir's expulsion from the *madrasah* has since been repealed. Muharrem's mother, Ayla, went to see the teacher Mursel el Emarat and asked him to readmit Demir. The instructor was amazed that Muharrem's mother would argue Demir's case against that of her own son. *Anneh* was jubilant and kissed Ayla's hands. Hamid grunted and told Ayla not to leave the house again without his permission. She grunted back and went about her business.

Demir and Murad walk the tight warren of the *Kapali Çarşi*, its groundwork first laid by Mehmet II after his conquest of the city. From the tiled floor to its arched ceiling, the market is an explosion of colour, scent, and sound. Walls are hung with carpets and stained glass lamps and Iznik plates. There are luxurious silks from Asia Minor, brightly painted wooden hookahs, and daggers inscribed with sacred Hadith. The air around the confectioner's stand is sweet enough to eat, his display of syrupy filo dough, sugared fruits, and roasted filberts dripping with honey, making Demir's mouth water. At every pace, a new debate is held in a different tongue: rapid-fire haggling over prices, oaths of a product's superiority over a rival vendor's. The script seldom varies: the merchant swears the buyer's offer will make beggars of him and all his descendants, the buyer makes the same claim of the merchant's price. The wrangling goes on this way, sometimes the buyer winning, other times the seller, the two often negotiating a price that satisfies both—though neither admits it.

Chained in one stall are human commodities as diverse as the spices on display across the aisle. There are Romanians and Hungarians, Bulgars and Poles, Italians and Spaniards, Russians and Circassians. Demir catches eyes with one, a tall man, muscular, with a thick yellow beard and long hair, his broad shoulders crisscrossed with whip marks. His face is kind, eyes light green. He returns Demir's gaze evenly. Slaves are part of the natural order, and Demir has often passed this quarter with indifference, but today, for reasons he cannot understand, he wishes he could free this man. Still, if slavery is his lot in life, he is lucky to be here—only in Istanbul can a slave rise to position. The Janissaries, elite of the Sultan's elite, are slaves, as is the Grand Vizier himself.

As the boys approach a purveyor of exotic birds, Murad points out one with a large, crooked beak. It looks like Muharrem. "So. I've been meaning to tell you. You hit your brother really good."

Demir smiles. "I'd throw him off the walls of Topkapi for what he did to you."

"How is the gazelle?" Murad asks, clearly embarrassed by sentiment.

"Strong. I think I'll have to set him free soon. In a week, maybe two."

Murad looks stricken. "Can't you keep him?"

"It wouldn't be fair. He was free when we met him, he should be free again," Demir reasons.

"Think if we go to the forest after you set him free he would remember us?" Murad looks down at his bad leg. "When I'm better, I mean. When I'm not a cripple anymore."

"Timu will like that." At the northwestern exit of the bazaar, Demir stops at a leather kiosk. The merchant is a large Turk with a fine moustache and hazel eyes bright beneath his yellow turban. Demir touches the stiff leather of a saddle, rich brown, sturdy and finely tooled. He loves it. He looks up at the merchant.

"I'll be a Sipahi, one day," Demir says. "Save this saddle for me until that day."

"I will *give* you this saddle on that day. Just remember my shop."

"I think I will take it now." Demir and Murad turn. It is Timurhan. They have not seen the young horseman in weeks, not since preparations for the campaign began. "It is a fine saddle, Demir. You should not wait to have it." Timurhan hands the merchant several coins.

Demir is ecstatic but feels guilty—first because he has nothing to offer Timurhan and second because apart from his crutch, Murad is leaving the bazaar empty-handed. The second concern is quickly addressed. There is a weaponsmith next to the leather stand, and from him, Timurhan procures a dagger. The blade is curved, engraved with *Qur'anic* poetry, its hilt inlaid with pearl. He presents it to Murad, whose eyes go wide. Finally, remembering courtesy, the two boys erupt:

"Our gratitude springs forth like sweet water from a desert fountain," Demir says.

"Your kindness shall be written in the golden book!" Murad proclaims. "*Askin cemal olsun!*"

And on they go, giving ornate voice to their appreciation for Timurhan's generosity. The Sipahi hoists the heavy saddle and asks the boys to follow him outside. Sun catches the golden crescents that top the minarets of the Beyazit mosque and reflects onto the cobbled square as delicate pools of light, suffusing Timurhan's face in warmth. "Demir, I was on my way to see your father."

At the mention of Hamid, Demir stiffens. He has only recently recovered fully from the beating the man had dealt him. Still, he would never deny Timurhan a request. "He is home today and will welcome you with pleasure."

***

In the foyer of Hamid's house, a footman greets Timurhan, who asks to see Hamid. The attendant disappears, reappearing minutes later with a tray of Turkish coffee and a plate of honey-soaked dates. "Master Al Hajji will be with you in a moment, my lord."

Timurhan nods and sits on one of many damask pillows in the antechamber. He sets down the new saddle, runs his hand over the embellished leather. Demir sits on the floor beside him.

"Timurhan?"

"Demir?"

"I want you to take this saddle with you."

Timurhan looks at him askance. "Is it not to your liking?"

Demir shakes his head. "No, no, I love it."

"Why do you wish to give it away?"

"I don't. I wish to lend it to you. That way, it will know victory before I come to use it. It will have inside it the spirit of the Sipahiyan, the spirit of Timurhan Yusuf al Salih."

The cavalryman is deeply moved by the words of the small boy. He wants to embrace the child, take him away from his brother and father— Timurhan knows of Hamid's legendary cruelty, just as he knows of the savage beating the man delivered Demir over his expulsion from the *madrasah*. Timurhan Yusuf al Salih, nephew of Mustafa Pasha, knows a great deal.

Al Hajji Hamid al Azm strides in with a swish of silk robes. On his head, he wears a crimson velvet fez. His fingers flash from his rings, his feet from the gems in his brocaded shoes. The man is money in motion. Timurhan rises from his cushion and bows low, despite his urge to unsheathe his sword and run it through the silken blob.

Hamid too gives a bow. "*Salaam aliekum.*"

"And peace be upon you. I am here on official business of the Sultan, bless his name. Mustafa Pasha has made the Padishah aware that the imperial cavalry could do with one hundred new horses for the campaign. More if you can spare them. He sent me to see about their immediate acquisition."

Hamid gives Timurhan a big smile. "The stables are at your disposal, lord and master." He claps his hands, and at once, there is a flurry of activity. Timurhan is impressed by how swiftly attendants and footmen rush into the hall. Hamid sends one to fetch Kemal from his shed, another to summon the bookkeeper, another, the scribe. Once assembled, he sends them ahead to the stables, and after offering Timurhan coffee and sweets, leads him to his horses.

***

Demir is not invited to join them. He knows this is because his father does not want him to hear how business is conducted. Hamid has remarked that the boy might wake up a man one morning and decide to cut his father's throat and take over the stables. This way, if the son is going to cut the father's throat, the son will fall into ruin. Demir thinks if Hamid needs to worry about anyone capable of cutting throats around here, he should worry about Muharrem.

Demir sits alone by the coal brazier and stares at the saddle that will soon bear a Sipahi of the Padishah. He cannot wait to tell his mother and Jameela and Kemal. But he doesn't want to leave the foyer just yet; he has to make sure Timurhan takes the saddle before leaving. Demir imagines the horseman, riding hard into battle, cutting down knights, those plunderers who do nothing but make trouble for the Sultan's empire. He imagines Timurhan returning to Istanbul, presenting him once more with this fine saddle.

The reverie is interrupted by an uneasy feeling. He looks up, sensing a presence. As if appearing out of thin air, Muharrem stands between hanging carpets. Demir starts—wherever Muharrem is, trouble is not far behind. As the older boy approaches, his expression is strangely docile.

"Brother, I come to apologise. I have treated you badly."

Demir looks at him guardedly, says nothing.

Muharrem sighs softly. "You do not trust me. I have worked hard to break your trust and must now work harder to repair it."

He seems sincere. His eyes do not waver, his voice steady. Demir remembers the first words Murad spoke the day he offered his hand in friendship: *Don't be so stupid as to trust your brother. You are smart in the ways of the text, but in the ways of the street, dumber than an ox.* Those words are no longer true. Demir narrows his eyes. "Why bother now?"

"Because we are brothers. The Messenger has said the bond of blood is as steel, and cannot be sundered. But before you can look to me as a brother, look to me as a friend."

Demir arcs an eyebrow. "You want to be my friend?"

"Yes." There is no menace in Muharrem's voice, no threat in his eyes. Perhaps the punch that bent his nose straightened out the rest of him.

"All right," Demir says.

Muharrem looks to the fat pillow next to Demir's cushion. "May I?"

"Of course."

The bigger boy sits down heavily as though standing has tired him out. They sit in silence a few moments, the heat of the brazier against their backs. Muharrem speaks quietly. "So. Your horseman friend is leaving soon to go kill some Christians. That's good. I hate them."

"He is going to kill knights," Demir says. "Not innocents."

"You think Christians are innocents?"

Demir contemplates the question. He has never spoken to a Christian but has seen them at the slave market. They certainly look nothing like the child-eating monsters his father described. He remembers the slave at the bazaar today, his kind green eyes. Sure, Christians are barbarians, but that doesn't make them *evil*. They have not yet seen Allah's light or felt its warmth. Naturally, Demir is relieved he is not one. "They believe they are on the right side, and I think that makes them innocent. They are like sheep, led by the wrong shepherd. They don't deserve to be slaughtered for it."

"Is that why you wish to become Sipahi? To *not* slaughter the enemies of Islam?"

"Only those who threaten Suleiman's empire," Demir replies.

"But are Christians not all witless sheep? How then can they threaten the empire?"

"It is not the sheep who trouble the Sultan. It is the wolves. The Knights of St John. They *do* know better. At Rhodos, for their lives, they swore they would never again rob from the Padishah's kingdom. They have made liars of themselves, and to lie is to know one has done wrong, therefore, a liar is not innocent and deserves no mercy."

Muharrem smiles, an act that seems to cause him physical discomfort. "You are very clever."

"Thank you." Demir debates returning the compliment, but as he just told Muharrem, it is not right to lie.

"Perhaps your wits may gain you acceptance to the devshirme when you are twelve."

Demir frowns. "The devshirme? That's the college where boys recruited from Christian villages are sent, where they train to become the slave soldiers of the Sultan, the Janissaries."

Muharrem nods. "Exactly right."

"Why would I go there?" Demir asks, certain his brother is merely puzzled by the complexity of the different factions.

"You mean you do not know?" Muharrem hesitates. "Hmm, for a moment, given your belief that Christians are not all evil, I thought you knew..."

Demir furrows his brow. "Knew what?"

"That you are half Christian," Muharrem replies evenly.

Demir jumps to his feet at the hideous charge. "That's not true!"

"It is, *kafir. Christian.*" Muharrem's tone makes an insult of the word.

"I am not Christian! I was born to Muslim parents in Istanbul!"

Muharrem speaks quietly. "Your *anneh* is no woman of Islam. She is the gutter filth of a Maltese sewer. I found a letter she wrote and took it to a scribe for translation. It is addressed to her daughter. Yes, that's right. You have a sister, who is no doubt every bit the whore your mother is. The impostor even has the name of an unbeliever. Graciela Tabone."

Tears spring to Demir's eyes. He thrusts an accusing finger at his brother. "You lie!"

"Your mother lies." Muharrem sits with cool poise on his cushion. "And she lies not only with her tongue, but her body, and her soul."

"*You are lying!*" Demir explodes, unable to contain his rage and his horror. This is just another of Muharrem's nasty tricks. It has to be.

So why does it cut him right to the core?

Muharrem leaps from his seat with a swiftness that belies his heavy frame and takes Demir by the shoulders. He struggles, no match for the bigger boy. Muharrem slams him hard against the wall, knocking the wind from his lungs. "You thought your attack on me would go unpunished?"

Demir spits at Muharrem. "I'm not afraid of you." And he really isn't, despite the pincers about to snap his clavicles. Demir's days of being afraid are over. "I hate you! Do you hear me? *I hate you!* Everyone hates you! Your own mother hates you!"

Muharrem's coolness vanishes with those last words. His eyes are turbulent, full of danger, his voice as threatening. He pulls Demir closer. They are nose to nose. Demir feels his spittle and his rage. "Do not speak of my mother."

"Then do not speak of mine."

The calmness creeps back into Muharrem's voice, making him ten times as frightening as when he foams with fury. "I think no person will be speaking of your whore mother ever again. Ever since I took her letter to my father, her embroidery has been empty, her bedchamber too. I wonder if Allah has at last taken his vengeance upon her for her lies… for as you said yourself, a liar is not innocent and deserves no mercy."

"*Where is she?*"

"You told me not to speak of her. I'll grant you that one request." He walks slowly, deliberately, almost gliding, towards the stairs. Behind him, Demir is rooted to the ground. His eyes catch fire as they glance to the poker next to the hot coal brazier. He could bash his brother to death with it. Demir takes a step towards the instrument. Something stops him. First, he will see what Muharrem wants in exchange for Yaminah… Graciela… whoever she is. *Anneh*—Mother—is the only name that matters right now. Demir chases after his brother, throws himself before him.

"Muharrem, please. I'm sorry for what I said. I take it back. Just don't hurt my mother."

"You're still on that?"

Demir has lost all composure. "*Where is she?* Tell me!"

"We are not to speak of mothers."

"Muharrem, I beg you!"

The bigger boy sneers. "Beg as a beggar should."

"What?"

"On your knees. Grovel like the dog you are for mercy and maybe you will have it."

Demir feels hatred strong inside him. He does as he's told, dropping to his knees.

"*Lower!*" Muharrem commands.

Again, Demir complies, bringing his chest to the floor.

"Now kiss my feet, mongrel." Muharrem sticks out his foot, points his toe. Demir stiffens. He takes his brother's foot in his hand and kisses it.

"Now, admit you are a snivelling Christian and I might be persuaded to tell you where your mother is. And as you wish her to live, you will address me henceforth as master."

"I am not Christian, master," Demir replies, shocked at his own boldness.

"According to your mother, I bring much joy when I go, so let me leave you to contemplate her fate as you await your own." Muharrem turns and starts up the stairs, pauses, turns back. "The servant girl Jameela missed her duties today." He is at the top of the staircase in a blink, Demir still abasing himself on the ground. He rises, trembling, and thinks again about going for the poker. Instead, he runs from the vestibule and flies up the stairs. He barrels down the corridor straight to his mother's room. Just as Muharrem had said, it is empty. Demir tears through the hallway, looks in every room, checks the servants' quarters.

Where is everybody? Servants? Chefs? Has Muharrem found letters from all of them? Demir runs blindly to the third storey, searches the çikma—a fully enclosed balcony. His mother likes to sit there sometimes and watch the outside world. Of course, now is not such a time. Where could she be? Has Hamid already sent her to be tortured? Demir's mind churns with the horrible images of his mother's torment all too vividly—he has seen torture done, forced by his father to watch. Muharrem loves it, but for Demir, it is unbearable. He once witnessed an errant servant being burned alive, tethered to a post between small fires. He must find *Anneh* before she can meet such a fate.

But why would Hamid hurt her? If she truly is a Christian from Malta, he must have known that before making her his wife. Why should he punish her for what he already knew? Perhaps there is more to this letter than that broken-nosed demon revealed.

The evening call to prayer floats down from the minarets. For the first time in his life, Demir ignores it. He prays as he runs, prays God will spare his mother. He looks in every passage, every room, behind hanging rugs and tapestries. In his frenzy, he even checks drawers and cupboards. He runs outside. It is dark, the sky a mess of purple and blue lines, faint white stars appearing across the great arcing rim. He makes it to the shed where Kemal sleeps and peeks inside. The stableman is in the middle of prayers. Demir wants badly to charge in and interrupt but that would be unforgivable. So he waits, pacing, sweating. Finally, Kemal rises and dusts dirty straw from his knees.

"Kemal!" Demir flies inside the small hut and throws his arms around the Moroccan's waist.

Kemal crouches. "In the name of the Prophet, what is wrong?"

"*Annem*—my mother. I can't find her. Something terrible has happened, and Muharrem is behind it."

A shadow passes over the stableman's face. "Perhaps she is busy with your father. He is in a celebratory mood, having just made a deal that will ensure fortune for his descendants and theirs."

Demir does not care about this new wealth. "My mother is not with Al Hajji."

"If only I could help you search your house. I am not permitted to enter."

"Can you search the stables?" Demir pleads. "The grounds? The bagnios?"

Kemal furrows his brow. "The bagnios? Why would she be in the Christian slave prison?"

"I don't know. I don't know why I said that," Demir lies. "I'm just worried."

"I will search every pace of the courtyard and the stables." Kemal rises to do just that. Demir runs back inside the house, heart pounding as he passes again through the vestibule to the wide, open stairs, taking them two, three at a time. He slows only to catch his breath. And that is when he hears it, from behind a doorway draped with a heavy carpet: the lovely strains of a flute.

Anneh! He bursts into the harem, rips past the mute eunuch standing guard to one side of the door. The eunuch starts, reaches for his blade, but recognizes the intruder. Males are forbidden from the harem, but right now, the Sultan himself could not stop Demir. He looks frantically around the dimly lit room. There is Ayla, the picture of serenity as she reclines on a long pillow of deep blue sussapine. The other wives lounge on fat cushions of orange and red damask, several female servants comfortable on soft pelt rugs. Young girls giggle at the entrance of a boy.

Demir is flooded with relief at the sight of Jameela, who is using a small taper to light wall sconces. Then, through thin white plumes rising from cones of incense, he sees his mother sitting cross-legged on a silk cushion, her flute at her lips. A million emotions hit him at once. He tears across the thick carpets towards her. His foot catches on one, sending him sprawling. He jumps up before anyone can come to his aid, and before anyone speaks, he throws himself before his mother.

"*Is it true?*"

The woman looks at him with starting eyes. "Is what true, my love?"

"Are you Christian? From Malta?"

She drops her flute. Everyone in the room is deathly silent, *Anneh* deathly pale. All eyes are on her, watching, studying. Ayla rises, puts her hands on Demir's shoulders and turns him around. She touches his hair, takes his chin in her hand and tilts his face.

"Child, you are flushed. Come, I will take you to bed." She takes his hand. He pulls it away.

"No." Demir turns back around. "Is it true?"

He can see the shock in his mother's colourless face. Somehow, she rises and picks him up. He stiffens at her touch. Ayla guides them to the door, turning to address the harem. "Poor child has taken ill. Something from the stables."

The wives and servants all coo with sympathy. All but Jameela.

***

Yaminah takes her son to her private room, sits him on the divan and kneels before him. Forcing sternness, she looks him in the eye.

"I'm sorry," he says. "I shouldn't have entered the sacred room. I had no right."

"Why did you?"

"Because... because Muharrem told me he found a letter you wrote to your daughter in Malta and you are a Christian and only pretending to be Muslim. He showed the letter to Father." *He showed the letter to Father.* To Al Hajji Hamid al Azm. Yaminah feels whatever blood is left in her face draining. Her tongue is dry, her stomach in turmoil. She fights to control her breathing. If that poisonous asp has the letter in his possession, there can be no lying, no denying. Yaminah curses her carelessness. She should have never made herself prey in a house where slithers the vilest snake she has ever known. She reaches for the pillow where she hid the letter and feels inside the damask case.

Nothing. In desperation, she rips open the pillow. There is an explosion of white feathers. Yaminah watches with despair as they float to the rug.

Muharrem has her letter. And so, has her, and her son.

***

An hour later, Demir sits alone on the corridor floor, back to the wall, knees to his chest. He knew simply by looking at his mother that everything Muharrem said was true. The one time Demir prayed Muharrem was lying, he was telling the truth. To the eye, the woman is the same beloved mother Demir has always known, and yet nothing is the same. He feels betrayed. He is not sure where to lay the blame for this betrayal—on her, on Muharrem, on Hamid, or on God.

Yesterday, Demir was Muslim, devout in his faith, a promising horseman, friend to a Sipahi, son of Yaminah, finally liked by his peers, and no longer afraid of anyone. Now, he does not know who he is. To which faith does he belong? Who among his peers will not use this to torture him? How can he remain in the *madrasah* with this mixed blood? Worse, how is he ever to enter the ranks of the Sipahiyan? Whose son is he? Yaminah does not even exist. Nothing of his old world exists. His entire life has been a lie. And worst of all, he is again afraid. So long as Muharrem has the letter, he has the power. His brother lied about one thing: that he gave the letter to Hamid. Had he, Mother would already have been punished severely. Even so, Demir must find the letter and burn it, or become his brother's slave. And he will never find it. Demir's misery descends upon him as heavily as the realisation: Muharrem wins.

CHAPTER FORTY-SIX

Yaminah manages to avoid Jameela's gentle questions with ease, telling her Demir had a nightmare and was frightened out of his senses. They both know she is lying, but also that it is not Jameela's place to push. Yaminah strokes the serving girl's hair and says, in all truth, that Demir is not himself, then, much as it pains her, sends Jameela away. Ayla, however, is not so easily dismissed.

"You are lying," she says, flat out. Truly, Yaminah wants to unburden herself; it is why she wrote that letter in the first place. But she cannot put another at risk.

Ayla crosses her arms. "Yaminah, I do not care which God hears your prayers. He sees inside your soul whether you face east and prostrate on your belly or cross yourself and drop to your knees. In a room lit by several lamps, there is only one indivisible light."

"If anyone hears such nonsense, you will lose your head."

Ayla gives Yaminah a look. "The only one who might hear is my sneak of a son, and I will die before fearing him. Muharrem is cruel and hard-hearted and impossible to love. He is a river of treachery that runs deep and long. Demir would not have come up with this on his own. I will end your troubles, but you must tell me the truth."

"As Allah is my witness," Yaminah says solemnly, "I cannot tell you anything. It is not safe, not for me, not for Demir, not for you. Let this be."

***

The past week has been the most horrible of Demir's life. It was bad enough finding out his entire life was a lie. But not enough for Muharrem, who has subjected him to every humiliation imaginable. Demir has always known his brother to be crafty and mean, but it astounds him to discover how twisted his mind really is. On the first day, Muharrem made Demir steal sweetmeats from confectioners inside the Grand Bazaar. Lucky for the younger boy, he found he was a rather skilled thief. Muharrem also insisted Demir address him permanently as *master* except in front of Hamid, Ayla, or the instructor at the *madrasah.* In front of classmates, servants, and *Anneh*, the title held. Muharrem ordered Demir to roll in horse manure, season his food with alum, cross himself in class, anything to degrade him and get him into trouble. If this goes on much longer, Demir's head will hang parboiled from the gate of Topkapi *saray.*

Today, Muharrem makes his worst demand yet: "You are no longer to be friends with the cripple, Murad."

Demir is devastated. "What? Why?"

Muharrem gives him a severe look.

"Why, master?" Demir corrects himself.

"Because I have said. And your role is to do as I say."

It is hopeless, but Demir tries anyway. "Master, please, can you not allow me this one thing? Murad is the only friend I have in the world."

Muharrem's mouth smiles, though his eyes do not. "Yes, I know. When you deliver him the news, you will do it exactly as I tell you."

After school, Murad clumps clumsily behind Demir, who is walking too fast for the injured boy to keep up. "Hold up a little."

Demir does not turn. He speaks in a clipped voice: "Why don't you hurry up?"

"You've been spending too much time with the gazelle, I think. You're becoming as fast," Murad jokes, though he struggles for breath. "Slow down."

"I don't want to slow down. You've been walking with that thing for so long now, and still, you don't know how to use it properly?"

"I'm sorry," Murad replies. "It's not so easy."

"Maybe you're just a stupid cripple." It is the nastiest thing Demir has ever said.

His friend stops. "I... I said I was sorry."

"And I said you are just a stupid cripple!" Demir shouts.

"You don't mean that."

Demir turns, walks right up to Murad. "Yes, I do! You can't walk two paces without needing rest. You are slower than a turtle." He hates himself, hates his half-brother for making him say these ugly things to his friend. Demir sees Murad's pain and feels the worst he has ever felt.

"Demir, what's wrong?"

"I am tired of you, that's what! I am the son of the Al Hajji Hamid al Azm. You are crippled riffraff unworthy of my acquaintance. I am done with you." And without awaiting the response that would surely cause his heart to cave in, Demir strides off, up the steep gradient of the narrow street. He can barely make out the road before him through the tears in his eyes.

Muharrem steps out from behind a tree. "Impressive."

"Shut up." Demir marches past. He stops, reconsiders. "I mean, shut up, *master.*

Now that he can no longer count Murad among his friends, Demir is right back to where he was when he first started at the *madrasah*—worse, because his strange, random antics have even made an enemy of the instructor. And Timurhan is leaving on the campaign against Malta at the end of this week. The only way for Demir to pass the time now is to mope and watch Kemal tend the few remaining horses. The stableman has noticed the darkening of the child's spirit, as Demir knew he would. Demir only shrugged when Kemal questioned him. No one can know the truth. Well, the gazelle can know; he will understand, since he is now half-horse, having been reared by a mare.

The days pass in lonely despair. Dazed, Demir has completely forgotten about the saddle he wanted Timurhan to have for the campaign. *The campaign.* It means so many different things now. What before he thought was a glorious movement against the Knights of St John is now the sacking of the land of his mother's birth, possibly the death of his unknown sister.

His sister. The notion still staggers him. What is she like? He wants to ask his mother, but cannot bring himself to talk to her about her other life. She never actually admitted to anything, so maybe it's not true.

Demir knows it is true. But it doesn't change the fact that he is a son of the Ottoman Empire, a son of Islam. The place of his mother's birth doesn't make a difference. He cannot look differently on the campaign now. Its objective remains the same. Besides, he doesn't know his sister, doesn't know Christ. And frankly, things were much better before he was forced to acknowledge the existence of either of them. He will bring the saddle to Timurhan.

Demir is supposed to ask his brother's permission before leaving the house, but Muharrem would never let him take the saddle to the Sipahi knowing how desperately he wants to. And it's not like Demir can hide the enormous leather contraption under his clothes. So, with a plan hatching, Demir goes to find his father.

Hamid sits in the dining hall, stuffing his face with griddled bread and spiced yoghurt and mutton. The man is a nasty eater, allowing the sauce to spill over his lip and dry on his chin. It turns Demir's stomach to watch his father devour his lunch, like a jackal with its bloody snout poking inside a dead antelope. Demir pities the pageboy, Hamid's ten-year-old *garzóne*, who silently attends the man as he demolishes his food.

Hamid talks with his mouth full. "Demir, do not bother me when I am eating."

"Forgiveness, I mean no bother," he says carefully. "It is just that Timurhan, the Sipahi, forgot his saddle here the night he came to buy all the horses. He had only just acquired the saddle from the market that afternoon, special for the campaign."

Hamid does not look up. "So? What do you want me to do? It's mine now."

Demir tries another approach. "It might be better for you to return it. He is very fond of it."

Bite. Chew. Swallow. Slurp. "Then he would not have forgotten it. Now leave me."

"If you return it to him, you will have earned his loyalty. I am sure he will reward you," Demir says, waiting a moment before adding: "He is, after all, of a noble and wealthy line."

This stops Hamid from his grotesque masticating, as Demir knew it would. His father is so hopelessly predictable. "Are the armies not assembling today, right now, ready for departure?"

"Yes, and that is why you must hurry."

Hamid growls. "*I* must do nothing. It is *you* who will hurry. Go. Fetch the saddle. It is in the stable with the rest."

Demir nods. "I will bring it to Kemal. It is big and heavy, perhaps he can take it to him."

"That slave does not have time to go running around Istanbul with a saddle! You take it. Now. Go! If he offers a reward, you return with it or my blackamoor will severe your hands."

Good old predictable Hamid. Demir bows and is off. Now that he has been given an order by his father, there is nothing Muharrem can do to stop him from leaving. Still, Demir knows he had better get out quickly, or Muharrem may yet find some way to sabotage him. This mission is too important to be thwarted by his sadistic brother.

In the stables, Demir greets Kemal politely but hurriedly and makes for the saddle room. There are over two hundred, each cushioned on a small dais of velvet. There is not enough time to search for the right one. Kemal, ever observant, strides over. He opens the boot closet and produces the exquisite saddle from its own velvet stand. "Best to grace this stable. You'll be returning it to your cavalryman friend?"

Demir feels his face flood with relief. "How did you know that's what I came here for?"

Kemal spreads his hands. "Because I know the Sultan's fleet departs today, and I know Timurhan forgot the saddle. Go, before your brother sees. He wants that saddle for his. Only because it is yours."

"Thank you, Kemal. *You* are the best to grace this stable."

"I know."

***

Muharrem looks out the window just in time to see his younger brother passing through the gates with that splendid saddle in his arms. He shoves Yaminah's letter, folded with its translation, into his pocket for safekeeping, and makes at once for the stables to question Kemal severely.

"Where is he going, you pile of horse dung with eyes?"

"Forgiveness, master, of whom do you speak?" Kemal asks.

"My brother, idiot!"

"I do not know."

"You are lying, filth. Tell me the truth, or face the consequences."

"The consequences, master?"

"Quit your stalling, dog!"

"Stalling? I work the stalls, yes. Alas, I cannot quit them, master."

Muharrem is ready to hit the man. "If you do not tell me at once where that worthless brother of mine is going, I will tell my father I caught you stealing from the vegetable garden."

Kemal sighs. "Your brother is gone by Al Hajji's command to return the saddle to a Sipahi."

Muharrem is furious. He wants that saddle. He does not care a lentil about stupid horses or stupid cavalries, but Demir prizes that saddle and that is reason enough to claim it. Now, the wretched little thief is giving it to the Sipahi. Worse, Muharrem cannot do anything about it because *Baba* is the one who told him to take it. Enraged, he gives Kemal a swift, sharp kick to his shin and storms off. He runs through the gates, down the street. In a few minutes, he sees his little brother, hurrying down the road with the enormous saddle in his arms.

"*Demir!*" Muharrem calls angrily.

The boy looks over his shoulder, eyes widening in surprise. Defiantly, he turns and starts running faster. This only heightens Muharrem's rage. The older boy is fat and out of shape, but because Demir is encumbered by the heavy saddle, he makes easy prey for Muharrem. He closes in as Demir struggles to get away, darting this way and that. He turns sharp corners, doubles back, runs uphill, down, looks over his shoulder.

"Give me the saddle!" Muharrem shouts.

"Go to hell!" Demir yells.

This shocks Muharrem to furious silence. That little rat is going to pay.

***

Demir dashes down a steep, narrow street, which leads away from the magnificent Fatih mosque. His foot catches on uneven cobblestone, the weight of the saddle throwing him off balance, and he hits the ground heavily. He eats dust and grit, tastes blood. He struggles to rise, but it is too late. Muharrem steps hard on his back, pinning him to the cobbles.

"Sneak! Dirty sneak!" He hoofs Demir in the side, once, twice. "How dare you defy me, you son of a Christian whore?" Demir curls into a ball to ward off the blows that keep coming. He thinks of the iron poker; how he wishes he had buried it in Muharrem's skull when he had the chance. Muharrem's foot finds Demir's cheek. He draws back enough that his assailant's big toe only manages to rip the flesh, not damage bone. The next kick lands between Demir's legs. Now the small boy thinks he is going to die. His hands, up protecting his face, go instinctively for his groin. He is going to vomit. Muharrem rears for another kick, this one aimed squarely at Demir's head.

This will be the deathblow. He shuts his eyes.

The kick never comes. Demir's eyes spring open in time to see Muharrem dropping to the ground, Murad behind him, his crutch poised in the after-swing.

"Go," he says. "He's not dead. He was clubbed and robbed by thieves. And maybe clubbed again, for good measure. He never saw me. He doesn't know who hit him."

"But—"

"Just go!" Murad cries. "We'll talk later."

Demir gathers up the saddle and with it, his bearings. Though his entire being screams with pain, he takes back to the road, though he can only hobble, turning once to smile gratefully at Murad, who is already on his knees raiding Muharrem's pockets, to make the robbery genuine.

Forty minutes later, Demir makes the walls of Topkapi. Most of the men have already boarded the ships. In this mass of soldiers, onlookers, and guards, he needs to find a vantage, and quick. There are trees all around, mighty ones with thick branches, but climbing with the saddle would be impossible, and leaving the saddle on the ground would be plain stupid. Demir looks around frantically. If only his brother had not delayed him, he might have managed a spot closer to the gates of Topkapi from which the men at arms stream in a beautiful parade of colour and plumes and silver.

To his joyful relief, there is a stone ledge protruding from the great wall enclosing the palace. It is high enough to put him over the heads of the crowd, but not so high that he would have to leave the saddle behind to climb there. He threads his way to it and hoists himself up. From this viewpoint, he can see over the crowd, right to the quay below the iron gate.

The harbour resounds with the heavy gait of the iron-spiked leather boots of the Janissaries, the clopping hooves of regiment upon regiment of magnificent cavalry, the rolling wheels of supply carts, the scraping fetters of the oarsmen. The water echoes with the thunder of drums, the ringing of brass trumpets. Sunlight glances off the swords and scimitars of the streaming lines. Mail shines dully under round helmets that gleam like the great domes of mosques, lances pointing skyward like a thousand minarets. These are the Sultan's sparkling jewels. Vibrant standards catch in the breeze off the water, flying proud with the colours of the empire. Below them, silk and velvet abound, robes of crimson and indigo, offset by white felt bonnets, fresh against the deep hues.

Following the Janissaries are Iayalars, a special corps trained by imams to hurl themselves into the breach regardless of certain death. They wear the skins of wild beasts, their heads covered in helmets of gilt steel. Behind the Iayalars come the screaming dervishes, horns blasting, camel hair streaming from tall Persian hats. They run naked, covered only by beaded aprons, shrieking *Qur'anic* war passages as they come. In their wake, march the mercenaries and levies from Rumelia and Anatolia, thugs called to arms by their feudal lords.

Behind them, ride the Sipahiyan, the royal cavalry, led by their Agha, his three-horsetail standard moving with the salty currents of air. While most men simply sit in their saddles, a Sipahi makes a throne of his. Each horseman is armed with a pistol and long knife in his girdle, scimitar, axe, and mace at his saddle, bow and quiver across his back. Every weapon is its own treasury, embellished from the flashing hilts of blades to the solid silver stirrups of the horses. Above the mounted squadron flutters its white banner, emblazoned gold with the poetry of the *Qur'an* and a flaming sword.

At last, amidst the plumes and the silver and the colour, Demir spots Timurhan Yusuf al Salih astride his spectacular Turkoman. If Demir runs his hardest, he will catch him. He tears through the crowd, down the slope towards the docks, stumbling as he goes. He will have to get Timurhan's attention, for the guards would sooner send the boy's head rolling than let him near this imperial procession. Demir struggles against the coppice of legs, finally making it to the latticed partition. There are guards stationed about the far perimeter. They are still and perfect, like marble statues.

"Timurhan!" Demir shouts in his loudest voice. He presses his face against the lattice. "*Timurhan!*" Demir has risked so much to be here, taken such a beating, he cannot bear the thought of failing when he is this close. He considers lobbing a stone at the horseman to get his attention. Of course, if he misses, it will mean catastrophe. Very well, he will *not* miss. He picks up a stone from the ground, sights his target, and prepares to launch the projectile. A guard reaches suddenly through the trellis. He seizes Demir by his shirt and pulls, slamming him hard against the fence. Stunned, Demir drops the stone.

"You would dare throw a rock at the men who mean to defend the empire of the Padishah? For this affront, you will lose your hands!"

"No! No!" Demir cries, squirming. "I needed to get the attention of a Sipahi, that's all!"

"By hitting him with a rock? Liar!" the guard lashes. "I will sever your tongue as well!"

"No, please! In the name of Allah!"

The guard does not release Demir. "What does a grubby bug want with a royal cavalryman?

"He forgot his saddle. I have it. See?"

The man looks down at the saddle. Demir sees the doubt in the guard's eyes, sees the horsemen disappearing aboard a galleass beyond, and knows he must talk quickly.

"Please, lord, my father is Al Hajji Hamid al Azm, the horse breeder. Many of these mounts are from his own stable. Timurhan Yusuf al Salih negotiated the sale. He forgot his saddle."

"You think I am so stupid? Every mounted man here sits in a saddle."

411

"But this one is special. Call him over, please!"

A fellow guard—higher ranking from his stride and his scowl—comes to see what the problem is.

"Caught this scruff of a boy about the throw a rock," the guard explains. "Says he has a saddle belonging to a Sipahi. I say we relieve him his hands."

Beyond the two men, Demir spots Timurhan, about to pass by. Timurhan glances in his direction at that moment. Now is Demir's only chance. He struggles furiously and shouts Timurhan's name. The guard reaches another arm through the lattice, both hands now clutching Demir. He instinctively forces his arms between the guard's and with a strong outward thrust, snaps the man's grip. Demir bends, picks up the saddle, and makes to throw it over the partition.

The guard, humiliated, draws his gun. Demir freezes.

"What's this?" a smooth voice asks.

The guard turns and is face to face with the flaring nostrils of a massive steed. He starts, making Demir snicker in spite of his own precarious situation.

"M-My lord Sipahi," the guard stammers, bowing low to the formidable cavalryman straddling the huge horse. The soldier's handsome face is stern, his bearing noble, the very picture of dignity. "Forgiveness. I am sorry for the disruption. It's just that this boy here was about to throw a rock at a member of the imperial cavalry. I moved to stop him."

"With a musket?" Timurhan asks dubiously.

"Well, no, not at first... He broke away, was going to make off. I just wanted to scare him."

"A fine job you did of it too," the horseman replies mildly. He looks to Demir. "You were going to throw a rock?"

"Yes."

"At who?"

"You."

"What have I done to earn a rock to the head?"

"Not hear me shouting your name."

At this, Timurhan laughs wholeheartedly, eyes bright as the blue topaz adorning his turban. "Forgive me. Next time I will listen harder. What is so important?"

"The saddle. You forgot it."

Demir shifts as Timurhan gazes at him, surely noticing the swollen, bloody lip, the gashes to his cheek. "I think you went to a lot of trouble to bring this to me."

Demir shrugs. He hoists the saddle over his head, its weight cramping his arms. "Take it."

Timurhan rises in his stirrups and leans over the partition. "Thank you, Demir. I know it will bear me well, to certain victory. El Saray will be

proud to wear it. Allah's blessings upon thee, little one. I will see you soon."
And with that, the cavalryman nudges the reins and rejoins his line. Demir stays
at the fence, watching until all the glorious Sipahiyan have embarked.

***

Muharrem seethes, playing everything over in his jarred brain. No matter how
he tries to sabotage that wretched pest, he can never fully succeed. Somehow,
someone came to his rescue today. Who? Who would dare strike the son of Al
Hajji Hamid? Whoever it was bashed him across his skull, stole his money.
Could it really have been common thieves? They would know Muharrem as the
renowned breeder's heir and therefore know his wealth. The attacker had also
moved him from the middle of the road and left him lying face down in horse
dung.

Demir will pay. Even if this latest humiliation is not his doing, it is his
fault. Had the little rat not run out and forced Muharrem to chase him, he
would not have been on the street in the first place. But what can he do to hurt
his brother further? He still has the letter. Yaminah is Christian, and Muharrem
has the proof. The perfect tool to bend Demir to his will. That letter can do
more damage than a bastinado and vivisection combined, burn more painfully
than a slow roast. A day will come when he can use that note to destroy Demir,
but today is not that day. He wishes to read it again, to revel in its scandal, and
reaches into his pocket. To his horror, it is empty. He feels again, checks every
pouch, every fold, patting himself and sweating. His very method of keeping
the letter safe has brought its loss—his attacker has stolen it! Why would some
stupid thief take it? Thieves can't even read! Perhaps in his haste, the robber
emptied the boy's pockets without heeding their contents. Muharrem swears
and rages, and determines to find the thief and retrieve the letter. The only
thing working in his favour is that Demir does not know Muharrem no longer
has it in his possession.

Fuelled by new fury, he works his brain to devise another way to make
his younger brother suffer. Muharrem already forced Demir to end his only
friendship. Who else is there? Jameela and Kemal. But a manoeuvre against
those two would take time to plan, and Muharrem needs satisfaction now. It
should be easy; Demir likes everyone. The sentimental fool even makes friends
with animals...

That's it.

It is the dinner hour. The wives are occupied in their dining quarters,
the servants in theirs, *Baba* in his. Lately, Ayla has been keeping a closer eye on
Muharrem than usual, but even she must eat. He creeps close to the wives'
dinner hall and listens at the doorway, covered by a hanging carpet to which
cling the scents of storax and spikenard. He hears his mother's voice. Pleased,
Muharrem steals to his father's sanctum and removes a dagger from its mount.
Sliding the blade into his belt, he leaves the house and heads to the stables.

They are empty of attendants. Only a few horses remain from the great transaction, and Hamid has yet to purchase new ones for breeding.

Muharrem enters, keeping low as he creeps. He does not want to alarm the horses, for a single whinny would alert that accursed Kemal to their distress.

There it is, at the end of the building, the stall of Dionysus, the pride of Hamid's stable and favourite of Demir. Friend of Demir. *Brother*, Muharrem has heard the boy call the horse. He reaches the stall gate, looks at the plaque inscribed with the horse's name. The charger is sleek, a rich chestnut, truly magnificent.

A shame Muharrem is going to cut its throat. He draws the dagger from his belt and coaxes Dionysus to the gate with a handful of grain. The horse's glossy neck is stretched over the partition, perfectly exposed for cutting. Muharrem adjusts his grip on the dagger. He presses it to the charger's throat, gently enough that it will not startle the beast. He holds the blade steadily, takes a deep breath.

Just as he is about to slice the edge across, he thinks of Hamid. If Muharrem kills this horse and is found out, his father will have him quartered. His mind works for a plan. Muharrem could blame the slaying on Kemal. No, that would never work. No one would believe him. *Damn it!* He will not soon have another opportunity as perfect as this.

A strange noise sounds from a stall three down from this one, followed by a shifting, a rustling. Muharrem goes to investigate. He peers into the compartment. Large, soft eyes return his gaze. It is the gazelle, Timu. A smile flickers across Muharrem's mouth.

***

Demir sits comfortably on a thick section of wall enclosing Topkapi palace. The Sublime Porte behind him, he is riveted by the scene before him. The Golden Horn is lit by the setting sun, the sky flaring the blazing red of the west, arcing into orange and copper and pink, melding into the purple of the eastern rim. The Sultan's ships below are another multitude of colour. The uniforms, turbans, pennons, and weapons of the great parade are now massed on the decks: twelve thousand fighting men on two hundred galleys and two galleasses.

Dragut Raïs and Sinan Pasha are at the helm of the flagship, her banners blazoned by a red and white ensign charged with a blue crescent. Demir wishes he could pick out Timurhan from the host, see el Saray saddled with *his* saddle. He squints, pretending he can see them, and waves. The hypnotic thrum of the oars fills the air, each blade moving in perfect unison, cutting the Bosphorus in beautiful lines. Dragut's flagship noses ahead of the rest, rounding Seraglio Point and pushing into open sea-lanes. Demir asks Allah to bless the fleet. His heart swells with pride.

A strange uneasiness fights that pride. It is the conflict of his two selves, which he has tried in vain to ignore. Demir looks to the swirling sky and asks Allah one more favour: "If it is true that I have a sister," he whispers aloud, "protect her too. It is not her fault she was born to unbelievers." He rests his head against a merlon and sighs, pleased he talked to God about his sister, confident God will not let harm come to her. He recalls a passage from the sacred book: *Whosoever puts his trust in Allah, He will suffice him.*

At this moment, Demir's world is almost right again. He made it to the quay and delivered the saddle to Timurhan—and, avoided getting himself shot by the guard in the process. Murad has forgiven him, and for that, Demir is deeply grateful. He will tell Murad everything. His friend deserves the truth, and if Murad decides he cannot be friends with a half-Christian, so be it.

Demir has another reason to smile: Muharrem took a good wallop to his ugly head today. *Another* good wallop. The small successes of the day have shown Demir that he is not powerless. In time, he will be able to talk to his mother again, when he comes to accept her truth. He just has to make sense of it first, and he wants to do that on his own, without anyone else swaying his thoughts. He finds some comfort in thinking she had already converted at the time of his birth. That might be enough to make him full Muslim.

Demir thinks of Dragut Raïs, born a peasant to Christian parents, standing now a proud lord of Islam at the helm of his own ship, the commander of the Sultan's fleet, the sea parting to his mighty stem. One day, Demir will be on that same ship as a Sipahi in service of Allah's Deputy on Earth, and he will know the exhilaration of riding his beloved Dionysus into battle.

He watches the armada and knows it is right for him to feel pride.

"Demir." He looks down, startled from his contemplations. It is Murad, limping towards him, folded parchment in his hand. Demir comes down from the wall, happy and worried to see his friend.

"Murad, I owe you my life. But you should not be here. If Muharrem sees, he will—"

"Stop talking." Demir's mouth clamps shut. Murad holds out the pages. "The whip your brother has used to torment you." This takes a moment to register on Demir's brain, though he sees the parchment and understands torment better than most. *The letter!* He struggles for breath, mind spinning with the possibilities. Could it be? Is he finally free? Is it really over? The notion staggers him—until he remembers the content of the letter, and knows if Murad has read it, the only thing over is their friendship. He should never have kept this from him.

Demir's internal dialogue must be transcribed on his face. Murad frowns. "Yes, I read it. Do you really think I would hobble all this way to return it if I cared about what it said? God knows it took me long enough to get here, and longer to find you. Take it. Burn it. And be done with it."

Demir accepts the letter and its translation into his shaking hands. He can scarcely believe the source of his misery has been recovered. He wants to eat it. Murad clumps off as if sensing Demir's need to be alone. Overwhelmed, he sits with his back to the wall of Topkapi, turning the folded sheets over and over. He did not know his mother could read or write, and now, he holds in his hands the proof of not only her abilities but her past life. Most important, he holds it all in *his* hands.

At last, he unfolds the letter, and gets to know his *Anneh*, one line at a time, and loves her just the same.

PART FOUR

EIGHT POINTED CROSS

CHAPTER FORTY-SEVEN

Malta, 16 July 1551

Dawn is newly broken on Birgu, the air already thick and hot and lazy. The sun penetrates the surface of the Grand Harbour, creating myriad shades of green and blue. Seagulls bob on tiny swells, occasionally nipping at mackerel.

Then, the gulls squawk and take flight, forced to make way for the massive wooden monsters bearing down on them. The imperial fleet of Sultan Suleiman has arrived, gliding steadily and unopposed over the harbour waters, hundreds of wooden wings beating in unison.

***

A red and white standard cut with the blue crescent of the Ottoman Empire flutters against the mast of the flagship. Under the lateen sails of the galleass, Dragut Raïs completes his ablutions. Facing the brilliant east, he kneels on his mat. The voice of the *mokkadem* carries the dawn prayer, the *salat al-fajr*, to the Faithful: "*Allahu Akbar! Allahu Akbar!* I bear witness that there is no god but God. *La ilaha il Allah.*" There is no rank to divide the men; they are all the slaves of God. The lord admirals pray next to the lowliest foot soldiers. Twelve thousand prostrate as one.

Dragut Raïs rises from his mat, shields his eyes and looks from the deck of his galleass to the fortress St Angelo standing at the peninsular tip of Birgu. The honey-coloured walls are strong, the bastions solid. Admiral Sinan Pasha, at Dragut's side, seems agitated. "*That* is it? *That* is the fortress the Sultan said would fall so easily?"

"Certainly no sparrow ever built his nest in a tree easier of access," Dragut replies.

From Sinan's wary expression, he does not share in this optimism. He looks at the triangular spit, and the massive limestone bulk guarding it. He turns to Dragut but does not get the chance to voice whatever thought is in his head.

419

***

At the tip of Mount Sciberras, the infant fortress of St Elmo is merely a star-shaped foundation with no garrison. On the slopes above it, however, Commander de Guimeran and his three hundred men stand armed and waiting. Word had reached Grand Master Juan d'Homedes by fast galley that the Ottoman fleet had landed on Sicily, and Sinan Pasha had demanded the surrender of Mahdia. When refused, Sinan took out his anger on Augusta, leaving the harbour a smoking ruin. A disoriented d'Homedes finally began scrambling to organise some sort of resistance. De Guimeran and his company were ferried across the harbour to Sciberras to lie in wait, while Sir Nicholas Upton, Englishman and Turcopilier, rode with his cavalry to the Marsa. A scout informed de Guimeran that Upton did not arrive in time to save the sentries; one Ottoman galley managed to make stealthy berth.

Now, from his elevated situation on the rise, Commander de Guimeran sights the flagship. "Fire!" he cries. Three hundred arquebusiers rain bullets on the starboard hand of the Turkish fleet.

***

Sinan Pasha hears the rattling. A second later, its terrible effect is visible: in an instant, most of the oarsmen are dead, hunched over their looms. Several foot soldiers are dead as well. Or dying. At so close a range, barely a shot did not break flesh. All eyes are on the slope of Sciberras. All but Sinan Pasha, whose eyes are on Dragut, the very picture of calm.

"*Innaa Lillaahi wa innaa ilayhi raaji'oon,*" Dragut says. "Truly, to Allah we belong and truly, to Him we shall return." The seaman orders the immediate landing of his men. But when they scale the rocky headland, it is deserted.

One in Dragut's number approaches. Beneath a turban of grimy beige, the corsair's face is etched deep with lines from exposure to the elements of the Middle Sea. "My lords, I once laboured in quarries under the yoke of the knights, after they drowned my galley and enslaved me. If we press for St Angelo, it will be winter before we take it."

Dragut frowns. "It is July."

"The fortress was strong when I was captive there. It will only be stronger now."

"What weaknesses?"

"None that an army this small could swiftly breach," the corsair replies.

"You have done a disservice to Islam," Dragut says. "You should have watered down the quicklime so the mortar would not set."

"Forgive me, effendi."

Sinan dismisses the corsair and turns to Dragut. "We cannot winter here. El Kanuni is determined to dislodge the Order from its stronghold on Tripoli. If St Angelo cannot be taken expeditiously then it cannot be taken at all. I say we march on Città Notabile."

Dragut shifts his gaze from the walls of St Angelo back to Sinan Pasha. "Agreed. Mdina is poorly defended. All but the Sipahi will advance on her. The horsemen will remain here to quell any resistance. The knights will send relief lines to Mdina. I want foot soldiers cutting those lines. Ambush will be met by ambush."

***

Timurhan Yusuf al Salih receives word from the Agha of the Sipahiyan that he is to join the squadron taking on the detachment of mounted knights. The soldier holds out a sweet carrot to his magnificent russet Turkoman, el Saray. He strokes the animal's neck with a loving hand, watching the sunlight catch in his mane. He runs his hands down the left foreleg, feeling knees, cannons, ankles, making sure everything is as it should be before moving to the next. Though Timurhan can saddle a horse with his hands tied behind his back, he checks and double-checks that the pad is centred, cinches not too tight, everything just so. He passes his hand along the smooth leather of Demir's saddle and smiles at the thought of the small boy anxiously awaiting tales of victory. Timurhan takes hold of the shiny pommel and swings himself up onto the horse. "It is time, Brother. Bear me well, el Saray, and, *insha'Allah*, bear me to triumph."

***

Nicholas Upton is a corpulent man. He is master of the *langue* of England and the Turcopilier of the Order. He is suffering mightily in his armour, the metal already hot to the touch, his fat body cooking inside it. The charger bearing his immensity must be suffering mightily too. The knight's face runs with sweat behind his visor. His breath comes in ragged gasps. And it is only just after dawn. The Englishman grumbles and swears.

Upton leads his cavalry of thirty knights and four hundred soldiers straight for the invading forces amassing at the Marsa. He hopes for a quick victory, but what he meets at the waterfront is not a band of riffraff on shabby nags. He meets the imperial cavalry of Suleiman the Magnificent. He meets the Sipahiyan. They are living treasuries, sunlight flashing in the rubies and sapphires and emeralds encrusted in their weapons and the silver trappings of their fine horses.

"They wish to dazzle us into surrender, is it?" Upton remarks to no one in particular as he kicks his horse into a full gallop. The shore erupts in battle cries and hooves. The Sipahiyan are battle-ready, lines neat, weapons drawn. At the order of their Agha, they spur their steeds into a charge.

Sword is raised to meet scimitar.

***

Angelica's *barnuża* is flung on the ground, spurned in the murderous heat. She takes some relief under the shade of a peach tree in the high-walled courtyard of the Predal mansion. Manoel is beside her, eyes half-closed. He yawns, and that makes her yawn. Angelica is trying to get him to focus on the ledger in her

421

lap but is having trouble doing so herself. Her eyes drift to the garlands of carnations, nodding lazily over the windowsills. Even the flowers are sleepy.

The oppressive heat is not the only thing driving Angelica from concentration. Ever since her uncle revealed the secret prison, she has not been able to rest easy. She worries not just for Robert but for her uncle, for Katrina, for Domenicus. She regards all persons of authority with suspicion, wondering if they know of the gaol and if they have put anyone in it. To cap it all, Katrina is angry with her for going to Marcello di Ruggieri. Although Katrina has no right to be angry—she only knows Angelica met with him because she herself went to see him too.

The swish of layered skirts turns Angelica's head. It is Elisabetta Predal, Lady of the manor, somehow still looking bright and fresh. A footman trails, carrying a silver tray, clear as a mirror, arranged with a porcelain pot and three cups, their gilt handles flashing with the morning. The attendant sets the tray on the glass table and bows. Elisabetta waves Angelica over.

"Come, try this. It's new and from far away. It's called coffee."

Angelica rises, leaving the ledger with Manoel. The back of her shift is wet and clings to her skin. The nape of her neck rolls with sweat, as do the dimples of her knees. She feels disgusting and hopes this coffee stuff is made of the ice Domenicus once described.

Suddenly, a tremendous blast rocks the foundation of the Predal home. Angelica stumbles, dropping her cup. The pot tips and spills boiling black water over pieces of broken porcelain. Manoel jumps up in terror. He runs to his mother and buries his face in her skirt.

"Sweet Jesus!" Elisabetta cries. "What was that?"

"I don't know," Angelica replies. She does not move, listening, waiting. The world resounds with another great boom. This time, a thick pall of smoke billows beyond the walls.

Elisabetta's eyes go round. "An explosion!" She crosses herself. Angelica runs to the wall and hops onto a bench to peer over. The perched situation of Mdina allows the entire island to be seen in one sweep. At once, her heart bucks, her blood chills, her mouth dries. To the north of Sciberras, in the glittering harbour of Marsamuscetto, is a fleet of moored galleys, a jungle of masts flapping not with Christian banners but with pennons of Islam. The slopes rising to the city range with black cannons and vibrant turbans. Angelica does not sense Elisabetta's approach and starts when the woman tugs her hand.

"*Kollox sew*? Everything all right? Has a ship exploded?"

"No, my lady," Angelica replies numbly as servants filter into the courtyard, staring and murmuring. "Muslims have landed. Hundreds. Thousands."

Elisabetta places her hand against the wall to steady herself. "...What?" she croaks. "*What*? How? How could they land without warning? Had the knights no word? Nothing?"

There is another blast, louder, closer, sending Angelica backwards and hard to the ground. Before she can recover, she feels Elisabetta taking hold of her and hauling her to her feet. The noblewoman picks up her son with one arm, and calling to the servants to follow, runs inside the house, slamming the doors behind them.

***

At the fortress St Angelo, on the second-floor study of the magisterial house, the knight Nico de Villegagnon stands before Grand Master d'Homedes in checked fury. He wants nothing more than to grab the senile old fool and shake him until his eyes roll back in his head. But that will accomplish nothing. No more than saying: *I told you so*, as every French knight in the Order would love to do.

"Excellency," de Villegagnon begins, "the ambush coordinated by de Guimeran was only partially successful. You must order a detachment to Mdina at once. Dragut will know the city is scarcely garrisoned. Fra Giorgio Adorno is there alone. We must act, and now."

D'Homedes looks down at his hands. "Mmm."

Nico de Villegagnon is ready to explode. A grunt? What good is a grunt? A Grand Master is supposed to lead! In his shocked bewilderment, this one can manage no more than a useless noise from his accursed lips. De Villegagnon takes a deep breath, glances in desperation to the Grand Master's lieutenant, Jean Parisot de Valette, standing quietly by. Valette is reputed never to gainsay authority. However, right now, the authority is saying nothing at all.

"Sire," he says carefully, "Allow de Villegagnon to take a relieving force to Mdina, and give him leave to defend it."

The Grand Master glances from one knight to the other. "You are both Frenchmen. Your homeland and mine are sworn enemies. Why should I trust you? Perhaps this Turkish raid is merely a conspiracy, organised by French knights. There are too many of you in the Order. Bloody French. A few francs paid to Dragut by Frenchmen provoked this attack. Bastards."

De Villegagnon blinks, unsure he heard the Grand Master correctly.

"Whatever the reason," d'Homedes continues, "Dragut Raïs is here, now. I have no choice." He looks with icy disfavour on the stunned de Villegagnon. "Take your detachment, and go."

***

"*Allahu Akbar!*" Timurhan rides el Saray hard into an advancing Christian soldier. From the lack of proper armour, this man is no knight. Timurhan would have preferred to dispatch a wasp from the Order's vile hive. He sees fear in the soldier's eyes. A moment later, the cavalryman is dead in his saddle, pierced in the heart by Timurhan's spear. It is mercy, a quick death. He rears his Turkoman and veers the beast round, galloping back into the fray. Sparks fly, metal clashing against metal. Sunlight conspires with armour and jewels to blind him momentarily. He unsheathes his scimitar and strikes off a man's head, which is quickly trampled by the hooves of his own horse.

The rocky shore of the Marsa is slippery with blood. The defending cavalry, under some fat knight, has managed to drive back a large number of the Sipahiyan and regain much of the shoreline. The battle rages, but many of the mounted Turks are now galloping around the flanks of the defenders to join the attack on Mdina.

Despite Timurhan's excellent physical condition, the heat is voracious, sapping his strength, parching him terribly. For a second, he imagines what the plump Christian commander must be feeling, but whatever it is, it will be nothing close to the heat the man will feel in hell. And although Timurhan has no pity for the knight, he does feel sorry for the man's horse. No creature should have to suffer like that.

***

Domenicus bursts into the chaos outside the apothecary shop just in time to catch Marcello di Ruggieri driving his mare through the street. The knight is fourth in a file of ten led by Nico de Villegagnon, all of them dressed in long leather jerkins covered by cuirasses, dull in the sunlight. This small detachment is heavily armed, five in its number carrying halberds, the others arquebuses. All have swords at their sides, long knives and maces at their saddles.

"Ruggieri!" Domenicus shouts.

Marcello reins his horse, the others riding on. "The enemy is upon us. Dragut leads, blast him! They march on Mdina. We ride now to the citadel."

Domenicus feels his heart career against his ribs. "Angelica is there. I'm coming with you."

"The hell you say," Marcello barks.

"I can help."

"*No.* You stay." The knight spurs his horse with a loud cry and is off.

"Wait!" Domenicus chases senselessly behind the galloping horse. "Wait, damn you!" Marcello falls easily back in stride with the rest of his squadron, soon lost in the haze of dust stirred by their chargers. Lungs burning, Domenicus stops, bends, catches his breath.

Birgu is bedlam. People rush this way and that, some taking refuge in their houses, others, the church. Mounted patrols trot the streets, shouting to confused villagers to get and stay indoors. Women weep and pray, holding their children as they run. Through billows of grey, a lone horseman rides from the direction of Corradino Heights. Domenicus straightens out, convinced it is Marcello, returning for him. But this man's hair is red, his mount's hindquarters draped with a heavy sack that jounces with each step. Domenicus jumps in front of the knight, forcing him to rein his horse.

"What the devil!" It is a robust Provençal, Gui de la Fon.

"I want to help at Mdina. What should I do? To whom do I report?" An arm flops out from the sack and hangs stiffly, dark blood trickling from the fingertips onto the dirt. Domenicus jumps back. "Jesus!"

"Those barbarians killed the sentries. Two at Marsamucetto lost their heads. And this one here," the Frenchman says grimly, jerking his head towards the red splotched sack, "This one was the Corradino sentry. Marco Vella. He still has his head, just barely."

***

The world must be ending, Katrina thinks. Her basket is knocked from her arms, fruits and vegetables rolling over the dirt, squashed under the feet of villagers. The noise is deafening. Guns boom and buildings tremble and people scream. Horses whinny their terror, bucking wildly against restraints. Goats and dogs and chickens run in every direction, tripping villagers in panicked flight. Katrina is swept violently into the crush. She tries desperately to keep upright, but in the pandemonium, loses her footing and sprawls to the cobbles. Fleeing villagers step on her hands, her legs, her back. She struggles to push herself up but is knocked back down. Her face slams into the road, and she tastes blood. She tries again. And again is trampled underfoot. The ground shakes with heavy hooves. She is going to die under the iron shoe of a horse.

At the last second, she rolls to the right. The enormous fore hoof lands a hand's breadth from her head. Two gloved hands slip under her arms and haul her to her feet. It is a young Aragonese, Cristoval Domingo.

"Make for St Lawrence," he shouts.

"What's happening?" she cries over her shoulder, already running for the conventual church.

"Dragut!" And he is off.

***

Angelica and the servants huddle together on the tiled floor of the antechamber, far from any windows. A strange noise cocks her head.

"What is it?" Elisabetta whispers, clinging to her son.

After a moment, Angelica replies, "Music." It is the song of a thousand Turkish gongs, trumpets, and horns, drowned only by the explosions that shake the walls. Angelica's hands are cold and damp with sweat. She breathes deep, forcing a calm head as she takes stock of the situation.

Mdina *wanted* to be isolated from the Order, so there are no knights stationed within the city save its governor, Giorgio Adorno, and scarce a garrison to defend its walls. Mdina's proud independence has secured its ruin. And from the intensity and frequency of the blasts, it will not be long before this imposing citadel is reduced to sand.

***

Domenicus runs all the way home on adrenaline. Once inside, he throws open the lid of his father's cedar chest. A sharp *whish* fills the room as he slides his blade into its metal-rimmed sheath. He digs out his father's breastplate, racing with it to the carpenter's stable. He tosses his saddle over Tramonto's back and fumbles with the cinch. He doubles his effort and succeeds only in doubling his time. Finally, the horse is rider ready. Domenicus mounts. He spurs with a swift kick and another to take Tramonto to a gallop.

He failed to protect Angelica once. He will *not* fail today.

***

The battle at the Marsa is all but finished, the clang of steel replaced by cheering from Christian throats. Timurhan sees he is outnumbered and outflanked. He will not surrender. He would die first, and what an honour, to do so in the service of Allah. But there is no honour in pointless suicide. The Christians have reclaimed the Marsa; he alone cannot drive them back. So he will swing the sword of God where it will do the most damage: on the walls of Città Notabile.

The Sipahi pats his horse on the neck. With a loud cry, he spurs el Saray headlong into the enemy lines, his great scimitar flashing as he forges his path.

***

Sweat drips into Nicholas Upton's eyes as he watches some lunatic Sipahi pound through the defensive ranks. The Englishman raises his arquebus, sighting down the shaft, waiting for the perfect moment to fire and knock the Moselman off his fine Turkoman. Upton's breath is laboured, his hefty body overheated. He narrows burning eyes and tries to focus.

Suddenly, a terrible pain shoots through his left arm. The Briton drops his gun. It clatters to the rocks. He gargles, clutching his chest. He slumps in his saddle. A moment later, he falls to the ground, armour clanking against the stone. One booted foot still locked in a stirrup, he is dragged some distance by his startled horse.

The first to arrive at the Turcopilier's side is Armand Debonnoel, a knight of Auvergne. The Frenchman bends to wrench Upton's leaden foot from the stirrup, then throws off the Englishman's helmet. He kneels, presses his fingers against the fallen knight's fleshy neck for a pulse.

Armand looks up at the gathering crowd. "*Merde.* He's dead."

***

There is anxious quiet within the dimly lit church. If it is hot outside, inside it is a kiln. The scent of hallowed incense hangs low. An arabesque of dust catches in the shafts of coloured light streaming through stained glass. The pews teem with peasants, some praying, some weeping, all sweating, all waiting.

An hour ago, Katrina overheard two villagers whispering about the death of the sentry, Marco Vella. In a frenzy of grief, his father Claudio took a truncheon and rushed upon the Turkish lines. The goatherd managed to kill a Janissary before being hacked to pieces himself.

Now, Katrina's limbs are still weak from the news. She is sick with the thought that Robert would be dead had he not been locked away in that hellish subterranean prison. And she is dazed by the sudden transformation of her hatred for Franco di Bonfatti into some measure of gratitude, for by his duplicity, he saved Robert's life.

She worries for her brother, having not seen him in her blind rush to the church. She prays Angelica is safe, knowing she is trapped in Mdina. Her last words to Angelica were spoken in anger, and if anything happens to her friend, Katrina will never forgive herself. She wishes her father were here, so she could bury her face in his chest until it is all over. But he is still on Gozo, with Belli. At least there, they are safe. Nothing exists on Gozo that Dragut and his pillagers could possibly want. She cradles her head in her hands and tries to shut everything out: the cannons, the crying, the thoughts that devil her. It is another hour before she looks up.

Across the nave, Father Anton Tabone sits with a group of village children separated from their parents in the mad dash for the church. He tells them stories, offering what comfort he can. He puts the sexton to work finding their mothers and fathers. Katrina crosses the church and sits near him, happy to hear a familiar voice. His back is to her, and it is a minute before he takes notice.

"Katrina," he says when he turns.

"Father Tabone."

He tilts his head. "Are you all right?"

"Yes. ...Not really. No."

"I am happy you are safe." The building shudders suddenly, glass rattling in tall stone casements. Katrina stiffens. "Cannon," the priest says calmly. "Don't worry, it's distant. Mere reverberation." He smiles at her. She smiles back. They do not mention Domenicus or Angelica.

"I was just telling my young friends here the story of David and Goliath."

"A good story," Katrina says. "A boy defeating a giant."

***

Marcello's mare lands her hooves with the slow cadence of caution. All around is evidence of invasion: smoking plots, razed crops, scorched lodgings. Visor lowered, Nico de Villegagnon leads his mounted cavalcade up the slope towards the fortress city of Mdina, taking his line through desiccated fields to keep off the main access.

Marcello grumbles. "If those idiot nobles had but allowed a proper garrison at Mdina, we would not be cooking in this armour or travelling up this bastard hill."

"Quiet," de Villegagnon hisses.

Suddenly, the ground shakes with hooves. As one, the knights whip round their heads, weapons raised. It is only by Marcello's quick reaction that the approaching man is not killed.

"Montesa!" he cries, half-furious, half-relieved.

"I want to help," Domenicus pants. The knights lower their blades.

"Son of a bitch," Marcello growls. "Almost got yourself killed. Hell, you *will* get yourself killed. If not by the infidel, then by me."

Nico de Villegagnon waves his hand for silence and addresses the newcomer. "You startled me. For that, I ought to shoot you. However, I haven't bullets to spare. If you can wield a blade, you are welcome. The rest of you, shut up."

Before prompting his mare, Marcello squints, sniffs. Something is not right. It is too quiet.

A lance flies at the knights. Nico de Villegagnon rears his horse onto its back legs, the animal taking the spear just below the neck. Villegagnon is violently thrown. The screaming horse writhes in agony on the ground, pink foam frothing from its mouth.

Twenty-five turbaned men, scimitars and daggers catching with sunlight, spring forth from a thicket of brush. It is a band of *yayas*, foot soldiers, whooping a shrill battle cry. Full of lightning and as fast, they are upon the cavalcade.

Marcello hops from his horse and pulls his two-handed sword from its scabbard. He prefers not to fight mounted. In an instant, a Turkish soldier meets him. Marcello sidesteps and slashes his bare-chested opponent down the middle, parting him navel to sternum. The mounted draw their weapons. It is fast a tangle of bright silks and silvery armour. To Marcello's right, a *yaya* slices his dagger deep into Tristan's arm and leaps back. Hollering, the Spaniard replies with a heavy swipe of his halberd. The foot soldier's body drops in a heap, his head rolling to Domenicus Montesa's feet.

***

In his dark nether world, Robert Falsone stands on his head, legs supported by the wall. He likes to see how long he can hold the position before his atrophied muscles tremble. He drops, disappointed. Didn't last a full minute. Lately, his body gives up sooner. Still, this game is something to pass the time, something to keep him sane. He remembers walking on his hands along the coastal rocks to make Katrina laugh. He wonders if that actually happened or if he had only imagined it. He wonders if he imagined it all. The months spent in this blackness have dulled his memory of the world outside. Now he questions whether there even is one.

No, he knows there is. The missing makes him know. The ribbon makes him know.

In that worn, tattered, faded ribbon, Robert finds refuge. In that frayed silken strip, he finds the strength to go on. It is everything to him. He holds it close to his face, trying to catch her in the thread. He does not talk to God. He talks to the ribbon. Talks to it as though it is Kat. He passes whole days with her that way. His fantasies are neither torment nor the beginnings of madness. They are hope. In his world of darkness, they are light.

Robert has long stopped trying to talk to the guards, especially after the incident with that fat Greek brute. The night Dr Callus came. The night he gave Robert the ribbon. The guard shot his fellow then demanded Robert identify his thwarted rescuers. He refused. The guard gave him the thrashing of his life. First, he broke Robert's arm. After that, he put a flaming match between the prisoner's fingers. Robert would not talk. The guard blackened Robert's eye and beat him with his pistol and slammed his head off the cold, solid ground. Still, Robert would not talk. That was the first ten minutes. The torture went on for two days. Costas Kiriakoulias brought Robert to the threshold of death with his savagery. In the end, the Greek gave up, and only because to push a prisoner across that threshold would be to cross it himself shortly thereafter.

For weeks, pain ran as a seamless fabric of bruises and abrasions all over Robert's body. He coughed blood. He sweated and had nightmares. He took a fever. He cursed God. He asked His forgiveness. He talked to his father. He cried for his mother.

Months later, Robert has still not fully recovered. Breath comes with a hitch, probably from the broken rib, and he knows frequent dizzy spells, probably from the severe concussion. He curls up on his side and rests his head in the nook of his arm. In his living grave, he holds the ribbon.

***

A foot soldier is immediately upon Domenicus, brandishing a bloody scimitar. The young man grips his sword, hands trembling. Swallowing hard, he prays they do not go soft. Everything he has learned of swordplay is a jumbled memory. *Never hesitate,* Franco once told him, *for in that split second, your enemy will have your life.*

The *yaya* swings. Domenicus parries clumsily, almost dropping his sword. His opponent swings again. He looks young, probably not much older than Domenicus—though with ten times the skill. The furious clang of steel on steel rings out, again and again. Hand-to-hand battles rage all around them. The foot soldier swipes at Domenicus, knocking him from his horse. He lands awkwardly, distracted in his struggle for balance. The *yaya* gives no quarter, striking mercilessly with his enormous curved blade. Domenicus dodges, jumps back. The fight goes on this way: the Turk always on the attack, advancing and slashing, the Maltese always on the defensive, retreating.

Domenicus has not managed a single swipe, his weapon warding off blows rather than delivering them. He is down on one knee, his arm heavy and cramping fast. Each deflection sends terrible waves through his bone; he cannot hold up his arm in defence much longer. His grip slackens, balance wavers. He closes his eyes, ready for the deathblow.

It does not come. Domenicus opens his eyes. The young Muslim's mouth is open, but no sound escapes. Something has taken his breath. The scimitar falls from his hand. His back is arched, fingers curled and stiff, eyes bulging. His chin drops, and blood trickles from his bottom lip to the tip of a sword poking through his chest. Standing behind the *yaya* is Marcello di Ruggieri. The knight rips his blade from the man's body, which falls lifeless to the ground.

Marcello hauls Domenicus to his feet. "It is wrong to kill a man engaged in combat with another. Don't make me do that again."

Domenicus can only nod. He is still trembling, so close did death shave him.

CHAPTER FORTY-EIGHT

Birgu holds her breath. A barrage on the village front has not come; still, the people are rattled by the distant rumble that is surely crushing Mdina. Katrina sits close to Father Tabone at a pew towards the back of the church. They endured the first few hours with stories, but after a time, the priest's voice grew tired. The pair then set about matching lost children with their parents, tending those sick with heat, comforting those sick with fear. The priest occupied one of the confessionals and listened to a long stream of sins from those certain this was their last chance.

Now, he and Katrina sit quietly together. She is desperately thirsty, almost enough to drink from the basin of holy water. If this goes on much longer, she will.

A few rows up and off to the side, a baby bawls, his shriek echoing in the loftiest alcoves and the deepest recesses. The wailing sets off other infants. Soon the nave is a chorus of crying babies.

"Father," Katrina whispers, her voice all but lost to the noise, "I need to talk to you."

"Of course. What is it?"

"Marco Vella is dead. If Robert were free, he'd be dead. I've spent these last months hating Franco di Bonfatti as no one has ever hated another. Now, how can I hate him? Only by his treachery is Robert alive."

"Sometimes, when we feel at our lowest, God is acting to spare us bigger pain."

Katrina bridles at that. "Forgive me, Father Tabone, but I will not honour Franco by believing for one second that he was doing God's work when he—" she cuts herself off, lowers her voice "...when he did what he did. If he could have foreseen the sentry's murder at the hand of those barbarians, surely Robert would have died today."

"I make no argument, Katrina. And truly, I am not telling you to look for God in Franco's intentions, but in the fact that his actions spared Robert's life. Robert in a cell is better than Robert in a grave. I understand you suffer terribly by his imprisonment but imagine your suffering had Robert been killed today. God spared you that grief."

"And was God sparing me grief when Franco killed Mea Falsone?"

"Perhaps God was sparing her grief," the priest replies.

Katrina faces him. "Want to do God's work? We can make things right if we act now."

Father Tabone crinkles his brow. "What are you talking about?"

"There is chaos all around us. It is almost a guarantee that no one will be guarding the prison. Together, you and I can free Robert. But we must move."

"Katrina, it is folly to venture outside."

She rises. "It is folly to miss this chance. I'll go alone if I must, but it will be easier with your help. You can slip away a few hours—there are a dozen priests here. I know where the prison is. I even know which cell holds Robert. All we need is a hatchet. Maybe a pair of daggers." She puts her hand on his shoulder. "Father, why let Marco's death be in vain?"

The priest inhales. He rises. "I know where to find a hatchet."

***

Domenicus finds himself next to Marcello in a cluster of ten knights surrounded by invading imperial soldiers.

"You would do well to surrender," Marcello says to the Muslims. He tosses his sword from hand to hand. None of the defenders remains mounted. Several horses bolt from the fray. Marcello breaks from the phalanx and wields his sword mightily against a spear-bearer. Two powerful strikes split the *yaya* in half.

"*Allahu Akbar!*" *God is great!* A Sipahi bursts from the main road and charges the knights. The horseman pierces Nico de Villegagnon's arm with a lance, then wheels to repeat the blow, but Villegagnon leaps upon him and stabs him with his own dagger. The knight flings the dead Sipahi from the horse and mounts the saddle in his place.

All around, swords and scimitars clash, flesh is torn, and blood mists the air. From the corner of his eye, Domenicus catches Etienne Charroux of Auvergne bringing his cutlass down on a *yaya's* head. The knight stumbles back in disbelief when the thick red turban does not yield. The Muslim soldier thrusts his pike, driving it deep into the Frenchman's shoulder. With a fierce cry, Etienne splinters the wooden spear, half of it still lodged in his flesh. The *yaya* whips a curved dagger from his sash and at the knight in the same liquid motion, severing his earlobe. The wound is not grave but bleeds as though it is. Etienne howls and jumps back, blood flowing down his neck in a weir of red.

The distraction costs Domenicus, for at that moment, a *yaya* leaps at him, arms raised above his head, hands gripping an Ottoman scythe. Without thinking, Domenicus thrusts his sword. The soldier still comes, propelled by his own momentum. They collide, and the two of them crash to the ground in a confusion of legs and arms, robes and armour. When they finally stop rolling, the infantryman is on top, eyes wide, the sword in his chest buried to the hilt. Domenicus snaps his hand away from the grip as though it burns.

He has just killed a man.

He pushes the body of his opponent off him and crawls away. Taking life is unlike anything Domenicus has ever imagined; it is not glorious as it was when he would slay pretend corsairs as a child. He does not feel brave. He feels like throwing up. On his knees, holding his stomach, he empties his gut onto the parched earth.

To his right, Nico de Villegagnon makes quick work of his turbaned adversary, delivering him a deep horizontal belly cut across the abdomen. The wound is mortal, and as the man falls dying to the ground, the words rasp on his last breath: "*Allahu Akbar!*"

One *yaya* remains. He runs but a shot from Tristan Galan's arquebus brings him down. The foot soldier is thrown forward, collapsing face down in a patch of wild fennel.

Domenicus is hunched over in the dirt, arms around his stomach. There is a pool of vomit before him, some of it on his hands. He is shaking, embarrassed. He glances to the strewn bodies, their young faces, the dusty earth, soaked crimson. Overwhelmed, he throws up again. He wipes his mouth on the back of his hand.

He rises to his knees and watches as most of the knights go to retrieve their mounts, de Villegagnon to end the suffering of his. The animal writhes on the ground, the spear broken but lodged deep inside. The knight dismounts the Sipahi's horse and crouches before his own. He strokes it gently, whispers to it, kisses it. He takes his long-knife into both hands and plunges it deep and swift, the charger's warm blood gushing out. De Villegagnon closes his eyes as the life drains from the animal and into the earth.

Tristan's horse did not make the dash with the others. He takes a skin from the saddle and tosses it to Domenicus, who accepts it gratefully as Marcello crouches before him, grinning and looking like an escaped madman with his blood-spattered face and bright eyes.

"Excellent. Not a single Christian wasted." The Florentine gives Domenicus a hearty pat on the shoulder. "First blood tastes the worst. Killing gets easier with practice, and tastes better." He rises, extends his hand. "On your feet, lad. That was nothing."

Marcello turns to Etienne Charroux, the most badly damaged of the lot. "I think we have erred in this violence. The Muslims only wanted *peace*—a piece of your ear, a piece of your arm..." he chuckles. "Let's yank that stick out of you and sew up that ear, quick-fast."

Villegagnon motions with his head for the men to mount. "Charroux, that sliver will not kill you. Make for the city, double time!"

***

Weapons range the slope rising towards Mdina, demi-cannon and culverin, musket and crossbow, instruments of war Dragut Raïs plays with magnificent precision.

The seaman is ebullient as he approaches Sinan Pasha, newly emerged from the Ottoman command tent. "Mdina chokes on our smoke."

Sinan frowns. "The Order will not abandon the noble city to certain death."

Dragut likes arguing little and likes sharing command less. "The Order has done."

"A relief force is inevitable," Sinan presses. "You allow vengeance to blind you. We are not here to avenge the brother of Dragut Raïs, but to carry out the will of the Sultan. If the city holds out much longer, we withdraw and launch the attack against Tripoli."

"Mdina will fall. We put our trust in Allah."

***

Plumes of smoke billow about Mdina's walls, obscuring the newly risen moon. Domenicus halts his horse at the edge of the moat that surrounds the city. He wonders if there is a gun trained on him, but pushes away the unnerving thought. The drawbridge is raised, the land eerily quiet, the heavy guns still. Perhaps the infidels will allow the city a break while they fall on their bellies for Allah.

Nico de Villegagnon's small, mounted troop swarms the counterscarp, the men calling for the bridge to be lowered. The band is flanked by mighty carobs, rooted in the dusty soil that carpets either side of the cobbled way.

Suddenly, a musket ball dents de Villegagnon's armour, sending him flying from his horse for a second time today.

"Snipers!" Domenicus cries. The knights rally and reply with arquebus fire, but as they shout to the bridge porters, enemy muskets speak again. Each shot flashes fiery orange light against the purple darkness. Domenicus is without a gun. He curses his stupidity, sorely aware he is nothing more than a hindrance to the men he wanted to help.

A hot iron ball penetrates the eye of Tristan Galan's horse. The animal is dead before hitting the ground, its master smashed beneath it. Domenicus races to pull him out from under the beast. Tristan is battered, but otherwise, in good condition, though devastated about his horse. His arquebus flashes, once, and again.

The defenders cluster. A lance flies towards them. Marcello jumps forward and slashes powerfully, breaking the spear with his two-handed sword. "We are assailed by ghosts, turbaned demons who have managed to surprise us twice today!"

Enemy muskets are now quiet. Domenicus strains to hear but catches only a distant rumble.

434

A twig snaps. Nico de Villegagnon gets a shot off. There is a thud.

Domenicus expects action now. None comes. When his blood has managed to cool some, a Sipahi bursts from among the trees. The imperial horseman is lightning, and as deadly, his scimitar flashing with stunning speed. Several knights fire their guns, but in the darkness, shoot wide or too high. Domenicus watches Tristan raise his arquebus and fire. The lead ball sails into the Sipahi's path, but connects only with his tightly wound turban. The great headdress is sent unravelling to the ground. The horseman disappears into the dark.

As the knights scramble to reload, the Sipahi returns for a second pass. He raises his scimitar, about to take Marcello's head. Domenicus throws himself at the Florentine, knocking him right over. In one fluid movement, he yanks Marcello's dagger from its scabbard and throws it at the Sipahi. This time, the devil is wounded, taking the large curved blade to his thigh. With a loud cry, the cavalryman swings round and disappears once more.

Seemingly unfazed, Marcello picks up the uncoiled turban. Amid the great lengths of fabric, he finds an exquisite blue topaz. He grins and tosses it to Domenicus.

"Lower the fucking bridge, curse and blast you!" de Villegagnon calls up, tunnelling his mouth.

Finally, there is a creaking, a groaning of wood. As one, the men look up. Using counterweights, two anxious porters work frantically to lower the drawbridge. Domenicus is the first across. He runs headlong into iron bars.

"For God's sake man, open the gates!" he cries, rubbing his nose.

A little red face peeks through two merlons. "No key. The governor has it. You'll have to climb." The porters toss ropes to the battered squadron. Domenicus scales the three-storey wall with his eyes and feels his heart sink.

✳✳✳

Angelica stares at the huge carving knife she took from the pantry. Its blade gleams bluish against the pale darkness. She prays there will be no need to use it. All she can do is worry. Worry for Domenicus. Was he caught in the attack? Could he have been killed? She pounds her head with her hands, beating the thought from her mind. She thinks of her uncle, of Katrina, and her worry is augmented. She longs for news, is going mad for news. Angelica Tabone is in the most beautiful house she has ever seen, its opulence beyond measure, its comforts without bounds, yet she wants nothing more than to be free of it.

Elisabetta Predal sits against the opposite wall, her son with his head in her lap. She is trembling. The chambermaid does her best to comfort the noblewoman, who seems deaf to solace. The Genoese gardener crawls slowly across the marble floor to Angelica. He sits next to her.

"I hope you do not mind me saying, but you are the image of your mother."

Angelica looks closely at the gardener. He is in his mid-forties, his brown hair streaked through with lines of grey. His face is kind, his bearing gentle. "You knew my mother?"

"As I know you," he whispers.

She tilts her head. "I have always found you familiar."

The gardener smiles. "We share a common enemy."

Angelica runs through her list of enemies. "Diana d'Alagona?"

He nods, eyes twinkling.

"You... you are the gardener who snuck me rags after she threw the water on me!"

"And I must say, we have all discussed it. We owe you great thanks," he says. "We know you are somehow behind Diana's wondrous and prolonged absence."

Angelica smiles, neither confirming nor denying.

The gardener turns solemn for a moment. "Your uncle says God loves all His children, even if we do not. But I don't think God loves Diana d'Alagona."

"That is because she is the spawn of Satan," Angelica replies. The two giggle together quietly, sharing a small moment of contentment. But the moment is swiftly shattered by a blast that shakes the house and jars its occupants to the core.

***

Eight villagers, sweat trailing over their temples, hold ropes for the knights as they scale the crenellated fortress wall two at a time. Domenicus has not even started the climb, yet sweat trails over his temple too. From below, he can see Marcello di Ruggieri is the first to make the top, and without taking a moment to catch his breath, lends his muscles to help pull up the others. They climb in the dark, each flash of light bringing them closer to the lip of the wall.

Finally, only Domenicus remains. He catches the end of the rope and, with a deep breath, starts the ascent. Midway, the muscles in his arms are screaming. Why is this so hard? Etienne Charroux made the climb with the end of a pike lodged in his shoulder! Domenicus can barely manage with scarce a scratch. Who does he think he is, anyway? Domenicus Montesa is no warrior; he is good at mixing herbs and making poultices, not scaling a wall amid a battle, not facing a real opponent in combat. He should just give up. He should never have come. *No! Stupid, selfish jackass!* Angelica is inside these walls. He has to... to what? Protect her? How? He can't even make it halfway up a wall. Can't even fight a man without throwing up all over himself.

The thoughts claw at him, make the top that much higher. He struggles for purchase. The knights call down encouragements, which have the opposite of their intended effect. The good-natured rallying only singles him out and makes him feel pathetic.

Domenicus blocks everything out, the shouts, the pain in his arms and chest, the thoughts that devil him. Only Angelica matters. He finds a rhythm to match his breathing to his climb: inhale, hand over hand, exhale, hand over hand, inhale. His muscles are on fire. He pushes himself harder.

At last, when he thinks he can go no more, he feels Marcello di Ruggieri's powerful hands take hold and haul him over the embrasure. The knight pats his back. "Not bad for a first climb." Marcello glances to Tristan Galan. "That's five *scudi* I owe you."

Domenicus looks up, chest heaving. "Five *scudi*? You bet against me?"

Nico de Villegagnon wastes no time. He summons a porter. "You, take me to the governor."

At once, the man obeys, leading the relief squadron down dark, narrow streets to the ramparts. The wrought-iron lanterns that line the walls have not been lit tonight. The thoroughfare is empty, the nobles locked up in their grand mansions, the peasants in their small quarters. Vines of red flowers move with the smoky breeze. At the ramparts, there are few fighting men. Fra Giorgio Adorno, the governor, meets the knights with jubilation and anger.

"Jesus Christ!" he cries.

"Not quite, but I see the resemblance," de Villegagnon remarks.

"I thought we had been abandoned to obliteration."

"Well, you are relieved. Command of this garrison is now mine."

"Take it with my compliments," Adorno replies.

De Villegagnon addresses his detachment. "We need men. Nobles, peasants, whomever you can find. Break down their doors. They have no choice in this. They must come with as many weapons as they can carry. More. Bring me men!" He sends three in his number on the errand. "And you," he says to Marcello, "You go fetch me some women. No one else has your knack at that. They will do the jobs I cannot spare men to do. Do not force them, the women are allowed the choice." De Villegagnon pauses, reconsiders. "Force them."

Marcello's expression of joyful disbelief reveals that never in his wildest dreams had he imagined he'd actually be given an *order* to fetch women.

Domenicus follows de Villegagnon to the most vulnerable position— the northern turret and its curtain wall. Bombardment wears on not only the villagers but the fortress they defend, especially its towers. As de Villegagnon inspects the walls, he picks up a small gang of peasant followers. They are a rough-looking lot, sooty and worn and untrained. But there is fire in their eyes. And when properly channelled, that fire is as formidable a weapon as any. They begin introducing themselves. Standing nearest to de Villegagnon is Alvarus, a short but tightly packed spindle of muscle, and Nardo, a large, soft man with big brown eyes. There is Barri, so called because he has the temper of a bull. The youngest among them is Francesco, Barri's son. The youth is his father's opposite, smiling and jovial and instantly likeable. Behind the first row of men are Dr Giuseppe Callus and his brother Antonio, the apothecary.

Domenicus is overjoyed to see the doctor, and bursts from the group to clasp arms with him. Callus's expression shows delight, surprise, and confusion all at once. "…Why are you…? How did you…? Where did you…? It's good to see you!"

The joyful reunion is short-lived. "Callus," de Villegagnon calls, "I've got a broken Frenchman here for you to fix."

Callus snickers. "You'll need a whole team to fix a Frenchman, but let's have a look just for fun." He inspects Etienne Charroux's shoulder, embedded still with the end of a pike. The doctor shakes his head. "We leave it where it is for the time being. To extract it will render him useless. I'll bandage it up to keep it still, and remove it later."

"Good enough," de Villegagnon says. Before Etienne can protest, de Villegagnon booms, "Men! Knights! Maltese brothers! Do you want to see crescent standards flapping from these walls?"

"No!"

"You want to see minarets where there once were steeples?"

"No!"

"Want to call that raggedy-ass Suleiman your Sultan?"

"No!"

"Nor I, lads! So we send them back to the Grand Turk with their guts stuffed in their mouths!" De Villegagnon points out five men, Alvarus and Nardo among them. "You, boil tar!" He smacks a meaty hand against Tristan's back. "Galan, station them on the ramparts. Spill tar through the holes onto any Muslim within range. Keep them back! Go!" No sooner are Tristan and his group off than de Villegagnon speaks again. "Masons and builders, any?"

Barri steps forward with a grunt. "Me. My boy, too."

"*Bon.* Go with this knight here—" he indicates the injured Etienne Charroux "—and assemble a team of stoneworkers. Repair the wall. It must withstand. *Allez! Allez!*" Domenicus waits, eager for orders. He must redeem himself. He hopes de Villegagnon will give him the opportunity.

By now, men summoned from their homes have begun to drift towards the walls. Some carry crossbows, some guns, but from the look of them, most have never lifted a weapon against another man in their lives. Barri the stonemason flashes at the sight of them. "About time, you mother whoring cowards! Ho there! Phillipu! Juliano! Blasius! Get over here. We have work to do."

De Villegagnon addresses those who remain. "You are strong hands! Hoist blocks to the masons. As you hope to live, you will do as they say. Knights! To the ramparts! Provide cover fire!" He tosses Domenicus an arquebus. "You, fire on the glacis, where the invaders are exposed. Go, go!" Domenicus is strangely thrilled that the commanding knight trusts him with such an important charge.

There are now fifty men assembled before de Villegagnon. He flings the back of his hand at a Castilian's chest. "Give these tenderfoots a quick lesson in firing arquebus and cannon. Set each man at an embrasure. Double time!" As Domenicus heads for the walls, he catches de Villegagnon muttering to himself: "…Now, where is that damned Florentine?"

***

Angelica picks at her fingernails. The maid, the gardener, and the footman sit in a cluster next to her. There is nothing to make the time pass, nothing to talk about. The waiting is dreadful. Not knowing what the waiting will bring, more so. The garrison is practically undefended, a breach almost guaranteed. So they wait for the breach and the inexorable raising of Muslim banners throughout the city that will follow. They wait for their capture, their slavery, their doom.

Manoel is fidgety, Elisabetta wringing her fingers, starting at every noise. She weeps aloud for her husband, who is away at Sicily. Angelica knows he had asked Elisabetta to join him, but she declined, citing seasickness. Now, it seems, she would happily swim the distance.

Suddenly, someone hits the ground in the courtyard outside. Angelica is seized by fear. Could it have happened? The walls breached? Angelica grabs her knife, the servants theirs. None would know how to use one against an armed soldier, but it is better than having nothing at all.

"My lady, take Manoel and go hide in the closet," Angelica orders.

"What about the rest of you?" Elisabetta whispers urgently. Angelica makes no reply. Then, she hears heavy footsteps. The gardener rises, steps before the women, his knife at the ready.

"Hide," he says. "All of you."

"No," Angelica replies. She moves towards the doors. There is a man in the courtyard.

***

All around Domenicus is ordered chaos. The invading guns, silent for a time, have come alive again, lacing smoky air with gunpowder, stinging his eyes. The noise is deafening. The men on the wall are black with soot. Tristan and his team keep gunfire off Etienne's by pouring boiling tar through holes in the machicolations, galleries supported on brackets. Cannonballs hurtle against the ramparts, breaking stone into fragments. Iron balls fly over the curtain wall and career across the cobbled ground, leaving debris in their wake.

Domenicus does not move from his spot, lying flat and working his arquebus hard to cut down as many Ottomans as he can. In the last hour, he has probably not dropped even one. Part of him wants to slip away and find Angelica, but right now, that is out of the question.

***

Armed with the bow Robert made, Katrina and Father Tabone run the back roads of Birgu and do not stop until well beyond the village boundaries. To their surprise, they meet no resistance. The rumours proved true—Mdina is the shield the Drawn Sword of Islam strikes. Still, they exercise caution, as there is no telling who the pair might encounter in the darkness.

439

"Katrina," Father Tabone whispers, maintaining a swift pace. "What is the plan?"

"Other than reaching the prison and breaking the door?"

The priest crosses himself. "Well, I am the idiot who kept asking God for a challenge."

In just over an hour, they reach the prison site. Although Katrina had been there only once, she knew the precise way. She takes Father Tabone behind the boulder where she met with Dr Callus before the first breakout attempt. They crouch in the darkness, waiting, listening. There is only the very distant rumble of cannon.

"The knights must have recruited the guards to help with defences," Katrina says.

"That, or the guards have taken refuge inside the prison."

"We're armed," she replies. Before Father Tabone might lose his nerve, Katrina hauls him to his feet, and together they cover the ground that lies between the boulder and where she remembers the prison door being. To her horror, the door is not there. She is instantly hot all over and cold all over. She drops to the ground and begins scouring the terrain. Has the prison been relocated because of the breakout attempt? Has it been shut down, all the prisoners killed? Her brow is dappled with sweat despite the cool night air. Father Tabone is on his knees, helping in the search.

"It was here. It was right here," Katrina whispers urgently as tiny rocks cut into her fingers. Before panic claims her, she bangs her hand against a metal grip. The door is covered by reeds, hidden in the guards' absence. "Father Tabone!" He is at her side in an instant. She closes her hand around the latch and pulls. The door does not budge. The priest produces a hatchet and begins hacking at the door. Each *thock* seems deafening. Father Tabone tires and hands the small axe to Katrina. The door is thick, its wood a challenge to hew. They trade off once more before the door finally gives. Immediately, a putrid smell escapes from below.

Katrina takes a step into the stale blackness.

***

Marcello returns to the ramparts with sixteen women. They walk an almost soldierly march, seemingly happy for the chance to do something. There are even a few noblewomen among them. Some carry kindling for the cauldron fires, others their husbands' extra guns, and all carry rocks in pockets and aprons and free hands.

Governor Giorgio Adorno brushes past Marcello, running and shouting at Nico de Villegagnon: "The magazine is near bare! Get men to collect errant cannonballs!" Adorno cradles a forty-pound iron ball and passes it, still hot, to a Maltese gunner.

"No lads to spare," de Villegagnon replies. "Take the women."

Marcello bends low as he runs along the parapet, setting newly trained arquebusiers into position around the masons.

"How do they handle the guns?" Marcello calls over the roar of battle.

"Terribly," the Castilian replies. He grins anyway.

"Ruggieri!" de Villegagnon shouts. "Send half the women to the cauldrons. Show them how to boil tar. Send the others to collect stray cannonballs! I need you now, a sharpshooter!"

One of the women, a tough, broad-shouldered mother of eight shoves Marcello forcefully away with one hand. "Get lost. Women know how to boil." Marcello backs off, a little frightened. He drops his visor over his face, races along the parapet, hops over Tristan, and finds a spot on the wall where he can safely crouch and prime his arquebus. He lies flat on his belly and peers through a double splayed embrasure.

And then, he remembers. Marcello crawls across a stone ledge to Domenicus and puts his hand on his back. "A gift awaits you. Go to where the women are boiling tar, that's where it is. Be careful of one though. She's a mean thing who would toss you in the cauldron as soon as look at you."

Domenicus gives him a quizzical look.

Marcello ignores the young man's confused air, turning his attention to the Turks advancing below. A flash illuminates a yellow turban. Marcello licks dry lips and fires.

***

"God is greater. God is greater. There is no god but God!"

The guns fall silent once more as the men of Islam fulfil the second pillar of their faith.

No sooner does Dragut Raïs complete his *raka'at* than Sinan Pasha approaches, his expression one of acute vexation. "A relief force has managed to penetrate Mdina. They answer fire with fire. We make for Tripoli, now, before expending another son of the empire."

Dragut frowns. "If we are to rid the world of the Knights of St John, we must take their headquarters. Malta, not Tripoli, is where the Order makes its convent. A body without an arm can still thrive; a body without a head cannot."

"It will be our bodies without heads if we fail."

For all his co-admiral's agitation, Dragut remains composed. "I will not suffer dissent to poison our lines," he says. "We are united under one banner. We will cool our guns but sustain a sporadic bombardment throughout the night, exhausting the defences. The citadel will have no rest. We unleash our greatest offensive in the morning when they have no resistance left in them."

***

Katrina and Father Tabone crawl slowly over ugly moving things. She concentrates on finding and freeing Robert from this subterranean hell.

441

"The seventh cell," she says to the priest, barely able to make out his form in the darkness.

"I say we break all the doors, free everyone."

"Robert first." She finds his cell and calls to him through the rusty grate. There is no reply. She and Father Tabone call again, pounding on the door. Katrina is seized by a second terror. There is no reason the guards would have moved him, so that leaves only one possibility.... Despite her gathering tears, she lifts the hatchet, strikes the door, once, again, and again. She is strong, but in her distress, lacks precision. The priest takes over. In ten minutes, he manages to make tinder of the heavy door. Inside, there is only blackness, no shapes to be discerned. The room is cold and dank, and entering it is like crossing into a nightmare.

"Robert," Katrina whispers loudly. "Robert, can you hear me?" She and Father Tabone stand perfectly still for several moments. She senses a presence, other than that of the priest, and follows the feeling blindly towards a corner of the chamber. She kneels, reaches out her hand.

Her fingers brush cold flesh.

***

The guns of Islam punch holes in the night. The blasts come fewer now, and farther between, but when they come, they are a dry thunderstorm. Domenicus slings his gun over his shoulder and makes for the cauldrons. He peers at the women as they fill smaller pots with bubbling liquid, pass them off to waiting hands. He has no idea why Marcello relieved him from his post.

Then he understands. There is no *gift* for him here. Domenicus was doing a bad job, unable to defend the fortress with his pitiful aim. Marcello sent him to the cauldrons where he would be out of the way! This is where the knights think he belongs? Standing around a pot waiting for tar to boil? Domenicus is filled with anger and humiliation.

He decides to go at once to de Villegagnon and ask to be put to work at the tower. He doesn't care if it's dangerous. He has to prove himself. After the incidents in the field and at the entrance wall, he has to show the commanding knight he is not useless.

Domenicus feels a hand slip around his waist. It startles him. He looks down and around.

Angelica! All the bad feelings are instantly washed away. She smiles. There are tears in her eyes. Her face is dirt-streaked and sweaty and beautiful. He throws his arms around her and kisses her and lifts her off her feet. "God, I love you!"

"I love you!"

He puts her down, squeezes her tight. Her body feels amazing against his. A piece of heaven in a battle-soaked hell. They stand this way a few wondrous moments, watching the terrible beauty of the night sky flash red with rippling blasts of cannon fire. He kisses her forehead, releases her.

"I was beyond worried for your safety," she says. "What are you doing here?"

"As if I was going to let you have all the fun without me." He grins. She does not.

"How did you enter the city? How did you make it past the Turkish lines? Domenicus, you could have gotten yourself killed."

"But I didn't, did I?" He smiles. "And you, *Signorina*, should be inside. It isn't safe here. I have plans to marry all of you, not just a piece."

"Marcello came for me. For all of us," Angelica says, indicating the women with a sweep of her hand. "We're following orders. He gave us the scare of our lives though."

"Oh?"

"The idiot climbed the garden wall and wandered around the Predal courtyard like a needle on a broken compass. The servants and I were ready to stab him to death, thinking he was some Muslim cur come to take us away. He identified himself just in time."

Domenicus laughs. "What do they have you doing?"

"Collecting cannon balls for the men."

"I'd prefer if you worked at the cauldrons. It's safer."

Angelica gives him a look. "Will you get off the wall and boil tar with me? It's safer." Now it is his turn to give a look. "I didn't think so," she says. "I'm just as vulnerable at the cauldrons as I am gathering cannonballs."

With all his heart, he wants to pull her back into his arms and stay here with her, but with all his heart, knows he cannot. So he allows himself a last kiss. He removes his breastplate. "Take this."

"What? No! You must wear it."

"Angelica, do as I ask. It will make tonight easier for me if I know you have it."

She sighs, takes it reluctantly. "You are foolish."

"And you are beautiful." As if to hurry him on, the citadel walls shudder.

Angelica takes his face in her hands and brushes aside damp strands from his forehead. "Be careful. Please."

"I'll see you after." Domenicus turns from her, turns back, and winks. With that, he goes back to his post, his stride full of purpose. He gives Marcello a nudge.

The knight grins. "Ah, Montesa. Did you like your present?"

"Yes, thank you. Did you know they were just about to stab you to death?"

***

Ecclesial chants rise with the walls of Mdina. Nico de Villegagnon turns, gives his head a shake. The city's vicar leads a procession of monks and nuns, priests and peasants. He and four others hoist an enormous banner emblazoned with the image of St Agatha.

De Villegagnon runs over. "You know, God would quite rightly think your parade a stupid idea at the moment. If you want to appeal to Him, do so in the safety of the cathedral."

"God has called us to action," the priest replies, his face a study in calm.

"Very well, Father. Find a gun and join the defences."

"First, hang this banner from the bastion wall." The fortress trembles, sending the pastor stumbling forward.

"We are about to be breached and your mind is on banners, priest?" de Villegagnon shouts, taking the man's arm to steady him.

"Saint Agatha appeared to a nun at the Abbey of Santa Scholastica and instructed her to display her image. I beseech you, *Honorabile*, we must not ignore this."

De Villegagnon is not a superstitious man, but right now, given the odds, if a saint wants to intervene, so be it. "Go," he says. "But soak the banner in water." The knight appraises the newest additions to his defensive line. He sends the men to the walls, but positions the Carmelites as far out of enemy range as possible, knowing his mother would take a swift paddle to his ass if he put a nun in harm's way. He orders them to gather debris from the city centre and pile everything at the foot of the bastion for gunners to cram into cannons. Finally, he marches behind a line of archers. "Incendiary weapons! At the ready!"

***

From the corner of his eye, Domenicus notices a small stable boy, torch in hand, lighting the tar-soaked hemp tips of arrows. Five knights and twelve unskilled villagers make up the team of bowmen. They are positioned atop the wall, arrows nocked and glowing. In unison, strings are pulled back and, as the banner of St Agatha unfurls over the face of the citadel, twenty arrows are released, flaming points lighting the sky with red stars. Though inexperience causes several darts to deflect, fire wreaks havoc on the tar-saturated hillside, igniting silk robes below, engulfing frontline invaders. Dying screams scale the wall.

Domenicus looks across his shoulder at the priest. Men of the cloth are not expected to take up arms. This one does so anyway, proving himself a deadly shot with the arquebus he picked up from a fallen Maltese. Domenicus marvels at him. The priest smiles. "Son, there is a time for everything! A time to laugh, a time to cry, a time to pray. And a time to shoot down turbaned bastards and send them to hell!" The Muslims respond in kind, shooting arrow and musket and bolt. Defenders scatter, regroup. Archers notch their arrows and wait for flame. None comes. Heads turn in all directions in search of the young fire-bearer.

"Haqq il-baghla," a blacksmith mutters. *Damn the bitch.* Domenicus follows the smithy's gaze. The fire-bearer, a stable boy, is dead, brought down by musket. Not a moment later, the son of a candle maker scampers along the parapet in the stable boy's place. The blacksmith drops, felled by an enemy arrow through the throat; a water seller, killed by a crossbow dart; next, a baker, crushed by flying masonry.

Domenicus takes the place of the blacksmith. He hoists the smithy's bow and quiver. The night sky is lighter now, having faded from black to purple to dove grey. Domenicus can make out the men below. He wishes he couldn't. While he cannot tell a Janissary from a dervish, the Ottoman lines are formidable, their numbers alarming. It is a sea of steel and silk, wave upon wave crashing against the trembling fortress. If they capture this city, all will be taken into slavery. He decides then that if the walls are breached, he will find Angelica and kill her himself.

Domenicus draws an arrow from his quiver, nocks it to his bow, and waits for the new fire bearer to light the tip. For some reason, the bow and arrow fall suddenly from his hands. An incredible force shoves him backwards. Has someone just delivered him a brutal punch to the ribs? Probably Robert—he's always doing silly things like that. Domenicus will pay him back later.

And where on earth did his bow and arrow go?

***

"Malta has tipped the balance of war in her favour," Sinan Pasha announces, just after dawn. "We take God's fight to Tripoli, the intended target of Suleiman's spear."

Dragut has tired of his co-admiral's cynicism. "The Sultan has many spears. His board is wide, his aim far-reaching."

"My lords!" calls a Janissary as he breaks through the lines at a full sprint. Both men turn.

"What is it?" Sinan snaps.

"We have captured a Sicilian galley, speeding here with a letter to the Grand Master from Messina, signed by the Receiver of the Order."

"Have you this letter on your person?" Dragut asks him.

"Yes, effendi." The Janissary produces the vellum.

Dragut reads it carefully, straining in the fragile light. He reads it twice.

"An evil omen," he says, handing the parchment to Sinan, whose eyes widen with each word they pass over. When he finishes, he lets the calfskin sheet fall from his hands, his expression bleak.

"Andrea Doria."

Dragut gives a pensive nod. The walls of Mdina hold true. Many of his men have not fared so well—broken, bleeding, dying. He meets his co-admiral's gaze. Convincing Sinan Pasha to press Mdina for another week would be difficult enough; to suggest extending their stay until September would end in mutiny. And now, there is the accursed Andrea Doria to deal with....

The Janissary, standing at perfect attention, addresses the admirals. "Orders, lords?"

Dragut looks past the Janissary to the sea, to Gozo beyond. Perhaps he may have his vengeance yet. "Departure."

***

In the Grand Master's study, Commander de Guimeran, the knight who orchestrated the surprise dawn attack on Dragut's fleet from the slopes of Sciberras, sits down and chuckles heartily. The Order's Receiver, bless him, sent a letter claiming Andrea Doria, Genoese admiral and Dragut's arch-nemesis, was sweeping towards Malta in a ship that headed a vast relief fleet.

The letter was a perfectly executed ruse on the part of the Receiver and contained not one smidgeon of truth. And the Ottoman Empire's finest fell for it. De Guimeran is delighted. The siege, if it can even be called that, has ended with minimal losses. Only one knight dead, and it was neither Muslim musket nor scimitar that did him in. It was the heat.

A shame, too—that fat Briton Nicholas Upton would have had a good laugh over this.

CHAPTER FORTY-NINE

The bells of Mdina's great cathedral clang in proclamation of the city's victory. Nico de Villegagnon allows himself a moment to smile. Morning shines on the northern slope, lighting a hillside charred from spot fires and strewn with Ottoman bodies, but clear of cannons. The threat is over. The villagers are joyous. Knights and peasants, nuns and nobles celebrate together, hugging, cheering, thanking God. Etienne and Tristan shake hands with Alvarus and Nardo, the two Maltese boasting how many Turks they killed, each with a number in the high hundreds. They laugh and clap each other on the back. Even Barri is beaming. He embraces his boy Francesco, and then pushes him away, cuffing him playfully across the head. Francesco takes the loving wallop with good humour.

For de Villegagnon, the fun soon ends. He walks the walls, meeting the dead. The stable boy, the blacksmith, the water seller. And there, lying on his back beneath the mound of a collapsed merlon, is Domenicus Montesa, his face barely visible from beneath the debris. De Villegagnon halts abruptly. He shouts for Marcello.

***

Now that everything is all right, Angelica wanders the ramparts, looking for Domenicus. She carries his breastplate in her arms, happy to return the cumbersome thing to its owner. A few paces away, Marcello and another knight work frantically to dig a body out from under some rubble. She climbs up onto the wall to help as they move broken stone from the man's chest.

Before either knight takes notice, Angelica gets a look at the victim's face. The breastplate falls from her grip and crashes against the cobbles. Her entire body is shaking.

"No, no… Please. No. It can't… he can't… Dear God, no!" Angelica crumples to her knees. She sobs, bent to the ground. All around her, church bells clang in triumph as voices proclaim joyful victory. It is terrible, abrasive noise. She feels herself being pulled into someone's arms. Maybe Marcello has come to comfort her. She pushes him away, tears across the wall to her fallen love. Once at his side, she throws the rocks off his body. *It can't be. Not my Domenicus. He came here for me. It is my fault. Why did he give me his armour? Why did I take it? Why? Oh God, no. Please. No.*

She sees his wound. It is horrific. A musket ball ripped through the flesh beneath his bottom rib and came out his back. The entry wound is bad, the exit worse. There is blood all over him, soaking the shreds of his shirt, splattered on his face. Angelica cradles his head in her arms, kissing his pale brow, her tears spilling over his face, dirt and dried blood running with the salty flood. She takes his hand in hers and squeezes. *Please. No. Not my Domenicus.*

Then... A pulse! Sweet merciful Jesus, there is a pulse!

"*Marcello!*" she screams. "Come quick! He is alive! Get a doctor! Get somebody! Anybody!"

***

To Angelica, it seems Marcello is purposely driving the cart into every rut in the road. Dr Callus struggles to keep his balance as he crouches over Domenicus.

"Angelica, it does not look good," the doctor says. On the walls of Mdina, he had acted fast, tearing his own shirt into strips and using them to pack the wounds and stem the bleeding. "Who knows how long he spent under the rubble after he was shot—an hour? Two?"

Angelica's eyes are heavy, her cheeks hot with twin streams of tears. "Please, Dr Callus, you are equal to the challenge. You cannot give up so quickly."

"I'm not giving up. But you must prepare yourself for the worst. He may not see out the hour. He is—" Callus cuts himself off. But he has already said too much. The words stab at her. *No, not again, not another. I will not allow it! Do you hear me, God? Damn it, do you hear? You will not take another from me!* She quickly recants. God might strike Domenicus dead for such a dare. *Forgive me. I am sorry! So sorry! Just don't take him. I will do anything. Anything! Please. He is my life.* Angelica holds his hand and does not move her eyes from his face. It is deathly pale and somehow still losing colour. She can feel the life slipping from him. She shouts at Marcello to drive the cart faster and more carefully.

They arrive at the *Sacra Infermeria* in superb time, but for Angelica, no ride has ever taken as excruciatingly long. Slowly, Marcello and Dr Callus place Domenicus on a narrow board and carry him to the gate, flung wide to allow the injured from the attack to be carted through. Callus walks backwards, Marcello forward, the knight shouting for people to make way. Angelica walks beside them, her eyes on Domenicus, always on Domenicus.

It comes as a tremendous shock when the hospital guard steps in front of her, stopping her mid-stride. She looks up in surprise and anger. "What? What is the problem?"

Marcello hesitates. "Let her pass," he says. "It's all right, she's with me."

448

"It's not all right, Ruggieri, and I don't care who she's with. Women are not permitted."

Angelica cannot believe this son of a bitch is enforcing rules at a time like this. "Please, my lord, he is to be my husband. You must—"

"I *must* do nothing. And if you don't let them go through without you, you'll be a widow before you are married."

She knows he's right. She wants to stave in his head. "Go," she says to Marcello and Callus, unable to say more because of the lump closing her throat.

"Wait here, I'll bring word." Angelica is not sure who just spoke, unable to see because of the tears blurring her vision. Then, they are gone.

Somehow, she makes her way to a bench outside the main gate and slumps heavily onto it. Her clothes are stained with his blood. Domenicus is going to die. And there is nothing she can do for him. He is going to die because of her, and all she can do for him is sit on a bench in the sun.

***

Father Tabone is at the rectory, hitching a cart to his mule. Now that the invaders have departed, and Robert is safe with Katrina, the priest is going to look for Angelica and Domenicus.

Hours earlier, in the underground cell, Katrina touched Robert, and by his cold, stiff flesh was convinced he was dead. Father Tabone went to smash down the remaining doors, leaving Katrina alone with Robert, his head in her lap. Suddenly, she felt movement, felt something being placed in her hand. It was her ribbon. She screamed for Father Tabone. Together, they carried Robert back to Birgu, barely stopping to rest. They had to dodge a small group of Turkish deserters tearing through the fields on the way back to the sea. A good sign for Malta—the siege was lifting.

Father Tabone and Katrina agreed the safest place for Robert would be his own home, where the curtains have been drawn for months and would remain so now. As soon as the young man was replenished with water and settled into his bed, the priest left to find his niece. He keeps his eye out for Dr Callus as well, who would be a great help to the terribly bruised and battered Robert Falsone.

Father Tabone passes now through the streets of Birgu, which look almost the same as they did two days ago. The word is that Mdina took all the bombardment. He is relieved to hear that although the wounded number in the hundreds, there were very few casualties—three sentries, eleven villagers in Mdina, and one knight, the fat Englishman. An attack of such measure, especially one that comes without warning, should have ended with casualties in the thousands.

"Makes you think they were using Malta as combat training," Father Tabone remarks jovially to a passer-by, who grins and nods. There is heavy foot traffic around the *Sacra Infermeria*, scores of wounded being carried in.

Father Tabone squints, to see if he recognizes any. Fortunately, no one. He decides to go to the Montesa house before Mdina, just in case they are there.

***

Angelica knocks on the Montesa door, but there is no answer. She needs to tell Katrina about Domenicus. Where could she be? Angelica lingers a few minutes more, but when no one turns up, she returns to the *Sacra Infermeria* to await word and to pray.

***

Ten minutes later, Father Tabone slows his mule to a stop just outside Augustine's house. He jumps down from the cart and goes inside. It is unoccupied. He gives one final sweeping glance, heads back outside.

***

In the operating theatre of the *Sacra Infermeria*, the surgeon knight Édouard de Gabriac looks grimly at the man on the table before him. He remembers the patient's mother dying on a similar table almost ten years ago. He must save her son.

Already two hours have passed since Callus and di Ruggieri brought Domenicus to the ward. Édouard de Gabriac was busy making rounds, tending the wounded, setting fractures, treating burns, when he came upon his former apprentice, near dead. Had it been someone other than Domenicus Montesa lying there, he would have sent him to the mortuary, to make room on the operating table for someone who actually had a chance. As long as Domenicus had a pulse, de Gabriac had to try.

And so, he and Callus worked feverishly on the patient, both convinced he was going to die any moment. Still, Domenicus managed to outlive the prognosis that he would expire within the hour.

Now, de Gabriac exposes the holes. The entry wound is a grisly opening to a bloody tunnel, but at its end, there is no light. The exit wound, cavernous and ridged, its edges gaping flaps, its smell putrid, is twice the size of the tunnel mouth and notably lower. The skin is discoloured, lacerated. Already the holes fester. His breath is so faint that three times de Gabriac has to bend to the patient's mouth to feel if the breeze of his life still blows.

He presses around the wounds for crepitus. Indeed, there is broken bone. The musket ball must have struck the floating rib and tumbled on its axis, altering the bullet track. That would explain why the wounds do not follow a linear path. De Gabriac probes further. The crooked trajectory led the ball through the lower end of the liver, though damage to the organ is luckily not too severe. More troublesome are the fragments of bone and pieces of his shirt still inside him, which present a new and ever more difficult challenge. The surgeon passes fresh, brine soaked linen around the edges of the wounds to clean them of blood and debris. He then uses long forceps to pick out the tiny pieces of fragmented bone and torn cloth.

De Gabriac shakes his head without meaning to. "Had the bullet the courtesy to pass through his leg or his arm, we could amputate, but this, this is impossible. Worse, the bone is in shards and the fabric in pieces. If even one is missed, he will die."

Callus gives no reply. De Gabriac can see in the doctor's face that he knows all too well what the outcome will be. So many ways for this young man to die—if not from the musket ball or the enormous loss of blood or the internal hemorrhage, then from his shattered rib or torn shirt.

Slowly, agonizingly so, de Gabriac and Callus remove piece after piece of bone and fabric. There are long hours ahead of them, and Domenicus may only have minutes.

***

Angelica remains on the bench outside the hospital. She has watched comings and goings all day, watched the village timidly returning to its normal paces. It seems she is the only one caught in the grey space between the whiteness of joy and the blackness of sorrow.

Marcello slipped outside to talk to her once, about four hours ago, and the news was not good. Still, so long as Domenicus clings to life, there is hope. Every time Angelica hears the heavy gait of boots passing through the loggia, her heart pounds. Is it someone coming to tell her he has succumbed? But it never is. She is desperate for news, but in the end, decides the longer it is taking, the better. It means he is putting up a fight. She prays and begs and prays harder. And when she thinks all her tears have dried up, fresh ones spring to her eyes.

At seven bells, she hears her name.

"Angelica!"

She looks up. It is Katrina. Her face is ashen, the picture of distress. She closes the space between them at a run. Father Tabone is a few paces behind, his expression equal parts relief and worry. He hangs quietly back.

Katrina is in a tear-streaked panic. "Tell me my brother is all right! Tell me he's alive."

"He's alive."

Katrina collapses onto the bench and hugs Angelica tight. "Oh thank God, thank God! A knight told your uncle what happened, and he came to Robert's house to tell me. The news tore me apart. But now, to hear he's all right... oh, thank God!" Angelica feels awful at Kat's mistaken joy and knows she must confess the seriousness of her brother's injury. But before she can bring herself to do so, Katrina puts her hand on Angelica's. "I am so sorry we quarrelled. You went to Marcello because you were trying to help Robert."

Angelica squeezes her friend's knee and keeps the conversation moving. "How did my uncle know to find you at Robert's house? Why were you there?"

"Later," Kat replies, smiling. "Too much to tell for now."

Angelica does not press, a decision she quickly regrets.

"What is it?" Katrina asks at the silence. "What aren't you telling me?"

Angelica looks at her hands. "Nothing... You asked if Domenicus is alive. He is. That's all."

Katrina jumps up from the bench. "No, it isn't! I can see it in your face. Tell me the truth!"

Angelica takes a deep breath, the air quivering inside her. "They... the doctors... they say the damage is grave. ...They say he's not going to make it. I... I'm sorry. So sorry."

CHAPTER FIFTY

A Gozitan farmer walks his rows. It will be a good year. It *is* a good year. Already, he has turned a profit. By this time, he is just barely breaking even but is content so long as he has enough to keep his wife and two daughters from starving. This year, however, he will be able to provide the older one with a dowry and marry her off. For the first time in a long time, the farmer's step is not as heavy as he treks uphill towards the cistern. The soil is a rich brown, lit with the morning, smelling fresh. A warm breeze blows off the sea, the air scented with salt and... he sniffs... salt and something else. Sweat and blood. He reaches the top of the knoll and looks to the bay.

The farmer drops his buckets. An enormous fleet, marked Turkish by crescent banners, plies the waters just off Marsalforn. Catastrophe has landed. Recovering from the shock, he sets off in a sprint, running full out through fields and glades, over fences and stone walls. He reaches his house in ten minutes flat and bursts through the door. His wife is sweeping ashes from the hearth, his two daughters washing linens, one scrubbing, the other wringing.

The younger one beams. "Pa!"

"Hello, my sweetheart," he replies fondly. He goes to the trunk next to the hearth and removes his sword from its place beneath the sheepskins. Without a word, he stabs his wife, killing her instantly and silently. He moves to his daughters. He kills them both.

With tears in his eyes, he lays their bodies together on one pallet, kisses their brows, takes up his bloody sword and goes to meet their murderers.

***

Timurhan Yusuf al Salih lies on the deck of a galley with the rest of the wounded. He has been instructed by a physician to keep his leg elevated. The Sipahi took a dagger deep to the thigh when he ambushed a pack of knights at the gate of Mdina. Surprisingly, the weapon that wreaked havoc on his leg was not thrown by a knight, but a mere Maltese foot soldier, whom the knights called Montesa. Timurhan made it back to his line with the dagger still embedded in his muscle, its tip poking out the back of his thigh. The blade missed his femur but plunged straight through his vastus lateralis, the flesh around the hilt red and blue and terribly inflamed. The wound wept viscous tears, and fever took Timurhan. He was carried on his horse to a galley, where a doctor removed the dagger and used a great length of catgut to suture muscle and vessel and flesh.

More upsetting—and possibly more painful—is the loss of his blue Ceylon topaz, given to him by his uncle Mustafa Pasha for its known power to bring strength. Worse still, Timurhan has been ordered off battle. What glory is there to be found in bed rest?

As he lies here, his thigh wrapped in fresh linen and bound with comfrey, he thinks of Demir. That day at the Grand Bazaar, he overheard the boy telling his friend he was certain Timurhan would slay five hundred knights. He did not slay one. Therefore, he will have to embellish the story a little—for Demir's benefit, of course. It *was* a knight that stabbed him with the dagger. And Timurhan ripped the dagger out of his own thigh and plunged it straight into the infidel's heart. That sounds better than the actual way of things.

Timurhan smiles. He will tell Demir the truth.

Discussion draws the cavalryman from his reveries. Dragut Raïs and Sinan Pasha are at the starboard gunwale. Timurhan can tell that Dragut is not happy about Mdina, but knows he is not a man to waste time brooding over that which is done. *Malish. Maktub. Never mind. It is written.*

"The fortress of Gozo will fall easily," Dragut says to his co-admiral.

Sinan's brow is etched with lines of consternation. He gives Dragut a cynical look. "As easily as that of Mdina?"

***

There are two watchtowers on Gozo. And their bells have been clanging the last twenty minutes, now drowned by the screams of villagers choking the streets. They run for the citadel, a neglected and poorly defended fortress perched upon the flat summit of a high plateau.

Augustine and Belli are among those making for the walls. They race up the steep gradient, the carpenter huffing and falling behind Augustine, who barely breaks a sweat charging up the narrow streets towards the stronghold. Villagers crowd about the embrasures between merlons and shout encouragements to those struggling to make it. Augustine turns, grabs Belli by the elbow and half-drags him uphill past the ravelin, over the ditch to the main gate, and finally through the sally port. They keep on running until they scale the seemingly endless flight of stairs. Belli, hand over heart, drops like a sack of grain at the top. Augustine goes on, straight to the walls. He looks through an arrow slit. There, in the glittering harbour, is a forest of masts, and fluttering from them, as leaves caught in the wind, are the banners of Islam.

Now, Augustine breaks into a sweat.

***

Galatian de Sesse, governor of Gozo, is accosted by a young sentry, Matheus Cumbo, who tears up the citadel stairs, taking them two, three at a time. "My lord! My lord! Dragut Raïs has landed! His men march on Marsalforn!"

Dragut Raïs. Galatian de Sesse starts at the name. The legendary corsair swore vengeance on the island after de Sesse ignored Muslim burial customs and had the body of Dragut's brother burned. The Spanish knight had heard rumours of the Ottoman fleet, but like the Grand Master, deemed the reports tenuous French drivel. Now, de Sesse frowns at the sentry.

Matheus shifts his weight. "Orders, lord?"

"Orders?"

The sentry furrows his brow. "What should we do? Are there guns? Crossbows? Orders, sir. Give bloody orders!"

De Sesse looks at his hands, contemplates. The citadel cannot endure a steady barrage. It is without a proper garrison. There is only one other knight here, an Englishman called William Tyrrel. De Sesse thinks of his subjects, their plight. The fate of five thousand rests in the hands he is now studying. The fortress magazine is poorly provisioned, and Dragut would have intercepted any reinforcement sent by galley from mainland Malta. That means de Sesse is alone in this fight. He considers capitulation. There is a loss of habit for any knight who surrenders his post to an enemy, the defrocking often accompanied by a prison sentence. Either way, Galatian de Sesse is doomed.

"My lord?" the sentry prompts.

De Sesse takes in the state of the men assembling along the walls— farmers, blacksmiths, fishermen, shepherds…. Indeed, he is alone. He looks a final time at Matheus before striding off to wait in the safety of his quarters until the Ottoman storm passes.

***

In an open field between sea and citadel, the Turkish command post is quickly set up. Sinan Pasha meets with the Aghas inside a tent. "Poison the cisterns and wells. Burn the houses. Bring me slaves. Kill those who resist." He casts a sideways glance on Dragut. "A quick business here."

***

Domenicus Montesa is dead. At least, from his pallor, he looks that way. He is unconscious, his body hot with fever. De Gabriac and Callus have laboured long hours on him, managing to extract the shreds of cloth. De Gabriac assigned Marcello to match them piece for piece until they filled the hole in the torn shift. The shards of rib presented a far more difficult challenge, as there was nothing with which to match up those.

Now, de Gabriac clips away dead skin around the ends of the wound track, rinsing his handiwork with white wine. He cuts bad muscle, ties ligatures until long after his fingers cramp. He uses more suturing thread on this patient than he recalls ever using before—at least three full spools. Next, he smears the holes with sarcocol, a gum resin from Persia reputed to seal wounds.

455

Domenicus never stirs. His heartbeat remains fluttery, breath faint. His life is fragile yet.

***

"All men and strong lads!" The voice belongs to the only other knight on Gozo, the Englishman, William Tyrrel. He booms in Italian at the host of peasants swarming him, Augustine among them. "Those able to bear arms, to the armoury! Women and children, back to the archways!"

Augustine falls in step with Tyrrel, who has assumed control of the defences following de Sesse's desertion. "Sir, I am a soldier of the Order. I fought at Rhodos. I sailed caravans with Gabriel Mercadal and Mathurin Romegas."

"*Bene*," the knight replies. "That makes four for the garrison. Get a weapon and blast anything turbaned." He smacks a meaty hand against Augustine's chest and strides on.

"Four? What do you mean?"

"Me, you, the sentry, and your big fellow there," Tyrrel says, indicating Belli.

Augustine furrows his brow. "Surely you can muster more than that."

The knight moves towards him. "Look around, sir. Farmers. Women. Children."

"Arm the farmers. Give them crossbows, they're easy enough to handle. The women and children can boil tar, throw rocks."

"*Rocks*? Throw rocks?" Tyrrel's tone suggests he is not sure whether to laugh or strike Augustine. "Rocks against muskets and heavy guns?" The knight spits at the ground. "Find a place along the northern wall." With that, he is off, swallowed by the mass of villagers. Matheus shoves the only available arquebus at Augustine, a crossbow at Belli, and then he too races off.

Augustine looks at Belli. "This is absurd. How could a fleet this size have passed unnoticed through the Middle Sea? Without word reaching the island? A campaign this determined requires months to plan and assemble. Malta should have been warned."

Belli shrugs. "It doesn't matter now. Let's survive the day. Then we'll question the Grand Master. And if I don't like his answers, I'll rip off his head and throw it at his dead body."

Augustine grunts. He leads Belli up a ramp, past the governor's palace, up another flight, and through a long narrow corridor of stone arches and wall lanterns, past the chapel of St Joseph. A final archway takes them to an unoccupied cleft in the north-eastern wall. There, they sit against a merlon. Augustine runs his hand over the notched, ancient stone. He turns away a moment, noticing as a great white-grey seagull alights atop a nearby cornice to preen his feathers; the bird seems pleased with himself and is not in the least bit troubled by the sorry state of the defences.

***

Father Tabone crouches before the bench neither Angelica nor Katrina has moved from these last hours. "Girls, come home," he says. "Katrina, I insist you and Robert stay with us, at least until your father returns. I'm sure he is already on his way. Please, both of you, I'll fix you something to eat. You must sleep."

"No," Angelica replies flatly. "I'm not going anywhere. I'm not hungry. I'm not tired." The darkness beneath her eyes betrays the truth, but the priest does not press.

Katrina leans forward. "Father, how is Robert? I try to divide the hours between watching over him and staying here, but it is difficult."

"I've checked in on him. He only sleeps. Katrina, give some of those hours to yourself. You too need rest."

She nods, but it is clear to him that she has no intention of obeying. "Father Tabone, will you go inside the hospital? To see about my brother?"

He rises, smoothes out his cassock, adjusts the strap of the pack on his shoulder. "Of course. That's why I'm here, to see about Domenicus. But afterwards, the two of you will return home with me, if just to eat and rest. Then you may come back."

Angelica looks him hard in the face. "*No.*"

He sighs, unwilling to argue with her, not now. He presents himself and his purpose at the loggia. The guard lets him through at once. Father Tabone is not surprised by the ease of his entry—what good Christian would deny access to a priest on his way to give last rites to a young man wounded on the walls of Mdina?

***

Outside the Ottoman command tent, Dragut Raïs reviews plans with the Agha of the Janissaries for the afternoon's attack. "The southern curtain wall is thick and stretches from the western ramparts to the eastern battery," Dragut says. "The main gates are weak. Breach those, the citadel is ours." His orders pass through the ranks as slaves drag cannons uphill towards the fortress.

Sinan Pasha approaches. "A Sipahi rode down some Gozitans fleeing the fortress. They claim governor de Sesse has barricaded himself inside his house. He has organized no resistance."

Dragut knows Galatian de Sesse, the knight who ignored the seaman's request and burned the body of his brother. The knight who, by doing so, brought vengeance upon his people. "He will want to hear terms."

Sinan flashes. "I will not treat with a coward."

"I did not say I would treat with him. I said he would want to hear terms. And these are my terms: he and every other citizen on this island are now the property of the Sultan."

***

William Tyrrel walks the parapet, shaking his head in dismay of his pathetic company. He sets what few peasants he has managed to equip with crossbows

457

at the crenels. He is the only man, besides governor de Sesse and the soldier-at-arms Montesa, who knows how to fire a cannon. De Sesse is a spineless coward locked up in his house, and Montesa the only other capable arquebusier. Tyrrel wholeheartedly regrets ceding his position on Malta as Turcopilier to his corpulent friend, Sir Nicholas Upton, who is probably right now enjoying a decadent meal. He smiles wryly at the notion, wishing he and Upton could trade places.

Although the lone gunner, Tyrrel decides to prime several cannons to give the illusion Gozo has more men on the guns than she actually does.

He is fully aware his efforts will make no difference—blasts will be too sporadic.

But it will annoy Dragut, so he'll do it anyway.

***

Gozo resounds with invasion. Augustine peers over the wall. A swarm of locusts, frenzied Iayalars leave only destruction in their wake, flattening the way for the Janissaries and their mounted rivals, the Sipahiyan. Behind the cavalry come screaming dervishes. Fields and houses burn. Villagers who did not make the citadel are fettered and marched towards the galleys.

Augustine looks over his shoulder. Huddled in the fortress cloisters are mothers holding their children. It is harder to look at them than at the waves of scimitars pressing forward in the sea of silver below. All he can do is thank God his own children are safe on Malta.

Seated next to him, Belli fiddles with his new crossbow. Augustine decides now is as good a time as any to give the carpenter a few pointers. "Hold the stock as you would an arquebus, like so." He takes the weapon from Belli and rests it on his shoulder. "Use the tip of your bolt as your sight."

"*Iż-żobb*," Belli grumps. "I thought I came to this stupid rock to build some bookshelves, not be murdered by Dragut, that left testicle of Satan." His voice is all but lost to the battle cry of the Iayalars as it streams over the walls like billowing smoke, and hangs about the air as thick as fog.

Belli spits. "May God eat them."

***

Domenicus Montesa's waxen face is damp, his body shivering. Everything earthly has been done, the wounds tended as best as they could be. Now, it is time to take care of the soul, in case the best is not good enough. And from the state of the patient, it likely is not.

The holes are dressed, and for that, Father Anton Tabone is thankful. Around the bandages are purple bruises, running in dark streaks up past the patient's chest and down beyond his navel. The contusions are the only signs of colour on his body. He is so pale he looks more dead than half the men occupying spaces in the mortuary.

Earlier, Father Tabone answered a knock on his door from Dr Callus. "Domenicus is going to die," the doctor said. "Come perform the Sacrament."

And so, the priest kneels beside the cot. He takes a small phial from his satchel and spreads some oil on his finger, which he crosses over the patient's brow. When the rite is complete, Father Tabone bows his head in prayer.

***

Augustine looks out through an arrow loop, watching with uninterrupted misery as fields are torched, green carpets reduced to ash. Smoke rises in thick plumes to the sky. Hosts of fire become flowing torrents, rivers of red.

He presses his back against the wall, and pours gunpowder into the muzzle of his arquebus, packing it firmly with a stick. He rams the iron ball into the barrel, fills the flash pan with powder. As he closes the cover, he glances across his shoulder. The seagull has not moved from the stone cornice, where he remains perched, sunning himself.

Augustine's gaze settles once on the advancing lines, the van now in range. He lights the slow match and carefully places it inside the serpentine. He sights down the barrel, squeezes, and, with a flash, the iron ball sails through a thick cloud of smoke. A Janissary falls.

Now, to do that a thousand more times.

***

Dragut Raïs is at the counterscarp in full view of the ravelin, a triangular stonework used to split an attacking force. He is all places if one, directing the assault, advising gunners. The rout will be complete in minutes. It comes as a great surprise when the citadel sends a cannonball his way. The seaman smiles, amused by the effort. It is almost a shame to deprive the defenders their one gunner.

Dragut raises his musket, sights his target and fires.

***

William Tyrrel, the lone cannon operator, takes a musket ball to the chest, and drops headfirst from the wall, his body turning as it tumbles silently. And so, the Englishman goes to reunite with his friend, Sir Nicholas Upton, and discuss trading places.

***

Enemy cannonballs hammer the walls. Augustine and Belli brace themselves on notches hewn into stone slabs. Whole sections of the stronghold begin slipping away, the foundation collapsing to rubble. "Down the stairs!" Augustine cries, hauling Belli to his feet. "To the sally port!"

The two men tear past the chapel, through an archway, down a stairway, past the governor's palace. Augustine's sights are on the last flight, but as he and Belli run the final stretch they are separated in the crush. Augustine feels the ground crumble beneath his feet.

The stone cornice remains strong to the wall, but the seagull has flown.

***

As Dragut predicted, the fortress is easily taken, the main gate swiftly breached. Random sections of the ramparts still stand, but the battery has been reduced to ruins. Iayalars swamp the *castello*, oblivious to everything but the lust to kill. Scores of corsairs flood the break, clustering densely, as scores more surround the citadel to catch anyone trying to flee.

Dragut is pleased—his galleys will be heavier by five thousand.

***

Father Tabone looks at the body before him. He does not want to lie to his niece, or to Katrina, but he cannot tell them he has just given Domenicus last rites. The priest touches the patient's hand, takes it in his, feels tears welling in his eyes. It is just too awful. This young man, so full of life, of promise, of... *My God!* The hand is squeezing back! Father Tabone is frantic. He looks wildly in all directions, not knowing what to do.

"De Gabriac! Callus! Someone! Anyone! Come quick!"

***

Out of bullets, Augustine presses his back to a fragment of wall and swings his arquebus at an Algerian. The corsair slashes at Augustine with a scimitar but the gun's barrel deflects the blow. The Algerian lunges, swinging his scythe mightily and knocking the makeshift club from Augustine's hand. The corsair swings again. His blade connects with soft limestone. In that fleeting second, Augustine dives for a discarded spear. With a great cry, he gores the corsair. The Algerian falls to the ground, still clutching the jewelled grip of his scimitar. Augustine feels the corsair's warm blood spattered on his face. He looks with frenzied desperation for Belli, but cannot find him in the mess of broken stone and bodies, dust and smoke. Through the chaos, he hears the voice of the governor, Galatian de Sesse, newly emerged from his apartments.

"Surrender! I surrender! I surrender the citadel and all within it!"

Augustine is dizzy. Across from him, he makes out a small girl, wandering out from the safety of a passageway into the violent fray. The sight of the vulnerable child clears his head. He wrenches the scimitar from the dead corsair and rips towards her, hopping over bodies as he goes. He scoops her into his arms and makes for the sally port.

Four paces from his destination he comes face to face with Sinan Pasha. Augustine puts the girl down and steps in front of her, using his own body as a shield. He raises his scimitar.

Suddenly, there is a flash of lightning, blinding, all-encompassing.

Lightning? How could there be lighting? There wasn't a cloud in the sky...

Then, the world goes black.

CHAPTER FIFTY-ONE

Domenicus stirs but does not wake as Dr Callus feeds him cold water with a spoon, passes a damp cloth over his burning face and neck. It is time to change the dressings. The wounds are painful to look at, even for a doctor—raw, oozing, the flesh contused blue and purple. Layers of skin come away in pieces. Callus uses rose oil and turpentine to clean the holes, wrapping them with bandages coated in honey. Domenicus shivers despite his fever. He cries out in his coma for his mother. He calls for Angelica, for Katrina.

He calls for his father.

***

Obscured by smoke, the sun strains to peek over the ruins of the *Gran Castello*, now a smouldering heap of rubble and bodies and ash. Face down in velvet dust, Belli lies motionless. His eyelids flutter him into waking. He tries to swallow, but his mouth is too dry. At his ankle, dull pain turns suddenly sharp. He twists round and, with an intake of powdery breath, jumps to his feet and kicks off the rat gnawing at his bloody flesh.

"You bastard. Go chew on someone dead." In the silence, his voice is thunder, reverberating on the rocks. His legs are shaky beneath him, his hands powdered dusty white. He has no idea how long he has been out. It seems to be morning. It was late afternoon when the wall fell.

The smell is sickening—blood and burned flesh. Much of what was once the curtain wall is now a cream-coloured wreckage festering with vermin—here a flank, there a merlon, here a buttress, there an archway. Bodies drape over stone, hang over walls. Some have pikes left in them, some arrows. Limbs, scattered. Belli is overwhelmed, unable to believe he alone survived the attack, to understand the destruction before him. There were not even that many enemy shots fired yesterday.

The wall—there must have been hundreds hiding in the passageways when it crumbled. Oh yes—he is starting to remember—and the breach, fighting in the breach. Thousands hauled into slavery.

"*Augustine!*" Belli calls, three and four times. No answer. He calls again, his voice echoing in every alcove, every rocky lee. He shouts himself hoarse.

Unsure if the blood on his face and dried brown on his arms is his own, he runs his hands over himself, feeling for cuts. Not until he touches his head does he wince. He looks at his fingers, wet with fresh blood from the gash in the back of his skull. He begins to despair and upbraids himself for it, furious at the tears stinging his eyes. He wipes them, smearing his cheeks with bloody dirt.

"Augustine!" he shouts. "*Anyone!*" He trudges over broken stone, stumbling in his search. He trips over a leg and crashes to the ground, lying there and groaning with his eyes closed. When at last he opens them, he is face to face with a woman. Her eyes are open too. They are turquoise, the waters of the Blue Lagoon. She is quite beautiful. And she is quite dead, crushed by the great blocks of the battery. This time, Belli allows himself to cry. He sobs for a full minute.

Eventually, he rises, gathering his bearing and with it, the will to keep looking. He bends next to a body and lifts the man's face from the ground by his thick, dark hair. It is not Augustine. Belli is flooded with guilty relief. He pulls another fistful of blood-matted hair, and this time recognizes the face. His eyes well with fresh tears. It is Matheus Cumbo, brave young sentry, a perfect, round hole in the centre of his brow where the musket ball passed. Belli lays the boy's face gently down.

There are bodies with heads missing altogether. The carpenter turns his attention to their hands, counting fingers, relieved when they tally ten. Some bodies are missing heads and hands—any one could be Augustine. Belli slumps to the ground and puts his aching head in his hands. It was he who had to break the news of Isabel's death to her children. Now, the awful task is his once more.

Then, there is a noise. A shifting of rubble. Belli is back on his feet, scrambling towards the sound. "*Hawn! Minn hemm?* Can you hear me?" He digs frantically, throwing rocks to the side. He bloodies his fingers and does not care. "*Ejja!* Say something!"

He stops, listens hard. No reply. It was just debris settling, or the wind playing tricks with sound. He kneels there before the mound of stone, probably nothing more now than a cairn.

Then, a noise. A shifting of rubble. And a muffled voice: "Oh! I'm here!"

Belli digs as a man possessed. Sweat burns as it seeps from open pores back into open cuts. Suddenly, a hand shoots through the fragmented stone. The carpenter grabs it and, throwing off remaining debris, pulls out the survivor.

A small, white-haired man emerges from the rocky prison. "God's blessings! God's thanks! *Grazzi sinjur*! *Grazzi hafna*!" Belli, not demonstrative by nature, hugs the man with enough strength to crush him.

"Easy. I did not survive the Turks to be killed by a Maltese."

Belli laughs. He feels guilty for it, surrounded as he is by the broken bodies of his countrymen. He releases his new companion and notices the man's face has gone pale, eyes haunted as they take in the grisly scene. "…Dragut's revenge," the old man whispers, barely audible.

"Let's go," Belli says quickly. "Perhaps there are others, hiding in the catacombs." He takes the man by the arm and leads him to the breach, where a dozen Iayalars are heaped. "So. What are you called?" Belli asks, stepping over bodies, grasping sections of wall for balance.

"Johannes."

"Pleased to meet you, Johannes. Now, let's get the hell out of here."

***

Most hours, Katrina kneels at Robert's bedside, alternately feeding him water and massaging his legs. He has lost much of his former self—his muscles diminished, face gaunt, eyes sunken. She talks to him, pours her heart out. She tells him about her brother.

Late one night, Dr Callus visited, and expressed great joy at Robert's rescue. The physician examined him, found that he had a broken rib, but told Katrina it would mend itself. All Robert needs is food to restore his body and comfort to restore his mind. Katrina is afraid, however, irreparable damage has been done to his senses. Occasionally, he opens his eyes but does not know her.

As much as she is unwilling to give her time to anything but Robert and Domenicus, she knows she must fetch food and water. She heads to her father's house to collect a few items, next to Belli's stable to feed the horse and the goat. After that, she makes a trip to the cistern.

Upon returning to the Falsone house, she stops cold in the doorway. Robert's bed is empty. Katrina drops the bucket of water at her feet, the crate of provisions on the tabletop, and runs outside to search the area around the house. There is no sign of him. She puts her hand against the wall to steady herself. Have *they* found out? Come to take him? She tears towards the rectory to find Father Tabone. Her chest burns as she pushes through the gate and pounds the path.

She need go no farther. There, in the churchyard, is Robert Falsone. He is on his knees, one arm resting loosely over the curve of Mea's tombstone, his head in the crook of his elbow. Kat crouches silently beside him and puts her hand on his. He looks up, meets her eyes, and buries his face in her neck as he sobs, there in the cool grass of the churchyard.

***

The sun burns bright and hot, baking Belli's wound. He is desperate for water. His entire being throbs, especially his head. It is a terrible hangover, but without the pleasure of drink.

He and Johannes walk an hour, the way strewn with dead goats that drank of poisoned cisterns. The Gozitan looks sadly at the animals, his eyes brimming. "That one was my goat. Or may as well have been. I kept goats, eight. Now they're gone. Like everything else."

Belli sweeps his surroundings. The land bears the scars of attack— razed fields, once carpeted with wildflowers, now black and smoking. The world seems empty of life. Could it be? Could it really be that of five thousand inhabitants, only two remain? It truly seems that way as they trudge the rolling terrain, taking the uphill slowly, the down cautiously. Johannes stops to rest against a low stone wall. His breathing has become increasingly laboured. Still, Belli is not keen on taking a break; if he stops now, he will collapse and not move again.

"We're almost there," he says.

"*Stenna*," Johannes pants. "One minute."

"You all right?"

"Yes. ...Not really. No. I think those blocks did some damage."

"Let me see." Belli helps Johannes to lift up his shirt. All along the man's chest and ribs are angry purple bruises. Belli does not know how to tell if anything is broken. He lets the shirt fall back into place. "It's not so bad," he lies. "You can make the harbour. One more hill. *Ejja*. I carry you."

The trek up the last hill to the harbour is painfully slow. There is nothing to motivate Belli or his companion, no promise of water, no promise of life. And while Johannes refuses to be carried, he still uses Belli as a crutch, further exhausting the carpenter. Ten minutes later, they make the summit.

The sight below takes Belli's breath: ten living men. He waves his free arm frantically and picks up his pace, all the time supporting Johannes. "Ho there! Over here!"

The men waiting by the waterfront look up in unison, and immediately head for the stone strewn spine of the slope. Behind them, the waters of Mġarr sparkle with the sun and ply with three galleys, the Order's red and white ensigns flapping against the masts.

Belli grunts. "Nice of those jackasses to show up."

By now, the ten survivors are mere paces away. "Hurry up!" one calls. "The feathered bastards of Mohammed have left and the feathered bastards of Christ are landing." He is a farmer, old and shrivelled, and the most colourful of a thoroughly motley looking crew. They are all old and sun-scorched, but that is where the commonalities end. The leader is short and sinewy. He wears a tattered brown *beritta* on his head and naked hostility in his small eyes. He introduces the other men, who range in height and girth: there is a tall, thin, tightly spooled glassblower; a muscular and scarred blacksmith; a one-eyed goatherd; a tiny fisherman with warm, green eyes; and a large grizzled one with a full grey beard.

"How in the hell did you lot escape Dragut?" Belli asks, incredulous.

"We didn't," the smithy replies. "Dragut didn't want us. He left us with a message for the Knights of St John. A warning of what comes to those who trouble Suleiman's realm."

CHAPTER FIFTY-TWO

Commotion in the streets startles Angelica into waking. She rises from the bench and rubs life back into her arm, numb from being pressed between her cheek and the hard surface.

Yesterday, she and Katrina spent all day outside the hospital, awaiting news. Shortly after dusk, Father Tabone brought them hope. Domenicus had squeezed his hand. Angelica jumped up from the bench, hugged her uncle and Katrina tight, and allowed herself a moment of relief. Father Tabone warned her to take caution in her joy—Domenicus has not broken the surface; there are fathoms yet.

The priest left, returning an hour later with bread and cheese, news that he had seen to Robert, and another request that the girls accompany him to the rectory. They thanked him for the bread and cheese and did not accompany him to the rectory.

Angelica and Katrina passed yet another night on the bench. Neither could sleep, so they began to reminisce, trading stories about Domenicus and even managing to laugh a little—until Angelica put a stop to it. "We talk about him as though he is dead. If we talk of him, we talk only of the present." An hour before dawn, she fell into broken sleep.

Now, Angelica is alone on the bench. Villagers make for the dockyard in droves. She is certain whatever draws them there is not another attack. No alarm has been raised, and in times of siege, people usually don't go running for the port to welcome the enemy. Whatever is happening, Kat will find out. Besides, nothing can make Angelica leave this spot, not for a second. In that second, someone might emerge from the infirmary with word.

She hates that she cannot be at her love's side, and wonders what would happen if she tried scaling the wall late at night. She would either fall and break her neck or get shot. Perhaps she can bribe the guard. But with what? She has nothing a nobleman of the Order could possibly want. She considers sneaking into the sacristy to steal the collection plate. But is gaining entry to the *Sacra Infermeria* really worth eternal damnation in hell?

She gives her head a good shake. Of course, it is.

***

The waterfront throngs with villagers and knights. Katrina stands in their midst, feeling more alone than she has ever felt in her life. Just when she thought she could bear no more worry, between her critically injured brother and Robert's fragile safety, along came news that managed to shatter all that was left of her world: massacre at Gozo.

So it is at the dockyard she has been waiting since. At the time of her arrival, people had already begun assembling. Now, with rumours of *Dragut's Revenge* coursing through the village, the crowd is five times what it was. She is tormented, feeling everything and nothing all at once. She tries shutting out the people around her, their morbid conversations and estimated death tolls.

It is another quarter-hour before the Order's galleys sweep into the harbour. Katrina almost reaches for the hand of the man next to her, just for something to hold onto. The crowd braces for the influx of Gozitan refugees about to flood the dock—there will be at least three thousand. Citizens of Birgu have brought wool blankets and barrels of fresh water. Surgeons and doctors await the new patients, now that those from the attack on Mdina have been tended.

Ten minutes later, the first galley shudders against the dock. Porters hurry to lower gangplanks. One by one, the survivors cross onto the dock. The twelfth to disembark is the carpenter.

Katrina's heart leaps with joy. "Belli!"

He looks up, searching the faces in the crowd for hers. "Katrina?"

"Over here!" she calls, pushing her way along. She makes it through and throws her arms around the big man. "Oh thank God!" He is bloody and battered and wonderful. "Are you hurt?"

"A few bruises."

Katrina looks beyond him to the gangplanks. Her father is usually first off a galley. He must have remained aboard to lend a hand with the wounded survivors. She stares at the dock, unable to turn away. But no other disembarks.

"…Where is he?" Her voice is stifled.

Belli shakes his head. His expression conveys what Katrina cannot bear to hear. Her breath comes rapid, shallow. She has been smashed in the chest with a board. Belli crouches, puts his hands on her shoulders, looks into her eyes.

"Your father is gone."

CHAPTER FIFTY-THREE

Angelica has barely moved from what has become *her* bench, going home only when Father Tabone carries her to the rectory in his cart as she sleeps. When she wakes, she is cross, tells him to leave her where she is. Then she hugs him and thanks him for his love and goes right back to her place outside the *Sacra Infermeria.*

Katrina is at her side whenever possible, worried sick about her brother, now further tortured by the likelihood of her father's death. Her eyes are dark, haunted with grief, her body too thin. Still, it astounds Angelica that her friend has managed to keep a sane head in the midst of all this. Especially when Angelica herself is falling apart after the news of Augustine.

✳✳✳

Upon returning from Sicily, the Protomedicus Alonso Predal hears about Domenicus from Dr Callus, a fellow resident of Mdina. As head of all medical practitioners, Alonso goes straight to the palace of the Grand Master to ask d'Homedes to relax the rules of the *Sacra Infermeria* and grant Angelica Tabone permission to enter. Alonso explains that she worked as a laundress at the hospital, and the man she wishes to see was once apprentice to the surgeon de Gabriac. The man's name is Domenicus Montesa.

The Grand Master does not glance up from his papers. "No."

So Angelica's employer pays Domenicus a visit himself. He is deeply under, somewhere between coma and sleep, but his face is no longer deathly pale. His fever has subsided, and the wounds, though grievous, do not fester. Alonso watches the patient's eyelids flutter. He thinks he can make out a smile.

Must be having a dream, he thinks. *A good dream.*

He tells Angelica about it. And she smiles, too.

✳✳✳

In the days that follow Alonso's visit, there are many more comings and goings—Father Tabone, the apothecary Antoni Zammit, and the knights beside whom Domenicus fought that awful day. But there is one person who

469

does not come. And with each day that passes, Angelica grows more puzzled by his absence—the carpenter, Belli.

Those who visit bring news of the young man's condition, which continues to improve: "His colour is returning." "The wounds no longer leak through his bandages." "His heart beats stronger."

Today, Dr Callus is Angelica's sunrise. "Domenicus opened his eyes. They stayed so less than two seconds, but were open nonetheless." Her heart swells with new hope.

She is only sorry that she was not there to greet her love when at last he looked.

***

A breeze carries the sweetness of twilight through one of many windows that cut the Florentine villa. Long white drapes flutter into the Count Raimondo di Bonfatti's bedchamber like tails of twin doves. Wall sconces give off fragile light, which flickers with the passage of warm air. Franco sits at his father's bedside, fingers tapping the plump velvet arms of his chair. He smells game cooking, but laced with the aroma of roasting meat is the sour smell of illness.

The count's faint breath is near hypnotising, *rasp, rasp, wheeze*, again and again. Eyes half-closed, Franco takes in the chamber, which is in every way opposite his austere bedroom at the *auberge*. Cornices are carved with apples and grapes tumbling in a delicious cascade. He follows the wooden cornucopia to the tall ceiling, painted with naked cherubs playing in the soft, pink folds of heaven. The fresco makes him think of his mother; the count had it drawn specially for her.

Franco drops his gaze onto his father, tucked beneath layers of fat, feathered quilts. The man looks dead. He will be soon. Franco is startled at how little he cares. Truly, the only reason he is even here is that his younger brother Dante sent a letter to the Grand Master begging Franco's return.

The Grand Master. Malta. *Damn it*. No matter how hard he tries to avoid thinking about it, he sees it in everything. No, not *it*. *Her*. Whether watching moonlight splay across the Arno or hearing bells toll in the distance or smelling smoke from the torches that line the walls of Cambio's Palazzo, he thinks of Katrina Montesa. He imagines her on his arm as he crosses the Ponte Vecchio, pictures her next to him at a pew in the cathedral. Each time, he smiles for a moment. Then, he remembers the awful thing he did, the thing he cannot undo, and his guilt rises like bile.

Franco finds some relief in the constant interruptions—physicians checking on the count, servants bringing food. They stop him from thinking, something he can rarely accomplish on his own.

So it was a queer thing this morning when he did not think of Malta at all. But around noon, as he crossed the open piazza surrounding Santa Maria del Fiore, he heard rumours of a vast Turkish fleet attacking the Maltese archipelago, sweeping thousands into captivity.

Franco's first thought was of Katrina. He prayed God kept her safe from the barbarians if the rumour proved true. His next thought was that it was probably false. A fleet the size of the one described would not have passed unnoticed over the Mediterranean. There would have been time to call the absent knights—including Franco—back to the island to help in its defence. Even if the rumour proved true, Dragut Raïs and his rats plundered throughout Franco's time on Malta, and the Order had always thwarted him. Why would the outcome be different this time? Perhaps there had been a small raid, but surely not the disaster of reports. Still, Franco will write to Marcello for word.

A knock recalls Franco to his surroundings. He rises from his chair and goes to see who calls. It is the count's doctor, physician to the ruling dei Medicis, here for his evening examination of the patient. He greets Raimondo di Bonfatti's eldest son with a bow and proceeds to the bed. Franco once again occupies the armchair. He turns his attention to his fingernails. They will soon need buffing.

"Count di Bonfatti," the doctor says quietly. Franco does not look up.

"Count di Bonfatti." This time, Franco lifts his gaze. He is surprised to see the physician, suddenly wan, looking directly at him. Even more surprising is the form of address—Franco is not the Count di Bonfatti.

"My lord, your father is dead."

Oh. Franco *is* the Count di Bonfatti. The realisation begins to take hold. The Grand Master may be moved to release him from the Order, now that this great responsibility has passed to him. And he no longer must answer to his father. He no longer must answer to anyone at all! He can do as he pleases. For a moment, Franco contents himself with this newfound liberty. But it dies as quickly as being born.

He still must answer to God.

***

Angelica waits at the hospital gate, anxious at her uncle's approach from the ward. She peppers him with questions. "Has he woke? Is he in pain? Has he spoken? Does he ask for me?"

"Domenicus is about to break the surface," Father Tabone announces happily. "He is peaceful. He said one word only."

"What word, Uncle?"

"Your name."

Angelica cries and smiles and cries some more. For the first time in many days, the tears are not of despair. Katrina arrives minutes later, and Angelica shares the wonderful news.

"Thank you," Katrina says, tearful. "Thank you for being here when I cannot."

"Of course," is all Angelica can manage past the lump in her throat. She wants desperately to say something to console Katrina in the loss of her father, but cannot bring herself to renew her friend's grief. So, she simply takes Katrina's hand into hers and squeezes.

***

Domenicus is conscious though still battling fever. A vaguely familiar man stands over him and smiles. Now that Domenicus is alert, the anaesthesia of delirium gives way to the terrible pain of his musket wounds. At first, the fire almost sends him back into his abyss. But he fights to stay awake. He grimaces and shuts his eyes, trying to stop the pain that stabs through his abdomen like a thousand serrated blades. He grits his teeth, opens his lids, two dams breaking to twin floods. He musters the strength to smile back at the man, who he thinks could be Dr Callus.

"I used to serve food here," Domenicus says. And with that, he passes out.

The next day, he awakens for a full hour. Father Tabone is beside him. The priest tells him of Angelica's unending vigil and Katrina's constant company. "My niece is heartsick she cannot be here with you. She will not move from the bench except when I abduct her after she is asleep."

"My guardian angel."

"Yes, in every way. On the walls of Mdina, it was she who insisted there was life left in you when others deemed you dead. But for her, truly you would be."

"I would give anything to see her. Is there no way?"

Father Tabone shakes his head. "Afraid not. She went behind my back and stole the collection money to bribe the guards. They took her coins and sent her away."

Domenicus takes a deep breath, already winded from talking. There are so many things he wants to know, so many people to ask about. For a moment, it overwhelms him, and he struggles for air, chest hitching with raspy breaths.

"Gently, Domenicus," Father Tabone says, putting a hand on his brow. "Rest easy."

"You must tell Angelica to take care of herself. I am well tended here."

"I will tell her. And she won't listen."

"So tell her if I worry too much about her, my stitches will come undone and I'll die."

"She is distressed and in love. She is not an idiot."

Domenicus laughs, and the pain that accompanies his laughter is so tremendous he almost cries. He pushes past it. "...My sister.... How is she?"

"When she heard the news that you were shot, she was more than devastated. But she has been brave, comforting Angelica despite her own pain. Truly, your sister adores you."

Domenicus smiles, though he aches knowing he cannot see her either. "And my father? This has been a difficult time for him. I'm sure he has barely left my side. I'm surprised he is not here now."

Father Tabone is silent for a moment. Finally, he says, "Your father loves you very much." The priest rises. "Rest. I have news of your progress to bring to Angelica and… your family."

***

In the bed next to Domenicus there is an old Gozitan named Johannes, being treated for fractured ribs. At first, that is all the young man learns about his neighbour. Each day, however, he pushes himself to stay up a little longer, hoping to see his father. Somehow, Augustine never comes when Domenicus is awake. Now, he speaks to Johannes in an effort to ward off sleep.

"You are from Gozo, you said? Good honey there."

"The best," Johannes replies.

"Why are you at a hospital here in Birgu?"

"I don't suppose you think I should be at one on Gozo?"

Domenicus furrows his brow. "Well… yes."

Johannes snickers. "Who would tend me? A goat? Even those are all gone."

Domenicus is confounded. Perhaps the old man is delirious. "I don't understand."

"My God, boy, how badly were you hurt? You really have not heard? It's been a month!" Johannes coughs, grimaces. "Gozo was sacked!"

"*What?*" Instinctively, Domenicus tries to sit upright, but pain forces him to stay on his back.

"Dragut came. Burned everything, took everyone. Left twelve of us behind. Well, left ten, but me and this fellow Belli survived the—"

"Belli?"

"Yes, a carpenter. Queer name, I know. Good lad though. Pulled me from the rubble."

Domenicus can barely follow. His mind is overworked, trying to make sense of the news while ignoring the fiery currents coursing through his body. "You and Belli, were you alone?"

"I was alone, but the carpenter was with his brother, I think, or cousin. He was killed. At least, that's what Belli thought. He never found the man's body."

***

The Baron d'Aramon, French Ambassador to the Ottoman Empire, arrived aboard a galley of France this morning and sits now at a desk across from Grand Master Juan d'Homedes.

"Naturally, his Excellency will be sending a relief force to Tripoli?" Aramon asks in a way that makes a statement of the question.

The Grand Master looks at the Ambassador as though he has just declared himself a raging necrophile. "No, monsieur le baron. The outpost will manage."

Aramon draws his eyebrows together. Has the lesson of the citadel already been lost on this old fool? "With all due respect, my lord, Tripoli will never bear up against a determined salvo from Dragut Raïs and Sinan Pasha. Sire, surely after the rape of Gozo—"

"That was the fault of her governor, Galatian de Sesse."

Aramon knows full well that it was the fault of the Grand Master for doing less than nothing to protect the tiny island, but saying so would be less than fruitless. "Very well, if your Grace allows me, I will sail to Tripoli and negotiate terms."

D'Homedes frowns. "You are on dangerous ground. If you succeed in negotiating the cessation of Ottoman hostilities, you will earn yourself the wrath of Sultan Suleiman, ally of your motherland France. If you do not succeed, it is the anger of Emperor Charles you will excite. And regardless of the outcome, your king will be displeased that you acted without his consent."

"King Henri will understand my need for haste," Aramon insists.

At length, Grand Mater Juan d'Homedes relents, though does so with ice in his eyes and frost in his tone. "Go, then. Treat with your Turkish allies."

***

"Why was this kept from me?" Domenicus demands, though his voice is still too weak to convey his true fury. He coughs and sputters.

"Easy," Dr Callus replies.

"Easy? *Easy*? My father is dead, goddamn it!"

"Shut up," surgeon de Gabriac snaps. "You apprenticed here long enough to know even the slightest upsetting of the humours could kill you." He glares at Johannes, in the bed next to Domenicus. "Of course we planned to tell you. We were waiting until you were strong enough."

"I *am* strong enough," he rasps.

"*Merde.* You may still die. It will be weeks, months, before you even walk."

Domenicus falls angrily silent for a moment. He looks from de Gabriac, whose face is set in stern lines, to Callus, whose expression is just concerned. And then, everything wells up inside. "I... I just... He was my father..." He breaks and cries. Hard. Tears streaming onto the pillow. "I'm sorry. So sorry. You saved my life, both of you. I just..." He turns his face to the side, embarrassed.

Callus crouches. "Easy," the doctor repeats. "*Kollox sew.* Everything is all right." But everything is not all right. Everything could not be farther from all right.

De Gabriac pats Domenicus gently on the shoulder. "I will bring you brandy, to ease the pain." He does not indicate which pain the brandy is supposed to ease.

Slowly, painfully, Domenicus lifts his hand and wipes his eyes. He sniffles and looks to Callus. "Are you sure my father is dead?"

"There is no certainty. But there is also no hope. Had he survived, he would be here, now."

"He could have been taken captive."

"Augustine would die before being led off in chains," Callus replies.

Domenicus shifts a little higher on the bed. "How long since the knights departed?"

The doctor furrows his brow. "Departed? For where?"

"To rescue the five thousand," Domenicus replies impatiently. "To avenge our dead."

"They have not gone."

"Not yet? Good Lord, what are they waiting for?"

"No, you misunderstand me. The knights are not going anywhere."

Domenicus struggles to raise himself on his elbows, cringing all the way. "But my father died for *their* fight. The knights are sworn to protect the people of Malta."

Callus looks down. "A knight cares more about the consistency of his horse's shit than he does the people of Malta."

Domenicus sinks back against the bed. The agony he feels at the loss of his father is ten times that of his musket wounds. He recalls his childhood awe of the knights. How he wished he could be one. *That pirate Dragut is no match for the Protectors of Malta!* he once declared to Robert.

Protectors of Malta—it is laughable.

Domenicus thinks of Robert, his best friend in the world, locked in some nameless hell, Mea dead, both at the hand of the Order. Now, he must accept that his beloved father has been abandoned to death by the very knights he spent his life serving.

"I am sorry," Callus says.

Domenicus flashes. "I'm sorry too. Sorry I ever had faith in this worthless Order. Sorry my father ever pledged it his service. ...Sorry the musket ball didn't finish its job."

"Talk sense, man."

Domenicus looks Callus in the face. "Thank you for everything Giuseppe, I owe you my life. I will never forget it. Now kindly help me out of this bed."

"Don't be so stupid."

"I'm not. I want to go. I will take nothing from the knights, their hospital, their food. I can lie in bed at home. And when I am well, I will find my father's body, and avenge his death."

"These are ravings."

Domenicus shakes his head. "I've never been of a clearer mind in my life, or of a more determined purpose. Now are you going to help me out of this bed, or not?"

Callus frowns. "Of course not."

"Fine." Domenicus pushes himself up and, through the nauseating pain, swings his legs over the side of the bed and places his feet on the floor.

A moment later, he is unconscious on the ground, wounds reopened and gushing through their dressings. Callus and de Gabriac labour two hours to redo what took as many seconds to undo.

***

As Belli watches Domenicus stir into waking, terrible guilt descends upon him—it is his fault Augustine was on Gozo in the first place. Because of this, he could not bring himself to face the man's son. When Callus ordered him to stay away from the hospital until Domenicus could bear news of his father's death, Belli was quite willing to comply.

Now, he recalls the day Isabel died. That day, Domenicus blamed him. Today, the blame will be laid upon him once again. The young man squints at Belli as if through a haze. Part of him hopes he will remain unrecognized. But Domenicus blinks, and the light of recognition dawns in his eyes. The light goes dark.

"I... I'm sorry," Belli stammers, struggling for the right words, saying the wrong ones.

"And I am tired of people telling me they're sorry," Domenicus lashes.

"You don't want me here. I don't blame you. I deserve your anger." Belli rises, turns to go.

"Wait." The carpenter turns back around, looks down at his big hands.

"What you deserve is my love," Domenicus says. "All my life you've been a second father to me and to Katrina. Pa went with you because he wanted to. Stay, please."

Belli sits down.

"Tell me of my father's last hours."

CHAPTER FIFTY-FOUR

18 August 1551

Every morning, Katrina goes to the dockyard to watch for a galley bearing her father—alive or dead. She clings to the remote hope that he is alive, and until she sees his body, will hold to that belief.

At the docks, knights just shoo her away. But today, the waterfront is in ferment. Today, even the Grand Master is among the rabble. And he is beyond furious.

The word is annihilation at Tripoli.

Katrina learns everything she can from conversations around her, piecing bits together to make the whole story: late yesterday, the French ambassador's galleys arrived from Tripoli—now the property of Sultan Suleiman—and attempted to enter the Maltese harbour. The Grand Master had them greeted as enemies, closing the mouth of the bay with a great chain raised only in times of siege. The guns of St Angelo boomed, not in welcome, but in threat. The galleys have not moved since.

Grand Master Juan d'Homedes is livid with Ambassador Amaron for negotiating safe passage for Tripoli's governor Gaspard de Valliers, whom the Grand Master believes should have been handed over to the Turks. The Sacred Council finally persuaded d'Homedes to permit Valliers and his knights ashore, but the Grand Master stood firm in denying Ambassador Amaron. D'Homedes declared him a traitor who sold Tripoli to the enemy and would likely barter a similar deal for Malta. The knight Valette was allowed to take ten small boats out to the anchored galleys and collect the refugees.

Now, Katrina watches as the first of these boats shudders against the dock. Gaspard de Valliers, bailiff of Auvergne, Grand Marshal of the Order, and former governor of Tripoli, climbs onto the pier.

Grand Master d'Homedes, trembling with rage, shoves through the crowd and assails him. "You were entrusted to protect Tripoli!" he explodes.

"Here is another title to add to your extensive collection: coward! You had an impregnable fortress, which you surrendered without a fight. You are stripped of habit and rank. The name de Valliers will be ripped from the wall!"

De Valliers looks stunned. "But, your Excellency, *you* abandoned us. For years, I have begged you to improve defences at Tripoli. The governors before me begged you. But you never sent money for fortifications, or even troops to defend what few bulwarks we had."

The Grand Master coils up, a snake about to strike. "*I sent men!*"

"Calabrian shepherd boys! Terrified children who panicked and tried to blow up the fortress!"

"Such mutiny is reason enough to have you court-martialed and hanged," d'Homedes snarls. He glares at de Valliers, the French knights beside him. "What of the Maltese foot soldiers?"

"Taken, Sire, by Dragut."

Juan d'Homedes goes white with fury. "You and your French compatriots are transported to Malta on the ambassador's galleys, while your troops are forsaken to Turkish captivity? *Despicable!*"

De Valliers balls fists at his sides. "You are the architect of this disaster! You are not fit for the office you hold."

The Grand Master strikes the knight to shocked gasps of the crowd. "How dare you! Emperor Charles will hear of this, King Henri too. Every monarch on the Continent will know the name de Valliers is a synonym for cowardice!" D'Homedes waves to one in his bodyguard. "Take this traitor to the dungeon to await trial. Flog him, ten lashes!"

The crowd explodes. Knights of the Spanish *langues* cheer as de Valliers is led away, while knights of France rally to his defence. "*Injuste!* De Valliers *est innocent!*" The Maltese don't seem to know whose side to take or to care. They are simply enjoying the spectacle. Katrina pushes her way through the madness and runs after the Grand Master, tightly surrounded by his guards.

"Grand Master!" she calls. "Grand Master!"

He swings round. "*What?* What do you want?"

"Sire, please, what is being done about the Gozitan captives?"

"What do *you* care?" he snaps.

"My father was on Gozo. He served the Order. He may have been captured."

"Do not bother me with this nonsense."

Nonsense? Pa is not *nonsense*. But before she can argue the point, d'Homedes speaks. "Your father is dead—whether he is in the rubble of the citadel or in the belly of Dragut's ship."

Katrina cannot believe the coldness of the man before her. She narrows her eyes. "De Valliers is right. You are not fit for the office you hold."

"*Guard!* Take her! Ten lashes!" A large, muscled man grabs hold of Katrina from behind. She cries out and struggles against his grip. D'Homedes calmly addresses all present: "The next person to address me in a manner less than reverent will know the taste of the chopping block."

At the flogging post, Katrina's wrists are tightly bound with rope and yanked above her head. Her back is bare, her shift torn down the middle. The sun beats mercilessly on her as she hangs like a slab of meat at the butcher shop. A gentle wind passes over her exposed flesh, raising tiny hairs. Her throat is tight, breath coming shallow and quick, then ragged and deep. Katrina stands on a small wooden platform, perfect for the gathering crowd to watch. She sees the faces, knows most of them. Some are filled with pity, some with amused contempt. She tries to shut them out, looks above the crowd, to the sea beyond, where gulls bob and play on its shimmering surface.

Heavy footsteps resound behind her. *Here comes the butcher.* She feels his breath on the back of her neck. She clenches her jaw and promises herself she will not cry out. Her gaze falls on the upturned faces once more. There, at the back, is Angelica, her eyes willing Katrina to be strong.

The flog is loosed from its tight coil. The whip snaps. Its bite is agonizing, sharp and deep and hot. Tears spring to her eyes, the faces before her running together. It snaps again, the audience cringing at the sound of leather cutting lines into her skin. Her only solace is that Robert is not here to watch, or surely he would end up dead trying to save her. The whip cracks a third time, harder, breaking her flesh excruciatingly and with it, her vow of silent endurance. She cries out, tears streaming down her sweaty face. Her back is on fire. She does not think she can endure seven more. Again the flog comes down, ripping the delicate fabric of her skin. She shuts her eyes and prays it will end soon. But it does not.

Katrina lies on her straw pallet, her exposed back a crisscross of bloody lines, her wrists scored from the rope, flesh puckered and oozing. Angelica bends over her, gently dabbing the weals with honey. Katrina inhales sharply, even such careful touch bringing fire to the raised lacerations.

She wants her father, wants to nestle in his warm embrace, wants to hear his wonderful voice. It tears her apart that she will never do those things again. She pries herself from the grip of self-pity—she still has Belli and, if the miracle holds, Domenicus too. She looks tearfully over her shoulder.

"I need to see my brother," she says.

Angelica sighs, brushes Katrina's hair behind her ear. "Then try not to get yourself executed."

CHAPTER FIFTY-FIVE

Angelica puts her hand on Domenicus, touching his face as if for the first time. Eight days after his disastrous attempt to leave the *Sacra Infermeria*, he was pronounced ready to go, provided he would be under constant supervision. Angelica was more than willing.

Now, he lies unconscious in the back of Father Tabone's small cart, thanks to a dosage of mandrake and belladonna given to ease his journey. Angelica watches the warm, autumn sunlight on his face and longs to kiss him. It will be a while yet—they are barely halfway home. She wants to hit her uncle with a stick. Good Lord, he drives slowly.

At the rectory, Father Tabone helps Angelica settle Domenicus comfortably into her bed. She will sleep on the floor in the storage room. As she covers him with a blanket, a knock sounds at the front door. Her uncle answers it. Alone at last, Angelica bends to kiss Domenicus, but at the approaching footsteps, bolts upright.

Katrina flies into the room, takes her brother's hand and presses it to her cheek. "He's going to be all right!"

Angelica smiles. "Yes, he is. Why don't you wake him? He'll be so happy to see you."

Katrina shakes her head. "No, I couldn't. He looks too peaceful. Besides, I'm sure he'd rather see you first anyway." She crouches, passes her hand over his brow. "I can't believe we almost lost you," she whispers. "Don't *ever* make me worry like that again, you bastard."

***

That evening, Domenicus awakens, starts at the unfamiliar surroundings. What happened to the ward? He must be dead. He is groggy and in pain, not exactly his idea of heaven. But, it is too comfortable to be hell. Then, he sees her sitting at the windowsill. His guardian angel, bathed in moonlight. So, he is in heaven, after all.

"Angelica," he whispers. She is at his side in an instant. For so long have they both imagined this moment that neither seems to know what to do. They hold each other in a gaze, lose themselves in it, find themselves in it. Domenicus could stay this way forever.

Angelica brushes his cheek with her fingers. "Hello, my love."

"Hello, back." A tear rolls from his eye. "How..." His voice is gruff. "How can I possibly thank you for saving my life?"

She smiles. "By living."

In the days that follow, Domenicus sees beauty in everything she does. The way she plumps his pillow, the way she flicks away a curl that falls in front of her eye, the way she blushes when she catches him staring. He watches her through the window when she is at work outside, sleeves rolled up past her elbows, tendrils slipping from her bun. She bends over a trough and scrubs the linens, often stopping to wipe sweat from her brow. She wrings the garments, flips them out, hangs them on the line. Little things. Mesmerizing things. As if touched by his gaze, she glances to the window. Her face instantly floods with worry. He smiles to allay her concern.

Every day, Domenicus grows stronger. He takes great pleasure from time spent with Angelica. But, his happiness fills him with shame. Augustine is gone. Domenicus loved the man more than anything and has not had the chance to mourn his loss. He can still feel the weight of his father's hand on his shoulder. The grief gnaws at him, dull and relentless. The knights will not avenge him, or anyone. As these angry thoughts spur Domenicus to toss restlessly, his own weakness reminds him that he can do nothing until he is strong enough.

***

Angelica finds great joy in tending him. When he is awake, she brings his meals and feeds him, though she knows he is quite capable of feeding himself. She reads to him and plays her flute, shaves him and brings him *qubbajt*. The fresh scent of baking bread regularly fills the rectory. She keeps his wounds clean and changes their dressings. If he is cold, she brings him all the blankets she can find; hot, she bathes away the heat. If he grows uncomfortable in one position, she helps him find a new one. If he is in pain, she holds him and gives him the medicine that takes it away.

As Angelica combs her patient's hair, her uncle pops his head into the room. "Hmph. My niece never fusses over me like this," he grumps. "I can't even recall the last time she baked *me* bread." But there is no sincerity in the complaint. With a parting nod, he leaves them.

"Angelica, rest," Domenicus says. "You do too much."

She raises an eyebrow. "Want me to stop?"

He gives a sheepish smile. "No."

She laughs. "Well, then? And don't worry. I rest plenty when you are under the herbs."

But that is not entirely true. It is when he is asleep, and her uncle snoring, that she does what she cannot with Domenicus watching. She takes a damp sponge and runs it gently over his face and neck, down his right arm, his left, across his chest, over the ripples of his stomach to the cave of his navel, down each leg. She massages the supple muscles of his thighs and calves as she goes. Mindful of virtue, she is always careful to keep *that* part of him covered.

Tonight, a sharp gust blows through her open window, slipping his blanket. Angelica gasps and averts her eyes. Something compels her to look again. She feels herself stir. It is wrong, and she knows it. She can't help it. Suddenly, he shifts. She fairly jumps, quickly throwing the sheet over him.

When Angelica passes the sponge over his skin the next night, his blanket does not slip by accident. Tonight, she takes a longer look, very aware of every sound—his breathing, her heart pounding, the crickets outside. She looks closely. Without thinking, she touches him. A shiver runs through her. Frightened, she snaps her hand back and runs off.

She forbids herself from taking any more advantage of the sleeping man. For most of the following morning and afternoon, she busies herself in the kitchen. *He knows. He must.* She is not sure if the thought terrifies or excites her. It does both.

Tonight, despite all contrary promises to herself, she allows her fingers to linger. Her touch is curious, gentle, her movement instinctive. She is amazed he does not wake. The drugs must be strong. As she sits on the edge of the bed, she closes her eyes, allowing her other senses to take over as she explores. A warm breeze, salted with surf, sweetened with wild grass, swirls around her with the darkness. His skin is delicate. She luxuriates in touching him. He shifts. This time, she does not run away. Instead, she leans forward, kisses him, feels herself on fire.

Suddenly, her uncle's rasping snore douses her flames. She sits straight up, swiftly covering Domenicus with three layers of blankets. She looks at his face, bathed in the bluish moonlight streaming through her window. She is certain there is a little smile on his lips.

The next morning, as Angelica serves Domenicus his breakfast, he props himself up on his elbows, squints at the brightness of the day. "I had a wonderful dream last night."

She almost drops the bowl, her voice a squeak. "Did you?"

He nods. "Yes. It was about you."

"Oh?"

He sighs. "A wonderful dream."

But the day turns out to be a nightmare. It is particularly painful for him, his dormant wounds seeming to come awake again. He throws up and cries and clings to Angelica. He pushes her away. A moment later, he reaches for her. She cleans his face and holds him close, and prepares the sedative sponge as de Gabriac showed her. She rocks him gently to sleep and does not move from his side. Father Tabone does a bad job with the linens, then ruins a meal over the hearth. Angelica can tell he is pleased with himself for having managed to cook something without burning down the rectory.

As the sun slips into its western cradle, Domenicus opens his eyes. In an instant, Angelica is on her knees at the bedside. "Are you comfortable? Do you want another blanket? Some water? What can I bring you? Anything you want."

"All I want is right here with me."

She smiles, checks his wounds. "They are healing well."

"Oh? And how do you know that?" he teases.

She shrugs. "I suppose since there is no evil smell about them, and you are no longer burning with fever, that they are healing, but," she winks, "what do I know?"

Domenicus grins. "Quite a bit, I think." He manages to sit up, his back supported by pillows.

"Not really, I'm just repeating what Callus said the last time he stopped in to check on you. Besides, he and de Gabriac told me what to look for."

"You are my guardian angel, truly."

Angelica recalls the last few nights. No guardian angel would have taken such liberties with a compromised man.

"Your sister was here again today," she says.

Domenicus brightens. "How is she? I miss her awfully."

"She comes every day, but you are always asleep. She refuses to wake you. I tell you, it has been difficult for her without you, and now, with the devastating news about your father... I'll go get her. She wants to see you." Angelica begins to rise but Domenicus stops her.

"Wait. Don't go. Not just yet. I want to enjoy you a little longer now that I feel better."

She looks down at his hand, closed around her wrist. She feels his strength. Unable to resist any longer, she bends, brings her mouth to his. The kiss is deep, a kiss of longing, a kiss of fulfilment. As their lips move slowly together, she reaches for the drawstring of his pants and gives a tug. Her hand slips inside, soon finds what it seeks. He inhales—almost a gasp. She pulls her hand away.

"Oh God, did I hurt you?"

"Only with desire."

And there are no more words. She takes his hands in hers, brings them to the frayed string that ties her creamy shift in a crisscross over her chest. Slowly, he pulls the string. He slides her blouse off her bare shoulders and down, pausing to kiss her throat, his breath soft on her skin. She runs her mouth along the trail of sparse, sandy-coloured hairs leading up from her lower abdomen to his navel. His breath comes faster. Her hair, her warmth, flows over him in a soft and fragrant wave. He pulls her close, her body melting against his. He runs his fingertips along a winding path up her legs, caressing the dimples of her knees, the length of her thighs. He kisses her mouth, one hand running down the slope of her back. She shudders, every part of her awake and wild to his touch.

A moment later, she is beneath him, clinging to him as the heat between them grows. Gentle currents swirl around them. Domenicus closes his eyes, moves with the rhythm of instinct, their hearts pounding with that same rhythm. Her hands are in his hair, brushing it back from his face. Their sweat runs and mingles. They hold each other, a hot flurry of lips and hands. It is sweet and warm, always growing in intensity, always rising to new heights.

Until, in a sudden burst, it all rushes together, as stars falling from the sky.

CHAPTER FIFTY-SIX

Now that Domenicus is nearly well again, Angelica has returned to her work in Mdina. He wakes, but the sight before him convinces him he is in a dream. Sitting in a chair at the end of the bed is Robert Falsone. Domenicus blinks. He says nothing, briefly lost of his ability to speak.

Robert grins. "See what happens when I'm not around to look after you?"

Domenicus sits up, shaking some, eyes misting. "No one told me... No one told me you were released. Robert! Is it really you? Robert! It's so good to see you!" Domenicus jumps from the bed, and the friends embrace, though, from the wincing, both are in pain and trying to hide it.

"A fine pair we make," Robert says. And they burst into laughter, laughing until it hurts, laughing through the pain, two broken boys whose spirits endure.

"I wanted more than anything to come to the hospital, but your sister would not allow it. My safety, she said. I think she just didn't want me to see you before she got to. I asked that no one tell you I'd been freed. I wanted to."

Domenicus smiles, shakes his head. "I can't believe you are here, now. It doesn't feel real." He squeezes Robert's arm, just to make sure. "Tell me what happened."

"It was your sister and Father Tabone. They came the night of the siege. The guards were summoned to the defences. I didn't even know there was an attack."

Domenicus raises his eyebrows in surprise. "Father Tabone? Really?"

Robert nods. "The priest can handle a hatchet, I tell you. He smashed all the doors in the prison. The cells were empty, apart from the bones in one. Poor bastard. That would have been me."

"Where have you been staying?"

"My house. Been a prisoner there too actually. I've left only twice— first to the churchyard and now. I know what you'll say. Same thing Katrina

487

does. It's not safe. But to live forever in fear, that is no life at all. I will be quiet, but not silent."

"Actually, for the time being, go ahead and shout." Domenicus pauses, reconsiders. "Well, not really, but the danger is in Italy. Franco is back in Florence. He's the only threat to you. No one else knew anything, and if anyone noticed your absence, no one would care about your return given recent events."

The two friends fall silent for a time. Robert speaks first. "I am overcome about your father. Augustine was the best of men. The very best."

Domenicus feels bitterness come over him. "The Order has taken our parents, all. In one way or another, the Knights of St John are responsible for all their deaths."

Robert sighs. "At least our parents are together now."

"How can you see any good in this? After what you've been through..."

"I've been dealt enough ugliness by the Order to make me full of hatred for three lifetimes, but hate will only make my soul heavy. I just want to be."

"But your mother... what they did to her..." Domenicus presses.

"I was heartbroken when Father Tabone told me. I am heartbroken still. But she is with my pa and brother now. She will never want for anything again."

Domenicus longs for Robert's acceptance. It will be a while yet.

There is a sudden pounding of steps in the hallway. The young men look to the door. Katrina bursts in, dispersing the now solemn air. By the time she reaches Domenicus, she is crying. She throws her arms tight around him. He hugs her back, burying his face in her shoulder.

"You look wonderful!" she says.

He wipes his tears. "You are beautiful. I'm sorry I scared you. And I'm sorry I was always asleep when you came to see me."

"It's all right." She squeezes his hands. "You are quite pleasant when you're unconscious."

Domenicus gives his sister's braid a gentle tug. He reaches into his pocket and produces the brilliant blue topaz Marcello tossed him at the gates of Mdina. It sparkles with the day. It dumbfounds Katrina and Robert. Domenicus laughs at their expressions, and repeats the words Augustine once said when they so sorely needed to hear them: "Our little family is going to be just fine, I promise."

CHAPTER FIFTY-SEVEN

The months that follow are quiet. Fully recovered, Domenicus prepares to travel to Sicily at the end of the harvest, to study at the apothecary school as his father hoped he would do. Augustine had spoken with great excitement about Etna, the volcano that rises up and up, an endless black wave. Domenicus will go see it first—Pa would like that. When his studies are complete, perhaps he and Angelica can venture to Spain, the land of his father's ancestors. He wonders if it snows in the northern realm of Aragon—Angelica would like that.

Before heading anywhere, however, Domenicus is determined to visit Gozo, the tiny island that is now but a massive grave. He will do his father the honour of finding his body and laying him to rest next to his beloved wife.

***

Robert and Katrina pass peaceful days together. He, too, is strong again and has found work as Belli's apprentice. Years earlier, upon seeing the bow Robert made for Katrina, Belli declared carpentry was in the young man's blood. Belli often remarks he is delighted he was right. Since taking on Robert, the carpenter's assignments have doubled. Together, they've been commissioned to build everything from formal dining tables to ornate bookcases that grace the spaces of knights and nobles alike. Several wealthier churches have contracted the pair to restore old pews. Robert loves his job. It is his business to create, and he is happy in his business.

One evening, he and Katrina take a walk along the copper coloured fields that unfold beyond Birgu. They bring along Robert's goat. It bleats and tramps and chews on hardy weeds. Robert breathes in everything, his senses awake to every nuance of his surroundings, especially Katrina next to him. The air is warm and safe and smells of salt. They pass through the countryside under a low sun. In this great patchwork, they find a soft, mossy spot and sit facing each other. Robert kisses Katrina's bent knee, rests his hand on it.

"Remember the day I told you I didn't need a castle?"

She nods. "That day on the rocks by the water."

489

He smiles. "Yes. That day, I said all I wanted was a simple plot for my goat and me. And a princess... a beautiful one... one with proper manners."

Katrina laughs. "The one who would teach *you* proper manners."

"Well, I have my plot and my goat." He produces Isabel's ribbon from his pocket, having taken it from Katrina a few days ago without her knowing. The ribbon is changed; it is still blue but has been tightly woven into a ring. A simple, exquisite ring. He takes Katrina's hand. "All I need now is my princess." Her eyes glisten as he slips the ring onto her finger. "So if you no longer have plans to marry the donkey, I'd like to spend my forever with you, *Qattusa*." Overcome with emotion, he takes her cheeks in his hands and brings his lips to hers. If heaven were an eternity spent in one perfect moment from life, this would be that moment. Right now, he is so happy, he is jealous of himself.

Right now, everything is right with the world.

EPILOGUE

Domenicus spends hours wandering the fallen Gozitan citadel. It is a fruitless search. Most of the dead have been carted away and tossed in a pit. The few remains are scattered and rotted. There is no way to identify his father now. He curses himself and the injuries that kept him away. He kneels near the breach and prays for the repose of Augustine's soul. He promises to look after Katrina and vows to avenge their father.

Domenicus leaves the site with a heavy heart, walking the long dirt road that rolls and curves towards the dockyard. As he nears the top of the final hill, something small and metallic, half-covered by sand and mottled with blood, flashes with the afternoon. He bends for a closer look.

It is a silver and turquoise eight-pointed cross on a thin, tarnished chain. Augustine's cross!

Domenicus pulls the necklace from its earthen cradle, hand trembling as he holds it up. He watches the cross twirl and catch with the light until it is made blurry by the tears in his eyes. His father passed this way. He is alive.

The sun will shine warmly upon your face one moment, be blocked behind clouds the next, Jean Parisot de Valette once said to him. *The test of a man is his ability to weather the storm.*

For his father, Domenicus Montesa would walk straight into the thunder. *I am going to find him*, he says to himself, more resolute now than ever. *I will, I swear to God, carry this cross until it is returned to its rightful owner.*

ABOUT THE AUTHOR

Marthese Fenech was born the youngest of five to Maltese parents in Toronto. She has travelled extensively across six continents, and in the course of researching for *Eight Pointed Cross*, toured Malta, Turkey, Italy, France—a wealth of fascinating places that introduced her to her characters and their cultures in a most authentic way.

When she was twelve, she lived in Malta for six months, enrolling in an all-girls private school run by nuns. She lasted three days before getting kicked out for talking too much. Back in Toronto, she started her own business recording, editing, and selling bootleg heavy metal concerts. While in high school, she took a position with a popular seafood chain as its first female dishwasher. She later worked with special needs children and adults, witnessing small miracles on a daily basis.

A former kickboxing instructor, Marthese currently teaches high school English and social science. She speaks fluent Maltese and French. As part of her research for *Eight Pointed Cross*, she took up archery and ended up accidentally becoming a certified instructor. She loves adventure, photography, running, surfing, snowboarding, and yoga.

Visit her website: marthesefenech.com

493

GLOSSARY

Al-fatihah: the first chapter of the Muslim holy book, the *Qur'an*. Its seven verses are a prayer for God's guidance

Apostates: people who renounce their faith, generally adopting the faith of their captors to secure more favourable treatment

Apothecary: a pharmacist trained in the art of preparing and dispensing drugs

Arquebus: an early muzzle-loaded trigger-based gun used in the fifteenth to seventeenth centuries, to which a burning match was applied, and from which the musket was later derived

Auberge: a hall of residence assigned to each tongue, or langue, where the knights lodged and took their meals

Barberot: barber-surgeon

Barnuża: a hood or cloak, typically worn by women in Malta

Bitha: a small courtyard usually behind or within a house

Bosun/boatswain: highest ranking petty officer in the deck department who has immediate charge of all deck hands and who in turn comes under the direct orders of the master or chief mate

Carrack: a large European sailing vessel of the fourteenth to the seventeenth centuries

Corsairs: privateers who operated in the Mediterranean. The most famous were the corsairs from the North African coast

Corsia: the gangway between rows of benches on a galley

Cortège: a solemn procession, especially for a funeral

Devshirme: the practice by which the Ottoman Empire conscripted boys from Christian families. The children were taken by force, converted to Islam, trained, and enrolled in one of the four royal institutions: the Palace, the Scribes, the Religious and the Military. The slave-soldiers of the Sultan, the Janissaries, were products of the devshirme

Galley: a sailing ship which could be propelled by oars when necessary

Galliot: smaller, swift galley, using sails and oars

Hadith: narrations originating from the words and deeds of the Islamic prophet Mohammad

hakem: head of the Università, or Maltese civil authority

Hocam: in Turkish, it is a combination of hoca, a term bestowed upon people who are devout Muslims and renowned for their wisdom as teachers. The m at the end of hocam denotes possession—not just teacher but my teacher

Hospitaller: A medieval Catholic military order founded in 1113 AD as the Knights of the Order of the Hospital of Saint John of Jerusalem

Janissaries: elite infantry units that formed the Ottoman Sultan's household troops and bodyguard. The force was created by the Sultan Murad I from Christian boys levied through the devshirme system

Langue: tongues or langues were the geographic-cultural sub-groupings of the members of the Knights of Saint John from the fourteenth to the eighteenth century. The Knights of St John hailed from the richest estates in civilized Europe. While serving in Malta, these young men were assigned to one of eight halls accommodating the various the langues, or tongues, depending upon their European homeland: Provence; Auvergne; France; Aragon; Castile; Italy; Germany; or England

Madrasah: translated as "a place where learning and studying are done." The term madrasah usually refers to the specifically Islamic institutions. In the Ottoman Empire, the study of hadiths (recorded sayings and deeds of Prophet Muhammad) was introduced by Süleyman I. In addition to religious studies, Ottoman madrasahs also taught styles of writing, grammar, syntax, poetry, composition, natural sciences, political sciences, and etiquette

Mokkadem: a holy man, prayer leader

Moor: North African Muslim of mixed Arab and Berber descent

Müderris: a madrasah teacher

Musket: a muzzle-loaded, smoothbore long gun, intended to be fired from the shoulder

Padishah: supreme royal title denoting the highest rank, and composed of the Persian pād (master) and shāh (king)

Pilier: each tongue, or langue, was headed by a Pilier, or Bailiff, who would also hold one of the high offices of the order: Grand Commander, Marshal, Hospitallier, Admiral, Turcopilier, Drapier. Only the Treasurer was independent of the Tongues. The Piliers were answerable only to the Grand Master, the supreme office each tongue always sought to gain for one of its own

Postulant: a person preparing to be admitted as a novice into a religious order

Sipahi: a fief-holding soldier of the elite imperial cavalry

Sobravestes or surcoat: a sleeveless garment worn as part of the insignia of an order of knighthood

Vizier: a high executive officer of the Ottoman Empire

From historians to rock stars, radio hosts to swordsmen, here's what some remarkable people are saying about *Eight Pointed Cross* and *Falcon's Shadow*, the first two novels in Fenech's *Siege of Malta* trilogy

"*Eight Pointed Cross* is everything a fan of historical fiction could hope for. ...And you're left confused about who to cheer for because there are great people on both sides, and isn't that the BEST kind of story?"
— **Fred Kennedy, Toronto radio personality on Q107 and host of the Issue Zero podcast**

"Over the decades I have read many novels with Malta as their setting. *Eight Pointed Cross* is the first one I have found to be accurate and factual in all of its cultural and historical details, while at the same time, having a thrilling and exciting plot depicted from both sides of the warring factions. Marthese Fenech is phenomenal!"
— **Knight Commander Richard S. Cumbo, Order of St. John, and Curator of the Maltese-Canadian Museum in Toronto**

"With a lyrical narrative that is as rich in historical detail as it is in story and a prose that is poetically pleasing to the ear, *Eight Pointed Cross* is the tautly gripping account of the clash of two great empires. *Eight Pointed Cross* is astoundingly ambitious, but it is in all ways an absolute triumph. Fenech has penned not only a dazzling account of the Knights Hospitaller and what life was like in Malta during this time but also what it was like to grow up in Istanbul. And by writing this book in third person subjective, Fenech has assured that *Eight Pointed Cross* will definitely stand out in a crowded bookcase."
— **Mary Anne Yarde, the Coffee Pot Book Club**

"Crystal-clear descriptive language … Ms. Fenech has recreated the compelling world of the Montesa family of Malta and the Knights of St. John as though she time-travelled back to the sixteenth century to do her research. An impressive debut!"
— **Karen Connelly, Governor General's Literary award recipient and author of *Burmese Lessons***

"Fenech's epic tapestry of a novel encompasses all the sights, sounds, and smells of the 16th-century Mediterranean: tender domestic scenes and blood-drenched battles, privilege and squalor. I believed every minute of it."
— **Carol Rasmussen, science writer at NASA and** former **book review** editor at *Library Journal*

"Marthese Fenech plunges you into her slice of history so deftly that you do not just read it, you live it."
— **Marsha Forchuk Skrypuch, award winning historical author of** *Don't Tell the Nazis* **and** *Stolen Girl*

"WOW! What a fantastic read! Great characters. Great imagery. Great story! The story takes you away. Exactly as a great book should. When one's dream is fueled by the passion to make it become a reality, Ms. Fenech's result here is nothing short of an amazing first effort. Congratulations on realizing your dream!
— **Rob Affuso, Soulsystem president, band leader, and drummer, former Skid Row drummer**

"Marthese Fenech's talent as a storyteller will not let you escape this enchanting tale, painfully detailed and a must to history lovers. You will fall in love with the characters and never forget them."
— **Claire Agius Ordway, producer and host of** *Dak li Jghodd, Ilsien in-nisa,* **and** *Travel and Taste*

"Many historical sagas have been published, but few convey the scale, complexity, and attention to historical detail of *Eight Pointed Cross*. Marthese Fenech creates intricate plots and multi-dimensional characters, whom she moves from one perilous situation to another, keeping readers avidly turning the pages. I found myself thoroughly immersed, a result of the stylistic traps awaiting the reader around every treacherous corner and the unabashed pathos of the tragedy subsumed in the plot. Ms Fenech must have been born with the narrative genetics in perfect order. I truly hope her relentless talent is acknowledged where it should be. Managing to weave a gripping storyline from the ordinary misadventures of love, envy, hate, cowardice and violence underscores her skills better than had she opted for a big story against an epic background."
— **Giovanni Bonello, historian, author, and former Judge of the European Courts of Human Rights**

"*Eight Pointed Cross* has all the ingredients that I consider important in a novel: a gripping plot, engaging, believable characters, stunning description, violence, love, sex, remarkable psychological insight, historical detail. The internal struggles of characters such as Augustine and Franco lend depth and substance to the characterization. A more recent literary giant, William Faulkner, in his speech upon receiving the Nobel Prize for literature in 1950, opined that the only thing worth writing about is the problems of the human heart in conflict with itself. Ms. Fenech has passed both tests with flying colours."
— **John Heighton, reviewer for the Porcupine's Quill**

"What a story! *Falcon's Shadow* is an emotional, tear-jerkingly brilliant novel that left me gasping for breath and begging for more. This is the kind of book that demands your attention from the opening sentence until the last full stop. It is a story of terrible suffering, but it is also one of desperate hope. "
— **Mary Anne Yarde, the Coffee Pot Book Club**

"*Falcon's Shadow* begins with a punch that leaves you breathless. Fenech excels at a number of different narrative facets, but for me, I was particularly engrossed by three aspects. The first is her characters: the good, bad, and morally grey are all equally interesting. The second is the engrossing battle scenes. The third is the deep critique of systematic power structures and how they affect even those who try to distance themselves. If you enjoy impressively researched history, realistic characters for whom you root and despair, and a story that dries out your eyes from compulsive reading, get *Falcon's Shadow*."
— **Tina S Beier, author of *the Burnt Ship* trilogy and producer of BookTube Channel *Sound and Fury***

Made in the USA
Middletown, DE
01 September 2022

70723914R00305